The Astounding-Analog Reader

The
ASTOUNDING ·
ANALOG
Reader

VOLUME ONE

edited by
Harry Harrison
·
Brian W. Aldiss

DOUBLEDAY & COMPANY, INC.
Garden City, New York · 1972

ACKNOWLEDGMENTS

All of the stories included in this volume were first published in *Astounding Science-Fiction*.

"Forgetfulness," by Don A. Stuart, copyright © 1937, 1964 by The Condé Nast Publications, Inc.; reprinted by permission of the Author's Estate and their agents, Scott Meredith Literary Agency, Inc.

"Seeds of the Dusk," by Raymond Z. Gallun, copyright © 1938 by Raymond Z. Gallun; reprinted by permission of the author.

"Farewell to the Master," by Harry Bates, copyright © 1940, 1966 by Harry Bates; reprinted by permission of the author.

"Trouble on Tantulus," by P. Schuyler Miller, copyright © 1941 by Street & Smith Publications, Inc.; reprinted by permission of the author.

"Time Wants a Skeleton," by Ross Rocklynne, copyright © 1941 by Street & Smith Publications, Inc.; copyright renewed 1969 by Ross Rocklynne; reprinted by permission of the author.

"Nightfall," by Isaac Asimov, copyright © 1941 by Street & Smith Publications, Inc.; copyright renewed 1968 by Isaac Asimov; reprinted by permission of the author.

"By His Bootstraps," by Anson MacDonald, copyright © 1941 by Street & Smith Publications, Inc.; copyright renewed 1968 by Robert A. Heinlein; reprinted by permission of the author's agent, Lurton Blassingame.

"The Push of a Finger," by Alfred Bester, copyright © 1942 by Street & Smith Publications, Inc.; reprinted by permission of the author.

"Clash by Night," by Lawrence O'Donnell, copyright © 1943 by Street & Smith Publications, Inc.; reprinted by permission of the Harold Matson Company, Inc.

"The Storm," by A. E. van Vogt, copyright © 1943 by Street & Smith Publications, Inc.; copyright renewed 1971 by A. E. van Vogt. Reprinted by permission of the author and his agent, Forrest J. Ackerman.

"City," by Clifford Simak, copyright © 1944 by Street & Smith Publications, Inc.; copyright renewed 1971 by Clifford D. Simak; reprinted by permission of the author.

"First Contact," by Murray Leinster, copyright © 1945 by Street & Smith Publications, Inc.; reprinted by permission of the author.

"Giant Killer," by A. Bertram Chandler, copyright © 1945 by Street & Smith Publications, Inc.; reprinted by permission of The Condé Nast Publications, Inc.

"Vintage Season," by Lawrence O'Donnell, copyright © 1946 by Street & Smith Publications, Inc.; reprinted by permission of the Harold Matson Company, Inc.

"Placet Is a Crazy Place," by Fredric Brown, copyright © 1946 by The Condé Nast Publications, Inc.; reprinted by permission of the author and his agents, Scott Meredith Literary Agency, Inc.

ISBN: 0-385-02334-0
Library of Congress Catalog Card Number 72-83145
Copyright © 1972 by Harry Harrison and Brian W. Aldiss
All Rights Reserved
Printed in the United States of America
First Edition

Contents

I

II

III

IV

Introduction

Astounding Stories of Super-Science *was conceived to fill a blank spot on a large sheet of color proofs of pulp magazine covers. Harry Bates, the founding editor of the magazine, tells this story and it has the ring of truth to it. The year was 1929 and the pulps were at the zenith of their garish-covered, untrimmed-edged, action-adventure existence. Printed on newspaper presses from reclaimed pulp their rough pages contained bits of ink and color from their previous existence on the wheel of magazine life. On the newsstands they fought for attention with the sulphur yellow, blood red and acid green of their covers; garish is an understatement. Since the covers were the selling point some real effort went into them. Competent artists were hired, impressive paintings executed, then printed in four colors on pure white glossy stock. For economy's sake all the different covers were printed at the same time, then bound about the proper magazines afterward. It was a proof sheet of these covers that hung in publisher William Clayton's office. Four across, four down, an eye-dazzling display of burning Fokkers, gun-blazing sheriffs, smooching lovers, bayoneted Germans, snap-brimmed detectives. Thirteen magazines in all— which by the inflexible laws of geometrics left three blank spaces in that heady array. Blank spaces that could be filled for almost no cost, if suitable magazines were found. Yet this display was so complete with war, western, love, air, adventure, detective, that there was just nothing left. But was there? What about those tentacled monsters and dirigible-like flying ships that zapped and boomed from the covers of the competition's Amazing Stories? What was the stuff called? Scientifiction, that was it. Why don't we publish it too?*

Conceived in the weeks preceding the 1929 stock market crash, the new magazine, Astounding Stories of Super-

Science, *was published in January 1930 just as the Great Depression began. One spare space was filled.*

The work of the early editors of this magazine cannot be faulted. This was a highly specialized field, they knew just what they wanted, and they paid good money for it, two cents a word on the barrelhead at a time when other magazines were paying a tenth of a cent on publication. There had to be action, adventure, and dazzle and there was indeed plenty of that. Harry Bates edited, rewrote and even wrote original stories to get what he wanted. For three years he followed this successful policy until, in 1933, the retitled Astounding Stories *ceased publication as the entire Clayton chain collapsed. Six months later the title was picked up by Street & Smith and the magazine resumed publication under the editorship of F. Orlin Tremaine. One of the most popular science fiction writers at the time was the young John W. Campbell, Jr., and Tremaine not only published his work but hired him as junior editor at Street & Smith when Tremaine became editorial director of a number of magazines in 1937. Campbell edited* Astounding *under the supervision of Tremaine until May 1938 when Tremaine left the firm. From that time until his death in 1971 John Campbell edited this magazine, shaping it, making it his own, shaping as well the writers who appeared in it, and in so doing he altered the entire course of this field. It can truthfully be said that he invented modern science fiction.*

The editors of this present volume, callow adolescents at the time, will never deny the mark it made upon their lives. Science fiction itself was the most colorful experience in those gray prewar, depression-deep days, and the other magazines paled beside the mind-blowing impact of Astounding. *Every issue was sought, read, coveted, reread, treasured. Eventually both editors were swept up by life and the war, sent around the world and shot at, carried home and returned to civilian life. And all of this time— unknown to each other—they were reading and saving this magazine,* Astounding Science-Fiction, *later to be retitled* Analog Science Fact—Science Fiction, *but referred to always as ASF. This anthology is perhaps more a product of that youthful and continuing enthusiasm than of our later roles as authors. It attempts, as far as possible, to recapture the sensation of reading this most singular of magazines down through the years.*

*Of necessity a good deal had to be left out, and even
the absolute residual minimum far exceeds our original
intent. But—can we complain of a wealth of riches? What
we have included here are the stories that impressed us
strongly when first read in those distant days, stories
that echoed in memory through the years—and stories that
still retained their strength upon rereading after two
decades or more. This is asking an awful lot to ask of fiction
published in pulp form by a magazine without the slightest
literary pretensions. Quite the opposite; periodically
through the years John Campbell would run small items
asking for stories from engineers, professional scientists,
people in the know with physical reality. He offered the lure of
extra money for a new camera or piece of equipment. He never
once mentioned access to a literary career. This is not to intimate
that the stories are without literary value; indeed the reverse
is true. Campbell himself was a fine writer, and when
he became an editor he exercised ruthless control over
content and story. Slipshod plotting and failure of technique
earned instant rejection. It might be said that he had a
literary feel for stories yet was hostile to literature. This
is understandable since he was a man with a mission—
or rather a number of missions. He was interested in
what was being communicated, not in how it was done.
In a way he very much resembled a young expatriate writer
we knew in a tropical part of the world. He wanted
very much to write, but his stories were mostly political
polemic since he was a dedicated member of the Communist
party. When faced with this he finally admitted that he
was more interested in communicating his political beliefs
than in perfecting the art or craft of writing. John Campbell
—though politically as far away as possible!—was pushed
on by an even more pressing enthusiasm. The entire
province of space and time was his oyster and he had
questions about all of it and answers about some of it.
Many times he only groped for an answer or guessed at
it; then he would phrase his groping and guessing as
forceful statement and make others contradict him and
prove their cases. Preferably in a story for his magazine.
His curiosity knew no bounds and when he communicated
this enthusiasm to his writers the result was the stories
represented here. At the same time his sense of humor
was of the roguish kind and many of his declarations
and editorials were designed to provoke cries of rage from*

*his readers. Characteristic is a statement he made just
a few months before he died. There was a group of us and
the talk came around to literature and the place of
science fiction in the greater whole of English letters. It
was pointed out that some enthusiastic aggrandizers
of SF stand on the barricades and declare that someday,
due to innate superiority, the short story and the novel
will be engulfed by science fiction and become a part
of it. Others, perhaps more realistically, say that SF is
one specialized part of the whole of literature. But not
John Campbell! With a sweep of one great hand he
dismissed these feckless arguments, then spread his arms
wide. "This is science fiction," he said, from open-armed
fingertip to fingertip. "It takes in all of time, from before
the universe was born, through the formation of suns and
planets, on through their destruction and forward to
the heat death of the universe. And after." His hands
came together so that his index fingers delimitated a
very tiny measure of space. "This is English Literature,
the most microscopic fraction of the whole."*

*That is the feeling that underlies these stories; eternity
is their province and science their guide. And the editor
always there to make sure that whatever was written
about would at least be written in a readable and entertaining
manner. More than that—the editor was always free with
ideas and suggestions and plots for more stories. The
perfect example is "First Contact" which appears here,
authored by Will Jenkins using the pen name Murray
Leinster. While we were obtaining rights from the author
he wrote back that for this particular anthology it would
be his first choice ". . . because I remember vividly when
John presented the idea of 'First Contact' to be written."
Will Jenkins had to say this, John Campbell never would.
Down through the years many other authors have come
forward with the same kind of statement.*

*Here are the stories. Space limitations ruled that more
had to be left out than were included. Harsh rules had to be
obeyed. Only one story by any single author; anything
else would be unfair to the many who could not be included.
The two Lawrence O'Donnell stories here are no exception
to this rule since this pen name conceals the identities of
the husband and wife team of Henry Kuttner and C. L.
Moore, each of whom wrote one of these stories. Then,
by virtue of length, the memorable serials had to be left out.*

*What remained after this refining process was the essence
of the magazine, the pure quill, the real thing that made
ASF a singular phenomenon.*

*When we go back to the beginning it is obvious that
science fiction has always been a family affair with the
same names appearing again and again in many roles. A
close examination of the ASF letter column,* Science
Discussions, *later to become* Brass Tacks, *reveals future
events casting their shadows before them. Here is the
correspondence of piping young fans like Isaac Asimov,
Donald Wollheim, and Frederik Pohl—Pohl's letter in
1937 proudly announcing the first World Science Fiction
Convention to be held in 1939. This was still in the pre-
Campbell era but authors who would later be associated
with his editorship were already represented in the
magazine; L. Sprague de Camp, Jack Williamson, Nat
Schachner, Willy Ley, E. E. Smith, Ph.D. These, and
others, proved capable enough of change and were carried
into the Campbell era. Others vanished from sight. What
they were writing at the dawn of this era is best exemplified
by this quote from Doc Smith's "Galactic Patrol" in the
September 1937 issue.*

He thrust out tractor beams of his own, and from the already
white-hot refractory throats of his projectors there raved out horribly
potent beams of annihilation, beams of dreadful power which tore
madly at the straining defensive screens of the patrol ship. Screens
flared vividly, radiating all the colors of the spectrum. Space itself
seemed a rainbow gone mad, for there were being exerted there
forces of a magnitude to stagger the imagination—forces to be
yielded only by the atomic might from which they sprang—forces
whose neutralization set up visible strains in the very fabric of the
ether itself.

*Gradually, the Campbell presence began to be felt. In
1938 Jack Williamson's "The Legion of Time" was published.
It was adventurous galaxy-leaping Williamson at his
best, but exploring the themes of probability and parallel
worlds far more than the far depths of space. And new
writers appeared this year, not yet masters of the medium
but ready to grow; L. Ron Hubbard, Malcolm Jameson,
Lester del Rey, H. L. Gold.*

*L. Ron Hubbard, already a pulp writer for magazines
like* Argosy, *was to become a regular contributor of short*

stories as well as a series about a spacegoing doctor written under the pen name René Lafayette, and finally the controversial but well received serial "Final Blackout" about the breakdown of Europe after the Second World War.

Malcolm Jameson, a retired Navy officer, is best remembered for his Bullard of the Space Patrol series, obviously drawn from his naval experiences and translated from ocean to space, a device much utilized by later writers. Lester del Rey's short stories are best represented by his "Helen O'Loy" in 1938, a sentimental blend of love and robotics. H. L. Gold was to later become the founding editor of Galaxy Science Fiction; but now the world was still young.

Clifford Simak, whom Kingsley Amis has referred to as the bucolic poet of science fiction, had been destroying universes with the best of them up until this time, but in this first Campbell year published his "Reunion on Ganymede," about Iowa farmers on Venus, which showed him on his way back from the galaxy's rim and almost to Earth again.

And Campbell himself. Writing as Don A. Stuart this first year also included "Who Goes There?", a story of a shape-changing alien that has been imitated, never equalled, later adapted for the movie The Thing.

Then, in 1939, began what readers of ASF have always referred to as the Golden Age of the magazine. And golden years they were indeed. Within twelve months Campbell had laid the groundwork for the successes to come. New writers who could produce the content-orientated stories were found, old writers re-educated in their thinking. The stories were of course the important part, yet at the same time Campbell was aware of the need to change the physical image of the magazine. On the cover the three-dimensional lettering of ASTOUNDING, apparently hewn from blocks of pine, vanished and a modern, neat bit of titling appeared in its place. In Times to Come department was introduced, a glimpse of future contents, and Science Discussions became Brass Tacks. Here were the letters from the readers, and the answers to them by the editor who, in a fine bit of time traveling, put his answer ahead of the letter, thereby getting in the last word first. New artists were found so that the interior and cover art improved markedly. Astronomical covers were featured, fine views of ruddy planets and burning suns, and the

*incomparable Hubert Rogers painted his first cover. Eventually
Campbell was even to control the advertisements that
went into the magazine, banishing forever the spotty youth
who proclaimed "Ugly blackheads out in seconds," or
his elder counterpart with the startled expression who
gasped "Did you say . . . RUPTURE?" All details were
part of the greater whole, this was John Campbell's
magazine and everyone involved marched to the sound
of his certain drum.*

*And what an inspiring beat it had! Space opera was still
there, nor was it ever absent for long until after the death
of E. E. Smith. Clifford Simak's "Cosmic Engineers" out-
Smithed Smith in 1939, but was well balanced by Campbell's
own "Cloak of Aesir." Not satisfied with writing and editing*
Astounding, *John Campbell also edited* Unknown *which
first appeared this year. We are tempted to digress and say
too much about this admirable magazine, but will resist and
simply state that it was unique as well as being
the best magazine of fantasy fiction ever published, going
on from victory to victory before being defeated by the
wartime paper shortage. But at this time the war was almost
three years in the future and the* Astounding *writers were
getting the beat of the Campbell drum. What a year 1939
was! Here was "Black Destroyer" by the new writer A. E. van
Vogt. Still an excellent story, a fit debut for this author of
classics still to come. Then there was "Trends," the
first story of the precocious teenager from New York,
Isaac Asimov. And a completely unknown ex-Navy officer
named Robert A. Heinlein with his first published story,
"Life-Line." A month after this another first story was
published, "Ether Breather" by Theodore Sturgeon. The
very earth was moving under the readers' feet! To round
out the year "Gray Lensman" was serialized, perhaps the
best of Doc Smith's Lensman series, its impact driven home
by the image of the stalwart Kimball Kinnison by Rogers
on the cover, with interior illustrations by Charles Schneeman,
the artist who best captured this era in black and white.*

*This was certainly the Golden Age. In 1940 we saw
Heinlein moving into longer work with the serial "If This
Goes On . . .", establishing a religious dictatorship in
America then overthrowing it. Strong stuff indeed; the
pulps are well behind us now. Then his "The Roads Must
Roll,"; what fine technology. "Requiem," followed "Coventry"
a sequel to "If This Goes On . . ." to be followed in turn by*

"*Blowups Happen*", *these blowups happening in an atomic energy plant—five years before the first atomic bomb was dropped. ASF readers surely did live in a different world. That other new writer, van Vogt, published "The Vault of the Beast," the monster this time a robot, then led us to the dizziest heights with his serial "Slan." For all its faults, never noticed at the time but discovered by critics years later, this novel of telepathic supermen is still a powerful book.*

The readers were hanging from the ropes—and enjoying every moment of it. Before 1940 closed they had more Asimov, Sturgeon, and Hubbard, and a real look at what it was like to be present during a revolution. "Fog" was written by Willy Ley, using the pen name Robert Willey, who knew the sensation from experience.

And so it went. From 1941 to 1946, where this present volume closes, the magic linkage of editor-author-reader continued. All were operating on the same wavelength and felt the same vibrations. The war was in progress now and soon many of the writers and illustrators would be in the armed forces, but before they went they produced a flood of still memorable work. Heinlein wrote "Universe," establishing forever the concept of the multi-generation starship, "Goldfish Bowl," and "Waldo"—a word that has since moved into our vocabulary. His serials are still in print as novels; "Sixth Column," "Methuselah's Children," and "Beyond This Horizon." We had Sturgeon's "Killdozer," and "Microcosmic God," Rocklynne's "Jackdaw," del Rey's "Nerves," to be amplified into a novel much later, and the young Asimov preparing his future with "Reason," the first positronic robot story, and "Foundation," the beginning of the series of that title.

Readers loved "series" stories, watching with fascination as they developed and grew. A. E. van Vogt had one going now, the Weapon Shop stories, and with "Co-operate—Or Else," the Rull series began. (The new writer, George O. Smith, was starting his Venus Equilateral series too.) Now van Vogt's serial, "The World of Ā," (pronounced "null-A" as we were quickly informed) converted us all to Korzybski and his general semantics theories.

Other new writers appeared, some new to ASF, some new to the world of letters; Raymond F. Jones, Anthony Boucher, and Alfred Bester. The old timers were still there too, Doc Smith continued his space-spanning saga with "Second Stage

Lensman." Fritz Leiber with "Gather Darkness," Lewis Padgett
with his "Fairy Chessmen," all serials that were destined to
be published as books.

ASF was a microcosm where creators and readers lived
together. "Final Blackout" by L. Ron Hubbard may be a
period piece now, but it was brutal and shockingly real in those
first years of the war when Hitler was blitzing across Europe.
Readers accused this serial of being either Communist or
Fascist propaganda—quite a sweep of opinion—and a poem
about its protagonist "The Lieutenant" by faithful-reader
H. K. Pruyn appeared in Brass Tacks. (A few lines from it:
"For here it is that once again/ He leads them through the
battle;/ Cheerful Frenchman, shaggy Scot,/ Like some roaming
cattle.")

Though many readers and authors went off to war they kept
their tight little world of ASF separate. The stories still escape
the outside world into a better—or at least a more interesting
one. However there was one brush between the worlds
that was not publicized until after the war. In March 1944
ASF published "Deadline" by Cleve Cartmill, which explained
in great detail how to build and drop an atomic bomb, and
it used terms like U-235 and critical mass. It must be
remembered that the first atomic bomb was not dropped until
August 6, 1945, so that in early 1944 this was the biggest and
best kept secret of the war. Military Intelligence appeared at
Cartmill's home in Manhattan Beach (Manhattan Beach—
Manhattan Project, they could not have enjoyed that
coincidence) and muttered about personal security, which
Cartmill countered by showing that all his facts came from
published sources. It is clear by hindsight that the arrival
of intelligence agents on the spot was a much greater breach
of security, indicating that there was something atomic
to be secretive about. John Campbell made this very point
when the agents suggested he stop printing atomic energy
and atomic bomb stories in the national interest. He showed
them that ASF had always printed this kind of story and
by dropping them ASF would be pointing in a very
obvious direction. (That the Campbell reasoning was
correct was proven by the later discovered fact that
Wernher Von Braun got his copy of ASF every month
through Sweden; surely other German scientists read the
magazine too.) Campbell and ASF were triumphant and
atomic stories stayed in. This anecdote was often used to
bolster the case for science fiction, in the days when it needed

support, and has gathered a great deal of mythology since in the telling. This was also one of the few cases where SF prediction came true since SF, like horoscope reading, shotguns the future with a wealth of predictions and only remembers the ones that work out. Most don't. As late as 1945 ASF writers were a little unsure about the details of rocket propulsion; ". . . when the first crude gasoline-driven rockets had struggled across space . . ." ("When the Rockets Come," Robert Abernathy.) We should settle for what SF is and not make too many claims for its prognosticative abilities.

There it was. A magazine, a world to escape to, a way of life. The stories we present here are representative of those first years, of the foundation, growth and blossoming of this singular magazine. It shaped the lives of its readers and contributors just as religion shaped the lives of the faithful during the ages of faith. The discovery of science fiction was, and still is, almost a matter of religious conversion, the entering of a new state. Every true reader can remember clearly the moment when he read his first SF story and fell into its embrace. A study done in Canada has even disclosed that deprivation of science fiction produces withdrawal symptoms in fanatic readers; this can be said for no other kind of literature. Now, with much of the predicted hardware of SF in existence, the casual reader may no longer feel the sense of conversion, martyrdom—even paranoia—that obsessed the early devotees. Though he may be able to understand it a bit better after he reads these stories.

The world was not a nice place to live in during those days, what with war, depression and deadly diseases without antibiotic cures. The world of ASF was indeed a preferable and far, far better one.

The Astounding-Analog Reader

ONE/

· Forgetfulness
· Seeds of the Dusk
· Farewell to the Master

Aldous Huxley says it in one of his essays—the Remote is the equivalent of the Future. Back in the thirties, ASF was one of the dwelling places of the Remote. The Remote was curiously accessible, possibly because Huxley's remark held good. Since then, the Future has come much nearer; any number of specialists have got at it, put their copyright on it, and made it loom ominously ahead of us, so that it now precludes those old-time golden vistas of the Remote.

For this phenomenon, for the construction of the Future as an almost tangible thing, ASF is itself partly to blame. It was the seriousness of ASF itself in deciding that science fiction was not just a realm of escape which brought about a gradual interest in the extrapolation of likely futures, and hence paved the way for the "think tanks" and the formidable contemporary array of futurologists. Nowadays, laymen think of the Future as a period maybe up to 2000 A.D. but little further; and most of the predictions in that region are pretty sombre, being concerned with urban decay, overpopulation, pollution, food shortage, and similar topics.

Happily, it was not always so. In the late thirties, a mellow calm hung over many ASF stories, a calm to be found in the Remote Future. Often this calm was the bittersweet one of the recession of civilization:

> *Far-called, our navies melt away;*
> *On dune and headland sinks the fire*

Nobody in ASF captured this wistful note better than John W. Campbell's other self, Don A. Stuart, many of whose stories—however mighty their machines—orbit about an essence of nostalgia.

The three tales that follow are all poignant. The era of

tough clamped-down endurance, fostered perhaps by the war years, is still to come. "Farewell to the Master"—the very title speaks of regret and calm. It was written by the first editor of Astounding Stories of Super-Science, *back in the Clayton days. In many respects, it remains one of the finest robot stories ever written, since it is about something more than robots themselves; it is about a possible evolution in man's relationship with creatures of his own inventing.*

Forgetfulness /

by DON A. STUART

"Space of our own? No—it is like the slogan: It rotates us to the end of time."

Ron Thule, the astronomer, stood in the lock gate and looked down across the sweep of gently rolling land. Slowly, he breathed in the strange, tangy odors of this planet. There was something of a vast triumph in his eyes, and something of sorrow. They had been here now scarcely five hours, and the sun was still low in the east, rising slowly. Out beyond, above the western horizon, a pale ghost of the strange twin world of this planet, less than a third of a million miles distant, seemed a faint, luminous cloud in the deep, serene blue of the sky.

It was triumph, for six long years of travel, at a speed close to that of light, lay behind them; three and a half light years distant was Pareeth, and the crowding people who had built and launched the mighty two-thousand-five-hundred foot, interstellar cruiser that had brought this little band of one hundred. Launched in hope and striving, seeking a new sun with new planets, new worlds to colonize. More than that, even, for this new-found planet was a stepping-stone to other infinities beyond. Ten years of unbroken travel was the maximum any ship they could build would endure. They had found a planet, in fact, nine planets. Now, the range they might explore for new worlds was extended by four light years.

And there was sorrow there, too, for there was a race here now. Ron Thule turned his eyes toward the little clustering village nestled in the swale of the hills, a village of simple, rounded domes of some opalescent, glassy material. A score of them straggled irregularly among the mighty, deep-green trees that shaded them from the morning sun, twenty-foot domes of pearl and rose and blue. The deep green of the trees and the soft green of the mosslike grass that covered all the low, rounded hills gave it a certain beauty; the sparkling colors of the little gardens about the domes added color and further beauty. It was a lovely spot, a spot where space-wearied, interstellar wanderers might rest in delight. A village, indeed, where anyone might rest in ease and enjoyment, after long, long labors.

Such it was. There was a race on this planet the men of Pareeth had found after six long years of space, six years of purring, humming atomic engines and echoing gray steel fabric that carried and protected them. Harsh utility of giant girders and rubbery flooring, the snoring drone of forty quadrillion horse power of atomic engines. It was replaced now by the soft coolness of the grassy land; the curving steel of the girders gave way to the brown of arching trees; the stern ceiling of steel plates gave way to the vast, blue arch of a planet's atmosphere. Sounds died away in infinitudes where there was no steel to echo them back; the unending drone of the mighty engines had become breezes stirring, rustling leaves—an invitation to rest.

The race that lived here had long since found it such, it seemed. Ron Thule looked across the little village of domes to the largest of them, perhaps thirty feet across. Commander Shor Nun was there with his archeologist and anthropologist—and a half score men of this planet. Rhth, they called it.

The conference was breaking up now. Shor Nun appeared, tall and powerful, his muscular figure in trim Interstellar Expedition uniform of utilitarian, silvery gray. Behind him came the other two in uniform—young, powerful men of Pareeth, selected for this expedition because of physical and mental perfection, as was every man of them.

Then came Seun, the man of Rhth. He was taller, slimmer, an almost willowy figure. His lean body was clothed in an elastic, close-fitting suit of golden stuff, while over his shoulders a glowing, magnificently shimmering cape of rich blue was thrown. Five more of these men came out, each in a golden suit, but the draped capes glowed in deep reds, and rich greens, blues and violets. They walked leisurely beside the men of Pareeth. An unconscious force made those trimly uniformed men walk in step between the great, arching trees.

They came near, and Shor Nun called out, "Is the expedition ready?"

From the forward lock, Toth Mour replied, "Aye, commander. Twenty-two men. What do these people say?"

Shor Nun shook his head slightly. "That we may look as we wish. The city is deserted. I cannot understand them. What arrangements have you made?"

"The men you mentioned are coming. Each head of department, save Ron Thule. There will be no work for the astronomer."

"I will come, Shor Nun," called out the astronomer, softly. "I can sketch; I would be interested."

"Well enough, as you like. Toth Mour, call the men into formation; we will start at once. The day varies in length, but is some thirteen hours long at this season, I am told."

Ron Thule leaped down to the soft turf and walked over toward the group. Seun looked at him slowly and smiled. The man of Rhth looked taller from this distance, nearly six and a third feet in height. His face was tanned to a golden color that came near to matching the gold of his clothing. His eyes were blue and very deep. They seemed uncertain—a little puzzled, curious about these men, curious about the vast, gray bulk that had settled like a grim shadow over the low hill. Half a mile in length, four hundred feet in diameter, it loomed nearly as large as the age-old, eroded hills it had berthed on. He ran a slim-fingered hand through the glinting golden hair that curled in unruly locks above a broad, smooth brow.

"There is something for an astronomer in all this world, I think." He smiled at Ron Thule. "Are not climate and soils and atmospheres the province of astronomy, too?"

"The chemists know it better," Ron Thule replied, and wondered slightly at his replying. He knew that the man of Rhth had not spoken, simply that the thought had come to be in his mind. "Each will have his special work, save for me. I will look at the city. They will look at the buildings and girders and the carvings or mechanisms, as is their choice. I will look at the city."

Uneasily, he moved away from the group, started alone across the field. Uneasiness settled on him when he was near this Seun, this descendant of a race that had been great ten millions of years before his own first sprang from the swamps. Cheated heir to a glory five million years lost.

The low, green roll of the hill fell behind him as he climbed the grassy flank. Very slowly before his eyes, the city lifted into view. Where the swelling curve of the hill faded softly into the infinite blue of the sky, first one little point, then a score, then hundreds appeared, as he walked up the crest—the city.

Then he stood on the crest. The city towered before him—five miles away across the gently rolling green swale. Titan city of a Titan race! The towers glowed with a sun-fired opalescence in the golden light of the sun. How long, great gods of this strange world, how long had they stood thus? Three thousand feet they rose from the level of age-sifted soil at their bases, three thousand feet of mighty mass, stupendous buildings of the giants long dead.

The strange little man from a strange little world circling a dim, forgotten star looked up at them, and they did not know, or care. He walked toward them, watched them climb into the blue of the sky. He crossed the broad green of the land, and they grew in their uncaring majesty.

Sheer, colossal mass, immeasurable weights and loading they were—and they seemed to float there on the grace of a line and a curve, half in the deep blue of the sky, half touching the warm, bright green of the land. They floated still on the strength of a dream dreamed by a man dead these millions of years. A brain had dreamed in terms of lines and curves and sweeping planes, and the brain had built in terms of opal crystal and vast masses. The mortal mind was buried under unknown ages, but an immortal idea had swept life into the dead masses it molded—they lived and floated still on the memory of a mighty glory. The glory of the race—

The race that lived in twenty-foot, rounded domes.

The astronomer turned. Hidden now by the rise of the verdant land was one of the villages that race built today. Low, rounded things, built, perhaps, of this same, strange, gleaming crystal, a secret half remembered from a day that must have been—

The city flamed before him. Across ten—or was it twenty—thousand millenniums, the thought of the builders reached to this man of another race. A builder who thought and dreamed of a mighty future, marching on, on forever in the aisles of time. He must have looked from some high, wind-swept balcony of the city to a star-sprinkled sky—and seen the argosies of space: mighty treasure ships that swept back to this remembered home, coming in from the legion worlds of space, from far stars and unknown, clustered suns; Titan ships, burdened with strange cargoes of unguessed things.

And the city peopled itself before him; the skies stirred in a moment's flash. It was the day of Rhth's glory then! Mile-long ships hovered in the blue, settling, slow, slow, home from worlds they'd circled. Familiar sights, familiar sounds, greeting their men again. Flashing darts of silver that twisted through mazes of the upper air, the soft, vast music of the mighty city. The builder lived, and looked out across his dream——

But, perhaps, from his height in the looming towers he could see across the swelling ground to the low, rounded domes of his people, his far descendants seeking the friendly shelter of the shading trees—

Ron Thule stood among the buildings of the city. He trod a pavement of soft, green moss, and looked behind to the swell of the land. The wind had laid this pavement. The moving air was the only force that maintained the city's walks. A thousand thousand years it has swept its gatherings across the plain, and deposited them as an offering at the base of these calm towers. The land had built up slowly, age on age, till it was five hundred feet higher than the land the builder had seen.

But his dream was too well built for time to melt away. Slowly time was burying it, even as, long since, time had buried him. The towers took no notice. They dreamed up to the blue of the skies and waited. They were patient; they had waited now a million, or was it ten million years? Some day, some year, the builders must return, dropping in their remembered argosies from the far, dim reaches of space, as they had once these ages gone. The towers waited; they were faithful to their trust. They had their memories, memories of a mighty age, when giants walked and worlds beyond the stars paid tribute to the city. Their builders would come again. Till then—naught bothered them in their silence.

But where the soft rains of a hundred thousand generations had drained from them, their infinite endurance softened to its gentle touch. Etched channels and rounded gutters, the mighty carvings dimming, rounding, their powerful features betrayed the slow effects. Perhaps—it had been so long—so long—even the city was forgetting what once it was. They had waited, these towers, for. . . .

And the builders walked in the shade of the trees, and built rounded domes. And a new race of builders was come, a race the city did not notice in its age-long quiet. Ron Thule looked up to them and wondered if it were to be that his people should carry on the dream begun so long ago.

Softened by the silence, voices from the expedition reached him. "—diamond won't scratch it, Shor Nun—more elastic than beryl steel. Tough——" That was Dee Lun, the metallurgist. He would learn that secret somehow. They would all learn. And Shor Nun, commander, executive, atomic engineer, would learn the secrets that their power plants must hold. The dream—the city's life—would go on!

Ron Thule wandered on. No duty his, today, no responsibility to study carefully the form and turn of sweeping line, the hidden art that floated ten millions of tons of mass on the grace of a line. That for the archeologist and the engineer. Nor his to study the cunning form of brace and girder, the making of the pearly walls. That for metallurgist and chemist.

Seun was beside him, looking slowly about the great avenues that swept away into slim canyons in the distance.

"Your people visited ours, once," said Ron Thule softly. "There are legends, the golden gods that came to Pareeth, bringing gifts of fire and the bow and the hammer. The myths have endured through two millions of our years—four and a half millions of yours. With fire and bow and hammer my people climbed to civilization. With atomic power they blasted themselves back to the swamps. Four times they climbed, discovered the secret of the atom, and blasted themselves back to the swamps. Yet all the changes could not efface the thankfulness to the golden gods, who came when Pareeth was young."

Seun nodded slowly. His unspoken thoughts formed clear and sharp in the astronomer's mind. "Yes, I know. The city builders, it was. Once, your sun and ours circled in a system as a double star. A wandering star crashed through that system, breaking it, and in the breaking making planets. Your sun circled away, the new-formed planets cooling; our sun remained, these worlds cooling till the day life appeared. We are twin races, born of the same stellar birth. The city builders found that, and sought your worlds. They were a hundred thousand light years distant, in that time, across all the width of the galaxy, as the two suns circled in separate orbits about the mass of the galaxy.

"The city builders went to see your race but once; they had meant to return, but before the return was made they had interfered in the history of another race, helping them. For their reward the city builders were attacked by their own weapons, by their own pupils. Never again have we disturbed another race."

"Across the galaxy, though. The Great Year—how could they—so many stars——"

"The problem of multiple bodies? The city builders solved it; they traced the orbits of all the suns of all space; they knew then what sun must once have circled with ours. The mathematics of it—I have forgotten—I cannot develop it. I am afraid I cannot answer your thoughts. My people have forgotten so many things the city builders knew.

"But your people seek entrance to the buildings. I know the city, all its ways and entrances. The drifting soil has covered every doorway, save those that once were used for the great airships. They are still unblocked. I know of one at this level, I think. Perhaps——"

II

Ron Thule walked slowly back toward the group. Seun was speaking with Shor Nun, and now they angled off across the city. Their voices hushed; their footfalls were lost in the silence that brooded forever over the towers. Down timeless avenues they marched, a tiny band in the valley of the Titans. The towers marched on and on, on either side, up over low hills, beyond the horizon. Then, before them, in the side of one of the milky walls a great opening showed. Some five feet above the level of the drifted soil, it led into the vast, black maw of the building. The little party grouped at the base, then, laboriously, one of the engineers boosted and climbed his way to the threshold and dropped a rope to a companion.

Seun stood a bit apart, till Shor Nun lifted himself up to the higher level and stood on the milky floor. Then the man of Rhth seemed to glow slightly; a golden haze surrounded him and he floated effortlessly up from the ground and into the doorway.

The engineers, Shor Nun, all stood frozen, watching him. Seun stopped, turned, half smiling. "How? It is the *lathan,* the suit I wear."

"It defies gravity?" asked Shor Nun, his dark eyes narrowing in keenest interest.

"Defies gravity? No, it does not defy, for gravity is a natural law. The city builders knew that. They made these suits shortly before they left the city. The *lathan* simply bends gravity to will. The mechanism is in the filaments of the back, servant to a wish. Its operation—I know only vague principles. I—I have forgotten so much. I will try to explain——"

Ron Thule felt the thoughts parading through his mind: Nodes and vibrations, atoms and less than atoms, a strange, invisible fabric of woven strains that were not there. His mind rebelled. Vague, inchoate stirrings of ideas that had no clarity; the thoughts were formless and indistinct, uncertain of themselves. They broke off.

"We have forgotten so much of the things the city builders knew, their arts and techniques," Seun explained. "They built things and labored that things might surround and protect them, as they thought. They labored generations that this city might be. They strove and thought and worked, and built fleets that sailed beyond the farthest star the clearest night reveals. They brought here their gains, their hard-won treasures—that they might build and make to protect these things.

"They were impermanent things, at best. How little is left of their five-million-year striving! We have no things today, nor any protecting of things. And we have forgotten the arts they developed to protect and understand these things. And with them, I am sorry, I have forgotten the thoughts that make the *lathan* understandable."

Shor Nun nodded slowly, turned to his party. Ron Thule looked back from this slight elevation, down the long avenue. And his eyes wandered aside to this descendant of the mighty dreamers, who dreamed no more.

"Seek passages to lower levels," said Shor Nun's voice. "Their records, their main interest must have centered near the ancient ground level. The engineers—we will seek the lowest, subsurface levels, where the powers and the forces of the city must have been generated. Come."

The opalescent light that filtered through the walls of the building faded to a rose dusk as they burrowed deeper into the vast pile. Corridors branched and turned; rooms and offices dust-littered and barren opened from them. Down the great two-hundred-foot corridor by which they had entered, ships had once floated, and at the heart of the building was a cavernous place where these ships had once rested—and rested still! Great, dim shapes, half seen in the misted light that filtered through wall on translucent wall.

The room blazed suddenly with the white light of half a dozen atomic torches, and the opalescent walls of the room reflected the flare across the flat, dusty sweep of the great floor. Twoscore smooth shapes of flowing lines clustered on the floor, a forgotten company of travelers that had stopped here once, when the city roared in triumphant life. A powdery, gray dust covered their crystal hulls.

Slowly, Shor Nun walked toward the nearest of them, a slim, thirty-foot-long private ship, waiting through eternity for a forgotten hand. The open lock at the side lighted suddenly at the touch of his foot, and soft lights appeared throughout the ship. Somewhere a soft, low humming began, and faded into silence in a moment. "Drus Nol—come with me. Seun, do you know the mechanism of these ships?"

The man of Rhth hesitated, then shook his head slowly. "I cannot explain it." He sighed. "They will not function now; they drew their power from the central plant of the city, and that has ceased operation. The last of the city builders shut it down as they left."

The men of Pareeth entered the ship hesitantly, and even while they walked toward the central control cabin at the nose, the white lighting dimmed through yellow, and faded out. Only their own torches remained. The stored power that had lain hidden in some cells aboard this craft was gone in a last, fitful glow. Somewhere soft, muffled thuds of relays acted, switching vainly to seek charged, emergency cells. The lights flared and died, flared and vanished. The questing relays relaxed with a tired click.

Dust-shrouded mechanism, etched in the light of flaring torches, greeted their eyes, hunched bulks, and gleaming tubes of glassy stuff that, by its sparkling, fiery life must be other than any glass they knew, more nearly kin to the brilliant refraction of the diamond.

"The power plant," said Shor Nun softly, "I think we had best look at that first. These are probably decayed; there might still be some stored power in the central plant they could pick up and give us a fatal shock. The insulation here——"

But the city builders had built well. There was no sign of frayed and age-rotted insulation. Only slight gray dust lay in torn blankets, tender fabric their movements had disturbed.

Seun walked slowly toward the far end of the room, rounding the silent, lightless bulks of the ancient ships. The dust of forgotten ages stirred softly in his wake, settled behind him. The men of Pareeth gathered in his steps, followed him toward the far wall.

A doorway opened there, and they entered a small room. The archeologist's breath whistled; the four walls were decorated with friezes of the history of the race that had built, conquered and sailed a universe—and lived in domes under sheltering trees.

Seun saw his interest, touched a panel at his side. Soundlessly, a door slid from the wall, clicked softly, and completed the frieze on that wall. The archeologist was sketching swiftly, speaking to the chemist and the photographer as he worked. The torches flared higher for a moment, and the men moved about in the twenty-foot room, making way for the remembering eye of the little camera.

As Seun touched another stud, the door slid back into the wall. The room of the ships was gone. Hastily, the men of Pareeth turned to Seun.

"Will that elevator work safely to raise us again? You said the power was cut off——"

"There is stored power. Nearly all had leaked away, but it was designed to be sufficient to run all this city and all its ships, wherever they might be, for seven days. There is power enough. And there are foot passages if you fear the power will not be sufficient. This is the lowest level; this is the level of the machines, the heart of the city—nearly one thousand feet below the level at which we entered."

"Are the machines, the power plant, in this building?"

"There is only one building, here beneath the ground. It is the city, but it has many heads. The power plant is off here, I think. It has been a long time since I came this way. I was young then, and the city builders fascinated me. Their story is interesting and——"

"Interesting——" The thought seemed to echo in Ron Thule's mind. The story of the conquest of a universe, the story of achievement such as his race dreamed of now. They had dreamed —and done. And that, to their descendants, that was—interesting. Interesting to this dark, strange labyrinth of branching corridors, and strange, hooded bulks. Production machinery, he knew, somehow, production machinery that forgotten workmen had hooded as they stepped away temporarily—for a year or two, perhaps till the waning population should increase again and make new demands on it. Then great storerooms, bundled things that might be needed, spare parts, and stored records and deeds. Libraries of dull metal under gray dust. The unneeded efforts of a thousand generations, rotting in this quiet dark that he, Ron Thule, and his companions had disturbed with the moment's rush of atomic flame.

Then the tortuous corridor branched, joined others, became suddenly a great avenue descending into the power room, the heart of the city and all that it had meant. They waited still, the mighty engines the last of the builders had shut down as he left, waited to start again the work they had dropped for the moment, taking a well-earned rest. But they must have grown tired in that rest, that waiting for the resurgence of their masters. They glowed dimly under the thin blankets of grayed dust, reflecting the clear brilliance of the prying light.

Shor Nun halted at the gate, his engineer beside him. Slowly, Seun of Rhth paced into the great chamber. "By the golden gods of Pareeth, Drus Nol, do you see that insulation—those buss-bars!"

"Five million volts, if it's no better than we build," the engineer said, "and I suppose they must be busses, though, by the stars of space, they look like columns! They're twenty-five feet through. But, man, man, the generator—for it must be a generator—it's no longer than the busses it energizes."

"When the generator operated," Seun's thoughts came, "the field it created ran through the bars, so that they, too, became nearly perfect conductors. The generator supplied the city, and its ships, wherever in all space they might be." And the further thought came into their minds, "It was the finest thing the city builders had."

Shor Nun stepped over the threshold. His eyes followed the immense busses, across in a great loop to a dimly sparkling switch panel, then across, and down to a thing in the center of the hall, a thing——

Shor Nun cried out, laughed and sobbed all at one moment. His hands clawed at his eyes; he fell to his knees, groaning. "Don't look—by the gods, don't look——" he gasped.

Drus Nol leaped forward, bent at his side. Shor Nun's feet moved in slow arcs through the dust of the floor, and his hands covered his face.

Seun of Rhth stepped over to him with a strange deliberation that yet was speed. "Shor Nun," came his thought, and the man of Pareeth straightened under it, "stand up."

Slowly, like an automatum, the commander of the expedition rose, twitching, his hands falling to his sides. His eyes were blank, white things in their sockets, and horrible to look at.

"Shor Nun, look at me, turn your eyes on me," said Seun. He stood half a head taller than the man of Pareeth, very slim and straight, and his eyes seemed to glow in the light that surrounded him.

As though pulled by a greater force, Shor Nun's eyes turned slowly, and first their brown edges, then the pupils showed again. The frozen madness in his face relaxed; he slumped softly into a more natural position—and Seun looked away.

Unsteadily, Shor Nun sat down on a great angling beam. "Don't look for the end of those busses, Drus Nol—it is not good. They knew all the universe, and the ends of it, long before they built this city. The things these men have forgotten embrace all the knowledge our race has, and a thousand thousand times more, and yet they have the ancient characteristics that made certain things possible to the city builders. I do not know what that thing may be, but my eyes had to follow it, and it went into another dimension. Seun, what is that thing?"

"The generator supplied the power for the city, and for the ships of the city, wherever they might be in space. In all the universe they could draw on the power of that generator, through that *sorgan* unit. That was the master unit; from it flowed the power of the generator, instantaneously, to any ship in all space,

so long as its corresponding unit was tuned. It created a field ro-
tating"—and the minds of his hearers refused the term—"which
involves, as well, time.

"In the first revolution it made, the first day it was built, it circled to the ultimate end of time and the universe, and back to the
day it was built. And in all that sweep, every *sorgan* unit tuned
to it must follow. The power that drove it died when the city
was deserted, but it is still making the first revolution, which it
made and completed in the first hundredth of a second it existed.

"Because it circled to the end of time, it passed this moment in
its swing, and every other moment that ever is to be. Were you to
wipe it out with your mightiest atomic blast, it would not be disturbed, for it is in the next instant, as it was when it was built.
And so it is at the end of time, unchanged. Nothing in space or
time can alter that, for it has already been at the end of time.
That is why it rotates still, and will rotate when this world dis-
solves, and the stars die out and scatter as dust in space. Only
when the ultimate equality is established, when no more change
is, or can be will it be at rest—for then other things will be equal
to it, all space equated to it, because space, too, will be unchanged through time.

"Since, in its first swing, it turned to that time, and back to the
day it was built, it radiated its power to the end of space and
back. Anywhere, it might be drawn on, and was drawn on by the
ships that sailed to other stars."

Ron Thule glanced very quickly toward and away from the
sorgan unit. It rotated motionlessly, twinkling and winking in
swift immobility. It was some ten feet in diameter, a round spheroid of rigidly fixed coils that slipped away and away in flashing
speed. His eyes twisted and his thoughts seemed to freeze as he
looked at it. Then he seemed to see beyond and through it, as
though it were an infinite window, to ten thousand other im-
mobile, swiftly spinning coils revolving in perfect harmony, and
beyond them to strange stars and worlds beyond the suns—a thousand cities such as this on a thousand planets: the empire of the
city builders!

And the dream faded—faded as that dream in stone and crystal and metal, everlasting reality, had faded in the softness of
human tissue.

III

The ship hung motionless over the towers for a long moment.
Sunlight, reddened as the stars sank behind the far hills, flushed

their opalescent beauty with a soft tint, softened even the harsh, utilitarian gray of the great, interstellar cruiser above them into an idle, rosy dream. A dream, perhaps, such as the towers had dreamed ten thousand times ten thousand times these long aeons they had waited?

Ron Thule looked down at them, and a feeling of satisfaction and fulfillment came to him. Pareeth would send her children. A colony here, on this ancient world, would bring a new, stronger blood to wash up in a great tide, to carry the ideals this race had forgotten to new heights, new achievements. Over the low hills, visible from this elevation, lay the simple, rounded domes of the people of Rhth—Seun and his little clan of half a hundred—the dwindling representatives of a once-great race.

It would mean death to these people—these last descendants. A new world, busy with a great work of reconquering this system, then all space! They would have no time to protect and care for these forgetful ones; these people of Rhth inevitably would dwindle swiftly in a strange, busy world. They who had forgotten progress five millions of years before; they who had been untrue to the dream of the city builders.

It was for Pareeth, and the sons of Pareeth to carry on the abandoned path again——

CONCLUSION OF THE REPORT TO THE COMMITTEE OF PAREETH SUBMITTED BY SHOR NUN, COMMANDER OF THE FIRST INTERSTELLAR EXPEDITION

—thus it seemed wise to me that we leave at the end of a single week, despite the objections of those members of the expedition personnel who had had no opportunity to see this world. It was better not to disturb the decadent inhabitants of Rhth in any further degree, and better that we return to Pareeth with these reports as soon as might be, since building operations would soon commence on the twelve new ships.

I suggest that these new ships be built of the new material *rhthite*, superior to our best previous materials. As has been shown by the incredible endurance of the buildings of the city, this material is exceedingly stable, and we have found it may be synthesized from the cheapest materials, saving many millions in the construction work to be undertaken.

It has been suggested by a certain member of the expedition, notable Thon Raul, the anthropologist, that we may underestimate the degree of civilization actually retained by the people of Rhth, specifically that it is possible that a type of civilization exists so radically divergent from our own, that it is to us unrecognizable as civilization. His suggestion of a purely mental civilization of a high order seems untenable in the face of the fact that Seun, a man well respected by his fellows, was unable to project his thoughts clearly at any time, nor was there any evidence that any large proportion of his thoughts were to himself of a high order of clarity. His answers were typified by "I have forgotten the development——" or "It is difficult for me to explain——" or "The exact mechanism is not understood by all of us—a few historians——"

It is, of course, impossible to disprove the assertion that such a civilization is possible, but there arises in my mind the question of advantage gained, it being a maxim of any evolutionary or advancing process that the change so made is, in some manner, beneficial to the modified organism of society. Evidently, on the statements made by Seun of Rhth, they have forgotten the knowledge once held by the mighty race that built the cities, and have receded to a state of repose without labor or progress of any kind.

Thon Raul has mentioned the effect produced on me by close observation of the *sorgan* mechanism, and further stated that Seun was able to watch this same mechanism without trouble, and able to benefit me after my unfortunate experience. I would point out that mental potentialities decline extremely slowly; it is possible that the present decadent people have the mental potentialities, still inherent in them, that permitted the immense civilization of the city builders.

It lies there, dormant. They are lost for lack of the driving will that makes it effective. The *Pareeth,* the greatest ship our race has ever built, is powered, fueled, potentially mighty now—and inert for lack of a man's driving will, since no one is at her helm.

So it is with them. Still, the mental capacity of the race overshadows us. But the divine fire of ambition has died. They rely wholly on materials and tools given them by a long-dead people, using even these in an automatic and uncomprehending way, as they do their curious flying suits.

Finally, it is our conclusion that the twelve ships under consideration should be completed with all possible speed, and the program as at present outlined carried out in full; *i.e.* seven thousand, six hundred and thirty-eight men and women between the ages of eighteen and twenty-eight will be selected on a basis of health, previous family history, personal character and ability as determined by psychological tests. These will be transported, together with a basic list of necessities, to the new planet, leaving in the early months of the coming year.

Six years will be required for this trip. At the end of the first year on the new planet, when some degree of organization has been attained, one ship, refueled, will return to Pareeth. At the end of the second year two ships will return from Rhth with all data accumulated in that period. Thereafter, two will sail each year.

On Pareeth, new ships will be manufactured at whatever rate seems practicable, that more colonists may be sent as swiftly as they desire. It is suggested, however, that, in view of the immense scientific advancements already seen in the cities of Rhth, no new ships be made until a ship returns with the reports of the first year's studies, in order that any resultant scientific advances may be incorporated.

The present crew of the *Pareeth* have proven themselves in every way competent, courageous and coöperative. As trained and experienced interstellar operators, it is further suggested that the one hundred men be divided among the thirteen ships to sail, the *Pareeth* retaining at least fifty of her present crew and acting as guide to the remainder of the fleet. Ron Thule, it is specifically requested, shall be astronomical commander of the fleet aboard the flagship. His astronomical work in positioning and calculating the new system has been of the highest order, and his presence is vitally needed.

> Signed by me, SHOR NUN, this
> thirty-second day after landing.

UNANIMOUS REPORT OF THE COMMITTEE OF PAREETH ON THE FIRST EXPEDITION TO THE PLANET RHTH

The Committee of Pareeth, after due consideration of the reports of Folder R127-s6-I1, entitled "Interstellar Exploration Reports, Expedition I" do send to commander of said expedition, Shor Nun, greetings.

The committee finds the reports highly satisfying, both in view of the successful nature of the expedition, and in that they represent an almost unanimous opinion.

In consequence, it is ordered that the ships designated by the department of engineering plan as numbers 18834-18846 be constructed with such expedition as is possible.

It is ordered that the seven thousand six hundred and thirty-eight young people be chosen in the manner prescribed in the attached docket of details.

It is ordered that in the event of the successful termination of the new colonizing expedition, such arrangements shall be made that the present decadent inhabitants of the planet Rhth shall be allowed free and plentiful land; that they shall be in no way molested or attacked. It is the policy of this committee of Pareeth that this race shall be wards of the newly founded Rhth State, to be protected and in all ways aided in their life.

We feel, further, a deep obligation to this race in that the archeological and anthropological reports clearly indicate that it was the race known to them as the city builders who first brought fire, the bow and the hammer to our race in mythological times. Once their race gave ours a foothold on the climb to civilization. It is our firm policy that these last decadent members of that great race shall be given all protection, assistance and encouragement possible to tread again the climbing path.

It is ordered that the first colony city on Rhth shall be established at the spot represented on the accompanying maps as N'yor, as called in the language of the Rhth people, near the point of landing of the first expedition. The near-by settlement of the Rhth people is not to be molested in any way, unless military action is forced upon the colonists.

It is ordered that if this condition shall arise, if the Rhth people object to the proposed settlement at the spot designated as N'yor, arbitration be attempted. Should this measure prove unsuccessful, military penalties shall be exacted, but only to the extent found necessary for effective action. The colonists shall aid in the moving of the settlement of the Rhth people, if the Rhth people do not desire to be near the city of the colonists.

In any case, it is ordered that the colonists shall, in every way within their aid, advance and inspire the remaining people of Rhth.

It is further ordered that Shor Nun, commander, shall be plenipotentiary representative of the committee of Pareeth, with all powers of a discretionary nature, his command to be military and of unquestioned authority until such time as the colony shall have been established for a period of two years. There shall then have been established a representative government of such nature and powers as the colonists themselves find suitable.

It is then suggested that this government, the State of Rhth, shall exchange such representatives with the committee of

Pareeth as are suitable in the dealings of two sovereign powers.

Until the establishment of the State of Rhth, it is further ordered that——

IV

The grassland rolled away very softly among the brown boles of scattered trees. It seemed unchanged. The city seemed unchanged, floating as it had a thousand thousand years halfway between the blue of the sky and the green of the planet. Only it was not alone in its opalescent beauty now; twelve great ships floated serene, motionless, above its towers, matching them in glowing color. And on the low roll of the hill, a thirteenth ship, gray and grim and scarred with eighteen years of nearly continuous space travel, rested. The locks moved; men stepped forth into the light of the low, afternoon sun.

To their right, the mighty monument of the city builders; to their left, the low, rounded domes of the great race's descendants. Ron Thule stepped down from the lock to join the eight department commanders who stood looking across toward the village among the trees.

Shor Nun turned slowly to the men with him, shook his head, smiling. "I did not think to ask. I have no idea what their life span may be. Perhaps the man we knew as Seun has died. When I first landed here, I was a young man. I am middle-aged now. That time may mean old age and extinction to these people."

"There is one man coming toward us now, Shor Nun," said Ron Thule softly. "He is floating on his—what was that name?—it is a long time since I heard it."

The man came nearer leisurely; time seemed to mean little to these people. The soft, blue glow of his suit grew, and he moved a bit more rapidly, as though conscious of their importance. "I—I think that is Seun," said the archeologist. "I have seen those pictures so many times——"

Seun stood before them again, smiling the slow, easy smile they had known twelve years before. Still he stood slim and straight, his face lined only with the easy gravings of humor and kindliness. He was as unchanged as the grassland, as the eternal city. The glow faded as he settled before them, noiselessly. "You have come back to Rhth, Shor Nun?"

"Yes, Seun. We promised you that when we left. And with some of our people as well. We hope to establish a colony here, near the ancient city; hope some day to learn again the secrets of the city builders, to roam space as they once did. Perhaps we will be able to occupy some of the long-deserted buildings of the city and bring life to it again."

"A permanent colony?" asked Seun thoughtfully.

"Yes, Seun."

"There are many other cities here, on this planet, nearly as large, equipped with all the things that made this city. To my race the quiet of the unstirred air is very dear; could you not as easily establish your colony in Shao—or Loun—any of the other places?"

Shor Nun shook his head slowly. "I am sorry, Seun. We had hoped to live near you, that we might both discover again those forgotten secrets. We must stay here, for this was the last city your people deserted; here in it are all the things they ever built, the last achievements of the city builders. We will aid you in moving your colony if you wish, to some other meadowland near the sea. All the world is the same to your people; only this city was built in this way; it was the last to be deserted."

Seun exhaled softly, looked at the ten men of Pareeth. His mind seemed groping, feeling for something. His deep blue eyes misted in thought, then cleared slowly as Ron Thule watched. Slowly, they moved from man to man of the group, pausing a moment at the anthropologist, catching Shor Nun's gaze for an instant, centering slowly on Ron Thule.

Ron Thule looked into the deep eyes for a moment, for a long eternity—deep, clear eyes, like mountain lakes. Subtly, the Rhthman's face seemed to change as he watched the eyes. The languor there changed, became a sense of timelessness, of limitlessness. The pleasant, carefree air became, somehow—different. It was the same, but as the astronomer looked into those eyes, a new interpretation came to him. A sudden, vast fear welled up in him, so that his heart contracted, and a sudden tremor came to his hands. "You have forgotten——" he mumbled unsteadily. "Yes —but you——"

Seun smiled, the firm mouth relaxing in approval. "Yes, Ron Thule. That is enough. I sought your mind. Someone must understand. Remember that only twice in the history of our race have we attempted to alter the course of another's history, for by that you will understand what I must do."

Seun's eyes turned away. Shor Nun was looking at him, and Ron Thule realized, without quite understanding his knowledge, that no time had elapsed for these others. Now he stood motionless, paralyzed with a new understanding.

"We must stay here," Seun's mind voice spoke softly. "I, too, had hoped we might live on this world together, but we are too different. We are too far apart to be so near."

"You do not wish to move?" asked Shor Nun sorrowfully.

Seun looked up. The twelve great interstellar cruisers hovered closer now, forming, almost, a roof over this conference ground. "That would be for the council to say, I know. But I think they would agree with me, Shor Nun."

Vague pictures and ideas moved through their minds, thoughts emanating from Seun's mind. Slowly, his eyes dropped from the twelve opalescent cruisers to the outstretched palm of his hand. His eyes grew bright, and the lines of his face deepened in concentration. The air seemed to stir and move; a tenseness of inaction came over the ten men of Pareeth and they moved restlessly.

Quite abruptly, a dazzling light appeared over Seun's hand, sparkling, myriad colors—and died with a tiny, crystalline clatter. Something lay in his upturned palm: a round, small thing of aquamarine crystal, shot through with veins and arteries of softly pulsing, silver light. It moved and altered as they watched, fading in color, changing the form and outline of light.

Again the tinkling, crystalline clatter came, and some rearrangement had taken place. There lay in his hand a tiny globe of ultimate night, an essence of darkness that no light could illumine, cased in a crystal surface. Stars shone in it, from the heart, from the borders, stars that moved and turned in majestic splendor in infinite smallness. Then faded.

Seun raised his eyes. The darkness faded from the crystal in his hand, and pulsing, little veins of light appeared in it. He raised it in his fingers, and nine of Pareeth's men fell back. Ron Thule looked on with frozen, wooden face.

A wave of blue haze washed out, caught and lifted the men and carried them effortlessly, intangibly back to the lock, through the lock. From the quiet of the grassland they were suddenly in the steel of the ship that clanged and howled with alarms. Great engines bellowed suddenly to life.

Ron Thule stood at the great, clear port light of the lock. Outside, Seun, in his softly glowing suit, floated a few feet from the ground. Abruptly, the great atomic engines of the *Pareeth* shrilled a chorus of ravening hate, and from the three great projectors the annihilating beams tore out, shrieking destruction through the air—and vanished. Seun stood at the junction of death, and his crystal glowed softly. Twelve floating ships screamed to the tortured shriek of overloaded atomics, and the planet below cursed back with quarter-mile-long tongues of lightning.

Somewhere, everywhere, the universe thrummed to a vast, crystalline note, and hummed softly. In that instant, the green meadowland of Rhth vanished; the eternal city dissolved into blackness. Only blackness, starless, lightless, shone outside the lock port light. The soft, clear note of the crystal hummed and beat and surged. The atomic engine's cry died full-throated. An utter, paralyzed quiet descended on the ship, so that the cry of a child somewhere echoed and reverberated noisily down the steel corridors.

The crystal in Seun's hand beat and hummed its note. The blackness beyond the port became gray. One by one, six opalescent ships shifted into view in the blackness beyond, moving with a slow deliberation, as though forced by some infinite power into a certain, predetermined configuration. Like atoms in a crystal lattice they shifted, seemed to click into place and hold steady—neatly, geometrically arranged.

Then noise came back to the ship, sounds that crept in, afraid of themselves, grew courageous and clamored; pounding feet of men, and women's screams.

"We're out of space," gasped Shor Nun. "That crystal—that thing in his hand——"

"In a space of our own," said Ron Thule. "Wait till the note of the crystal dies down. It is weakening, weakening slowly, to us, but it will be gone, and then——"

Shor Nun turned to him, his dark eyes shadowed, his face pale, and drawn. "What do you know—how——"

Ron Thule stood silent. He did not know. Somewhere, a crystal echoed for a moment in rearrangement and tinkling sound; the universe echoed to it softly, as the last, faint tone died away.

"Shor Nun—Shor Nun——" a slow, wailing cry was building up in the ship. Scampering feet on metal floors became a march.

Shor Nun sobbed once. "That crystal—they had not lost the weapons of the city builders. Space of our own? No—it is like the *sorgan:* It rotates us to the end of time! This is the space we knew —when all time has died, and the stars are gone and the worlds are dust. This is the end of the nothingness. The city builders destroyed their enemies thus—by dumping them at the end of time and space. I know. They must have. And Seun had the ancient weapon. When the humming note of the crystal dies—the lingering force of translation——

"Then we shall die, too. Die in the death of death. Oh, gods— Sulon—Sulon, my dear—our son——" Shor Nun, commander, seemed to slump from his frozen rigidity. He turned abruptly away from the port light toward the inner lock door. It opened before him suddenly, and a technician stumbled down, white-faced and trembling.

"Commander—Shor Nun—the engines are stopped. The atoms will not explode; no power can be generated. The power cells are supplying emergency power, but the full strength of the drive does not move nor shake the ship! What—what is this?"

Shor Nun stood silent. The ship thrummed and beat with the softening, dying note of the universe-distant crystal that held all the beginnings and the endings of time and space in a man's hand. The note was fading; very soft and sweet, it was. Through the ship the hysterical cry of voices had changed; it was softening with the thrum, softening, listening to the dying thread of infinitely sweet sound.

Shor Nun shrugged his shoulders, turned away. "It does not matter. The force is fading. Across ten million years the city buildings have reached to protect their descendants."

The note was very low—very faint; a quivering hush bound the ship. Beyond the port light, the six sister ships began to move again, very stealthily away, retreating toward the positions they had held when this force first seized them. Then—

Shor Nun's choked cry was drowned in the cries of the others in the lock. Blinding white light stabbed through the port like a solid, incandescent bar. Their eyes were hot and burning.

Ron Thule, his astronomer's eyes accustomed to rapid, extreme changes of light, recovered first. His word was indistinct, a cross between a sob and a chuckle.

Shor Nun stood beside him, winking tortured eyes. The ship was waking, howling into a mad, frightened life; the children screamed in sympathetic comprehension of their elders' terror.

White, blazing sunlight on green grass and brown dirt. The weathered gray of concrete, and the angular harshness of great building cradles. A sky line of white-tipped, blue mountains, broken by nearer, less-majestic structures of steel and stone and glass, glinting in the rays of a strong, warm sun with a commonness, a familiarity that hurt. A vast nostalgia welled up in them at the sight—

And died before another wave of terror. "Darun Tara," said Shor Nun. "Darun Tara, on Pareeth. I am mad—this is mad. A crazy vision in a crazy instant as the translating force collapses. Darun Tara as it was when we left it six long years ago. Changed —that half-finished shed is still only three quarters finished. I can see Thio Roul, the portmaster there, coming toward us. I am mad. I am five light years away——"

"It is Darun Tara, Shor Nun," Ron Thule whispered. "And the city builders could never have done this. I understand now. I——"

He stopped. The whole great ship vibrated suddenly to thwang like the plucked bass string of a Titan's harp. Creaks and squeals, and little grunting readjustments, the fabric of the cruiser protested.

"My telescope——" cried Ron Thule. He was running toward the inner lock door, into the dark mouth of the corridor.

Again the ship thrummed to a vibrant stroke. The creaking of the girders and strakes protested bitterly; stressed rivets grunted angrily.

Men pounded on the lock door from without. Thio Roul, Ton Gareth, Hol Brawn—familiar faces staring anxiously in. Shor Nun moved dully toward the gate controls——

V

Shor Nun knocked gently at the closed metal door of the ship's observatory. Ron Thule's voice answered, muffled, vague, from beyond.

The commander opened the door; his breath sucked in sibilantly. "Space!" he gasped.

"Come and see, come and see," the astronomer called softly.

Shor Nun instinctively felt his way forward on tiptoe. The great observatory room was space; it was utter blackness, and the corridor lights were swallowed in it the instant the man crossed the threshold. Blackness, starred by tiny, brilliant points, scattered very sparsely, in every direction.

"Seun took the telescope, but he left me this, instead. I understand now; he said that only twice had they attempted to alter a race's history.

"This is space, and *that* is Troth, our own star. Watch——"

The star expanded; the whole of this imageless space exploded outward and vanished through the unseen walls of the observatory. Troth floated alone, centered in the invisible room. Seven tiny dots of light hung near it, glowing in its reflected light.

"And that is our system. Now this is the star of Rhth——"

Space contracted, shifted and exploded, leaving one shining, yellowish star, attended by five brightly visible worlds.

"The other planets are too small or too dimly illuminated to see. When I came there was a new system displayed. This one."

Another planetary system appeared.

"That is the system of Prothor."

"Prothor!" Shor Nun stared. "Five and a half light years away —and planets?"

"Planets. Uninhabited, for I can bring each planet as near as I will. But, Shor Nun"—sorrow crept into the astronomer's voice— "though I can see every detail of each planet of that system, though I can see each outline of the planets of Rhth's system— only those three stars can I see, close by."

"No other planetary systems!"

"No other planetary system that Seun will reveal to us. I understand. One we won on the right of our own minds, our own knowledge; we reached his worlds. We had won a secret from nature by our own powers; it was part of the history of our race. They do not want to molest, or in any way influence the history of a race—so they permitted us to return, if only we did not disturb them. They could not refuse us that, a breach in their feelings of justice.

"But they felt it needful to dispossess us, Shor Nun, and this Seun did. But had he done no more, our history was altered, changed vitally. So—this he gave us; he has shown us another, equally near planetary system that we may use. We have not lost vitally. That is his justice."

"His justice. Yes, I came to you, Ron Thule, because you seemed to know somewhat of the things that happened." Shor Nun's voice was low in the dark of the observatory. He looked at the floating planets of Prothor. "What is—Seun? How has this happened? Do you know? You know that we were greeted by our friends—and they turned away from us.

"Six years have passed for us. They wanted to know what misfortune made us return at the end—of a single year. One year has passed here on Pareeth. My son was born, there in space, and he has passed his fourth birthday. My daughter is two. Yet these things have not happened, for we were gone a single year. Seun has done it, but it cannot be; Seun, the decadent son of the city builders; Seun, who has forgotten the secrets of the ships that sailed beyond the stars and the building of the Titan Towers, opalescent in the sun; Seun, whose people live in a tiny village sheltered from the rains and the sun by a few green trees.

"What are these people of Rhth?"

Ron Thule's voice was a whisper from the darkness. "I come from a far world, by what strange freak we will not say. I am a savage, a rising race that has not learned the secret of fire, nor bow, nor hammer. Tell me, Shor Nun, what is the nature of the two dry sticks I must rub, that fire may be born? Must they be hard, tough oak, or should one be a soft, resinous bit of pine? Tell me how I may make fire."

"Why—with matches or a heat ra— No, Ron Thule. Vague thoughts, meaningless ideas and unclear. I—I have forgotten the ten thousand generations of development. I cannot retreat to a level you, savage of an untrained world, would understand. I—I have forgotten."

"Then tell me, how I must hold the flint, and where must I press with a bit of deer horn that the chips shall fly small and even, so that the knife will be sharp and kill my prey for me? And how shall I rub and wash and treat the wood of the bow, or the skin of the slain animal that I may have a coat that will not be stiff, but soft and pliable?"

"Those, too, I have forgotten. Those are unnecessary things. I cannot help you, savage. I would greet you, and show you the relics of our deserted past in museums. I might conduct you through ancient caves, where mighty rock walls defended my ancestors against the wild things they could not control.

"Yes, Ron Thule. I have forgotten the development."

"Once"—Ron Thule's voice was tense—"the city builder made atomic generators to release the energy bound in that violent twist of space called an atom. He made the *sorgan* to distribute its power to his clumsy shells of metal and crystal—the caves that protected him from the wild things of space.

"Seun has forgotten the atom; he thinks in terms of space. The powers of space are at his direct command. He created the crystal that brought us here from the energy of space, because it made easy a task his mind alone could have done. It was no more needful than is an adding machine. His people have no ships; they are anywhere in space they will without such things. Seun is not a decadent son of the city builders. His people never forgot the dream that built the city. But it was a dream of childhood, and his people were children then. Like a child with his broomstick horse, the mind alone was not enough for thought; the city builders, just as ourselves, needed something of a solid metal and crystal, to make their dreams tangible."

"My son was born in space, and is four. Yet we were gone a single year from Pareeth." Shor Nun sighed.

"Our fleet took six years to cross the gulf of five light years. In thirty seconds, infinitely faster than light, Seun returned us, that there might be the minimum change in our racial history. Time is a function of the velocity of light, and five light years of distance is precisely equal to five years of time multiplied by the square root of minus one. When we traversed five light years of space in no appreciable time, we dropped back, also, through five years of time.

"You and I have spent eighteen years of effort in this exploration, Shor Nun—eighteen years of our manhood. By this hurling us back Seun has forever denied us the planets we earned by those long years of effort. But now he does not deny us wholly.

"They gave us this, and by it another sun, with other planets. This Seun gave not to me, as an astronomer; it is his gift to the race. Now it is beyond us ever to make another. And this which projects this space around us will cease to be, I think, on the day we land on those other planets of that other sun, where Seun will be to watch us—as he may be here now, to see that we understand his meanings.

"I know only this—that sun I can see, and the planets circling it. The sun of Rhth I can see, and those planets, and our own. But —though these others came so near at the impulse of my thoughts, no other sun in all space can I see so near.

"That, I think, is the wish of Seun and his race."

The astronomer stiffened suddenly.

Shor Nun stood straight and tense.

"Yes," whispered Seun, very softly, in their minds.

Ron Thule sighed.

1932

Seeds of the Dusk/

by RAYMOND Z. GALLUN

A novelette of the days when Earth grows old and cold—when all Earth's folk are keening wits to survive—

It was a spore, microscopic in size. Its hard shell—resistant to the utter dryness of interplanetary space—harbored a tiny bit of plant protoplasm. That protoplasm, chilled almost to absolute zero, possessed no vital pulsation now—only a grim potentiality, a savage capacity for revival, that was a challenge to Fate itself.

For years the spore had been drifting and bobbing erratically between the paths of Earth and Mars, along with billions of other spores of the same kind. Now the gravity of the Sun drew it a few million miles closer to Earth's orbit, now powerful magnetic radiations from solar vortices forced it back toward the world of its origin.

It seemed entirely a plaything of chance. And, of course, up to a point it was. But back of its erratic, unconscious wanderings, there was intelligence that had done its best to take advantage of the law of averages.

The desire for rebirth and survival was the dominant urge of this intelligence. For this was during the latter days, when Earth itself was showing definite signs of senility, and Mars was near as dead as the Moon.

Strange, intricate spore-pods, conceived as a man might conceive a new invention, but put into concrete form by a process of minutely exact growth control, had burst explosively toward a black, spacial sky. In dusty clouds the spores had been hurled upward into the vacuum thinness that had once been an extensive atmosphere. Most of them had, of course, dropped back to the red, arid soil; but a comparative few, buffeted by feeble air currents, and measured numerically in billions, had found their way from the utterly tenuous upper reaches of Mars' gaseous envelope into the empty ether of the void.

With elements of a conscious purpose added, the thing that was taking place was a demonstration of the ancient Arrhenius

Spore Theory, which, countless ages ago, had explained the prop-
agation of life from world to world.

The huge, wonderful parent growths were left behind, to continue a hopeless fight for survival on a burnt-out world. During
succeeding summer seasons they would hurl more spores into
the interplanetary abyss. But soon they themselves would be only
brown, mummied relics—one with the other relics of Mars; the
gray, carven monoliths; the strange, hemispherical dwellings,
dotted with openings arranged like the cells of a honeycomb.
Habitations of an intelligent animal folk, long perished, who had
never had use for halls or rooms, as such things are known to
men on Earth.

The era of utter death would come to Mars, when nothing
would move on its surface except the shadows shifting across
dusty deserts, and the molecules of sand and rock vibrating with
a little warmth from the hot, though shrunken, Sun. Death—complete death! But the growths which were the last civilized beings
of Mars had not originated there. Once they had been on the
satellites of Jupiter, too. And before that—well, perhaps even the
race memory of their kind had lost the record of those dim, distant ages. Always they had waited their chance, and when the
time came—when a world was physically suited for their development—they had acted.

A single spore was enough to supply the desired foothold on
a planet. Almost inevitably—since chance is, in fundamentals, a
mathematical element depending on time and numbers and rep-
etition—that single spore reached the upper atmosphere of Earth.

For months, it bobbed erratically in tenuous, electrified gases.
It might have been shot into space again. Upward and downward
it wandered; but with gravity to tug at its insignificant mass,
probability favored its ultimate descent to the harsh surface.

It found a resting place, at last, in a frozen desert gully.
Around the gully were fantastic, sugar-loaf mounds. Near-by was
one thin, ruined spire of blue porcelain—an empty reminder of
a gentler era, long gone.

The location thus given to it seemed hardly favorable in its
aspect. For this was the northern hemisphere, locked now in the
grip of a deadly winter. The air, depleted through the ages, as
was the planet's water supply, was arid and thin. The temperature, though not as rigorous and deadening as that of interplanetary space, ranged far below zero. Mars in this age was near
dead; Earth was a dying world.

But perhaps this condition, in itself, was almost favorable. The spore belonged to a kind of life developed to meet the challenge of a generally much less friendly environment than that of even this later-day Earth.

There was snow in that desert gully—maybe a quarter-inch depth of it. The rays of the Sun—white and dwarfed after so many eons of converting its substance into energy—did not melt any of that snow even at noon. But this did not matter. The life principle within the spore detected favorable conditions for its germination, just as, in spring, the vital principle of Earthly seeds had done for almost incalculable ages.

By a process parallel to that of simple fermentation, a tiny amount of heat was generated within the spore. A few crystals of snow around it turned to moisture, a minute quantity of which the alien speck of life absorbed. Roots finer than spiderweb grew, groping into the snow. At night they were frozen solid, but during the day they resumed their brave activity.

The spore expanded, but did not burst. For its shell was a protecting armor which must be made to increase in size gradually without rupture. Within it, intricate chemical processes were taking place. Chlorophyl there was absorbing sunshine and carbon dioxide and water. Starch and cellulose and free oxygen were being produced.

So far, these processes were quite like those of common terrestrial flora. But there were differences. For one thing, the oxygen was not liberated to float in the atmosphere. It had been ages since such lavish waste had been possible on Mars, whose thin air had contained but a small quantity of oxygen in its triatomic form, ozone, even when Earth was young.

The alien thing stored its oxygen, compressing the gas into the tiny compartments in its hard, porous, outer shell. The reason was simple. Oxygen, combining with starch in a slow, fermentive combustion, could produce heat to ward off the cold that would otherwise stop growth.

The spore had become a plant now. First, it was no bigger than a pinhead. Then it increased its size to the dimensions of a small marble, its fuzzy, green-brown shape firmly anchored to the soil itself by its long, fibrous roots. Like any terrestrial growth, it was an intricate chemical laboratory, where transformations took place that were not easy to comprehend completely.

And now, perhaps, the thing was beginning to feel the first glimmerings of a consciousness, like a human child rising out of the blurred, unremembering fog of birth. Strange, oily nodules, scattered throughout its tissues, connected by means of a complex network of delicate, white threads, which had the functions of a nervous system, were developing and growing—giving to the sporeplant from Mars the equivalent of a brain. Here was a sentient vegetable in the formative stage.

A sentient vegetable? Without intelligence it is likely that the ancestors of this nameless invader from across the void would long ago have lost their battle for survival.

What senses were given to this strange mind, by means of which it could be aware of its environment? Undoubtedly it possessed faculties of sense that could detect things in a way that was as far beyond ordinary human conception as vision is to those individuals who have been born blind. But in a more simple manner it must have been able to feel heat and cold and to hear sounds, the latter perhaps by the sensitivity of its fine, cilia-like spines. And certainly it could see in a way comparable to that of a man.

For, scattered over the round body of the plant, and imbedded deep in horny hollows in its shell, were little organs, lensed with a clear vegetable substance. These organs were eyes, developed, perhaps, from far more primitive light-sensitive cells, such as many forms of terrestrial flora possess.

But during those early months, the spore plant saw little that could be interpreted as a threat, swiftly to be fulfilled. Winter ruled, and the native life of this desolate region was at a standstill.

There was little motion except that of keen, cutting winds, shifting dust, and occasional gusts of fine, dry snow. The white, shrunken Sun rose in the east, to creep with protracted slowness across the sky, shedding but the barest trace of warmth. Night came, beautiful and purple and mysterious, yet bleak as the crystalline spirit of an easy death.

Through the ages, Earth's rate of rotation had been much decreased by the tidal drag of Solar and Lunar gravities. The attraction of the Moon was now much increased, since the satellite was nearer to Terra than it had been in former times. Because of the decreased rate of rotation, the days and nights were correspondingly lengthened.

All the world around the spore plant was a realm of bleak, unpeopled desolation. Only once, while the winter lasted, did anything happen to break the stark monotony. One evening, at moonrise, a slender metal car flew across the sky with the speed of a bullet. A thin propelling streamer of fire trailed in its wake, and the pale moonglow was reflected from its prow. A shrill, mechanical scream made the rarefied atmosphere vibrate, as the craft approached to a point above the desert gully, passed, and hurtled away, to leave behind it only a startling silence and an aching memory.

For the spore plant did remember. Doubtless there was a touch of fear in that memory, for fear is a universal emotion, closely connected with the law of self-preservation, which is engrained in the texture of all life, regardless of its nature or origin.

Men. Or rather, the cold, cruel, cunning little beings who were the children of men. The Itorloo, they called themselves. The invader could not have known their form as yet, or the name of the creatures from which they were descended. But it could guess something of their powers from the flying machine they had built. Inherited memory must have played a part in giving the queer thing from across the void this dim comprehension. On other worlds its ancestors had encountered animal folk possessing a similar science. And the spore plant was surely aware that here on Earth the builders of this speeding craft were its most deadly enemies.

The Itorloo, however, inhabiting their vast underground cities, had no knowledge that their planet had received an alien visitation—one which might have deadly potentialities. And in this failure to know, the little spore plant, hidden in a gully where no Itorloo foot had been set in a thousand years, was safe.

Now there was nothing for it to do but grow and prepare to reproduce its kind, to be watchful for lesser enemies, and to develop its own peculiar powers.

It is not to be supposed that it must always lack, by its very nature, an understanding of physics and chemistry and biological science. It possessed no test tubes, or delicate instruments, as such things were understood by men. But it was gifted with something—call it an introspective sense—which enabled it to study in minute detail every single chemical and physical process that went on within its own substance. It could feel not only the juices coursing sluggishly through its tissues, but it could feel, too, in a kind of atomic pattern, the change of water and carbon dioxide into starch and free oxygen.

Gift a man with the same power that the invader's kind had acquired, perhaps by eons of practice and directed will—that of feeling vividly even the division of cells, and the nature of the protoplasm in his own tissues—and it is not hard to believe that he would soon delve out even the ultimate secret of life. And in the secret of life there must be involved almost every conceivable phase of practical science.

The spore plant proceeded with its marvelous self-education, part of which must have been only recalling to mind the intricate impressions of inherited memories.

Meanwhile it studied carefully its bleak surroundings, prompted not only by fear, but by curiosity as well. To work effectively, it needed understanding of its environment. Intelligence it possessed beyond question; still it was hampered by many limitations. It was a plant, and plants have not an animal's capacity for quick action, either of offense or defense. Here, forever, the entity from across the void was at a vast disadvantage, in this place of pitiless competition. In spite of all its powers, it might now have easily been destroyed.

The delicate, ruined tower of blue porcelain, looming up from the brink of the gully— The invader, scrutinizing it carefully for hours and days, soon knew every chink and crack and fanciful arabesque on its visible side. It was only a ruin, beautiful and mysterious alike by sunshine and moonlight, and when adorned with a fine sifting of snow. But the invader, lost on a strange world, could not be sure of its harmlessness.

Close to the tower were those rude, high, sugar-loaf mounds, betraying a sinister cast. They were of hard-packed Earth, dotted with many tiny openings. But in the cold, arid winter, there was no sign of life about them now.

All through those long, arctic months, the spore plant continued to develop, and to grow toward the reproductive stage. And it was making preparations too—combining the knowledge acquired by its observations with keen guesswork, and with a science apart from the manual fabrication of metal and other substances.

II

A milder season came at last. The Sun's rays were a little warmer now. Some of the snow melted, moistening the ground enough to germinate Earthly seeds. Shoots sprang up, soon to develop leaves and grotesque, devilish-looking flowers.

In the mounds beside the blue tower a slow awakening took place. Millions of little, hard, reddish bodies became animated once more, ready to battle grim Nature for sustenance. The ages had done little to the ants, except to increase their fierceness and cunning. Almost any organic substances could serve them as food, and their tastes showed but little discrimination between one dainty and another. And it was inevitable, of course, but presently they should find the spore plant.

Nor were they the latter's only enemies, even in this desert region. Of the others, Kaw and his black-feathered brood were the most potent makers of trouble. Not because they would attempt active offense themselves, but because they were able to spread news far and wide.

Kaw wheeled alone now, high in the sunlight, his ebon wings outstretched, his cruel, observant little eyes studying the desolate terrain below. Buried in the sand, away from the cold, he and his mate and their companions had slept through the winter. Now Kaw was fiercely hungry. He could eat ants if he had to, but there should be better food available at this time of year.

Once, his keen eyes spied gray movement far below. As if his poised and graceful flight was altered by the release of a trigger, Kaw dived plummet-like and silent toward the ground.

His attack was more simple and direct than usual. But it was successful. His reward was a large, long-tailed rodent, as clever as himself. The creature uttered squeaks of terror as meaningful as human cries for help. In a moment, however, Kaw split its intelligently rounded cranium with a determined blow from his strong, pointed beak. Bloody brains were devoured with indelicate gusto, to be followed swiftly by the less tasty flesh of the victim. If Kaw had ever heard of table manners, he didn't bother with them. Kaw was intensely practical.

His crop full, Kaw was now free to exercise the mischievous curiosity which he had inherited from his ancient forbears. They who had, in the long-gone time when Earth was young, uprooted many a young corn shoot, and had yammered derisively from distant treetops when any irate farmer had gone after them with a gun.

With a clownish skip of his black, scaly feet, and a show-offish swerve of his dusty ebon wings, Kaw took to the air once more. Upward he soared, his white-lidded eyes directed again toward the ground, seeking something interesting to occupy his attention and energies.

Thus, presently, he saw a brownish puff that looked like smoke or dust in the gully beside the ruined blue tower at the pinnacle of which he and his mate were wont to build their nest in summer. Sound came then—a dull, ringing pop. The dusty cloud expanded swiftly upward, widening and thinning until its opacity was dissipated into the clearness of the atmosphere.

Kaw was really startled. That this was so was evinced by the fact that he did not voice his harsh, rasping cry, as he would have done had a lesser occurrence caught his attention. He turned back at first, and began to retreat, his mind recognizing only one possibility in what had occurred. Only the Itorloo, the Children of Men, as far as he knew, could produce explosions like that. And the Itorloo were cruel and dangerous.

However, Kaw did not go far in his withdrawal. Presently—since there were no further alarming developments—he was circling back toward the source of the cloud and the noise. But for many minutes he kept what he considered a safe distance, the while he tried to determine the nature of the strange, bulging, grayish-green thing down there in the gully.

A closer approach, he decided finally, was best made from the ground. And so he descended, alighting several hundred yards distant from the narrow pocket in the desert.

Thence he proceeded to walk cautiously forward, taking advantage of the cover of the rocks and dunes, his feathers gleaming with a dusty rainbow sheen, his large head bobbing with the motion of his advance like any fowl's. His manner was part laughably ludicrous, part scared, and part determined.

And then, peering from behind a large boulder, he saw what he had come to see. It was a bulging, slightly flattened sphere, perhaps a yard across. From it projected flat, oval things of a gray-green color, like the leaves of a cactus. And from these, in turn, grew clublike protuberances of a hard, horny texture—spore-pods. One of them was blasted open, doubtless by the pressure of gas accumulated within it. These spore-pods were probably not as complexly or powerfully designed as those used by the parent growths on Mars, for they were intended for a simpler purpose. The entire plant bristled with sharp spines, and was furred with slender hairs, gleaming like little silver wires.

Around the growth, thousands of ant bodies lay dead, and from its vicinity other thousands of living were retreating. Kaw eyed these evidences critically, guessing with wits as keen as those of a man of old their sinister significance. He knew, too, that presently other spore-pods would burst with loud, disturbing noises.

Kaw felt a twinge of dread. Evolution, working through a process of natural selection—and, in these times of hardship and pitiless competition, putting a premium on intelligence—had given to his kind a brain power far transcending that of his ancestors. He could observe, and could interpret his observations with the same practical comprehension which a primitive human being might display. But, like those primitives, he had developed, too, a capacity to feel superstitious awe.

That gray-green thing of mystery had a fantastic cast which failed to identify it with—well—with naturalness. Kaw was no botanist, certainly; still he could recognize the object as a plant of some kind. But those little, bright, eye-lenses suggested an unimaginable scrutiny. And those spines, silvery in sheen, suggested ghoulish animation, the existence of which Kaw could sense as a nameless and menacing unease.

He could guess, then, or imagine—or even know, perhaps—that here was an intruder who might well make itself felt with far-reaching consequences in the future. Kaw was aware of the simple fact that most of the vegetation he was acquainted with grew from seeds or the equivalent. And he was capable of concluding that this flattened spheroid reproduced itself in a manner not markedly unfamiliar. That is, if one was to accept the evidence of the spore-pods. Billions of spores, scattering with the wind! What would be the result?

Kaw would not have been so troubled, were it not for those crumpled thousands of ant bodies, and the enigma of their death. It was clear that the ants had come to feed on the invader—but they had perished. How? By some virulent plant poison, perhaps?

The conclusions which intelligence provides can produce fear where fear would otherwise be impossible. Kaw's impulse was to seek safety in instant departure, but horror and curiosity fascinated him. Another deeper, more reasoned urge commanded him. When a man smells smoke in his house at night, he does not run away; he investigates. And so it was with Kaw.

He hopped forward cautiously toward the invader. A foot from its rough, curving side he halted. There, warily, as if about to attack a poisonous lizard, he steeled himself. Lightly and swiftly his beak shot forward. It touched the tip of a sharp spine.

The result left Kaw dazed. It was as though he had received a stunning blow on the head. A tingling, constricting sensation shot through his body, and he was down, flopping in the dust.

Electricity. Kaw had never heard of such a thing. Electricity generated chemically in the form of the invader, by a process analogous to that by which, in dim antiquity, it had been generated in the bodies of electric eels and other similar creatures.

However, there was a broad difference here between the subject and the analogy. Electric eels had never understood the nature of their power, for they were as unresponsible for it as they were unresponsible for the shape of the flesh in which they had been cast. The spore plant, on the other hand, comprehended minutely. Its electric organs had been minutely preplanned and conceived before one living cell of their structure had been caused to grow on another. And these organs were not inherited, but were designed to meet the more immediate needs of self-protection. During the winter, the invader, studying its surroundings, had guessed well.

Slowly Kaw's brain cleared. He heard an ominous buzzing, and knew that it issued from the plant. But what he did not know was that, like the electric organs, the thing's vocal equipment was invented for possible use in its new environment. For days, since the coming of spring, the invader had been listening to sounds of various kinds, and had recognized their importance on Earth.

Now Kaw had but one thought, and that was to get away. Still dazed and groggy, he leaped into the air. From behind him, in his hurried departure, he heard a dull plop. More billions of spores, mixing with the wind, to be borne far and wide.

But now, out of his excitement, Kaw drew a reasoned and fairly definite purpose. He had a fair idea of what he was going to do, even though the course of action he had in mind might involve him with the greatest of his enemies. Yet, when it came to a choice, he would take the known in preference to the unknown.

He soared upward toward the bright blue of the heavens. The porcelain tower, the ant hills, and the low mounds which marked the entrances to the rodent colonies slipped swiftly behind. As if the whole drab landscape were made to move on an endless belt.

Kaw was looking for his mate, and for the thirty-odd, black-winged individuals who formed his tribe. Singly and in small groups, he contacted and collected them. Loud, raucous cries, each with a definite verbal meaning, were exchanged. Menace was on the Earth—bizarre, nameless menace. Excitement grew to fever pitch.

Dusk, beautiful and soft and forbidding, found the bird clan assembled in a chamber high-placed in a tremendous edifice many miles from where Kaw had made his discovery. The building belonged to the same gentle culture which had produced the blue porcelain tower. The floor of the chamber was doubtless richly mosaiced. But these were relics of departed splendor now thickly masked with dust and filth.

From the walls, however, painted landscapes of ethereal

beauty, and the faces of a happy humankind of long ago peeped through the gathering shadows. They were like ghosts, a little awed at what had happened to the world to which they had once belonged. Those gentle folk had dwelt in a kindlier climate which was now stripped forever from the face of the Earth. And they had been wiped out by creatures who were human too, but of a different, crueler race.

Through delicately carven screens of pierced marble, far up on the sides of the chamber's vast, brooding rotunda, the fading light of day gleamed, like a rose glow through the lacework of fairies.

But this palace of old, dedicated to laughter and fun and luxury, and to the soaring dreams of the fine arts, was now only a chill, dusty gathering place for a clan of black-winged, gruesome harpies.

They chuckled and chattered and cawed, like the crows of dead eras. But these sounds, echoing eerily beneath cloistered arches, dim and abhorrent in the advancing gloom of night, differed from that antique yammering. It constituted real, intelligent conversation.

Kaw, perched high on a fancifully wrought railing of bronze, green with the patina of age, urged his companions with loud cries, and with soft, pleading notes. In his own way, he had some of the qualities of a master orator. But, as all through an afternoon of similar arguing, he was getting nowhere. His tribe was afraid. And so it was becoming more and more apparent that he must undertake his mission alone. Even Teka, his mate, would not accompany him.

At last Kaw ruffled his neck feathers, and shook his head violently in an avian gesture of disgust. He leaped from his perch and shot through a glassless window with an angry scream that was like the curse of a black ghoul.

It was the first time that he had ever undertaken a long journey at night. But in his own judgment, necessity was such that no delay could be tolerated.

The stars were sharp and clear, the air chill and frosty. The ground was dotted sparsely with faint glimmerings from the chimneys of the crude furnaces which, during the colder nights of spring and fall, warmed the underground rodent colonies.

After a time the Moon rose, huge and yellow, like the eye of a monster. In that bloom and silence, Kaw found it easy to feel the creeping and imperceptible, yet avalanching, growth of horror. He could not be sure, of course, that he was right in his guess that the mission he had undertaken was grimly important. But his savage intuition was keen.

The Itorloo—the Children of Men—he must see them, and tell them what he knew. Kaw was aware that the Itorloo had no love for any but themselves. But they were more powerful than the winds and the movements of the Sun and Moon themselves. They would find a swift means to defeat the silent danger.

And so, till the gray dawn, Kaw flew on and on, covering many hundreds of miles, until he saw a low dome of metal, capping a hill. The soft half-light of early morning sharpened its outlines to those of a beautiful, ebon silhouette, peaceful and yet forbidding. Beneath it, as Kaw knew, was a shaft leading down to the wonderous underworld of the Itorloo, as intriguing to his mind as a shadowland of magic.

Fear tightened its constricting web around Kaw's heart—but retreat was something that must not be. There was too much at stake ever to permit a moment of hesitation.

Kaw swung into a wide arc, circling the dome. His long wings, delicately poised for a soaring glide, did not flap now, but dipped and rose to capture and make use of the lifting power of every vagrant wisp of breeze. And from his lungs issued a loud, raucous cry.

"Itorloo!" he screamed. "Itorloo!"

The word, except for its odd, parrot-like intonation, was pronounced in an entirely human manner. Kaw, in common with his crow ancestors, possessed an aptitude for mimicry of the speech of men.

Tensely he waited for a sign, as he swung lower and nearer to the dome.

III

Zar felt irritable. He did not like the lonely surface vigil and the routine astronomical checkings that constituted his duty. All night he'd sat there at his desk with signal lights winking around him, helping surface watchers at the other stations check the position of a new meteor swarm by means of crossing beams of probe rays.

Angles, distances, numbers! Zar was disgusted. Why didn't the construction crews hurry? The whole race could have been moved to Venus long ago, and might just as well have been. For as far as Zar could see, there was no real reason to retain a hold on the burnt-out Earth. The native Venusians should have been crushed a century back. There wasn't any reason why this pleasant task shouldn't have been accomplished then—no reason except stupid, official inertia!

The sound of a shrill bird cry, throbbing from the pickup diaphragm on the wall, did not add any sweetening potion to Zar's humor. At first he paid no attention; but the insistent screaming of the name of his kind—"Itorloo! Itorloo!"—at length aroused him to angry action.

His broad, withered face, brown and hideous and goblinlike, twisted itself into an ugly grimace. He bounded up from his chair, and seized a small, pistol-like weapon.

A moment later he was out on the sandy slopes of the hill, looking up at the black shape that swooped and darted timidly, close to his head. On impulse Zar raised his weapon, no thought of compassion in his mind.

But Kaw screamed again: "Itorloo! Loaaah!"

In Zar's language, "Loaaah!" meant "Danger!" very emphatically. Zar's hand, bent on execution, was stayed for the moment at least. His shrewd little eyes narrowed, and from his lips there issued yammering sounds which constituted an understandable travesty of the speech of Kaw's kind.

"Speak your own tongue, creature!" he ordered sharply. "I can understand!"

Still swooping and darting nervously, Kaw screamed forth his story, describing in quaint manner the thing he had seen, employing comparisons such as any primitive savage would use. In this way the invader was like a boulder, in that way it was like a thorn cactus, and in other ways it resembled the instruments of death which the Itorloo employed. In all ways it was strange, and unlike anything ever seen before.

And Zar listened with fresh and calculated attention, getting from this bird creature the information he required to locate the strange miracle. Kaw was accurate and clear enough in giving his directions.

Zar might have forgotten his inherent ruthlessness where his feathered informer was concerned, had not Kaw become a trifle too insistent in his exhortations to action. He lingered too long and screamed too loudly.

Irritated, Zar raised his weapon. Kaw swept away at once, but there was no chance for him to get out of range. Invisible energy shot toward him. Black feathers were torn loose, and floated aflame in the morning breeze. Kaw gave a shrill shriek of agony and reproach. Erratically he wavered to the ground.

Zar did not even glance toward him, but retraced his way leisurely into the surface dome. An hour later, however, having received permission from his superiors, he had journeyed across those hundreds of miles to the gully beside the blue porcelain tower. And there he bent over the form of the invader. Zar was somewhat awed. He had never been to Mars. For two hundred thousand years or more, no creature from Earth had ever visited that planet. The Itorloo were too practical to attempt such a useless venture, and their more recent predecessors had lacked some of the adventurous incentive required for so great and hazardous a journey.

But Zar had perused old records, belonging to an era half a million years gone by. He knew that this gray-green thing was at least like the flora of ancient Mars. Into his mind, matter-of-fact for the most part, came the glimmerings of a mighty romance, accentuating within him a consciousness of nameless dread, and of grand interplanetary distances.

Spines. Bulging, hard-shelled, pulpy leaves that stored oxygen under pressure. Chlorophyl that absorbed sunshine and made starch, just as in an ordinary Earthly plant. Only the chlorophyl of this growth was beneath a thick, translucent shell, which altered the quality of the light it could reflect. That was why astronomers in the pre-interplanetary era had doubted the existence of vegetation on Mars. Green plants of Terra, when photographed with infra red light, looked silvery, like things of frost. But—because of their shells—Martian vegetation could not betray its presence in the same manner.

Zar shuddered, though the morning air was not chill by his standards. The little gleaming orbs of the invader seemed to scrutinize him critically and coldly, and with a vast wisdom. Zar saw the shattered spore-pods, knowing that their contents now floated in the air, like dust—floated and settled—presenting a subtle menace whose tool was the unexpected, and against which—because of the myriad numbers of the widely scattered spores—only the most drastic methods could prevail.

Belatedly, then, anger came. Zar drew a knife from his belt. Half in fury and half in experiment, he struck the invader, chipping off a piece of its shell. He felt a sharp electric shock, though by no means strong enough to kill a creature of his size. From the wound he made in the plant, oxygen sizzed softly. But the invader offered no further defense. For the present it had reached the end of its resources.

Zar bounded back. His devilish little weapon flamed then, for a full two minutes. When he finally released pressure on its trigger, there was only a great, smouldering, glowing hole in the ground where the ghoulish thing from across space had stood.

Such was Zar's and the entire Itorloo race's answer to the intruder. Swift destruction! Zar chuckled wickedly. And there were ways to rid Earth of the treacherous menace of the plant intelligences of Mars entirely, even though they would take time.

Besides there was Venus, the world of promise. Soon half of the Itorloo race would be transported there. The others certainly could be accommodated if it became necessary.

Necessary? Zar laughed. He must be getting jittery. What had the Itorloo to fear from those inert, vegetable things? Now he aimed his weapon toward the blue tower, and squeezed the trigger. Weakened tiles crumbled and fell down with a hollow, desolate rattle that seemed to mock Zar's ruthlessness.

Suddenly he felt sheepish. To every intelligent being there is a finer side that prompts and criticizes. And for a moment Zar saw himself and his people a little more as they really were.

Unlike the lesser creatures, the Children of Men had not advanced very much mentally. The ups and downs of history had not favored them. War had reversed the benefits of natural selection, destroying those individuals of the species best suited to carry it on to greater glory. Zar knew this, and perhaps his senseless assault upon the ruined building was but a subconscious gesture of resentment toward the people of long ago who had been kinder and wiser and happier.

Zar regretted his recent act of destroying the spore plant. It should have been preserved for study. But now—well—what was done could not be changed.

He entered his swift, gleaming rocket car. When he closed its cabin door behind him, it seemed that he was shutting out a horde of mocking, menacing ghosts.

In a short while he was back at the surface station. Relieved there of his duty by another little brown man, he descended the huge cylindrical shaft which dropped a mile to the region that was like the realm of the Cyclops. Thrumming sounds, winking lights, shrill shouts of the workers, blasts of incandescent flame, and the colossal majesty of gigantic machines, toiling tirelessly.

In a vast, pillared plaza the keels of spaceships were being laid —spaceships for the migration and the conquest. In perhaps a year—a brief enough time for so enormous a task—they would soar away from Earth, armed to the teeth. There would be thousands of the craft then, for all over the world, in dozens of similar underground places, they were in process of construction.

Zar's vague fears were dissipated in thoughts of conquest to come. The Venus folk annihilated in withering clouds of flame. The glory of the Itorloo carried on and on——

IV

Kaw was not dead. That this was so was almost a miracle, made possible, perhaps, by a savage, indomitable will to live. In his small bird body there was a fierce, burning courage that compensated for many of his faults.

For hours he lay there on the desert sand, a pathetic and crumpled bundle of tattered feathers, motionless except for his labored breathing, and the blinking of his hate-filled eyes. Blood dripped slowly from the hideous, seared wound on his breast, and his whole body ached with a vast, dull anguish.

Toward sundown, however, he managed to hobble and flutter forward a few rods. Here he buried himself shallowly in the sand, where his chilled body would be protected from the nocturnal cold.

For three days he remained thus interred. He was too weak and sick to leave his burrow. Bitterness toward Zar and the other cruel Itorloo, he did not feel. Kaw had lived too long in this harsh region to expect favors. But a black fury stormed within him, nevertheless—a black fury as agonizing as physical pain. He wanted revenge. No, he needed revenge as much as he needed the breath of life. He did not know that Itorloo plans directed against the intruding spores from Mars were already under way, and that—as a by-product—they would destroy his own kind, and all primitive life on the surface of the Earth.

Kaw left his hiding place on the fourth day. Luck favored him, for he found a bit of carrion—part of the dead body of an antelopelike creature.

Somehow, through succeeding weeks and days, he managed to keep alive. The mending of his injured flesh was slow indeed, for the burnt wound was unclean. But he started toward home, hopping along at first, then flying a little, a hundred yards at a time. Tedium and pain were endless. But the fiendish light of what must seem forever fruitless hatred, never faded in those wicked, white-lidded eyes. Frequently Kaw's long, black beak snapped in a vicious expression of boundless determination.

Weeks of long days became a month, and then two months. Starved to a black-clad skeleton, and hopeless of ever being fit to hunt again, Kaw tottered into a deep gorge one evening. Utterly spent, he sank to the ground here, his brain far too weary to take note of any subtle unusualness which the deepening shadows half masked.

He scarcely saw the rounded things scattered here. Had he

noticed them, his blurred vision would have named them small boulders and nothing more. Fury, directed at the Itorloo, had made him almost forget the spore plants. He did not know that this was to be a place of magic. Chance and the vagrant winds had made it so. A hundred spores, out of many millions, had lodged here. Conditions had been just right for their swift development. It was warm, but not too warm. And there was moisture too. Distantly Kaw heard the trickle of water. He wanted to get to it, but his feebleness prevented him.

He must have slept, then, for a long time. It seemed that he awoke at the sound of an odd buzzing, which may have possessed hypnotic properties. He felt as weak and stiff as before, but he was soothed and peaceful now, in spite of his thirst and hunger.

He looked about. The gorge was deep and shadowy. A still twilight pervaded it, though sunshine gilded its bulging, irregular lips far above. These details he took in in a moment.

He looked, then, at the grotesque shapes around him—things which, in the deeper darkness, he had thought to be only boulders. But now he saw that they were spore plants, rough, eerie, brooding, with their little, lensed light-sensitive organs agleam.

The excitement of terror seized him, and he wanted to flee, as from a deadly enemy. But this urge did not last long. The hypnotic buzz, which issued from the diaphragmic vocal organs of the plants, soothed and soothed and soothed, until Kaw felt very relaxed.

There were dead ants around him, doubtless the victims of electrocution. Since no better food was within reach, Kaw hopped here and there, eating greedily.

After that he hobbled to the brackish spring that dripped from the wall, and drank. Next he dropped to the ground, his fresh drowsiness characterized by sleepy mutterings about himself, his people, and the all-wise Itorloo. And it seemed, presently, that the buzzing of the invaders changed in character at last, seeming to repeat his own mutterings clumsily, like a child learning to talk.

"Kaw! Itorloo!" And other words and phrases belonging to the speech of the crow clans.

It was the beginning of things miraculous and wonderful for Kaw, the black-feathered rascal. Many suns rose and set, but somehow he felt no urge to wander farther toward his home region. He did not know the Lethean fascination of simple hypnotism. True, he sallied afield farther and farther, as his increasing strength permitted. He hunted now, eating bugs and beetles for the most part. But always he returned to the gorge, there to listen to the weird growths, buzzing, chattering, speaking to him in his own tongue. In them there seemed somehow to be a vague suggestion of the benignance of some strange, universal justice, in spite of their horror.

And night and day, rocket cars, streamlined and gleaming, swept over the desert. Now and then beams of energy were unleashed from them, whipping the sand into hot flame, destroying the invading spore plants that had struck root here and there. Only the law of chance kept them away from the gorge, as doubtless it allowed them to miss other hiding places of alien life. For the wilderness was wide.

But this phase of the Itorloo battle against the invading spore plants was only a makeshift preliminary, intended to keep the intruders in check. Only the Itorloo themselves knew about the generators now being constructed far underground—generators which, with unseen emanations, could wipe out every speck of living protoplasm on the exposed crust of the planet. Theirs was a monumental task, and a slow one. But they meant to be rid, once and for all, of the subtle threat which had come perhaps to challenge their dominion of the Earth. Kaw and his kind, the rodents, the ants, and all the other simple People of the Dusk of Terra's Greatness, were seemingly doomed.

Kaw's hatred of the Children of Men was undimmed, more justly than he was aware. Thus it was easy for him to listen when he was commanded: "Get an Itorloo! Bring him here! Alone! On foot!"

Zar was the logical individual to produce, for he was the nearest, the most readily available. But summer was almost gone before Kaw encountered the right opportunity, though he watched with care at all times.

Evening, with Venus and the Moon glowing softly in the sky. Kaw was perched on a hilltop, close to the great surface dome, watching as he had often watched before. Out of its cylindrical hangar, Zar's flier darted, and then swung in a slow arc. Presently it headed at a leisurely pace into the northwest. For once its direction was right, and it was not traveling too fast for Kaw to keep pace with it. Clearly its pilot was engaged in a rambling pleasure jaunt, which had no definite objective.

Kaw, pleased and excited, fell in behind at a safe distance. There he remained until the craft was near the gorge. Now there was danger, but if things were done right——

He flapped his wings violently to catch up with his mechanical quarry. He screamed loudly: "Itorloo! Itorloo! Descend! Descend! I am Kaw, who informed you of the unknowns long ago! I would show you more! More! More!" All this in shrill, avian chatterings.

Kaw's trickery was naively simple. But Zar heard, above the noise of his rocket blasts. Suspicion? He felt it, of course. There was no creature in this era who accepted such an invitation without question. Yet he was well armed. In his own judgment he should be quite safe. Curiosity led him on.

He shut off his rocket motors, and uttered the bird jargon, questioning irritably: "Where? What is it, black trickster?"

Kaw skittered about defensively. "Descend!" he repeated. "Descend to the ground. The thing that bears you cannot take you where we must go!"

The argument continued for some little time, primitive with matching curiosity and suspicion.

And meanwhile, in the gloomy gorge cut in vague geologic times by some gushing stream, entities waited patiently. Sap flowed in their tissues, as in the tissues of any other vegetation, but the fine hairs on their forms detected sounds, and their light-sensitive cells served as eyes. Within their forms were organs equivalent to human nerve and brain. They did not use tools or metals, but worked in another way, dictated by their vast disadvantages when compared to animal intelligences. Yet they had their advantages, too.

Now they waited, dim as bulking shadows. They detected the excited cries of Kaw, who was their instrument. And perhaps they grew a little more tense, like a hunter in a blind, when he hears the quacking of ducks through a fog.

There was a grating of pebbles and a little brown man, clad in a silvery tunic, stepped cautiously into view. There was a weapon clutched in his slender hand. He paused, as if suddenly awed and fearful. But no opportunity to retreat was given him.

A spore-pod exploded with a loud plop in the confined space. A mass of living dust filled the gorge, like a dense, opaque cloud, choking, blinding. Zar squeezed the trigger of his weapon impulsively. Several of the invaders were blasted out of existence. Stones clattered down from where the unaimed beam of energy struck the wall.

Panic seized the little man, causing him to take one strangling breath. In a few moments he was down, writhing helpless on the ground. Choked by the finely divided stuff, his consciousness seemed to drop into a black hole of infinity. He, Zar, seemed

about to pay for his misdeeds. With a mad fury he heard the derisive screams of Kaw, who had tricked him. But he could not
curse in return, and presently his thoughts vanished away to
nothing.

Awareness of being alive came back to him very slowly and
painfully. At first he felt as though he had pneumonia—fever, suffocation, utter vagueness of mind. Had the spores germinated
within his lungs, he would surely have died. But they did not,
there; conditions were too moist and warm for them. Gradually
he coughed them up.

He felt cold with a bitter, aching chill, for the weather had
changed with the lateness of the season. Fine snow sifted down
into the gorge from clouds that were thin and pearly and sun-
gilded. Each tiny crystal of ice glittered with a thousand prismatic
hues as it slowly descended. And the silence was deathly, bearing
a burden of almost tangible desolation. In that burden there
seemed to crowd all the antique history of a world—history whose
grand movement shaded gradually toward stark, eternal death.

Zar wanted to flee this awful place that had become like part
of another planet. He jerked his body as if to scramble feebly to
his feet. He found then that he was restrained by cordlike tendrils,
hard as horn, and warm with a faint, fermentive, animal-like heat.
Like the beat of a nameless pulse, tiny shocks of electricity
tingled his flesh in a regular rhythm.

It was clear to Zar that while he had been inert the tendrils had
fastened themselves slowly around him, in a way that was half
like the closing of an ancient Venus Flytrap, carnivorous plant of
old, and half like the simple creeping of a vine on a wall.

Those constricting bonds were tightening now. Zar could feel
the tiny thorns with which they were equipped biting into his
flesh. He screamed in horror and pain. His cries echoed hollowly
in the cold gorge. The snow, slowly sifting, and the silence, both
seemed to mock—by their calm, pitiless lack of concern—the
plight in which he found himself.

And then a voice, chattering faintly in the language of Kaw the
Crow: "Be still. Peace. Peace. Peace. Peace. Peace——"

Gradually the sleepy tone quieted Zar, even though he was
aware that whatever the invaders might do to him could bring
him no good.

Plants with voices. Almost human voices! Some sort of tym-
panic organs, hidden, perhaps, in some of those pulpy leaves, Zar
judged. From the records of the old explanations of Mars, he
knew a little about these intruders, and their scheme of life.
Organs, with the functions of mechanical contrivances, conceived

and grown as they were needed! An alien science, adapted to the abilities and limitations of vegetative intelligences—intelligences that had never controlled the mining and smelting and shaping of metal!

Zar, tight in the clutch of those weird monstrosities, realized some of their power. Strangely it did not affect the hypnotic calm that wrapped him.

Mars. These wondrous people of the dusk of worlds had survived all animal life on the Red Planet. They had spanned Mars in a vast, irregularly formed network, growing along dry river beds, and the arms of vanished seas. They had not been mere individuals, for they had cooperated to form a civilization of a weird, bizarre sort. Great, hollow roots, buried beneath the ground, had drawn water from melting polar snows. Those roots had been like water conduits. A rhythmic pulsation within them had pumped the water across thousands of miles of desert, providing each plant along the way with moisture, even on that dying and almost dehydrated world. The canals of Mars! Yes, a great irrigation system, a great engineering feat—but out of the scope of Itorloo methods entirely.

And through the living texture of those immense joining roots, too, had doubtless flown the impulses of thoughts and commands —the essence of leadership and security. Even now, when Mars was all but dead, its final civilization must still be trying to fight on.

Strange, wonderful times those old explorers had seen. Cold sunlight on bizarre ruins, left by extinct animal folk. Thin air and arctic weather, worse than that of Earth in the present age. Death everywhere, except for those vegetative beings grouped in immense, spiny, ribbonlike stretches. Dim shapes at night under hurtling Phobos, the nearer moon, and Deimos, her leisurely sister. Zar did not know just how it had happened, but he had heard that only a few of those human adventurers had escaped from the people of Mars with their lives.

Zar's thought rambled on in a detached way that was odd for him. Perhaps Nature had a plan that she used over and over again. On Terra the great reptiles of the Mesozoic period had died out to be replaced by mammals. Men and the Children of Men had become supreme at last.

Succession after succession, according to some well-ordered scheme? In the desolate quiet of falling snow, tempered only by the muted murmur of the frigid wind, it was easy for Zar to fall prey to such a concept, particularly since he was held powerless in the grasp of the invaders. Tendrils, thorny, stinging tendrils, which must have been grown purposely to receive an Itorloo captive! Zar could realize, then, a little of the fantastic introspective sense which gave these beings a direct contact with the physical secrets of their forms. And in consequence a knowledge of chemistry and biology that was clearer than anything that an Itorloo might be expected to attain along similar lines.

Zar wanted to shriek, but his awe and his weakness strangled him beyond more than the utterance of a gasping sigh.

Then the mighty spirit of his kind reasserted itself. Zar was aware that most probably he himself would presently perish; but the Itorloo, his kind, his real concern, could never lose! Not with all the mighty forces at their command! To suppose that they could be defeated by the sluggish intruders was against reason! In a matter of months—when the preparations for the vast purification process had been completed—Earth would be free of those intruders once more. Zar's brown face contracted into a leer of defiance that had a touch of real greatness. Brutality, force, cunning, and the capacity for quick action—those were the tools of the Itorloo, but they had strength too. Zar was no fool—no shortsighted individual who leaps to hasty, optimistic conclusions—but in a contest between the Itorloo and the invaders there could be but a single outcome by any standard within Zar's reach.

In this belief, he was comforted, and his luck, presently, after long hours of suffering, seemed far better than he had any reason to hope for. The hard, thorny tendrils unquestionably were relaxing from about him a very little. He could not guess why, and in consequence he suspected subtle treachery. But he could find no reason to suppose that some hidden motive was responsible.

All his avid energies were concentrated, now, on escape. He concluded that perhaps the cold had forced the slight vegetable relaxation, and he proceeded to make the best possible use of his chances. Some time during the night his straining hands reached the hilt of his knife. Not long afterward Zar clutched his blast gun.

Zar limped stiffly to his flier, cursing luridly; while behind him in the gorge, red firelight flickered, and wisps of smoke lanced into the frigid wind.

Zar wished that Kaw was somewhere in sight, to receive his wrath too. The ebon rascal had vanished.

Winter deepened during succeeding days. The Itorloo in their buried cities felt none of its rigors, however.

Zar had submitted to a physical examination after his weird

adventure, and had been pronounced fit. And of all his people he seemed to toil the most conscientiously.

The Venus project. Soon the Children of Men would be masters of that youthful, sunward planet. The green plains and jungles, and the blue skies of Venus. Soon! Soon! Soon! Zar was full of dreams of adventure and brutal pleasure.

Periodically the rocket craft of the Itorloo sallied forth from the cities to stamp out the fresh growth of the invaders. The oxygen-impregnated substance of their forms flamed in desert gullies, and along the rims of shrivelled salt seas, where the spore plants were trying to renew their civilization. Most of them did not get a chance, even, to approach maturity. But because even one mature survivor could pollute the Earth with billions of spores, impossible to destroy otherwise, the purification process must be carried through.

Spring again, and then mid-summer. The spaceships were almost ready to leap Venus-ward on the great adventure. The generators, meant to spread life-destroying emanations over the crust and atmosphere above, stood finished and gleaming in the white-domed caverns that housed them.

Zar looked at the magnificent, glittering array in the spaceship construction chamber of his native community with pride and satisfaction.

"Tomorrow," he said to a companion, a fierce light in his eyes.

The other nodded, the white glare of the atomic welding furnaces lighting up his features, and betraying there a wolfish grin of pleasure.

"Tomorrow," Zar repeated, an odd sort of vagueness in his tone.

V

Kaw had long ago rejoined his tribe. Life, during those recent months, had been little different from what had been usual in the crow clans for thousands of years. For purposes of safety, Kaw had led his flock into a desert fastness where patrolling Itorloo fliers were seldom seen, and where only a few spore plants had yet appeared.

His first intimation that all was not well was a haunting feeling of unease, which came upon him quite suddenly one day just before noon. His body burned and prickled uncomfortably, and he felt restless. Other than these dim evidences, there was nothing to betray the invisible hand of death.

Emanations, originating in the generators of the Itorloo, far underground. But Kaw was no physicist. He knew only that he and his fellows were vaguely disturbed.

With Teka, his mate, and several of their companions, he soared high into the sky. There, for a time, he felt better. Far overhead, near the Sun's bright disc, he glimpsed the incandescent streamers of Itorloo vessels, distant in space. And presently, with little attention, he saw those vessels—there were five in the group —turn back toward Earth.

The advance in the strength of the deadly emanations was slow. Vast masses of rock, covering the upper crust of the planet in a thin shell, had to develop a kind of resonance to them before they could reach their maximum power.

By nightfall Kaw felt only slightly more uncomfortable. By the following dawn, however, he was definitely droopy and listless. The gradual, world-wide process of purification advanced, directed at the invaders, but promising destruction to the less favored native life of Earth, too.

Four days. Huddled in a pathetic group in a ruined structure of antiquity, Kaw's tribe waited. Their features were dull and ruffled, and they shivered as if with cold. Some of them uttered low, sleepy twitterings of anguish.

That evening Kaw watched the pale Moon rise from a battered window embrasure. He was too weak to stand, but rested slumped forward on his breast. His eyes were rheumy and heavy-lidded, but they still held a savage glitter of defiance, which perhaps would burn in them even after they had ceased to live and see. And Kaw's clouded mind could still hazard a guess as to the identity of the author of his woes. Brave but impotent, he could still scream a hoarse challenge inspired by a courage as deathless as the ages.

"Itorloo! Itorloo!——"

Some time before the first group of spaceships, headed for Venus, had been recalled to Earth, Zar, assigned to the second group, which had not yet entered the launching tubes, had collapsed against his instrument panels.

His affliction had come with a suddenness that was utterly abrupt. Recovering from his swoon, he found himself lying on a narrow pallet in the hospital quarters of the city. His vision was swimming and fogged, and he felt hot and cold by turns.

But he could see the silvery tunic'd figure of the physician standing close to him.

"What is wrong?" he stammered. "What is it that has happened to me? A short time ago I was well!"

"Much is wrong," the physician returned quietly. "And you have not really been well for a long time. A germ disease—a type of thing which we thought our sanitation had stamped out millenniums ago—has been ravaging your brain and nerves for months! Only its insidiousness prevented it from being discovered earlier. During its incipient stages the poisons of it seem actually to stimulate mental and physical activity, giving a treacherous impression of robust health. And we know, certainly, that this disease is extremely contagious. It does not reveal itself easily, but I and others have examined many apparently healthy individuals with great care. In each there is the telltale evidence that the disease is not only present, but far advanced. Hundreds have collapsed as you have. More, surely, will follow. It is my belief that the entire race has been afflicted. And the plague has a fatal look. Panic has broken out. There is a threatened failure of power and food supplies. Perhaps an antitoxin can be found—but there is so little time."

Half delirious, Zar could still grasp the meaning of the physician's words, and could understand the origin of the disease.

He began to mutter with seeming incoherence: "The changing Earth. Reptiles. Mammals. Men—— Succession. Nature——"

His voice took on a fiercer tone. "Fight, Itorloo!" he screamed. "Fight!"

Cruel he was, as were all his people, but he had pluck. Suddenly he arose to a sitting posture on his bed. His eyes flamed. If his act represented the final dramatic gesture of all the hoary race of man, still it was magnificent. Nor were any tears to be shed, for extinction meant only a task completed.

"Fight!" he shouted again, as if addressing a limitless multitude. "Fight, Itorloo! Study! Learn! Work! It is the only hope! Keep power flowing in the purification generators if you can. The old records of the explorations of Mars—those plants! Their approach to problems is different from our own. No metals. No machines as we know them. But in hidden compartments in their tissues it was easy for them to create the bacteria of death! They *invented* those bacteria, and grew them, breaking them away from their own substance. Some way, when I was a captive, I was infected. The thorns on the tendrils that held me! I was the carrier! Find an antitoxin to fight the plague, Itorloo! Work——"

VI

One year. Two. Three. The sunshine was brilliant, the air almost warm. The rusty desert hills in the distance were the same.

Ancient ruins brooded in the stillness, as they had for so long. On the slopes ant hordes were busy. Rodent colonies showed similar evidence of population. In the sky, Kaw and his companions wheeled and turned lazily.

This was the same Earth, with several changes. Bulbous, spiny things peopled the gorges, and were probing out across the desert, slowly building—with hollow, connecting roots—the water pipes of a tremendous irrigation system. Like that of Mars, and like that of Ganymede, moon of Jupiter, in former ages. Saline remnants of seas and polar snows could alike provide the needed moisture.

Thoughts traveled swiftly along connecting roots. Little orbs and wicked spines gleamed. The invaders were at peace now. Only the Itorloo could have threatened their massed might. There was no danger in the lesser native life.

The subterranean cities of the former rulers of Earth were inhabited only by corpses and by intruding ants, who, like the other fauna of this planet, were immune to the plague, which had been directed and designed for the Itorloo alone. The last race of men was now one with the reptiles of the Mesozoic. But all was peace.

Kaw screamed out his contentment in loud, lazy cries, as he circled in the clear air. He seldom thought of the past any more. If the new masters were not truly benignant, they were indifferent. They left him alone. Kaw, creature of Earth's dusk, was happy.

The great surface dome where Zar, the Itorloo, had once kept watch, was already surrounded by crowded growths. The plants had achieved a great, but an empty, victory. For Earth was a dying planet. Within the dome an astronomical telescope gleamed dully, collecting dust. Often Zar had directed it toward Venus, goal of shattered Itorloo dreams.

But who knew? Out of the void to Ganymede the invaders had come. Across space to Mars. Riding light to Earth. Perhaps when the time came—when Venus was growing old——

1938

Farewell to the Master /

by HARRY BATES

The robot was harmless, in fact couldn't be moved in any way what-ever—till a newsman stuck his nose in where it didn't belong!

From his perch high on the ladder above the museum floor, Cliff Sutherland studied carefully each line and shadow of the great robot, then turned and looked thoughtfully down at the rush of visitors come from all over the Solar System to see Gnut and the traveler for themselves and to hear once again their amazing, tragic story.

He himself had come to feel an almost proprietary interest in the exhibit, and with some reason. He had been the only free-lance picture reporter on the Capitol grounds when the visitors from the Unknown had arrived, and had obtained the first pro-fessional shots of the ship. He had witnessed at close hand every event of the next mad few days. He had thereafter photographed many times the eight-foot robot, the ship, and the beautiful slain ambassador, Klaatu, and his imposing tomb out in the center of the Tidal Basin, and, such was the continuing news value of the event to the billions of persons throughout habitable space, he was there now once more to get still other shots and, if possible, a new "angle."

This time he was after a picture which showed Gnut as weird and menacing. The shots he had taken the day before had not given quite the effect he wanted, and he hoped to get it today; but the light was not yet right and he had to wait for the after-noon to wane a little.

The last of the crowd admitted in the present group hurried in, exclaiming at the great pure green curves of the mysterious time-space traveler, then completely forgetting the ship at sight of the awesome figure and great head of the giant Gnut. Hinged robots of crude manlike appearance were familiar enough, but never had Earthling eyes lain on one like this. For Gnut had almost ex-actly the shape of a man—a giant, but a man—with greenish metal for man's covering flesh, and greenish metal for man's bulging muscles. Except for a loin cloth, he was nude. He stood like the powerful god of the machine of some undreamed-of scientific civilization, on his face a look of sullen, brooding thought. Those who looked at him did not make jests or idle remarks, and those nearest him usually did not speak at all. His strange, internally illuminated red eyes were so set that every observer felt they were fixed on himself alone, and he engendered a feeling that he might at any moment step forward in anger and perform unimaginable deeds.

A slight rustling sound came from speakers hidden in the ceiling above, and at once the noises of the crowd lessened. The recorded lecture was about to be given. Cliff sighed. He knew the thing by heart; had even been present when the recording was made, and met the speaker, a young chap named Stillwell.

"Ladies and gentlemen," began a clear and well-modulated voice—but Cliff was no longer attending. The shadows in the hollows of Gnut's face and figure were deeper; it was almost time for his shot. He picked up and examined the proofs of the pictures he had taken the day before and compared them critically with the subject.

As he looked a wrinkle came to his brow. He had not noticed it before, but now, suddenly, he had the feeling that since yesterday something about Gnut was changed. The pose before him was the identical one in the photographs, every detail on comparison seemed the same, but nevertheless the feeling persisted. He took up his viewing glass and more carefully compared subject and photographs, line by line. And then he saw that there *was* a difference.

With sudden excitement, Cliff snapped two pictures at different exposures. He knew he should wait a little and take others, but he was so sure he had stumbled on an important mystery that he had to get going, and quickly folding his accessory equipment he descended the ladder and made his way out. Twenty minutes later, consumed with curiosity, he was developing the new shots in his hotel bedroom.

What Cliff saw when he compared the negatives taken yesterday and today caused his scalp to tingle. Here was a slant indeed! And apparently no one but he knew! Still, what he had discovered, though it would have made the front page of every paper in the Solar System, was after all only a lead. The story, what really had happened, he knew no better than anyone else. It must be his job to find out.

And that meant he would have to secrete himself in the build-

ing and stay there all night. That very night; there was still time
for him to get back before closing. He would take a small, very
fast infrared camera that could see in the dark, and he would get
the real picture and the story.

He snatched up the little camera, grabbed an aircab and hurried back to the museum. The place was filled with another section of the ever-present queue, and the lecture was just ending.
He thanked Heaven that his arrangement with the museum permitted him to go in and out at will.

He had already decided what to do. First he made his way to
the "floating" guard and asked a single question, and anticipation
broadened on his face as he heard the expected answer. The second thing was to find a spot where he would be safe from the eyes
of the men who would close the floor for the night. There was
only one possible place, the laboratory set up behind the ship.
Boldly he showed his press credentials to the second guard, stationed at the partitioned passageway leading to it, stating that he
had come to interview the scientists; and in a moment was at the
laboratory door.

He had been there a number of times and knew the room well.
It was a large area roughly partitioned off for the work of the
scientists engaged in breaking their way into the ship, and full of
a confusion of massive and heavy objects—electric and hot-air
ovens, carboys of chemicals, asbestos sheeting, compressors,
basins, ladles, a microscope, and a great deal of smaller equipment common to a metallurgical laboratory. Three white-
smocked men were deeply engrossed in an experiment at the
far end. Cliff, waiting a good moment, slipped inside and hid himself under a table half buried with supplies. He felt reasonably
safe from detection there. Very soon now the scientists would
be going home for the night.

From beyond the ship he could hear another section of the
waiting queue filing in—the last, he hoped, of the day. He settled
himself as comfortably as he could. In a moment the lecture
would begin. He had to smile when he thought of one thing the
recording would say.

Then there it was again—the clear, trained voice of the chap
Stillwell. The foot scrapings and whispers of the crowd died
away, and Cliff could hear every word in spite of the great bulk
of the ship lying interposed.

"Ladies and gentlemen," began the familiar words, "the Smithsonian Institution welcomes you to its new Interplanetary Wing
and to the marvelous exhibits at this moment before you."

A slight pause. "All of you must know by now something of what happened here three months ago, if indeed you did not see it for yourself in the telescreen," the voice went on. "The few facts are briefly told. A little after 5:00 p. m. on September 16th, visitors to Washington thronged the grounds outside this building in their usual numbers and no doubt with their usual thoughts. The day was warm and fair. A stream of people was leaving the main entrance of the museum, just outside in the direction you are facing. This wing, of course, was not here at that time. Everyone was homeward bound, tired no doubt from hours on their feet, seeing the exhibits of the museum and visiting the many buildings on the grounds nearby. And then it happened.

"On the area just to your right, just as it is now, appeared the time-space traveler. It appeared in the blink of an eye. It did not come down from the sky; dozens of witnesses swear to that; it just appeared. One moment it was not here, the next it was. It appeared on the very spot it now rests on.

"The people nearest the ship were stricken with panic and ran back with cries and screams. Excitement spread out over Washington in a tidal wave. Radio, television, and newspapermen rushed here at once. Police formed a wide cordon around the ship, and army units appeared and trained guns and ray projectors on it. The direst calamity was feared.

"For it was recognized from the very beginning that this was no spaceship from anywhere in the Solar System. Every child knew that only two spaceships had ever been built on Earth, and none at all on any of the other planets and satellites; and of those two, one had been destroyed when it was pulled into the Sun, and the other had just been reported safely arrived on Mars. Then, the ones made here had a shell of a strong aluminum alloy, while this one, as you see, is of an unknown greenish metal.

"The ship appeared and just sat here. No one emerged, and there was no sign that it contained life of any kind. That, as much as any single thing, caused excitement to sky-rocket. Who, or what, was inside? Were the visitors hostile or friendly? Where did the ship come from? How did it arrive so suddenly right on this spot without dropping from the sky?

"For two days the ship rested here, just as you now see it, without motion or sign that it contained life. Long before the end of that time the scientists had explained that it was not so much a spaceship as a space-time traveler, because only such a ship could arrive as this one did—materialize. They pointed out that such a traveler, while theoretically understandable to us Earthmen, was far beyond attempt at our present state of knowledge, and that this one, activated by relativity principles, might well have come from the far corner of the Universe, from a distance which light itself would require millions of years to cross.

"When this opinion was disseminated, public tension grew until it was almost intolerable. Where had the traveler come from? Who were its occupants? Why had they come to Earth? Above all, why did they not show themselves? Were they perhaps preparing some terrible weapon of destruction?

"And where was the ship's entrance port? Men who dared go look reported that none could be found. No slightest break or crack marred the perfect smoothness of the ship's curving ovoid surface. And a delegation of high-ranking officials who visited the ship could not, by knocking, elicit from its occupants any sign that they had been heard.

"At last, after exactly two days, in full view of tens of thousands of persons assembled and standing well back, and under the muzzles of scores of the army's most powerful guns and ray projectors, an opening appeared in the wall of the ship, and a ramp slid down, and out stepped a man, godlike in appearance and human in form, closely followed by a giant robot. And when they touched the ground the ramp slid back and the entrance closed as before.

"It was immediately apparent to all the assembled thousands that the stranger was friendly. The first thing he did was to raise his right arm high in the universal gesture of peace; but it was not that which impressed those nearest so much as the expression on his face, which radiated kindness, wisdom, the purest nobility. In his delicately tinted robe he looked like a benign god.

"At once, waiting for this appearance, a large committee of high-ranking government officials and army officers advanced to greet the visitor. With graciousness and dignity the man pointed to himself, then to his robot companion, and said in perfect English with a peculiar accent, 'I am Klaatu,' or a name that sounded like that, 'and this is Gnut.' The names were not well understood at the time, but the sight-and-sound film of the television men caught them and they became known to everyone subsequently.

"And then occurred the thing which shall always be to the shame of the human race. From a treetop a hundred yards away came a wink of violet light and Klaatu fell. The assembled multitude stood for a moment stunned, not comprehending what had happened. Gnut, a little behind his master and to one side, slowly turned his body a little toward him, moved his head twice, and stood still, in exactly the position you now see him.

"Then followed pandemonium. The police pulled the slayer of Klaatu out of the tree. They found him mentally unbalanced; he kept crying that the devil had come to kill every one on Earth. He was taken away, and Klaatu, although obviously dead, was rushed to the nearest hospital to see if anything could be done to revive him. Confused and frightened crowds milled about the Capitol grounds the rest of the afternoon and much of that night. The ship remained as silent and motionless as before. And Gnut, too, never moved from the position he had come to rest in.

"Gnut never moved again. He remained exactly as you see him all that night and for the ensuing days. When the mausoleum in the Tidal Basin was built, Klaatu's burial services took place where you are standing now, attended by the highest functionaries of all the great countries of the world. It was not only the most appropriate but the safest thing to do, for if there should be other living creatures in the traveler, as seemed possible at that time, they had to be impressed by the sincere sorrow of us Earthmen at what had happened. If Gnut was still alive, or perhaps I had better say functionable, there was no sign. He stood as you see him during the entire ceremony. He stood so while his master was floated out to the mausoleum and given to the centuries with the tragically short sight-and-sound record of his historic visit. And he stood so afterward, day after day, night after night, in fair weather and in rain, never moving or showing by any slightest sign that he was aware of what had gone on.

"After the interment, this wing was built out from the museum to cover the traveler and Gnut. Nothing else could very well have been done, it was learned, for both Gnut and the ship were far too heavy to be moved safely by any means at hand.

"You have heard about the efforts of our metallurgists since then to break into the ship, and of their complete failure. Behind the ship now, as you can see from either end, a partitioned workroom has been set up where the attempt still goes on. So far its wonderful greenish metal has proved inviolable. Not only are they unable to get in, but they cannot even find the exact place from which Klaatu and Gnut emerged. The chalk marks you see are the best approximation.

"Many people have feared that Gnut was only temporarily deranged, and that on return to function might be dangerous, so the scientists have completely destroyed all chance of that. The greenish metal of which he is made seemed to be the same as that of the ship and could no more be attacked, they found, nor could they find any way to penetrate to his internals; but they had other means. They sent electrical currents of tremendous voltages and amperages through him. They applied terrific heat to all parts of his metal shell. They immersed him for days in gases and acids and strongly corroding solutions, and they have bombarded him with every known kind of ray. You need have no fear of him now. He cannot possibly have retained the ability to function in any way.

"But—a word of caution. The officials of the government know that visitors will not show any disrespect in this building. It may be that the unknown and unthinkably powerful civilization from which Klaatu and Gnut came may send other emissaries to see what happened to them. Whether or not they do, not one of us must be found amiss in our attitude. None of us could very well anticipate what happened, and we all are immeasurably sorry, but we are still in a sense responsible, and must do what we can to avoid possible retaliations.

"You will be allowed to remain five minutes longer, and then, when the gong sounds, you will please leave promptly. The robot attendants along the wall will answer any questions you may have.

"Look well, for before you stand stark symbols of the achievement, mystery, and frailty of the human race."

The recorded voice ceased speaking. Cliff, carefully moving his cramped limbs, broke out in a wide smile. If they knew what he knew!

For his photographs told a slightly different story from that of the lecturer. In yesterday's a line of the figured floor showed clearly at the outer edge of the robot's near foot; in today's, *that line was covered*. Gnut had moved!

Or been moved, though this was very unlikely. Where was the derrick and other evidence of such activity? It could hardly have been done in one night, and all signs so quickly concealed. And why should it be done at all?

Still, to make sure, he had asked the guard. He could almost remember verbatim his answer:

"No, Gnut has neither moved nor been moved since the death of his master. A special point was made of keeping him in the position he assumed at Klaatu's death. The floor was built in under him, and the scientists who completed his derangement erected their apparatus around him, just as he stands. You need have no fears."

Cliff smiled again. He did not have any fears.

Not yet.

II

A moment later the big gong above the entrance doors rang the closing hour, and immediately following it a voice from the speakers called out, "Five o'clock, ladies and gentlemen. Closing time, ladies and gentlemen."

The three scientists, as if surprised it was so late, hurriedly washed their hands, changed to their street clothes and disappeared down the partitioned corridor, oblivious of the young picture man hidden under the table. The slide and scrape of the feet on the exhibition floor rapidly dwindled, until at last there were only the steps of the two guards walking from one point to another, making sure everything was all right for the night. For just a moment one of them glanced in the doorway of the laboratory, then he joined the other at the entrance. Then the great metal doors clanged to, and there was silence.

Cliff waited several minutes, then carefully poked his way out from under the table. As he straightened up, a faint tinkling crash sounded at the floor by his feet. Carefully stooping, he found the shattered remains of a thin glass pipette. He had knocked it off the table.

That caused him to realize something he had not thought of before: A Gnut who had moved might be a Gnut who could see and hear—and really be dangerous. He would have to be very careful.

He looked about him. The room was bounded at the ends by two fiber partitions which at the inner ends followed close under the curving bottom of the ship. The inner side of the room was the ship itself, and the outer was the southern wall of the wing. There were four large high windows. The only entrance was by way of the passage.

Without moving, from his knowledge of the building, he made his plan. The wing was connected with the western end of the museum by a doorway, never used, and extended westward toward the Washington Monument. The ship lay nearest the southern wall, and Gnut stood out in front of it, not far from the northeast corner and at the opposite end of the room from the entrance of the building and the passageway leading to the laboratory. By retracing his steps he would come out on the floor at the point farthest removed from the robot. This was just what he wanted, for on the other side of the entrance, on a low platform, stood a paneled table containing the lecture apparatus, and this table was the only object in the room which afforded a place for him to lie concealed while watching what might go on. The only other objects on the floor were the six manlike robot attendants in fixed stations along the northern wall, placed there to answer visitors' questions. He would have to gain the table.

He turned and began cautiously tiptoeing out of the laboratory and down the passageway. It was already dark there, for what light still entered the exhibition hall was shut off by the great bulk of the ship. He reached the end of the room without making a sound. Very carefully he edged forward and peered around the bottom of the ship at Gnut.

He had a momentary shock. The robot's eyes were right on him!—or so it seemed. Was that only the effect of the set of his eyes, he wondered, or was he already discovered? The position of Gnut's head did not seem to have changed, at any rate. Probably everything was all right, but he wished he did not have to cross that end of the room with the feeling that the robot's eyes were following him.

He drew back and sat down and waited. It would have to be totally dark before he essayed the trip to the table.

He waited a full hour, until the faint beams from the lamps on the grounds outside began to make the room seem to grow lighter; then he got up and peeped around the ship once more. The robot's eyes seemed to pierce right at him as before, only now, due no doubt to the darkness, the strange internal illumination seemed much brighter. This was a chilling thing. Did Gnut know he was there? What were the thoughts of the robot? What *could* be the thoughts of a man-made machine, even so wonderful a one as Gnut?

It was time for the cross, so Cliff slung his camera around on his back, went down on his hands and knees, and carefully moved to the edge of the entrance wall. There he fitted himself as closely as he could into the angle made by it with the floor and started inching ahead. Never pausing, not risking a glance at Gnut's unnerving red eyes, moving an inch at a time, he snaked along. He took ten minutes to cross the space of a hundred feet, and he was wet with perspiration when his fingers at last touched the one-foot rise of the platform on which the table stood. Still slowly, silently as a shadow, he made his way over the edge and melted behind the protection of the table. At last he was there.

He relaxed for a moment, then, anxious to know whether he had been seen, carefully turned and looked around the side of the table.

Gnut's eyes were now full on him! Or so it seemed. Against the general darkness, the robot loomed a mysterious and still darker shadow that, for all his being a hundred and fifty feet away, seemed to dominate the room. Cliff could not tell whether the position of his body was changed or not.

But if Gnut were looking at him, he at least did nothing else. Not by the slightest motion that Cliff could discern did he appear to move. His position was the one he had maintained these last three months, in the darkness, in the rain, and this last week in the museum.

Cliff made up his mind not to give away to fear. He became conscious of his own body. The cautious trip had taken something out of him—his knees and elbows burned and his trousers were no doubt ruined. But these were little things if what he hoped for came to pass. If Gnut so much as moved, and he could catch him with his infrared camera, he would have a story that would buy him fifty suits of clothes. And if on top of that he could learn the purpose of Gnut's moving—provided there was a purpose— that would be a story that would set the world on its ears.

He settled down to a period of waiting; there was no telling when Gnut would move, if indeed he would move that night. Cliff's eyes had long been adjusted to the dark and he could make out the larger objects well enough. From time to time he peered out at the robot—peered long and hard, till his outlines wavered and he seemed to move, and he had to blink and rest his eyes to be sure it was only his imagination.

Again the minute hand of his watch crept around the dial. The inactivity made Cliff careless, and for longer and longer periods he kept his head back out of sight behind the table. And so it was that when Gnut did move he was scared almost out of his wits. Dull and a little bored, he suddenly found the robot out on the floor, halfway in his direction.

But that was not the most frightening thing. It was that when he did see Gnut he did not catch him moving! He was stopped as still as a cat in the middle of stalking a mouse. His eyes were now much brighter, and there was no remaining doubt about their direction: he was looking right at Cliff!

Scarcely breathing, half hypnotized, Cliff looked back. His thoughts tumbled. What was the robot's intention? Why had he stopped so still? Was he being stalked? How could he move with such silence?

In the heavy darkness Gnut's eyes moved nearer. Slowly but in perfect rhythm the almost imperceptible sound of his foot- steps beat on Cliff's ears. Cliff, usually resourceful enough, was this time caught flatfooted. Frozen with fear, utterly incapable of fleeing, he lay where he was while the metal monster with the fiery eyes came on.

For a moment Cliff all but fainted, and when he recovered, there was Gnut towering over him, legs almost within reach. He was bending slightly, burning his terrible eyes right into his own!

Too late to try to think of running now. Trembling like any cornered mouse, Cliff waited for the blow that would crush him. For an eternity, it seemed, Gnut scrutinized him without moving. For each second of that eternity Cliff expected annihilation, sudden, quick, complete. And then suddenly and unexpectedly it was over. Gnut's body straightened and he stepped back. He turned. And then, with the almost jerkless rhythm which only he among robots possessed, he started back toward the place from which he came.

Cliff could hardly believe he had been spared. Gnut could have crushed him like a worm—and he had only turned around and gone back. Why? It could not be supposed that a robot was capable of human considerations.

Gnut went straight to the other end of the traveler. At a certain place he stopped and made a curious succession of sounds. At once Cliff saw an opening, blacker than the gloom of the building, appear in the ship's side, and it was followed by a slight sliding sound as a ramp slid out and met the floor. Gnut walked up the ramp and, stooping a little, disappeared inside the ship.

Then, for the first time, Cliff remembered the picture he had come to get. Gnut had moved, but he had not caught him! But at least now, whatever opportunities there might be later, he could get the shot of the ramp connecting with the opened door; so he twisted his camera into position, set it for the proper exposure, and took a shot.

A long time passed and Gnut did not come out. What could he be doing inside? Cliff wondered. Some of his courage returned to him and he toyed with the idea of creeping forward and peeping through the port, but he found he had not the courage for that. Gnut had spared him, at least for the time, but there was no telling how far his tolerance would go.

An hour passed, then another, Gnut was doing something inside the ship, but what. Cliff could not imagine. If the robot had been a human being, he knew he would have sneaked a look, but as it was, he was too much of an unknown quantity. Even the simplest of Earth's robots under certain circumstances were inexplicable things; what, then, of this one, come from an unknown and even unthinkable civilization, by far the most wonderful construction ever seen—what superhuman powers might he not possess? All that the scientists of Earth could do had not served to derange him. Acid, heat, rays, terrific crushing blows—he had withstood them all; even his finish had been unmarred. He might be able to see perfectly in the dark. And right where he was, he might be able to hear or in some way sense the least change in Cliff's position.

More time passed, and then, some time after two o'clock in the morning, a simple homely thing happened, but a thing so unexpected that for a moment it quite destroyed Cliff's equilibrium. Suddenly, through the dark and silent building, there was a faint whir of wings, soon followed by the piercing, sweet voice of a bird. A mocking bird. Somewhere in the gloom above his head. Clear and full throated were its notes; a dozen little songs it sang, one after the other without pause between—short insistent calls, twirrings, coaxings, cooings—the spring love song of perhaps the finest singer in the world. Then, as suddenly as it began, the voice was silent.

If an invading army had poured out of the traveler, Cliff would have been less surprised. The month was December; even in Florida the mocking birds had not yet begun their song. How had one gotten into that tight, gloomy museum? How and why was it singing there?

He waited, full of curiosity. Then suddenly he was aware of Gnut, standing just outside the port of the ship. He stood quite still, his glowing eyes turned squarely in Cliff's direction. For a moment the hush in the museum seemed to deepen; then it was broken by a soft thud on the floor near where Cliff was lying.

He wondered. The light in Gnut's eyes changed, and he started his almost jerkless walk in Cliff's direction. When only a little away, the robot stopped, bent over, and picked something from the floor. For some time he stood without motion and looked at a little object he held in his hand. Cliff knew, though he could not see, that it was the mocking bird. Its body, for he was sure that it had lost its song forever. Gnut then turned, and without a glance at Cliff, walked back to the ship and again went inside.

Hours passed while Cliff waited for some sequel to this surprising happening. Perhaps it was because of his curiosity that his fear of the robot began to lessen. Surely if the mechanism was unfriendly, if he intended him any harm, he would have finished him before, when he had such a perfect opportunity. Cliff began to nerve himself for a quick look inside the port. And a picture;

he must remember the picture. He kept forgetting the very reason he was there.

It was in the deeper darkness of the false dawn when he got sufficient courage and made the start. He took off his shoes, and in his stockinged feet, his shoes tied together and slung over his shoulder, he moved stiffly but rapidly to a position behind the nearest of the six robot attendants stationed along the wall, then paused for some sign which might indicate that Gnut knew he had moved. Hearing none, he slipped along behind the next robot attendant and paused again. Bolder now, he made in one spurt all the distance to the farthest one, the sixth, fixed just opposite the port of the ship. There he met with a disappointment. No light that he could detect was visible within; there was only darkness and the all-permeating silence. Still, he had better get the picture. He raised his camera, focused it on the dark opening, and gave the film a comparatively long exposure. Then he stood there, at a loss what to do next.

As he paused, a peculiar series of muffled noises reached his ears, apparently from within the ship. Animal noises—first scrapings and pantings, punctuated by several sharp clicks, then deep, rough snarls, interrupted by more scrapings and pantings, as if a struggle of some kind were going on. Then suddenly, before Cliff could even decide to run back to the table, a low, wide, dark shape bounded out of the port and immediately turned and grew to the height of a man. A terrible fear swept over Cliff, even before he knew what the shape was.

In the next second Gnut appeared in the port and stepped unhesitatingly down the ramp toward the shape. As he advanced it backed slowly away for a few feet; but then it stood its ground, and thick arms rose from its sides and began a loud drumming on its chest, while from its throat came a deep roar of defiance. Only one creature in the world beat its chest and made a sound like that. The shape was a gorilla!

And a huge one!

Gnut kept advancing, and when close, charged forward and grappled with the beast. Cliff would not have guessed that Gnut could move so fast. In the darkness he could not see the details of what happened; all he knew was that the two great shapes, the titanic metal Gnut and the squat but terrifically strong gorilla, merged for a moment with silence on the robot's part and terrible, deep, indescribable roars on the other's; then the two separated, and it was as if the gorilla had been flung back and away.

The animal at once rose to its full height and roared deafeningly. Gnut advanced. They closed again, and the separation of before was repeated. The robot continued inexorably, and now the gorilla began to fall back down the building. Suddenly the beast darted at a manlike shape against the wall, and with one rapid side movement dashed the fifth robot attendant to the floor and decapitated it.

Tense with fear, Cliff crouched behind his own robot attendant. He thanked Heaven that Gnut was between him and the gorilla and was continuing his advance. The gorilla backed farther, darted suddenly at the next robot in the row, and with strength almost unbelievable picked it from its roots and hurled it at Gnut. With a sharp metallic clang, robot hit robot, and the one of Earth bounced off to one side and rolled to a stop.

Cliff cursed himself for it afterward, but again he completely forgot the picture. The gorilla kept falling back down the building, demolishing with terrific bursts of rage every robot attendant that he passed and throwing the pieces at the implacable Gnut. Soon they arrived opposite the table, and Cliff now thanked his stars he had come away. There followed a brief silence. Cliff could not make out what was going on, but he imagined that the gorilla had at last reached the corner of the wing and was trapped.

If he was, it was only for a moment. The silence was suddenly shattered by a terrific roar, and the thick, squat shape of the animal came bounding toward Cliff. He came all the way back and turned just between Cliff and the port of the ship. Cliff prayed frantically for Gnut to come back quickly, for there was now only the last remaining robot attendant between him and the madly dangerous brute. Out of the dimness Gnut did appear. The gorilla rose to its full height and again beat its chest and roared its challenge.

And then occurred a curious thing. It fell on all fours and slowly rolled over on its side, as if weak or hurt. Then panting, making frightening noises, it forced itself again to its feet and faced the oncoming Gnut. As it waited, its eye was caught by the last robot attendant and perhaps Cliff, shrunk close behind it. With a surge of terrible destructive rage, the gorilla waddled sideward toward Cliff, but this time, even through his panic, he saw that the animal moved with difficulty, again apparently sick or severely wounded. He jumped back just in time; the gorilla pulled out the last robot attendant and hurled it violently at Gnut, missing him narrowly.

That was its last effort. The weakness caught it again; it dropped heavily on one side, rocked back and forth a few times, and fell to twitching. Then it lay still and did not move again.

The first faint pale light of the dawn was seeping into the room. From the corner where he had taken refuge, Cliff watched closely the great robot. It seemed to him that he behaved very queerly. He stood over the dead gorilla, looking down at him with what in a human would be called sadness. Cliff saw this clearly; Gnut's heavy greenish features bore a thoughtful, grieving expression new to his experience. For some moments he stood so, then as might a father with his sick child, he leaned over, lifted the great animal in his metal arms and carried it tenderly within the ship.

Cliff flew back to the table, suddenly fearful of yet other dangerous and inexplicable happenings. It struck him that he might be safer in the laboratory, and with trembling knees he made his way there and hid in one of the big ovens. He prayed for full daylight. His thoughts were chaos. Rapidly, one after another, his mind churned up the amazing events of the night, but all was mystery; it seemed there could be no rational explanation for them. That mocking bird. The gorilla. Gnut's sad expression and his tenderness. What could account for a fantastic melange like that!

Gradually full daylight did come. A long time passed. At last he began to believe he might yet get out of that place of mystery and danger alive. At 8:30 there were noises at the entrance, and the good sound of human voices came to his ears. He stepped out of the oven and tiptoed to the passageway.

The noises stopped suddenly and there was a frightened exclamation and then the sound of running feet, and then silence. Stealthily Cliff sneaked down the narrow way and peeped fearfully around the ship.

There Gnut was in his accustomed place, in the identical pose he had taken at the death of his master, brooding sullenly and alone over a space traveler once again closed tight and a room that was a shambles. The entrance doors stood open and, heart in his mouth, Cliff ran out.

A few minutes later, safe in his hotel room, completely done in, he sat down for a second and almost at once fell asleep. Later, still in his clothes and still asleep, he staggered over to the bed. He did not wake up till midafternoon.

III

Cliff awoke slowly, at first not realizing that the images tumbling in his head were real memories and not a fantastic dream.

It was recollection of the pictures which brought him to his feet. Hastily he set about developing the film in his camera.

Then in his hands was proof that the events of the night were real. Both shots turned out well. The first showed clearly the ramp leading up to the port as he had dimly discerned it from his position behind the table. The second, of the open port as snapped from in front, was a disappointment, for a blank wall just back of the opening cut off all view of the interior. That would account for the fact that no light had escaped from the ship while Gnut was inside. Assuming Gnut required light for whatever he did.

Cliff looked at the negatives and was ashamed of himself. What a rotten picture man he was to come back with two ridiculous shots like these! He had had a score of opportunities to get real ones—shots of Gnut in action—Gnut's fight with the gorilla—even Gnut holding the mocking bird—spine-chilling stuff!—and all he had brought back was two stills of a doorway. Oh, sure, they were valuable, but he was a Grade A ass.

And to top this brilliant performance, he had fallen asleep!

Well, he'd better get out on the street and find out what was doing.

Quickly he showered, shaved, and changed his clothes, and soon was entering a nearby restaurant patronized by other picture and newsmen. Sitting alone at the lunch bar, he spotted a friend and competitor.

"Well, what do *you* think?" asked his friend when he took the stool at his side.

"I don't think anything until I've had breakfast," Cliff answered.

"Then haven't you heard?"

"Heard what?" fended Cliff, who knew very well what was coming.

"You're a fine picture man," was the other's remark. "When something really big happens, you are asleep in bed." But then he told him what had been discovered that morning in the museum, and of the world-wide excitement at the news. Cliff did three things at once, successfully—gobbled a substantial breakfast, kept thanking his stars that nothing new had transpired, and showed continuous surprise. Still chewing, he got up and hurried over to the building.

Outside, balked at the door, was a large crowd of the curious, but Cliff had no trouble gaining admittance when he showed his press credentials. Gnut and the ship stood just as he had left them, but the floor had been cleaned up and the pieces of the demolished robot attendants were lined up in one place along the wall. Several other competitor friends of his were there.

"I was away; missed the whole thing," he said to one of them—Gus. "What's supposed to be the explanation for what happened?"

"Ask something easy," was the answer. "Nobody knows. It's thought maybe something came out of the ship, maybe another robot like Gnut. Say—where have you been?"

"Asleep."

"Better catch up. Several billion bipeds are scared stiff. Revenge for the death of Klaatu. Earth about to be invaded."

"But that's—"

"Oh, I know it's all crazy, but that's the story they're being fed; it sells news. But there's a new angle just turned up, very surprising. Come here."

He led Cliff to the table where stood a knot of people looking with great interest at several objects guarded by a technician. Gus pointed to a long slide on which were mounted a number of short dark-brown hairs.

"Those hairs came off a large male gorilla," Gus said with a certain hard-boiled casualness. "Most of them were found among the sweepings of the floor this morning. The rest were found on the robot attendants."

Cliff tried to look astounded. Gus pointed to a test tube partly filled with a light amber fluid.

"And that's blood, diluted—gorilla blood. It was found on Gnut's arms."

"Good Heaven!" Cliff managed to exclaim. "And there's no explanation?"

"Not even a theory. It's your big chance, wonder boy."

Cliff broke away from Gus, unable to maintain his act any longer. He couldn't decide what to do about his story. The press services would bid heavily for it—with all his pictures—but that would take further action out of his hands. In the back of his mind he wanted to stay in the wing again that night, but—well, he simply was afraid. He'd had a pretty stiff dose, and he wanted very much to remain alive.

He walked over and looked a long time at Gnut. No one would ever have guessed that he had moved, or that there had rested on his greenish metal face a look of sadness. Those weird eyes! Cliff wondered if they were really looking at him, as they seemed, recognizing him as the bold intruder of last night. Of what unknown stuff were they made—those materials placed in his eye sockets by one branch of the race of man which all the science of his own could not even serve to disfunction? What was Gnut thinking? What could be the thoughts of a robot—a mechanism of metal poured out of man's clay crucibles? Was he angry at him? Cliff thought not. Gnut had had him at his mercy—and had walked away.

Dared he stay again?

Cliff thought perhaps he did.

He walked about the room, thinking it over. He felt sure Gnut would move again. A Mikton ray gun would protect him from another gorilla—or fifty of them. He did not yet have the real story. He had come back with two miserable architectural stills!

He might have known from the first that he would stay. At dusk that night, armed with his camera and a small Mikton gun, he lay once more under the table of supplies in the laboratory and heard the metal doors of the wing clang to for the night.

This time he would get the story—and the pictures.

If only no guard was posted inside!

IV

Cliff listened hard for a long time for any sound which might tell him that a guard had been left, but the silence within the wing remained unbroken. He was thankful for that—but not quite completely. The gathering darkness and the realization that he was now irrevocably committed made the thought of a companion not altogether unpleasant.

About an hour after it reached maximum darkness he took off his shoes, tied them together and slung them around his neck, down his back, and stole quietly down the passageway to where it opened into the exhibition area. All seemed as it had been the preceding night. Gnut looked an ominous, indistinct shadow at the far end of the room, his glowing red eyes again seemingly right on the spot from which Cliff peeped out. As on the previous night, but even more carefully, Cliff went down on his stomach in the angle of the wall and slowly snaked across to the low platform on which stood the table. Once in its shelter, he fixed his shoes so that they straddled one shoulder, and brought his camera and gun holster around, ready on his breast. This time, he told himself, he would get pictures.

He settled down to wait, keeping Gnut in full sight every minute. His vision reached maximum adjustment to the darkness. Eventually he began to feel lonely and a little afraid. Gnut's red-glowing eyes were getting on his nerves; he had to keep assuring himself that the robot would not harm him. He had little doubt but that he himself was being watched.

Hours slowly passed. From time to time he heard slight noises at the entrance, on the outside—a guard, perhaps, or maybe curious visitors.

At about nine o'clock he saw Gnut move. First his head alone; it turned so that the eyes burned stronger in the direction where Cliff lay. For a moment that was all; then the dark metal form stirred slightly and began moving forward—straight toward himself. Cliff had thought he would not be afraid—much—but now his heart stood still. What would happen this time?

With amazing silence, Gnut drew nearer, until he towered an ominous shadow over the spot where Cliff lay. For a long time his red eyes burned down on the prone man. Cliff trembled all over; this was worse than the first time. Without having planned it, he found himself speaking to the creature.

"You would not hurt me," he pleaded. "I was only curious to see what's going on. It's my job. Can you understand me? I would not harm or bother you. I . . . I couldn't if I wanted to! Please!"

The robot never moved, and Cliff could not guess whether his words had been understood or even heard. When he felt he could not bear the suspense any longer, Gnut reached out and took something from a drawer of the table, or perhaps he put something back in; then he stepped back, turned, and retraced his steps. Cliff was safe! Again the robot had spared him!

Beginning then, Cliff lost much of his fear. He felt sure now that this Gnut would do him no harm. Twice he had had him in his power, and each time he had only looked and quietly moved away. Cliff could not imagine what Gnut had done in the drawer of the table. He watched with the greatest curiosity to see what would happen next.

As on the night before, the robot went straight to the end of the ship and made the peculiar sequence of sounds that opened the port, and when the ramp slid out he went inside. After that Cliff was alone in the darkness for a very long time, probably two hours. Not a sound came from the ship.

Cliff knew he should sneak up to the port and peep inside, but he could not quite bring himself to do it. With his gun he could handle another gorilla, but if Gnut caught him it might be the end. Momentarily he expected something fantastic to happen—he knew not what; maybe the mocking bird's sweet song again, maybe a gorilla, maybe—anything. What did at last happen once more caught him with complete surprise.

He heard a sudden muffled sound, then words—human words—every one familiar.

"Gentlemen," was the first, and then there was a very slight pause. "The Smithsonian Institution welcomes you to its new Interplanetary Wing and to the marvelous exhibits at this moment before you."

It was the recorded voice of Stillwell! But it was not coming through the speakers overhead, but much muted, from within the ship.

After a slight pause it went on:

"All of you must . . . must—" Here it stammered and came to a stop. Cliff's hair bristled. That stammering was not in the lecture!

For just a moment there was silence; then came a scream, a hoarse man's scream, muffled, from somewhere within the heart of the ship; and it was followed by muted gasps and cries, as of a man in great fright or distress.

Every nerve tight, Cliff watched the port. He heard a thudding noise within the ship, then out the door flew the shadow of what was surely a human being. Gasping and half stumbling, he ran straight down the room in Cliff's direction. When twenty feet away, the great shadow of Gnut followed him out of the port.

Cliff watched, breathless. The man—it was Stillwell, he saw now—came straight for the table behind which Cliff himself lay, as if to get behind it, but when only a few feet away, his knees buckled and he fell to the floor. Suddenly Gnut was standing over him, but Stillwell did not seem to be aware of it. He appeared very ill, but kept making spasmodic futile efforts to creep on to the protection of the table.

Gnut did not move, so Cliff was emboldened to speak.

"What's the matter, Stillwell?" he asked. "Can I help? Don't be afraid. I'm Cliff Sutherland; you know, the picture man."

Without showing the least surprise at finding Cliff there, and clutching at his presence like a drowning man would a straw, Stillwell gasped out:

"Help me! Gnut . . . Gnut—" He seemed unable to go on.

"Gnut what?" asked Cliff. Very conscious of the fire-eyed robot looming above, and afraid even to move out to the man, Cliff added reassuringly: "Gnut won't hurt you. I'm sure he won't. He doesn't hurt me. What's the matter? What can I do?"

With a sudden accession of energy, Stillwell rose on his elbows.

"Where am I?" he asked.

"In the Interplanetary Wing," Cliff answered. "Don't you know?"

Only Stillwell's hard breathing was heard for a moment. Then hoarsely, weakly, he asked:

"How did I get here?"

"I don't know," said Cliff.

"I was making a lecture recording," Stillwell said, "when suddenly I found myself here . . . or I mean in there—"

He broke off and showed a return of his terror.

"Then what?" asked Cliff gently.

"I was in that box—and there, above me, was Gnut, the robot. Gnut! But they made Gnut harmless! He's never moved!"

"Steady, now," said Cliff. "I don't think Gnut will hurt you." Stillwell fell back on the floor.

"I'm very weak," he gasped. "Something— Will you get a doctor?"

He was utterly unaware that towering above him, eyes boring down at him through the darkness, was the robot he feared so greatly.

As Cliff hesitated, at a loss what to do, the man's breath began coming in short gasps, as regular as the ticking of a clock. Cliff dared to move out to him, but no act on his part could have helped the man now. His gasps weakened and became spasmodic, then suddenly he was completely silent and still. Cliff felt for his heart, then looked up to the eyes in the shadow above.

"He is dead," he whispered.

The robot seemed to understand, or at least to hear. He bent forward and regarded the still figure.

"What is it, Gnut?" Cliff asked the robot suddenly. "What are you doing? Can I help you in any way? Somehow I don't believe you are unfriendly, and I don't believe you killed this man. But what happened? Can you understand me? Can you speak? What is it you're trying to do?"

Gnut made no sound or motion, but only looked at the still figure at his feet. In the robot's face, now so close, Cliff saw the look of sad contemplation.

Gnut stood so several minutes; then he bent lower, took the limp form carefully—even gently, Cliff thought—in his mighty arms, and carried him to the place along the wall where lay the dismembered pieces of the robot attendants. Carefully he laid him by their side. Then he went back into the ship.

Without fear now, Cliff stole along the wall of the room. He had gotten almost as far as the shattered figures on the floor when he suddenly stopped motionless. Gnut was emerging again.

He was bearing a shape that looked like another body, a larger one. He held it in one arm and placed it carefully by the body of Stillwell. In the hand of his other arm he held something that Cliff could not make out, and this he placed at the side of the body he had just put down. Then he went to the ship and returned once more with a shape which he laid gently by the others; and when this last trip was over he looked down at them all for a moment, then turned slowly back to the ship and stood motionless, as if in deep thought, by the ramp.

Cliff restrained his curiosity as long as he could, then slipped forward and bent over the objects Gnut had placed there. First in the row was the body of Stillwell, as he expected, and next was the great shapeless furry mass of a dead gorilla—the one of last night. By the gorilla lay the object the robot had carried in his free hand—the little body of the mocking bird. These last two had remained in the ship all night, and Gnut, for all his surprising gentleness in handling them, was only cleaning house. But there was a fourth body whose history he did not know. He moved closer and bent very low to look.

What he saw made him catch his breath. Impossible!—he thought; there was some confusion in his directions; he brought his face back, close to the first body. Then his blood ran cold. The first body was that of Stillwell, but the last in the row was Stillwell, too; there were two bodies of Stillwell, both exactly alike, both dead.

Cliff backed away with a cry, and then panic took him and he ran down the room away from Gnut and yelled and beat wildly on the door. There was a noise on the outside.

"Let me out!" he yelled in terror. "Let me out! Let me out! Oh, hurry!"

A crack opened between the two doors and he forced his way through like a wild animal and ran far out on the lawn. A belated couple on a nearby path stared at him with amazement, and this brought some sense to his head and he slowed down and came to a stop. Back at the building, everything looked as usual, and in spite of his terror, Gnut was not chasing him.

He was still in his stockinged feet. Breathing heavily, he sat down on the wet grass and put on his shoes; then he stood and looked at the building, trying to pull himself together. What an incredible melange! The dead Stillwell, the dead gorilla, and the dead mocking bird—all dying before his eyes. And then that last frightening thing, the second dead Stillwell whom he had *not* seen die. And Gnut's strange gentleness, and the sad expression he had twice seen on his face.

As he looked, the grounds about the building came to life. Several people collected at the door of the wing, above sounded the siren of a police copter, then in the distance another, and from all sides people came running, a few at first, then more and more. The police planes landed on the lawn just outside the door of the wing, and he thought he could see the officers peeping inside. Then suddenly the lights of the wing flooded on. In control of himself now, Cliff went back.

He entered. He had left Gnut standing in thought at the side of the ramp, but now he was again in his old familiar pose in the usual place, as if he had never moved. The ship's door was closed, and the ramp gone. But the bodies, the four strangely assorted bodies, were still lying by the demolished robot attendants where he had left them in the dark.

He was startled by a cry behind his back. A uniformed museum guard was pointing at him.

"This is the man!" the guard shouted. "When I opened the door this man forced his way out and ran like the devil!"

The police officers converged on Cliff.

"Who are you? What is all this?" one of them asked him roughly.

"I'm Cliff Sutherland, picture reporter," Cliff answered calmly. "And I was the one who was inside here and ran away, as the guard says."

"What were you doing?" the officer asked, eyeing him. "And where did these bodies come from?"

"Gentlemen, I'd tell you gladly—only business first," Cliff answered. "There's been some fantastic goings on in this room, and I saw them and have the story, but"—he smiled—"I must decline to answer without advice of counsel until I've sold my story to one of the news syndicates. You know how it is. If you'll allow me the use of the radio in your plane—just for a moment, gentlemen— you'll have the whole story right afterward—say in half an hour, when the television men broadcast it. Meanwhile, believe me, there's nothing for you to do, and there'll be no loss by the delay."

The officer who had asked the questions blinked, and one of the others, quicker to react and certainly not a gentleman, stepped toward Cliff with clenched fists. Cliff disarmed him by handing him his press credentials. He glanced at them rapidly and put them in his pocket.

By now half a hundred people were there, and among them were two members of a syndicate crew whom he knew, arrived by copter. The police growled, but they let him whisper in their ear and then go out under escort to the crew's plane. There, by radio, in five minutes, Cliff made a deal which would bring him more money than he had ever before earned in a year. After that he turned over all his pictures and negatives to the crew and gave them the story, and they lost not one second in spinning back to their office with the flash.

More and more people arrived, and the police cleared the building. Ten minutes later a big crew of radio and television men forced their way in, sent there by the syndicate with which he had dealt. And then a few minutes later, under the glaring lights set up by the operators and standing close by the ship and not far from Gnut—he refused to stand underneath him—Cliff gave his story to the cameras and microphones, which in a fraction of a second shot it to every corner of the Solar System.

Immediately afterward the police took him to jail. On general principles and because they were pretty blooming mad.

V

Cliff stayed in jail all that night—until eight o'clock the next morning, when the syndicate finally succeeded in digging up a lawyer and got him out. And then, when at last he was leaving, a Federal man caught him by the wrist.

"You're wanted for further questioning over at the Continental Bureau of Investigation," the agent told him. Cliff went along willingly.

Fully thirty-five high-ranking Federal officials and "big names" were waiting for him in an imposing conference room—one of the president's secretaries, the undersecretary of state, the underminister of defense, scientists, a colonel, executives, department heads, and ranking "C" men. Old gray-mustached Sanders, chief of the CBI, was presiding.

They made him tell his story all over again, and then, in parts, all over once more—not because they did not believe him, but because they kept hoping to elicit some fact which would cast significant light on the mystery of Gnut's behavior and the happenings of the last three nights. Patiently Cliff racked his brains for every detail.

Chief Sanders asked most of the questions. After more than an hour, when Cliff thought they had finished, Sanders asked him several more, all involving his personal opinions of what had transpired.

"Do you think Gnut was deranged in any way by the acids, rays, heat, and so forth applied to him by the scientists?"

"I saw no evidence of it."

"Do you think he can see?"

"I'm sure he can see, or else has other powers which are equivalent."

"Do you think he can hear?"

"Yes, sir. That time when I whispered to him that Stillwell was dead, he bent lower, as if to see for himself. I would not be surprised if he also understood what I said."

"At no time did he speak, except those sounds he made to open the ship?"

"Not one word, in English or any other language. Not one sound with his mouth."

"In your opinion, has his strength been impaired in any way by our treatment?" asked one of the scientists.

"I have told you how easily he handled the gorilla. He attacked the animal and threw it back, after which it retreated all the way down the building, afraid of him."

"How would you explain the fact that our autopsies disclosed no mortal wound, no cause of death, in any of the bodies—gorilla, mocking bird, or the two identical Stillwells?"—this from a medical officer.

"I can't."

"You think Gnut is dangerous?"—from Sanders.

"Potentially very dangerous."

"Yet you say you have the feeling he is not hostile."

"To me, I meant. I do have that feeling, and I'm afraid that I can't give any good reason for it, except the way he spared me twice when he had me in his power. I think maybe the gentle way he handled the bodies had something to do with it, and maybe the sad, thoughtful look I twice caught on his face."

"Would you risk staying in the building alone another night?"

"Not for anything." There were smiles.

"Did you get any pictures of what happened last night?"

"No, sir." Cliff, with an effort, held on to his composure, but he was swept by a wave of shame. A man hitherto silent rescued him by saying:

"A while ago you used the word 'purposive' in connection with Gnut's actions. Can you explain that a little?"

"Yes, that was one of the things that struck me: Gnut never seems to waste a motion. He can move with surprising speed when he wants to; I saw that when he attacked the gorilla; but most other times he walks around as if methodically completing some simple task. And that reminds me of a peculiar thing: at times he gets into one position, any position, maybe half bent over, and stays there for minutes at a time. It's as if his scale of time values was eccentric, compared to ours; some things he does surprisingly fast, and others surprisingly slow. This might account for his long periods of immobility."

"That's very interesting," said one of the scientists. "How would you account for the fact that he recently moves only at night?"

"I think he's doing something he wants no one to see, and the night is the only time he is alone."

"But he went ahead even after finding you there."

"I know. But I have no other explanation, unless he considered me harmless or unable to stop him—which was certainly the case."

"Before you arrived, we were considering incasing him in a large block of glasstex. Do you think he would permit it?"

"I don't know. Probably he would; he stood for the acids and rays and heat. But it had better be done in the daytime; night seems to be the time he moves."

"But he moved in the daytime when he emerged from the traveler with Klaatu."

"I know."

That seemed to be all they could think of to ask him. Sanders slapped his hand on the table.

"Well, I guess that's all Mr. Sutherland," he said. "Thank you for your help, and let me congratulate you for a very foolish, stubborn, brave young man—young businessman." He smiled very faintly. "You are free to go now, but it may be that I'll have to call you back later. We'll see."

"May I remain while you decide about that glasstex?" Cliff asked. "As long as I'm here I'd like to have the tip."

"The decision has already been made—the tip's yours. The pouring will be started at once."

"Thank you, sir," said Cliff—and calmly asked more: "And will you be so kind as to authorize me to be present outside the building tonight? Just outside. I've a feeling something's going to happen."

"You want still another scoop, I see," said Sanders not unkindly, "then you'll let the police wait while you transact your business."

"Not again, sir. If anything happens, they'll get it at once."

The chief hesitated. "I don't know," he said. "I'll tell you what. All the news services will want men there, and we can't have that; but if you can arrange to represent them all yourself, it's a go.

Nothing's going to happen, but your reports will help calm the hysterical ones. Let me know."

Cliff thanked him and hurried out and phoned his syndicate the tip—free—then told them Sanders' proposal. Ten minutes they called him back, said all was arranged, and told him to catch some sleep. They would cover the pouring. With light heart, Cliff hurried over to the museum. The place was surrounded by thousands of the curious, held far back by a strong cordon of police. For once he could not get through; he was recognized, and the police were still sore. But he did not care much; he suddenly felt very tired and needed that nap. He went back to his hotel, left a call, and went to bed.

He had been asleep only a few minutes when his phone rang. Eyes shut, he answered it. It was one of the boys at the syndicate, with peculiar news. Stillwell had just reported, very much alive—the real Stillwell. The two dead ones were some kind of copies; he couldn't imagine how to explain them. He had no brothers.

For a moment Cliff came fully awake, then he went back to bed. Nothing was fantastic any more.

VI

At four o'clock, much refreshed and with an infrared viewing magnifier slung over his shoulder, Cliff passed through the cordon and entered the door of the wing. He had been expected and there was no trouble. As his eyes fell on Gnut, an odd feeling went through him, and for some obscure reason he was almost sorry for the giant robot.

Gnut stood exactly as he had always stood, the right foot advanced a little, and the same brooding expression on his face; but now there was something more. He was solidly incased in a huge block of transparent glasstex. From the floor on which he stood to the top of his full eight feet, and from there on up for an equal distance, and for about eight feet to the left, right, back, and front, he was immured in a water-clear prison which confined every inch of his surface and would prevent the slightest twitch of even his amazing muscles.

It was absurd, no doubt, to feel sorry for a robot, a man-made mechanism, but Cliff had come to think of him as being really alive, as a human is alive. He showed purpose and will; he performed complicated and resourceful acts; his face had twice clearly shown the emotion of sadness, and several times what appeared to be deep thought; he had been ruthless with the gorilla, and gentle with the mocking bird and the other two bodies, and he had twice refrained from crushing Cliff when there seemed every reason that he might. Cliff did not doubt for a minute that he was still alive, whatever that "alive" might mean.

But outside were waiting the radio and television men; he had work to do. He turned and went to them and all got busy.

An hour later Cliff sat alone about fifteen feet above the ground in a big tree which, located just across the walk from the building, commanded through a window a clear view of the upper part of Gnut's body. Strapped to the limbs about him were three instruments—his infrared viewing magnifier, a radio mike, and an infrared television eye with sound pickup. The first, the viewing magnifier, would allow him to see in the dark with his own eyes, as if by daylight, a magnified image of the robot, and the others would pick up any sights and sounds, including his own remarks, and transmit them to the several broadcast studios which would fling them millions of miles in all directions through space. Never before had a picture man had such an important assignment, probably—certainly not one who forgot to take pictures. But now that was forgotten, and Cliff was quite proud, and ready.

Far back in a great circle stood a multitude of the curious—and the fearful. Would the plastic glasstex hold Gnut? If it did not, would he come out thirsting for revenge? Would unimaginable beings come out of the traveler and release him, and perhaps exact revenge? Millions at their receivers were jittery; those in the distance hoped nothing awful would happen, yet they hoped something would, and they were prepared to run.

In carefully selected spots not far from Cliff on all sides were mobile ray batteries manned by army units, and in a hollow in back of him, well to his right, there was stationed a huge tank with a large gun. Every weapon was trained on the door of the wing. A row of smaller, faster tanks stood ready fifty yards directly north. Their ray projectors were aimed at the door, but not their guns. The grounds about the building contained only one spot—the hollow where the great tank was—where, by close calculation, a shell directed at the doorway would not cause damage and loss of life to some part of the sprawling capital.

Dusk fell; out streamed the last of the army officers, politicians and other privileged ones; the great metal doors of the wing clanged to and were locked for the night. Soon Cliff was alone, except for the watchers at their weapons scattered around him.

Hours passed. The moon came out. From time to time Cliff reported to the studio crew that all was quiet. His unaided eyes could now see nothing of Gnut but the two faint red points of his eyes, but through the magnifier he stood out as clearly as if in daylight from an apparent distance of only ten feet. Except for his eyes, there was no evidence that he was anything but dead and unfunctionable metal.

Another hour passed. Now and again Cliff thumbed the levels of his tiny radio-television watch—only a few seconds at a time because of its limited battery. The air was full of Gnut and his own face and his own name, and once the tiny screen showed the tree in which he was then sitting and even, minutely, himself. Powerful infrared long-distance television pickups were even then focused on him from nearby points of vantage. It gave him a funny feeling.

Then, suddenly, Cliff saw something and quickly bent his eye to the viewing magnifier. Gnut's eyes were moving; at least the intensity of the light emanating from them varied. It was as if two tiny red flashlights were turned from side to side, their beams at each motion crossing Cliff's eyes.

Thrilling, Cliff signaled the studios, cut in his pickups, and described the phenomenon. Millions resonated to the excitement in his voice. Could Gnut conceivably break out of that terrible prison?

Minutes passed, the eye flashes continued, but Cliff could discern no movement or attempted movement of the robot's body. In brief snatches he described what he saw. Gnut was clearly alive; there could be no doubt he was straining against the transparent prison in which he had at last been locked fast; but unless he could crack it, no motion should show.

Cliff took his eye from the magnifier—and started. His unaided eye, looking at Gnut shrouded in darkness, saw an astonishing thing not yet visible through his instrument. A faint red glow was spreading over the robot's body. With trembling fingers he readjusted the lens of the television eye, but even as he did so the glow grew in intensity. It looked as if Gnut's body was being heated to incandescence!

He described it in excited fragments, for it took most of his attention to keep correcting the lens. Gnut passed from a figure of dull red to one brighter and brighter, clearly glowing now even through the magnifier. And then he moved! Unmistakably he moved!

He had within himself somehow the means to raise his own body temperature, and was exploiting the one limitation of the plastic in which he was locked. For glasstex, Cliff now remembered, was a thermoplastic material, one that set by cooling and conversely would soften again with heat. Gnut was melting his way out!

In three-word snatches, Cliff described this. The robot became cherry-red, the sharp edges of the icelike block rounded, and the whole structure began to sag. The process accelerated. The robot's body moved more widely. The plastic lowered to the crown of his head, then to his neck, then his waist, which was as far as Cliff could see. His body was free! And then, still cherry-red, he moved forward out of sight!

Cliff strained eyes and ears, but caught nothing but the distant roar of the watchers beyond the police lines and a few low, sharp commands from the batteries posted around him. They, too, had heard, and perhaps seen by telescreen, and were waiting.

Several minutes passed. There was a sharp, ringing crack; the great metal doors of the wing flew open, and out stepped the metal giant, glowing no longer. He stood stockstill, and his red eyes pierced from side to side through the darkness.

Voices out in the dark barked orders and in a twinkling Gnut was bathed in narrow crisscrossing rays of sizzling, colored light. Behind him the metal doors began to melt, but his great green body showed no change at all. Then the world seemed to come to an end; there was a deafening roar, everything before Cliff seemed to explode in smoke and chaos, his tree whipped to one side so that he was nearly thrown out. Pieces of debris rained down. The tank gun had spoken, and Gnut, he was sure, had been hit.

Cliff held on tight and peered into the haze. As it cleared he made out a stirring among the debris at the door, and then dimly but unmistakably he saw the great form of Gnut rise to his feet. He got up slowly, turned toward the tank, and suddenly darted toward it in a wide arc. The big gun swung in an attempt to cover him, but the robot side-stepped and then was upon it. As the crew scattered, he destroyed its breech with one blow of his fist, and then he turned and looked right at Cliff.

He moved toward him, and in a moment was under the tree. Cliff climbed higher. Gnut put his two arms around the tree and gave a lifting push, and the tree tore out at the roots and fell crashing to its side. Before Cliff could scramble away, the robot had lifted him in his metal hands.

Cliff thought his time had come, but strange things were yet in store for him that night. Gnut did not hurt him. He looked at him from arm's length for a moment, then lifted him to a sitting position on his shoulders, legs straddling his neck. Then, holding one ankle, he turned and without hesitation started down the path which led westward away from the building.

Cliff rode helpless. Out over the lawns he saw the muzzles of the scattered field pieces move as he moved, Gnut—and himself—their one focus. But they did not fire. Gnut, by placing him on his shoulders, had secured himself against that—Cliff hoped.

The robot bore straight toward the Tidal Basin. Most of the field pieces throbbed slowly after. Far back, Cliff saw a dark tide of confusion roll into the cleared area—the police lines had broken. Ahead, the ring thinned rapidly off to the sides; then, from all directions but the front, the tide rolled in until individual shouts and cries could be made out. It came to a stop about fifty yards off, and few people ventured nearer.

Gnut paid them no attention, and he no more noticed his burden than he might a fly. His neck and shoulders made Cliff a seat hard as steel, but with the difference that their underlying muscles with each movement flexed, just as would those of a human being. To Cliff, this metal musculature became a vivid wonder.

Straight as the flight of a bee, over paths, across lawns and through thin rows of trees Gnut bore the young man, the roar of thousands of people following close. Above droned copters and darting planes, among them police cars with their nerve-shattering sirens. Just ahead lay the still waters of the Tidal Basin, and in its midst the simple marble tomb of the slain ambassador, Klaatu, gleaming black and cold in the light of the dozen searchlights always trained on it at night. Was this a rendezvous with the dead?

Without an instant's hesitation, Gnut strode down the bank and entered the water. It rose to his knees, then waist, until Cliff's feet were under. Straight through the dark waters for the tomb of Klaatu the robot made his inevitable way.

The dark square mass of gleaming marble rose higher as they neared it. Gnut's body began emerging from the water as the bottom shelved upward, until his dripping feet took the first of the rising pyramid of steps. In a moment they were at the top, on the narrow platform in the middle of which rested the simple oblong tomb.

Stark in the blinding searchlights, the giant robot walked once around it, then, bending, he braced himself and gave a mighty push against the top. The marble cracked; the thick cover slipped askew and broke with a loud noise on the far side. Gnut went to his knees and looked within, bringing Cliff well up over the edge.

Inside, in sharp shadow against the converging light beams, lay a transparent plastic coffin, thick walled and sealed against the centuries, and containing all that was mortal of Klaatu, unspoken visitor from the great Unknown. He lay as if asleep, on his face the look of godlike nobility that had caused some of the ignorant to believe him divine. He wore the robe he had arrived in. There were no faded flowers, no jewelry, no ornaments; they would have seemed profane. At the foot of the coffin lay the small sealed box, also of transparent plastic, which contained all of Earth's records of his visit—a description of the events attending his arrival, pictures of Gnut and the traveler, and the little roll of sight-and-sound film which had caught for all time his few brief motions and words.

Cliff sat very still, wishing he could see the face of the robot. Gnut, too, did not move from his position of reverent contemplation—not for a long time. There on the brilliantly lighted pyramid, under the eyes of a fearful, tumultuous multitude, Gnut paid final respect to his beautiful and adored master.

Suddenly, then, it was over. Gnut reached out and took the little box of records, rose to his feet and started down the steps.

Back through the water, straight back to the building, across lawns and paths as before, he made his irresistible way. Before him the chaotic ring of people melted away, behind they followed as close as they dared, trampling each other in their efforts to keep him in sight. There are no television records of his return. Every pickup was damaged on the way to the tomb.

As they drew near the building, Cliff saw that the tank's projectile had made a hole twenty feet wide extending from the roof to the ground. The door still stood open, and Gnut, hardly varying his almost jerkless rhythm, made his way over the debris and went straight for the port end of the ship. Cliff wondered if he would be set free.

He was. The robot set him down and pointed toward the door; then, turning, he made the sounds that opened the ship. The ramp slid down and he entered.

Then Cliff did the mad, courageous thing which made him famous for a generation. Just as the ramp started sliding back in he skipped over it and himself entered the ship. The port closed.

VII

It was pitch dark, and the silence was absolute. Cliff did not move. He felt that Gnut was close, just ahead, and it was so.

His hard metal hand took him by the waist, pulled him against his cold side, and carried him somewhere ahead. Hidden lamps suddenly bathed the surroundings with bluish light.

He set Cliff down and stood looking at him. The young man already regretted his rash action, but the robot, except for his always unfathomable eyes, did not seem angry. He pointed to a stool in one corner of the room. Cliff quickly obeyed this time and sat meekly, for a while not even venturing to look around.

He saw he was in a small laboratory of some kind. Complicated metal and plastic apparatus lined the walls and filled several small tables; he could not recognize or guess the function of a single piece. Dominating the center of the room was a long metal table on whose top lay a large box, much like a coffin on the outside, connected by many wires to a complicated apparatus at the far end. From close above spread a cone of bright light from a many-tubed lamp.

One thing, half covered on a near-by table, did look familiar—and very much out of place. From where he sat it seemed to be a brief case—an ordinary Earthman's brief case. He wondered.

Gnut paid him no attention, but at once, with the narrow edge of a thick tool, sliced the lid off the little box of records. He lifted out the strip of sight-and-sound film and spent fully half an hour adjusting it within the apparatus at the end of the big table. Cliff watched, fascinated, wondering at the skill with which the robot used his tough metal fingers. This done, Gnut worked for a long time over some accessory apparatus on an adjoining table. Then he paused thoughtfully a moment and pushed inward a long rod.

A voice came out of the coffinlike box—the voice of the slain ambassador.

"I am Klaatu," it said, "and this is Gnut."

From the recording!—flashed through Cliff's mind. The first and only words the ambassador had spoken. But, then, in the very next second he saw that it was not so. There was a man in the box! The man stirred and sat up, and Cliff saw the living face of Klaatu!

Klaatu appeared somewhat surprised and spoke quickly in an unknown tongue to Gnut—and Gnut, for the first time in Cliff's experience, spoke himself in answer. The robot's syllables tumbled out as if born of human emotion, and the expression on Klaatu's face changed from surprise to wonder. They talked for several minutes. Klaatu, apparently fatigued, then began to lie down, but stopped midway, for he saw Cliff. Gnut spoke again,

at length. Klaatu beckoned Cliff with his hand, and he went to
him.

"Gnut has told me everything," he said in a low, gentle voice,
then looked at Cliff for a moment in silence, on his face a faint,
tired smile.

Cliff had a hundred questions to ask, but for a moment hardly
dared open his mouth.

"But you," he began at last—very respectfully, but with an escaping excitement—"you are not the Klaatu that was in the tomb?"

The man's smile faded and he shook his head.

"No." He turned to the towering Gnut and said something in
his own tongue, and at his words the metal features of the robot
twisted as if with pain. Then he turned back to Cliff. "I am dying,"
he announced simply, as if repeating his words for the Earthman.
Again to his face came the faint, tired smile.

Cliff's tongue was locked. He just stared, hoping for light.
Klaatu seemed to read his mind.

"I see you don't understand," he said. "Although unlike us,
Gnut has great powers. When the wing was built and the lectures
began, there came to him a striking inspiration. Acting on it at
once, in the night, he assembled this apparatus . . . and now he
has made me again, from my voice, as recorded by your people.
As you must know, a given body makes a characteristic sound.
He constructed an apparatus which reversed the recording process, and from the given sound made the characteristic body."

Cliff gasped. So that was it!

"But you needn't die!" Cliff exclaimed suddenly, eagerly. "Your
voice recording was taken when you stepped out of the ship,
while you were well! You must let me take you to a hospital! Our
doctors are very skillful!"

Hardly perceptibly, Klaatu shook his head.

"You still don't understand," he said slowly and more faintly.
"Your recording had imperfections. Perhaps very slight ones, but
they doom the product. All of Gnut's experiments died in a few
minutes, he tells me . . . and so must I."

Suddenly, then, Cliff understood the origin of the "experiments." He remembered that on the day the wing was opened a
Smithsonian official had lost a brief case containing film strips recording the speech of various world fauna. There, on that table,
was a brief case! And the Stillwells must have been made from
strips kept in the table drawer!

But his heart was heavy. He did not want this stranger to die.

Slowly there dawned on him an important idea. He explained it with growing excitement.

"You say the recording was imperfect, and of course it was. But the cause of that lay in the use of an imperfect recording apparatus. So if Gnut, in his reversal of the process, had used exactly the same pieces of apparatus that your voice was recorded with, the imperfections could be studied, canceled out, and you'd live, and not die!"

As the last words left his lips, Gnut whipped around like a cat and gripped him tight. A truly human excitement was shining in the metal muscles of his face.

"Get me that apparatus!" he ordered—in clear and perfect English! He started pushing Cliff toward the door, but Klaatu raised his hand.

"There is no hurry," Klaatu said gently; "it is too late for me. What is your name, young man?"

Cliff told him.

"Stay with me to the end," he asked. Klaatu closed his eyes and rested; then, smiling just a little, but not opening his eyes, he added: "And don't be sad, for I shall now perhaps live again . . . and it will be due to you. There is no pain—" His voice was rapidly growing weaker. Cliff, for all the questions he had, could only look on, dumb. Again Klaatu seemed to be aware of his thoughts.

"I know," he said feebly, "I know. We have so much to ask each other. About your civilization . . . and Gnut's—"

"And yours," said Cliff.

"And Gnut's," said the gentle voice again. "Perhaps . . . some day . . . perhaps I will be back—"

He lay without moving. He lay so for a long time, and at last Cliff knew that he was dead. Tears came to his eyes; in only these few minutes he had come to love this man. He looked at Gnut. The robot knew, too, that he was dead, but no tears filled his red-lighted eyes; they were fixed on Cliff, and for once the young man knew what was in his mind.

"Gnut," he announced earnestly, as if taking a sacred oath, "I'll get the original apparatus. I'll get it. Every piece of it, the exact same things."

Without a word, Gnut conducted him to the port. He made the sounds that unlocked it. As it opened, a noisy crowd of Earthmen outside trampled each other in a sudden scramble to get out of the building. The wing was lighted. Cliff stepped down the ramp.

The next two hours always in Cliff's memory had a dreamlike quality. It was as if that mysterious laboratory with the peacefully sleeping dead man was the real and central part of his life, and his scene with the noisy men with whom he talked a gross and barbaric interlude. He stood not far from the ramp. He told only part of his story. He was believed. He waited quietly while all the pressure which the highest officials in the land could exert was directed toward obtaining for him the apparatus the robot had demanded.

When it arrived, he carried it to the floor of the little vestibule behind the port. Gnut was there, as if waiting. In his arms he held the slender body of the second Klaatu. Tenderly he passed him out to Cliff, who took him without a word, as if all this had been arranged. It seemed to be the parting.

Of all the things Cliff had wanted to say to Klaatu, one remained imperatively present in his mind. Now, as the green metal robot stood framed in the great green ship, he seized his chance.

"Gnut," he said earnestly, holding carefully the limp body in his arms, "you must do one thing for me. Listen carefully. I want you to tell your master—the master yet to come—that what happened to the first Klaatu was an accident, for which all Earth is immeasurably sorry. Will you do that?"

"I have known it," the robot answered gently.

"But will you promise to tell your master—just those words—as soon as he is arrived?"

"You misunderstand," said Gnut, still gently, and quietly spoke four more words. As Cliff heard them a mist passed over his eyes and his body went numb.

As he recovered and his eyes came back to focus he saw the great ship disappear. It just suddenly was not there any more. He fell back a step or two. In his ears, like great bells, rang Gnut's last words. Never, never was he to disclose them till the day he came to die.

"You misunderstand," the mighty robot had said. "I am the master."

1940

TWO/

· Trouble on Tantalus
· Time Wants a Skeleton
· Nightfall

Much of the hokum which appeared in ASF's rival science fiction magazines was forbidden in its sacrosanct pages. The romantic, the exotic, was kept within bounds; slowly, indeed, it withered and died entirely. But in the early forties—in the Golden Age—a balance between sheer fantasy and sheer nonsense was delicately maintained.

Look, for example, at "Trouble on Tantalus," written by a gentleman who has been Analog's resident book reviewer for many years. What happens there? Why, some lone spaceman on some ghastly planet far out in the galaxy gets caught by a Stalker. He rouses to consciousness to find himself in a windowless place confronted by some extremely odd beings, among them an ill-intentioned Blueskin and a nightmare creature that croaks the kind of croak which rattles in a young reader's memory for ages: "I am Shag, a Murath."

This fine animal reveals that they are all captive within the incubation pouch of a Stalker! Miller's story, on reflection, may owe a certain debt to Edgar Rice Burroughs and Stanley Weinbaum; but it has an authority of its own.

The same may be said for "Time Wants a Skeleton," by that grand old writer of magazine sf, Ross Rocklynne. A strangely circular plot-line, a story heavy with fate, and a dramatic setting on a planet about to break up . . . it was irresistible, and at least one young reader cherished it for many years as the best piece of sf he had ever read.

To read the story today is to see how heavily it tends toward melodrama. But belief remains in the discovery of that sinister cave which—deserted, transformed— will reappear millions of years later in such different circumstances! And the irresistible approach of destruction

*is there still . . . But memory is as much an artist as a
mere recorder; and Rocklynne's simple descriptive line,
"Heavy, dully coloured birds fought their way overhead,"
first received in 1941, had grown over the years into
a whole volume on the doomed fauna and flora of a planet
predestined to be strewn across the skies of the solar system.
The story's great to read now—far greater to have read
it "way back when!"*

*"Nightfall" made almost as great an impression.
What a romantic theme!—Darkness falling only once in two
thousand, and forty-nine years! Hubert Rogers spread the terror
of it across the cover, with a madman dashing into the great
observatory with a burning brand and, far in the background,
the cities of Lagash going up in flames!*

*Alas, life is long, art short, and we can see now how stagey is
the unlikely character-conflict between the director of the
university and a young newspaperman; but the theme still
retains its gloomy splendour and the situation its tragedy.*

*In many other ways, too, "Nightfall" lays claim to our
attention. The other two grand old stories in this section look
back toward the past history of science fiction; "Nightfall"
points towards the future of ASF. For Asimov is, in many ways,
the Astounding writer par excellence. He may utilise
phenomena familiar to an earlier generation of writers, but
Asimov's mode of operation is more calculated and intellectual.
One may guess that a typical thirties writer, using the
"Nightfall" theme, would have Lagash's light eclipsed by a
"runaway planet" (the skies of thirties sf are full of 'em!);
but Lagash's doom, in Asimov's hands, is the result of an eclipse
which can be predicted, a cyclic event, one yielding to
rational calculation.*

*Precisely this new factor marked the best years of
Campbell's Astounding, and nowhere is it more evident than in
the writings of Asimov. That he has become (somewhat in the
manner of H. G. Wells) a law-giver rather than a story-teller
does not detract from his achievement in introducing
something of scientific method into the very unfolding of
his stories. By the time of "Nightfall", he had begun his long-
lasting robot series, and here again the old mad hordes of
cyclopean-eyed tin menaces have been banished by the
formulation of laws, on the basis of which things are
predictable, and the universe in consequence habitable to
reason.*

This scientific spirit pervades Asimov's fiction and compensates for lack of psychological understanding. It rises to its greatest in the Foundation series which, in many ways, interestingly embodies Asimov's own attitude to sf; it is itself about prediction. Psycho-history is the laws of robotics applied to human populations.

Trouble on Tantalus /

by P. SCHUYLER MILLER

There was a mystery somewhere on that little-known planet, and like it or not, Moran was being carried into the heart of it!

The mutter of the bull drums throbbed through the dripping blackness. Moran pushed his face deeper into the muck of the forest floor and listened.

VUB, vub, vub, vub. VUB, vub, vub, vub.

They were on three sides of him now. To east, and south, and north of him the Blueskin shamans were thumping their mocking challenge, dancing their frenzied dances, promising their young men his skull for the village pyramid and his skin for a drum that would outroar, outbluster and outbrag any drum in all the reeking jungles of Tantalus.

To east and south and north—the road ahead was clear. There lay the great sky-reaching crags of the Mountains of the Night, blanketed in everlasting clouds, cleft by bottomless chasms, drenched by the endless rains that were slishing into the mire in which he lay, rattling on the forest roof above him. There, somewhere, was the mysterious Black Hole that had sucked a score of ether ships into oblivion since men first found this God-forsaken planet. There—

Somewhere ahead of him another drum began to beat. *Tap, tap, tap.* A little drum—a shrill drum—a drum headed with human skin. *Tap, tap, tap.* A drum that jeered and mocked and dared him to come and fight. He knew that drum. He knew the blue-skinned devil who was hammering Pete Davis' stretched pelt with Pete Davis' bleached white shinbone, and by the same token, old Wallagash knew him. The withered ear that was nailed to the wall of his shack back in Talus was mate to the one that was out there in the blackness, listening to the tap, tap, tapping of Pete's shin on Pete's tanned belly. The evil, slanted eye that was peering through the murk was mate to the one his knuckles had found the night Pete Davis died. North and south, east and west. They had him, and they knew it. Well, by Heaven they'd see fighting before he went!

Six feet six of him reared out of the stinking muck. Black mud matted his red beard and his red mane. Black ooze trickled down the white barrel of his chest. One huge fist closed on the thorn branch that arched over him and ripped it down. He broke it across his knee and hefted it approvingly. With a shillelagh like that in his hand Paddy Moran could bash heads till they cut the guts out of him, and maybe a bit longer if his legs held.

VUB, vub, vub, vub. VUB, vub, vub, vub.

They'd make no drum of his skin, by the saints! They'd carve no obscene runes on his boiled shins to make magic against white men of Earth. They'd finish him, like enough, but what they got wouldn't be cat meat. He shivered. There was a tale told that the Morans had a banshee to wail them into the place of Death when the time came, but like enough she'd lost her way after the first few million miles of empty space. Sirius was not a far star, as stars went, but it was far enough, and Tantalus was by a long way the least pleasant of its many planets.

He made no attempt to be quiet now. The sooner it was done the better. He plowed his way steadily through the dripping undergrowth toward that mocking tapping in the west. It grew louder as he approached, and he could hear the echo of it rattling against the naked rock of the escarpment beyond. Then suddenly it stopped.

He stood stock-still, head up like a listening stag. Far to the north a single drum still mumbled; it broke off in midbeat, and the only sound was the hiss of rain through the branches and the drip of water in liquid mud. His grip on the thorn club tightened until he felt the skin stretch on his knuckles. The short hairs prickled along his spine. What deviltry was afoot now?

And then he heard it.

Rather, he felt it. Under his spread feet the ground trembled with a slow, rhythmic shock. One—and two—and three—and four. Like a marching army. Like the slow pacing of a giant cat. Like—

Saints above! *The Stalkers!*

Sweat came out on him in trickling beads. Blueskins he could fight. Blueskins were men. But the Stalkers were legend—horrible legend!

He listened, not breathing. They moved like cats, with a cat's stealth, with a cat's cruel sureness. They were black as the pit of hell, invisible in the night. They were ogres, demons, vampires. They were Death!

Somewhere behind him a Blueskin screamed in terror—the high, mad yammer of a frightened beast. It was too far—there must be more than one. They hunted in pairs, legend said. Up through his legs, from the quaking bog to his prickling brain, thudded the slow rhythm of the approaching footsteps. One—and two—and three—and four—

Off to the right a tree ripped down through the tangle of vines and branches to crash with echoing thunder in the mud. He wheeled, stared vainly into the blackness. Was it there?

There was a trickle of light from above. Silver highlights shone on the sprawling roots of a forest giant. Slowly, settling each foot in the mire with infinite care, he moved into their shadow. Squeezed into a crevice in the trunk he stared at the ghostly column of light that filtered down from above. It must cross that to reach him. He would see it, silhouetted against the gleam from that glistening pool. Magnified by the resonant wood on which he stood, the footsteps shook his whole tensed body. Thud! And thud! And thud!

They stopped. A foul, animal reek stifled him. Then claws thick as a man's body closed on him and lifted him struggling into the treetops.

Moran regained consciousness. The reek of musk was still in his nostrils. The air was saturated with it. It made his head swim. He lay still in the dark, trying to gauge his whereabouts. There was a carpet of thick velvet under his spread fingers. It was dry, and hot, and it swayed under him with a slow rhythm that matched the swing of the thudding footsteps.

He got unsteadily to his feet, stood with spread legs. He put out his hand, and touched naked, wrinkled flesh that shrank away with a shriek. Something went scuttling past him in the darkness. Something whispered behind him. There was a slow, methodical sucking that brought the goose pimples on him. He took one cautious step ahead.

His foot struck something, spun it aside. He stooped and groped for it, found it. It was his club. Then he remembered the pouch at his waist. There was a white light in it. His fingers fumbled with the flap, opened it, found the little metal cylinder with its crystal bulb. As the tiny flame blazed up his jaw sagged in amazement.

He was in a narrow, windowless room lined with black velvet. A great scarlet egg twice his height filled all the far end. And cowering against its base was such an assemblage as only the mad, black jungles of Tantalus could have spawned.

Two little things like naked pink Teddy bears huddled together against the scarlet shell. Their huge, opalescent eyes sparkled with blind terror in the bright light. A creature like a wingless, boat-billed stork, with a bristling bright-blue mustache fringing its horny beak, stood morosely on one leg, regarding him with one oval eye. There was a flat pancake disk of mottled flesh, pegged around the edge with short red legs, that seemed to be trying to burrow under the egg. And almost at his feet a thing like a giant black weasel, with six stubby legs and a tubular snout, was sucking avidly at the throat of a Blueskin woman.

Some sixth sense warned him. He ducked as an eight-inch glass blade snicked past his ear and shattered against the egg. He spun on bent legs, his club raised. Old Wallagash crouched there against the wall, a snarl on his wrinkled face, red hatred in his single slanted eye. In his withered claw was a thing like a barbed steel skewer, three feet long and needle-sharp. With a cackling screech he leaped, just as Moran's club came down with a splintering crash.

The shaman's arm fell limp, broken at the elbow. Moran's fist caught him under his receding chin. The second blow smashed into his naked belly; the third crunched full into his grinning, black-lipped mouth. Then Moran had him by the scrawny throat, worrying him like a dog with a bone.

Wallagash went limp. Moran got to his feet and retrieved his light. Ugly old devil! All Blueskins were ugly, with their pointed ears and slant eyes, their grinning, toothy mouths, their bodies made in grotesque imitation of humanity. There was a story that they were the creation of the demented scientist who had first landed on this insane planet that the space hogs call Tantalus. Certainly they resembled nothing in this mud hole so much as man. A filthy tuft of hair hung at the dead sachem's waist. Blond hair. A woman's hair! Moran knew those bleached locks—knew them intimately. So that was why Pete Davis had launched his mad crusade against the Blueskins. Moran shrugged. Much good it had done him. You could get other women, but a man had only one skin.

He turned his back on what was left of Wallagash. There was other danger here. That weasel-thing—he'd heard of them before. Rumor had it that they followed you until you slept, then sucked the life out of you while you dreamed pretty dreams. He'd learned to respect rumor in such matters. He picked up the dead Blueskin's needle-sword.

"O, Man."

The voice came from above. It was like the croak of a Martian raven. He looked up. Perched on top of the great scarlet egg was the damnedest creature he had ever seen.

It was the size of a bulldog, with a face like a vampire bat and a head of spiky black hair growing between two spreading ears. It was as black as sin, with short, kinky wool growing all over its potbellied body down to the ankles of its double-jointed legs. Its feet were two-toed claws, bare black skin over knuckly bone. And wrapping it like a leather cape were two huge bat's wings whose hooked wrists stuck up above its head like furled flags.

It had eyes like blood-red soup plates with pin-prick pupils. One of them swiveled to stare up into the shadows above them; the other regarded him unwinkingly.

"I am Shag, a Murath," the thing croaked.

Moran had heard of the Muraths. "Gollywogs," space hogs called them. They were the true native race of Tantalus, held in slavery by the few semicivilized Blueskins who had their black stone cities on the strip of fen land beyond the Mountains of the Night. Few humans had ever visited them, and fewer had returned, for while the citified Blueskins lacked some of the unpleasant habits of their savage brethren, they were inclined to be touchy and had some unpleasant tendencies toward atavism.

"Do not touch the sheetag," the clipped voice went on. "It will scream and arouse the Stalker. I can escape. I can bring help."

Sheetag—that was the weasel thing. But what did this padded cell have to do with the Stalkers? What had happened, anyway?

"Where are we?" Moran demanded. "What's this all about?"

The little creature rustled its wings impatiently. "Must we talk?" it asked. "Very well. This is the egg of a Stalker. This is its incubation pouch. Perhaps the egg will hatch and the young of the Stalker will eat us. Perhaps it will do something else. I do not know. Nobody knows. I know that I can escape if you will help. You will come here please."

Moran shrugged. Half his life had been spent in space and the planets that rattled around in space. He'd given up balking at screwy situations long ago. He crammed his shoulders into the space behind the big red egg, wedged his knee against its pebbly surface, and began to climb.

Against his back the black plush wall of the room pulsed with a rhythm quite different from the lurch and sway he had felt before. It was like a great artery, throbbing with the incessant pulse of life. What if it *was* an artery? What if this *was* the brooding pouch of a Stalker, as Shag had said? Then what in the name of Heaven must a Stalker be like?

The Murath thrust out a long-toed foot and hauled him up on the rounded top of the egg. It had no hands, only the two great wings. They must have had a spread of twenty feet. No wonder the creature's chest stuck out like the keel of a yacht.

He had to stoop because of the ceiling. The black fur lining stopped opposite his knees. Leathery black skin covered two bands of muscle that closed the pouch. He put his hand up. They were warm, like flesh. They were flesh. It was true.

The gollywog's hideous face swiveled toward him. "You can make an opening," it observed passionlessly. "You are strong. I will crawl out. I am small. I will bring help. I can fly."

One scrawny claw kicked at the bands of muscle above his head. "The pouch is weak here. You are strong. You will make it open. You will hold it until I escape. I can fly. I will bring help."

Moran stiffened his legs, and braced both hands where the gollywog had pointed. Sure—he'd open up, if it could be done. As for letting the little rat make his getaway alone, that was something else. He gritted his teeth and heaved. With surprising ease the walls of muscle parted. He thrust his shoulders into the gap, hitched his knees against the opposite side, and shoved.

He was in starlight. Fifty feet below drifted a sea of swirling, heaving clouds. Above, a vast black naked body blotted out the stars. This was a Stalker! This thing that walked on mountains!

The Murath's bristling head pushed up beside his legs. It climbed out and perched precariously on the lip of the pouch, staring owlishly out over the panorama of mountain crags that rose about them. The Stalker was deep in the heart of the unknown ranges, and every swing stride was bearing them farther. Then below sounded a shrill, piercing scream of rage. The *sheetag!* The Stalker stopped.

Two vast bat wings spread before him and Shag dived spinning into space. His tiny body swung like a grape between his great black wings. They flapped slowly, ponderously, lifting him higher and higher above the encircling peaks, carrying him with each beat farther from the colossal body of the Stalker. Then out of the rolling cloud-sea burst a shape from nightmare—the second Stalker!

Two hundred feet—three hundred—how could he measure it in that phantom light? Only the weak gravity of Tantalus could spawn so monstrous a thing. The mists boiled about its shoulders, about its waist, about its plodding legs. Legs like the massive columns of centuries-old trees. A body broad as an ether ship, squat, bent, blotting out the sky. A head peaked and misshapen, with glowing yellow eyes like gibbous moons. And arms like the flails of Death himself, striking like mighty serpents at the tiny winging shape!

Some updraft from the steepled crags caught the Murath and spun him upward like a leaf. The smiting talons swept harmlessly beneath him; he rocked dizzily in the boiling air currents, then tilted his giant wings and slid like a drifting shadow into the abyss.

Again that vast claw struck—and missed. The winged dot swerved deftly from its path. The black wings folded and Shag fell like a plummet into the seething mists. Only the furrows left by raking talons showed where he had been.

A spasm shook the wall of muscle against which Moran was braced. Spurted like a melon seed from between the closing lips of the pouch, he sprawled over emptiness while the clouds rushed up to meet him. Then out of nowhere came a giant, glistening hand that caught him, crushed him, thrust him kicking into oblivion.

It seemed that he came swimming up out of unfathomable depths. A glassy wall stretched over him, barring him from the light. He beat at it with his fists—burst through and yelled with all the pent-up agony of bursting lungs. His feet were under him, firm on solid stone, and he shouted blind defiance at God and man.

He saw the sprawling city of the Stalkers.

Walls of splintered rock soared upward into the clouds. He stood a thousand feet above the valley floor, on a terrace of cut stone, with the grotesque hovels spread before him like children's blocks rolled on a table top. Slabs of gray granite, toppled together and chinked with blocks of softer stone. Barrows of heaped boulders, covered with baked mud. Walled in crannies of the living rock, black with damp and dirt and decay. And beyond an endless labyrinth of smooth-cut blocks, ruined and desolate, stretching out mile after mile across the valley floor.

A city—and the memory of a city.

Giants had built it when Tantalus was young. Giants dwelt now in the hovels that huddled in the shadow of its colossal walls. Giants vaster and more terrible than anything in men's dreams, dwarfed by a glory that was dead and forever lost.

Steps climbed from the valley, each tread thrice a tall man's height. At their foot the Stalkers stood. There was a score of them —all that remained of the race that had raised the city of the plain. Their bodies were a mockery of man's, their arms dangling, simian things with three-clawed hands, their feet splayed, cloven hoofs. Their heads were like the twisted wedge of an earthly Brazil nut, the flat, curved bases turned ahead, the sloping sides meeting in a bony ridge that ran in a frill of jagged bone down their massive backs. An eye was set in each slant-face, great faceted yellow jewels peering out of pockets in the rubbery black flesh. A beaklike mouth split the forward apex of the wedge, and from its scarlet lips came a humming like the purr of a giant cat.

Behind him sounded an answering trill, shrill, sweet—and terrible!

Moran spun in his tracks. Pylons of cut stone rose on either hand, framing a mighty gateway in the cliffs. Beyond them, cut out of the gorge's floor, was a pit, blocking it from wall to wall. A pit—and in the pit a toad!

Great webbed paws were bowed under its bleached white belly. Its flat, warty head hung level with the terrace where he stood. Its golden eyes blinked sleepily, hypnotically, at the little group that cowered at the pit's edge—the creatures of the pouch.

Fear froze them in their tracks—fear and the fascination of those burning eyes. They swayed on their feet to the murmuring rhythm of the Stalkers, to the shrill piping of the monster toad. But now that crooning trill stopped short. Instantly one of the little pink things turned and ran. Faster than sight the toad's pale tongue licked out—and it was gone. Again from the valley he heard the exultant mutter of the Stalkers.

Pictures were racing through Moran's brain. Pictures of Earth, and he a boy, sprawled flat in the cool green grass beside a little stream, watching a toad eat ants. Time after time that lightning-swift tongue had struck, and each time an ant vanished. But always an ant that moved!

An ant that moved! Moran's muscles tensed. Billion on billions of miles separated this colossal monster from the little, harmless toads of Earth, but perhaps the force of evolution that had given them life had acted in the same way on this mad, black world. Perhaps this toad too saw only things that moved.

Slowly, slowly his fingers crept across his thigh, behind his back, where his knife should be. It came loose in his fingers and that hand crept slowly back. Eyes on the toad's great jeweled ones, he waited for that moment when its deadly trill would cease. Soon now—

Before it came he flipped the knife. It spun in a shining arc, stood quivering in the furry shoulder of the weasel-thing. With a scream of rage it spun, leaping like a black arrow toward him, but the toad was quicker. Its tongue licked out—was gone—and with it the *sheetag*. In that instant Moran sprang.

Five great strides took him to the pit's edge. Legs that had not faltered under accelerations of five gravities flung him into space. Feet first he struck between the toad's great, staring eyes. He slipped, fell to his knees, then before the monster's sluggish brain could know what had happened was on his feet and running, leaping, rolling on the gorge's rocky floor. Behind him the purring of the Stalkers rose to an angry buzz. He heard their great hoofs pounding on the stairs, the slap of the toad's webbed paws on the pit's walls as it turned. Scrambling to his feet he began to run.

The ravine twisted upward between sheer walls of solid rock. The floor was worn smooth by the tread of countless naked feet during endless years. Two hundred feet above him he could see the black smears where generations of Stalkers had rubbed their sooty shoulders against the rock. Below, at a man's height, were other smears where other, smaller things had gone. What was it that drew them, here in the desolate heart of the ranges?

As he climbed he began to feel the wind. The valley of the Stalkers was sheltered, but now he was rising above the level of the bounding cliffs, close under the cloud blanket, and as he advanced the force of the wind increased until he was leaning against a howling gale. It was raining again, a slow drizzle, and the fine droplets stung his face and bare body, washing away the mud that had caked on them.

By the time he reached the summit of the pass he was crawling on all fours, digging his fingers into crannies of the rock, hugging the walls of the ravine for what little shelter they afforded. He was in the midst of the clouds now, so that he groped his way through an impenetrable fog, lit from above by the weird blue light of distant Sirius.

On and on he crawled, driven now by a blind determination that seemed to have been born of the wind and the fog. Whatever happened, he would not turn back. Something there ahead called him as it had called countless other beings of many worlds through untold centuries.

At last the path led down. An icy rivulet ran ankle-deep in the groove that was worn in the soft slate by the plodding of many feet through many years. Soon he was below the clouds again, and the gorge was widening and deepening into a canyon whose fluted walls were a great harp on which the winds played dolefully. How far he had come from the valley of the Stalkers and their monstrous toad-god, he did not know. Nor did he care. There ahead, near now, was—something.

Ahead a natural archway spanned the gorge. It had been shaped into a gateway through which the wind screamed, a window above emptiness through which poured a flood of violet light. Battling his way foot by foot against the tempest, Moran came to the gateway and looked through.

Another valley lay below him, carved out of many-colored sandstone by the fury of the winds. Weird columns of red and orange rose from its barren floor, and the black slits of dry arroyos channeled its painted walls. Dykes of volcanic rock angled across it in an insane labyrinth, the softer shales and sandstones eaten away from around them, leaving them like the cyclopean tumbled ramparts of a city of the winds.

He did not see the weird beauty of that painted garden. He did not see the black dots that were caves in the gray limestone that underlay the painted rocks. He looked beyond, at the Black Hole of Tantalus—and the thing that gave it birth.

Opposite him the wind-carved minarets drew back from a road of purple quartz that formed a slowly rising ramp across the valley floor. Closing the valley's eastern end rose a cliff of black obsidian, splintered into a myriad of knife-edged facets by the terrific forces that had raised it from the depths of the planet. At its foot gaped the abyss.

Ten miles it must have been, between the obsidian wall and the rock of its nearer lip. Out of it poured a torrent of violet light, striking back with countless scintillant spear-shafts from the broken cliff. Above it the clouds spun back in the mighty whirlpool of the Black Hole, through which streamed the cosmic forces of the abyss that could suck a ship out of space against all the power of a hundred drumming jets. And where the road of amethyst met its edge there rose a shaft of clear crystal, six-sided, blunt-tipped, thirty feet and more from base to tip, through which the light from the planet's heart beat in a shower of fiery radiance. A giant crystal of pure, clear quartz, and at its heart a cavity, a bubble, in which floated a thin black speck that was—something.

The path led down through the maze of steepled rocks. At the first turn the abyss was lost to sight. It was then he saw the dwellers in the caves.

There were perhaps thirty of them, of a dozen races and worlds. There were Blueskins from Tantalus' own reeking jungles, and leather-bellied dwarfs from the red deserts of Mars. There were three-eyed, six-armed drogas from the twin worlds of Alpha Centauri, and octopus-armed lizards who inhabited the last of the six planets that circled Sirius. There was the tiny form of a Murath, one great wing burned away by a ray-blast. And old and young, short and tall, there were men of Earth!

They stood on the slope in front of the caves, gaunt and silent, eyeing him dourly. Moran tugged at his belt where a gun should be and squared his naked shoulders. They didn't seem overjoyed at the sight of him. Food was probably scarce here, and he was another mouth to cut down their rations. Well—they'd take him, and they'd like it!

As he came down from the rocks their line split to let him through. He felt a prickling at his spine as he passed between them, but no one moved to harm him. At the mouth of the largest cave he turned, his arms folded, his back to a great block of fallen stone.

"Now then," he demanded, "let's have it."

One man stepped forward from the rest, a Negro with the fine features and silky hair that meant Venusian blood.

"You're new here," he said tonelessly. "You're big and maybe you feel big. Maybe you'll have ideas about doing things, and about who'll do them. I wouldn't if I was you."

A grin came on Moran's bronzed face. He knew this kind of talk. "I might at that," he admitted. "And what would you gentlemen be thinking you might do about it?"

Three others aligned themselves with the black man. One was a Martian, with the shoulders and dangling arms of a bull ape. The other two were men his own size, or bigger.

"We've laws here," the Martian hissed. "We have ways of keeping them. There are four of us who see to that. You will eat when we tell you and what we tell you. You will sleep where we say and do what work we say. That is the law here, and you will obey it."

"Is it now?" Moran's thumbs were in his belt, and he teetered appraisingly on his toes. "So that's the way of it—little to eat and a devil of a lot too many to eat it. There'll be rations, I'm thinking, and the four of you to share them out when the time comes." He let his gaze wander insolently over the sullen faces of the crowd and back to the four who confronted him. "Now then, have you ever held the thought to make it five?"

The taller of the two white men answered. He had a knife scar on his cheek, and one ear had been mutilated by a ray-blast. "You're new here, fella," he sneered. "There's meat on your bones and blood in your guts. You'll take new men's rations till we and the boss say different. You'll do what we say, when we say it, or we'll pare you down a size in the collar and a couple more in the head."

Moran's grin was insulting. "Oh my, oh my," he deplored. "Is there no sportsmanship left in the race of man? Four of you against one, and you with your sour-looking friends to boot. Yah!" He spat contemptuously. "Come on, the four of you! I'll take any one of you with my hands tied and bend you into knots! I'll take all four of you—yes, and your friends besides—and show you who'll make the laws in this place from now on! Show me this skulking boss of yours, and by the saints I'll—"

"You will what?"

A man stood in the cave mouth, an old man, with white hair and beard, taller than Moran. He wore shorts and a jerkin of leather, and his arms were folded on the hilt of a mighty broadsword.

Moran turned to face him. Here was a man of another sort, a man he could treat as an equal.

"You'll be the boss, I think," he sneered. "And you a man past your best years. Faith, it must be no trick at all, to handle this gang of bezabors you have here."

"Do you think so?" There was a queer light in the old man's eyes. They were eagle eyes, peering under snow-white brows into Moran's face. The steely ring had gone out of his voice when he answered. "You have a name, I think. What, among friends, might it be?"

"Friends is it?" Moran snorted. "You talk softer than the boys here. It's maybe different if you've a man to buck, in the place of a lot of starved bilge rats with no starch in their knees. There's no secret to it, though—friend or foe it's Moran."

"Danny! My boy!" The great sword fell clanging on the rock. Tears were in the old man's eyes and his hands were outstretched. "Danny Moran—have you forgot your father?"

Moran gripped the oldster's two shoulders. The grin was back on his face and twice as broad.

"Paddy Moran is the way of it," he said, "not Danny. Patrick Terence Aloysius Moran is the whole of it, and a name that's known from here to Capella and maybe farther. Danny Moran was my father, God rest his soul, before the drink got him and he went off by his lone self after chib-bugs on Pluto. Is there a chance at all that you would be that teetotalin', horse-stealin', space-blisterin' old reprobate of the world, my esteemed old spalpeen of a grandfather?"

He knew it before he asked. The Moran face was there, under the white beard, and the Moran eyes, and the muscles of the Morans rippled under his fingers in shoulders that were eighty years old and more besides. It was thirty years ago that Michael Moran had steered his ship into the black gulf that is between the stars, and vanished like dust into space. Thirty years ago Patrick Moran was but a likely glint in his father's eye as he surveyed the pretty girls of Dublin. There had been tales told of the teetotaling giant with ready fists and a readier tongue who seemed always to have scrip in his wallet and a chip on each of his broad shoulders, but they ended where they began, in emptiness. Old Michael Moran was a legend among space hogs, and another Moran was fast becoming one in his own right.

A grin stood on the old man's face. His gnarled fist smote Moran's chest with a blow that would fell an ox. His arm went around the younger man's shoulder as he turned to his watching men.

"Ye've a Moran to deal with here, ye blaggards!" he roared. "Blood of my blood, and by the feel of him bone of my bone. He'll whip any five of you with his two hands tied and a quart of liquor in him, but by the Lord Harry if he touches a drop in my presence I'll have the hide off his back for it! Zagar—Moses—come here, the pack of you. Wolves that ye are, you've a better wolf than any of you to fawn on and ye'll feel his fangs too if need be, as ye've felt mine! He's new, but he's a Moran, and we'll stew the fatted calf in his honor, and be damned to tomorrow!"

The Martian's face was dark. "The ration's too short now," he hissed. "There's ten days before we'll get more. By what right do you break the law for a new man?"

Moran felt the old man stiffen beside him. One foot came down on the great sword, so that it clanged faintly on the rock.

"I made the law," the calm voice said. "I'll make new ones if need be. Would you, perhaps, care to make a trial of it?"

Zagar's glance fell. "You have the sword," he mumbled.

"I have indeed." The old man picked it up and stood again with his hands clasped on its massive hilt. It was beaten out of a strange gray steel, tempered blue at the edges, and as broad as a man's thigh. "With my own two hands I made it out of the star that fell, and as ye've cause to know I've used it. Are there, maybe, some of you that think it has grown too heavy for me to swing?"

"The law's for you, not us." It was Moses, the Negro. "You made it to suit yourself and you break it to make a feast for a man who has no need of food. You've kept us to a ration that a dog would starve on. You've kept us weak and sick, so you could lord it over us with your loud mouth and your big sword. We're thirty men, hungry, and you'll swill away our food!"

"And what will you do?" Moran felt the old man's elbow against him, pushing him back.

"We're bare-handed and you have the sword. All right. You asked if we thought you could still swing it. Well—can you?"

Quick as was the Negro's spring, the boss was quicker. The great blade fell in an arc of blue light. Split to the breastbone, Moses dropped at his feet. Then before he could free the sword the Martian was upon him.

The glint of battle shone in the old man's eyes. He caught the squat form in his two hands and swung it above his head, then hurled it, twisting and sprawling, into the mob. At his side Moran was slugging knee to knee with the bigger of Zagar's two companions. He felt the man's ribs come under his fist, saw bright red blood spurt from his lips, and stepped over him to meet the charge of the half-mad pack.

Months of starvation had told on them. In bloody glee Moran smashed at their bony faces, kicked at their crowding bodies, before the tide closed over him. He dug his thumbs into the throat of a snarling Blueskin uglier than old Wallagash. He ducked past the six flailing arms of a Centaurian and pushed back his scaly, three-eyed skull until his bull neck cracked. Then a tentacle as thick as his arm twined round his throat and began to tighten. As he raised his hands to tear it away, a second twisting tendril fastened on his wrists. A bloody haze thickened before his eyes. A pulse of spent air throbbed and hacked at his throat. Then with the clang of steel on iron-hard scales the tentacles loosened and he fell to his knees. He heard a great voice roaring somewhere near him. The mist cleared and he saw the old man, his sword red to the hilt, standing spread-legged over the cloven body of the lizard-man and shouting his defiance at the mob.

"Come on!" he cried. "Show me the stuff in you! There's but the two of us here, and me a grandfather to boot. Can I swing the sword yet, did you ask? Can I prove the law, who made it? Rats is what you are—crawling, squeaking rats! Is it food you're wanting? There's carrion for you! Fill your bellies so you can crawl into your holes like the rats ye are and dream of the day when you'll pull down Michael Moran. Or will you go to *her* and get your fill of what she'll give you?"

They quailed before him. Six of them were dead and Zagar lay writhing with a broken back. They retreated as the old man strode to where the crippled Martian lay.

"You know the law," he said quietly. "There's only death for you, the way you are, and you've got the choice. Which is it, the sword—or her?"

Moran saw black venom in Zagar's eyes. The flat brown face twisted in a leer of hate. "I claim the law!" the Martian hissed. "Take me to her!"

Dead silence followed his reply. Leaning on his sword, the old man stared into the hate-filled eyes. He shook himself like a great, shaggy dog.

"Pick him up, Paddy Moran," he commanded. "You'll be with us a long time, and you may as well know the whole of it now as later. Follow behind me now, and remember—kin of mine or not, I'm boss!"

Shouldering his bloody sword like a rifle, the old man strode down the broken slope in front of the caves. Picking up Zagar, Moran followed. An impulse came over him to crush the life out of that hate-filled dwarfish body and fling it away among the rocks, but the Martian's whisper stopped him:

"I claim the law!"

Following paths which old Michael seemed to know well, they wound their way through the labyrinth of wind-worn, gaudy stone, forcing their way against the howling gusts of wind that buffeted them from every side. They came to a little stream, a mere trickle of icy water running in a groove in the soft rock, and stopped to wash the blood from their faces and bodies and to clean the great sword. At last, through an avenue in the rock, Moran saw the amethyst dyke rising before them, its top a good fifty feet above the rock of the valley floor. Blocks of broken crystal made a steep way to its top, and up that broken away they climbed until they stood side by side on its bare summit, that ran like a great smoky purple road to the east.

Here in the open they were exposed to the full force of the wind. The dyke was glassy-smooth, and Moran had all he could do to keep his footing as he followed the old man along its top toward the abyss. He tried to speak, but the wind snatched the words from his mouth. He bowed his shoulders over the now unconscious Martian and struggled on.

Straight as a drawn line the purple causeway ran, splitting the valley in two halves. As they struggled on, the giant clear crystal at its end loomed ever higher before them and the dazzling radiance from the abyss beat ever brighter upon them, until they were forced to shield their eyes. A sudden gust spun Moran around and flung him to his knees, and as he rose he saw that the others were close behind them.

The old man walked cradling the sword in his arms like a child, his white head bowed. Moran could feel the fierce light on his skin, burning deep into it. Then it was welling up through the rock under his feet, beating in on all sides, so that it seemed that he walked on a ribbon of purple ice, flung out in a great projecting frost-tongue over the abyss.

The old man stopped. The dyke was narrow here, barely eight feet across, and the mutter of the wind had died until Moran could hear his voice.

"Lay him there at her feet."

Moran strode forward, one pace, two and three, and laid the body of the Martian at the base of the crystal shaft. He stepped back and looked up.

He saw her floating there.

She was a woman, taller than most, and slim. Her hair streamed in a red glory over her bare white shoulders, covering her body with a veil of silken flame. Her hands were pressed flat against her body, each pink fingernail showing as though lit from within. Her head was bent a little to look down, her red lips parted breathlessly. Her eyes were closed and the long dark lashes lay gently on her cheeks that were soft as white velvet.

She floated in a hollow in the quartz, an oval casket filled with violet radiance that surrounded her like a halo. The light from the abyss seemed somehow collected, curdled, compressed into the intangible medium in which she swam, her little feet pressed close together, her ten pink toes treading on emptiness. She was woman as men have dreamed of her since time began, and in him Moran felt the hot desire flooding up through his veins and bringing all the savage fury of love out of him in a mighty shout.

His grandfather's hand was on his shoulder and he shook it off. He stepped forward, stiff-legged, like a robot walking. He heard the Martian's cackle of mad glee.

He saw her green eyes open and look down at him.

Out of the world went everything but the love and the glory of her. Out of the world went everything but the red, red welcome of her parted lips, and the warm pleasure of her burning hair. Into his soul swam the glory of her sea-green eyes, calling him, drawing his life out to mingle with her life in a Nirvana never known to man.

In a world where the grass was springing emerald flame, where the trees drooped with clustered pearls for fruit and the streams were molten sapphire he wandered at her side under seething purple skies, and drank from the silver cup she held for him, feeling a flame of radiant fire surging through his veins as he sank with her into the clinging purple mists from which she drew her immortality—and his.

In a world where soft, perfumed breezes blew over spindrift of apple-jade and slow waves curled along coral sands, he lay dreaming under a moon of argent and shadowy purple, under a sky studded with diamond stars. In shadowed darkness, arched over with the filmy fronds of giant ferns, bedded on tufted mosses, he lay and played at love with maidens who ran from him through the pulsing darkness and danced among the silver moonbeams, mockingly, whose ringing voices called him, lured him, over hill and dale until in the cool gray light of dawn he came upon them bowered among orchids and saw them melt and merge into a shining, yielding One.

Flesh of her flesh he hung in the void above the Universe and saw it spread in a shining cloud beneath his spurning feet, saw it receding to a pin point of misty light as he rushed on and up and out into the utter blackness of space, held in her slim, warm arms, bathed in her fiery hair, drinking the sweetness of her crimson lips—until in all Eternity were only they two, and the hungry, feasting love that made them one, man and woman, until the end of time.

Soul of her soul he swam in a place of fires that burned without warmth, of tiny glowing motes that drifted up out of nowhere and swirled about his head like perfumed smoke. He caught one between finger and thumb and held it up for his mind to probe it and know it for a universe of universes, infinitely small, infinitely remote, where the lifetime of a world was but the ticking of a pulse. Yet in that microcosm he lived as he lived in the place of flame, and she with him, holding her to him with the green promise of her half-closed eyes, weaving a web with the copper glory of her hair, drawing him down, down, down into unfathomable blackness where there was only the green, cold light of her two eyes, staring, staring out of nothingness.

And then her soft hand was in his, drawing him away into a place where there was only herself and the beauty of her, like a thing alive and breathing, where he was but a hungering, longing atom of her being, merging in her, looking out through her eyes upon a world of mad, warped shapes that filled him with fear and loathing, and with a hate that came into him out of her and filled him with blinding rage—rage that eclipsed all save the smile on her soft, warm lips and the half-closed eyes that regarded him under drooping lashes—hate that split him in two parts, a part that fought and slew and a part that watched.

He saw one who wore his shape wrest the great sword from the old man's hand and buffet him to the ground. He saw that one charge berserker upon the huddled crowd of men, hewing at them like a woodsman at a tree, beating at them as with a flail of steel, driving them before him like milling sheep. A silver thread ran from him to that one whom he saw, and over it came surging a great, cold glee, and the slippery stickiness of fresh blood warm on his hands, and the salt taste of blood on his lips, that were her lips, licked by her pointed tongue. He felt the evil joy welling up in her at the odor of death that was in the air, and the sight of death in her eyes, and it seemed that it drove out the self that was in her, and made it one with he who stood and slew.

He was that one, there on the purple path, with the great sword in his bloody hands and the blood of slaughtered men wet on his face. And behind him, where the witch-woman swam in her crystal sepulcher, he heard the rasping, vengeful cackle of Zagar, the Martian.

All the lusts of his man's body had been sucked up by the witch's gaze—the lust of man for woman, and the lust of man for gold, and the bloody lust of man for war and death. Those lusts were gone from him, and he stood, now, cold and empty, staring at the old man, his grandfather, where he lay senseless at the abyss' edge. He saw the Martian, twisted with pain at the crystal's base. And he saw again the woman floating in her mist, with the dark evil standing naked in her green eyes.

The red sword swung in an arc of steel and smote at the crystal's face. Again—again—and the whole world rang with the clamor of steel on quartz. But the walls of the bubble that held her were thin, and with the third mighty blow they shivered and rained about him like needles of clear ice. Again he raised his dripping sword—and met her clear green eyes.

Slowly his arms fell limp at his sides and the sword fell at his feet unheeded. Her small bare feet stepped daintily down among the broken shards. Her red hair flowed back over her round white shoulders, revealing all the loveliness of her witch's body, and her two slim hands were held out to him in invitation.

It seemed that an icy draft blew on his chest as he took her hands in his. Uncomprehending he saw the long white welts that rose where her fingers touched him. Her hands were on his arms now, sapping away their strength, and her red lips were raised to his, her pointed tongue licking out between her sharp white teeth. There was a perfume on her hair and her body, pungent and intoxicating, that filled his brain and drugged his reeling senses. He felt her body against his, and all its promise poured through him in a numbing, chilling wave that left in him a single core of searing fire. Her eyes were closed, but now they opened slowly and he plunged recklessly, hopelessly into their fathomless green depths.

In him a bubble burst. An atom of white fire exploded in his brain, scourging him, cleansing him. He looked into his grandfather's steely eyes, over the sundered, bloodless body of the woman-thing, cleft by a single blow of the great gray sword. He raised her body up in his two hands, and it was light as a husk of shadow and cold as the touch of Death. He hurled it out into the sea of violet flame, and saw it drift and spin and sink like a feather into the abyss. Then the fury of the winds burst over them and he was flat on his face at the abyss' edge, clinging with bleeding fingers to the jagged quartz.

Inch by inch he dragged himself back from the verge, along the ribbon of amethyst to a place where he could scramble down into the shelter of the rocks. His grandfather was there, with the others who were still alive. The old man's hand seized his arm in a grip of iron.

"You did it, boy! You did what every man of us has tried to do since we were spilled into this hell's paradise! You went to her freely, and you broke her spell and her power with it. We've only the Stalkers to face now, and with her gone I'm thinking it will be a different tale."

Moran shuddered. If the old man's arm had not been strong and his eye sure, those full red lips would have touched his. What lay beyond he dared not guess. What had she been—she with her woman's shape, a woman's allure, yet dry and bloodless like a husk of cast skin? What manner of unnatural force kept the life in her, there in her crystal tomb and after? What would have been the price of that last kiss—or its reward?

"Tell me about it," he said huskily. "What's it all about?"

"She was the answer," the old man told him. "Once there was a reason for it. They had brains, those old Stalkers that built the city and put her here. They knew what they were doing, but now"—he spat contemptuously—"these things that've come down from them do what they do because it's habit, because their parents did, and theirs before them, because their pint-size brains haven't room for anything but the things they've always done. Maybe she was a goddess, if things like that can have goddesses. Anyway, every time things were fixed so that Sirius' companion star

shone through the Black Hole they'd bring food and leave it by
the crystal. We lived on that, and men like us have lived on it
for Heaven knows how long. She never touched it—not her. *We*
were the food she craved!

"I don't know if they found her here, those old Stalkers, or if
she was from another star, maybe another universe, and they put
her there in the crystal to keep her from getting at them. She'd
have taken them, all right. She drew no lines, but she liked her
own kind best. She took them when she could. You've been
through it—you know, maybe, what it was—but she left them dead
and drawn, with something gone out of them—and smiling. It was
the choice we gave to them that broke the law—quick death by
the sword, or her. Some of 'em took her—

"That's where the toad came in. She needed strong men, big
men, men with brains that could fight her, that she could play
like a fish before she took the life out of them. The Stalkers would
bring what they could get, and them that got past the toad were
fit for her. There's been a lot of us, since I came here. It took a
quick brain and a strong body to make it, and she got the best
there was."

"Why did you stay here?" Moran demanded. "There must be
some way out."

"Hell, we've all tried that!" It was a scarred half-caste from one
of Earth's stray colonies. "There's no way, only the way we came,
and there you've got the toad to pass and the Stalkers if you make
it. With her dead we'll starve here. There was worse things than
goin' to her!"

Moran's eyes narrowed. "Are you man enough to risk the Stalkers if I handle the toad?" They stared at him blankly. "They're
big but they're stupid; some of us'll get through. Do you have the
guts to try?"

They shuffled forward, one by one, until they were crowding
around him. "All right," he told them, "you've got leather—make
me two ropes, strong ones, and get together whatever you've got
to fight with. Grandpa and me'll do the rest."

It was night when they crossed the summit of the pass and crept
down the gorge through the eternal rains—a dozen men, armed
with broken stones, knives of chipped flint, or their bare hands.
Ahead of them went Moran, his eyes and ears alert for any
sign of danger, and at his side marched the old man, fondling his
beloved sword.

Shortly after dawn Moran gave the word. They lashed the
ropes securely about his body and snubbed them about projec-

tions of the cliff. He walked slowly toward the edge of the pit. The toad was waiting. Slowly its flat head rose, its golden eyes blinked, and that hypnotic trill began to throb from its swollen throat. A chill of horror brought the cold sweat out on Moran's skin. What if the ropes should break?

He was at the limit of his tether now. Fascinated, he stared at the hideous face that hovered at the pit's edge. Gritting his teeth, Moran waved his arms. The trilling stopped; the great toad's muscles tensed. With a shout Moran leaped back.

At once the pallid tongue licked out. He felt its sticky mass envelop him, felt the leather thongs cutting into his flesh as they resisted its pull. He was suffocating, strangling, the breath crushed out of his bursting lungs. Then came the scramble of feet on the stone and old Michael Moran was at his side. He heard the clang of steel on stone, and the severed tongue dropped at his feet. A second blow and the ropes were cut, and the two men sprang forward into the pit. Side by side they stood on the toad's broad skull. Seizing the sword, Moran raised it high above his head and smote with all his strength. Blood and brain pulp spurted from the cleft in the monster's skull, and the last dying kick of the great creature flung them from its back. Then it was still, and they were clambering up over its colossal bulk, out of the pit, with their crew close at their heels.

The Stalkers were aroused. In the half light of dawn Moran could see their ungainly forms scrambling out of their barrows, hear them calling out to each other in their purring voices. He saw their eyes glowing in the darkness like golden moons as they stalked across the valley toward the stairs.

Moran looked at his grandfather. The old man's legs were braced, his white locks whipping in the wind. The others were close behind—ten grim-faced men, armed with chipped stones and bits of wood, waiting to die fighting against inhuman giants thirty times their size. With room to run, to dodge, to hide among the ruined buildings of the deserted city, they might have escaped. Here, penned on this narrow ledge, they had no chance. Even the great sword could do nothing against those giant bodies.

He took the old man gently by the arm. "Give me the blade," he said. "You've had your fun, now. Let it be Paddy Moran that shows the creatures the welcome we have for them."

Cradling the sword in his arms as his grandfather had done, he watched them coming up the steps. Their heads towered far above him; they were almost within reach. He flung a curt order over his shoulder: "Wait—then run for their legs. They'll be a bit busy at the first, and you'll maybe get through."

Grounding the sword's point, he tensed for the first futile blow.

Black hail screamed down across his vision. Great sweeping wings—long, shining lances—ray guns spitting out their needles of white fire. In hundreds and thousands, streaming from the clouds like rain in a headlong dive, the Muraths came.

Bewildered, the Stalkers stood in a huddle, midway of the stairs, their misshapen heads cocked upward, their vast arms hanging limp. Then they were in retreat, stumbling across the plain to the shelter of the ruined city, striking vainly at the buzzing, darting mites that zoomed and banked about their heads striking death with rays and stabbing spears. Five of them lay dead and others were staggering, falling, to lie still on the bare stone.

Out of the winged horde one tiny figure dropped toward the watching men. It braked deftly and landed at Moran's feet. "Greetings, O Man," it croaked. "Shag holds his word. Life for life—that is law."

It was Shag, the Murath, who showed them the road through the Mountains of the Night before he returned to complete the slaughter which his winged legions had begun. From time immemorial Stalkers and Muraths had warred, and many of Shag's kinsfolk had gone to feed the great toad in the Stalkers' pit. Never before had one of them escaped, to lead his race back to the hidden stronghold of the giants and to their vengeance.

1941

Time Wants a Skeleton/

by ROSS ROCKLYNNE

Six people thrown back in Time knew that one of them had to supply a skeleton to lie a million years on an asteroid—

Asteroid No. 1007 came spinning relentlessly up.

Lieutenant Tony Crow's eyes bulged. He released the choked U-bar frantically, and pounded on the auxiliary underjet controls. Up went the nose of the ship, and stars, weirdly splashed across the heavens, showed briefly.

Then the ship fell, hurling itself against the base of the mountain. Tony was thrown from the control chair. He smacked against the wall, grinning twistedly. He pushed against it with a heavily shod foot as the ship teetered over, rolled a bit, and then was still—still, save for the hiss of escaping air.

He dived for a locker, broke out a pressure suit, perspiration pearling his forehead. He was into the suit, buckling the helmet down, before the last of the air escaped. He stood there, pained dismay in his eyes. His roving glance rested on the wall calendar.

"Happy December!" he snarled.

Then he remembered. Johnny Braker was out there, with his two fellow outlaws. By now, they'd be running this way. All the more reason why Tony should capture them now. He'd need their ship.

He acted quickly, buckling on his helmet, working over the air lock. He expelled his breath in relief as it opened. Nerves humming, he went through, came to his feet, inclosed by the bleak soundlessness of a twenty-mile planetoid more than a hundred million miles removed from Earth.

To his left the mountain rose sharply. Good. Tony had wanted to put the ship down there anyway. He took one reluctant look at the ship. His face fell mournfully. The stern section was caved in and twisted so much it looked ridiculous. Well, that was *that*.

He quickly drew his Hampton and moved soundlessly around the mountain's shoulder. He fell into a crouch as he saw the gleam of the outlaw ship, three hundred yards distant across a plain, hovering in the shadow thrown by an overhanging ledge.

Then he saw the three figures leaping toward him across the plain. His Hampton came viciously up. There was a puff of rock to the front left of the little group. They froze.

Tony left his place of concealment, snapping his headset on.

"Stay where you are!" he bawled.

The reaction was unexpected. Braker's voice came blasting back.

"The hell you say!"

A tiny crater came miraculously into being to Tony's left. He swore, jumped behind his protection, came out a second later to send another projectile winging its way. One of the figures pitched forward, to move no more, the balloon rotundity of its suit suddenly lost. The other two turned tail, only to halt and hole up behind a boulder gracing the middle of the plain. They proceeded to pepper Tony's retreat.

Tony shrank back against the mountainside, exasperated beyond measure. His glance, roving around, came to rest on a cave, a fault in the mountain that tapered out a hundred feet up.

He stared at the floor of the cave unbelievingly.

"I'll be double-damned," he muttered.

What he saw was a human skeleton.

He paled. His stomach suddenly heaved. Outrageous, haunting thoughts flicked through his consciousness. The skeleton was— horror!

And it had existed in the dim, unutterably distant past, before the asteroids, before the human race had come into existence!

The thoughts were gone, abruptly. Consciousness shuddered back. For a while, his face pasty white, his fingers trembling, he thought he was going to be sick. But he wasn't. He stood there, staring. Memories! If he knew where they came from— His very mind revolted suddenly from probing deeper into a mystery that tore at the very roots of his sanity!

"It existed before the human race," he whispered. "Then where did the skeleton come from?"

His lips curled. Illusion! Conquering his maddening revulsion, he approached the skeleton, knelt near it. It lay inside the cave. Colorless starlight did not allow him to see it as well as he might. Yet, he saw the gleam of gold on the long, tapering finger. Old yellow gold, untarnished by atmosphere; and inset with an emerald, with a flaw, a distinctive, ovular air bubble, showing through its murky transparency.

He moved backward, away from it, face set stubbornly. "Illusion," he repeated.

Chips of rock, flaked off the mountainside by the exploding bullets of a Hampton, completed the transformation. He risked stepping out, fired.

The shot struck the boulder, split it down the middle. The two halves parted. The outlaws ran, firing back to cover their hasty retreat. Tony waited until the fire lessened, then stepped out and sent a shot over their heads.

Sudden dismay showed in his eyes. The ledge overhanging the outlaw ship cracked—where the bullet had struck it.

"What the hell—" came Braker's gasp. The two outlaws stopped stock-still.

The ledge came down, its ponderousness doubled by the absence of sound. Tony stumbled panting across the plain as the scene turned into a churning hell. The ship crumbled like clay. Another section of the ledge descended to bury the ship inextricably under a small mountain.

Tony Crow swore blisteringly. But ship or no ship, he still had a job to do. When the outlaws finally turned, they were looking into the menacing barrel of his Hampton.

"Get 'em up," he said impassively.

With studied insolence, Harry Jawbone Yates, the smaller of the two, raised his hands. A contemptuous sneer merely played over Braker's unshaved face and went upward to his smoky eyes.

"Why should I put my hands up? We're all pals, now—theoretically." His natural hate for any form of the law showed in his eyes. "You sure pulled a prize play, copper. Chase us clear across space, and end up getting us in a jam it's a hundred-to-one shot we'll get out of."

Tony held them transfixed with the Hampton, knowing what Braker meant. No ship would have reason to stop off on the twenty-mile mote in the sky that was Asteroid 1007.

He sighed, made a gesture. "Hamptons over here, boys. And be careful." The weapons arced groundward. "Sorry. I was intending to use your ship to take us back. I won't make another error like that one, though. Giving up this early in the game, for instance. Come here, Jawbone."

Yates shrugged. He was blond, had pale, wide-set eyes. By nature, he was conscienceless. A broken jawbone, protruding at a sharp angle from his jawline, gave him his nickname.

He held out his wrists. "Put 'em on." His voice was an effortless affair which did not go as low as it could; rather womanish, therefore. Braker was different. Strength, nerve, and audacity showed in every line of his heavy, compact body. If there was one thing that characterized him it was his violent desire to live. These were men with elastic codes of ethics. A few of their more unscrupulous activities had caught up with them.

Tony put cuffs over Yates' wrist.

"Now you, Braker."

"Damned if I do," said Braker.

"Damned if you don't," said Tony. He waggled the Hampton, his normally genial eyes hardening slightly. "I mean it, Braker," he said slowly.

Braker sneered and tossed his head. Then, as if resistance was below his present mood, he submitted.

He watched the cuffs click silently. "There isn't a hundred-to-one chance, anyway," he growled.

Tony jerked slightly, his eyes turned skyward. He chuckled.

"Well, what's so funny?" Braker demanded.

"What you just said." Tony pointed. "The hundred-to-one shot —there she is!"

Braker turned.

"Yeah," he said. "Yeah. Damnation!"

A ship, glowing faintly in the starlight, hung above an escarpment that dropped to the valley floor. It had no visible support, and, indeed, there was no trace of the usual jets.

"Well, that's an item!" Yates muttered.

"It is at that," Tony agreed.

The ship moved. Rather, it simply disappeared, and next showed up a hundred feet away on the valley floor. A valve in the side of the cylindrical affair opened and a figure dropped out, stood looking at them.

A metallic voice said, "Are you the inhabitants or just people?"

The voice was agreeably flippant, and more agreeably feminine. Tony's senses quickened.

"We're people," he explained. "See?" He flapped his arms like wings. He grinned. "However, before you showed up, we had made up our minds to be—inhabitants."

"Oh. Stranded." The voice was slightly chilly. "Well, that's too bad. Come on inside. We'll talk the whole thing over. Say, are those handcuffs?"

"Right."

"Hm-m-m. Two outlaws—and a copper. Well, come on inside and meet the rest of us."

An hour later, Tony, agreeably relaxed in a small lounge, was smoking his third cigarette, pressure suit off. Across the room was Braker and Yates. The girl, whose name, it developed, was Laurette, leaned against the door jamb, clad in jodhpurs and white silk blouse. She was blond and had clear, deep-blue eyes. Her lips were pursed a little and she looked angry. Tony couldn't keep his eyes off her.

Another man stood beside her. He was dark in complexion and looked as if he had a short temper. He was snapping the finger-nails of two hands in a manner that showed characteristic impatience and nervousness. His name was Erle Masters.

An older man came into the room, fitting glasses over his eyes. He took a quick look around the room. Tony came to his feet.

Laurette said tonelessly, "Lieutenant, this is my father. Daddy, Lieutenant Tony Crow of the IPF. Those two are the outlaws I was telling you about."

"Outlaws, eh?" said Professor Overland. His voice seemed deep enough to count the separate vibrations. He rubbed at a stubbled jaw. "Well, that's too bad. Just when we had the DeTosque strata 1007 fitting onto 70. And there were ample signs to show a definite dovetailing of apex 1007 into Morrell's fourth crater on Ceres, which would have put 1007 near the surface, if not on it. If we could have followed those up without an interruption—"

"Don't let this interrupt you," Masters broke in. His nails clicked. "We'll let these three sleep in the lounge. We can finish up the set of indications we're working on now, and then get rid of them."

Overland shook his graying head doubtfully. "It would be un-thinkable to subject those two to cuffs for a full month."

Masters said irritably, "We'll give them a parole. Give them their temporary freedom if they agree to submit to handcuffs again when we land on Mars."

Tony laughed softly. "Sorry. You can't trust those two for five minutes, let alone a month." He paused. "Under the circumstances, professor, I guess you realize I've got full power to enforce my request that you take us back to Mars. The primary concern of the government in a case like this would be placing these two in custody. I suggest if we get under way now, you can devote more time to your project."

Overland said helplessly, "Of course. But it cuts off my chances of getting to the Christmas banquet at the university." Disappointment showed in his weak eyes. "There's a good chance they'll give me Amos, I guess, but it's already December third. Well, anyway, we'll miss the snow."

Laurette Overland said bitterly, "I wish we hadn't landed on 1007. You'd have got along without us then, all right."

Tony held her eyes gravely. "Perfectly, Miss Overland. Except

that we would have been inhabitants. And, shortly, very, very
dead ones."

"So?" She glared.

Erle Masters grabbed the girl's arm with a muttered word and
led her out of the room.

Overland grasped Tony's arm in a friendly squeeze, eyes twinkling. "Don't mind them, son. If you or your charges need anything, you can use my cabin. But we'll make Mars in forty-eight
hours, seven or eight of it skimming through the Belt."

Tony shook his head dazedly. "Forty-eight hours?"

Overland grinned. His teeth were slightly tobacco-stained.
"That's it. This is one of the new ships—the H-H drive. They zip
along."

"Oh! The Fitz-Gerald Contraction?"

Overland nodded absently and left. Tony stared after him. He
was remembering something now—the skeleton.

Braker said indulgently, "What a laugh."

Tony turned.

"What," he asked patiently, "is a laugh?"

Braker thrust out long, heavy legs. He was playing idly with
a gold ring on the third finger of his right hand.

"Oh," he said carelessly, "a theory goes the rounds the asteroids
used to be a planet. They're not sure the theory is right, so they
send a few bearded long faces out to trace down faults and strata
and striations on one asteroid and link them up with others. The
girl's old man was just about to nail down 1007 and 70 and Ceres.
Good for him. But what the hell! They prove the theory and the
asteroids still play ring around the rosy and what have they got
for their money?"

He absently played with his ring.

Tony as absently watched him turning it round and round on
his finger. Something peculiar about— He jumped. His eyes
bulged.

That ring! He leaped to his feet, away from it.

Braker and Yates looked at him strangely.

Braker came to his feet, brows contracting. "Say, copper, what
ails you? You gone crazy? You look like a ghost."

Tony's heart began a fast, insistent pounding. Blood drummed
against his temples. So he looked like a ghost? He laughed
hoarsely. Was it imagination that suddenly stripped the flesh from
Braker's head and left nothing but—a skull?

"I'm not a ghost," he chattered senselessly, still staring at the
ring.

He closed his eyes tight, clenched his fists.

"He's gone bats?" said Yates, incredulously.

"Bats! Absolutely bats!"

Tony opened his eyes, looked carefully at Braker, at Yates, at the tapestried walls of the lounge. Slowly, the tensity left him. Now, no matter what developed he would have to keep a hold on himself.

"I'm all right, Braker. Let me see that ring." His voice was low, controlled, ominous.

"You take a fit?" Braker snapped suspiciously.

"I'm all right." Tony deliberately took Braker's cuffed hands into his own, looked at the gold band inset with the flawed emerald. Revulsion crawled in his stomach, yet he kept his eyes on the ring.

"Where'd you get the ring, Braker?" He kept his glance down.

"Why—'29, I think it was; or '28." Braker's tone was suddenly angry, resentful. He drew away. "What is this, anyway? I got it legal, and so what?"

"What I really wanted to know," said Tony, "was if there was another ring like this one—ever. I hope not . . . I don't know if I do. Damn it!"

"And I don't know what you're talking about," snarled Braker. "I still think you're bats. Hell, flawed emeralds are like fingerprints, never two alike. You know that yourself."

Tony slowly nodded and stepped back. Then he lighted a cigarette, and let the smoke inclose him.

"You fellows stay here," he said, and backed out and bolted the door behind him. He went heavily down the corridor, down a short flight of stairs, then down another short corridor.

He chose one of two doors, jerked it open. A half dozen packages slid from the shelves of what was evidently a closet. Then the other door opened. Tony staggered backward, losing his balance under the flood of packages. He bumped into Laurette Overland. She gasped and started to fall. Tony managed to twist around in time to grab her. They both fell anyway. Tony drew her to him on impulse and kissed her.

She twisted away from him, her face scarlet. Her palm came around, smashed into his face with all her considerable strength. She jumped to her feet, then the fury in her eyes died. Tony came erect, smarting under the blow.

"Sportsmanlike," he snapped angrily.

"You've got a lot of nerve," she said unsteadily. Her eyes went past him. "You clumsy fool. Help me get these packages back on the shelves before daddy or Erle come along. They're Christmas presents, and if you broke any of the wrappings— Come on, can't you help?"

Tony slowly hoisted a large carton labeled with a "Do Not Open Before Christmas" sticker, and shoved it onto the lower rickety shelf, where it stuck out, practically ready to fall again. She put the smaller packages on top to balance it.

She turned, seeming to meet his eyes with difficulty.

Finally she got out, "I'm sorry I hit you like that, lieutenant. I guess it was natural—your kissing me I mean." She smiled faintly at Tony, who was ruefully rubbing his cheek. Then her composure abruptly returned. She straightened.

"If you're looking for the door to the control room, that's it."

"I wanted to see your father," Tony explained.

"You can't see him now. He's plotting our course. In fifteen minutes—" She let the sentence dangle. "Erle Masters can help you in a few minutes. He's edging the ship out of the way of a polyhedron."

"Polyhedron?"

"Many-sided asteroid. That's the way we designate them." She was being patronizing now.

"Well, of course. But I stick to plain triangles and spheres and cubes. A polyhedron is a sphere to me. I didn't know we were on the way. Since when? I didn't feel the acceleration."

"Since ten minutes ago. And naturally there wouldn't be any acceleration with an H-H drive. Well, if you want anything, you can talk to Erle." She edged past him, went swinging up the corridor. Tony caught up with her.

"You can help me," he said, voice edged. "Will you answer a few questions?"

She stopped, her penciled brows drawn together. She shrugged. "Fire away, lieutenant."

She leaned against the wall, tapping it patiently with one manicured fingernail.

Tony said, "All I know about the Hoderay-Hammond drive, Miss Overland, is that it reverses the Fitz-Gerald Contraction principle. It makes use of a new type of mechanical advantage. A moving object contracts in the direction of motion. Therefore a stationary object, such as a ship, can be made to move if you contract it in the direction you want it to move. How that's accomplished, though, I don't know."

"By gravitons— Where have you been all your life?"

"Learning," said Tony, "good manners."

She flushed. Her fingers stopped drumming. "If you realized you were interrupting important work, you'd know why I forget my manners. We were trying to finish this up so daddy could get back to his farewell dinner at the university. I guess the professors guessed right when they sent his— Well, why should I explain that to you?"

"I'm sure," said Tony, "I don't know."

"Well, go on," she said coldly.

Tony lighted a cigarette, offered her one with an apology. She shook her head impatiently.

Tony eyed her through the haze of smoke. "Back there on 1007 I saw a skeleton with a ring on its finger."

She seemed nonplused. "Well. Was it a pretty ring?"

Tony said grimly, "The point is, Braker never got near that skeleton after I saw it, but that same ring is now on his finger."

Startlement showed in her eyes. "That doesn't sound very plausible, lieutenant!"

"No, of course it doesn't. Because then the same ring is in two different places at the same time."

"And of course," she nodded, "that would be impossible. Go on. I don't know what you're getting at, but it certainly is interesting."

"Impossible?" said Tony. "Except that it happens to be the truth. I'm not explaining it away, Miss Overland, if that's your idea. Here's something else. The skeleton is a human skeleton, but it existed before the human race existed."

She shoved herself away from her indolent position. "You must be crazy."

Tony said nothing.

"How did you know?" she said sharply.

"I *know*. Now *you* explain the H-H drive, if you will."

"I will!" She said: "Gravitons are the ultimate particle of matter. There are 1846 in a proton, one in an electron, which is the reason why a proton is 1846 times as heavy as an electron.

"Now you can give me a cigarette, lieutenant. I'm curious about this thing, and if I can't get to the bottom of it, my father certainly will."

After a while, she blew out smoke nervously.

She continued, speaking rapidly: "A Wittenberg disrupter tears atoms apart. The free electrons are shunted off into accumulators, where we get power for lighting, cooking, heating and so forth. The protons go into the proton analyzer, where the gravitons are ripped out of them and stored in a special type of spherical field.

When we want to move the ship, the gravitons are released. They spread through the ship and everything in the ship.

"The natural place for a graviton is in a proton. The gravitons rush for the protons—which are already saturated with 1846 gravitons. Gravitons are unable to remain free in three-dimensional space. They escape along the time line, into the past. The reaction contracts the atoms of the ship and everything in the ship, and shoves it forward along the opposite space-time line—forward into the future and forward in space. In the apparent space of a second, therefore, the ship can travel thousands of miles, with no acceleration effects.

"Now, there you have it, lieutenant. Do what you can with it."

Tony said, "What would happen if the gravitons were forced into the future rather than the past?"

"Lieutenant, I would have been surprised if you hadn't said that! Theoretically, it's an impossibility. Anybody who knows gravitons would say so. But if Braker is wearing a ring that a skeleton older than the human race is also wearing— *Ugh!*"

She put her hands to her temples in genuine distaste. "We'll have to see my father," she said wearily. "He'll be the one to find out whether or not you make this up as you go along."

Erle Masters looked from Tony to Laurette.

"You believe this bilge he's been handing you?"

"I'm not interested in what you think, Erle. But I am in what you do, daddy."

Overland looked uneasy, his stubbled jaws barely moving over a wad of rough-cut.

"It does sound like . . . er . . . bilge," he muttered. "If you weren't an IPF man, I'd think you were slightly off-center. But— one thing, young man. How did you know the skeleton was older than the human race?"

"I said it existed *before* the human race."

"Is there any difference?"

"I think there is—somehow."

"Well," said Overland patiently, "how do you know it?"

Tony hesitated. "I don't really know. I was standing at the mouth of the cave, and something—or someone—told me."

"*Someone!*" Masters blasted the word out incredulously.

"I don't know!" said Tony. "All I know is what I'm telling you. It couldn't have been supernatural—could it?"

Overland said quickly, "Don't let it upset you, son. Of course it wasn't supernatural. There's a rational explanation somewhere, I guess. But it's going to be hard to come by."

He nodded his head abstractedly, and kept on nodding it like a marionette. Then he smiled peculiarly.

"I'm old now, son—you know? And I've seen a lot. I don't disbelieve anything. There's only one logical step for a scientist to take now, and that's to go back and take a look at that skeleton."

Masters' breath sounded. "You can't do that!"

"But we're going to. And remember that I employ *you*, because Laurette asked me to. Now turn this ship back to 1007. This might be more important than patching up a torn-up world at that." He chuckled.

Laurette shook her blond head. "You know," she said musingly, "this might be the very thing we *shouldn't* do, going back like this. On the other hand, if we went on our way, *that* might be the thing we shouldn't do."

Masters muttered, "You're talking nonsense, Laurette."

He ostentatiously grabbed her bare arm, and led her from the room after her father, throwing Tony a significant glance as he passed.

Tony expelled a long breath. Then, smiling twistedly, he went back to the lounge, to wait—for what? His stomach contracted again with revulsion—or was it a premonition?

Braker came sharply to his feet. "What's up, Crow?"

"Let me see that ring again," Tony said. After a minute he raised his eyes absently. "It's the same ring," he muttered.

"I wish to hell," Braker exploded, "I knew what you were talking about!"

Tony looked at him obliquely, and said under his breath, "Maybe it's better you don't."

He sat down and lighted a cigarette. Braker swore, and finally wandered to the window. Tony knew what he was thinking: of Earth; of the cities that teemed; of the vast stretches of open space between the planets. Such would be his thoughts. Braker, who loved life and freedom.

Braker, who wore a ring—

Then the constellations showing through the port abruptly changed pattern.

Braker leaped back, eyes bulging. "What the—"

Yates, sitting sullenly in the corner, came alertly to his feet. Braker mutely pointed at the stars.

"I could have sworn," he said thickly.

Tony came to his feet. He had seen the change. But his thoughts flowed evenly, coldly, a smile frozen on his lips.

"You saw right, Braker," he said coldly, then managed to grab the guide rail as the ship bucked. Braker and Yates sailed across the room, faces ludicrous with surprise. The ship turned the other way. The heavens spun, the stars blurring. Something else Tony saw beside blurred stars: a dull-gray, monstrous landscape, a horizon cut with mountains, a bright, small Sun fringing tumbled clouds with reddish, ominous silver. Then stars again, rushing past the port, simmering through an atmosphere—

Blackness crushed its way through Tony Crow's consciousness, occluding it until, finally, his last coherent thought had gone. Yet he seemed to know what had happened. There was a skeleton in a cave on an asteroid—millions of years from now. And the ship had struck.

Tony moved, opened his eyes. The lights were out, but a pale shaft of radiance was streaming through the still-intact port. Sounds insinuated themselves into his consciousness. The wet drip of rain, the low murmur of a spasmodic wind, a guttural *kutakikchkut* that drifted eerily, insistently, down the wind.

Tony slowly levered himself to his feet. He was lying atop Braker. The man was breathing heavily, a shallow gash on his forehead. Involuntarily, Tony's eyes dropped to the ring. It gleamed—a wicked eye staring up at him. He wrenched his eyes away.

Yates was stirring, mumbling to himself. His eyes snapped open, stared at Tony.

"What happened?" he said thickly. He reeled to his feet. *"Phew!"*

Tony smiled through the gloom. "Take care of Braker," he said, and turned to the door, which was warped off its hinges. He loped down the corridor to the control room, slowing down on the lightless lower deck ramp. He felt his way into the control room. He stumbled around until his foot touched a body. He stooped, felt a soft, bare arm. In sudden, stifling panic, he scooped Laurette's feebly breathing body into his arms. She might have been lead, as his feet seemed made of lead. He forced himself up to the upper corridor, kicked open the door of her father's room, placed her gently on the bed. There was light here, probably that of a moon. He scanned her pale face anxiously, rubbing her arms toward the heart. Blood came to her cheeks. She gasped, rolled over. Her eyes opened.

"Lieutenant," she muttered.

"You all right?"

Tony helped her to her feet.

"Thanks, lieutenant. I'll do." She tensed. "What about my father?"

"I'll bring him up," said Tony.

Five minutes later, Overland was stretched on the bed, pain in his open eyes. Three ribs were broken. Erle Masters hovered at the foot of the bed, dabbing at one side of his face with a reddened handkerchief, a dazed, scared look in his eyes. Tony knew what he was scared of, but even Tony wasn't playing with that thought now.

He found a large roll of adhesive in the ship's medicine closet. He taped Overland's chest. The breaks were simple fractures. In time, they would do a fair job of knitting. But Overland would have to stay on his back.

Masters met Tony's eyes reluctantly.

"We'll have to get pressure suits and take a look outside."

Tony shrugged. "We won't need pressure suits. We're already breathing outside air, and living under this planet's atmospheric pressure. The bulkheads must be stowed in some place."

Overland's deep voice sounded, slowly. "I think we've got an idea where we are, Erle. You can feel the drag of this planet—a full-size planet, too. Maybe one and a half gravities. I can feel it pulling on my ribs." A bleak expression settled on his stubbled face. He looked at Tony humorlessly. "Maybe I'm that skeleton, son."

Tony caught his breath. "Nonsense. Johnny Braker's wearing the ring. If anybody's that skeleton, he is. *Not* that I wish him any bad luck, of course." He nodded once, significantly, then turned toward the door with a gesture at Masters. Masters, plainly resenting the soundless command, hesitated, until Laurette made an impatient motion at him.

They prowled through the gloomy corridor toward the small engine room, pushed the door open. The overpowering odor of ozone and burning rubber flung itself at them.

Masters uttered an expressive curse as Tony played a beam over what was left of the reversed Fitz-Gerald Contraction machinery. His nails clicked startlingly loud in the heavy silence.

"Well, that's that," he muttered.

"What d'you mean—that's that?" Tony's eyes bored at him through the darkness.

"I mean that we're stuck here, millions of years ago." He laughed harshly, unsteadily.

Tony said without emotion, "Cut it out. Hasn't this ship got auxiliary rocket blasts?"

"Naturally. But this is a one and a half gravity planet. Anyway, the auxiliary jets won't be in such good condition after a fifty-foot drop."

"Then we'll fix 'em," said Tony sharply. He added, "What makes you so sure it's millions of years ago, Masters?"

Masters leaned back against the door jamb, face as cold and hard as stone.

"Don't make me bow to you any more than I have to, lieutenant," he said ominously. "I didn't believe your story before, but I do now. You predicted this crack-up—it had to happen. So I'm ready to concede it's millions of years ago; mainly because there wasn't any one and a half gravity planet within hundreds of millions of miles of the asteroid belt. But there *used* to be one."

Tony said, lips barely moving, "Yes?"

"There used to be one—*before the asteroids.*"

Tony smiled twistedly. "I'm glad you realize that."

He turned and went for the air lock, but, since the entire system of electric transmission had gone wrong somewhere, he abandoned it and followed a draft of wet air. He jerked open the door of a small storage bin, and crawled through. There was a hole here, that had thrust boxes of canned goods haphazardly to one side. Beyond was the open night.

Tony crawled out, stood in the lee of the ship, occasional stinging drops of rain lashing at their faces. Wind soughed across a rocky plain. A low roar heralded a nearby, swollen stream. A low *kutakikchkut* monotonously beat against the night, night-brooding bird, Tony guessed, nested in the heavy growth flanking a cliff that cut a triangular section from a heavily clouded sky. Light from a probable moon broke dimly through clouds on the leftward horizon.

Masters' teeth chattered in the cold.

Tony edged his way around the ship, looking the damage over. He was gratified to discover that although the auxiliary rocket jets were twisted and broken, the only hole was in the storage bin bulkheads. That could be repaired, and so, in time, could the jets.

They started to enter the ship when Masters grasped his arm. He pointed up into the sky, where a rift in the clouds showed.

Tony nodded slowly. Offsetting murkily twinkling stars, there was another celestial body, visible as a tiny crescent.

"A planet?" muttered Tony.

"Must be." Masters' voice was low.

They stared at it for a moment, caught up in the ominous, baleful glow. Then Tony shook himself out of it, went for the storage bin.

Walking down the corridor with Masters, Tony came upon Braker and Yates.

Braker grinned at him, but his eyes were ominous.

"What's this I hear about a skeleton?"

Tony bit his lip. "Where'd you hear it?"

"From the girl and her old man. We stopped outside their room a bit. Well, it didn't make sense, the things they were saying. Something about an emerald ring and a skeleton and a cave." He took one step forward, an ugly light in his smoky eyes. "Come clean, Crow. How does this ring I've got on my finger tie up with a skeleton?"

Tony said coldly, "You're out of your head. Get back to the lounge."

Braker sneered. "Why? You can't make us stay there with the door broken down."

Masters made an impatient sound. "Oh, let them go, lieutenant. We can't bother ourselves about something as unimportant as this. Anyway, we're going to need these men for fixing up the ship."

Tony said to Yates, "You know anything about electricity? Seems to me you had an E.E. once."

Yates' thin face lighted, before he remembered his sullen pose. "O. K., you're right," he muttered. He looked at Braker interrogatively.

Braker said: "Sorry. We're not obligated to work for you. As prisoners, you're responsible for us and our welfare. We'll help you or whoever's bossing the job *if* we're not prisoners."

Tony nodded. "Fair enough. But tonight, you stay prisoners. Tomorrow, maybe not," and he herded them back into the lounge. He cuffed them to the guide rail, and so left them, frowning a little. Braker had been too acquiescent.

The reason for that struck Tony hard. Walking back along the corridor, he saw something gleaming on the floor. He froze. Revulsion gripping him, he slowly picked up the ring.

Masters turned, said sharply, "What's up?"

Tony smiled lopsidedly, threw the ring into the air twice, speculatively, catching it in his palm. He extended it to Masters. "Want a ring?"

Masters' face went white as death. He jumped back.

"Damn you!" he said violently. "Take that thing away!"

"Braker slipped it off his finger," said Tony, his voice edging into the aching silence. Then he turned on his heel, and walked back to the lounge. He caught Braker's attention.

He held the ring out.

"You must have dropped it," he said.

Braker's lips opened in a mirthful, raucous laugh.

"You can have it, copper," he gasped. "*I* don't want to be any damned skeleton!"

Tony slipped the ring into his pocket and walked back down the corridor with a reckless swing to his body.

He knocked on the door to Overland's room, opened it when Laurette's voice sounded.

Masters and Laurette looked at him strangely.

Overland looked up from the bed.

"Lieutenant," he said, an almost ashamed look on his face, "sometimes I wonder about the human mind. Masters seems to think that now *you've* got the ring, *you're* going to be the skeleton."

Masters' nails clicked. "It's true, isn't it? The outlaws know about the ring. We know about it. But Crow *has* the ring, and it's certain none of us is going to take it."

Overland made an exasperated clicking sound.

"It's infantile," he snapped. "Masters, you're acting like a child, not like a scientist. There's only one certainty, that one of us is going to be the skeleton. But there's no certainty which one. And there's even a possibility that all of us will die." His face clouded angrily. "And the most infantile viewpoint possible seems to be shared by all of you. You've grown superstitious about the ring. Now it's—a ring of death! Death to him who wears the ring! *Pah!*"

He stretched forth an imperative hand.

"Give it to me, lieutenant! I'll tell you right now that no subterfuge in the universe will change the fact of my being a skeleton if I *am* the skeleton; and vice versa."

Tony shook his head. "I'll be keeping it—for a while. And you might as well know that no scientific argument will convince anybody the ring is not a ring of death. For, you see, it is."

Overland sank back, lips pursed. "What are you going to do with it?" he charged. When Tony didn't answer, he said pettishly, "Oh, what's the use! On the face of it, the whole situation's impossible." Then his face lighted. "What did you find out?"

Tony briefly sketched his conclusions. It would be two or three weeks before they could repair the rocket jets, get the electric transmission system working properly.

Overland nodded absently. "Strange, isn't it!" he mused. "All that work DeTosque, Bodley, Morrell, Haley, the Farr brothers and myself have done goes for nothing. Our being here proves the theory they were working on."

Laurette smiled lopsidedly at Tony.

"Lieutenant," she said, "maybe the skeleton was a woman."

"A woman!" Masters' head snapped around, horror on his face. "Not you, Laurette!"

"Why not? Women have skeletons, too—or didn't you know?" She kept her eyes on Tony. "Well, lieutenant? I put a question up to you."

Tony kept his face impassive. "The skeleton," he said, without a tremor, "was that of a man."

"Then," said Laurette Overland, stretching out her palm, cup-shaped, "give me the ring."

Tony froze, staring. That his lie should have this repercussion was unbelievable. Out of the corner of his eye he saw Overland's slowly blanching face. On Masters, Laurette's statement had the most effect.

"Damn you, Crow!" he said thickly. "This is just a scheme of yours to get rid of the ring!" He lunged forward.

The action was unexpected. Tony fell backward under the impact of the man's fist. He sprawled on his back. Masters threw himself at him.

"Erle, you utter fool!" That was Laurette's wail.

Disgust settled on Tony's face. He heaved, by sheer muscular effort, and threw Masters over on his back. His fist came down with a brief but pungent *crack*. Masters slumped, abruptly lifeless.

Tony drew himself to his feet, panting. Laurette was on her knees beside Masters, but her dismayed eyes were turned upward to Tony.

"I'm sorry, lieutenant!" she blurted.

"What have you got to be sorry about?" he snapped. "Except for being in love with a fool like that one."

He was sorry for it the second he said it. He didn't try to read Laurette's expression, but turned sullen eyes to Overland.

"It's night," he said abruptly, "and it's raining. Tomorrow, when the Sun comes up, it'll probably be different. We can figure out the situation then, and start our plans for—" He let the sentence dangle. Plans for what? He concluded, "I suggest we all get some sleep," and left.

He arranged some blankets on the floor of the control room, and instantly went to sleep, though there were times when he stirred violently. The skeleton was in his dreams—

There were five of them at the breakfast table. Laurette serving; Masters beside her, keeping his eyes sullenly on the food; Braker, eating as heartily as his cuffed hands would allow; Yates, picking at his food with disinterest.

Tony finished his second cup of coffee, and scraped his chair back.

"I'll be taking a look around," he told Laurette in explanation. He turned to the door.

Braker leaned back in his chair until it was balanced on two legs, and grinned widely.

"Where you going, Mr. Skeleton?"

Tony froze.

"After a while, Braker," he said, eyes frigid, "the ring will be taken care of."

Yates' fork came down. "If you mean you're going to try to get rid of it, you know you can't do it. It'll come back." His eyes were challenging.

Masters looked up, a strange, milling series of thoughts in his sullen eyes. Then he returned to his food.

Tony, wondering what that expression had meant, shrugged and left the room; and shortly, the ship, by way of the cavity in the storage bin.

He wandered away from the ship, walking slowly, abstractedly, allowing impressions to slip into his mind without conscious resistance. There was a haunting familiarity in this tumbled plain, though life had no place in the remembrance. There was some animal life, creatures stirring in the dank humus, in long, thick grass, in gnarled tree tops. This was mountain country and off there was a tumbling mountain stream.

He impelled himself toward it, the tiny, yet phenomenally bright Sun throwing a shadow that was only a few inches long. It was high "noon."

He stood on the brink of the rocky gorge, spray prismatically alive with color, dashing up into his face. His eyes followed the stream up to the mountain fault where water poured downward to crush at the rocks with the steady, pummeling blow of a giant. He stood there, lost in abstraction, other sounds drowned out.

All except the grate of a shoe behind him. He tried to whirl; too late! Hands pushed against his back—in the next second, he had tumbled off the brink of the chasm, clutching wildly, vainly, at thick spray. Then, an awful moment of freezing cold, and the waters had inclosed him. He was borne away, choking for air, frantically flailing with his arms.

He was swept to the surface, caught a chaotic glimpse of Sun and clouded sky and rock, and then went under again, with a half lungful of air. He tensed, striving to sweep away engulfing panic. A measure of reason came back. Hands and feet began to work in purposeful unison. The surface broke around him. He stayed on top. But that was only because the stream was flowing darkly, swiftly, evenly. He was powerless to force himself against this current.

He twisted, savagely looking for some sign of release. A scaly, oily tree limb came at him with a rush. One wild grab, and the limb was bending downstream, straining against the pressure his body was exerting. He dashed hair from his eyes with one trembling hand, winced as he saw the needle-bed of rapids a hundred feet downstream. If that limb hadn't been there— His mind shuddered away from the thought.

Weakly, he drew himself hand over hand upward, until the tree trunk was solidly below him. He dropped to the ground, and lay there, panting. Then he remembered the hands on his back. With a vicious motion, he jerked out his key ring. That was the answer —the key to the cuffs was gone, taken during the night, of course! Erle Masters, then, had pulled this prize play, or perhaps one of the outlaws, after Masters released him.

After a while, he came to his feet, took stock of his surroundings. Off to his left, a cliff side, and scarcely a half mile distant, the pathetically awry hulk of the ship, on the top of the slope that stretched away.

The cliff side came into his vision again. A fault in the escarpment touched a hidden spot in his memory. He involuntarily started toward it. But he slowed up before he got to the fault— which was really a cave that tapered out to nothingness as its sides rose.

The cave!

And this sloping plain, these mountains, composed the surface of Asteroid 1007, millions of years from now.

Tony dropped emotionlessly to his knees at the mouth of the cave. Not so long ago, he had done the same thing. Then there had been a complete, undisjointed skeleton lying there. Somehow, then, he had known the skeleton existed before the human race— as if it were someone—the skeleton?—that had spoken to him across the unutterable years. The skeleton? That could not be! Yet, whence had come the memory?

He took the ring from his pocket and put it on his finger. It gleamed.

He knelt there for minutes, like a man who worships at his own grave, and he was not dead. Not dead! He took the ring from his finger, then, a cold, bleak smile growing on his face.

He came to his feet, a rising wind whipping at his hair. He took a half dozen running steps toward the river, brought his arm over his shoulder in a throwing gesture.

Somehow the ring slipped from his fingers and fell.

He stooped, picked it up. This time, he made it leave his hand. It spun away, twinkling in the faint sunlight. But the gravity had hold of it, and it fell on the brink of the river, plainly visible.

A dry, all-gone feeling rose in Tony's throat. Grimly, he went forward, picked it up again. Keeping his eyes on it, he advanced to the brink of the river gorge. He held the ring over the darkly swirling waters, slowly released it.

It struck the river like a plummet. The waters inclosed it and it was gone. He looked at the spot where it had disappeared, half expecting it to spring back up into his hand. But it was gone. Gone for good!

He started dazedly back to the ship, moving in an unreal dream. Paradoxical that he had been able to get rid of it. It had dropped from his hand once, fallen short of the river once. The third time it had given up trying!

When he came up to the ship, Masters was standing at the stern, looking at the broken rocket jets. He turned, and saw Tony, water still dripping from his uniform. He fell back a step, face turned pallid.

Tony's lips curled. "Who did it?"

"D-did what?"

"You know what I mean," Tony bit out. He took three quick steps forward.

Masters saw that, and went reckless. Tony side-stepped him, brought his left arm around in a short arc. Masters went down cursing. Tony knelt, holding Masters down by the throat. He felt through his pockets, unearthed the key to the cuffs. Then he hauled Masters to his feet and shook him. Masters' teeth clicked.

"Murderer!" Tony snapped, white with rage.

Masters broke loose. "I'd do it again," he said wildly, and swung. He missed. Tony lashed out with the full power of his open palm, caught Masters on the side of the head. Masters went reeling back, slammed against the side of the ship. Tony glared at him, and then turned on his heel.

He met Laurette Overland coming down the stairs to the upper corridor.

"Lieutenant!" Her eyes danced with excitement. "I've been looking for you. Where in the world have you been?"

"Ask Masters." He urged himself down the corridor, jaw set. She fell into step beside him, running to keep up with his long strides.

"You're all wet!" she exclaimed. "Can't you tell me what happened? Did you go swimming?"

"Involuntarily." He kept on walking.

She grabbed his arm, and slowed him to a stop. An ominous glint replaced her excitement.

"What," she said, "did you mean when you said I should ask Erle about it? Did he push you in? If he did, I'll—" She was unable to speak.

Tony laughed humorlessly. "He admitted it. He stole my key to the handcuffs with the idea that it would be easier to free Braker and Yates that way after I was . . . uh . . . properly prepared to be a skeleton."

Her head moved back and forth. "That's horrible," she said lowly. "Horrible."

He held her eyes. "Perhaps I shouldn't have told you about it," he said, voice faintly acid. "He's your fiancé, isn't he?"

She nodded, imperceptibly, studying him through the half gloom. "Yes. But maybe I'll change my mind, lieutenant. Maybe I will. But in the meantime, come along with me. Daddy's discovered something wonderful."

Professor Overland's head was propped up. He had a pencil and paper on his pyramided legs.

"Oh. Lieutenant! Come in." His face lighted. "Look here! Gravitons *can* thrust their way through to the future, giving the ship a thrust into the past. But only if it happened to enter the spherical type of etheric vacuum. This vacuum would be minus everything—electrons, photons, cosmic rays and so forth, except under unusual circumstances. At some one time, in either the past or future, there might be a stream of photons bridging the vacuum. Now, when gravitons are ejected into the past, they grab hold of light photons, and become ordinary negative electrons. Now say the photons are farther away in the past than they are in the future. The gravitons therefore follow the line of least resistance and hook up with photons of the future. The photons in this case were perhaps hundreds of millions of years away in the vacuum. In traveling that time-distance, the gravitons kicked the ship back for a proportionate number of years, burned up our machinery, and wrecked us on this suddenly appearing before-the-asteroid world."

Laurette said brightly, "But that isn't the important part, daddy."

"I can find another of those etheric vacuums," Overland went on, preoccupiedly, pointing out a series of equations. "Same type, same structure. But we have to go to the planet Earth in order to rebuild the reversed contraction machinery. We'll find the materials we need there." He glanced up. "But we have to get off this world before it cracks up, lieutenant."

Tony started. "Before this world cracks up?"

"Certainly. Naturally. You can—" His heavy brows came down abruptly. "You didn't know about that, did you? Hm-m-m." He stroked his jaw, frowning. "You recall the crescent planet you and Masters saw? Well, he took some readings on that. It's wonderful, son!" His eyes lighted. "It's an ill wind that blows nobody good. Not only do we know now that the asteroid evolved from a broken-up planet, but we also know the manner in which that planet broke up. Collision with a heavy, smaller body."

Tony paled. "You mean—" he said huskily. "Good heavens!" Sweat stood out on his forehead. "How soon will that happen?" he said ominously.

"Well, Erle has the figures. Something over eighteen or nineteen days. It'll be a crack-up that'll shake the Sun. And we'll be here to witness it." He smiled wryly. "I'm more scientist than man, I guess. I never stop to think we might die in the crack-up, and furnish six skeletons instead of one."

"There'll be no skeletons," Tony said, eyes narrowed. "For one thing, we can repair the ship, though we'll have to work like mad. For another—I threw the ring into the river. It's gone."

Laurette seemed to pale. "I . . . I don't see how that could be done," she stammered. "You couldn't get rid of it, not really—could you?"

"It's gone," Tony said stubbornly. "For good. And don't forget it. There'll be no skeleton. And you might try to impress that on Masters, so he doesn't try to produce one," he added significantly.

He left the room with a nod, a few seconds later stepped into the lounge. Braker and Yates turned around. Both were cuffed.

Tony took the key from his pocket and the cuffs fell away. In brief, pungent tones, then, he explained the situation, the main theme being that the ship had to be well away from the planet before the crack-up. Yates would go over the wiring system. Braker, Masters and Tony would work with oxyacetylene torches and hammers over the hole in the hull and the rocket jets.

Then he explained about the ring.

Yates ran a thin hand through his yellow hair.

"You don't do it that easy," he said in his soft, effortless voice. "There's a skeleton up there, and it's got Braker's ring on its finger. It's got to be accounted for, don't it? It's either me or you or Braker or the girl or her old man or Masters. There ain't any use trying to avoid it, either." His voice turned sullen. He looked at Braker, then at Tony. "Anyway, I'm keeping my back turned the right way so there won't be any dirty work."

Braker's breath sounded. "Why, you dirty rat," he stated. He took a step toward Yates. "You would think of that. And probably you'd try it on somebody else, too. Well, don't go pulling it on me, understand." He scowled. "And you better watch him, too, Crow. He's pure poison—in case you got the idea we were friends."

"Oh, cut it out," Tony said wearily. He added, "If we get the ship in working order, there's no reason why all six of us shouldn't get off—alive." He turned to the door, waved Braker and Yates after him. Yet he was sickeningly aware that *his* back was turned to men who admittedly had no conscience to speak of.

A week passed. The plain rang with sledge-hammer strokes directed against the twisted tubes. Three were irreplaceable.

Tony, haggard, tired, unbelievably grimed from his last trip up the twisted, hopeless-looking main blast tube, was suddenly shocked into alertness by sounds of men's voices raised in fury outside the ship. He ran for the open air lock, and urged himself toward the ship's stern. Braker and Yates were tangling it.

"I'll kill him!" Braker raged. He had a rock the size of his fist in his hand. He was attempting, apparently, to knock Jawbone Yates' brains out. Erle Masters stood near, chewing nervously at his upper lip.

With an oath, Tony wrenched the rock from Braker's hand, and hauled the man to his feet. Yates scrambled erect, whimpering, mouth bleeding.

Braker surged wildly toward him. "The dirty —!" he snarled. "Comes up behind me with an oxy torch!"

Yates shrilled, backing up, "That's a lie!" He pointed a trembling hand at Braker. "It was *him* that was going to use the torch on *me!*"

"Shut up!" Tony bawled. He whirled on Masters. "You've got a nerve to stand there," he snarled. "But then you *want* a skeleton! Damned if you're going to get one! Which one did it?"

Masters stammered, "I didn't see it! I . . . I was just—"

"The hell you say!" Tony whirled on the other two, transfixing them with cold eyes.

"Cut it out," he said, lips barely moving. "Either you're letting your nerves override you, or either one or both of you is blaming the other for a move he made himself. You might as well know the skeleton I saw was intact. What do you think a blow torch would do to a skeleton?" His lips curled.

Braker slowly picked up his torch with a poisonous glance at Yates. Yates as slowly picked his sledge hammer. He turned on Tony.

"You said the skeleton was intact?" Eagerness, not evident from his carefully sullen voice, was alive in his eyes.

Tony's glance passed over the man's broken, protruding jaw. "The head," he replied, "was in shadow."

He winced. The passing of hope was a hard thing to watch, even in a man like Jawbone Yates.

He turned, releasing his breath in a long, tired sigh. What a man-sized job this was. Outwitting fate—negating what *had* happened!

Tony worked longer than he expected that day, tracing down the web of asbestos-covered rocket fuel conduits, marking breaks down on the chart. The Sun sank slowly. Darkness swept over the plain, along with a rising wind. He turned on the lights, worked steadily on, haggard, nerves worn. Too much work to allow a slowing up. The invading planet rose each night a degree or more larger. Increasing tidal winds and rainstorms attested to a growing gravitational attraction.

He put an x-mark on the check—and then froze. A scream had gone blasting through the night.

Tony dropped pencil and chart, went flying up the ramp to the upper corridor. He received the full impact of Masters' second scream. Masters had left his room, was running up the corridor, clad in pajamas. There was a knife sticking out of his shoulder.

Tony, gripped with horror, impelled himself after the man, caught up with him as he plunged face downward. He dropped to one knee, staring at a heavy meat knife that had been plunged clear through the neck muscles on Masters' left shoulder, clearly a bid for a heart stroke.

Masters turned on his side. He babbled, face alive with horror. Tony rose, went with the full power of his legs toward the lounge.

A figure showed, running ahead of him. He caught up with it, whipped his arm around the man's neck.

"You!"

Yates squirmed tigerishly. He turned, broke loose, face alive with fury. Tony's open palm lashed out, caught Yates full on the face. Yates staggered and fell. He raised himself to one elbow.

"Why'd you do it?" Tony rasped, standing over him.

Yates' face was livid. "Because I'd rather live than anything else I can think of!" His booted foot lashed out. Tony leaped back. Yates rose. Tony brought his bunched fist up from his knees with all the ferocity he felt. Yates literally rose an inch off the floor, sagged, and sopped to the floor.

Tony picked him up in one arm, and flung him bodily into the lounge.

Braker rose from his sleeping position on a cushioned bench, blinking.

Tony said cuttingly, "Your pal ran a knife through Masters' shoulder."

"Huh?" Braker was on his feet. "Kill him?" In the half-light his eyes glowed.

"You'd be glad if he did!"

Braker looked at Yates. Then, slowly, "Listen, copper. Don't make the mistake of putting me in the same class with a rat like Yates. I don't knife people in the back. But if Masters was dead, I'd be glad of it. It might solve a problem that's bothering the rest of us. What you going to do with him?"

"I already did it. But tell Yates he better watch out for Masters, now."

Braker grunted scornfully. "Huh. Masters'll crack up and down his yellow back."

Tony left.

Laurette and Overland were taking care of Masters in his room. The wound was clean, hardly bleeding.

Overland, somewhat pale, was hanging onto the door. "It's not serious, honey," he said, as her fingers nimbly wound bandages.

"Not serious?" She turned stricken eyes up to Tony. "Look at him. And daddy says it's not serious!"

Tony winced. Masters lay face down on the bed, babbling hysterically to himself, his eyes preternaturally wide. His skin was a pasty white, and horror had etched flabby lines around his lips.

"Knifed me," he gasped. "Knifed me. I was sleeping, that was the trouble. But I heard him—" He heaved convulsively, and buried his face in his pillow.

Laurette finished her job, face pale.

"I'll stay here the rest of the night," Tony told her.

Overland gnawed painfully at his lower lip.

"Who did it?"

Tony told him.

"Can't we do something about it?"

"What?" Tony laughed scornfully. "Masters had the same trick pulled on him that he pulled on me. He isn't any angel himself."

Overland nodded wearily. His daughter helped him out of the room.

During the night, Masters tossed and babbled. Finally he fell into a deep sleep. Tony leaned back in a chair, moodily listening to the sough of the wind, later on watching the Sun come up, staining the massed clouds with running, changing streaks of color.

Masters awoke. He rolled over. He saw Tony, and went rigid. He came to his feet, and huddled back against the wall.

"Get out," he gasped, making a violent motion with his hand.

"You're out of your head," said Tony angrily. "It was Yates."

Masters panted, "I know it was. What difference does it make? You're all in the same class. I'm going to watch myself after this. I'm going to keep my back turned the right way. I'm going to be sure that none of you—"

Tony put his hands on his hips, eyes narrowed.

"If you've got any sense, you'll try to forget this and act like a human being. Better to be dead than the kind of man you'll turn into."

"Get out. Get out!" Masters waved his hand again, shuddering.

Tony left, shaking his head slowly.

Tony stood outside the ship, smoking a cigarette. It was night. He heard a footstep behind him. He fell back a step, whirling.

"Nerves getting you, too?" Laurette Overland laughed shakily, a wool scarf blowing back in the heavy, unnatural wind.

Tony relaxed. "After two weeks of watching everybody watching everybody else, I guess so."

She shivered. He sensed it was not from the bite of the wind. "I suppose you mean Erle."

"Partly. Your father's up and around today, isn't he? He shouldn't have gotten up that night."

"He can get around all right."

"Maybe he better lock himself in his room." He smiled with little amusement. "The others are certain the ring will come back."

She was silent. Through the ominous gloom, lit now by a crescent planet that was visible as a small moon, and growing steadily larger, he saw a rueful, lopsided smile form on her face. Then it was gone.

She said, "Erle was telling me the jets are in bad condition. A trial blast blew out three more."

"That's what happened."

She went on: "He also told me there was a definite maximum

weight the jets could lift in order to get us free of the gravity. We'll have to throw out everything we don't need. Books, rugs, clothing, beds." She drew a deep breath. "And in the end, maybe a human being."

Tony's smile was frozen. "Then the prophecy would come true."

"Yes. It is a prophecy, isn't it?" She seemed childishly puzzled. She added, "And it looks like it has to come true. Because— Excuse me, lieutenant," she said hurriedly, and vanished toward the air lock.

Tony stared after her, his mind crawling with unpleasant thoughts. It was unbelievable, fantastic. So you couldn't outwit fate. The ship would have to be lightened. Guesswork might easily turn into conviction. There might be one human being too many—

Professor Overland came slowly from the air lock, wincing from the cold after his two weeks of confinement. His haggard eyes turned on Tony. He came forward, looking up at the growing planet of destruction.

"Erle has calculated three days, eight hours and a few minutes. But it's ample time, isn't it, lieutenant?"

"One jet will straighten out with some man-size labor. Then we can start unloading extra tonnage. Lots of it."

"Yes. Yes. I know." He cleared his throat. His eyes turned on Tony, filled with a peculiar kind of desperation. "Lieutenant," he said huskily, "there's something I have to tell you. The ring came back."

Tony's head jerked. "It came back?" he blurted.

"In a fish."

"*Fish?*"

Overland ran a trembling hand across his brow. "Yesterday a week ago, Laurette served fried fish. She used an old dress for a net. I found the ring in what she brought to my room. Well, I'm not superstitious about the ring. One of us *is* the skeleton—up there. We can't avoid it. I put the ring on—more bravado than anything else. But this morning"—his voice sank to a whisper— "the ring was gone. Now I'm becoming superstitious, unscientifically so. Laurette is the only one who could—or would—have taken it. The others would have been glad it was on my finger rather than theirs. Even Erle."

Tony stared through him. He was remembering Laurette's peculiar smile. Abruptly, he strode toward the ship, calling back hurriedly:

"Better go inside, sir."

In the ship, he knocked sharply on Laurette's door.

She answered nervously, "Yes."

"May I come in?"

"No. No. Do you have to?"

He thought a moment, then opened the door and stepped inside. She was standing near her bed, her eyes haunted.

Tony extended a hand imperatively. "Give me the ring."

She said, her voice low, controlled, "Lieutenant, I'll keep the ring. You tell that to the others. Then there won't be any of this nervous tension and this murder plotting."

He said ominously, "You may wind up a skeleton."

"You said the skeleton was not a woman."

"I was lying."

"You mean," she said, "it *was* a woman?"

Tony said patiently, "I mean that I don't know. I couldn't tell. Do I get the ring, or don't I?"

She drew a deep breath. "Not in the slightest can it decide who will eventually die."

Tony advanced a step. "Even your father doesn't believe that now," he grated.

She winced. "I'll keep the ring and stay in my room except when I cook. You can keep everybody out of the ship. Then there won't be anybody to harm me."

Footsteps sounded in the corridor. Masters entered the room. Tension had drawn hollow circles under eyes that refused to stay still.

"You," he said to Tony, his voice thin, wavering. He stood with his back to the wall. He wet his lips. "I was talking with your father."

"All right, all right," she said irritably. "I've got the ring, and I'm keeping it."

"No, you can't, Laurette. We're going to get rid of it, this time. The six of us are going to watch."

"You can't get rid of it!" Then, abruptly, she snatched it off her finger. "Here!"

Imperceptibly, he shrank back against the wall.

"There's no use transferring it now. You've got it, you might as well carry it." His eyes swiveled, lighted with a sudden burst of inspiration. "Better yet, let Crow carry it. He represents the law. That would make it proper."

She seemed speechless.

"Can you imagine it? Can you imagine a sniveling creature like him— I'll keep the ring. First my father gets weak in the knees, and then—" She cast a disdainful look at Masters. "I wish you'd both leave me alone, please."

Tony shrugged, left the room, Masters edging out after him. Tony stopped him.

"How much time have we got left?"

Masters said jerkily, "We've been here fourteen days. It happens on the twenty-fifth. That's eleven days from now, a few hours either way."

"How reliable are your figures?"

Masters muttered, "Reliable enough. We'll have to throw out practically everything. Doors, furniture, clothes. And then—"

"Yes?"

"I don't know," Masters muttered, and slunk away.

It was the twenty-fourth of December.

Tidal winds increased in savagery in direct proportion to the growing angular diameter of the invading planet. Heavy, dully colored birds fought their way overhead. On the flanks of abruptly rising cliff edges, gnarled trees lashed. Rain fell spasmodically. Clouds moved in thoroughly indiscriminate directions. Tentacular leaves whirlpooled. Spray, under the wind's impact, cleared the river gorge. The waterfall was muted.

Rushing voluminous air columns caught at the growing pile emerging from the ship's interior, whisked away clothing, magazines, once a mattress. It did not matter. Two worlds were to crash in that momentous, before-history forming of the asteroids. There was but one certainty. This plain, these mountains—and a cave—were to stay intact through the millions of years.

Inside the air lock, Masters stood beside a heavy weight scale. Light bulbs, dishes, silverware, crashed into baskets indiscriminately, the results weighed, noted, discarded. Doors were torn off their hinges, floors ripped up. Food they would keep, and water, for though they eventually reached Earth, they could not know whether it yet supported life.

The ship, devoid of furnishings, had been a standard eleven tons for an H-H drive. Furnishings, food, et cetera, brought her to over thirteen tons. Under a one and a half gravity, it was twenty tons. Masters' figures, using the firing area the ship now had, with more than half the jets beyond use, were exact enough. The maximum lift the jets would or could afford was plus or minus a hundred pounds of ten and three quarter tons.

Masters looked up from his last notation, eyes red-rimmed, lips twitching. Braker and Yates and Tony were standing in the air lock, watching him.

Fear flurried in Masters' eyes. "What are you looking at me like that for?" he snarled. Involuntarily, he fell back a step.

Yates giggled.

"You sure do take the fits. We was just waiting to see how near we was to the mark. There ain't anything else to bring out."

"Oh, there isn't?" Masters glared. "We're still eight hundred pounds on the plus side. How about the contraction machinery?"

Tony said: "It's our only hope of getting back to the present. Overland needs it to rebuild the drive."

"Pressure suits!"

"We're keeping six of them, in case the ship leaks."

"Doors!" said Masters wildly. "Rugs!"

"All," said Tony, "gone."

Masters' nails clicked. "Eight hundred pounds more," he said hoarsely. He looked at his watch, said, "Eleven hours plus or minus," took off his watch and threw it out. He made a notation on his pad, grinning crookedly. "Another ounce gone."

"I'll get Overland," Tony decided.

"Wait!" Masters thrust up a pointing finger. "Don't leave me alone with those two wolves. They're waiting to pounce on us. Four times one hundred and fifty is six hundred."

"You're bats," said Braker coldly.

"Besides," said Yates, "where would we get the other two hundred pounds?"

Masters panted at Tony, "You hear that? He wants to know where they'd get the other two hundred pounds!"

"I was joking," said Yates.

"Joking! *Joking!* When he tried to knife me once!"

"Because," concluded Yates, "the cards call for only one skeleton. *I'll* get him."

He came back shortly with Laurette and her father.

Overland fitted his glasses over his weak eyes while he listened, glancing from face to face.

"It would be suicidal to get rid of the machinery, what's left of it. I have another suggestion. We'll take out all the direct-vision ports. They might add up to eight hundred pounds."

"Not a bad idea," said Braker slowly. "We can wear pressure suits. The ship might leak anyway."

Masters waved a hand. "Then get at it! Laurette, come here. You've got the ring. *You* don't want to be the skeleton, do you? Put your back to this wall with me."

"Oh, Erle," she said in disgust, and followed her father out.

Tony brought three hack saws from the pile of discarded tools. Working individual rooms, the three of them went through the ship, sawing the ports off at the hinges, pulling out the port packing material. The ship was now a truly denuded spectacle, the floors a mere grating of steel.

The ports and packing were placed on the scale.

"Five hundred—five twenty-five—five sixty-one. That's all!" Masters sounded as if he were going to pieces.

Tony shoved him aside. "Five sixty-one it is. There may be a margin of error, though," he added casually. "Braker, Yates—out with this scale."

The two stooped, heaved. The scale, its computed weight already noted, went out—

Tony said, "Come on, Masters."

Masters trotted behind, doglike, as if he had lost the power of thought. Tony got the six pressure suits out of the corner of the control room, and gestured toward them. Everybody got into the suits.

Tony buckled his helmet down. "Now give her the gun."

Masters stood at the auxiliary rocket control board, face pale, eyes unnaturally wide.

He made numerous minor adjustments. He slowly depressed a plunger. A heavy, vibrating roar split the night. The ship leaped. There was a sensation of teetering motion. In the vision plates, the plain moved one step nearer, as if a new slide had been inserted in a projector. The roar swept against them voluminously. The picture remained the same.

Masters wrenched up the plunger, whirled.

"You see?" he panted. "I could have told you!"

Professor Overland silenced him with a wave of the hand, pain showing in his eyes.

"I make this admission almost at the expense of my sanity," he said slowly. "Events have shaped themselves—incredibly. Backward. In the future, far away, in a time none of us may ever see again, lies a skeleton with a ring on its finger.

"Now which causes which—the result or its cause?"

He took off his glasses, blinked, fitted them back on.

"You see," he said carefully, "some of the things that have happened to us are a little bit incredible. There is Lieutenant Crow's —*memory* of these events. He saw the skeleton and it brought back memories. From where? From the vast storehouse of the past? That does not seem possible. Thus far it is the major mystery, how he *knew* that the skeleton existed before the human race.

"Other things are perhaps more incredible. Three shipwrecks! Incredible coincidence! Then there is the incident of the ring.

It is—a ring of death. I say it who thought I would never say it. Lieutenant Crow even had some difficulty throwing it into the river. A fish swallowed it and it came back to me. Then my daughter stole it from me. And she refused to give it up, or let us know what her plans for disposition of it are.

"I do not know whether we are shaping a future that is, or whether a future that is is shaping us.

"And finally we come to the most momentous occurrence of this whole madness. An utterly ridiculous thing like two hundred or two hundred and fifty pounds.

"So we must provide a skeleton. The future that *is* says so."

Silence held. The roar of the river, and the growing violence of the tidal wind rushed in at them. Braker's breath broke loose.

"He's right. Somebody has to get off—and stay off! And it isn't going to be the old man, him being the only one knows how to get us back."

"That's right," said Yates. "It ain't going to be the old man."

Masters shrank back. "Well, don't look at me!" he snarled.

"I wasn't looking at you," Yates said mildly.

Tony's stomach turned rigid. This was what you had to go through to choose a skeleton to die on an asteroid, its skin and flesh to wear and evaporate away and finally wind up millions of years later as a skeleton in a cave with a ring on its finger. These were some of the things you had to go through before you became that skeleton yourself—

"Laurette," he said, "isn't in this lottery."

Braker turned on him. "The hell she isn't!"

Laurette said, voice edged, "I'm in. I might be the straw that broke the camel's back."

Overland said painfully, "Minus a hundred and five might take us over the escarpment. Gentlemen, I'll arrange this lottery, being the only non-participant."

Masters snarled, eyes glittering, "You're prejudiced in favor of your daughter!"

Overland looked at him mildly, curiously, as he would some insect. He made a clicking sound with his lips.

Masters pursued his accusation.

"We'll cut for high man, low card to take the rap!"

"Yah!" jeered Yates. "With your deck, I suppose."

"Anybody's deck!" said Masters.

"All the cards were thrown out. Why weren't yours?"

"Because I knew it would come to this."

"Gentlemen," said Overland wearily. "It won't be a deck. Laurette, the ring."

She started, paled. She said, "I haven't got it."

"Then," said her father, without surprise, "we'll wait around until it shows up."

Braker whirled on him. "You're crazy! We'll draw lots anyway. Better still, we'll find where she put the ring."

"I buried it," said the girl, and her eyes fluttered faintly. "You better leave it buried. You're just proving—"

"Buried it!" blasted Masters. "When she could have used a hammer on it. When she could have melted it in an oxyacetylene torch. When she could—"

"When she could have thrown it in the river and have a fish bring it back! Shut up, Masters." Braker's jawline turned ominous. "Where's the ring? The skeleton's got to have a ring and it's going to have one."

"I'm not going to tell you." She made a violent motion with her hand. "This whole thing is driving me crazy. We don't need the ring for the lottery. Leave it there, can't you?" Her eyes were suddenly pleading. "If you dig it up again, you'll just complete a chain of coincidence that couldn't possibly—"

Overland said, "We won't use the ring in the lottery. It'll turn up later and the skeleton will wear it. We don't have to worry about it, Braker."

Yates said, "Now we're *worrying* about it!"

"Well, it has to be there, doesn't it?" Braker charged.

Tony interrupted by striking a match. He applied flame to a cigarette, sucked in the nerve-soothing smoke.

His eyes were hard, watchful. "Ten hours to get out of range of the collision," his lips said.

"Then we'll hold the lottery now," said Overland. He turned and left the room. Tony heard his heavy steps dragging up the ramp.

The five stood statuesque until he came back. He had a book in one hand. Five straws stuck out from between the pages, their ends making an even line parallel with the book.

Overland's extended hand trembled slightly.

"Draw," he said. "My daughter may draw last, so you may be sure I am not tricking anybody. Lieutenant? Braker? Anybody. And the short straw loses."

Tony pulled a straw.

"Put it down on the floor at your feet," said Overland, "since someone may have previously concealed a straw."

Tony put it down, face stony.

The straw was as long as the book was wide.

Braker said, in an ugly tone, "Well, I'll be damned!"

Braker drew a shorter one. He put it down.

Yates drew a still shorter one. His smile of bravado vanished. Sweat stood suddenly on his pale forehead.

"Go ahead, Masters!" he grated. "The law of averages says you'll draw a long one."

"I don't believe in the law of averages," said Masters sulkily. "Not on this planet, anyway— I'll relinquish the chance to Laurette."

"That," said Laurette, "is sweet of you."

She took a straw without hesitation.

Masters said nervously, "It's short, isn't it?"

"Shorter than mine." Yates' breath came out in a long sigh. "Go ahead, Masters. Only one straw left, so you don't have to make a decision."

Masters jerked it out.

He put it on the floor. It was long.

A cry burst from Overland's lips. "Laurette!"

She faced their silent stares with curled lips.

"That's that. I hope my hundred and five helps."

Tony dropped his cigarette. "It won't," he snapped. "We were fools for including you."

Suddenly he was watching Braker out of the corner of his eye, his nerves tense.

Overland said in a whisper, "How could I suggest leaving my daughter out? I said a hundred pounds *might* be the margin. If I'd have suggested leaving her out, you'd have accused me of favoritism."

Braker said casually, "There's only going to be one lottery held here."

Yates looked dumfounded. "Why, you blasted fool," he said. "What if we're stuck back here before the human race and there ain't any women?"

"That's what I mean. I thought we'd include the girl. If she was drawn, then we could ask some gentleman to volunteer in her place."

He made a sudden motion. Tony made a faster one. His Hampton came out and up.

"Drop it!" he rasped. "I said—*drop it!*"

Braker's eyes bulged. He looked at the Hampton as if he were unable to comprehend it. He cursed rackingly and dropped the automatic as if it were infested with a radioactive element. It clattered on the metal grating of the denuded floor.

A smile froze on Tony's lips. "Now you can explain where you got that automatic."

Braker, eyes fuming like those of a trapped animal, involuntarily shot a glance at Masters.

Tony turned his head slightly toward Masters. "It would be you," he said bitterly.

He whirled—too late. Yates hurtled toward him, struck him in a flying tackle. Tony fell audibly. He tangled furiously with Yates. No good! Braker, face contorted with glee, leaped on top of him, struggled mightily, and then with the main force of his two gloved hands wrenched the Hampton away, rolled from Tony's reach, then snapped himself to his feet, panting.

"Thanks, Yates!" he exclaimed. "Now get up, Crow. Get up. What a man. What a big hulking man. Weighs two hundred if he weighs an ounce." His lips curled vengefully. "Now get up and get out!"

Overland made a step forward, falteringly.

Braker waved the weapon all-inclusively.

"Back, you," he snarled. "This is my party, and it's a bad-taste party, too. Yates, corner the girl. Masters, stand still—you're my friend if you want to be. All right, lieutenant, get going—and dig! For the ring!" His face screwed up sadistically. "Can't disappoint that skeleton, can we?"

Tony came to his feet slowly, heart pounding with what seemed like long-spaced blows against his ribs. Painfully, his eyes ran from face to face, finally centered on Laurette's.

She surged forward against Yates' retaining grip.

"Don't let them do it, lieutenant," she cried. "It's a dirty trick. You're the one person out of the four who doesn't deserve it. I'll—" She slumped back, her voice fading, her eyes burning. She laughed jerkily. "I was just remembering what you did when all the Christmas packages came tumbling down on us. You kissed me, and I slapped you, but I really wanted you to kiss me again."

Yates laughed nastily. "Well, would you listen to that. Masters, you going to stand there and watch them two making love?"

Masters shuddered, his face graying. He whispered, "It's all right. I wish—"

"Cut out the talk!" Braker broke in irritably.

Tony said, as if the other conversation had not intervened, "I wanted to kiss you again, too." He held her wide, unbelieving eyes for a long moment, then dropped his and bit at his shuddering lower lip. It seemed impossible to stand here and realize that this was defeat and that there was no defense against it! He shivered with an unnatural jerk of the shoulders.

"All right," Braker said caustically, "get going."

Tony stood where he was. Braker and everybody else except Laurette Overland faded. Her face came out of the mist, wild, tense, lovely and lovable. Tears were coming from her eyes, and her racking sobs were muted. For a long moment, he hungrily drank in that last glimpse of her.

"Lieutenant!"

He said dully, his eyes adding what his lips did not, "Good-by, Laurette."

He turned, went toward the air lock with dragging feet, like a man who leaves the death house only to walk toward a worse fate. He stopped at the air lock. Braker's gun prodded him.

He stood faintly in the air lock until Braker said, "Out, copper! Get moving."

And then he stepped through, the night and the wild wind inclosing him, the baleful light of the invading planet washing at him.

Faintly he heard Braker's jeering voice, "So long, copper." Then, with grim, ponderous finality, came the wheeze of the closing air lock.

He wandered into the night for a hundred feet, somehow toward the vast pile that had been extracted from the ship's interior. He seemed lost in unreality. This was the pain that went beyond all pains, and therefore numbed.

He turned. A blast of livid flame burst from the ship's main tube. Smaller parallels of fire suddenly ringed it. The ship moved. It slid along the plain on its runners, hugged the ground for two hundred feet, plummeting down the slope. Tony found himself tense, praying staccato curses. Another hundred feet. The escarpment loomed.

He thrust his arms forcefully upward.

"Lift!" he screamed. *"Lift!"*

The ship's nose turned up, as her short wings caught the force of the wind. Then it roared up from the plain, cleared the escarpment by a scant dozen feet. The echoes of the blast muted the very howl of the wind. The echoes died. Then there was nothing but a bright jewel of light receding. Then there was—nothing.

Tony looked after it, conscious that the skin was stretched dry and tight across his cheekbones. His upflung arms dropped. A little laugh escaped his lips. He turned on his heels. The wind was so furious he could lean against it. It was night, and though the small moon this before-the-asteroids world boasted was invisible, the heavens overflowed with the baleful, pale-white glow of the invading planet.

It was still crescent. He could clearly see the ponderous immensity the lighted horns embraced. The leftward sky was occluded a full two fifth by the falling monster, and down in the seas, the shores would be overborne by tidal waves.

He stood motionless. He was at a loss in which direction to turn. An infinity of directions, and there could be no purpose in any. What type of mind could choose a direction?

That thought was lost. He moved toward the last link he had with humanity—with Laurette. He stood near the trembling pile. There was a cardboard carton, addressed to Professor Henry Overland, a short chain of canceled stamps staring up at him, pointing to the nonexistence of everything that would be. America and Christmas and the post office.

He grinned lopsidedly. The grin was lost. It was even hard to know what to do with one's face. He was the last man on a lost world. And even though he was doomed to death in this unimaginably furious crack-up, he should have some goal, something to live for up to the very moment of death!

He uttered a soft, trapped cry, dashed his gloves to his helmeted face. Then a thought simmered. Of course! The ring! He had to find the ring, and he would. The ring went with the skeleton. And the skeleton went with the ring. Lieutenant Tony Crow —and there could be no doubt of this whatsoever—was to be that skeleton which had grinned up at him so many years ago—no, not ago, acome.

A useless task, of course. The hours went past, and he wandered across the tumbled, howling plain, traversing each square foot, hunting for a telltale, freshly turned mound of earth. He went to the very brink of the river gorge, was immersed in leaping spumes of water. Of the ring that he must have there was no trace.

Where would she have buried it? How would her mind work? Surely, she could not have heartlessly buried the ring, hiding it forever, when Tony Crow needed it for the skeleton he was to turn into!

He knew the hours were flying. Yet, better to go mad with this tangible, positive purpose, than with the intangible, negative one of waiting spinelessly for death from the lowering monster who now owned the heavens.

How convenient this was. One time-traveled. One witness to the origin of the asteroids. Similarly, one might time-travel and understand at last the unimaginable, utterly baffling process by which the solar system came into being. Nothing as simple as a collision. Or a binary sweeping past a single. Or a whirling nebula. It would be connected with the expanding universe, in some outrageously simple manner. But everything was simple once one knew the answer. For instance—

The ring! Yes, it was as simple as that. Even Laurette Overland would be forced to yield to the result that was influencing its own cause!

Tenseness gave way to relief. One could not baffle the future. Naturally, she'd buried the ring in the cave. Unless she wanted to be perverse. But she would *not* be perverse in a matter like this. Future and present demanded co-operation, if there was to be a logical future!

Forcing himself against a wind that blew indiscriminately, he reached the funnel in the mountainside. The skeleton was not here, naturally. But it would be—with the necessary ring on its finger. Unbelievable how the future shaped its own past! It was as if his own skeleton, which existed millions of years *acome,* on which his own healthy flesh rode *now,* were plainly telling him what he should do.

He dug with a cold methodicity, starting from the rear of the cave. No sign of the ring, and no sign of recently turned earth. He discarded his gloves, placed them carefully to one side, and dug with a sharp rock.

No sign of the ring! The hours passed. What was he to do? His thoughts sharpened with desperation. An hour, little more, remained. Then would come the smash—and death.

He was in the cave! He, the skeleton!

He lay on his back, head propped up in locked hands. Trees and limbs and leaves hurtled by in a tempestuous wind. Soon, out in the sky, would float the remnants of this very substantial world. The millions of years would pass. A Lieutenant Tony Crow, on the trail of three criminals, would land here, look into this cave, and see his own skeleton—only he would not know it.

He lay there, tense, waiting. The wind would dig up the ring, whip it through the air. He would hear a tinkling sound. That would be the ring, striking against the wall of the cave. He would pick it up and put it on his finger. In a few moments after that would come the sound—the heavy vibration—the ear-splitting concussion—the cosmic clash—the . . . the . . . *bang* of a world breaking up. *Bang!*

He listened, waiting for the ring.

He listened, and heard a voice, screaming down the wind.

He impelled himself to his feet, in one surge of motion. He stood there, blood pounding against his temples, his lips parted and trembling. There could be no sound like that. Not when he was the last human being on this world. Not when the scream could be that of Laurette Overland, calling to him.

Of course, it was not she. Of course, it could not be. This was merely one of those things previewing the preparation of a skeleton with a ring in a— *Stop!*

He moved from the cave, out into the wind, and stood there. He heard nothing—did he? A pound of feet—such as death running might make.

A scream!

He ran around the shoulder of the mountain, stood there, panting, clasping his helmeted head between his trembling, cold hands.

"Lieutenant!"

A voice, whipped into his imagination by the ungodly wind! He would not believe it.

A form, stumbling out of the pale night! Running toward him, its lips moving, saying words that the wind took away. And it was Laurette Overland, forming in his imagination now that he had gone completely mad.

He waited there, in cold amusement. There was small use in allowing himself to be fooled. And yet—and yet—the ring had to come back; to him. This was Laurette Overland, and she was bringing it—for him to wear. That was selfish of her. If *she* had the ring, if *she* had dug it up, why didn't *she* wear it?

Then she would be the skeleton.

Then there would be two skeletons!

His mind froze, then surged forward into life and sanity. A cold cry of agony escaped him. He stumbled forward and caught the girl up in his arms. He could feel the supple firmness of her body even through the folds of her undistended pressure suit.

Laurette's lips, red and full against the ghastly induced paleness of her face, parted and words came out. Yet he could make no sense of it, for the unimaginable wind, and the cold horror lancing through his mind occluded words and sentences.

"—had to . . . out. A hundred pounds." He felt her hysterical laugh. So the ship had started to fall. She had bailed out, had swept to solid ground on streams of flame shooting from the rocket jets in the shoulders of her suit. This much he knew. Hours and hours she had fought her way—toward the plain. Because, she remembered something. The ship was gone. Safe. She remembered something that was important and it had to do with the skeleton and the ring. She had to get out. It was her part in the ghastly across-the-millions-of-years stage play. She had to dig up the ring.

He held her out at arm's length and looked down at her gloved hands. Yes, there was mud on them. So the ring had not been in the cave.

His eyes shuddered upward to hers.

"Give me the ring." His lips formed the words slowly.

"No, no, lieutenant," she blurted out. "It's not going to be *that* way. Don't you see? It's Amos! Amos!"

"You must be crazy to have come back!" he panted. He shook in sudden overwhelming, maddening fury. "You're crazy anyway!"

He suddenly wrenched at her hands, forced them open. But there was no ring. He shook her madly.

"Where's the ring? Give it to me, you damned little fool! If you're wearing it—if you think for one moment—you can't do this—"

The wind whipped the words away from her, she knew, even as that which she was saying was lost to him.

He stopped talking, and with a cold ferocity wrapped one arm around her, and with the other started to unbuckle her gloves with his own bare hands. She struggled suddenly, tigerishly. She wrenched herself away from him. She ran backward three steps. She looked up into the sky for one brief second, at the growing monster. He could see the cold, frantic horror settling on her face. Collision! And it was a matter of moments! And he, the true skeleton, did not have the ring!

He moved toward her, one slow step at a time, his eyes wild, his jaw set with purpose.

She darted past him. He whirled, panting, went frantically after her. And every step he took grew more leaden, for the moment was here. The collision was about to occur. And the girl was running toward the cave.

Laurette vanished around the shoulder of the mountain. The cave swallowed her. His steps slowed down. He stood there, drew a deep, tremulous breath. Then he entered the cave, and stood facing her, the wind's howl diminishing.

She said, coldly, "We haven't much time to talk or fight, lieutenant. You're acting like a madman. Here." She stooped and picked up his gloves. She held them out. "Put these on."

He said, "Give me the ring."

She stared at him through the gloom, at his preternaturally wide eyes.

"All right," she said. She unbuckled the glove of her right hand. She moved close to him, holding his eyes with her own. "If you want to be the skeleton, you may."

He felt her fingers touch his right hand. He felt something cold traveling up his fingers. He felt the ring inclosing his finger. Yes, the ring was on there, where it should be. He felt it—coldly. It could not very well be his imagination—could it? Of course not. She would not try to fool him. Yet her eyes were hypnotic, and he was in a daze. Feebly, he knew he should resist. But she forced his glove over his right hand, and he heard the buckles click. Then the left hand glove went on, and was buckled.

Her arms crept up around his neck. Tears glinted unashamedly in her eyes.

"Hold me tight, lieutenant," she whispered huskily. "You know . . . you know, there may be a chance."

"No, there isn't, Laurette. There can't be. I've got the ring on my finger."

He could feel her drawing a deep breath. "Of course—you've got the ring on your finger! I think it can't be very far away, lieutenant. Hold me." Her voice was a whimper. "Maybe we'll live."

"Not I. Perhaps you."

"This cave, this very mountain, lived through the holocaust. And perhaps we will, too. Both of us."

She was being illogical, he knew. But he had sunk into a dull, apathetic state of mind. Let her try to believe what was impossible. He had the ring on his finger. He *did*.

Did he?

He jerked. He had felt the cold of its metal encircling his finger. He had *thought* he had felt it! His fingers moved. A dull, sickening sense of utter defeat engulfed him. This was defeat. *She* had the ring! *She* was the skeleton!

And there was no time to change it. There would be no time. The blood rushed in his head, giddily. He caught her eyes, and held them, and tried to let her know in that last moment that he knew what she had done. She bit her lip and smiled. Then—her face clouded. Clouded as his thoughts clouded. It was like that.

He heard no monstrous sound, for here was sound that was no sound. It was simply the ponderous headlong meeting of two planets. They had struck. They were flattening out against each other, in the immeasurable second when consciousness was whipped away, and fragments of rock, some large, some small, were dribbling out in a fine frothy motion from underneath the circle of collision. The planet was yawning mightly. A jigsaw of pieces, a Humpty Dumpty that all the king's horses and all the king's men could never put together again. This was the mighty prelude to the forming of an asteroid belt, and of a girl skeleton on Asteroid No. 1007.

He was alive.
Alive and thinking.
It did not seem possible.
He was wedged into the back of the cave. A boulder shut off light, and a projecting spur of it reached out and pinioned him with gentle touch against the wall at his back. He was breathing. His suit was inflated with ten pounds of pressure. Electric coils were keeping his body warm. He was alive and the thoughts were beginning in his brain. Slow, senseless thoughts. Thoughts that were illogical. He could not even bring himself to feel emotion. He was pinioned here in the darkness, and out there was an asteroid of no air, small gravity, and a twenty-mile altitude.

Laurette Overland would be dead, and she would be wearing the ring. Tears, unashamed, burned at his eyes.

How long had he been here, wedged in like this: minutes, hours, days? Where were Overland, Masters, Braker and Yates? Would they land and move this boulder away?

Something suddenly seemed to shake the mountain. He felt the vibration rolling through his body. What had caused that? Some internal explosion, an aftermath of the collision? That did not seem likely, for the vibration had been brief, barely perceptible.

He stood there, wedged, his thoughts refusing to work except with a monotonous regularity. Mostly he thought of the skeleton; so that skeleton *had* existed before the human race!

After a while, it might have been five minutes or an hour or more, he became aware of arms and legs and a sluggishly beating heart. He raised his arms slowly, like an automaton that has come to life after ages of motionlessness, and pushed against the boulder that hemmed him in. It seemed to move away from him easily. He stepped to one side and imparted a ponderous, rocking motion to the boulder. It fell forward and stopped. Light, palely emanating from the starry, black night that overhung Asteroid No. 1007, burst through over the top of the boulder. Good.

There was plenty of room to crawl through—after a while. He leaned against the boulder, blood surging weakly in his veins.

He felt a vibration so small that it might have been imagination. Then again, it might have been the ship, landing on the asteroid. At least, there was enough likelihood of that to warrant turning his headset receiver on.

He listened, and heard the dull undertone of a carrier wave; or was that the dull throb of blood against his temples? No, it couldn't be. He strained to listen, coherent thoughts at last making headway in his mind.

Then:

"Go on, professor—Masters." That was Braker's voice! "We'll all go crazy if we don't find out who the skeleton is."

Then Braker had landed the ship, after escaping the holocaust that had shattered that before-the-asteroids world! Tony almost let loose a hoarse breath, then withheld it, savagely. If Braker heard that, he might suspect something. Whatever other purpose Tony had in life now, the first and most important was to get the Hampton away from Braker.

Overland muttered, his voice lifeless, "If it's my daughter, I'd rather you'd go first, Braker."

Masters spoke. "I'll go ahead, professor. I'd do anything to—" His voice broke.

Overland muttered, "Don't take it so hard, son. We all have our bad moments. It couldn't be a skeleton, anyway."

"Why not?" That was Yates. Then, "Oh, hell, yes! It couldn't be, could it, professor? You know, this is just about the flukiest thing that has ever happened I guess. Sometimes it makes me laugh! On again, off again!"

"Finnegan," finished Braker absently. "Say, I don't get it. This time business. You say the gravity of that planet was holding us back in time like a rubber band stretched tight. When the planet went, the rubber band broke—there wasn't that gravity any more. And then we snapped back to our real time. But what if Crow and your daughter weren't released like that? Then we ought to find the skeleton—maybe two of 'em."

"The gravity of the asteroid would not be enough to hold them back," Overland said wearily.

"Then I don't get it," Braker snapped with exasperation. "This is the present, our real present. Back there is the ledge that cracked our ship up, so it has to be the present. Then how come Crow said he saw a skeleton? Say," he added, in a burst of anger, "do you think that copper was pulling the wool over our eyes? Well, I'll be—"

Yates said, "Grow up! Crow was telling the truth."

Overland said, "The skeleton will be there. The lieutenant saw it."

Masters: "Maybe he saw his own skeleton."

Yates: "Say, that's right!"

Braker: "Well, why not? The same ring was in two different places at the same time, so I guess the same skeleton could be in Crow at the same time as in the cave. It's a fact, and you don't talk yourself out of it."

Tony's head was whirling. What in heaven were they talking about? Were they intimating that the release of gravity, when the planet broke up, released everything back to the real present, as if some sort of bond had been broken? His hands started to tremble. Of course. It was possible. The escapage of gravitons had thrust them back into the past. Gravitons, the very stuff of gravity, had held them there. And when that one and a half gravity had dispersed, when the gravitons were so far distant that they no longer exerted that tension, everything had snapped back—to the present!

Everything! His thoughts turned cold. Somewhere, somehow, something was terribly wrong. His head ached. He clenched his hands, and listened again. For a full minute, there was no voice. Tony could envision them walking along, Masters and Overland in front, Braker and Yates behind, making their slow way to the cave, Overland dreading what he was to find there.

Then: "Hurry it up, professor. Should be right around here."

Overland whispered, throatily, "There it is, Braker. My God!" He sounded as if he were going all to pieces.

"The skeleton!" Yates blurted out, burs in his voice. "Ye gods, professor, d'you suppose— Why sure—they just weren't snapped back."

Shaking, pasty white of face, Tony clawed his way halfway up the boulder. He hung there, just able to look outside. The whole floor of the cave was visible. And the skeleton lay there, gleaming white, and the ring shone on its tapering finger!

Laurette.

He lifted his head, conscious that his eyes were smarting painfully. Through a blur, he saw Braker, Yates, Masters and Overland, standing about thirty feet distant from the cave, silent, speechless, staring at the skeleton.

Braker said, his voice unsteady, "It's damned strange, isn't it? We knew it was going to be there, and there it is, and it robs you of your breath."

Yates cleared his throat, and said firmly, "Yeah, but who is it? Crow or the girl?"

Overland took a step forward, his weak eyes straining.

"It's not a very long skeleton, is it?" he whispered.

Braker said, harshly, "Now don't try talking yourself into anything, professor. You can't see the skeleton well enough from here to tell who it is. Masters, stop shaking." His words were implicit with scorn. "Move over there and don't try any funny stuff like you did on the ship a while ago. I should have blasted you then. I'm going to take a look at that skeleton."

He went forward sideways, hand on his right hip where the Hampton was holstered.

He came up to the mouth of the cave, stood looking down on the skeleton, frowning. Then he knelt. Tony could see his face working with revulsion, but still he knelt there, as if fascinated.

Tony's lips stretched back from his teeth. Here's where Braker got his! He worked his way up to the top of the boulder, tensed, slid over to the other side on his feet. He took one step forward and bent his knees.

Braker raised his head.

His face contorted into a sudden mask of horror.

"*You!*" he screamed. His eyes bulged.

Tony leaped.

Braker fell backward, face deathly pale, clawing at the Hampton. Tony was on top of him before he could use it. He pinned Braker down, going for the Hampton with hands, feet, and blistering curses. His helmet was a sudden madhouse of consternated voices. Overland, Masters, and Yates swept across his vision. And Yates was coming forward.

He caught hold of the weapon, strained at it mightily, the muscles of his stomach going rigid under the exertion.

Braker kicked at Tony's midriff with heavy boots, striving to puncture the pressure suit. Tony was forced over on his back, saw Braker's sweating face grinning mirthlessly into his.

Stars were suddenly occluded by Yates' body. The man fell to his knees, pinned Tony down, and with Braker's help broke Tony's hold on the Hampton.

"Give it to me!" That was Masters' voice, blasting out shrilly. By sheer surprise, he wrenched the weapon from Yates. Tony flung himself to his feet as the outlaw hurled himself at Masters with a snarl, made a grab for Yates' foot. Yates tried to shake him off, hopped futilely, then stumbled forward, falling. But he

struck against Masters. Masters' hold on the weapon was weak.
It went sailing away in an arc, fell at the mouth of the cave.

"Get it!" Braker's voice blasted out as he struggled to his feet.
Masters was ahead of him. Wildly, he thrust Braker aside. Yates
reached out, tripped Masters. Braker went forward toward the
Hampton, and then stopped, stock-still.

A figure stepped from the cave, picked up the weapon, and
said, in cold, unmistakable tones.

"Up with them. You, Braker. Yates!"

Braker's breath released in a long shuddering sigh, and he
dropped weakly, helplessly to his knees.

His voice was horrible. "I'm crazy," he said simply, and continued to kneel there and continued to look up at the figure as if it
were a dead figure come to life at which he stared.

The blood drummed upward in Tony's temples, until it was a
wild, crazy, diapason. His shuddering hands raised to clasp his
helmet.

Then:

"Laurette," he whispered brokenly. *"Laurette!"*

There were six human beings here.

And *one skeleton on the floor of the cave.*

How long that tableau held, Tony had no way of knowing.
Professor Overland, standing off to Tony's left, arms half raised,
a tortured, uncomprehending look on his face. Masters, full
length on his stomach, pushing at the ground with his clawed
hands to raise his head upward. Yates, in nearly the same position, turned to stone. Braker, his breath beginning to sound out
in little, bottled-up rasps.

And the girl, Laurette, she who should have been the skeleton,
standing there at the mouth of the cave, her face indescribably
pale, as she centered the Hampton on Braker and Yates.

Her voice edged into the aching silence.

"It's Amos," she said. She was silent, looking at her father's
haggard face, smiling twistedly.

"Amos," said Overland hoarsely, saying nothing else, but in
that one word showing his utter, dismaying comprehension. He
stumbled forward three steps. "We thought— We thought—" He
seemed unable to go on. Tears sounded in his voice. He said hum-
bly, "We thought you were the— But no. It's Amos!" His voice
went upward hysterically.

"Stop it!" Laurette's voice lashed out. She added softly, tenderly, "No, I'm not the skeleton. Far from it, daddy. Amos is the
skeleton. He was the skeleton all along. I didn't realize it might

be that way until the ship lifted. Then it seemed that the ship was going to fall and I thought my hundred and five might help after all and anyway, I decided that the lieutenant was all alone down there. And that somehow made me think of the time all the Christmas packages tumbled down on him and how I slapped him." She laughed unsteadily. "That made me remember that the university sent your present with a 'Do Not Open Before Christmas' sticker on it. I remembered you were leaving the university and they were giving you a combination farewell gift and Christmas present. You didn't know, but I did, that the professors decided you couldn't possibly be back before Christmas and so they sent it to the ship. You had always told them you admired—Amos. He hung on the biology classroom wall. It seemed I suddenly knew how things *had* to be. I put two and two together and I took a chance on it."

She fell silent, and the silence held for another full, shocking minute. She went on, as if with an effort.

"We threw everything out of the ship, remember? The Christmas presents, too. When I dropped from the ship later, I reached the plain and I broke open the carton with the 'Do Not Open' sticker on it, and there was Amos, as peaceful as you please. I put the ring on his finger and left him there, because I knew that some way the wind or crack-up or *something* would drop him in the cave. He *had* to turn up in the cave.

"Anyway," she added, her lips quirking roguishly, "by our time, back there, it was December 25th."

Masters clawed his way to his knees, his lips parted unnaturally.

"A Christmas present!" he croaked. "A Christmas present!" His face went white.

The girl said unsteadily, "Cut it out, Erle!"

She leaned weakly against the wall of the cave. "Now come up here, lieutenant, and take this gun out of my hands and don't stare at me as if you've lost your senses."

Tony forced himself to his feet, and like an automaton skirted around Braker and Yates and took the suddenly shaking weapon from her.

She uttered a weary sigh, smiled at him faintly, bemusedly, and whispered, "Merry Christmas, lieutenant!" She slumped slowly to the ground.

Tony gestured soundlessly at Masters. Masters, face abject and ashamed, picked her up in tender arms.

"Come up here, professor," Tony said dully. He felt as if all the life had been pumped from his bones.

Overland came forward, shaking his head with emotion. "Amos!" he whispered. He broke in a half-hysterical chuckle, stopped himself. He hovered Laurette, watching her tired face. "At least my girl lives," he whispered brokenly.

"Get up, Braker," said Tony. "You, too, Yates."

Yates rose, vaguely brushing dust from his pressure suit, his lips working over words that refused to emerge.

Braker's voice was a hoarse, unbelieving whisper. His eyes were abnormally wide and fixed hypnotically on the skeleton. "So that's what we went through—for a damned classroom skeleton." He repeated it. "For a damned classroom skeleton!"

He came to his feet, fighting to mold his strained face back to normal. "Just about back where we started, eh? Well," he added in a shaking, bitter tone, "Merry Christmas." He forced his lips into half-hearted cynicism.

Tony's face relaxed. He drew in a full, much-needed breath of air. "Sure. Sure— Merry Christmas. Everybody. Including Amos —whoever he used to be."

Nobody seemed to have anything to say. Or perhaps their thoughts were going back for the moment to a pre-asteroid world. Remembering. At least Masters was remembering, if the suffering, remorseful look on his face meant anything.

Tony broke it. "That's that, isn't it? Now we can go back to the ship. From there to Earth. Professor—Masters—start off." He made a tired gesture.

Masters went ahead, without a backward look, carrying the gently breathing, but still unconscious girl. Overland stole a last look at the skeleton, at Amos, where he lay, unknowing of the chaos the mere fact of his being there, white and perfect and wired together, and with a ring on his perfect tapering finger, had caused. Overland walked away hurriedly after Masters. Amos would stay where he was.

Tony smiled grimly at Braker. He pointed with his free hand. "Want your ring back, Braker?"

Braker's head jerked minutely. He stared at the ring, then back at Tony. His fists clenched at his sides. "*No!*"

Tony grinned—for the first time in three weeks.

"Then let's get going."

He made a gesture. Braker and Yates, walking side by side, went slowly for the ship, Tony following behind. He turned only once, and that was to look at his wrecked patrol ship, where it lay against the base of the mountain. A shudder passed down his spine. There was but one mystery that remained now. And its solution was coming to Tony Crow, in spite of his effort to shove its sheerly maddening implications into the back of his mind—

Professor Overland and Masters took Laurette to her room. Tony took the two outlaws to the lounge, wondering how he was going to secure them. Masters solved his problem by entering with a length of insulated electric wire. He said nothing, but wordlessly went to work securing Braker and Yates to the guide rail while Tony held the Hampton on them. After he had finished, Tony bluntly inspected the job. Masters winced, but he said nothing.

After they were out in the hall, going toward Laurette's room, Masters stopped him. His face was white, strained in the half-darkness.

"I don't know how to say this," he began huskily.

"Say what?"

Masters' eyes shifted, then, as if by a deliberate effort of will, came back.

"That I'm sorry."

Tony studied him, noted the lines of suffering around his mouth, the shuddering pain in his eyes.

"Yeah, I know how you feel," he muttered. "But I guess you made up for it when you tackled Braker and Yates. They might have been using electric wire on us by now." He grinned lopsidedly, and clapped Masters on the arm. "Forget it, Masters. I'm with you all the way."

Masters managed a smile, and let loose a long breath. He fell into step beside Tony's hurrying stride. "Laurette's O. K."

"Well, lieutenant," said Laurette, stretching lazily, and smiling up at him, "I guess I got weak in the knees at the last minute."

"Didn't we all!" He smiled ruefully. He dropped to his knees. She was still in her pressure suit and lying on the floor. He helped her to a sitting position, and then to her feet.

Overland chuckled, though there was a note of uneasy reminiscence in his tone. "Wait till I tell the boys at Lipton U. about this."

"You'd better not," Laurette warned. She added, "You broke down and admitted the ring was an omen. When a scientist gets superstitious—"

Tony broke in. "Weren't we all?"

Masters said, dropping his eyes, "I guess we had good enough reason to be superstitious about it." His hand went absently upward to his shoulder.

Overland frowned, and, hands behind his back, walked to the empty porthole. "All that work DeTosque, the Farr brothers, Morrell and myself put in. There's no reason to patch up the asteroids and try to prove they were all one world. But at the same time, there's no proof—no absolute proof—" He clicked his tongue. Then he swung on Tony, biting speculatively at his lower lip, his eyes sharpening.

"There's one thing that needs explaining which probably never will be explained, I guess. It's too bad. Memory? Bah! That's not the answer, lieutenant. You stood in the cave there, and you saw the skeleton, and somehow you *knew* it had existed before the human race, but was not *older* than the human race. It's something else. You didn't pick up the memory from the past—not over a hundred million years. What then?" He turned away, shaking his head, came back abruptly as Tony spoke, eyes sharpening.

"I'll tell you why," Tony said evenly.

His head moved up and down slowly, and his half-lidded eyes looked lingeringly out the porthole toward the mountain where his wrecked patrol ship lay. "Yes, I'll tell you why."

Laurette, Masters and Overland were caught up in tense silence by the strangeness of his tone.

He said faintly: "Laurette and I were trapped alive in the back of the cave when the two worlds crashed. We lived through it. I didn't know she was back there, of course; she recovered consciousness later—at the right time, I'd say!" He grinned at her obliquely, then sobered again. "I saw the skeleton and somehow I was too dazed to realize it couldn't be Laurette. Because when the gravity was dispersed, the tension holding everything back in time was released, and everything went back to the present— just a little less than the present. I'll explain that later."

He drew a long breath.

"This is hard to say. I was in the back of the cave. I felt something strike the mountainside.

"That was my patrol ship—with me in it."

His glance roved around. Overland's breath sucked in audibly.

"Careful now, boy," he rumbled warningly, alarm in his eyes.

Tony's lips twisted. "It happens to be the truth. After my ship crashed I got out. A few minutes later I stood at the mouth of the cave, looking at the skeleton. For a minute, I—remembered. Fragmentary things. The skeleton was—horror.

"And why not? I was also in the back of the cave, thinking that

Laurette was dead and that she was a skeleton. The Tony Crow at the mouth of the cave and the Tony Crow trapped in the rear of the cave were *en rapport* to an infinite degree. They were the same person, in two different places at the same time, and their brains were the same."

He stopped.

Masters whispered through his clenched teeth, "Two Tony Crows. It couldn't be."

Tony leaned back against the wall. "There were two rings, at the same time. There were two skeletons, at the same time. Braker had the skeleton's ring on his finger. Amos was wrapped up in a carton with a Christmas sticker on it. They were both some place else. You all know that and admit it. Well, there were two Tony Crows, and if I think about it much longer, it'll drive me—"

"Hold it, boy!" Overland's tone was sharp. Then he said mildly, "It's nothing to get excited about. The mere fact of time-travel presupposes duplicity of existence. Our ship and everything in it was made of electrons that existed somewhere else at the same time—a hundred million years ago, on the pre-asteroid world. You can't get away from it. And you don't have to get scared just because two Tony Crows were a few feet distant from each other. Remember that all the rest of us were duplicated, too. Ship A was thrust *back* into time just an hour or so before Ship B landed here after being thrust *forward*. You see?"

Laurette shuddered. "It's clear, but it's—" She made a confused motion.

Overland's tired, haggard eyes twinkled. "Anyway, there's no danger of us running across ourselves again. The past is done for. That's the main thing."

Neither Laurette nor Tony said anything. They were studying each other, and a smile was beginning at the corner of Laurette's lips. Erle Masters squirmed uncomfortably.

Overland continued, speculatively: "There was an energy loss some place. We weren't snapped back to the real present at all. We should have come back to the present that we left, *plus* the three weeks we stayed back in time. Back there it was Christmas —and Laurette was quite correct when she broke open my package." He grinned crookedly. "But it's still more than three weeks to Christmas here. It was a simple energy loss, I guess. If I had a penc—"

Erle Masters broke in on him, coughing uncomfortably and grinning wryly at the same time. "We'd better get down to the control room and plot out our course, professor."

"What?" Overland's eyes widened. He looked around at the

man and girl. "Oh." He studied them, then turned, and clapped Masters on the back. "You're dead right, son. Let's get out!"

"I'm glad you weren't Amos," Tony told the girl.

"I couldn't very well have been, lieutenant."

He grinned, coloring slightly.

Then he took her hands in his, and put his head as close to hers as the helmets would allow.

He said, "When we get back to Earth, I'm going to put a r—" He stopped, biting at his lip. Remembrances of another time, on a pre-asteroid world, flooded back with the thought.

She started, paled. Involuntarily, her eyes turned to the open port, beyond which was a mountain, a cave, a skeleton, a ring.

She nodded, slowly, faintly. "It's a good idea," she murmured. She managed a smile. "But not—an emerald."

1941

Nightfall /

by ISAAC ASIMOV

How would a people who saw the stars but once in two thousand years react—"If the stars should appear one night in a thousand years, how would men believe and adore, and preserve for many generations the remembrance of the city of God!"—Emerson

Aton 77, director of Saro University, thrust out a belligerent lower lip and glared at the young newspaperman in a hot fury.

Theremon 762 took that fury in his stride. In his earlier days, when his now widely syndicated column was only a mad idea in a cub reporter's mind, he had specialized in "impossible" interviews. It had cost him bruises, black eyes, and broken bones; but it had given him an ample supply of coolness and self-confidence.

So he lowered the outthrust hand that had been so pointedly ignored and calmly waited for the aged director to get over the worst. Astronomers were queer ducks, anyway, and if Aton's actions of the last two months meant anything, this same Aton was the queer-duckiest of the lot.

Aton 77 found his voice, and though it trembled with restrained emotion, the careful, somewhat pedantic, phraseology, for which the famous astronomer was noted, did not abandon him.

"Sir," he said, "you display an infernal gall in coming to me with that impudent proposition of yours."

The husky telephotographer of the Observatory, Beenay 25, thrust a tongue's tip across dry lips and interposed nervously, "Now, sir, after all—"

The director turned to him and lifted a white eyebrow. "Do not interfere, Beenay. I will credit you with good intentions in bringing this man here; but I will tolerate no insubordination now."

Theremon decided it was time to take a part. "Director Aton, if you'll let me finish what I started saying I think—"

"I don't believe, young man," retorted Aton, "that anything you could say now would count much as compared with your daily columns of these last two months. You have led a vast newspaper campaign against the efforts of myself and my colleagues to organize the world against the menace which it is now too late to avert. You have done your best with your highly personal attacks to make the staff of this Observatory objects of ridicule."

The director lifted the copy of the Saro City *Chronicle* on the table and shook it at Theremon furiously. "Even a person of your well-known impudence should have hesitated before coming to me with a request that he be allowed to cover today's events for his paper. Of all newsmen, you!"

Aton dashed the newspaper to the floor, strode to the window and clasped his arms behind his back.

"You may leave," he snapped over his shoulder. He stared moodily out at the skyline where Gamma, the brightest of the planet's six suns, was setting. It had already faded and yellowed into the horizon mists, and Aton knew he would never see it again as a sane man.

He whirled. "No, wait, come here!" He gestured peremptorily. "I'll give you your story."

The newsman had made no motion to leave, and now he approached the old man slowly. Aton gestured outward, "Of the six suns, only Beta is left in the sky. Do you see it?"

The question was rather unnecessary. Beta was almost at zenith; its ruddy light flooding the landscape to an unusual orange as the brilliant rays of setting Gamma died. Beta was at aphelion. It was small; smaller than Theremon had ever seen it before, and for the moment it was undisputed ruler of Lagash's sky.

Lagash's own sun, Alpha, the one about which it revolved, was at the antipodes; as were the two distant companion pairs. The red dwarf Beta—Alpha's immediate companion—was alone, grimly alone.

Aton's upturned face flushed redly in the sunlight. "In just under four hours," he said, "civilization, as we know it, comes to an end. It will do so because, as you see, Beta is the only sun in the sky." He smiled grimly. "Print that! There'll be no one to read it."

"But if it turns out that four hours pass—and another four—and nothing happens?" asked Theremon softly.

"Don't let that worry you. Enough will happen."

"Granted! And *still*—if nothing happens?"

For a second time, Beenay 25 spoke, "Sir, I think you ought to listen to him."

Theremon said, "Put it to a vote, Director Aton."

There was a stir among the remaining five members of the Observatory staff, who till now had maintained an attitude of wary neutrality.

"That," stated Aton flatly, "is not necessary." He drew out his pocket watch. "Since your good friend, Beenay, insists so urgently, I will give you five minutes. Talk away."

"Good! Now, just what difference would it make if you allowed me to take down an eyewitness account of what's to come? If your prediction comes true, my presence won't hurt; for in that case my column would never be written. On the other hand, if nothing comes of it, you will just have to expect ridicule or worse. It would be wise to leave that ridicule to friendly hands."

Aton snorted. "Do you mean yours when you speak of friendly hands?"

"Certainly!" Theremon sat down and crossed his legs. "My columns may have been a little rough at times, but I gave you people the benefit of the doubt every time. After all, this is not the century to preach 'the end of the world is at hand' to Lagash. You have to understand that people don't believe the 'Book of Revelations' any more, and it annoys them to have scientists turn about face and tell us the Cultists are right after all—"

"No such thing, young man," interrupted Aton. "While a great deal of our data has been supplied us by the Cult, our results contain none of the Cult's mysticism. Facts are facts, and the Cult's so-called 'mythology' has certain facts behind it. We've exposed them and ripped away their mystery. I assure you that the Cult hates us now worse than you do."

"I don't hate you. I'm just trying to tell you that the public is in an ugly humor. They're angry."

Aton twisted his mouth in derision. "Let them be angry."

"Yes, but what about tomorrow?"

"There'll be no tomorrow!"

"But if there is. Say that there is—just to see what happens. That anger might take shape into something serious. After all, you know, business has taken a nose dive these last two months. Investors don't really believe the world is coming to an end, but just the same they're being cagy with their money until it's all over. Johnny Public doesn't believe you, either, but the new spring furniture might as well wait a few months—just to make sure.

"You see the point. Just as soon as this is all over, the business interests will be after your hide. They'll say that if crackpots—begging your pardon—can upset the country's prosperity any time they want simply by making some cockeyed prediction—it's up to the planet to prevent them. The sparks will fly, sir."

The director regarded the columnist sternly. "And just what were you proposing to do to help the situation?"

"Well," grinned Theremon, "I was proposing to take charge of the publicity. I can handle things so that only the ridiculous side will show. It would be hard to stand, I admit, because I'd have to make you all out to be a bunch of gibbering idiots, but if I can get people laughing at you, they might forget to be angry. In return for that, all my publisher asks is an exclusive story."

Beenay nodded and burst out, "Sir, the rest of us think he's right. These last two months we've considered everything but the million-to-one chance that there is an error somewhere in our theory or in our calculations. We ought to take care of that, too."

There was a murmur of agreement from the men grouped about the table, and Aton's expression became that of one who found his mouth full of something bitter and couldn't get rid of it.

"You may stay if you wish, then. You will kindly refrain, however, from hampering us in our duties in any way. You will also remember that I am in charge of all activities here, and in spite of your opinions as expressed in your columns, I will expect full co-operation and full respect—"

His hands were behind his back, and his wrinkled face thrust forward determinedly as he spoke. He might have continued indefinitely but for the intrusion of a new voice.

"Hello, hello, hello!" It came in a high tenor, and the plump cheeks of the newcomer expanded in a pleased smile. "What's this morgue-like atmosphere about here? No one's losing his nerve, I hope."

Aton started in consternation and said peevishly, "Now what the devil are you doing here, Sheerin? I thought you were going to stay behind in the Hideout."

Sheerin laughed and dropped his tubby figure into a chair. "Hideout be blowed! The place bored me. I wanted to be here, where things are getting hot. Don't you suppose I have my share of curiosity? I want to see these Stars the Cultists are forever speaking about." He rubbed his hands and added in a soberer tone, "It's freezing outside. The wind's enough to hang icicles on your nose. Beta doesn't seem to give any heat at all, at the distance it is."

The white-haired director ground his teeth in sudden exasperation, "Why do you go out of your way to do crazy things, Sheerin? What kind of good are you around here?"

"What kind of good am I around there?" Sheerin spread his palms in comical resignation. "A psychologist isn't worth his salt in the Hideout. They need men of action and strong, healthy women that can breed children. Me? I'm a hundred pounds too heavy for a man of action, and I wouldn't be a success at breeding children. So why bother them with an extra mouth to feed? I feel better over here."

Theremon spoke briskly, "Just what is the Hideout, sir?"

Sheerin seemed to see the columnist for the first time. He frowned and blew his ample cheeks out, "And just who in Lagash are you, redhead?"

Aton compressed his lips and then muttered sullenly, "That's Theremon 762, the newspaper fellow. I suppose you've heard of him."

The columnist offered his hand. "And, of course, you're Sheerin 501 of Saro University. I've heard of *you*." Then he repeated, "What is this Hideout, sir?"

"Well," said Sheerin, "we have managed to convince a few people of the validity of our prophecy of—er—doom, to be spectacular about it, and those few have taken proper measures. They consist mainly of the immediate members of the families of the Observatory staff, certain of the faculty of Saro University and a few outsiders. Altogether, they number about three hundred, but three quarters are women and children."

"I see! They're supposed to hide where the Darkness and the—er—Stars can't get at them, and then hold out when the rest of the world goes poof."

"If they can. It won't be easy. With all of mankind insane; with the great cities going up in flames—environment will not be conducive to survival. But they have food, water, shelter, and weapons—"

"They've got more," said Aton. "They've got all our records, except for what we will collect today. Those records will mean everything to the next cycle, and *that's* what must survive. The rest can go hang."

Theremon whistled a long, low whistle and sat brooding for several minutes. The men about the table had brought out a multichess board and started a six-member game. Moves were made rapidly and in silence. All eyes bent in furious concentration on the board. Theremon watched them intently and then rose and approached Aton, who sat apart in whispered conversation with Sheerin.

"Listen," he said, "let's go somewhere where we won't bother the rest of the fellows. I want to ask some questions."

The aged astronomer frowned sourly at him, but Sheerin chirped up, "Certainly. It will do me good to talk. It always does. Aton was telling me about your ideas concerning world reaction to a failure of the prediction—and I agree with you. I read your column pretty regularly, by the way, and as a general thing I like your views."

"Please, Sheerin," growled Aton.

"Eh? Oh, all right. We'll go into the next room. It has softer chairs, anyway."

There were softer chairs in the next room. There were also thick red curtains on the windows and a maroon carpet on the floor. With the bricky light of Beta pouring in, the general effect was one of dried blood.

Theremon shuddered, "Say, I'd give ten credits for a decent dose of white light for just a second. I wish Gamma or Delta were in the sky."

"What are your questions?" asked Aton. "Please remember that our time is limited. In a little over an hour and a quarter we're going upstairs, and after that there will be no time for talk."

"Well, here it is." Theremon leaned back and folded his hands on his chest. "You people seem so all-fired serious about this that I'm beginning to believe you. Would you mind explaining what it's all about?"

Aton exploded, "Do you mean to sit there and tell me that you've been bombarding us with ridicule without even finding out what we've been trying to say?"

The columnist grinned sheepishly. "It's not that bad, sir. I've got the general idea. You say that there is going to be a world-wide Darkness in a few hours and that all mankind will go violently insane. What I want now is the science behind it."

"No, you don't. No, you don't," broke in Sheerin. "If you ask Aton for that—supposing him to be in the mood to answer at all—he'll trot out pages of figures and volumes of graphs. You won't make head or tail of it. Now if you were to ask me, I could give you the layman's standpoint."

"All right; I ask you."

"Then first I'd like a drink." He rubbed his hands and looked at Aton.

"Water?" grunted Aton.

"Don't be silly!"

"Don't you be silly. No alcohol today. It would be too easy to get my men drunk. I can't afford to tempt them."

The psychologist grumbled wordlessly. He turned to Theremon, impaled him with his sharp eyes, and began.

"You realize, of course, that the history of civilization on Lagash displays a cyclic character—but I mean, *cyclic!*"

"I know," replied Theremon cautiously, "that that is the current archeological theory. Has it been accepted as a fact?"

"Just about. In this last century it's been generally agreed upon. This cyclic character is—or, rather, was—one of *the* great mysteries. We've located series of civilizations, nine of them definitely, and indications of others as well, all of which have reached heights comparable to our own, and all of which, without exception, were destroyed by fire at the very height of their culture.

"And no one could tell why. All centers of culture were thoroughly gutted by fire, with nothing left behind to give a hint as to the cause."

Theremon was following closely. "Wasn't there a Stone Age, too?"

"Probably, but as yet, practically nothing is known of it, except that men of that age were little more than rather intelligent apes. We can forget about that."

"I see. Go on!"

"There have been explanations of these recurrent catastrophes, all of a more or less fantastic nature. Some say that there are periodic rains of fire; some that Lagash passes through a sun every so often; some even wilder things. But there is one theory, quite different from all of these, that has been handed down over a period of centuries."

"I know. You mean this myth of the 'Stars' that the Cultists have in their 'Book of Revelations.'"

"Exactly," rejoined Sheerin with satisfaction. "The Cultists said that every two thousand and fifty years Lagash entered a huge cave, so that all the suns disappeared, and there came *total darkness all over the world!* And then, they say, things called Stars appeared, which robbed men of their souls and left them unreasoning brutes, so that they destroyed the civilization they themselves had built up. Of course, they mix all this up with a lot of religio-mystic notions, but that's the central idea."

There was a short pause in which Sheerin drew a long breath. "And now we come to the Theory of Universal Gravitation." He pronounced the phrase so that the capital letters sounded—and at that point Aton turned from the window, snorted loudly, and stalked out of the room.

The two stared after him, and Theremon said, "What's wrong?"

"Nothing in particular," replied Sheerin. "Two of the men were due several hours ago and haven't shown up yet. He's terrifically shorthanded, of course, because all but the really essential men have gone to the Hideout."

"You don't think the two deserted, do you?"

"Who? Faro and Yimot? Of course not. Still, if they're not back within the hour, things would be a little sticky." He got to his feet suddenly, and his eyes twinkled. "Anyway, as long as Aton is gone—"

Tiptoeing to the nearest window, he squatted, and from the low window box beneath withdrew a bottle of red liquid that gurgled suggestively when he shook it.

"I *thought* Aton didn't know about this," he remarked as he trotted back to the table. "Here! We've only got one glass so, as the guest, you can have it. I'll keep the bottle." And he filled the tiny cup with judicious care.

Theremon rose to protest, but Sheerin eyed him sternly. "Respect your elders, young man."

The newsman seated himself with a look of pain and anguish on his face. "Go ahead, then, you old villain."

The psychologist's Adam's apple wobbled as the bottle upended, and then, with a satisfied grunt and a smack of the lips, he began again.

"But what do you know about gravitation?"

"Nothing, except that it is a very recent development, not too well established, and that the math is so hard that only twelve men in Lagash are supposed to understand it."

"*Tcha!* Nonsense! Boloney! I can give you all the essential math in a sentence. The Law of Universal Gravitation states that there exists a cohesive force among all bodies of the universe, such that the amount of this force between any two given bodies is proportional to the product of their masses divided by the square of the distance between them."

"Is that all?"

"That's enough! It took four hundred years to develop it."

"Why that long? It sounded simple enough, the way you said it."

"Because great laws are not divined by flashes of inspiration, whatever you may think. It usually takes the combined work of a world full of scientists over a period of centuries. After Genovi 41 discovered that Lagash rotated about the sun Alpha, rather than vice versa—and that was four hundred years ago—astronomers have been working. The complex motions of the six suns were recorded and analyzed and unwoven. Theory after theory was advanced and checked and counterchecked and modified and abandoned and revived and converted to something else. It was a devil of a job."

Theremon nodded thoughtfully and held out his glass for more liquor. Sheerin grudgingly allowed a few ruby drops to leave the bottle.

"It was twenty years ago," he continued after remoistening his own throat, "that it was finally demonstrated that the Law of Universal Gravitation accounted exactly for the orbital motions of the six suns. It was a great triumph."

Sheerin stood up and walked to the window, still clutching his bottle, "And now we're getting to the point. In the last decade, the motions of Lagash about Alpha were computed according to gravity, and *it did not account for the orbit observed;* not even when all perturbations due to the other suns were included. Either the law was invalid, or there was another, as yet unknown, factor involved."

Theremon joined Sheerin at the window and gazed out past the wooded slopes to where the spires of Saro City gleamed bloodily on the horizon. The newsman felt the tension of uncertainty grow within him as he cast a short glance at Beta. It glowered redly at Zenith, dwarfed and evil.

"Go ahead, sir," he said softly.

Sheerin replied, "Astronomers stumbled about for years, each proposed theory more untenable than the one before—until Aton had the inspiration of calling in the Cult. The head of the Cult, Sor 5, had access to certain data that simplified the problem considerably. Aton set to work on a new track.

"What if there were another nonluminous planetary body such as Lagash? If there were, you know, it would shine only by reflected light, and if it were composed of bluish rock, as Lagash itself largely is, then, in the redness of the sky, the eternal blaze of the suns would make it invisible—drown it out completely."

Theremon whistled, "What a screwy idea!"

"You think *that's* screwy? Listen to this: Suppose this body rotated about Lagash at such a distance and in such an orbit and had such a mass that its attraction would exactly account for the deviations of Lagash's orbit from theory—do you know what would happen?"

The columnist shook his head.

"Well, sometimes this body would get in the way of a sun." And Sheerin emptied what remained in the bottle at a draft.

"And it does, I suppose," said Theremon flatly.

"Yes! But only one sun lies in its plane of revolutions." He jerked a thumb at the shrunken sun above. "Beta! And it has been shown that the eclipse will occur only when the arrangement of the suns is such that Beta is alone in its hemisphere and at maximum distance, at which time the moon is invariably at minimum distance. The eclipse that results, with the moon seven times the apparent diameter of Beta, covers all of Lagash and lasts well over half a day, so that no spot on the planet escapes the effects. *That eclipse comes once every two thousand and forty-nine years."*

Theremon's face was drawn into an expressionless mask. "And that's my story?"

The psychologist nodded. "That's all of it. First the eclipse—which will start in three quarters of an hour—then universal Darkness, and, maybe, these mysterious Stars—then madness, and end of the cycle."

He brooded. "We had two months' leeway—we at the Observatory—and that wasn't enough time to persuade Lagash of the danger. Two centuries might not have been enough. But our records are at the Hideout, and today we photograph the eclipse. The next cycle will *start off* with the truth, and when the *next* eclipse comes, mankind will at last be ready for it. Come to think of it, that's part of your story, too."

A thin wind ruffled the curtains at the window as Theremon opened it and leaned out. It played coldly with his hair as he stared at the crimson sunlight on his hand. Then he turned in sudden rebellion.

"What is there in Darkness to drive *me* mad?"

Sheerin smiled to himself as he spun the empty liquor bottle with abstracted motions of his hand. "Have you ever experienced Darkness, young man?"

The newsman leaned against the wall and considered. "No. Can't say I have. But I know what it is. Just—uh—" He made vague motions with his fingers, and then brightened. "Just no light. Like in caves."

"Have you ever been in a cave?"

"In a *cave!* Of course not!"

"I thought not. *I* tried last week—just to see—but I got out in a hurry. I went in until the mouth of the cave was just visible as a blur of light, with black everywhere else. I never thought a person my weight could run that fast."

Theremon's lip curled. "Well, if it comes to that, I guess I wouldn't have run, if I had been there."

The psychologist studied the young man with an annoyed frown.

"My, don't you talk big! I dare you to draw the curtain."

Theremon looked his surprise and said, "What for? If we had

four or five suns out there we might want to cut the light down
a bit for comfort, but now we haven't enough light as it is."

"That's the point. Just draw the curtain; then come here and
sit down."

"All right." Theremon reached for the tasseled string and
jerked. The red curtain slid across the wide window, the brass
rings hissing their way along the crossbar, and a dusk-red shadow
clamped down on the room.

Theremon's footsteps sounded hollowly in the silence as he
made his way to the table, and then they stopped halfway. "I
can't see you, sir," he whispered.

"Feel your way," ordered Sheerin in a strained voice.

"But I can't see you, sir." The newsman was breathing harshly.
"I can't see anything."

"What did you expect?" came the grim reply. "Come here and
sit down!"

The footsteps sounded again, waveringly, approaching slowly.
There was the sound of someone fumbling with a chair. Theremon's voice came thinly, "Here I am. I feel . . . *ulp* . . . all right."

"You like it, do you?"

"N-no. It's pretty awful. The walls seem to be—" He paused.
"They seem to be closing in on me. I keep wanting to push them
away. But I'm not going *mad!* In fact, the feeling isn't as bad
as it was."

"All right. Draw the curtain back again."

There were cautious footsteps through the dark, the rustle of
Theremon's body against the curtain as he felt for the tassel, and
then the triumphant *ro-o-o-osh* of the curtain slithering back. Red
light flooded the room, and with a cry of joy Theremon looked
up at the sun.

Sheerin wiped the moistness off his forehead with the back of
a hand and said shakily, "And that was just a dark room."

"It can be stood," said Theremon lightly.

"Yes, a dark room can. But were you at the Jonglor Centennial
Exposition two years ago?"

"No, it so happens I never got around to it. Six thousand miles
was just a bit too much to travel, even for the exposition."

"Well, I was there. You remember hearing about the 'Tunnel
of Mystery' that broke all records in the amusement area—for the
first month or so, anyway?"

"Yes. Wasn't there some fuss about it?"

"Very little. It was hushed up. You see, that Tunnel of Mystery
was just a mile-long tunnel—with no lights. You got into a little

open car and jolted along through Darkness for fifteen minutes. It was very popular—while it lasted."

"Popular?"

"Certainly. There's a fascination in being frightened *when it's part of a game.* A baby is born with three instinctive fears: of loud noises, of falling, and of the absence of light. That's why it's considered so funny to jump at someone and shout 'Boo!' That's why it's such fun to ride a roller coaster. And that's why that Tunnel of Mystery started cleaning up. People came out of that Darkness shaking, breathless, half dead with fear, but they kept on paying to get in."

"Wait a while, I remember now. Some people came out dead, didn't they? There were rumors of that after it shut down."

The psychologist snorted. "Bah! Two or three died. That was nothing! They paid off the families of the dead ones and argued the Jonglor City Council into forgetting it. After all, they said, if people with weak hearts want to go through the tunnel, it was at their own risk—and besides, it wouldn't happen again. So they put a doctor in the front office and had every customer go through a physical examination before getting into the car. That actually *boosted* ticket sales."

"Well, then?"

"But, you see, there was something else. People sometimes came out in perfect order, except that they refused to go into buildings—any buildings; including palaces, mansions, apartment houses, tenements, cottages, huts, shacks, lean-tos, and tents."

Theremon looked shocked. "You mean they refused to come in out of the open. Where'd they sleep?"

"In the open."

"They should have *forced* them inside."

"Oh, they did, they did. Whereupon these people went into violent hysterics and did their best to bat their brains out against the nearest wall. Once you got them inside, you couldn't keep them there without a strait jacket and a shot of morphine."

"They must have been crazy."

"Which is exactly what they were. One person out of every ten who went into that tunnel came out that way. They called in the psychologists, and we did the only thing possible. We closed down the exhibit." He spread his hands.

"What was the matter with these people?" asked Theremon finally.

"Essentially the same thing that was the matter with you when you thought the walls of the room were crushing in on you in the dark. There is a psychological term for mankind's instinctive fear of the absence of light. We call it 'claustrophobia,' because the lack of light is always tied up with inclosed places, so that fear of one is fear of the other. You see?"

"And those people of the tunnel?"

"Those people of the tunnel consisted of those unfortunates whose mentality did not quite possess the resiliency to overcome the claustrophobia that overtook them in the Darkness. Fifteen minutes without light is a long time; you only had two or three minutes, and I believe you were fairly upset.

"The people of the tunnel had what is called a 'claustrophobic fixation.' Their latent fear of Darkness and inclosed places had crystallized and become active, and, as far as we can tell, permanent. *That's* what fifteen minutes in the dark will do."

There was a long silence, and Theremon's forehead wrinkled slowly into a frown. "I don't believe it's that bad."

"You mean you don't want to believe," snapped Sheerin. "You're afraid to believe. Look out the window!"

Theremon did so, and the psychologist continued without pausing, "Imagine Darkness—everywhere. No light, as far as you can see. The houses, the trees, the fields, the earth, the sky—*black!* And Stars thrown in, for all I know—whatever *they* are. Can you conceive it?"

"Yes, I can," declared Theremon truculently.

And Sheerin slammed his fist down upon the table in sudden passion. "You lie! You can't conceive that. Your brain wasn't built for the conception any more than it was built for the conception of infinity or of eternity. You can only talk about it. A fraction of the reality upsets you, and when the real thing comes, your brain is going to be presented with a phenomenon outside its limits of comprehension. You will go mad, completely and permanently! There is no question of it!"

He added sadly, "And another couple of millenniums of painful struggle comes to nothing. Tomorrow there won't be a city standing unharmed in all Lagash."

Theremon recovered part of his mental equilibrium. "That doesn't follow. I still don't see that I can go loony just because there isn't a Sun in the sky—but even if I did, and everyone else did, how does that harm the cities? Are we going to blow them down?"

But Sheerin was angry, too. "If you were in Darkness, what would you want more than anything else; what would it be that every instinct would call for? Light, damn you, *light!*"

"Well?"

"And how would you get light?"

"I don't know," said Theremon flatly.

"What's the *only* way to get light, short of the sun?"

"How should I know?"

They were standing face to face and nose to nose.

Sheerin said, "You burn something, mister. Ever see a forest fire? Ever go camping and cook a stew over a wood fire? Heat isn't the only thing burning wood gives off, you know. It gives off light, and people know that. And when it's dark they want light, and they're going to *get it*."

"So they burn wood?"

"So they burn whatever they can get. They've got to have light. They've got to burn something, and wood isn't handy—so they'll burn whatever is nearest. They'll have their light—and every center of habitation goes up in flames!"

Eyes held each other as though the whole matter were a personal affair of respective will powers, and then Theremon broke away wordlessly. His breathing was harsh and ragged, and he scarcely noted the sudden hubbub that came from the adjoining room behind the closed door.

Sheerin spoke, and it was with an effort that he made it sound matter-of-fact. "I think I heard Yimot's voice. He and Faro are probably back. Let's go in and see what kept them."

"Might as well!" muttered Theremon. He drew a long breath and seemed to shake himself. The tension was broken.

The room was in an uproar, with members of the staff clustering about two young men who were removing outer garments even as they parried the miscellany of questions being thrown at them.

Aton bustled through the crowd and faced the newcomers angrily. "Do you realize that it's less than half an hour before deadline? Where have you two been?"

Faro 24 seated himself and rubbed his hands. His cheeks were red with the outdoor chill. "Yimot and I have just finished carrying through a little crazy experiment of our own. We've been trying to see if we couldn't construct an arrangement by which we could simulate the appearance of Darkness and Stars so as to get an advance notion as to how it looked."

There was a confused murmur from the listeners, and a sudden look of interest entered Aton's eyes. "There wasn't anything said of this before. How did you go about it?"

"Well," said Faro, "the idea came to Yimot and myself long ago, and we've been working it out in our spare time. Yimot knew of a low one-story house down in the city with a domed roof—it had once been used as a museum, I think. Anyway, we bought it—"

"Where did you get the money?" interrupted Aton peremptorily.

"Our bank accounts," grunted Yimot 70. "It cost two thousand credits." Then, defensively, "Well, what of it? Tomorrow, two thousand credits will be two thousand pieces of paper. That's all."

"Sure," agreed Faro. "We bought the place and rigged it up with black velvet from top to bottom so as to get as perfect a Darkness as possible. Then we punched tiny holes in the ceiling and through the roof and covered them with little metal caps, all of which could be shoved aside simultaneously at the close of a switch. At least, we didn't do that part ourselves; we got a carpenter and an electrician and some others—money didn't count. The point was that we could get the light to shine through those holes in the roof, so that we could get a starlike effect."

Not a breath was drawn during the pause that followed. Aton said stiffly:

"You had no right to make a private—"

Faro seemed abashed. "I know, sir—but, frankly, Yimot and I thought the experiment was a little dangerous. If the effect really worked, we half expected to go mad—from what Sheerin says about all this, we thought that would be rather likely. We wanted to take the risk ourselves. Of course, if we found we could retain sanity, it occurred to us that we might develop immunity to the real thing, and then expose the rest of you to the same thing. But things didn't work out at all—"

"Why, what happened?"

It was Yimot who answered. "We shut ourselves in and allowed our eyes to get accustomed to the dark. It's an extremely creepy feeling because the total Darkness makes you feel as if the walls and ceiling are crushing in on you. But we got over that and pulled the switch. The caps fell away and the roof glittered all over with little dots of light—"

"Well?"

"Well—nothing. That was the whacky part of it. Nothing happened. It was just a roof with holes in it, and that's just what it looked like. We tried it over and over again—that's what kept us so late—but there just isn't any effect at all."

There followed a shocked silence, and all eyes turned to Sheerin, who sat motionless, mouth open.

Theremon was the first to speak. "You know what this does to this whole theory you've built up, Sheerin, don't you?" He was grinning with relief.

But Sheerin raised his hand. "Now wait a while. Just let me think this through." And then he snapped his fingers, and when he lifted his head there was neither surprise nor uncertainty in his eyes. "Of course—"

He never finished. From somewhere up above there sounded a sharp clang, and Beenay, starting to his feet, dashed up the stairs with a "What the devil!"

The rest followed after.

Things happened quickly. Once up in the dome, Beenay cast one horrified glance at the shattered photographic plates and at the man bending over them; and then hurled himself fiercely at the intruder, getting a death grip on his throat. There was a wild threshing, and as others of the staff joined in, the stranger was swallowed up and smothered under the weight of half a dozen angry men.

Aton came up last, breathing heavily. "Let him up!"

There was a reluctant unscrambling and the stranger, panting harshly, with his clothes torn and his forehead bruised, was hauled to his feet. He had a short yellow beard curled elaborately in the style affected by the Cultists.

Beenay shifted his hold to a collar grip and shook the man savagely. "All right, rat, what's the idea? These plates—"

"I wasn't after *them,*" retorted the Cultist coldly. "That was an accident."

Beenay followed his glowering stare and snarled, "I see. You were after the cameras themselves. The accident with the plates was a stroke of luck for you, then. If you had touched Snapping Bertha or any of the others, you would have died by slow torture. As it is—" He drew his fist back.

Aton grabbed his sleeve. "Stop that! Let him go!"

The young technician wavered, and his arm dropped reluctantly. Aton pushed him aside and confronted the Cultist. "You're Latimer, aren't you?"

The Cultist bowed stiffly and indicated the symbol upon his hip. "I am Latimer 25, adjutant of the third class to his serenity, Sor 5."

"And"—Aton's white eyebrows lifted—"you were with his serenity when he visited me last week, weren't you?"

Latimer bowed a second time.

"Now, then, what do you want?"

"Nothing that you would give me of your own free will."

"Sor 5 sent you, I suppose—or is this your own idea?"

"I won't answer that question."

"Will there be any further visitors?"

"I won't answer that, either."

Aton glanced at his timepiece and scowled. "Now, man, what is it your master wants of me? I have fulfilled my end of the bargain."

Latimer smiled faintly, but said nothing.

"I asked him," continued Aton angrily, "for data only the Cult could supply, and it was given to me. For that, thank you. In return, I promised to prove the essential truth of the creed of the Cult."

"There was no need to prove that," came the proud retort. "It stands proven by the 'Book of Revelations.'"

"For the handful that constitute the Cult, yes. Don't pretend to mistake my meaning. I offered to present scientific backing for your beliefs. And I did!"

The Cultist's eyes narrowed bitterly. "Yes, you did—with a fox's subtlety, for your pretended explanation backed our beliefs, and at the same time removed all necessity for them. You made of the Darkness and of the Stars a natural phenomenon, and removed all its real significance. That was blasphemy."

"If so, the fault isn't mine. The facts exist. What can I do but state them?"

"Your 'facts' are a fraud and a delusion."

Aton stamped angrily. "How do *you* know?"

And the answer came with the certainty of absolute faith. "I *know!*"

The director purpled and Beenay whispered urgently. Aton waved him silent. "And what does Sor 5 want us to do? He still thinks, I suppose, that in trying to warn the world to take measures against the menace of madness, we are placing innumerable souls in jeopardy. We aren't succeeding if that means anything to him."

"The attempt itself has done harm enough, and your vicious effort to gain information by means of your devilish instruments must be stopped. We obey the will of their Stars, and I only regret that my clumsiness prevented me from wrecking your infernal devices."

"It wouldn't have done you too much good," returned Aton. "All our data, except for the direct evidence we intend collecting right now, is already safely cached and well beyond possibility of harm." He smiled grimly. "But that does not affect your present status as an attempted burglar and criminal."

He turned to the men behind him. "Someone call the police at Saro City."

There was a cry of distaste from Sheerin. "Damn it, Aton, what's wrong with you? There's no time for that. Here"—he bustled his way forward—"let me handle this."

Aton stared down his nose at the psychologist. "This is not the time for your monkeyshines, Sheerin. Will you please let me handle this my own way? Right now you are a complete outsider here, and don't forget it."

Sheerin's mouth twisted eloquently. "Now why should we go to the impossible trouble of calling the police—with Beta's eclipse a matter of minutes from now—when this young man here is perfectly willing to pledge his word of honor to remain and cause no trouble whatsoever?"

The Cultist answered promptly, "I will do no such thing. You're free to do what you want, but it's only fair to warn you that just as soon as I get my chance I'm going to finish what I came out here to do. If it's my word of honor you're relying on, you'd better call the police."

Sheerin smiled in a friendly fashion. "You're a determined cuss, aren't you? Well, I'll explain something. Do you see that young man at the window? He's a strong, husky fellow, quite handy with his fists, and he's an outsider besides. Once the eclipse starts there will be nothing for him to do except keep an eye on you. Besides him, there will be myself—a little too stout for active fisticuffs, but still able to help."

"Well, what of it?" demanded Latimer frozenly.

"Listen and I'll tell you," was the reply. "Just as soon as the eclipse starts, we're going to take you, Theremon and I, and deposit you in a little closet with one door, to which is attached one giant lock and no windows. You will remain there for the duration."

"And afterward," breathed Latimer fiercely, "there'll be no one to let me out. I know as well as you do what the coming of the Stars means—I know it far better than you. With all your minds gone, you are not likely to free me. Suffocation or slow starvation, is it? About what I might have expected from a group of scientists. But I don't give my word. It's a matter of principle, and I won't discuss it further."

Aton seemed perturbed. His faded eyes were troubled. "Really, Sheerin, locking him—"

"Please!" Sheerin motioned him impatiently to silence. "I don't think for a moment things will go that far. Latimer has just tried a clever little bluff, but I'm not a psychologist just because I like the sound of the word." He grinned at the Cultist. "Come now, you don't really think I'm trying anything as crude as slow starvation. My dear Latimer, if I lock you in the closet, you are not going to see the Darkness, and you are not going to see the Stars. It does not take much of a knowledge of the fundamental creed of the Cult to realize that for you to be hidden from the Stars when they appear means the loss of your immortal soul. Now, I believe you to be an honorable man. I'll accept your word of honor to make no further effort to disrupt proceedings if you'll offer it."

A vein throbbed in Latimer's temple, and he seemed to shrink within himself as he said thickly, "You have it!" And then he added with swift fury, "But it is my consolation that you will all be damned for your deeds of today." He turned on his heel and stalked to the high three-legged stool by the door.

Sheerin nodded to the columnist. "Take a seat next to him, Theremon—just as a formality. Hey, Theremon!"

But the newspaperman didn't move. He had gone pale to the lips. "Look at that!" The finger he pointed toward the sky shook, and his voice was dry and cracked.

There was one simultaneous gasp as every eye followed the pointing finger and, for one breathless moment, stared frozenly.

Beta was chipped on one side!

The tiny bit of encroaching blackness was perhaps the width of a fingernail, but to the staring watchers it magnified itself into the crack of doom.

Only for a moment they watched, and after that there was a shrieking confusion that was even shorter of duration and which gave way to an orderly scurry of activity—each man at his prescribed job. At the crucial moment there was no time for emotion. The men were merely scientists with work to do. Even Aton had melted away.

Sheerin said prosaically, "First contact must have been made fifteen minutes ago. A little early, but pretty good considering the uncertainties involved in the calculation." He looked about him and then tiptoed to Theremon, who still remained staring out the window, and dragged him away gently.

"Aton is furious," he whispered, "so stay away. He missed first contact on account of this fuss with Latimer, and if you get in his way he'll have you thrown out the window."

Theremon nodded shortly and sat down. Sheerin stared in surprise at him.

"The devil, man," he exclaimed, "you're shaking."

"Eh?" Theremon licked dry lips and then tried to smile. "I don't feel very well, and that's a fact."

The psychologist's eyes hardened. "You're not losing your nerve?"

"No!" cried Theremon in a flash of indignation. "Give me a chance, will you? I haven't really believed this rigmarole—not way down beneath, anyway—till just this minute. Give me a chance to get used to the idea. *You've* been preparing yourself for two months or more."

"You're right, at that," replied Sheerin thoughtfully. "Listen! Have you got a family—parents, wife, children?"

Theremon shook his head. "You mean the Hideout, I suppose. No, you don't have to worry about that. I have a sister, but she's two thousand miles away. I don't even know her exact address."

"Well, then, what about yourself? You've got time to get there, and they're one short anyway, since I left. After all, you're not needed here, and you'd make a darned fine addition—"

Theremon looked at the other wearily. "You think I'm scared stiff, don't you? Well, get this, mister, I'm a newspaperman and I've been assigned to cover a story. I intend covering it."

There was a faint smile on the psychologist's face. "I see. Professional honor, is that it?"

"You might call it that. But, man, I'd give my right arm for another bottle of that sockeroo juice even half the size of the one *you* hogged. If ever a fellow needed a drink, I do."

He broke off. Sheerin was nudging him violently. "Do you hear that? Listen!"

Theremon followed the motion of the other's chin and stared at the Cultist, who, oblivious to all about him, faced the window, a look of wild elation on his face, droning to himself the while in singsong fashion.

"What's he saying?" whispered the columnist.

"He's quoting 'Book of Revelations,' fifth chapter," replied Sheerin. Then, urgently, "Keep quiet and listen, I tell you."

The Cultist's voice had risen in a sudden increase of fervor:

"'And it came to pass that in those days the Sun, Beta, held lone vigil in the sky for ever longer periods as the revolutions passed; until such time as for full half a revolution, it alone, shrunken and cold, shone down upon Lagash.

"'And men did assemble in the public squares and in the highways, there to debate and to marvel at the sight, for a strange depression had seized them. Their minds were troubled and their speech confused, for the souls of men awaited the coming of the Stars.

"'And in the city of Trigon, at high noon, Vendret 2 came forth and said unto the men of Trigon, "Lo, ye sinners! Though ye scorn the ways of righteousness, yet will the time of reckoning come. Even now the Cave approaches to swallow Lagash; yea, and all it contains.

"'And even as he spoke the lip of the Cave of Darkness passed the edge of Beta so that to all Lagash it was hidden from sight. Loud were the cries of men as it vanished, and great the fear of soul that fell upon them.

"'It came to pass that the Darkness of the Cave fell upon Lagash, and there was no light on all the surface of Lagash. Men were even as blinded, nor could one man see his neighbor, though he felt his breath upon his face.

"'And in this blackness there appeared the Stars, in countless numbers, and to the strains of ineffable music of a beauty so wondrous that the very leaves of the trees turned to tongues that cried out in wonder.

"'And in that moment the souls of men departed from them, and their abandoned bodies became even as beasts; yea, even as brutes of the wild; so that through the blackened streets of the cities of Lagash they prowled with wild cries.

"'From the Stars there then reached down the Heavenly Flame, and where it touched, the cities of Lagash flamed to utter destruction, so that of man and of the works of man nought remained.

"'Even then—'"

There was a subtle change in Latimer's tone. His eyes had not shifted, but somehow he had become aware of the absorbed attention of the other two. Easily, without pausing for breath, the timbre of his voice shifted and the syllables became more liquid.

Theremon, caught by surprise, stared. The words seemed on the border of familiarity. There was an elusive shift in the accent, a tiny change in the vowel stress; nothing more—yet Latimer had become thoroughly unintelligible.

Sheerin smiled slyly. "He shifted to some old-cycle tongue, probably their traditional second cycle. That was the language in which the 'Book of Revelations' had originally been written, you know."

"It doesn't matter; I've heard enough." Theremon shoved his

chair back and brushed his hair back with hands that no longer shook. "I feel much better now."

"You do?" Sheerin seemed mildly surprised.

"I'll say I do. I had a bad case of jitters just a while back. Listening to you and your gravitation and seeing that eclipse start almost finished me. But this"—he jerked a contemptuous thumb at the yellow-bearded Cultist—"*this* is the sort of thing my nurse used to tell me. I've been laughing at that sort of thing all my life. I'm not going to let it scare me *now*."

He drew a deep breath and said with a hectic gaiety, "But if I expect to keep on the good side of myself, I'm going to turn my chair away from the window."

Sheerin said, "Yes, but you'd better talk lower. Aton just lifted his head out of that box he's got it stuck into and gave you a look that should have killed you."

Theremon made a mouth. "I forgot about the old fellow." With elaborate care he turned the chair from the window, cast one distasteful look over his shoulder and said, "It has occurred to me that there must be considerable immunity against this Star madness."

The psychologist did not answer immediately. Beta was past its zenith now, and the square of bloody sunlight that outlined the window upon the floor had lifted into Sheerin's lap. He stared at its dusky color thoughtfully and then bent and squinted into the sun itself.

The chip in its side had grown to a black encroachment that covered a third of Beta. He shuddered, and when he straightened once more his florid cheeks did not contain quite as much color as they had had previously.

With a smile that was almost apologetic, he reversed his chair also. "There are probably two million people in Saro City that are all trying to join the Cult at once in one gigantic revival." Then, ironically, "The Cult is in for an hour of unexampled prosperity. I trust they'll make the most of it. Now, what was it you said?"

"Just this. How do the Cultists manage to keep the 'Book of Revelations' going from cycle to cycle, and how on Lagash did it get written in the first place? There must have been some sort of immunity, for if everyone had gone mad, who would be left to write the book?"

Sheerin stared at his questioner ruefully. "Well, now, young man, there isn't any eyewitness answer to that, but we've got a few damned good notions as to what happened. You see, there are three kinds of people who might remain relatively unaffected.

First, the very few who don't see the Stars at all; the blind, those who drink themselves into a stupor at the beginning of the eclipse and remain so to the end. We leave them out—because they aren't really witnesses.

"Then there are children below six, to whom the world as a whole is too new and strange for them to be too frightened at Stars and Darkness. They would be just another item in an already surprising world. You see that, don't you?"

The other nodded doubtfully. "I suppose so."

"Lastly, there are those whose minds are too coarsely grained to be entirely toppled. The very insensitive would be scarcely affected—oh, such people as some of our older, work-broken peasants. Well, the children would have fugitive memories, and that, combined with the confused, incoherent babblings of the half-mad morons, formed the basis for the 'Book of Revelations.'

"Naturally, the book was based, in the first place, on the testimony of those least qualified to serve as historians; that is, children and morons; and was probably extensively edited and re-edited through the cycles."

"Do you suppose," broke in Theremon, "that they carried the book through the cycles the way we're planning on handing on the secret of gravitation?"

Sheerin shrugged. "Perhaps, but their exact method is unimportant. They do it, somehow. The point I was getting at was that the book can't help but be a mass of distortion, even if it is based on fact. For instance, do you remember the experiment with the holes in the roof that Faro and Yimot tried—the one that didn't work?"

"Yes."

"You know why it didn't w—" He stopped and rose in alarm, for Aton was approaching, his face a twisted mask of consternation. "*What's happened?*"

Aton drew him aside and Sheerin could feel the fingers on his elbow twitching.

"Not so loud!" Aton's voice was low and tortured. "I've just gotten word from the Hideout on the private line."

Sheerin broke in anxiously, "They are in trouble?"

"Not *they.*" Aton stressed the pronoun significantly. "They sealed themselves off just a while ago, and they're going to stay buried till day after tomorrow. They're safe. But the *city*, Sheerin —it's a shambles. You have no idea—" He was having difficulty in speaking.

"Well?" snapped Sheerin impatiently. "What of it? It will get worse. What are you shaking about?" Then, suspiciously, "How do you feel?"

Aton's eyes sparked angrily at the insinuation, and then faded to anxiety once more. "You don't understand. The Cultists are active. They're rousing the people to storm the Observatory—promising them immediate entrance into grace, promising them salvation, promising them anything. What are we to do, Sheerin?"

Sheerin's head bent, and he stared in long abstraction at his toes. He tapped his chin with one knuckle, then looked up and said crisply, "Do? What is there to do? Nothing at all! Do the men know of this?"

"No, of course not!"

"Good! Keep it that way. How long till totality?"

"Not quite an hour."

"There's nothing to do but gamble. It will take time to organize any really formidable mob, and it will take more time to get them out here. We're a good five miles from the city—"

He glared out the window, down the slopes to where the farmed patches gave way to clumps of white houses in the suburbs; down to where the metropolis itself was a blur on the horizon—a mist in the waning blaze of Beta.

He repeated without turning, "It will take time. Keep on working and pray that totality comes first."

Beta was cut in half, the line of division pushing a slight concavity into the still-bright portion of the Sun. It was like a gigantic eyelid shutting slantwise over the light of a world.

The faint clatter of the room in which he stood faded into oblivion, and he sensed only the thick silence of the fields outside. The very insects seemed frightened mute. And things were dim.

He jumped at the voice in his ear. Theremon said, "Is something wrong?"

"Eh? Er—no. Get back to the chair. We're in the way." They slipped back to their corner, but the psychologist did not speak for a time. He lifted a finger and loosened his collar. He twisted his neck back and forth but found no relief. He looked up suddenly.

"Are you having any difficulty in breathing?"

The newspaperman opened his eyes wide and drew two or thee long breaths. "No. Why?"

"I looked out the window too long, I suppose. The dimness got me. Difficulty in breathing is one of the first symptoms of a claustrophobic attack."

Theremon drew another long breath. "Well, it hasn't got me yet. Say, here's another of the fellows."

Beenay had interposed his bulk between the light and the pair in the corner, and Sheerin squinted up at him anxiously. "Hello, Beenay."

The astronomer shifted his weight to the other foot and smiled feebly. "You won't mind if I sit down awhile and join in on the talk? My cameras are set, and there's nothing to do till totality." He paused and eyed the Cultist, who fifteen minutes earlier had drawn a small, skin-bound book from his sleeve and had been poring intently over it ever since. "That rat hasn't been making trouble, has he?"

Sheerin shook his head. His shoulders were thrown back and he frowned his concentration as he forced himself to breathe regularly. He said, "Have you had any trouble breathing, Beenay?"

Beenay sniffed the air in his turn. "It doesn't seem stuffy to me."

"A touch of claustrophobia," explained Sheerin apologetically.

"Oh-h-h! It worked itself differently with me. I get the impression that my eyes are going back on me. Things seem to blur and—well, nothing is clear. And it's cold, too."

"Oh, it's cold, all right. That's no illusion." Theremon grimaced. "My toes feel as if I've been shipping them cross country in a refrigerating car."

"What we need," put in Sheerin, "is to keep our minds busy with extraneous affairs. I was telling you a while ago, Theremon, why Faro's experiments with the holes in the roof came to nothing."

"You were just beginning," replied Theremon. He encircled a knee with both arms and nuzzled his chin against it.

"Well, as I started to say, they were misled by taking the 'Book of Revelations' literally. There probably wasn't any sense in attaching any physical significance to the Stars. It might be, you know, that in the presence of total Darkness, the mind finds it absolutely necessary to create light. This illusion of light might be all the Stars there really are."

"In other words," interposed Theremon, "you mean the Stars are the results of the madness and not one of the causes. Then, what good will Beenay's photographs be?"

"To prove that it is an illusion, maybe; or to prove the opposite, for all I know. Then again—"

But Beenay had drawn his chair closer, and there was an expression of sudden enthusiasm on his face. "Say, I'm glad you two got on to this subject." His eyes narrowed and he lifted one finger. "I've been thinking about these Stars and I've got a really cute notion. Of course, it's strictly ocean foam, and I'm not trying to advance it seriously, but I think it's interesting. Do you want to hear it?"

He seemed half reluctant, but Sheerin leaned back and said, "Go ahead! I'm listening."

"Well, then, supposing there were other suns in the universe." He broke off a little bashfully. "I mean suns that are so far away that they're too dim to see. It sounds as if I've been reading some of that fantastic fiction, I suppose."

"Not necessarily. Still, isn't that possibility eliminated by the fact that, according to the Law of Gravitation, they would make themselves evident by their attractive forces?"

"Not if they were far enough off," rejoined Beenay, "really far off—maybe as much as four light years, or even more. We'd never be able to detect perturbations then, because they'd be too small. Say that there were a lot of suns that far off; a dozen or two, maybe."

Theremon whistled melodiously. "What an idea for a good Sunday supplement article. Two dozen suns in a universe eight light years across. Wow! That would shrink *our* universe into insignificance. The readers would eat it up."

"Only an idea," said Beenay with a grin, "but you see the point. During eclipse, these dozen suns would become visible, because there'd be no *real* sunlight to drown them out. Since they're so far off, they'd appear small, like so many little marbles. Of course, the Cultists talk of millions of Stars, but that's probably exaggeration. There just isn't any place in the universe you could put a million suns—unless they touch one another."

Sheerin had listened with gradually increasing interest. "You've hit something there, Beenay. And exaggeration is just exactly what would happen. Our minds, as you probably know, can't grasp directly any number higher than five; above that there is only the concept of 'many.' A dozen would become a million just like that. A damn good idea!"

"And I've got another cute little notion," Beenay said. "Have you ever thought what a simple problem gravitation would be if only you had a sufficiently simple system? Supposing you had a universe in which there was a planet with only one sun. The planet would travel in a perfect ellipse and the exact nature of the gravitational force would be so evident it could be accepted as an axiom. Astronomers on such a world would start off with gravity probably before they even invent the telescope. Naked-eye observation would be enough."

"But would such a system be dynamically stable?" questioned Sheerin doubtfully.

"Sure! They call it the 'one-and-one' case. It's been worked out mathematically, but it's the philosophical implications that interest me."

"It's nice to think about," admitted Sheerin, "as a pretty abstraction—like a perfect gas or absolute zero."

"Of course," continued Beenay, "there's the catch that life would be impossible on such a planet. It wouldn't get enough heat and light, and if it rotated there would be total Darkness half of each day. You couldn't expect life—which is fundamentally dependent upon light—to develop under those conditions. Besides—"

Sheerin's chair went over backward as he sprang to his feet in a rude interruption. "Aton's brought out the lights."

Beenay said, "Huh," turned to stare, and then grinned halfway around his head in open relief.

There were half a dozen foot-long, inch-thick rods cradled in Aton's arms. He glared over them at the assembled staff members.

"Get back to work, all of you. Sheerin, come here and help me!"

Sheerin trotted to the older man's side and, one by one, in utter silence, the two adjusted the rods in makeshift metal holders suspended from the walls.

With the air of one carrying through the most sacred item of a religious ritual, Sheerin scraped a large, clumsy match into spluttering life and passed it to Aton, who carried the flame to the upper end of one of the rods.

It hesitated there a while, playing futilely about the tip, until a sudden, crackling flare cast Aton's lined face into yellow highlights. He withdrew the match and a spontaneous cheer rattled the window.

The rod was topped by six inches of wavering flame! Methodically, the other rods were lighted, until six independent fires turned the rear of the room yellow.

The light was dim, dimmer even than the tenuous sunlight. The flames reeled crazily, giving birth to drunken, swaying shadows. The torches smoked devilishly and smelled like a bad day in the kitchen. But they emitted yellow light.

There is something to yellow light—after four hours of somber, dimming Beta. Even Latimer had lifted his eyes from his book and stared in wonder.

Sheerin warmed his hands at the nearest, regardless of the soot that gathered upon them in a fine, gray powder, and muttered ecstatically to himself. "Beautiful! Beautiful! I never realized before what a wonderful color yellow is."

But Theremon regarded the torches suspiciously. He wrinkled

his nose at the rancid odor, and said, "What are those things?"

"Wood," said Sheerin shortly.

"Oh, no, they're not. They aren't burning. The top inch is charred and the flame just keeps shooting up out of nothing."

"That's the beauty of it. This is a really efficient artificial-light mechanism. We made a few hundred of them, but most went to the Hideout, of course. You see"—he turned and wiped his blackened hands upon his handkerchief—"you take the pithy core of coarse water reeds, dry them thoroughly and soak them in animal grease. Then you set fire to it and the grease burns, little by little. These torches will burn for almost half an hour without stopping. Ingenious, isn't it? It was developed by one of our own young men at Saro University."

After the momentary sensation, the dome had quieted. Latimer had carried his chair directly beneath a torch and continued reading, lips moving in the monotonous recital of invocations to the Stars. Beenay had drifted away to his cameras once more, and Theremon seized the opportunity to add to his notes on the article he was going to write for the Saro City *Chronicle* the next day—a procedure he had been following for the last two hours in a perfectly methodical, perfectly conscientious and, as he was well aware, perfectly meaningless fashion.

But, as the gleam of amusement in Sheerin's eyes indicated, careful note taking occupied his mind with something other than the fact that the sky was gradually turning a horrible deep purple-red, as if it were one gigantic, freshly peeled beet; and so it fulfilled its purpose.

The air grew, somehow, denser. Dusk, like a palpable entity, entered the room, and the dancing circle of yellow light about the torches etched itself into ever-sharper distinction against the gathering grayness beyond. There was the odor of smoke and the presence of little chuckling sounds that the torches made as they burned; the soft pad of one of the men circling the table at which he worked, on hesitant tiptoes; the occasional indrawn breath of someone trying to retain composure in a world that was retreating into the shadow.

It was Theremon who first heard the extraneous noise. It was a vague, unorganized *impression* of sound that would have gone unnoticed but for the dead silence that prevailed within the dome.

The newsman sat upright and replaced his notebook. He held his breath and listened; then, with considerable reluctance, threaded his way between the solarscope and one of Beenay's cameras and stood before the window.

The silence ripped to fragments at his startled shout:

"Sheerin!"

Work stopped! The psychologist was at his side in a moment. Aton joined him. Even Yimot 70, high in his little lean-back seat at the eyepiece of the gigantic solarscope, paused and looked downward.

Outside, Beta was a mere smoldering splinter, taking one last desperate look at Lagash. The eastern horizon, in the direction of the city, was lost in Darkness, and the road from Saro to the Observatory was a dull-red line bordered on both sides by wooded tracts, the trees of which had somehow lost individuality and merged into a continuous shadowy mass.

But it was the highway itself that held attention, for along it there surged another, and infinitely menacing, shadowy mass.

Aton cried in a cracked voice, "The madmen from the city! They've come!"

"How long to totality?" demanded Sheerin.

"Fifteen minutes, but . . . but they'll be here in five."

"Never mind, keep the men working. We'll hold them off. This place is built like a fortress. Aton, keep an eye on our young Cultist just for luck. Theremon, come with me."

Sheerin was out the door, and Theremon was at his heels. The stairs stretched below them in tight, circular sweeps about the central shaft, fading into a dank and dreary grayness.

The first momentum of their rush had carried them fifty feet down, so that the dim, flickering yellow from the open door of the dome had disappeared and both up above and down below the same dusky shadow crushed in upon them.

Sheerin paused, and his pudgy hand clutched at his chest. His eyes bulged and his voice was a dry cough. "I can't . . . breathe . . . go down . . . yourself. Close all doors—"

Theremon took a few downward steps, then turned. "Wait! Can you hold out a minute?" He was panting himself. The air passed in and out his lungs like so much molasses, and there was a little germ of screeching panic in his mind at the thought of making his way into the mysterious Darkness below by himself.

Theremon, after all, was afraid of the dark!

"Stay here," he said. "I'll be back in a second." He dashed upward two steps at a time, heart pounding—not altogether from the exertion—tumbled into the dome and snatched a torch from its holder. It was foul smelling, and the smoke smarted his eyes almost blind, but he clutched that torch as if he wanted to kiss it for joy, and its flame streamed backward as he hurtled down the stairs again.

Sheerin opened his eyes and moaned as Theremon bent over him. Theremon shook him roughly. "All right, get a hold on yourself. We've got light."

He held the torch at tiptoe height and, propping the tottering psychologist by an elbow, made his way downward in the middle of the protecting circle of illumination.

The offices on the ground floor still possessed what light there was, and Theremon felt the horror about him relax.

"Here," he said brusquely, and passed the torch to Sheerin. "You can hear *them* outside."

And they could. Little scraps of hoarse, wordless shouts.

But Sheerin was right; the Observatory *was* built like a fortress. Erected in the last century, when the neo-Gavottian style of architecture was at its ugly height, it had been designed for stability and durability, rather than for beauty.

The windows were protected by the grillework of inch-thick iron bars sunk deep into the concrete sills. The walls were solid masonry that an earthquake couldn't have touched, and the main door was a huge oaken slab reinforced with iron at the strategic points. Theremon shot the bolts and they slid shut with a dull clang.

At the other end of the corridor, Sheerin cursed weakly. He pointed to the lock of the back door which had been neatly jimmied into uselessness.

"That must be how Latimer got in," he said.

"Well, don't stand there," cried Theremon impatiently. "Help drag up the furniture—and keep that torch out of my eyes. The smoke's killing me."

He slammed the heavy table up against the door as he spoke, and in two minutes had built a barricade which made up for what it lacked in beauty and symmetry by the sheer inertia of its massiveness.

Somewhere, dimly, far off, they could hear the battering of naked fists upon the door; and the screams and yells from outside had a sort of half reality.

That mob had set off from Saro City with only two things in mind: the attainment of Cultist salvation by the destruction of the Observatory, and a maddening fear that all but paralyzed them. There was no time to think of ground cars, or of weapons, or of leadership, or even of organization. They made for the Observatory on foot and assaulted it with bare hands.

And now that they were there, the last flash of Beta, the last ruby-red drop of flame, flickered feebly over a humanity that had left only stark, universal fear!

Theremon groaned, "Let's get back to the dome!"

In the dome, only Yimot, at the solarscope, had kept his place. The rest were clustered about the cameras, and Beenay was giving his instructions in a hoarse, strained voice.

"Get it straight, all of you. I'm snapping Beta just before totality and changing the plate. That will leave one of you to each camera. You all know about . . . about times of exposure—"

There was a breathless murmur of agreement.

Beenay passed a hand over his eyes. "Are the torches still burning? Never mind, I see them!" He was leaning hard against the back of a chair. "Now remember, don't . . . don't try to look for good shots. Don't waste time trying to get t-two stars at a time in the scope field. One is enough. And . . . and if you feel yourself going, *get away from the camera.*"

At the door, Sheerin whispered to Theremon, "Take me to Aton. I don't see him."

The newsman did not answer immediately. The vague forms of the astronomers wavered and blurred, and the torches overhead had become only yellow splotches.

"It's dark," he whimpered.

Sheerin held out his hand, "Aton." He stumbled forward. "Aton!"

Theremon stepped after and seized his arm. "Wait, I'll take you." Somehow he made his way across the room. He closed his eyes against the Darkness and his mind against the chaos within it.

No one heard them or paid attention to them. Sheerin stumbled against the wall. "Aton!"

The psychologist felt shaking hands touching him, then withdrawing, and a voice muttering, "Is that you, Sheerin?"

"Aton!" He strove to breathe normally. "Don't worry about the mob. The place will hold them off."

Latimer, the Cultist, rose to his feet, and his face twisted in desperation. His word was pledged, and to break it would mean placing his soul in mortal peril. Yet that word had been forced from him and had not been given freely. The Stars would come soon; he could not stand by and allow— And yet his word was pledged.

Beenay's face was dimly flushed as it looked upward at Beta's last ray, and Latimer, seeing him bend over his camera, made his decision. His nails cut the flesh of his palms as he tensed himself.

He staggered crazily as he started his rush. There was nothing before him but shadows; the very floor beneath his feet lacked substance. And then someone was upon him and he went down with clutching fingers at his throat.

He doubled his knee and drove it hard into his assailant. "Let me up or I'll kill you."

Theremon cried out sharply and muttered through a blinding haze of pain, "You double-crossing rat!"

The newsman seemed conscious of everything at once. He heard Beenay croak, "I've got it. At your cameras, men!" and then there was the strange awareness that the last thread of sunlight had thinned out and snapped.

Simultaneously he heard one last choking gasp from Beenay, and a queer little cry from Sheerin, a hysterical giggle that cut off in a rasp—and a sudden silence, a strange, deadly silence from outside.

And Latimer had gone limp in his loosening grasp. Theremon peered into the Cultist's eyes and saw the blankness of them, staring upward, mirroring the feeble yellow of the torches. He saw the bubble of froth upon Latimer's lips and heard the low animal whimper in Latimer's throat.

With the slow fascination of fear, he lifted himself on one arm and turned his eyes toward the blood-curdling blackness of the window.

Through it shone the Stars!

Not Earth's feeble thirty-six hundred Stars visible to the eye— Lagash was in the center of a giant cluster. Thirty thousand mighty suns shown down in a soul-searing splendor that was more frighteningly cold in its awful indifference than the bitter wind that shivered across the cold, horribly bleak world.

Theremon staggered to his feet, his throat constricting him to breathlessness, all the muscles of his body writhing in a tensity of terror and sheer fear beyond bearing. He was going mad, and knew it, and somewhere deep inside a bit of sanity was screaming, struggling to fight off the hopeless flood of black terror. It was very horrible to go mad and know that you were going mad—to know that in a little minute you would be here physically and yet all the real essence would be dead and drowned in the black madness. For this was the Dark—the Dark and the Cold and the Doom. The bright walls of the universe were shattered and their awful black fragments were falling down to crush and squeeze and obliterate him.

He jostled someone crawling on hands and knees, but stumbled somehow over him. Hands groping at his tortured throat, he limped toward the flame of the torches that filled all his mad vision.

"Light!" he screamed.

Aton, somewhere, was crying, whimpering horribly like a terribly frightened child. "Stars—all the Stars—we didn't know at all. We didn't know anything. We thought six stars is a universe is something the Stars didn't notice is Darkness forever and ever and ever and the walls are breaking in and we didn't know we couldn't know and anything—"

Someone clawed at the torch, and it fell and snuffed out. In the instant, the awful splendor of the indifferent Stars leaped nearer to them.

On the horizon outside the window, in the direction of Saro City, a crimson glow began growing, strengthening in brightness, that was not the glow of a sun.

The long night had come again.

1941

THREE/

· By His Bootstraps
· The Push of a Finger
· Clash by Night

*In each section now, more young giants spring out of the
ground!*

*After Asimov, Heinlein writing as Anson MacDonald, Henry
Kuttner writing as Lawrence O'Donnell, and Alfred Bester
writing as Alfred Bester!*

*They are three very different kinds of writer. Like Asimov,
Heinlein will always be regarded as an author moulded by
ASF, and it is at least arguable that once he was free of the
Campbellian mould he tended to sprawl and lose that first
fine-honed precision of his. (Asimov's best novels, on the other
hand, appeared beyond the pages on ASF—Caves of Steel
and The Naked Sun.)*

*By general consent, "By His Bootstraps" is the most effective
story of time-travel after H. G. Wells's The Time Machine. It
is as inward-turned as The Time Machine is outward-looking.
And this is curious because the striding young Heinlein of
these days was nothing if not outward-looking—but in the
involvements of one man caught in the toils of several roles,
though not of more than one sex, we catch here an airy prelude
to later Heinlein. Such considerations apart, what a piece of
ingenuity "Bootstraps" is!*

*Like Asimov's, Heinlein's was a cool fiction. For Kuttner,
glamour and excitement came first, and science second or third.
His ability to tell a story seems much more natural than theirs.
By this date, he was prolific and well-known, writing under
many names; in "Clash by Night" we can watch the great, the
ingenious Kuttner, diving and darting in and out of the
mythological seas of his imagining in yet another disguise.*

*This magical potion of Kuttner was a rarity among the
simulated realisms of ASF in any year, and would become a*

deal rarer as the years went by and orthodoxy set in. It quoted from poets, even borrowing its title from a line of Matthew Arnold's Dover Beach—a habit frowned on in a rather anti-literary magazine until Mark Clifton arrived to work his way through Pope's Essay on Man! More to the point, "Clash by Night" was a prelude to one of ASF's great serials, "Fury!" This was our first glimpse of the Keeps in that mighty undersea world of Venus.

And then there is Alfred Bester's "The Push of a Finger"! The authors represented so far have been old-timers, the Men who dwell in the Mountains. Bester is one of the modern masters, and it is a surprise to find him appearing so early in the science fictional day. Like another of the modern masters, Ray Bradbury, Bester probably was not entirely at home in ASF. Only three stories of his ever appeared there; and only one of Ray Bradbury's. We should not let nostalgia blind us to the fact that even the unique "Astounding" was never everyone's meat.

But "Push of a Finger" is a miracle: very Campbellian in many ways, and yet entirely Besterish, with all his love of the towering and the just plain damned unlikely (which is nevertheless expertly justified). It is Besterish in its tale of obsessional love, in its gallant battle against the statistics of chance, in its rich humour, and even in its love of a jingle which, in this case, goes

> *Neon*
> *Crypton*
> *Ammoniated*
> *FitzJohn*
> *Neon*
> *Crypton*
> *Ammoniated*
> *FitzJohn*

And it is Campbellian in the theme of something being hunted down, in the detail of a vast organisation, in the secrecy, and the pace being stepped up towards an awful and unexpected revelation. Later in time, the institutions seem to have closed in on Campbell; "The Push of a Finger" is a reminder of the way the man dearly loved a good joke. And Bester's is a good one.

None of these remarkable stories yield much deference to probability. Indeed, their relish is drawn from telling us an improbable story for maximum effect. The parallel is with the

♥

Hollywood of the time, also enjoying a Golden Age. Confidence was what succeeded, and verve always took precedence over likelihood. Moreover, confidence was to be depended on—it is the secret of ASF's Golden Age. The authors start in without frills, knowing they will have their audience by its collective ears.

Just savour the opening lines of "By His Bootstraps" and "Clash by Night" (discounting the introduction): "Bob Wilson did not see the circle grow"; "Scott drank stinging usiqueplus and glowered across the smoky tavern". Very little hesitation observable there.

With science fiction as with Hollywood, such confidence often betokened the serving of absolute hokum. No doubt of it, many virtues have emerged since the early forties which were not always present then. But, by God, the old confidence is greatly missed. The loss is in part to do with the fragmentation of audiences; but Campbell at this period knew every one of his readers. He had his own private electrode plugged into the center of their little sizzling brains—and kept madly activating it with stories like these every month!

By His Bootstraps/

by ANSON MACDONALD

Concerning the man who not only met himself, but stood by while hisself fought himself!

Bob Wilson did not see the circle grow.

Nor, for that matter, did he see the stranger who stepped out of the circle and stood staring at the back of Wilson's neck—stared, and breathed heavily, as if laboring under strong and unusual emotion.

Wilson had no reason to suspect that anyone else was in his room; he had every reason to expect the contrary. He had locked himself in his room for the purpose of completing his thesis in one sustained drive. He *had* to—tomorrow was the last day for submission, yesterday the thesis had been no more than a title: "An Investigation into Certain Mathematical Aspects of a Rigor of Metaphysics."

Fifty-two cigarettes, four pots of coffee, and thirteen hours of continuous work had added seven thousand words to the title. As to the validity of his thesis he was far too groggy to give a damn. Get it done, turn it in, take three stiff drinks and sleep for a week.

He glanced up and let his eyes rest on his wardrobe door, behind which he had cached a gin bottle, nearly full. No, he admonished himself, one more drink and you'll never finish it, Bob, old son.

The stranger behind him said nothing.

Wilson resumed typing. "—nor is it valid to assume that a conceivable proposition is necessarily a possible proposition, even when it is possible to formulate mathematics which describes the proposition with exactness. A case in point is the concept 'Time Travel.' Time travel may be imagined and its necessities may be formulated under any and all theories of time, formulae which resolve the paradoxes of each theory. Nevertheless, we know certain things about the empirical nature of time which preclude the possibility of the conceivable proposition. Duration is an attribute of consciousness and not of the plenum. It has no *ding an sicht*. Therefore—"

A key of the typewriter stuck, three more jammed up on top of it. Wilson swore duly and reached forward to straighten out the cantankerous machinery. "Don't bother with it," he heard a voice say. "It's a lot of utter hogwash anyhow."

Wilson sat up with a jerk, then turned his head slowly around. He fervently hoped that there was someone behind him. Otherwise—

He perceived the stranger with relief. "Thank God," he said to himself. "For a moment I thought I had come unstuck." His relief turned to extreme annoyance. "What the devil are you doing in my room?" he demanded. He shoved back his chair, got up and strode over to the one door. It was still locked, and bolted on the inside.

The windows were no help; they were adjacent to his desk and three stories above a busy street. "How *did* you get in?" he added.

"Through that," answered the stranger, hooking a thumb toward the circle. Wilson noticed it for the first time, blinked his eyes and looked again. There it hung between them and the wall, a great disk of nothing, of the color one sees when the eyes are shut tight.

Wilson shook his head vigorously. The circle remained. "Gosh," he thought, "I was right the first time. I wonder when I slipped my trolley?" He advanced toward the disk, put out a hand to touch it.

"Don't!" snapped the stranger.

"Why not?" said Wilson edgily. Nevertheless he paused.

"I'll explain. But let's have a drink first." He walked directly to the wardrobe, opened it, reached in and took out the bottle of gin without looking.

"Hey!" yelled Wilson. "What are you doing there? That's *my* liquor."

"*Your* liquor—" The stranger paused for a moment. "Sorry. You don't mind if I have a drink, do you?"

"I suppose not," Bob Wilson conceded in a surly tone. "Pour me one while you're about it."

"O. K.," agreed the stranger, "then I'll explain."

"It had better be good," Wilson said ominously. Nevertheless he drank his drink and looked the stranger over.

He saw a chap about the same size as himself and much the same age—perhaps a little older, though a three-day growth of beard may have accounted for that impression. The stranger had a black eye and a freshly cut and badly swollen upper lip. Wilson decided he did not like the chap's face. Still, there was something familiar about the face; he felt that he should have recognized it, that he had seen it many times before under different circumstances.

"Who are you?" he asked suddenly.

"Me?" said his guest. "Don't you recognize me?"

"I'm not sure," admitted Wilson. "Have I ever seen you before?"

"Well—not exactly," the other temporized. "Skip it—you wouldn't know about it."

"What's your name?"

"My name? Uh . . . just call me Joe."

Wilson set down his glass. "O. K., Joe Whatever-your-name-is, trot out that explanation and make it snappy."

"I'll do that," agreed Joe. "That dingus I came through"—he pointed to the circle—"that's a Time Gate."

"A what?"

"A Time Gate. Time flows along side by side on each side of the Gate, but some thousands of years apart—just how many thousands I don't know. But for the next couple of hours that Gate is open. You can walk into the future just by stepping through that circle." The stranger paused.

Bob drummed on the desk. "Go ahead. I'm listening. It's a nice story."

"You don't believe me, do you? I'll show you." Joe got up, went again to the wardrobe and obtained Bob's hat, his prized and only hat, which he had mistreated into its present battered grandeur through six years of undergraduate and graduate life. Joe chucked it toward the impalpable disk.

It struck the surface, went on through with no apparent resistance, disappeared from sight.

Wilson got up, walked carefully around the circle, and examined the bare floor. "A neat trick," he conceded. "Now I'll thank you to return to me my hat."

The stranger shook his head. "You can get it yourself when you pass through."

"Huh?"

"That's right. Listen—" Briefly the stranger repeated his explanation about the Time Gate. Wilson, he insisted, had an opportunity that comes once in a millennium—if he would only hurry up and climb through that circle. Furthermore, though Joe could not explain in detail at the moment, it was very important that Wilson go through.

Bob Wilson helped himself to a second drink, and then a third. He was beginning to feel both good and argumentative. "Why?" he said flatly.

Joe looked exasperated. "Dammit, if you'd just step through once, explanations wouldn't be necessary. However—" According to Joe, there was an old guy on the other side who needed Wilson's help. With Wilson's help the three of them would run the country. The exact nature of the help Joe could not or would not specify. Instead he bore down on the unique possibilities for high adventure. "You don't want to slave your life away teaching numskulls in some fresh-water college," he insisted. "This is your chance. Grab it!"

Bob Wilson admitted to himself that a Ph.D. and an appointment as an instructor was not his ideal of existence. Still, it beat working for a living. His eye fell on the gin bottle, its level now deplorably lowered. That explained it. He got up unsteadily.

"No, my dear fellow," he stated, "I'm not going to climb on your merry-go-round. You know why?"

"Why?"

"Because I'm drunk, that's why. You're not there at all. *That* ain't there." He gestured widely at the circle. "There ain't anybody here but me, and I'm drunk. Been working too hard," he added apologetically. "I'm goin' to bed."

"You're not drunk."

"I *am* drunk. Peter Piper pepped a pick of pippered peckles." He moved toward his bed.

Joe grabbed his arm. "You can't do that," he said.

"Let him alone!"

They both swung around. Facing them, standing directly in front of the circle, was a third man. Bob looked at the newcomer, looked back at Joe, blinked his eyes and tried to focus them. The two looked a good bit alike, he thought, enough alike to be brothers. Or maybe he was seeing double. Bad stuff, gin. Should've switched to rum a long time ago. Good stuff, rum. You could drink it, or take a bath in it. No, that was gin—he meant Joe.

How silly! Joe was the one with the black eye. He wondered why he had ever been confused.

Then who was this other lug? Couldn't a couple of friends have a quiet drink together without people butting in?

"Who are you?" he said with quiet dignity.

The newcomer turned his head, then looked at Joe. "*He* knows me," he said meaningly.

Joe looked him over slowly. "Yes," he said, "yes, I suppose I

do. But what the deuce are you here for? And why are you trying
to bust up the plan?"

"No time for long-winded explanations. I know more about it
than you do—you'll concede that—and my judgment is bound to
be better than yours. He doesn't go through the Gate."

"I don't concede anything of the sort—"

The telephone rang.

"Answer it!" snapped the newcomer.

Bob was about to protest the peremptory tone, but decided he
wouldn't. He lacked the phlegmatic temperament necessary to ignore a ringing telephone. "Hello?"

"Hello," he was answered. "Is that Bob Wilson?"

"Yes. Who is this?"

"Never mind. I just wanted to be sure you were there. I *thought*
you would be. You're right in the groove, kid, right in the groove."

Wilson heard a chuckle, then the click of disconnection.
"Hello," he said. "Hello!" He jiggled the bar a couple of times,
then hung up.

"What was it?" asked Joe.

"Nothing. Some nut with a misplaced sense of humor." The
telephone bell rang again. Wilson added, "There he is again," and
picked up the receiver. "Listen, you butterfly-brained ape! I'm a
busy man, and this is *not* a public telephone."

"Why, Bob!" came a hurt feminine voice.

"Huh? Oh, it's you, Genevieve. Look—I'm sorry. I apologize—"

"Well, I should think you would!"

"You don't understand, honey. A guy has been pestering me
over the phone and I thought it was him. You know I wouldn't
talk that way to you, Babe."

"Well, I should think not. Particularly after all you said to
me this afternoon, and all we *meant* to each other."

"Huh? This afternoon? Did you say this afternoon?"

"Of course. But what I called up about was this: You left your
hat in my apartment. I noticed it a few minutes after you had
gone and just thought I'd call and tell you where it is. Anyhow,"
she added coyly, "it gave me an excuse to hear your voice again."

"Sure. Fine," he said mechanically. "Look, babe, I'm a little
mixed up about this. Trouble I've had all day long, and more
trouble now. I'll look you up tonight and straighten it out. But
I *know* I didn't leave your hat in my apartment—"

"*Your* hat, silly!"

"Huh? Oh, sure! Anyhow, I'll see you tonight. 'By." He rang

off hurriedly. Gosh, he thought, that woman is getting to be a problem. Hallucinations. He turned to his two companions.

"Very well, Joe. I'm ready to go if you are." He was not sure just when or why he had decided to go through the time gadget, but he had. Who did this other mug think he was, anyhow, trying to interfere with a man's freedom of choice?

"Fine!" said Joe, in a relieved voice. "Just step through. That's all there is to it."

"No, you don't!" It was the ubiquitous stranger. He stepped between Wilson and the Gate.

Bob Wilson faced him. "Listen, you! You come butting in here like you think I was a bum. If you don't like it, go jump in the lake—and I'm just the kind of guy who can do it! You and who else?"

The stranger reached out and tried to collar him. Wilson let go a swing, but not a good one. It went by nothing faster than parcel post. The stranger walked under it and let him have a mouthful of knuckles—large, hard ones. Joe closed in rapidly, coming to Bob's aid. They traded punches in a free-for-all, with Bob joining in enthusiastically but inefficiently. The only punch he landed was on Joe, theoretically his ally. However, he had intended it for the third man.

It was this *faux pas* which gave the stranger the opportunity to land a clean left jab on Wilson's face. It was inches higher than the button, but in Bob's bemused condition it was sufficient to cause him to cease taking part in the activities.

Bob Wilson came slowly to awareness of his surroundings. He was seated on a floor which seemed a little unsteady. Someone was bending over him. "Are you all right?" the figure inquired.

"I guess so," he answered thickly. His mouth pained him; he put his hand to it, got it sticky with blood. "My head hurts."

"I should think it would. You came through head over heels. I think you hit your head when you landed."

Wilson's thoughts were coming back into confused focus. Came through? He looked more closely at his succorer. He saw a middle-aged man with gray-shot bushy hair and a short, neatly trimmed beard. He was dressed in what Wilson took to be purple lounging pajamas.

But the room in which he found himself bothered him even more. It was circular and the ceiling was arched so subtly that it was difficult to say how high it was. A steady glareless light filled the room from no apparent source. There was no furniture save for a high dais or pulpit-shaped object near the wall facing him. "Came through? Came through what?"

"The Gate, of course." There was something odd about the man's accent. Wilson could not place it, save for a feeling that English was not a tongue he was accustomed to speaking.

Wilson looked over his shoulder in the direction of the other's gaze, and saw the circle.

That made his head ache even more. "Oh Lord," he thought, "now I really am nuts. Why don't I wake up?" He shook his head to clear it.

That was a mistake. The top of his head did not quite come off—not quite. And the circle stayed where it was, a simple locus hanging in the air, its flat depth filled with the amorphous colors and shapes of no-vision. "Did I come through that?"

"Yes."

"Where am I?"

"In the Hall of the Gate in the High Palace of Norkaal. But what is more important is *when* you are. You have gone forward a little more than thirty thousand years."

"Now I know I'm crazy," thought Wilson. He got up unsteadily and moved toward the Gate.

The older man put a hand on his shoulder. "Where are you going?"

"Back!"

"Not so fast. You will go back all right—I give you my word on that. But let me dress your wounds first. And you should rest. I have some explanations to make to you, and there is an errand you can do for me when you get back—to our mutual advantage. There is a great future in store for you and me, my boy—a great future!"

Wilson paused uncertainly. The elder man's insistence was vaguely disquieting. "I don't like this."

The other eyed him narrowly. "Wouldn't you like a drink before you go?"

Wilson most assuredly would. Right at the moment a stiff drink seemed the most desirable thing on earth—or in time. "O. K."

"Come with me." The older man led him back of the structure near the wall and through a door which led into a passageway. He walked briskly; Wilson hurried to keep up.

"By the way," he asked, as they continued down the long passage, "what is your name?"

"My name? You may call me Diktor—everyone else does."

"O. K., Diktor. Do you want my name?"

"Your name?" Diktor chuckled. "I know your name. It's Bob Wilson."

"Huh? Oh—I suppose Joe told you."

"Joe? I know no one by that name."

"You don't? He seemed to know you. Say—maybe you aren't the guy I was supposed to see."

"But I am. I have been expecting you—in a way, Joe . . . Joe— Oh!" Diktor chuckled. "It had slipped my mind for a moment. He told you to call him Joe, didn't he?"

"Isn't it his name?"

"It's as good a name as any other. Here we are." He ushered Wilson into a small, but cheerful, room. It contained no furniture of any sort, but the floor was soft and warm as live flesh. "Sit down. I'll be back in a moment."

Bob looked around for something to sit on, then turned to ask Diktor for a chair. But Diktor was gone, furthermore the door through which they had entered was gone. Bob sat down on the comfortable floor and tried not to worry.

Diktor returned promptly. Wilson saw the door dilate to let him in, but did not catch on to how it was done. Diktor was carrying a carafe, which gurgled pleasantly, and a cup. "Mud in your eye," he said heartily and poured a good four fingers. "Drink up."

Bob accepted the cup. "Aren't you drinking?"

"Presently. I want to attend to your wounds first."

"O. K." Wilson tossed off the first drink in almost indecent haste—it was good stuff, a little like Scotch, he decided, but smoother and not as dry—while Diktor worked deftly with salves that smarted at first, then soothed. "Mind if I have another?"

"Help yourself."

Bob drank more slowly the second cup. He did not finish it; it slipped from relaxed fingers, spilling a ruddy, brown stain across the floor. He snored.

Bob Wilson woke up feeling fine and completely rested. He was cheerful without knowing why. He lay relaxed, eyes still closed, for a few moments and let his soul snuggle back into his body. This was going to be a good day, he felt. Oh, yes—he had finished that double-damned thesis. No, he hadn't either! He sat up with a start.

The sight of the strange walls around him brought him back into continuity. But before he had time to worry—at once, in fact —the door relaxed and Diktor stepped in. "Feeling better?"

"Why, yes, I do. Say what is this?"

"We'll get to that. How about some breakfast?"

In Wilson's scale of evaluations breakfast rated just after life itself and ahead of the chance of immortality. Diktor conducted him to another room—the first that he had seen possessing windows. As a matter of fact half the room was open, a balcony hanging high over a green countryside. A soft, warm, summer breeze wafted through the place. They broke their fast in luxury, Roman style, while Diktor explained.

Bob Wilson did not follow the explanations as closely as he might have done, because his attention was diverted by the maidservants who served the meal. The first came in bearing a great tray of fruit on her head. The fruit was gorgeous. So was the girl. Search as he would he could discern no fault in her.

Her costume lent itself to the search.

She came first to Diktor, and with a single, graceful movement dropped to one knee, removed the tray from her head, and offered it to him. He helped himself to a small, red fruit and waved her away. She then offered it to Bob in the same delightful manner.

"As I was saying," continued Diktor, "it is not certain where the High Ones came from or where they went when they left Earth. I am inclined to think they went away into Time. In any case they ruled more than twenty thousand years and completely obliterated human culture as you knew it. What is more important to you and to me is the effect they had on the human psyche. One twentieth-century style go-getter can accomplish just about anything he wants to accomplish around here— Aren't you listening?"

"Huh? Oh, yes, sure. Say, that's one mighty pretty girl." His eyes still rested on the exit through which she had disappeared.

"Who? Oh, yes, I suppose so. She's not exceptionally beautiful as women go around here."

"That's hard to believe. I could learn to get along with a girl like that."

"You like her? Very well, she is yours."

"Huh?"

"She's a slave. Don't get indignant. They are slaves by nature. If you like her, I'll make you a present of her. It will make her happy." The girl had just returned. Diktor called to her in a language strange to Bob. "Her name is Arma," he said in an aside, then spoke to her briefly.

Arma giggled. She composed her face quickly, and, moving over to where Wilson reclined, dropped on both knees to the floor and lowered her head, with both hands cupped before her. "Touch her forehead," Diktor instructed.

Bob did so. The girl arose and stood waiting placidly by his side. Diktor spoke to her. She looked puzzled, but moved out of the room. "I told her that, notwithstanding her new status, you wished her to continue serving breakfast."

Diktor resumed his explanations while the service of the meal continued. The next course was brought in by Arma and another girl. When Bob saw the second girl he let out a low whistle. He realized he had been a little hasty in letting Diktor give him Arma. Either the standard of pulchritude had gone up incredibly, he decided, or Diktor went to a lot of trouble in selecting his servants.

"—for that reason," Diktor was saying, "it is necessary that you go back through the Time Gate at once. Your first job is to bring this other chap back. Then there is one other task for you to do, and we'll be sitting pretty. After that it is share and share alike for you and me. And there is plenty to share, I— You aren't listening!"

"Sure I was, chief. I heard every word you said." He fingered his chin. "Say, have you got a razor I could borrow? I'd like to shave."

Diktor swore softly in two languages. "Keep your eyes off those wenches and listen to me! There's work to be done."

"Sure, sure. I understand that—and I'm your man. When do we start?" Wilson had made up his mind some time ago—just shortly after Arma had entered with the tray of fruit, in fact. He felt as if he had walked into some extremely pleasant dream. If cooperation with Diktor would cause that dream to continue, so be it. To hell with an academic career!

Anyhow, all Diktor wanted was for him to go back where he started and persuade another guy to go through the Gate. The worst that could happen was for him to find himself back in the twentieth century. What could he lose?

Diktor stood up. "Let's get on with it," he said shortly, "before you get your attention diverted again. Follow me." He set off at a brisk pace with Wilson behind him.

Diktor took him to the Hall of the Gate and stopped. "All you have to do," he said, "is to step through the Gate. You will find yourself back in your own room, in your own time. Persuade the man you find there to go through the Gate. We have need of him. Then come back yourself."

Bob held up a hand and pinched thumb and forefinger together. "It's in the bag, boss. Consider it done." He started to step through the Gate.

"Wait!" commanded Diktor. "You are not used to time travel.

I warn you that you are going to get one hell of a shock when you step through. This other chap—you'll recognize him."

"Who is he?"

"I won't tell you because you wouldn't understand. But you will when you see him. Just remember this— There are some very strange paradoxes connected with time travel. Don't let anything you see throw you. You do what I tell you to and you'll be all right."

"Paradoxes don't worry me," Bob said confidently. "Is that all? I'm ready."

"One minute." Diktor stepped behind the raised dais. His head appeared above the side a moment later. "I've set the controls. O. K. Go!"

Bob Wilson stepped through the locus known as the Time Gate.

There was no particular sensation connected with the transition. It was like stepping through a curtained doorway into a darker room. He paused for a moment on the other side and let his eyes adjust to the dimmer light. He was, he saw, indeed in his own room.

There was a man in it, seated at his own desk. Diktor had been right about that. This, then, was the chap he was to send back through the Gate. Diktor had said he would recognize him. Well, let's see who it is.

He felt a passing resentment at finding someone at *his* desk in *his* room, then thought better of it. After all, it was just a rented room; when he disappeared no doubt it had been rented again. He had no way of telling how long he had been gone—shucks, it might be the middle of next week!

The chap did look vaguely familiar, although all he could see was his back. Who was it? Should he speak to him, cause him to turn around? He felt vaguely reluctant to do so until he knew who it was. He rationalized the feeling by telling himself that it *was* desirable to know with whom he was dealing before he attempted anything as outlandish as persuading this man to go through the Gate.

The man at the desk continued typing, paused to snuff out a cigarette by laying it in an ash tray, then stamping it with a paper weight.

Bob Wilson knew that gesture.

Chills trickled down his back. "If he lights his next one," he whispered to himself, "the way I think he is going to—"

The man at the desk took out another cigarette, tamped it on one end, turned it and tamped the other, straightened and crimped the paper on one end carefully against his left thumbnail and placed that end in his mouth.

Wilson felt the blood beating in his neck. *Sitting there with his back to him was himself, Bob Wilson!*

He felt that he was going to faint. He closed his eyes and steadied himself on a chair back. "I knew it," he thought, "the whole thing is absurd. I'm crazy. I know I'm crazy. Some sort of split personality. I shouldn't have worked so hard."

The sound of typing continued.

He pulled himself together, and reconsidered the matter. Diktor had warned him that he was due for a shock, a shock that could not be explained ahead of time, because it could not be believed. "All right—suppose I'm not crazy. If time travel can happen at all, there is no reason why I can't come back and see myself doing something I did in the past. If I'm sane, that is what I'm doing.

"And if I am crazy, it doesn't make a damn bit of difference what I do!

"And furthermore," he added to himself, "if I'm crazy, maybe I can stay crazy and go back through the Gate! No, that does not make sense. Neither does anything else—the hell with it!"

He crept forward softly and peered over the shoulder of his double. "Duration is an attribute of the consciousness," he read, "and not of the plenum."

"That tears it," he thought, "right back where I started, and watching myself write my thesis."

The typing continued. "It has no *ding an sicht*. Therefore—" A key stuck, and others piled up on top of it. His double at the desk swore and reached out a hand to straighten the keys.

"Don't bother with it," Wilson said on sudden impulse. "It's a lot of utter hogwash anyhow."

The other Bob Wilson sat up with a jerk, then looked slowly around. An expression of surprise gave way to annoyance. "What the devil are you doing in my room?" he demanded. Without waiting for an answer he got up, went quickly to the door and examined the lock. "How did you get in?"

"This," thought Wilson, "is going to be difficult."

"Through that," Wilson answered, pointing to the Time Gate. His double looked where he had pointed, did a double take, then advanced cautiously and started to touch it.

"Don't!" yelled Wilson.

The other checked himself. "Why not?" he demanded.

Just why he must not permit his other self to touch the Gate was not clear to Wilson, but he had had an unmistakable feeling of impending disaster when he saw it about to happen. He tem-

porized by saying, "I'll explain. But let's have a drink." A drink
was a good idea in any case. There had never been a time when
he needed one more than he did right now. Quite automatically
he went to his usual cache of liquor in the wardrobe and took
out the bottle he expected to find there.

"Hey!" protested the other. "What are you doing there? That's
my liquor."

"*Your* liquor—" Hell's bells! It was *his* liquor. No, it wasn't; it
was—*their* liquor. Oh, the devil! It was much too mixed up to
try to explain. "Sorry. You don't mind if I have a drink, do you?"

"I suppose not," his double said grudgingly. "Pour me one while
you're about it."

"O. K.," Wilson assented, "then I'll explain." It was going to
be much, much too difficult to explain until he had had a drink,
he felt. As it was, he couldn't explain it fully to himself.

"It had better be good," the other warned him, and looked Wilson over carefully while he drank his drink.

Wilson watched his younger self scrutinizing him with confused and almost insupportable emotions. Couldn't the stupid fool
recognize his own face when he saw it in front of him? If he
could not *see* what the situation was, how in the world was he
ever going to make it clear to him?

It had slipped his mind that his face was barely recognizable
in any case, being decidedly battered and unshaven. Even more
important, he failed to take into account the fact that a person
does not look at his own face, even in mirrors, in the same frame
of mind with which he regards another's face. No sane person
ever expects to see his own face hanging on another.

Wilson could see that his companion was puzzled by his appearance, but it was equally clear that no recognition took place.
"Who are you?" the other man asked suddenly.

"Me?" replied Wilson. "Don't you recognize me?"

"I'm not sure. Have I ever seen you before?"

"Well—not exactly," Wilson stalled. How did you go about telling another guy that the two of you were a trifle closer than
twins? "Skip it—you wouldn't know about it."

"What's your name?"

"My name? Uh—" Oh, oh! This was going to be sticky! The
whole situation was utterly ridiculous. He opened his mouth, tried
to form the words "Bob Wilson," then gave up with a feeling of
utter futility. Like many a man before him, he found himself
forced into a lie because the truth simply would not be believed.
"Just call me Joe," he finished lamely.

He felt suddenly startled at his own words. It was at this point that he realized that he was *in fact,* "Joe," the Joe whom he had encountered once before. That he had landed back in his own room at the very time at which he had ceased working on his thesis he already realized, but he had not had time to think the matter through. Hearing himself refer to himself as Joe slapped him in the face with the realization that this was not simply a similar scene, but the *same* scene he had lived through once before—save that he was living through it from a different viewpoint.

At least he thought it was the same scene. Did it differ in any respect? He could not be sure, as he could not recall, word for word, what the conversation had been.

For a complete transcript of the scene that lay dormant in his memory he felt willing to pay twenty-five dollars cash, plus sales tax.

Wait a minute now—he was under no compulsion. He was sure of that. Everything he did and said was the result of his own free will. Even if he couldn't remember the script, there were some things he *knew* "Joe" hadn't said. "Mary had a little lamb," for example. He would recite a nursery rhyme and get off this damned repetitious treadmill. He opened his mouth—

"O. K., Joe Whatever-your-name-is," his alter ego remarked, setting down a glass which had contained, until recently, a quarter pint of gin, "trot out that explanation and make it snappy."

He opened his mouth again to answer the question, then closed it. "Steady, son, steady," he told himself. "You're a free agent. You want to recite a nursery rhyme—go ahead and do it. Don't answer him; go ahead and recite it—and break this vicious circle."

But under the unfriendly, suspicious eye of the man opposite him he found himself totally unable to recall any nursery rhyme. His mental processes stuck on dead center.

He capitulated. "I'll do that. That dingus I came through—that's a Time Gate."

"A what?"

"A Time Gate. Time flows along side by side on each side—" As he talked he felt sweat breaking out on him; he felt reasonably sure that he was explaining in exactly the same words in which explanation had first been offered to *him.* "—into the future just by stepping through that circle." He stopped and wiped his forehead.

"Go ahead," said the other implacably. "I'm listening. It's a nice story."

Bob suddenly wondered if the other man *could* be himself. The stupid arrogant dogmatism of the man's manner infuriated him. All right, all right! He'd show him. He strode suddenly over to the wardrobe, took out his hat and threw it through the Gate.

His opposite number watched the hat snuff out of existence with expressionless eyes, then stood up and went around in back of the Gate, walking with the careful steps of a man who is a little bit drunk, but determined not to show it. "A neat trick," he applauded, after satisfying himself that the hat was gone, "now I'll thank you to return to me my hat."

Wilson shook his head. "You can get it for yourself when you pass through," he answered absent-mindedly. He was pondering the problem of how many hats there were on the other side of the Gate.

"Huh?"

"That's right. Listen—" Wilson did his best to explain persuasively what it was he wanted his earlier *persona* to do. Or rather to cajole. Explanations were out of the question, in any honest sense of the word. He would have preferred attempting to explain tensor calculus to an Australian aborigine, even though he did not understand that esoteric mathematics himself.

The other man was not helpful. He seemed more interested in nursing the gin than he did in following Wilson's implausible protestations.

"Why?" he interrupted pugnaciously.

"Dammit," Wilson answered, "if you'd just step through once, explanations wouldn't be necessary. However—" He continued with a synopsis of Diktor's proposition. He realized with irritation that Diktor had been exceedingly sketchy with *his* explanations. He was forced to hit only the high spots in the logical parts of his argument, and bear down on the emotional appeal. He was on safe ground there—no one knew better than he did himself how fed up the earlier Bob Wilson had been with the petty drudgery and stuffy atmosphere of an academic career. "You don't want to slave your life away teaching numskulls in some freshwater college," he concluded. "This is your chance. Grab it!"

Wilson watched his companion narrowly and thought he detected a favorable response. He definitely seemed interested. But the other set his glass down carefully, stared at the gin bottle, and at last replied:

"My dear fellow, I am not going to climb on your merry-go-round. You know why?"

"Why?"

"Because I'm drunk, that's why. You're not there at all. *That* ain't there." He gestured widely at the Gate, nearly fell, and recovered himself with effort. "There ain't anybody here but me, and I'm drunk. Been working too hard," he mumbled, "'m goin' to bed."

"You're not drunk," Wilson protested unhopefully. "Damnation," he thought, "a man who can't hold his liquor shouldn't drink."

"I am drunk. Peter Piper pepped a pick of pippered peckles." He lumbered over toward the bed.

Wilson grabbed his arm. "You can't do that."

"Let him alone!"

Wilson swung around, saw a third man standing in front of the Gate—recognized him with a sudden shock. His own recollection of the sequence of events was none too clear in his memory, since he had been somewhat intoxicated—damned near boiled, he admitted—the first time he had experienced this particular busy afternoon. He realized that he should have anticipated the arrival of a third party. But his memory had not prepared him for who the third party would turn out to be.

He recognized himself—another carbon copy.

He stood silent for a minute, trying to assimilate this new fact and force it into some reasonable integration. He closed his eyes helplessly. This was just a little too much. He felt that he wanted to have a few plain words with Diktor.

"Who the hell are you?" He opened his eyes to find that his other self, the drunk one, was addressing the latest edition. The newcomer turned away from his interrogator and looked sharply at Wilson.

"*He* knows me."

Wilson took his time about replying. This thing was getting out of hand. "Yes," he admitted, "yes, I suppose I do. But what the deuce are you here for? And why are you trying to bust up the plan?"

His facsimile cut him short. "No time for long-winded explanations. I know more about it than you do—you'll concede that—and my judgment is bound to be better than yours. He doesn't go through the Gate."

The offhand arrogance of the other antagonized Wilson. "I don't concede anything of the sort—" he began.

He was interrupted by the telephone bell. "Answer it!" snapped Number Three.

The tipsy Number One looked belligerent but picked up the handset. "Hello. . . . Yes. Who is this? . . . Hello. . . . Hello!"

He tapped the bar of the instrument, then slammed the receiver back into its cradle.

"Who was that?" Wilson asked, somewhat annoyed that he had not had a chance to answer it himself.

"Nothing. Some nut with a misplaced sense of humor." At that instant the telephone rang again. "There he is again!" Wilson tried to answer it, but his alcoholic counterpart beat him to it, brushed him aside. "Listen, you butterfly-brained ape! I'm a busy man and this is *not* a public telephone. . . . Huh? Oh, it's you, Genevieve. Look—I'm sorry. I apologize— . . . You don't understand, honey. A guy has been pestering me over the phone and I thought it was him. You know I wouldn't talk to you that way, Babe. . . . Huh? This afternoon? Did you say *this* afternoon? . . . Sure. Fine. Look, Babe, I'm a little mixed up about this. Trouble I've had all day long and more trouble now. I'll look you up tonight and straighten it out. But I *know* I didn't leave your hat in my apartment— . . . Huh? Oh, sure! Anyhow, I'll see you tonight. 'By."

It almost nauseated Wilson to hear his earlier self catering to the demands of that clinging female. Why didn't he just hang up on her? The contrast with Arma—there was a dish!—was acute; it made him more determined than ever to go ahead with the plan, despite the warning of the latest arrival.

After hanging up the phone his earlier self faced him, pointedly ignoring the presence of the third copy. "Very well, Joe," he announced. "I'm ready to go if you are."

"Fine!" Wilson agreed with relief. "Just step through. That's all there is to it."

"No, you don't!" Number Three barred the way.

Wilson started to argue, but his erratic comrade was ahead of him. "Listen, you! You come butting in here like you think I was a bum. If you don't like it, go jump in the lake—and I'm just the kind of a guy who can do it! You and who else?"

They started trading punches almost at once. Wilson stepped in warily, looking for an opening that would enable him to put the slug on Number Three with one decisive blow.

He should have watched his drunken ally as well. A wild swing from that quarter glanced off his already damaged features and caused him excruciating pain. His upper lip, cut, puffy, and tender from his other encounter, took the blow and became an area of pure agony. He flinched and jumped back.

A sound cut through his fog of pain, a dull *Smack!* He forced his eyes to track and saw the feet of a man disappear through the Gate. Number Three was still standing by the Gate. "Now you've done it!" he said bitterly to Wilson, and nursed the knuckles of his left hand.

The obviously unfair allegation reached Wilson at just the wrong moment. His face still felt like an experiment in sadism. "Me?" he said angrily. "*You* knocked him through. I never laid a finger on him."

"Yes, but it's your fault. If you hadn't interfered, I wouldn't have had to do it."

"*Me* interfere? Why, you baldfaced hypocrite—*you* butted in and tried to queer the pitch. Which reminds me—you owe me some explanations and I damn well mean to have 'em. What's the idea of—"

But his opposite number cut in on him. "Stow it," he said gloomily. "It's too late now. He's gone through."

"Too late for what?" Wilson wanted to know.

"Too late to put a stop to this chain of events."

"Why should we?"

"Because," Number Three said bitterly, "Diktor has played me —I mean has played *you* . . . *us*—for a dope, for a couple of dopes. Look, he told you that he was going to set you up as a big shot over *there*"—he indicated the Gate—"didn't he?"

"Yes," Wilson admitted.

"Well, that's a lot of malarkey. All he means to do is to get us so incredibly tangled up in this Time Gate thing that we'll never get straightened out again."

Wilson felt a sudden doubt nibbling at his mind. It *could* be true. Certainly there had not been much sense to what had happened so far. After all, why should Diktor want his help, want it bad enough to offer to split with him, even-Stephen, what was obviously a cushy spot? "How do you know?" he demanded.

"Why go into it?" the other answered wearily. "Why don't you just take my word for it?"

"Why should I?"

His companion turned a look of complete exasperation on him. "If you can't take my word, whose word can you take?"

The inescapable logic of the question simply annoyed Wilson. He resented this interloping duplicate of himself anyhow; to be asked to follow his lead blindly irked him. "I'm from Missouri," he said. "I'll see for myself." He moved toward the Gate.

"Where are you going?"

"Through! I'm going to look up Diktor and have it out with him."

"Don't!" the other said. "Maybe we can break the chain even now." Wilson felt and looked stubborn. The other sighed. "Go ahead," he surrendered. "It's your funeral. I wash my hands of you."

Wilson paused as he was about to step through the Gate. "It is, eh? Hm-m-m—how can it be *my* funeral unless it's *your* funeral, too?"

The other man looked blank, then an expression of apprehension raced over his face. That was the last Wilson saw of him as he stepped through.

The hall of the Gate was empty of other occupants when Bob Wilson came through on the other side. He looked for his hat, but did not find it, then stepped around back of the raised platform, seeking the exit he remembered. He nearly bumped into Diktor.

"Ah, there you are!" the older man greeted him. "Fine! Fine! Now there is just one more little thing to take care of, then we will be all squared away. I must say I am pleased with you, Bob, very pleased indeed."

"Oh, you are, are you?" Bob faced him truculently. "Well, it's too bad I can't say the same about you! I'm not a damn bit pleased. What was the idea of shoving me into that . . . that daisy chain without warning me? What's the meaning of all this non-sense? Why didn't you warn me?"

"Easy, easy," said the older man, "don't get excited. Tell the truth now—if I had told you that you were going back to meet yourself face to face, would you have believed me? Come now, 'fess up."

Wilson admitted that he would not have believed it.

"Well, then," Diktor continued with a shrug, "there was no point in my telling you, was there? If I had told you, you would not have believed me, which is another way of saying that you would have believed false data. Is it not better to be in ignorance than to believe falsely?"

"I suppose so, but—"

"Wait! I did not intentionally deceive you. I did not deceive you at all. But had I told you the full truth, you would have been deceived because you would have rejected the truth. It was better for you to learn the truth with your own eyes. Otherwise—"

"Wait a minute! Wait a minute!" Wilson cut in. "You're getting me all tangled up. I'm willing to let bygones be bygones, if you'll come clean with me. Why did you send me back at all?"

"'Let bygones be bygones.'" Diktor repeated. "Ah, if we only could! But we can't. That's why I sent you back—in order that you might come through the Gate in the first place."

"Huh? Wait a minute—I already *had* come through the Gate."

Diktor shook his head. "Had you, now? Think a moment. When you got back into your own time and your own place you found your earlier self there, didn't you?"

"Mmmm—yes."

"*He*—your earlier self—had not yet been through the Gate, had he?"

"No. I—"

"How could you have *been* through the Gate, unless you persuaded him to *go* through the Gate?"

Bob Wilson's head was beginning to whirl. He was beginning to wonder who did what to whom and who got paid. "But that's impossible! You are telling me that I did something because I was going to do something."

"Well, didn't you? You were there."

"No I didn't—no . . . well, maybe I did, but it didn't *feel* like it."

"Why should you expect it to? It was something totally new to your experience."

"But . . . but—" Wilson took a deep breath and got control of himself. Then he reached back into his academic philosophical concepts and produced the notion he had been struggling to express. "It denies all reasonable theories of causation. You would have me believe that causation can be completely circular. I went through because I came back from going through to persuade myself to go through. That's silly."

"Well, didn't you?"

Wilson did not have an answer ready for that one. Diktor continued with, "Don't worry about it. The causation you have been accustomed to is valid enough in its own field but is simply a special case under the general case. *Causation in a plenum need not be and is not limited by a man's perception of duration.*"   ·

Wilson thought about that for a moment. It sounded nice, but there was something slippery about it. "Just a second," he said. "How about entropy? You can't get around entropy."

"Oh, for Heaven's sake," protested Diktor, "shut up, will you? You remind me of the mathematicians that proved that airplanes couldn't fly." He turned and started out the door. "Come on. There's work to be done."

Wilson hurried after him. "Dammit, you can't do this to me. What happened to the other two?"

"The other two what?"

"The other two of me? Where are they? How am I ever going to get unsnarled?"

"You aren't snarled up. You don't feel like more than one person, do you?"

"No, but—"

"Then don't worry about it."

"But I've got to worry about it. What happened to the guy that came through just ahead of me?"

"You remember, don't you? However—" Diktor hurried on ahead, led him down a passageway, and dilated a door. "Take a look inside," he directed.

Wilson did so. He found himself looking into a small windowless unfurnished room, a room that he recognized. Sprawled on the floor, snoring steadily, was another edition of himself.

"When you first came through the Gate," explained Diktor at his elbow, "I brought you in here, attended to your hurts, and gave you a drink. The drink contained a soporific which will cause you to sleep about thirty-six hours, sleep that you badly needed. When you wake up, I will give you breakfast and explain to you what needs to be done."

Wilson's head started to ache again. "Don't do that," he pleaded. "Don't refer to that guy as if he were me. *This is me*, standing here."

"Have it your own way," said Diktor. "That is the man you *were*. You remember the things that are about to happen to him, don't you?"

"Yes, but it makes me dizzy. Close the door, please."

"O. K.," said Diktor, and complied. "We've got to hurry, anyhow. Once a sequence like this is established there is no time to waste. Come on." He led the way back to the Hall of the Gate.

"I want you to return to the twentieth century and obtain certain things for us, things that can't be obtained on this side but which will be very useful to us in, ah, developing—yes, that is the word—developing this country."

"What sort of things?"

"Quite a number of items. I've prepared a list for you—certain reference books, certain items of commerce. Excuse me, please. I must adjust the controls of the Gate." He mounted the raised platform from the rear. Wilson followed him and found that the structure was boxlike, open at the top, and had a raised floor. The Gate could be seen by looking over the high sides.

The controls were unique.

Four colored spheres the size of marbles hung on crystal rods arranged with respect to one another as the four major axes of a tetrahedron. The three spheres which bounded the base of the tetrahedron were red, yellow, and blue; the fourth at the apex was white. "Three spatial controls, one time control," explained Diktor. "It's very simple. Using here-and-now as zero reference, displacing any control away from the center moves the other end of the Gate farther from here-and-now. Forward or back, right or left, up or down, past or future—they are all controlled by moving the proper sphere in or out on its rod."

Wilson studied the system. "Yes," he said, "but how do you tell where the other end of the Gate is? Or when? I don't see any graduations."

"You don't need them. You can see where you are. Look." He touched a point under the control framework on the side toward the Gate. A panel rolled back and Wilson saw there was a small image of the Gate itself. Diktor made another adjustment and Wilson found that he could see through the image.

He was gazing into his own room, as if through the wrong end of a telescope. He could make out two figures, but the scale was too small for him to see clearly what they were doing, nor could he tell which editions of himself were there present—if they were in truth himself! He found it quite upsetting. "Shut it off," he said.

Diktor did so and said, "I must not forget to give you your list." He fumbled in his sleeve and produced a slip of paper which he handed to Wilson. "Here—take it."

Wilson accepted it mechanically and stuffed it into his pocket. "See here," he began, "everywhere I go I keep running into myself. I don't like it at all. It's disconcerting. I feel like a whole batch of guinea pigs. I don't half understand what this is all about and now you want to rush me through the Gate again with a bunch of half-baked excuses. Come clean. Tell me what it's all about."

Diktor showed temper in his face for the first time. "You are a stupid and ignorant young fool. I've told you all that you are able to understand. This is a period in history entirely beyond your comprehension. It would take weeks before you would even begin to understand it. I am offering you half a world in return for a few hours' co-operation and you stand there arguing about it. Stow it, I tell you. Now—where shall we set you down?" He reached for the controls.

"Get away from those controls!" Wilson rapped out. He was getting the glimmering of an idea. "Who are you, anyhow?"

"Me? I'm Diktor."

"That's not what I mean and you know it. How did you learn English?"

Diktor did not answer. His face became expressionless.

"Go on," Wilson persisted. "You didn't learn it here; that's a cinch. You're from the twentieth century, aren't you?"

Diktor smiled sourly. "I wondered how long it would take you to figure that out."

Wilson nodded. "Maybe I'm not bright, but I'm not as stupid as you think I am. Come on. Give me the rest of the story."

Diktor shook his head. "It's immaterial. Besides, we're wasting time."

Wilson laughed. "You've tried to hurry me with that excuse once too often. How can we waste time when we have *that?*" He pointed to the controls and to the Gate beyond it. "Unless you lied to me, we can use any slice of time we want to, any time. No, I think I know why you tried to rush me. Either you want to get me out of the picture here, or there is something devilishly dangerous about the job you want me to do. And I know how to settle it—you're going with me!"

"You don't know what you're saying," Diktor answered slowly. "That's impossible. I've got to stay here and manage the controls."

"That's just what you aren't going to do. You could send me through and lose me. I prefer to keep you in sight."

"Out of the question," answered Diktor. "You'll have to trust me." He bent over the controls again.

"Get away from there!" shouted Wilson. "Back out of there before I bop you one." Under Wilson's menacing fist Diktor withdrew from the control pulpit entirely. "There. That's better," he added when both of them were once more on the floor of the hall.

The idea which had been forming in his mind took full shape. The controls, he knew, were still set on his room in the boarding-house where he lived—or had lived—back in the twentieth century. From what he had seen through the speculum of the controls, the time control was set to take him right back to the day in 1942 from which he had started. "Stand there," he commanded Diktor, "I want to see something."

He walked over to the Gate as if to inspect it. Instead of stopping when he reached it, he stepped on through.

He was better prepared for what he found on the other side than he had been on the two earlier occasions of time translation —"earlier" in the sense of sequence in his memory track. Nevertheless it is never too easy on the nerves to catch up with one's self.

For he had done it again. He was back in his own room, but there were two of himself there before him. They were very much preoccupied with each other; he had a few seconds in which to get them straightened out in his mind. One of them had a beautiful black eye and a badly battered mouth. Beside that he was very much in need of a shave. That tagged him. He had been through the Gate at least once. The other, though somewhat in need of shaving himself, showed no marks of a fist fight.

He had them sorted out now, and knew where and *when* he was. It was all still most damnably confusing, but after former—no, not *former*, he amended—*other* experiences with time translation he knew better what to expect. He was back at the beginning again; this time he would put a stop to the crazy nonsense once and for all.

The other two were arguing. One of them swayed drunkenly toward the bed. The other grabbed him by the arm. "You can't do that," he said.

"Let him alone!" snapped Wilson.

The other two swung around and looked him over. Wilson watched the more sober of the pair size him up, saw his expression of amazement change to startled recognition. The other, the earliest Wilson, seemed to have trouble in focusing on him at all. "This is going to be a job," thought Wilson. "The man is positively stinking." He wondered why anyone would be foolish enough to drink on an empty stomach. It was not only stupid, it was a waste of good liquor.

He wondered if they had left a drink for him.

"Who are you?" demanded his drunken double.

Wilson turned to "Joe." "*He* knows me," he said significantly.

"Joe," studied him. "Yes," he conceded, "yes, I suppose I do. But what the deuce are you here for? And why are you trying to bust up the plan?"

Wilson interrupted him. "No time for long-winded explanations. I know more about it than you do—you'll concede that—and my judgment is bound to be better than yours. He doesn't go through the Gate."

"I don't concede anything of the sort—"

The ringing of the telephone checked the argument. Wilson greeted the interruption with relief, for he realized that he had started out on the wrong tack. Was it possible that he was really as dense himself as this lug appeared to be? Did *he* look that way to other people? But the time was too short for self-doubts and soul-searching. "Answer it!" he commanded Bob (Boiled) Wilson.

The drunk looked belligerent, but acceded when he saw that Bob (Joe) Wilson was about to beat him to it.

"Hello. . . . Yes. Who is this? . . . Hello. . . . Hello!"

"Who was that?" asked "Joe."

"Nothing. Some nut with a misplaced sense of humor." The telephone rang again. "There he is again." The drunk grabbed the phone before the others could reach it. "Listen, you butterfly-brained ape! I'm a busy man and this is *not* a public telephone. . . . Huh? Oh, it's you, Genevieve—" Wilson paid little attention to the telephone conversation—he had heard it too many times before, and he had too much on his mind. His earliest *persona* was much too drunk to be reasonable, he realized; he must concentrate on some argument that would appeal to "Joe"—otherwise he was outnumbered. "—Huh? Oh, sure!" the call concluded. "Anyhow, I'll see you tonight. 'By."

Now was the time, thought Wilson, before this dumb yap can open his mouth. What would he say? What would sound convincing?

But the boiled edition spoke first. "Very well, Joe," he stated, "I'm ready to go if you are."

"Fine!" said "Joe." "Just step through. That's all there is to it."

This was getting out of hand, not the way he had planned it at all. "No, you don't!" he barked and jumped in front of the Gate. He would have to make them realize, and quickly.

But he got no chance to do so. The drunk cussed him out, then swung on him; his temper snapped. He knew with sudden fierce exultation that he had been wanting to take a punch at someone for some time. Who did they think they were to be taking chances with his future?

The drunk was clumsy; Wilson stepped under his guard and hit him hard in the face. It was a solid enough punch to have convinced a sober man, but his opponent shook his head and came back for more. "Joe" closed in. Wilson decided that he would have to put his original opponent away in a hurry, and give his attention to "Joe"—by far the more dangerous of the two.

A slight mix-up between the two allies gave him his chance. He stepped back, aimed carefully, and landed a long jab with his left, one of the hardest blows he had ever struck in his life. It lifted his target right off his feet.

As the blow landed Wilson realized his orientation with respect to the Gate, knew with bitter certainty that he had again played through the scene to its inescapable climax.

He was alone with "Joe"; their companion had disappeared through the Gate.

His first impulse was the illogical but quite human and very common feeling of look-what-you-made-me-do. "Now you've done it!" he said angrily.

"Me?" "Joe" protested. "You knocked him through. I never laid a finger on him."

"Yes," Wilson was forced to admit. "But it's your fault," he added, "if you hadn't interfered, I wouldn't have had to do it."

"*Me* interfere? Why, you baldfaced hypocrite, you butted in and tried to queer the pitch. Which reminds me—you owe me some explanations and I damn well mean to have them. What's the idea of—"

"Stow it," Wilson headed him off. He hated to be wrong and he hated still more to have to admit that he was wrong. It had been hopeless from the start, he now realized. He felt bowed down by the utter futility of it. "It's too late now. He's gone through."

"Too late for what?"

"Too late to put a stop to this chain of events." He was aware now that it always had been too late, regardless of what time it was, what year it was, or how many times he came back and tried to stop it. He *remembered* having gone through the first time, he had *seen* himself asleep on the other side. Events would have to work out their weary way.

"Why should we?"

It was not worth while to explain, but he felt the need for self-justification. "Because," he said, "Diktor has played me—I mean has played *you* . . . us—for a dope, for a couple of dopes. Look, he told you that he was going to set you up as a big shot over there, didn't he?"

"Yes—"

"Well, that's a lot of malarkey. All he means to do is to get us so incredibly tangled up in this Gate thing that we'll never get straightened out again."

"Joe" looked at him sharply. "How do you know?"

Since it was largely hunch, he felt pressed for reasonable explanation. "Why go into it?" he evaded. "Why don't you just take my word for it?"

"Why should I?"

Why should you? Why, you lunk, can't you see? I'm yourself, older and more experienced—you *have* to believe me. Aloud he answered, "If you can't take my word, whose word can you take?"

"Joe" grunted. "I'm from Missouri," he said. "I'll see for myself."

Wilson was suddenly aware that "Joe" was about to step through the Gate. "Where are you going?"

"Through! I'm going to look up Diktor and have it out with him."

"Don't!" Wilson pleaded. "Maybe we can break the chain even

now." But the stubborn sulky look on the other's face made him realize how futile it was. He was still enmeshed in inevitability; it *had* to happen. "Go ahead," he shrugged. "It's your funeral. I wash my hands of you."

"Joe" paused at the Gate. "It is, eh? Hm-m-m—how can it be my funeral unless it's *your* funeral, too?"

Wilson stared speechlessly while "Joe" stepped through the Gate. Whose funeral? He had not thought of it in quite that way. He felt a sudden impulse to rush through the Gate, catch up with his alter ego, and watch over him. The stupid fool might do anything. Suppose he got himself killed? Where would that leave Bob Wilson? Dead, of course.

Or would it? Could the death of a man thousands of years in the future kill *him* in the year 1942? He saw the absurdity of the situation suddenly, and felt very much relieved. "Joe's" actions could not endanger him; he remembered everything that "Joe" had done—was going to do. "Joe" would get into an argument with Diktor and, in due course of events, would come back through the Time Gate. No, *had* come back through the Time Gate. He was "Joe." It was hard to remember that.

Yes, he was "Joe." As well as the first guy. They would thread their courses, in and out and roundabout, and end up here, with *him*. Had to.

Wait a minute—in that case the whole crazy business was straightened out. He had gotten away from Diktor, had all of his various personalities sorted out, and was back where he started from, no worse for the wear except for a crop of whiskers and, possibly, a scar on his lip. Well, he knew when to let well enough alone. Shave, and get back to work, kid.

As he shaved he stared at his face and wondered why he had failed to recognize it the first time. He had to admit that he had never looked at it objectively before. He had always taken it for granted.

He acquired a crick in his neck from trying to look at his own profile through the corner of one eye.

On leaving the bathroom the Gate caught his eye forcibly. For some reason he had assumed that it would be gone. It was not. He inspected it, walked around it, carefully refrained from touching it. Wasn't the damned thing ever going to go away? It had served its purpose; why didn't Diktor shut it off?

He stood in front of it, felt a sudden surge of the compulsion that leads men to jump from high places. What would happen if he went through? What would he find? He thought of Arma.

And the other one—what was her name? Perhaps Diktor had not told him. The other maidservant, anyhow, the second one.

But he restrained himself and forced himself to sit back down at the desk. If he was going to stay here—and of course he was, he was resolved on that point—he must finish the thesis. He had to eat; he needed the degree to get a decent job. Now where was he?

Twenty minutes later he had come to the conclusion that the thesis would have to be rewritten from one end to the other. His prime theme, the application of the empirical method of the problems of speculative metaphysics and its expression in rigorous formulae, was still valid, he decided, but he had acquired a mass of new and not yet digested data to incorporate in it. In rereading his manuscript he was amazed to find how dogmatic he had been. Time after time he had fallen into the pathetic fallacy of DesCartes, mistaking clear reasoning for correct reasoning.

He tried to brief a new version of the thesis, but discovered that there were two problems he was forced to deal with which were decidedly not clear in his mind: the problem of the ego and the problem of free will. When there had been three of him in the room, which one was the ego—was *himself*? And how was it that he had been unable to change the course of events?

An absurdly obvious answer to the first question occurred to him at once. The ego was himself. Self is self, an unproved and unprovable first statement, directly experienced. What, then, of the other two? Surely they had been equally sure of ego-being—he remembered it. He thought of a way to state it: Ego is the point of consciousness, the latest term in a continuously expanding series along the line of memory duration. That sounded like a general statement, but he was not sure; he would have to try to formulate it mathematically before he could trust it. Verbal language had such queer booby traps in it.

The telephone rang.

He answered it absent-mindedly. "Yes?"

"Is that you, Bob?"

"Yes. Who is this?"

"Why, it's Genevieve, of course, darling. What's come over you today? That's the second time you've failed to recognize my voice."

Annoyance and frustration rose up in him. Here was another problem he had failed to settle—well, he'd settle it now. He ignored her complaint. "Look here, Genevieve, I've told you not to telephone me while I'm working. Good-by!"

"Well, of all the— You can't talk that way to me, Bob Wilson! In the first place, you weren't working today. In the second place, what makes you think you can use honey and sweet words on me and two hours later snarl at me? I'm not any too sure I want to marry you."

"Marry you? What put that silly idea in your head?"

The phone sputtered for several seconds. When it had abated somewhat he resumed with, "Now just calm down. This isn't the Gay Nineties, you know. You can't assume that a fellow who takes you out a few times intends to marry you."

There was a short silence. "So that's the game, is it?" came an answer at last in a voice so cold and hard and completely shrewish that he almost failed to recognize it. "Well, there's a way to handle men like you. A woman isn't unprotected in this State!"

"You ought to know," he answered savagely. "You've hung around the campus enough years."

The receiver clicked in his ear.

He wiped the sweat from his forehead. That dame, he knew, was quite capable of causing him lots of trouble. He had been warned before he ever started running around with her, but he had been so sure of his own ability to take care of himself. He should have known better—but then he had not expected anything quite as raw as this.

He tried to get back to work on his thesis, but found himself unable to concentrate. The deadline of 10 a. m. the next morning seemed to be racing toward him. He looked at his watch. It had stopped. He set it by the desk clock—four fifteen in the afternoon. Even if he sat up all night he could not possibly finish it properly.

Besides there was Genevieve—

The telephone rang again. He let it ring. It continued; he took the receiver off the cradle. He would *not* talk to her again.

He thought of Arma. There was a proper girl with the right attitude. He walked over to the window and stared down into the dusty, noisy street. Half subconsciously he compared it with the green and placid countryside he had seen from the balcony where he and Diktor had breakfasted. This was a crummy world full of crummy people. He wished poignantly that Diktor had been on the up-and-up with him.

An idea broke surface in his brain and plunged around frantically. The Gate was still open. *The Gate was still open!* Why worry about Diktor? He was his own master. Go back and play it out—everything to gain, nothing to lose.

He stepped up to the Gate, then hesitated. Was he wise to do it? After all, how much did he know about the future?

He heard footsteps climbing the stairs, coming down the hall, no—yes, stopping at his door. He was suddenly convinced that it was Genevieve; that decided him. He stepped through.

The hall of the Gate was empty on his arrival. He hurried around the control box to the door and was just in time to hear, "Come on. There's work to be done." Two figures were retreating down the corridor. He recognized both of them and stopped suddenly.

That was a near thing, he told himself; I'll just have to wait until they get clear. He looked around for a place to conceal himself, but found nothing but the control box. That was useless; they were coming back. Still—

He entered the control box with a plan vaguely forming in his mind. If he found that he could dope out the controls, the Gate might give him all the advantage he needed. First he needed to turn on the speculum gadget. He felt around where he recalled having seen Diktor reach to turn it on, then reached in his pocket for a match.

Instead he pulled out a piece of paper. It was the list that Diktor had given him, the things he was to obtain in the twentieth century. Up to the present moment there had been too much going on for him to look it over.

His eyebrows crawled up his forehead as he read. It was a funny list, he decided. He had subconsciously expected it to call for technical reference books, samples of modern gadgets, weapons. There was nothing of the sort. Still, there was a sort of mad logic to the assortment. After all, Diktor knew these people better than he did. It might be just what was needed.

He revised his plans, subject to being able to work the Gate. He decided to make one more trip back and do the shopping Diktor's list called for—but for his own benefit, not Diktor's. He fumbled in the semidarkness of the control booth, seeking the switch or control for the speculum. His hand encountered a soft mass. He grasped it, and pulled it out.

It was his hat.

He placed it on his head, guessing idly that Diktor had stowed it there, and reached again. This time he brought forth a small notebook. It looked like a find—very possibly Diktor's own notes on the operation of the controls. He opened it eagerly.

It was not what he had hoped. But it did contain page after page of handwritten notes. There were three columns to the page; the first was in English, the second in international phonetic symbols, the third in a completely strange sort of writing. It took no brilliance for him to identify it as a vocabulary. He slipped it into a pocket with a broad smile; it might have taken Diktor months or even years to work out the relationship between the two languages; he would be able to ride on Diktor's shoulders in the matter.

The third try located the control and the speculum lighted up. He felt again the curious uneasiness he had felt before, for he was gazing again into his own room and again it was inhabited by two figures. He did not want to break into that scene again, he was sure. Cautiously he touched one of the colored beads.

The scene shifted, panned out through the walls of the boardinghouse and came to rest in the air, three stories above the campus. He was pleased to have gotten the Gate out of the house, but three stories was too much of a jump. He fiddled with the other two colored beads and established that one of them caused the scene in the speculum to move toward him or away from him while the other moved it up or down.

He wanted a reasonably inconspicuous place to locate the Gate, some place where it would not attract the attention of the curious. This bothered him a bit; there was no ideal place, but he compromised on a blind alley, a little court formed by the campus powerhouse and the rear wall of the library. Cautiously and clumsily he maneuvered his flying eye to the neighborhood he wanted and set it down carefully between the two buildings. He then readjusted his position so that he stared right into a blank wall. Good enough!

Leaving the controls as they were, he hurried out of the booth and stepped unceremoniously back into his own period.

He bumped his nose against the brick wall. "I cut that a little too fine," he mused as he slid cautiously out from between the confining limits of the wall and the Gate. The Gate hung in the air, about fifteen inches from the wall and roughly parallel to it. But there was room enough, he decided—no need to go back and readjust the controls. He ducked out of the areaway and cut across the campus toward the Students' Co-op, wasting no time. He entered and went to the cashier's window.

"Hi, Bob."

"H'lo, Soupy. Cash a check for me?"

"How much?"

"Twenty dollars."

"Well—I suppose so. Is it a good check?"

"Not very. It's my own."

"Well, I might invest in it as a curiosity." He counted out a ten, a five, and five ones.

"Do that," advised Wilson. "My autographs are going to be rare collectors' items." He passed over the check, took the money, and proceeded to the bookstore in the same building. Most of the books on the list were for sale there. Ten minutes later he had acquired title to:

"The Prince," by Niccolo Machiavelli.

"Behind the Ballots," by James Farley.

"Mein Kampf" (unexpurgated), by Adolf Schicklegruber.

"How to Win Friends and Influence People," by Dale Carnegie.

The other titles he wanted were not available in the bookstore; he went from there to the university library where he drew out "Real Estate Broker's Manual," "History of Musical Instruments," and a quarto titled "Evolution of Dress Styles." The latter was a handsome volume with beautiful colored plates and was classified as reference. He had to argue a little to get a twenty-four hour permission for it.

He was fairly well loaded down by then; he left the campus, went to a pawnshop and purchased two used, but sturdy, suitcases into one of which he packed the books. From there he went to the largest music store in the town and spent forty-five minutes in selecting and rejecting phonograph records, with emphasis on swing and boogie-woogie—highly emotional stuff, all of it. He did not neglect classical and semi-classical, but he applied the same rule to those categories—a piece of music had to be sensuous and compelling, rather than cerebral. In consequence his collection included such strangely assorted items as the "Marseillaise," Ravel's "Bolero," four Cole Porter's, and "L'Après-midi d'un Faune."

He insisted on buying the best mechanical reproducer on the market in the face of the clerk's insistence that what he needed was an electrical one. But he finally got his own way, wrote a check for the order, packed it all in his suitcases, and had the clerk get a taxi for him.

He had a bad moment over the check. It was pure rubber, as the one he had cashed at the Students' Co-op had cleaned out his balance. He had urged them to phone the bank, since that was what he wished them not to do. It had worked. He had established, he reflected, the all-time record for kiting checks—thirty thousand years.

When the taxi drew up opposite the court where he had located the Gate, he jumped out and hurried in.

The Gate was gone.

He stood there for several minutes, whistling softly, and assessing—unfavorably—his own abilities, mental processes, et cetera. The consequences of writing bad checks no longer seemed quite so hypothetical.

He felt a touch at his sleeve. "See here, Bud, do you want my hack, or don't you? The meter's still clicking."

"Huh? Oh, sure." He followed the driver, climbed back in.

"Where to?"

That was a problem. He glanced at his watch, then realized that the usually reliable instruments had been through a process which rendered its reading irrelevant. "What time is it?"

"Two fifteen." He reset his watch.

Two fifteen. There would be a jamboree going on in his room at that time of a particularly confusing sort. He did not want to go *there*—not yet. Not until his blood brothers got through playing happy fun games with the Gate.

The Gate!

It would be in his room until sometime after four fifteen. If he timed it right— "Drive to the corner of Fourth and McKinley," he directed, naming the intersection closest to his boardinghouse.

He paid off the taxi driver there, and lugged his bags into the filling station at that corner, where he obtained permission from the attendant to leave them and assurance that they would be safe. He had nearly two hours to kill. He was reluctant to go very far from the house for fear some hitch would upset his timing.

It occurred to him that there was one piece of unfinished business in the immediate neighborhood—and time enough to take care of it. He walked briskly to a point two streets away, whistling cheerfully, and turned in at an apartment house.

In response to his knock the door of Apartment 211 was opened a crack, then wider. "Bob darling! I thought you were working today."

"Hi, Genevieve. Not at all—I've got time to burn."

She glanced back over her shoulder. "I don't know whether I should let you come in—I wasn't expecting you. I haven't washed the dishes, or made the bed. I was just putting on my make-up."

"Don't be coy." He pushed the door open wide, and went on in.

When he came out he glanced at his watch. Three thirty—plenty of time. He went down the street wearing the expression of the canary that ate the cat.

He thanked the service station salesman and gave him a quarter for his trouble, which left him with a lone nickel. He looked at this coin, grinned to himself, and inserted it in the pay phone in the office of the station. He dialed his own number.

"Hello," he heard.

"Hello," he replied. "Is that Bob Wilson?"

"Yes. Who is this?"

"Never mind," he chuckled. "I just wanted to be sure you were there. I thought you would be. You're right in the groove, kid, right in the groove." He replaced the receiver with a grin.

At four ten he was too nervous to wait any longer. Struggling under the load of the heavy suitcases he made his way to the boardinghouse. He let himself in and heard a telephone ringing upstairs. He glanced at his watch—four fifteen. He waited in the hall for three interminable minutes, then labored up the stairs and down the upper hallway to his own door. He unlocked the door and let himself in.

The room was empty, the Gate still there.

Without stopping for anything, filled with apprehension lest the Gate should flicker and disappear while he crossed the floor, he hurried to it, took a firm grip on his bags, and strode through it.

The Hall of the Gate was empty, to his great relief. What a break, he told himself thankfully. Just five minutes, that's all I ask. Five uninterrupted minutes. He set the suitcases down near the Gate to be ready for a quick departure. As he did so he noticed that a large chunk was missing from a corner of one case. Half a book showed through the opening, sheared as neatly as with a printer's trimmer. He identified it as "Mein Kampf."

He did not mind the loss of the book but the implications made him slightly sick at his stomach. Suppose he had not described a clear arc when he had first been knocked through the Gate, had hit the edge, half in and half out? Man Sawed in Half—and no illusion!

He wiped his face and went to the control booth. Following Diktor's simple instructions he brought all four spheres together at the center of the tetrahedron. He glanced over the side of the booth and saw that the Gate had disappeared entirely. "Check!" he thought. "Everything on zero—no Gate." He moved the white sphere slightly. The Gate reappeared. Turning on the speculum he was able to see that the miniature scene showed the inside of the Hall of the Gate itself. So far so good—but he would not be able to tell what time the Gate was set for by looking into the Hall. He displaced a space control slightly; the scene flickered past the walls of the palace and hung in the open air. Returning the white time control to zero he then displaced it very, very slightly. In the miniature scene the sun became a streak of brightness across the sky; the days flickered past like light from a low frequency source of illumination. He increased the displacement a little, saw the ground become sear and brown, then snow covered, and finally green again.

Working cautiously, steadying his right hand with his left, he made the seasons march past. He had counted ten winters when he became aware of voices somewhere in the distance. He stopped and listened, then very hastily returned the space controls to zero, leaving the time control as it was—set for ten years in the past—and rushed out of the booth.

He hardly had time to grasp his bags, lift them, and swing them through the Gate, himself with them. This time he was exceedingly careful not to touch the edge of the circle.

He found himself, as he had planned to, still in the Hall of the Gate, but, if he had interpreted the controls correctly, ten years away from the events he had recently participated in. He had intended to give Diktor a wider berth than that, but there had been no time for it. However, he reflected, since Diktor was, by his own statement and the evidence of the little notebook Wilson had lifted from him, a native of the twentieth century, it was quite possible that ten years was enough. Diktor might not be in this era. If he was, there was always the Time Gate for a gateway. But it was reasonable to scout out the situation first before making any more jumps.

It suddenly occurred to him that Diktor might be looking at him through the speculum of the Time Gate. Without stopping to consider that speed was no protection—since the speculum could be used to view *any* time sector—he hurriedly dragged his two suitcases into the cover of the control booth. Once inside the protecting walls of the booth he calmed down a bit. Spying could work both ways. He found the controls set at zero; making use of the same process he had used once before, he ran the scene in the speculum forward through ten years, then cautiously hunted with the space controls on zero. It was a very difficult task; the time scale necessary to hunt through several months in a few minutes caused any figure which might appear in the speculum to flash past at an apparent speed too fast for his eye to follow. Several times he thought he detected flitting shadows which might be human beings but he was never able to find them when he stopped moving the time control.

He wondered in great exasperation why whoever had built the

double-damned gadget had failed to provide it with graduations and some sort of delicate control mechanism—a vernier, or the like. It was not until much later that it occurred to him that the creator of the Time Gate might have no need of such gross aids to his senses. He would have given up, was about to give up, when, purely by accident, one more fruitless scanning happened to terminate with a figure in the field.

It was himself, carrying two suitcases. He saw himself walking directly into the field of view, grow large, disappear. He looked over the rail, half expecting to see himself step out of the Gate.

But nothing came out of the Gate. It puzzled him, until he recalled that it was the setting at *that* end, ten years in the future, which controlled the time of egress. But he had what he wanted; he sat back and watched. Almost immediately Diktor and another edition of himself appeared in the scene. He recalled the situation when he saw it portrayed in the speculum. It was Bob Wilson number three, about to quarrel with Diktor and make his escape back to the twentieth century.

That was that—Diktor had not seen him, did not know that he had made unauthorized use of the Gate, did not know that he was hiding ten years in the "past," would not look for him there. He returned the controls to zero, and dismissed the matter.

But other matters needed his attention—food, especially. It seemed obvious, in retrospect, that he should have brought along food to last him for a day or two at least. And maybe a .45. He had to admit that he had not been very foresighted. But he easily forgave himself—it was hard to be foresighted when the future kept slipping up behind one. "All right, Bob, old boy," he told himself aloud, "let's see if the natives are friendly—as advertised."

A cautious reconnoiter of the small part of the Palace with which he was acquainted turned up no human beings, nor life of any sort, not even insect life. The place was dead, sterile, as static and unlived-in as a window display. He shouted once, just to hear a voice. The echoes caused him to shiver; he did not do it again.

The architecture of the place confused him. Not only was it strange to his experience—he had expected that—but the place, with minor exceptions, seemed totally unadapted to the uses of human beings. Great halls large enough to hold ten thousand people at once—had there been floors for them to stand on. For there frequently were no floors in the accepted meaning of a level or reasonably level platform. In following a passageway he came suddenly to one of the great mysterious openings in the structure and almost fell in before he realized that his path had terminated. He crawled gingerly forward and looked over the edge. The mouth of the passage debouched high up on a wall of the place; below him the wall was cut back so that there was not even a vertical surface for the eye to follow. Far below him, the wall curved back and met its mate of the opposite side—not decently, in a horizontal plane, but at an acute angle.

There were other openings scattered around the walls, openings as unserviceable to human beings as the one in which he crouched. "The High Ones," he whispered to himself. All his cockiness was gone out of him. He retraced his steps through the fine dust and reached the almost friendly familiarity of the Hall of the Gate.

On his second try he attempted only those passages and compartments which seemed obviously adapted to men. He had already decided what such parts of the Palace must be—servants' quarters, or, more probably, slaves' quarters. He regained his courage by sticking to such area. Though deserted completely, by contrast with the rest of the great structure a room or a passage which seemed to have been built for men was friendly and cheerful. The sourceless ever-present illumination and the unbroken silence still bothered him, but not to the degree to which he had been upset by the Gargantuan and mysteriously convoluted chambers of the "High Ones."

He had almost despaired of finding his way out of the Palace and was thinking of retracing his steps when the corridor he was following turned and he found himself in bright sunlight.

He was standing at the top of a broad steep ramp which spread fanlike down to the base of the building. Ahead of him and below him, distant at least five hundred yards, the pavement of the ramp met the green of sod and bush and tree. It was the same placid, lush, and familiar scene he had looked out over when he breakfasted with Diktor—a few hours ago and ten years in the future.

He stood quietly for a short time, drinking in the sunshine, soaking up the heart-lifting beauty of the warm, spring day. "This is going to be all right," he exulted. "It's a grand place."

He moved slowly down the ramp, his eyes searching for human beings. He was halfway down when he saw a small figure emerge from the trees into a clearing near the foot of the ramp. He called out to it in joyous excitement. The child—it was a child he saw—looked up, stared at him for a moment, then fled back into the shelter of the trees.

"Impetuous, Robert—that's what you are," he chided himself.

"Don't scare 'em. Take it easy." But he was not made down-hearted by the incident. Where there were children there would be parents, society, opportunities for a bright, young fellow who took a broad view of things. He moved on down at a leisurely pace.

A man showed up at the point where the child had disappeared. Wilson stood still. The man looked him over and advanced hesitantly a step or two. "Come here!" Wilson invited in a friendly voice. "I won't hurt you."

The man could hardly have understood his words, but he advanced slowly. At the edge of the pavement he stopped, eyed it and would not proceed farther.

Something about the behavior pattern clicked in Wilson's brain, fitted in with what he had seen in the Palace, and with the little that Diktor had told him. "Unless," he told himself, "the time I spent in 'Anthropology I' was totally wasted, this Palace is tabu, and the ramp I'm standing on is tabu, and, by contagion, I'm tabu. Play your cards, son, play your cards!"

He advanced to the edge of the pavement, being careful not to step off it. The man dropped to his knees and cupped his hands in front of him, head bowed. Without hesitation Wilson touched him on the forehead. The man got back to his feet, his face radiant.

"This isn't even sporting," Wilson said. "I ought to shoot him on the rise."

His Man Friday cocked his head, looked puzzled, and answered in a deep, melodious voice. The words were liquid and strange and sounded like a phrase from a song. "You ought to commercialize that voice," Wilson said admiringly. "Some stars get by on less. However— Get along now, and fetch something to eat. Food." He pointed to his mouth.

The man looked hesitant, spoke again. Bob Wilson reached into his pocket and took out the stolen notebook. He looked up "eat," then looked up "food." It was the same word. "Blellan," he said carefully.

"Blellaaaan?"

"Blellaaaaaaaan," agreed Wilson. "You'll have to excuse my accent. Hurry up." He tried to find "hurry" in the vocabulary, but it was not there. Either the language did not contain the idea or Diktor had not thought it worth while to record it. But we'll soon fix that, Wilson thought—if there isn't such a word, I'll give 'em one.

The man departed.

Wilson sat himself down Turk-fashion and passed the time by studying the notebook. The speed of his rise in these parts, he decided, was limited only by the time it took him to get into full communication. But he had only time enough to look up a few common substantives when his first acquaintance returned, in company.

The procession was headed by an extremely elderly man, white-haired but beardless. All of the men were beardless. He walked under a canopy carried by four male striplings. Only he of all the crowd wore enough clothes to get by anywhere but on a beach. He was looking uncomfortable in a sort of toga effect which appeared to have started life as a Roman-striped awning. That he was the head man was evident.

Wilson hurriedly looked up the word for "chief."

The word for chief was "Diktor."

It should not have surprised him, but it did. It was, of course, a logical probability that the word "Diktor" was a title rather than a proper name. It simply had not occurred to him.

Diktor—*the* Diktor—had added a note under the word. "One of the few words," Wilson read, "which shows some probability of having been derived from the dead languages. This word, a few dozen others, and the grammatical structure of the language itself, appear to be the only link between the language of the 'Forsaken Ones' and the English language."

The chief stopped in front of Wilson, just short of the pavement. "O. K., Diktor," Wilson ordered, "kneel down. You're not exempt." He pointed to the ground. The chief knelt down. Wilson touched his forehead.

The food that had been fetched along was plentiful and very palatable. Wilson ate slowly and with dignity, keeping in mind the importance of face. While he ate he was serenaded by the entire assemblage. The singing was excellent, he was bound to admit. Their ideas of harmony he found a little strange and the performance, as a whole, seemed primitive, but their voices were all clear and mellow and they sang as if they enjoyed it.

The concert gave Wilson an idea. After he had satisfied his hunger he made the chief understand, with the aid of the indispensable little notebook, that he and his flock were to wait where they were. He then returned to the Hall of the Gate and brought back from there the phonograph and a dozen assorted records. He treated them to a recorded concert of "modern" music.

The reaction exceeded his hopes. "Begin the Beguine" caused tears to stream down the face of the old chief. The first movement of Tschaikowsky's "Concerto Number One in B Flat Minor" practically stampeded them. They jerked. They held their heads and moaned. They shouted their applause. Wilson refrained from giving them the second movement, tapered them off instead with the compelling monotony of the "Bolero."

"Diktor," he said—he was not thinking of the old chief—"Diktor, old chum, you certainly had these people doped out when you sent me shopping. By the time you show up—if you ever do—I'll own the place."

This is not an account of how Boosterism came to Arcadia. Wilson's rise to power was more in the nature of a triumphal progress than a struggle for supremacy; it contained little that was dramatic. Whatever it was that the High Ones had done to the human race it had left them with only physical resemblance and with temperament largely changed. The docile friendly children with whom Wilson dealt had little in common with the brawling, vulgar, lusty, dynamic swarms who had once called themselves the People of the United States.

The relationship was like that of Jersey cattle to longhorns, or cocker spaniels to wolves. The fight was gone out of them. It was not that they lacked intelligence, nor civilized arts; it was the competitive spirit that was gone, the will-to-power.

Wilson had a monopoly on that.

But even he lost interest in playing a game that he always won. Having established himself as boss man by taking up residence in the Palace and representing himself as the viceroy of the departed High Ones, he, for a time, busied himself in organizing certain projects intended to bring the culture "up-to-date"—the reinvention of musical instruments, establishment of a systematic system of mail service, redevelopment of the idea of styles in dress and a tabu against wearing the same fashion more than one season. There was cunning in the latter project. He figured that arousing a hearty interest in display in the minds of the women-folk would force the men to hustle to satisfy their wishes. What the culture lacked was drive—it was slipping downhill. He tried to give them the drive they lacked.

His subjects co-operated with his wishes, but in a bemused fashion, like a dog performing a trick, not because he understands it, but because his master and godhead desires it.

He soon tired of it.

But the mystery of the High Ones, and especially the mystery of their Time Gate, still remained to occupy his mind. His was a mixed nature, half hustler, half philosopher. The philosopher had his inning.

It was intellectually necessary to him that he be able to construct in his mind a physio-mathematical model for the phenomena exhibited by the Time Gate. He achieved one, not a good one perhaps, but one which satisfied all of the requirements. Think of a plane surface, a sheet of paper, or, better yet, a silk handkerchief—silk, because it has no rigidity, folds easily, while maintaining all of the relational attributes of a two-dimensional continuum on the surface of the silk itself. Let the threads of the woof be the dimension—or direction—of time; let the threads of the warp represent all three of the space dimensions.

An ink spot on the handkerchief becomes the Time Gate. By folding the handkerchief that spot may be superposed on any other spot on the silk. Press the two spots together between thumb and forefinger; the controls are set, the Time Gate is open, a microscopic inhabitant of this piece of silk may crawl from one fold to the other without traversing any other part of the cloth.

The model is imperfect; the picture is static—but a physical picture is necessarily limited by the sensory experience of the person visualizing it.

He could not make up his mind whether or not the concept of folding the four-dimensional continuum—three of space, one of time—back on itself so that the Gate was "open" required the concept of higher dimensions through which to fold it. It seemed so, yet it might simply be an intellectual shortcoming of the human mind. Nothing but empty space was required for the "folding," but "empty space" was itself a term totally lacking in meaning—he was enough of a mathematician to know that.

If higher dimensions were required to "hold" a four-dimensional continuum, then the number of dimensions of space and of time were necessarily infinite; each order requires the next higher order to maintain it.

But "infinite" was another meaningless term. "Open series" was a little better, but not much.

Another consideration forced him to conclude that there was probably at least one more dimension than the four his senses could perceive—the Time Gate itself. He became quite skilled in handling its controls, but he never acquired the foggiest notion of how it worked, or how it had been built. It seemed to him that the creatures who built it must necessarily have been able to stand outside the limits that confined him in order to anchor the Gate to the structure of space time. The concept escaped him.

He suspected that the controls he saw were simply the part that stuck through into the space he knew. The very Palace itself

might be no more than a three-dimensional section of a more involved structure. Such a condition would help to explain the
otherwise inexplicable nature of its architecture.

He became possessed of an overpowering desire to know more
about these strange creatures, the "High Ones," who had come
and ruled the human race and built this Palace and this Gate,
and gone away again—and in whose backwash he had been flung
out of his setting some thirty millennia. To the human race they
were no more than a sacred myth, a contradictory mass of tradition. No picture of them remained, no trace of their writing, nothing of their works save the High Palace of Norkaal and the Gate.
And a sense of irreparable loss in the hearts of the race they had
ruled, a loss expressed by their own term for themselves—the Forsaken Ones.

With controls and speculum he hunted back through time,
seeking the Builders. It was slow work, as he had found before.
A passing shadow, a tedious retracing—and failure.

Once he was sure that he had seen such a shadow in the miniature Hall reflected in the speculum. He set the controls back
far enough to be sure that he had repassed it, armed himself with
food and drink, and waited.

He waited three weeks.

The shadow might have passed during the hours he was forced
to take out for sleep. But he felt sure that he was in the right
period; he kept up the vigil.

He saw it.

It was moving toward the Gate.

When he pulled himself together he was halfway down the passageway leading away from the Hall. He realized that he had
been screaming. He still had an attack of the shakes.

Somewhat later he forced himself to return to the Hall, and,
with eyes averted, enter the control booth and return the spheres
to zero. He backed out hastily and left the Hall for his apartment.
He did not touch the controls nor enter the Hall for more than
two years.

It had not been fear of physical menace that had shaken his
reason, nor the appearance of the creature—he could recall nothing of *how* it looked. It had been a feeling of sadness infinitely
compounded which had flooded through him at the instant, a
sense of tragedy, of grief insupportable and unescapable, of infinite weariness. He had been flicked with emotions many times
too strong for his spiritual fiber and which he was no more fitted
to experience than an oyster is to play a violin.

He felt that he had learned all about the High Ones a man

could learn and still endure. He was no longer curious. The shadow of that vicarious emotion ruined his sleep, brought him sweating out of dreams.

One other problem bothered him—the problem of himself and his meanders through time. It still worried him that he had met himself coming back, so to speak, had talked with himself, fought with himself.

Which one was *himself?*

He was all of them, he knew, for he remembered being each one. How about the times when there had been more than one present?

By sheer necessity he was forced to expand the principle of nonidentity—"Nothing is identical with anything else, not even with itself"—to include the ego. In a four-dimensional continuum each event is an absolute individual, it has its space co-ordinates and its date. The Bob Wilson he was right now was *not* the Bob Wilson he had been ten minutes ago. Each was a discrete section of a four-dimensional process. One resembled the other in many particulars, as one slice of bread resembles the slice next to it. But they were *not* the same Bob Wilson—they differed by a length of time.

When he had doubled back on himself, the difference had become apparent, for the separation was now in space rather than in time, and he happened to be so equipped as to be able to see a space length, whereas he could only remember a time difference. Thinking back he could remember a great many different Bob Wilsons, baby, small child, adolescent, young man. They were all different—he knew that. The only thing that bound them together into a feeling of identity was continuity of memory.

And that was the same thing that bound together the three—no, four, Bob Wilsons on a certain crowded afternoon, a memory track that ran through all of them. The only thing about it that remained remarkable was time travel itself.

And a few other little items—the nature of "free will," the problem of entropy, the law of the conservation of energy and mass. The last two, he now realized, needed to be extended or generalized to include the cases in which the Gate, or something like it, permitted a leak of mass, energy, or entropy from one neighborhood in the continuum to another. They were otherwise unchanged and valid. Free will was another matter. It could not be laughed off, because it could be directly experienced—yet his own free will had worked to create the same scene over and over again. Apparently human will must be considered as one of the factors which make up the processes in the continuum—"free" to the ego, mechanistic from the outside.

And yet his last act of evading Diktor had apparently changed the course of events. He was here and running the country, had been for many years, but Diktor had not showed up. Could it be that each act of "true" free will created a new and different future? Many philosophers had thought so.

This future appeared to have no such person as Diktor—*the* Diktor—in it, anywhere or anywhen.

As the end of his first ten years in the future approached, he became more and more nervous, less and less certain of his opinion. Damnation, he thought, if Diktor is going to show up it was high time that he did so. He was anxious to come to grips with him, establish which was to be boss.

He had agents posted throughout the country of the Forsaken Ones with instructions to arrest any man with hair on his face and fetch him forthwith to the Palace. The Hall of the Gate he watched himself.

He tried fishing the future for Diktor, but had no significant luck. He thrice located a shadow and tracked it down; each time it was himself. From tedium and partly from curiosity he attempted to see the other end of the process; he tried to relocate his original home, thirty thousand years in the past.

It was a long chore. The further the time button was displaced from the center, the poorer the control became. It took patient practice to be able to stop the image within a century or so of the period he wanted. It was in the course of this experimentation that he discovered what he had once looked for, a fractional control—a vernier, in effect. It was as simple as the primary control, but twist the bead instead of moving it directly.

He steadied down on the twentieth century, approximated the year by the models of automobiles, types of architecture, and other gross evidence, and stopped in what he believed to be 1942. Careful displacement of the space controls took him to the university town where he had started—after several false tries; the image did not enable him to read road signs.

He located his boardinghouse, brought the Gate into his own room. It was vacant, no furniture in it.

He panned away from the room, and tried again, a year earlier. Success—his own room, his own furniture, but empty. He ran rapidly back, looking for shadows.

There! He checked the swing of the image. There were three figures in the room, the image was too small, the light too poor for him to be sure whether or not one of them was himself. He leaned over and studied the scene.

He heard a dull thump outside the booth. He straightened up and looked over the side.

Sprawled on the floor was a limp human figure. Near it lay a crushed and battered hat.

He stood perfectly still for an uncounted time, staring at the two redundant figures, hat and man, while the winds of unreason swept through his mind and shook it. He did not need to examine the unconscious form to identify it. He knew . . . *he knew*—it was his younger self, knocked willy-nilly through the Time Gate.

It was not that fact in itself which shook him. He had not particularly expected it to happen, having come tentatively to the conclusion that he was living in a different, an alternative, future from the one in which he had originally transmitted the Time Gate. He had been aware that it might happen, nevertheless, that it did happen did not surprise him.

When it did happen, *he himself had been the only spectator!*

He was Diktor. He was *the* Diktor. He was *the only* Diktor!

He would never find Diktor, nor have it out with him. He need never fear his coming. There never had been, never would be, any other person called Diktor, because Diktor never had been nor ever would be anyone but himself.

In review, it seemed obvious that he must be Diktor; there were so many bits of evidence pointing to it. And yet it had not been obvious. Each point of similarity between himself and the Diktor, he recalled, had arisen from rational causes—usually from his desire to ape the gross characteristics of the "other" and thereby consolidate his own position of power and authority before the "other" Diktor showed up. For that reason he had established himself in the very apartments that "Diktor" had used—so that they would be "his" first.

To be sure his people called him Diktor, but he had thought nothing of that—they called anyone who ruled by that title, even the little subchieftains who were his local administrators.

He had grown a beard, such as Diktor had worn, partly in imitation of the "other" man's precedent, but more to set him apart from the hairless males of the Forsaken Ones. It gave him prestige, increased his tabu. He fingered his bearded chin. Still, it seemed strange that he had not recalled that his own present appearance checked with the appearance of "Diktor." "Diktor" had been an older man. He himself was only thirty-two, ten here, twenty-two *there*.

Diktor he had judged to be about forty-five. Perhaps an unprejudiced witness would believe himself to be that age. His hair and beard were shot with gray—had been, ever since the year he had succeeded too well in spying on the High Ones. His face was lined. Uneasy lies the head and so forth. Running a country, even a peaceful Arcadia, will worry a man, keep him awake nights.

Not that he was complaining—it had been a good life, a grand life, and it beat anything the ancient past had to offer.

In any case, he had been looking for a man in his middle forties, whose face he remembered dimly after ten years and whose picture he did not have. It had never occurred to him to connect that blurred face with his present one. Naturally not.

But there were other little things. Arma, for example. He had selected a likely-looking lass some three years back and made her one of his household staff, renaming her Arma in sentimental memory of the girl he had once fancied. It was logically necessary that they were the same girl, not two Armas, but one.

But, as he recalled her, the "first" Arma had been much prettier.

Hm-m-m—it must be his own point of view that had changed. He admitted that he had had much more opportunity to become bored with exquisite female beauty than his young friend over there on the floor. He recalled with a chuckle how he had found it necessary to surround himself with an elaborate system of tabus to keep the nubile daughters of his subjects out of his hair—most of the time. He had caused a particular pool in the river adjacent to the Palace to be dedicated to his use in order that he might swim without getting tangled up in mermaids.

The man on the floor groaned, but did not open his eyes.

Wilson, the Diktor, bent over him but made no effort to revive him. That the man was not seriously injured he had reason to be certain. He did not wish him to wake up until he had had time to get his own thoughts entirely in order.

For he had work to do, work which must be done meticulously, without mistake. Everyone, he thought with a wry smile, makes plans to provide for their future.

He was about to provide for his past.

There was the matter of the setting of the Time Gate when he got around to sending his early self back. When he had tuned in on the scene in his room a few minutes ago, he had picked up the action just before his early self had been knocked through. In sending him back he must make a slight readjustment in the time setting to an instant around two o'clock of that particular afternoon. That would be simple enough; he need only search a short sector until he found his early self alone and working at his desk.

But the Time Gate had appeared in that room at a later hour; he had just caused it to do so. He felt confused.

Wait a minute, now—if he changed the setting of the time control, the Gate would appear in his room at the earlier time, remain there, and simply blend into its "reappearance" an hour or so later. Yes, that was right. To a person in the room it would simply be as if the Time Gate had been there all along, from about two o'clock.

Which it had been. He would see to that.

Experienced as he was with the phenomena exhibited by the Time Gate, it nevertheless required a strong and subtle intellectual effort to think other than in durational terms, to take an *eternal* viewpoint.

And there was the hat. He picked it up and tried it on. It did not fit very well, no doubt because he was wearing his hair longer now. The hat must be placed where it would be found— Oh, yes, in the control booth. And the notebook, too.

The notebook, the notebook— Mm-m-m— Something funny, there. When the notebook he had stolen had become dog-eared and tattered almost to illegibility some four years back, he had carefully recopied its contents in a new notebook—to refresh his memory of English rather than from any need for it as a guide. The worn-out notebook he had destroyed; it was the new one he intended to obtain, and leave to be found.

In that case, *there never had been two notebooks*. The one he had now would become, after being taken through the Gate to a point ten years in the past, the notebook from which he had copied it. They were simply different segments of the same physical process, manipulated by means of the Gate to run concurrently, side by side, for a certain length of time.

As he had himself—one afternoon.

He wished that he had not thrown away the worn-out notebook. If he had it at hand, he could compare them and convince himself that they were identical save for the wear and tear of increasing entropy.

But when had he learned the language, in order that he might prepare such a vocabulary? To be sure, when he copied it he then *knew* the language—copying had not actually been necessary.

But he *had* copied it.

The physical process he had all straightened out in his mind, but the intellectual process it represented was completely circular. His older self had taught his younger self a language which the older self knew because the younger self, after being taught, grew up to be the older self and was, therefore, capable of teaching.

But where had it started?

Which comes first, the hen or the egg?

You feed the rats to the cats, skin the cats, and feed the carcasses of the cats to the rats who are in turn fed to the cats. The perpetual motion fur farm.

If God created the world, who created God?

Who wrote the notebook? Who started the chain?

He felt the intellectual desperation of any honest philosopher. He knew that he had about as much chance of understanding such problems as a collie has of understanding how dog food gets into cans. Applied psychology was more his size—which reminded him that there were certain books which his early self would find very useful in learning how to deal with the political affairs of the country he was to run. He made a mental note to make a list.

The man on the floor stirred again, sat up. Wilson knew that the time had come when he must insure his past. He was not worried; he felt the sure confidence of the gambler who is "hot," who *knows* what the next roll of the dice will show.

He bent over his alter ego. "Are you all right?" he asked.

"I guess so," the younger man mumbled. He put his hand to his bloody face. "My head hurts."

"I should think it would," Wilson agreed. "You came through head over heels. I think you hit your head when you landed."

His younger self did not appear fully to comprehend the words at first. He looked around dazedly, as if to get his bearings. Presently he said, "Came through? Came through what?"

"The Gate, of course," Wilson told him. He nodded his head toward the Gate, feeling that the sight of it would orient the still groggy younger Bob.

Young Wilson looked over his shoulder in the direction indicated, sat up with a jerk, shuddered and closed his eyes. He opened them again after what seemed to be a short period of prayer, looked again, and said, "Did I come through that?"

"Yes," Wilson assured him.

"Where am I?"

"In the Hall of the Gate in the High Palace of Norkaal. But what is more important," Wilson added, "is *when* you are. You have gone forward a little more than thirty thousand years."

The knowledge did not seem to reassure him. He got up and stumbled toward the Gate. Wilson put a restraining hand on his shoulder. "Where are you going?"

"Back!"

"Not so fast." He did not dare let him go back yet, not until the Gate had been reset. Besides he was still drunk—his breath was staggering. "You will go back all right—I give you my word on that. But let me dress your wounds first. And you should rest. I have some explanations to make to you, and there is an errand you can do for me when you get back—to our mutual advantage. There is a great future in store for you and me, my boy—a great future!"

A great future!

1941

The Push of a Finger /

by ALFRED BESTER

*—or a careless word, for that matter, can wreck the entire universe.
Think not? Well, if it happened this way—*

I think it's about time someone got all those stories together and
burned them. You know the kind I mean—X, the mad scientist,
wants to change the world; Y, the ruthless dictator, wants to rule
the world; Z, the alien planet, wants to destroy the world.

Let me tell you a different kind of story. It's about a whole
world that wanted to rule one man—about a planet of people who
hunted down a single individual in an effort to change his life,
yes, and even destroy him, if it had to be. It's a story about one
man against the entire Earth, but with the positions reversed.

They've got a place in Manhattan City that isn't very well
known. Not known, I mean, in the sense that the cell-nucleus
wasn't known until scientists began to get the general idea. This
was an undiscovered cell-nucleus, and still is, I imagine. It's the
pivot of our Universe. Anything that shakes the world comes out
of it; and, strangely enough, any shake that does come out of it
is intended to prevent worse upheavals.

Don't ask questions now. I'll explain as I go along.

The reason the average man doesn't know about this particular
nucleus is that he'd probably go off his nut if he did. Our officials
make pretty sure it's kept secret, and although some nosybodies
would scream to high heaven if they found out something was
being kept from the public, anyone with sense will admit it's for
the best.

It's a square white building about ten stories high and it looks
like an abandoned hospital. Around nine o'clock in the morning
you can see a couple of dozen ordinary looking citizens arriving,
and at the end of the workday some of them leave. But there's a
considerable number that stay overtime and work until dawn or
until the next couple of dawns. They're cautious about keeping
windows covered so that high-minded citizens won't see the light

and run to the controller's office yawping about overtime and breaking down Stability. Also they happen to have permission.

Yeah, it's real big-time stuff. These fellas are so important, and their work is so important they've got permission to break the one unbreakable law. They can work overtime. In fact as far as they're concerned they can do any damned thing they please, Stability or no Stability—because it so happens they're the babies that maintain Stability. How? Take it easy. We've got plenty of time—and I'll tell you.

It's called the Prog Building and it's one of the regular newspaper beats, just like the police courts used to be a couple of hundred years ago. Every paper sends a reporter down there at three o'clock. The reporters hang around and bull for a while and then some brass hat interviews them and talks policy and economics and about how the world is doing and how it's going to do. Usually it's dull stuff but every once in a while something really big comes out, like the time they decided to drain the Mediterranean. They—

What?

You never heard of that? Say, who is this guy anyway? Are you kidding? From the Moon, hey, all your life? Never been to the home planet? Never heard about what goes on? A real cosmic hick. Baby, you can roll me in a rug. I thought your kind died out before I was born. O. K., you go ahead and ask questions whenever you want. Maybe I'd better apologize now for the slang. It's part and parcel of the newspaper game. Maybe you won't be able to understand me sometimes, but I've got a heart of gold.

Anyway—I had the regular three o'clock beat at the Prog Building and this particular day I got there a little early. Seems the *Trib* had a new reporter on the beat, guy by the name of Halley Hogan, whom I'd never met. I wanted to get together with him and talk policy. For the benefit of the hermit from the Moon I'll explain that no two newspapers in any city are permitted to share the same viewpoint or opinion.

I thought all you boys knew that. Well, sure—I'm not kidding. Look. Stability is the watchword of civilization. The world must be Stable, right? Well, Stability doesn't mean stasis. Stability is reached through an equipoise of opposing forces that balance each other. Newspapers are supposed to balance the forces of public opinion so they have to represent as many different points of view as possible. We reporters always got together before a story, or after, and made sure none of us would agree on our attitudes. You know—some would say it was a terrible thing and some would say it was a wonderful thing and some would say it didn't mean a thing and so on. I was with the *Times* and our natural competitor and opposition was the *Trib*.

The newspaper room in the Prog Building is right next to the main offices, just off the foyer. It's a big place with low-beamed ceiling and walls done in synthetic wood panels. There was a round table in the center surrounded by hardwood chairs, but we stood the chairs along the wall and dragged up the big deep leather ones. We all would sit with our heels on the table and every chair had a groove on the table in front of it. There was an unwritten law that no shop could be talked until every groove was filled with a pair of heels. That's a newspaper man's idea of a pun.

I was surprised to find almost everybody was in. I slipped into my place and upped with my feet and then took a look around. Every sandal showed except the pair that should have been opposite me, so I settled back and shut my eyes. That was where the *Trib* man should have been parked, and I certainly couldn't talk without my opposition being there to contradict me.

The *Post* said: "What makes, Carmichael?"

I said: "Ho-hum—"

The *Post* said: "Don't sleep, baby, there's big things cookin'."

The *Ledger* said: "Shuddup, you know the rules—" He pointed to the vacant segment of the table.

I said: "You mean the law of the jungle."

The *Record*, who happened to be the *Ledger's* opposition, said: "Old Bobbus left. He ain't coming in no more."

"How come?"

"Got a Stereo contract. Doing comedy scenarios."

I thought to myself: "Oi, that means another wrestling match." You see, whenever new opposition reporters get together, they're supposed to have a symbolic wrestling match. I said supposed. It always turns into a brawl with everybody else having the fun.

"Well," I said, "this new Hogan probably doesn't know the ropes yet. I guess I'll have to go into training. Anybody seen him? He look strong?" They all shook their heads and said they didn't know him. "O. K., then let's gab without him—"

The *Post* said: "Your correspondent has it that the pot's a-boilin'. Every bigwig in town is in there." He jabbed his thumb toward the main offices.

We all gave the door a glance, only, like I always did, I tried to knock it in with a look. You see, although all of us came down to the Prog Building every day, none of us knew what was inside.

Yeah, 's' fact. We just came and sat and listened to the big shots and went away. Like specters at the feast. It griped all of us, but me most of all.

I would dream about it at night. How there was a Hyperman living in the Prog Building, only he breathed chlorine and they kept him in tanks. Or that they had the mummies of all the great men of the past which they reanimated every afternoon to ask questions. Or it would be a cow in some dreams that was full of brains and they'd taught it to "moo" in code. There were times when I thought that if I didn't get upstairs into the Prog Building I'd burst from frustration.

So I said: "You think they're going to fill up the Mediterranean again?"

The *Ledger* laughed. He said: "I hear tell they're going to switch poles. North to south and vice versa."

The *Record* said: "You don't think they could?"

The *Ledger* said: "I wish they would—if it'd improve my bridge."

I said: "Can it, lads, and let's have the dope."

The *Journal* said: "Well, all the regulars are in—controller, vice con and deputy vice con. But there also happens to be among those present—the chief stabilizer."

"No!"

He nodded and the others nodded. "Fact. The C-S himself. Came up by pneumatic from Washington."

I said: "Oh, mamma! Five'll get you ten they're digging up Atlantis this time."

The *Record* shook his head. "The C-S didn't wear a digging look."

Just then the door to the main office shoved open and the C-S came thundering out. I'm not exaggerating. Old Groating had a face like Moses, beard and all, and when he frowned, which was now, you expected lightning to crackle from his eyes. He breezed past the table with just one glance from the blue quartz he's got for eyes, and all our legs came down with a crash. Then he shot out of the room so fast I could hear his rep tunic swish with quick whistling sounds.

After him came the controller, the vice con and the deputy vice con, all in single file. They were frowning, too, and moving so rapidly we had to jump to catch the deputy. We got him at the door and swung him around. He was short and fat and trouble didn't sit well on his pudgy face. It made him look slightly lop-sided.

He said: "Not now, gentlemen."

"Just a minute, Mr. Klang," I said, "I don't think you're being fair to the press."

"I know it," the deputy said, "and I'm sorry, but I really cannot spare the time."

I said: "So we report to fifteen million readers that time can't be spared these days—"

He stared at me, only I'd been doing some staring myself and I knew I had to get him to agree to give us a release.

I said: "Have a heart. If anything's big enough to upset the stability of the chief stabilizer, we ought to get a look-in."

That worried him, and I knew it would. Fifteen million people would be more than slightly unnerved to read that the C-S had been in a dither.

"Listen," I said. "What goes on? What were you talking about upstairs?"

He said: "All right. Come down to my office with me. We'll prepare a release."

Only I didn't go out with the rest of them. Because, you see, while I'd been nudging the deputy I'd noticed that all of them had rushed out so fast they'd forgotten to close the office door. It was the first time I'd seen it unlocked and I knew I was going to go through it this time. That was why I'd wheedled that release out of the deputy. I was going to get upstairs into the Prog Building because everything played into my hands. First, the door being left open. Second, the man from the *Trib* not being there.

Why? Well, don't you see? The opposition papers always paired off. The *Ledger* and the *Record* walked together and the *Journal* and the *News* and so on. This way I was alone with no one to look for me and wonder what I was up to. I pushed around in the crowd a little as they followed the deputy out, and managed to be the last one in the room. I slipped back behind the door jamb, waited a second and then streaked across to the office door. I went through it like a shot and shut it behind me. When I had my back against it I took a breath and whispered: "Hyperman, here I come!"

I was standing in a small hall that had synthetic walls with those fluorescent paintings on them. It was pretty short, had no doors anywhere, and led toward the foot of a white staircase. The only way I could go was forward, so I went. With that door locked behind me I knew I would be slightly above suspicion—but only slightly, my friends, only slightly. Sooner or later someone was going to ask who I was.

The stairs were very pretty. I remember them because they were the first set I'd ever seen outside the Housing Museum. They had white even steps and they curved upwards like a conic section. I ran my fingers along the smooth stone balustrade and trudged up expecting anything from a cobra to one of Tex Richard's Fighting Robots to jump out at me. I was scared to death.

I came to a square railed landing and it was then I first sensed the vibrations. I'd thought it was my heart whopping against my ribs with that peculiar *bam-bam-bam* that takes your breath away and sets a solid lump of cold under your stomach. Then I realized this pulse came from the Prog Building itself. I trotted up the rest of the stairs on the double and came to the top. There was a sliding door there. I took hold of the knob and thought: "Oh, well, they can only stuff me and put me under glass"—so I shoved the door open.

Boys, this was it—that nucleus I told you about. I'll try to give you an idea of what it looked like because it was the most sensational thing I've ever seen—and I've seen plenty in my time. The room took up the entire width of the building and it was two stories high. I felt as though I'd walked into the middle of a clock. Space was literally filled with the shimmer and spin of cogs and cams that gleamed with the peculiar highlights you see on a droplet of water about to fall. All of those thousands of wheels spun in sockets of precious stone—just like a watch only bigger— and those dots of red and yellow and green and blue fire burned until they looked like a painting by that Frenchman from way back. Seurat was his name.

The walls were lined with banks of Computation Integraphs— you could see the end-total curves where they were plotted on photoelectric plates. The setting dials for the Integraphs were all at eye level and ran around the entire circumference of the room like a chain of enormous white-faced periods. That was about all of the stuff I could recognize. The rest just looked complicated and bewildering.

That *bam-bam-bam* I told you about came from the very center of the room. There was a crystal octahedron maybe ten feet high, nipped between vertical axes above and below. It was spinning slowly so that it looked jerky, and the vibration was the sound of the motors that turned it. From way high up there were shafts of light projected at it. The slow turning facets caught those beams and shattered them and sent them dancing through the room. Boys—it was really sensational.

I took a couple of steps in and then a little old coot in a white jacket bustled across the room, saw me, nodded, and went about his business. He hadn't taken more than another three steps when he stopped and came back to me. It was a real slow take.

He said: "I don't quite—" and then he broke off doubtfully. He had a withered, faraway look, as though he'd spent all his life trying to remember he was alive.

I said: "I'm Carmichael."

"O yes!" he began, brightening a little. Then his face got dubious again.

I played it real smart. I said: "I'm with Stabilizer Groating."

"Secretary?"

"Yeah."

"You know, Mr. Mitchell," he said, "I can't help feeling that despite the gloomier aspects there are some very encouraging features. The Ultimate Datum System that we have devised should bring us down to surveys of the near future in a short time—" He gave me a quizzical glance like a dog begging for admiration on his hind legs.

I said: "Really?"

"It stands to reason. After all, once a technique has been devised for pushing analysis into the absolute future, a comparatively simple reversal should bring it as close as tomorrow."

I said: "It should at that"—and wondered what he was talking about. Now that some of the fright had worn off I was feeling slightly disappointed. Here I expected to find the Hyperman who was handing down Sinai Decrees to our bosses and I walk into a multiplied clock.

He was rather pleased. He said: "You think so?"

"I think so."

"Will you mention that to Mr. Groating? I feel it might encourage him—"

I got even smarter. I said: "To tell you the truth, sir, the Stabilizer sent me up for a short review. I'm new to the staff and unfortunately I was delayed in Washington."

He said: "*Tut-Tut*, forgive me. Step this way, Mr. . . . Mr. Ahh—"

So I stepped his way and we went weaving through the clockworks to a desk at one side of the room. There were half a dozen chairs behind it and he seated me alongside himself. The flat top of the desk was banked with small tabs and push buttons so that it looked like a stenotype. He pressed one stud and the room darkened. He pressed another and the *bam-bam* quickened until it was a steady hum. The octahedron crystal whirled so quickly that it became a shadowy mist of light under the projectors.

"I suppose you know," the old coot said in rather self-conscious tones, "that this is the first time we've been able to push our definitive analysis to the ultimate future. We'd never have done it if Wiggons hadn't developed his self-checking data systems."

I said: "Good for Wiggons," and I was more confused than ever. I tell you, boys, it felt like waking up from a dream you couldn't quite remember. You know that peculiar sensation of having everything at the edge of your mind so to speak and not being able to get hold of it—I had a thousand clues and inferences jangling around in my head and none of them would interlock. But I knew this was big stuff.

Shadows began to play across the crystal. Off-focus images and flashes of color. The little old guy murmured to himself and his fingers plucked at the keyboard in a quick fugue of motion. Finally he said: "Ah!" and sat back to watch the crystal. So did I.

I was looking through a window in space, and beyond that window I saw a single bright star in the blackness. It was sharp and cold and so brilliant it hurt your eyes. Just beyond the window, in the foreground, I saw a spaceship. No, none of your cigar things or ovate spheroids or any of that. It was a spaceship that seemed to have been built mostly in afterthoughts. A great rambling affair with added wings and towers and helter-skelter ports. It looked like it'd been built just to hang there in one place.

The old coot said: "Watch close now, Mr. Muggins, things happen rather quickly at this tempo."

Quickly? They practically sprinted. There was a spurt of activity around the spaceship. Towers went up and came down; the bug-like figures of people in space armor bustled about; a little cruiser, shaped like a fat needle, sped up to it, hung around a while and then sped away. There was a tense second of waiting and then the star blotted out. In another moment the spaceship was blotted out, too. The crystal was black.

My friend, the goofy professor, touched a couple of studs and we had a long view. There were clusters of stars spread before me, sharply, brilliantly in focus. As I watched, the upper side of the crystal began to blacken. In a few swift moments the stars were blacked out. Just like that. Blooey! It reminded me of school when we added carbon ink to a drop under the mike just to see how the amoebae would take it.

He punched the buttons like crazy and we had more and more views of the Universe, and always that black cloud crept along, blotting everything out. After a while he couldn't find any more stars. There was nothing but blackness. It seemed to me that it wasn't more than an extra-special Stereo Show, but it chilled me nevertheless. I started thinking about those amoebae and feeling sorry for them.

The lights went on and I was back inside the clock again. He turned to me and said: "Well, what do you think?"

I said: "I think it's swell."

That seemed to disappoint him. He said: "No, no—I mean, what do you make of it? Do you agree with the others?"

"With Stabilizer Groating, you mean?"

He nodded.

I said: "You'll have to give me a little time to think it over. It's rather—startling."

"By all means," he said, escorting me to the door, "do think it over. Although"—he hesitated with his hand on the knob—"I shouldn't agree with your choice of the word 'startling.' After all, it's only what we expected all along. The Universe must come to an end one way or another."

Think? Boys, the massive brain practically fumed as I went back downstairs. I went out into the press room and I wondered what there was about a picture of a black cloud that could have upset the Stabilizer. I drifted out of the Prog Building and decided I'd better go down to the controller's office for another bluff, so I didn't drift any more. There was a pneumatic pick-up at the corner. I caught a capsule and clicked off the address on the dial. In three and a half minutes I was there.

As I turned the overhead dome back and started to step out of my capsule, I found myself surrounded by the rest of the newspaper crowd.

The *Ledger* said: "Where you been, my friendly, we needed your quick brain but bad."

I said: "I'm still looking for Hogan. I can't cover a thing until I've seen him. What's this need for brains?"

"Not just any brains. Your brain."

I got out of the capsule and showed my empty pocket.

The *Ledger* said: "We're not soaping you for a loan—we needed interpolation."

"Aha?"

The *Record* said: "The dope means interpretation. We got one of those official releases again. All words and no sense."

"I mean interpolation," the *Ledger* said. "We got to have some one read implications into this barren chaff."

I said: "Brothers, you want exaggeration and I'm not going to be it this time. Too risky."

So I trotted up the ramp to the main floor and went to the deputy vice's office and then I thought: "I've got a big thing here, why bother with the small fry?" I did a turnabout and went

straight to the controller's suite. I knew it would be tough to get
in because the controller has live secretaries—no voders. He also
happens to have four receptionists. Beautiful, but tough.

The first never saw me. I breezed right by and was in the second anteroom before she could say: "What is it, pa-lee-azz?" The
second was warned by the bang of the door and grabbed hold of
my arm as I tried to go through. I got past anyway, with two of
them holding on, but number three added her lovely heft and I
bogged down. By this time I was within earshot of the controller
so I screamed: "Down with Stability!"

Sure I did. I also shouted: "Stability is all wrong! I'm for Chaos.
Hurray for Chaos!" and a lot more like that. The receptionists
were shocked to death and one of them put in a call for emergency and a couple of guys hanging around were all for boffing
me. I kept on downing with Stability and fighting toward the
sanctum sanctorum et cetera and having a wonderful time because the three girls hanging on to me were strictly class and I
happily suffocated on Exuberant No. 5. Finally the controller
came out to see what made.

They let go of me and the controller said: "What's the meaning of this? . . . Oh, it's you."

I said: "Excuse it, please."

"Is this your idea of a joke, Carmichael?"

"No, sir, but it was the only quick way to get to you."

"Sorry, Carmichael, but it's a little too quick."

I said: "Wait a minute, sir."

"Sorry, I'm extremely busy." He looked worried and impatient
all at once.

I said: "You've got to give me a moment in private."

"Impossible. See my secretary." He turned toward his office.
"Please, sir—"

He waved his hand and started through the door. I took a
jump and caught him by the elbow. He was sputtering furiously
when I swung him around, but I got my arms around him and
gave him a hug. When my mouth was against his ear I whispered: "I've been upstairs in the Prog Building. *I know!*"

He stared at me and his jaw dropped. After a couple of vague
gestures with his hands he motioned me in with a jerk of
his head. I marched straight into the controller's office and almost
fell down dead. The stabilizer was there. Yeah, old Jehovah
Groating himself, standing before the window. All he needed was
the stone tablets in his arms—or is it thunderbolts?

I felt very, very sober, my friends, and not very smart any more
because the stabilizer is a sobering sight no matter how you kid

about him. I nodded politely and waited for the controller to
shut the door. I was wishing I could be on the other side of the
door. Also I was wishing I'd never gone upstairs into the Prog
Building.

The controller said: "This is John Carmichael, Mr. Groating,
a reporter for the *Times*."

We both said: "How-d'you-do?" only Groating said it out loud.
I just moved my lips.

The controller said: "Now, Carmichael, what's this about the
Prog Building?"

"I went upstairs, sir."

He said: "You'll have to speak a little louder."

I cleared my throat and said: "I went upstairs, sir."

"You what!"

"W-went upstairs."

This time lightning really did flash from the C-S's eyes.

I said: "If I've made trouble for anyone, I'm sorry. I've been
wanting to get up there for years and . . . and when I got the
chance today, I couldn't resist it—" Then I told them how I
sneaked up and what I did.

The controller made a terrible fuss about the whole affair, and
I knew—don't ask me how, I simply knew—that something drastic was going to be done about it unless I talked plenty fast. By
this time, though, the clues in my head were beginning to fall
into place. I turned directly to the C-S and I said: "Sir, Prog
stands for Prognostication, doesn't it?"

There was silence. Finally Groating nodded slowly.

I said: "You've got some kind of fortuneteller up there. You
go up every afternoon and get your fortune told. Then you come
out and tell the press about it as though you all thought it up
by yourselves. Right?"

The controller sputtered, but Groating nodded again.

I said: "This afternoon the end of the Universe was prognos-
ticated."

Another silence. At last Groating sighed wearily. He shut the
controller up with a wave of his hand and said: "It seems Mr.
Carmichael does know enough to make things awkward all
around."

The controller burst out: "It's no fault of mine. I always insisted on a thorough guard system. If we had guarded the—"

"Guards," Groating interrupted, "would only have upset existing Stability. They would have drawn attention and suspicion.

We were forced to take the chance of a slip-up. Now that it's happened we must make the best of it."

I said: "Excuse me, sir. I wouldn't have come here just to boast. I could have kept quiet about it. What bothers me is what bothered you?"

Groating stared at me for a moment, then turned away and began to pace up and down the room. There was no anger in his attitude; if there had been, I wouldn't have been as scared as I was. It was a big room and he did a lot of pacing and I could see he was coldly analyzing the situation and deciding what was to be done with me. That frigid appraisal had me trembling.

I said: "I'll give you my word not to mention this again—if that'll do the trick."

He paid no attention—merely paced. My mind raced crazily through all the nasty things that could happen to me. Like solitary for life. Like one-way exploration. Like an obliterated memory track which meant I would have lost my twenty-eight years, not that they were worth much to anyone but me.

I got panicky and yelled: "You can't do anything to me. Remember Stability—" I began to quote the Credo as fast as I could remember: "The *status quo* must be maintained at all costs. Every member of society is an integral and essential factor of the *status quo*. A blow at the Stability of any individual is a blow aimed at the Stability of society. Stability that is maintained at the cost of so much as a single individual is tantamount to Chaos—"

"Thank you, Mr. Carmichael," the C-S interrupted. "I have already learned the Credo."

He went to the controller's desk and punched the teletype keys rapidly. After a few minutes of horrible waiting the answer came clicking back. Groating read the message, nodded and beckoned to me. I stepped up to him and, boys, I don't know how the legs kept from puddling on the floor.

Groating said: "Mr. Carmichael, it is my pleasure to appoint you confidential reporter to the Stability Board for the duration of this crisis."

I said: "Awk!"

Groating said: "We've maintained Stability, you see, and insured your silence. Society cannot endure change—but it can endure and welcome harmless additions. A new post has been created and you're it."

I said: "Th-thanks."

"Naturally, there will be an advance in credit for you. That is the price we pay, and gladly. You will attach yourself to me.

All reports will be confidential. Should you break confidence, society will exact the usual penalty for official corruption. Shall I quote the Credo on that point?"

I said: "No, sir!" because I knew that one by heart. The usual penalty isn't pleasant. Groating had me beautifully hog-tied. I said: "What about the *Times*, sir?"

"Why," Groating said, "you will continue your usual duties whenever possible. You will submit the official releases as though you had no idea at all of what was really taking place. I'm sure I can spare you long enough each day to make an appearance at your office."

Suddenly he smiled at me and in that moment I felt better. I realized that he was far from being a Jehovian menace—in fact that he'd done all he could to help me out of the nasty spot my curiosity had got me into. I grinned back and on impulse shoved out my hand. He took it and gave it a shake. Everything was fine.

The C-S said: "Now that you're a fellow-official, Mr. Carmichael, I'll come to the point directly. The Prog Building, as you've guessed, is a Prognostication Center. With the aid of a complete data system and a rather complex series of Integraphs we have been able to . . . to tell our fortunes, as you put it."

I said: "I was just shooting in the dark, sir. I really don't believe it."

Groating smiled. He said: "Nevertheless it exists. Prophecy is far from being a mystical function. It is a very logical science based on experimental factors. The prophecy of an eclipse to the exact second of time and precise degree of longitude strikes the layman with awe. The scientist knows it is the result of precise mathematical work with precise data."

"Sure," I began, "but—"

Groating held up his hand. "The future of the world line," he said, "is essentially the same problem magnified only by the difficulty of obtaining accurate data—and enough data. For example: Assuming an apple orchard, what are the chances of apples being stolen?"

I said: "I couldn't say. Depends, I suppose, on whether there are any kids living in the neighbourhood."

"All right," Groating said, "that's additional data. Assuming the orchard and the small boys, what are the chances of stolen apples?"

"Pretty good."

"Add data. A locust plague is reported on the way."

"Not so good."

"More data. Agriculture reports a new efficient locust spray."

"Better."

"And still more data. In the past years the boys have stolen apples and been soundly punished. Now what are the chances?"

"Maybe a little less."

"Continue the experimental factors with an analysis of the boys. They are headstrong and will ignore punishment. Add also the weather forecasts for the summer; add the location of the orchard and attitude of owner. Now sum up: Orchard plus boys plus thefts plus punishment plus character plus locusts plus spray plus—"

I said: "Good heavens!"

"You're overwhelmed by the detail work," Groating smiled, "but not by the lack of logic. It is possible to obtain all possible data on the orchard in question and integrate the factors into an accurate prophecy not only as to the theft, but as to the time and place of theft. Apply this example to our own Universe and you can understand the working of the Prognosis Building. We have eight floors of data analyzers. The sifted factors are fed into the Integrators and—presto, prophecy!"

I said: "Presto, my poor head!"

"You'll get used to it in time."

I said: "The pictures?"

Groating said: "The solution of a mathematical problem can take any one of a number of forms. For Prognosis we have naturally selected a picturization of the events themselves. Any major step in government that is contemplated is prepared in data form and fed into the Integrator. The effect of that step on the world line is observed. If it is beneficial, we take that step; if not, we abandon it and search for another—"

I said: "And the picture I saw this afternoon?"

Groating sobered. He said: "Up until today, Mr. Carmichael, we have not been able to integrate closer to the present than a week in the future—or deeper into the future than a few hundred years. Wiggon's new data technique has enabled us to push to the end of our existence, and it is perilously close. You saw the obliteration of our Universe take place less than a thousand years from now. This is something we must prevent at once."

"Why all the excitement? Surely something will happen during the next ten centuries to avoid it."

"What will happen?" Groating shook his head. "I don't think you understand our problem. On the one hand you have the theory of our society. Stability. You yourself have quoted the Credo. A society which must maintain its Stability at the price of instability is Chaos. Keep that in mind. On the other hand we cannot wait while our existence progresses rapidly toward extinction. The closer it draws to that point, the more violent the change will have to be to alter it.

"Think of the progress of a snowball that starts at the top of a mountain and rolls down the slopes, growing in bulk until it smashes an entire house at the bottom. The mere push of a finger is sufficient to alter its future when it starts—a push of a finger will save a house. But if you wait until the snowball gathers momentum you will need violent efforts to throw the tons of snow off the course."

I said: "Those pictures I saw were the snowball hitting our house. You want to start pushing the finger now—"

Groating nodded. "Our problem now is to sift the billions of factors stored in the Prog Building and discover which of them is that tiny snowball."

The controller, who had been silent in a state of wild suppression all the while, suddenly spoke up. "I tell you it's impossible, Mr. Groating. How can you dig the one significant factor out of all those billions?"

Groating said: "It will have to be done."

"But there's an easier way," the controller cried. "I've been suggesting it all along. Let's attempt the trial and error method. We instigate a series of changes at once and see whether or not the future line is shifted. Sooner or later we're bound to strike something."

"Impossible," Groating said. "You're suggesting the end of Stability. No civilization is worth saving if it must buy salvation at the price of its principles."

I said: "Sir, I'd like to make a suggestion."

They looked at me. The C-S nodded.

"It seems to me that you're both on the wrong track. You're searching for a factor from the present. You ought to start in the future."

"How's that?"

"It's like if I said old maids were responsible for more clover. You'd start investigating the old maids. You ought to start with the clover and work backwards."

"Just what are you trying to say, Mr. Carmichael?"

"I'm talking about *a posteriori* reasoning. Look, sir, a fella by the name of Darwin was trying to explain the balance of nature. He wanted to show the chain of cause and effect. He said in so many words that the number of old maids in a town governed the growth of clover, but if you want to find out how, you've got to work it out *a posteriori;* from effect to cause. Like this: Only bumblebees can fertilize clover. The more bumblebees, the more clover. Field mice attack bumblebee nests, so the more field mice, the less clover. Cats attack mice. The more cats, the more clover. Old maids keep cats. The more old maids . . . the more clover. Q. E. D."

"And now," Groating laughed, "construe."

"Seems to me you ought to start with the catastrophe and follow the chain of causation, link by link, back to the source. Why not use the Prognosticator backwards until you locate the moment when the snowball first started rolling?"

There was a very long silence while they thought it over. The controller looked slightly bewildered and he kept muttering: Cats—clover—old maids— But I could see the C-S was really hit. He went to the window and stood looking out, as motionless as a statue. I remember staring past his square shoulder and watching the shadows of the helios flicking noiselessly across the façade of the Judiciary Building opposite us.

It was all so unreal—this frantic desperation over an event a thousand years in the future; but that's Stability. It's strictly the long view. Old Cyrus Brennerhaven of the *Morning Globe* had a sign over his desk that read: If you take care of the tomorrows, the todays will take care of themselves.

Finally Groating said: "Mr. Carmichael, I think we'd better go back to the Prog Building—"

Sure I felt proud. We left the office and went down the hall toward the pneumatics and I kept thinking: "I've given an idea to the Chief Stabilizer. He's taken a suggestion from *me!*" A couple of secretaries had rushed down the hall ahead of us when they saw us come out, and when we got to the tubes, three capsules were waiting for us. What's more, the C-S and the controller stood around and waited for *me* while I contacted my city editor and gave him the official release. The editor was a little sore about my disappearance, but I had a perfect alibi. I was still looking for Hogan. That, my friends, was emphatically that.

At the Prog Building we hustled through the main offices and back up the curved stairs. On the way the C-S said he didn't think we ought to tell Yarr, the little old coot I'd hoodwinked, the real truth. It would be just as well, he said, to let Yarr go on thinking I was a confidential secretary.

So we came again to that fantastic clockwork room with its myriad whirling cams and the revolving crystal and the hypnotic *bam-bam* of the motors. Yarr met us at the door and escorted us to the viewing desk with his peculiar absent-minded subservience. The room was darkened again, and once more we watched the cloud of blackness seep across the face of the Universe. The sight chilled me more than ever, now that I knew what it meant.

Groating turned to me and said: "Well, Mr. Carmichael, any suggestions?"

I said: "The first thing we ought to find out is just what that spaceship has to do with the black cloud . . . don't you think so?"

"Why yes, I do." Groating turned to Yarr and said: "Give us a close-up of the spaceship and switch in sound. Give us the integration at normal speed."

Yarr said: "It would take a week to run the whole thing off. Any special moment you want, sir?"

I had a hunch. "Give us the moment when the auxiliary ship arrives."

Yarr turned back to his switchboard. We had a close-up of a great round port. The sound mechanism clicked on, running at high speed with a peculiar *wheetledy-woodledey-weedledy* garble of shrill noises. Suddenly the cruiser shot into view. Yarr slowed everything down to normal speed.

The fat needle nosed into place, the ports clanged and hissed as the suction junction was made. Abruptly, the scene shifted and we were inside the lock between the two ships. Men in stained dungarees, stripped to the waist and sweating, were hauling heavy canvas-wrapped equipment into the mother ship. To one side two elderly guys were talking swiftly:

"You had difficulty?"

"More than ever. Thank God this is the last shipment."

"How about credits?"

"Exhausted."

"Do you mean that?"

"I do."

"I can't understand it. We had over two millions left."

"We lost all that through indirect purchases and—"

"And what?"

"Bribes, if you must know."

"Bribes?"

"My dear sir, you can't order cyclotrons without making people suspicious. If you so much as mention an atom today, you accuse yourself."

"Then we all stand accused here and now."

"I'm not denying that."

"What a terrible thing it is that the most precious part of our existence should be the most hated."

"You speak of—"

"The atom."

The speaker gazed before him meditatively, then sighed and turned into the shadowy depths of the spaceship.

I said: "All right, that's enough. Cut into the moment just before the black-out occurs. Take it inside the ship."

The integrators quickened and the sound track began its shrill babble again. Quick scenes of the interior of the mother ship flickered across the crystal. A control chamber, roofed with a transparent dome passed repeatedly before us, with the darting figures of men snapping through it. At last the Integrator fixed on that chamber and stopped. The scene was frozen into a still-photograph—a tableau of half a dozen half-naked men poised over the controls, heads tilted back to look through the dome.

Yarr said: "It doesn't take long. Watch closely."

I said: "Shoot."

The scene came to life with a blurp.

"—ready on the tension screens?"

"Ready, sir."

"Power checked?"

"Checked and ready, sir."

"Stand by, all. Time?"

"Two minutes to go."

"Good—" The graybeard in the center of the chamber paced with hands clasped behind him, very much like a captain on his bridge. Clearly through the sound mechanism came the thuds of his steps and the background hum of waiting mechanism.

The graybeard said: "Time?"

"One minute forty seconds."

"Gentlemen: In these brief moments I should like to thank you all for your splendid assistance. I speak not so much of your technical work, which speaks for itself, but of your willingness to exile yourselves and even incriminate yourselves along with me— Time?"

"One twenty-five."

"It is a sad thing that our work which is intended to grant the greatest boon imaginable to the Universe should have been driven into secrecy. Limitless power is so vast a concept that even I cannot speculate on the future it will bring to our worlds. In a few minutes, after we have succeeded, all of us will be universal heroes. Now, before our work is done, I want all of you to know that to me you are already heroes— Time?"

"One ten."

"And now, a warning. When we have set up our spacial partition membrane and begun the osmotic transfer of energy from hyperspace to our own there may be effects which I have been unable to predict. Raw energy pervading our space may also pervade our nervous systems and engender various unforeseen conditions. Do not be alarmed. Keep well in mind the fact that the change cannot be anything but for the better— Time?"

"Fifty seconds."

"The advantages? Up to now mathematics and the sciences have merely been substitutes for what man should do for himself. So FitzJohn preached in his first lecture, and so we are about to prove. The logical evolution of energy mechanics is not toward magnification and complex engineering development, but toward simplification—toward the concentration of all those powers within man himself— Time?"

"Twenty seconds."

"Courage, my friends. This is the moment we have worked for these past ten years. Secretly. Criminally. So it has always been with those who have brought man his greatest gifts."

"Ten seconds."

"Stand by, all."

"Ready all, sir."

The seconds ticked off with agonizing slowness. At the moment of zero the workers were galvanized into quick action. It was impossible to follow their motions or understand them, but you could could see by the smooth timing and interplay that they were beautifully rehearsed. There was tragedy in those efforts for us who already knew the outcome.

As quickly as they had begun, the workers stopped and peered upward through the crystal dome. Far beyond them, crisp in the velvet blackness, that star gleamed, and as they watched, it winked out.

They started and exclaimed, pointing. The graybeard cried:

"It's impossible!"

"What is it, sir?"

"I—"

And in that moment blackness enveloped the scene.

I said: "Hold it—"

Yarr brought up the lights and the others turned to look at me. I thought for a while, idly watching the shimmering cams and cogs around me. Then I said: "It's a good start. The reason I imagine you gentlemen have been slightly bewildered up to now is that you're busy men with no time for foolishness. Now I'm not so busy and very foolish, so I read detective stories. This is going to be a kind of backward detective story."

"All right," Groting said. "Go ahead."

"We've got a few clues. First, the Universe has ended through an attempt to pervade it with energy from hyperspace. Second, the attempt failed for a number of reasons which we can't discover yet. Third, the attempt was made in secrecy. Why?"

The controller said: "Why not? Scientists and all that—"

"I don't mean that kind of secrecy. These men were plainly outside the law, carrying on an illicit experiment. We must find out why energy experiments or atomic experiments were illegal. That will carry us back quite a few decades toward the present."

"But how?"

"Why, we trace the auxiliary cruiser, of course. If we can pick them up when they're purchasing supplies, we'll narrow our backward search considerably. Can you do it, Dr. Yarr?"

"It'll take time."

"Go ahead—we've got a thousand years."

It took exactly two days. In that time I learned a lot about the Prognosticator. They had it worked out beautifully. Seems the future is made up solely of probabilities. The Integrator could push down any one of these possible avenues, but with a wonderful check. The less probable the avenue of future was, the more off-focus it was. If a future event was only remotely possible, it was pictured as a blurred series of actions. On the other hand, the future that was almost positive in the light of present data, was sharply in focus.

When we went back to the Prog Building two days later, Yarr was almost alive in his excitement. He said: "I really think I've got just the thing you're looking for."

"What's that?"

"I've picked up an actual moment of bribery. It has additional data that should put us directly on the track."

We sat down behind the desk with Yarr at the controls. He had a slip of paper in his hand which he consulted with much muttering as he adjusted co-ordinates. Once more we saw the preliminary off-focus shadows, then the sound blooped on like a hundred Stereo records playing at once. The crystal sharpened abruptly into focus.

The scream and roar of a gigantic foundry blasted our ears. On both sides of the scene towered the steel girder columns of the foundry walls, stretching deep into the background like the grim pillars of a satanic cathedral. Overhead cranes carried enormous blocks of metal with a ponderous gait. Smoke—black, white and fitfully flared with crimson from the furnaces, whirled around the tiny figures.

Two men stood before a gigantic casting. One, a foundryman in soiled overalls, made quick measurements which he called off to the other carefully checking a blueprint. Over the roar of the foundry the dialogue was curt and sharp:

"One hundred three point seven."

"Check."

"Short axis. Fifty-two point five."

"Check."

"Tangent on ovate diameter. Three degrees point oh five two."

"Check!"

"What specifications for outer convolutions?"

"Y equals cosine X."

"Then that equation resolves to X equals minus one half Pi."

"Check."

The foundryman climbed down from the casting, folding his three-way gauge. He mopped his face with a bit of waste and eyed the engineer curiously as the latter carefully rolled up the blueprint and slid it into a tube of other rolled sheets. The foundryman said: "I think we did a nice job."

The engineer nodded.

"Only what in blazes do you want it for? Never saw a casting like that."

"I could explain, but you wouldn't understand. Too complicated."

The foundryman flushed. He said: "You theoretical guys are too damned snotty. Just because I know how to drop-forge doesn't mean I can't understand an equation."

"Mebbeso. Let it go at that. I'm ready to ship this casting out at once."

As the engineer turned to leave, rapping the rolled blueprints nervously against his calf, a great pig of iron that had been sailing up from the background swung dangerously toward his head. The foundryman cried out. He leaped forward, seized the engineer by the shoulder and sent him tumbling to the concrete floor. The blueprints went flying.

He pulled the engineer to his feet immediately and tried to straighten the dazed man who could only stare at the tons of iron that sailed serenely on. The foundryman picked up the scattered sheets and started to sort them. Abruptly he stopped and examined one of the pages closely. He began to look through the others, but before he could go any further, the blueprints were snatched from his hands.

He said: "What's this casting for?"

The engineer rolled the sheets together with quick, intense motions. He said: "None of your blasted business."

"I think I know. That's one-quarter a cyclotron. You're getting the other parts made up in different foundries, aren't you?"

There was no answer.

"Maybe you've forgotten Stabilization Rule 930."

"I haven't forgotten. You're crazy."

"Want me to call for official inspection?"

The engineer took a breath, then shrugged. He said: "I suppose the only way to convince you is to show you the master drafts. Come on—"

They left the foundry and trudged across the broad concrete of a landing field to where the fat needle of the auxiliary ship lay. They mounted the ramp to the side port and entered the ship. Inside, the engineer called: "It's happened again, boys. Let's go!"

The port swung shut behind them. Spacemen drifted up from the surrounding corridors and rooms. They were rangy and tough-looking and the snub-nosed paralyzers glinted casually in their hands as though they'd been cleaning them and merely happened to bring them along. The foundryman looked around for a long time. At last he said: "So it's this way?"

"Yes, it's this way. Sorry."

"I'd like you to meet some of my friends, some day—"

"Perhaps we will."

"They'll have an easier time with you than you're gonna have with me!" He clenched fists and poised himself to spring.

The engineer said: "Hey—wait a minute. Don't lose your head. You did me a good turn back there. I'd like to return the favor. I've got more credit than I know what to do with."

The foundryman gave him a perplexed glance. He relaxed and began to rub his chin dubiously.

He said: "Damn if this isn't a sociable ship. I feel friendlier already—"

The engineer grinned.

I called: "O. K., that's enough. Cut it," and the scene vanished.

"Well?" Yarr asked eagerly.

I said: "We're really in the groove now. Let's check back and locate the Stabilization debates on Rule 930." I turned to the C-S. "What's the latest rule number, sir?"

Groating said: "Seven fifteen."

The controller had already been figuring. He said: "Figuring the same law-production rate that would put Rule 930 about six hundred years from now. Is that right, Mr. Groating?"

The old man nodded and Yarr went back to his keyboard. I'm not going to bother you with what we all went through because a lot of it was very dull. For the benefit of the hermit from the Moon I'll just mention that we hung around the Stability Library until we located the year S. R. 930 was passed. Then we shifted to Stability headquarters and quick-timed through from January 1st until we picked up the debates on the rule.

The reasons for the rule were slightly bewildering on the one hand, and quite understandable on the other. It seems that in the one hundred and fifty years preceding, almost every Earthwide university had been blown up in the course of an atomic-energy experiment. The blowups were bewildering—the rule understandable. I'd like to tell you about that debate because—well, because things happened that touched me.

The Integrator selected a cool, smooth foyer in the Administration Building at Washington. It had a marble floor like milky ice flecked with gold. One side was broken by a vast square window studded with a thousand round-bottle panes that refracted the afternoon sunlight into showers of warm color. In the background were two enormous doors of synthetic oak. Before those doors stood a couple in earnest conversation—a nice-looking boy with a portfolio under his arm, and a stunning girl. The kind with sleek-shingled head and one of those clean-cut faces that look fresh and wind-washed.

The controller said: "Why, that's the foyer to the Seminar Room. They haven't changed it at all in six hundred years."

Groating said: "Stability!" and chuckled.

Yarr said: "The debate is going on inside. I'll shift scene—"

"No—wait," I said. "Let's watch this for a while." I don't know why I wanted to—except that the girl made my pulse run a little faster and I felt like looking at her for a couple of years.

She was half crying. She said: "Then, if for no other reason—for my sake."

"For yours!" The boy looked harassed.

She nodded. "You'll sweep away his life work with a few words and a few sheets of paper."

"My own work, too."

"Oh, but won't you understand? You're young. I'm young. Youth loves to shatter the old idols. It feasts on the broken shards of destruction. It destroys the old ideas to make way for its own. But he's not young like us. He has only his past work to live on. If you shatter that, he'll have nothing left but a futile resentment. I'll be pent up with a broken old man who'll destroy me along with himself. Darling, I'm not saying you're wrong—I'm only asking you to wait a little."

She was crying openly now. The boy took her by the arm and led her to the crusted window. She turned her face away from the light—away from him. The boy said: "He was my teacher. I worship him. What I'm doing now may seem like treachery, but it's only treachery to his old age. I'm keeping faith with what he was thirty years ago—with the man who would have done the same thing to his teacher."

She cried: "But are you keeping faith with me? You, who will have all the joy of destroying and none of the tedious sweeping away the pieces. What of my life and all the weary years to come when I must coddle him and soothe him and lead him through the madness of forgetting what you've done to him?"

"You'll spend your life with me. I break no faith with you, Barbara."

She laughed bitterly. "How easily you evade reality. I shall spend my life with you—and in that short sentence, *poof!*"—she flicked her hand—"you dismiss everything. Where will he live? Alone? With us? Where?"

"That can be arranged."

"You're so stubborn, so pig-headed in your smug, righteous truth-seeking. Steven—for the very last time—please. Wait until he's gone. A few years, that's all. Leave him in peace. Leave us in peace."

He shook his head and started toward the oaken doors. "A few years waiting to salvage the pride of an old man, a few more catastrophes, a few more thousand lives lost—it doesn't add up."

She sagged against the window, silhouetted before the riot of color, and watched him cross to the doors. All the tears seemed drained out of her. She was so limp I thought she would fall to the floor at any instant. And then, as I watched her, I saw her stiffen and I realized that another figure had entered the foyer and was rushing toward the boy. It was an oldish man, bald and with an ageless face of carved ivory. He was tall and terribly thin. His eyes were little pits of embers.

He called: "Steven!"

The boy stopped and turned.

"Steven, I want to talk to you."

"It's no use, sir!"

"You're headstrong, Steven. You pit a few years' research against my work of a lifetime. Once I respected you. I thought you would carry on for me as I've carried on for the generations that came before me."

"I am, sir."

"You are not." The old man clutched at the boy's tunic and spoke intensely. "You betray all of us. You will cut short a line of research that promises the salvation of humanity. In five minutes you will wipe out five centuries of work. You owe it to those who slaved before us not to let their sweat go in vain."

The boy said: "I have a debt also to those who may die."

"You think too much of death, too little of life. What if a thousand more are killed—ten thousand—in the end it will be worth it."

"It will never be worth it. There will never be an end. The theory has always been wrong, faultily premised."

"You fool!" the old man cried. "You damned, blasted young fool. You can't go in there!"

"I'm going, sir. Let go."

"I won't let you go in."

The boy pulled his arm free and reached for the doorknob. The old man seized him again and yanked him off balance. The boy muttered angrily, set himself and thrust the old man back. There was a flailing blur of motion and a cry from the girl. She left the window, ran across the room and thrust herself between the two. And in that instant she screamed again and stepped back. The boy sagged gently to the floor, his mouth opened to an O of astonishment. He tried to speak and then relaxed. The girl dropped to her knees alongside him and tried to get his head on her lap. Then she stopped.

That was all. No shot or anything. I caught a glimpse of a metallic barrel in the old man's hand as he hovered frantically over the dead boy. He cried: "I only meant to— I—" and kept on whimpering.

After a while the girl turned her head as though it weighed a ton, and looked up. Her face was suddenly frostbitten. In dull tones she said: "Go away, father."

The old man said: "I only—" His lips continued to twitch, but he made no sound.

The girl picked up the portfolio and got to her feet. Without glancing again at her father, she opened the doors, stepped in and closed them behind her with a soft click. The debating voices broke off at the sight of her. She walked to the head of the table, set the portfolio down, opened it and took out a sheaf of typescript. Then she looked at the amazed men who were seated around the table gaping at her.

She said: "I regret to inform the stabilizers that Mr. Steven Wilder has been unavoidably detained. As his fiancée and co-worker, however, I have been delegated to carry on his mission and present his evidence to the committee—" She paused and went rigid, fighting for control.

One of the stabilizers said: "Thank you. Will you give your evidence, Miss . . . Miss?"

"Barbara Leeds."

"Thank you, Miss Leeds. Will you continue?"

With the gray ashes of a voice she went on: "We are heartily in favor of S. R. 930 prohibiting any further experimentation in atomic energy dynamics. All such experiments have been based on—almost inspired by the FitzJohn axioms and mathematic. The catastrophic detonations which have resulted must invariably result since the basic premises are incorrect. We shall prove that the backbone of FitzJohn's equations is entirely in error. I speak of

$$i = (b/a) \; \pi \; i \; e/\mu \; . \; . \; ."$$

She glanced at the notes, hesitated for an instant, and then continued: "FitzJohn's errors are most easily pointed out if we consider the Leeds Derivations involving transfinite cardinals—"

The tragic voice droned on.

I said: "C-cut."

There was silence.

We sat there feeling bleak and cold, and for no reason at all, the icy sea-green opening bars of Debussy's "La Mer" ran through my head. I thought: "I'm proud to be a human—not because I think or I am, but because I can feel. Because humanity can reach out to us across centuries, from the past or future, from facts or imagination, and touch us—move us."

At last I said: "We're moving along real nice now."

No answer.

I tried again: "Evidently that secret experiment that destroyed existence was based on this FitzJohn's erroneous theory, eh?"

The C-S stirred and said: "What? Oh— Yes, Carmichael, quite right."

In low tones the controller said: "I wish it hadn't happened. He was a nice-looking youngster, that Wilder—promising."

I said: "In the name of heaven, sir, it's not going to happen if we pull ourselves together. If we can locate the very beginning and change it, he'll probably marry the girl and live happily ever after."

"Of course—" The controller was confused. "I hadn't realized." I said: "We've got to hunt back a lot more and locate this Fitz-John. He seems to be the key man in this puzzle."

And how we searched. Boys, it was like working a four-dimensional jig saw, the fourth dimension in this case being time. We located a hundred universities that maintained chairs and departments exclusively devoted to FitzJohn's mathematics and theories. We slipped back a hundred years toward the present and found only fifty and in those fifty were studying the men whose pupils were to fill the chairs a century later.

Another century back and there were only a dozen universities that followed the FitzJohn theories. They filled the scientific literature with trenchant, belligerent articles on FitzJohn, and fought gory battles with his opponents. How we went through the libraries. How many shoulders we looked over. How many pages of equations we snap-photographed from the whirling octahedron for future reference. And finally we worked our way back to Bowdoin College, where FitzJohn himself had taught, where he worked out his revolutionary theories and where he made his first converts. We were on the home stretch.

FitzJohn was a fascinating man. Medium height, medium color, medium build—his body had the rare trick of perfect balance. No matter what he was doing, standing, sitting, walking, he was always exquisitely poised. He was like the sculptor's idealization of the perfect man. FitzJohn never smiled. His face was cut and chiseled as though from a roughish sandstone; it had the noble dignity of an Egyptian carving. His voice was deep, unimpressive in quality, yet unforgettable for the queer, intense stresses it laid on his words. Altogether he was an enigmatic creature.

He was enigmatic for another reason, too, for although we traced his career at Bowdoin backward and forward for all its forty years, although we watched him teach the scores and scores of disciples who afterward went out into the scholastic world to take up the fight for him—we could never trace FitzJohn back into his youth. It was impossible to pick him up at any point earlier than his first appearance on the physics staff of the college. It seemed as though he were deliberately concealing his identity.

Yarr raged with impotent fury. He said: "It's absolutely aggravating. Here we follow the chain back to less than a half century from today and we're blocked—" He picked up a small desk phone and called upstairs to the data floors. "Hullo, Cullen? Get me all available date on the name FitzJohn. FitzJOHN. What's the matter, you deaf? F-I-T-Z . . . That's right. Be quick about it."

I said: "Seems as if FitzJohn didn't want people to know where he came from."

"Well," Yarr said pettishly, "that's impossible. I'll trace him backward, second by second, if I have to!"

I said: "That would take a little time, wouldn't it?"

"Yes."

"Maybe a couple of years?"

"What of it; You said we had a thousand."

"I didn't mean you to take me seriously, Dr. Yarr."

The small pneumatic at Yarr's desk whirred and clicked. Out popped a cartridge. Yarr opened it and withdrew a list of figures, and they were appalling. Something like two hundred thousand FitzJohns on the Earth alone. It would take a decade to check the entire series through the Integrator. Yarr threw the figures to the floor in disgust and swiveled around to face us.

"Well?" he asked.

I said: "Seems hopeless to check FitzJohn back second by second. At that rate we might just as well go through all the names on the list."

"What else is there to do?"

I said: "Look, the Prognosticator flirted twice with something interesting when we were conning FitzJohn's career. It was something mentioned all through the future, too."

"I don't recall—" the C-S began.

"It was a lecture, sir," I explained. "FitzJohn's first big lecture when he set out to refute criticism. I think we ought to pick that up and go through it with a fine comb. Something is bound to come out of it."

"Very well."

Images blurred across the spinning crystal as Yarr hunted for the scene. I caught fuzzy fragments of a demolished Manhattan City with giant crablike creatures mashing helpless humans, their scarlet chiton glittering. Then an even blurrier series of images. A city of a single stupendous building towering like Babel into the heavens; a catastrophic fire roaring along the Atlantic seaboard; then a sylvan civilization of odd, naked creatures flitting from one giant flower to another. But they were all so far off focus they made my eyes ache. The sound was even worse.

Groating leaned toward me and whispered: "Merely vague possibilities—"

I nodded and then riveted my attention to the crystal, for it held a clear scene. Before us lay an amphitheater. It was modeled on the ancient Greek form, a horseshoe of gleaming whitestone terraces descending to a small square white rostrum. Behind the rostrum and surrounding the uppermost tiers of seats was a simple colonnade. The lovely and yet noble dignity was impressive.

The controller said: "Hel-lo, I don't recognize this."

"Plans are in the architectural offices," Groating said. "It isn't due for construction for another thirty years. We intend placing it at the north end of Central Park—"

It was difficult to hear them. The room was filled with the bellow and roar of shouting from the amphitheater. It was packed from pit to gallery with quick-jerking figures. They climbed across the terraces; they fought up and down the broad aisles; they stood on their seats and waved. Most of all they opened their mouths into gaping black blots and shouted. The hoarse sound rolled like slow, thunderous waves, and there was a faint rhythm struggling to emerge from the chaos.

A figure appeared from behind the columns, walked calmly up to the platform and began arranging cards on the small table. It was FitzJohn, icy and self-possessed, statuesque in his white tunic. He stood alongside the table, carefully sorting his notes, utterly oblivious of the redoubled roar that went up at his appearance. Out of that turmoil came the accented beats of a doggerel rhyme:

> Neon
> Crypton
> Ammoniated
> FitzJohn
> Neon
> Crypton
> Ammoniated
> FitzJohn

When he was finished, FitzJohn straightened and, resting the fingertips of his right hand lightly on top of the table, he gazed out at the rioting—unsmiling, motionless. The pandemonium was reaching unprecedented heights. As the chanting continued, costumed figures appeared on the terrace tops and began fighting down the aisles toward the platform. There were men wearing metal-tubed frameworks representing geometric figures. Cubes, spheres, rhomboids and tesseracts. They hopped and danced outlandishly.

Two young boys began unreeling a long streamer from a drum concealed behind the colonnade. It was of white silk and an endless equation was printed on it that read:

$$eia = 1 + ia - a_2! + a_3! - a_4! \ldots$$

and so on, yard after yard after yard. It didn't exactly make sense, but I understood it to be some kind of cutting reference to Fitz-John's equations.

There were hundreds of others, some surprising and many obscure. Lithe contortionists, made up to represent Möbius Strips, grasped ankles with their hands and went rolling down the aisles. A dozen girls appeared from nowhere, clad only in black net, representing giant Aleph-Nulls, and began an elaborate ballet. Great gas-filled balloons, shaped into weird topological manifolds were dragged in and bounced around.

It was utter insanity and utterly degrading to see how these mad college kids were turning FitzJohn's lecture into a Mardi Gras. They were college kids, of course, crazy youngsters who probably couldn't explain the binomial theorem, but nevertheless were giving their own form of expression to their teachers' antagonism to FitzJohn. I thought vaguely of the days centuries back when a thousand Harvard undergraduates did a very similar thing when Oscar Wilde came to lecture. Undergraduates whose entire reading probably consisted of the *Police Gazette*.

And all the while they danced and shouted and screamed, Fitz-John stood motionless, fingertips just touching the table, waiting for them to finish. You began with an admiration for his composure. Then suddenly you realized what a breathtaking performance was going on. You glued your eyes to the motionless figure and waited for it to move—and it never did.

What?

You don't think that was so terrific, eh? Well, one of you get up and try it. Stand alongside a table and rest your fingertips lightly on the top—not firmly enough to bear the weight of your arm—but just enough to make contact. Maybe it sounds simple. Just go ahead and try it. I'll bet every credit I ever own no one of you can stand there without moving for sixty seconds. Any takers? I thought not. You begin to get the idea, eh?

They began to get the same idea in the amphitheater. At first the excitement died down out of shame. There's not much fun making a holy show of yourself if your audience doesn't react. They started it up again purely out of defiance, but it didn't last long. The chanting died away, the dancers stopped cavorting, and at last that entire audience of thousands stood silent, uneasily watching FitzJohn. He never moved a muscle.

After what seemed like hours of trying to outstare him, the kids suddenly gave in. Spatters of applause broke out across the terraces. The clapping was taken up and it rose to a thunder of beating palms. No one is as quick to appreciate a great performance as a youngster. These kids sat down in their seats and applauded like mad. FitzJohn never moved until the applause, too, had died down, then he picked up his card and, without preamble—as though nothing at all had happened—he began his lecture.

"Ladies and gentlemen, I have been accused of creating my theory of energy-dynamics and my mathematics out of nothing—and my critics cry: 'From nothing comes nothing.' Let me remind you first that man does not create in the sense of inventing what never existed before. Man only discovers. The things we seem to invent, no matter how novel and revolutionary, we merely discover. They have been waiting for us all the time.

"Moreover, I was not the sole discoverer of this theory. No scientist is a lone adventurer, striking out into new fields for himself. The way is always led by those who precede us, and we who seem to discover all, actually do no more than add our bit to an accumulated knowledge.

"To show you how small my own contribution was and how much I inherited from the past, let me tell you that the basic equation of my theory is not even my own. It was discovered some fifty years prior to this day—some ten years before I was born.

"For on the evening of February 9, 2909, in Central Park, on the very site of this amphitheater, my father, suddenly struck with an idea, mentioned an equation to my mother. That equation:

$$i = (b/a)\ \pi\ i\ e/\mu\ \ldots\text{"}$$

was the inspiration for my own theory. So you can understand just how little I have contributed to the 'invention' of The Tension Energy-Dynamics Equations—"

FitzJohn glanced at the first card and went on: "Let us consider, now, the possible permutations on the factor

$$e/\mu\ \ldots\text{"}$$

I yelled: "That's plenty. Cut!" and before the first word was out of my mouth the controller and the C-S were shouting, too. Yarr blanked out the crystal and brought up the lights. We were all on our feet, looking at each other excitedly. Yarr jumped up so fast his chair went over backward with a crash. We were in a fever because, boys, that day happened to be February 9, 2909, and we had just about two hours until evening.

The controller said: "Can we locate these FitzJohns?"

"In two hours? Don't be silly. We don't even know if they're named FitzJohn today."

"Why not?"

"They may have changed their name—it's getting to be a fad nowadays. The son may have changed his name as a part of that cover-up of his past. Heaven only knows why not—"

"But we've got to split them up—whoever they are."

The C-S said: "Take hold of yourself. How are we going to separate eleven million married people? Didn't you ever hear of Stability?"

"Can't we publish a warning and order everybody out of the park?"

"And let everybody know about the Prog Building?" I said. "You keep forgetting Stability."

"Stability be damned! We can't let them have that conversation—and if they do anyway, we can't let them have that boy!"

Groating was really angry. He said: "You'd better go home and read through the Credo. Even if it meant the salvation of the Universe I would not break up a marriage—nor would I harm the boy."

"Then what do we do?"

"Have patience. We'll think of something."

I said: "Excuse me, sir—I've got an idea."

"Forget ideas," the controller yelled, "we need action."

"This is action."

The C-S said: "Go ahead, Carmichael."

"Well, obviously the important thing is to keep all married couples out of the north sector of Central Park tonight. Suppose we get a special detail of police together at once. Then we beat through the park and get everyone out. We can quarantine it—set up a close cordon around the park and guard it all night."

The controller yelled: "It may be one of the policemen."

"O. K., then we pick the unmarried ones. Furthermore, we give strict orders that all women are to stay away."

The C-S said: "It might work—it'll have to work. We can't let that conversation take place."

I said: "Excuse me, sir, do you happen to be married?"

He grinned: "My wife's in Washington. I'll tell her to stay there."

"And the controller, sir?"

The controller said: "She'll stay home. What about yourself?"

"Me? Strictly bachelor."

Groating laughed. "Unfortunate, but excellent for tonight. Come, let's hurry."

We took the pneumatic to headquarters and let me tell you, stuff began to fly, but high! Before we were there ten minutes, three companies were reported ready for duty. It seemed to satisfy the controller, but it didn't satisfy me. I said: "Three's not enough. Make it five."

"Five hundred men? You're mad."

I said: "I wish it could be five thousand. Look, we've knocked our brains out digging through a thousand years for this clue. Now that we've got it I don't want us to muff the chance."

The C-S said: "Make it five."

"But I don't think we've got that many unmarried men in the service."

"Then get all you can. Get enough so they can stand close together in the cordon—close enough so no one can wander through. Look—this isn't a case of us hunting down a crook who knows we're after him. We're trying to pick up a couple who are perfectly innocent—who may wander through the cordon. We're trying to prevent an accident, not a crime."

They got four hundred and ten all told. The whole little regiment was mustered before headquarters and the C-S made a beautifully concocted speech about a criminal and a crime that had to be prevented and hoopusgadoopus, I forget most of it. Naturally we couldn't let them know about the Prog Building any more than we could the citizens—and I suppose you understand why the secret had to be kept.

You don't, eh? Well, for the benefit of the hermit from the Moon I'll explain that, aside from the important matter of Stability, there's the very human fact that the Prog would be besieged by a million people a day looking for fortunetelling and hot tips on the races. Most important of all, there's the question of death. You can't let a man know when and how he's going to die. You just can't.

There wasn't any sense keeping the news from the papers because everyone around Central Park was going to know something was up. While the C-S was giving instructions, I slipped into a booth and asked for multidial. When most of the reporters' faces were on segments of the screen, I said: "Greetings, friendlies!"

They all yelled indignantly because I'd been out of sight for three days.

I said: "No more ho-hum, lads. Carmichael sees all and tells all. Hot-foot it up to the north end of Central Park in an hour or so. Big stuff!"

The *Journal* said: "Take you three days to find that out?"

"Yep."

The *Post* said: "Can it, Carmichael. The last time you sent us north, the south end of the Battery collapsed."

"This is no gag. I'm giving it to you straight."

"Yeah?" The *Post* was belligerent. "I say Gowan!"

"Gowan yourself," the *Ledger* said. "This side of the opposition is credible."

"You mean gullible."

I said: "The word this time is sensational. Four hundred police on the march. Tramp-tramp-tramp—the beat of the drum—boots —et cetera. Better get moving if you want to tag along."

The *News* gave me a nasty smile and said: "Brother, for your sake it better be good—because I'm preparing a little sensation of my own to hand over."

I said: "Make it a quick double cross, Newsy. I'm in a hurry," and I clicked off. It's funny how sometimes you can't get along with wrong people.

You know how fast night comes on in February. The blackness gathers in the sky like a bunched cape. Then someone lets it drop and it sinks down over you with swiftly spreading black folds. Those dusky folds were just spreading out toward the corners of the sky when we got to the park. The cops didn't even bother to park their helios. They vaulted out and left them blocking the streets. In less than half a minute, two hundred were beating through the park in a long line, driving everyone out. The rest were forming the skeleton of the cordon.

It took an hour to make sure the park was clear. Somehow, if you tell a hundred citizens to do something, there will always be twenty who'll fight you—not because they really object to doing what they're told, but just out of principle or curiosity or cantankerousness.

The all-clear came at six o'clock, and it was just in time because it was pitch dark. The controller, the C-S and myself stood before the high iron gates that open onto the path leading into the rock gardens. Where we stood we could see the jet masses of foliage standing crisp and still in the chill night. To either side of us stretched the long, wavering lines of police glow lamps. We could see the ring of bright dots drawn around the entire north end of the park like a necklace of glowing pearls.

The silence and the chill waiting was agonizing. Suddenly I said: "Excuse me, sir, but did you tell the police captain to O. K. the reporters?"

The C-S said: "I did, Carmichael—" and that was all. It wasn't so good because I'd hoped we'd have a little talk to ease the tension.

Again there was nothing but the cold night and the waiting. The stars overhead were like bits of radium and so beautiful you wished they were candy so you could eat them. I tried to imagine them slowly blotted out, and I couldn't. It's impossible to visualize the destruction of any lovely thing. Then I tried counting the police lamps around the park. I gave that up before I reached twenty.

At last I said: "Couldn't we go in and walk around a bit, sir?"

The C-S said: "I don't see why not—"

So we started through the gate, but we hadn't walked three steps into the park when there was a shout behind us and the sharp sounds of running feet.

But it was only old Yarr running up to us with a couple of cops following him. Yarr looked like a banshee with his coat flying and an enormous muffler streaming from his neck. He dressed real old-fashioned. He was all out of breath and just gasped while the C-S told the cops it was all right.

Yarr panted: "I . . . I—"

"Don't worry, Dr. Yarr, everything is safe so far."

Yarr took an enormous breath, held it for a moment and then let it out with a *woosh*. In natural tones he said: "I wanted to ask you if you'd hold on to the couple. I'd like to examine them for a check on the Prognosticator."

Gently, the C-S explained: "We're not trying to catch them, Dr. Yarr. We don't know who they are and we may never know. All we want to do is to prevent this conversation."

So we forgot about taking a walk through the gardens and there was more cold and more silence and more waiting. I clasped my hands together and I was so chilled and nervous it felt like I had ice water between the palms. A quick streak of red slanted up through the sky, the rocket discharges of the Lunar Transport, and ten seconds later I heard the *wham* of the take-off echoing from Governor's Island and the follow-up drone. Only that drone kept on sounding long after it should have died away and it was too thin—too small—

I looked up, startled, and there was a helio making lazy circles over the center of the rock gardens. Its silhouette showed clearly against the stars and I could see the bright squares of its cabin windows. Suddenly I realized there was a stretch of lawn in the center of the gardens where a helio could land—where a couple could get out to stretch their legs and take an evening stroll.

I didn't want to act scared, so I just said: "I think we'd better go inside and get that helio out of there."

So we entered the gate and walked briskly toward the gardens, the two cops right at our heels. I managed to keep on walking for about ten steps and then I lost all control. I broke into a run and the others ran right behind me—the controller, the C-S, Yarr and the cops. We went pelting down the gravel path, circled a dry fountain and climbed a flight of steps three at a clip.

The helio was just landing when I got to the edge of the lawn. I yelled: "Keep off! Get out of here!" and started toward them across the frozen turf. My feet pounded, but not much louder than my heart. I guess the whole six of us must have sounded like a herd of buffalo. I was still fifty yards off when dark figures started climbing out of the cabin. I yelled: "Didn't you hear me? Get out of this park!"

And then the *Post* called: "That you, Carmichael? What goes on?"

Sure—it was the press.

So I stopped running and the others stopped and I turned to the C-S and said: "Sorry about the false alarm, sir. What shall I do with the reporters—have them fly out or can they stay? They think this is a crime hunt."

Groating was a little short of breath. He said: "Let them stay, Carmichael, they can help us look for Dr. Yarr. He seems to have lost himself somewhere in the woods."

I said: "Yes, sir," and walked up to the helio.

The cabin door was open and warm amber light spilled out into the blackness. All the boys were out by this time, getting into their coveralls and stamping around and making the usual newspaper chatter. As I came up, the *Post* said: "We brung your opposition along, Carmichael—Hogan of the *Trib*."

The *News* said: "Now's as good a time as any for the wrasslin' match, eh? You been in training, Carmichael?" His voice had a nasty snigger to it and I thought: "Oh-ho, this Hogan probably scales two twenty and he'll mop me up, but very good—to the great satisfaction, no doubt, of my confrere from the *News*."

Only when they shoved Hogan forward, he wasn't so big, so I thought: "At a time like this—let's get it over with fast." I took a little spring through the dark and grabbed Hogan around the chest and dumped him to the ground.

I said: "O. K., opposition, that's—"

Suddenly I realized this Hogan'd been soft—soft but firm, if you get me. I looked down at her, full of astonishment and she looked up at me, full of indignation, and the rest of the crowd roared with laughter.

I said: "I'll be a pie-eyed emu."

And then, my friends, six dozen catastrophes and cataclysms and volcanoes and hurricanes and everything else hit me. The

C-S began shouting and then the controller and after a moment, the cops. Only by that time the four of them were on top of me and all over me, so to speak. Little Yarr came tearing up, screaming at Groating and Groating yelled back and Yarr tried to bash my head in with his little fists. They yanked me to my feet and marched me off while the reporters and this Halley Hogan girl stared. I can't tell you much about what happened after that—the debating and the discussing and the interminable sound and fury, because most of the time I was busy being locked up. All I can tell you is that I was it. Me. I. I was the one man we were trying to stop. I—innocent me. I was X, the mad scientist and Y, the ruthless dictator and Z, the alien planet—all rolled into one. I was the one guy the Earth was looking to stop.

Sure—because you see if you twist "I'll be a pie-eyed emu" enough, you get FitzJohn's equation:

$$i = (b/a) \, \pi \, i \, e/\mu \ldots "$$

I don't know how my future son is going to figure I was talking mathematics. I guess it'll just be another one of those incidents that turn into legend and get pretty well changed in the process. I mean the way an infant will "goo" and by the time his pop gets finished telling about it it's become the Preamble to the Credo.

What?

No, I'm not married—yet. In fact, that's why I'm stationed up here editing a two-sheet weekly on this God-forsaken asteroid. Old Groating, he calls it protective promotion. Well, sure, it's a better job than reporting. The C-S said they wouldn't have broken up an existing marriage, but he was going to keep us apart until they can work something out on the Prognosticator.

No—I never saw her again after that time I dumped her on the turf, but, boys, I sure want to. I only got a quick look, but she reminded me of that Barbara Leeds girl, six hundred years from now. That lovely kind with shingled hair and a clean-cut face that looks fresh and wind-washed—

I keep thinking about her and I keep thinking how easy it would be to stow out of here on an Earth-bound freighter—change my name—get a different kind of job. To hell with Groating and to hell with Stability and to hell with a thousand years from now. I've to see her again—soon.

I keep thinking how I've got to see her again.

1942

Clash by Night/

by LAWRENCE O'DONNELL

*The whole system of which he was a part was doomed, he knew—a
mercenary army that fought other mercenary armies for cities that
lay beneath the seas of Venus. Yet—there was a fascination and a reasonless loyalty to that futile system that held him.*

INTRODUCTION

*A half mile beneath the shallow Venusian Sea the black imper-
vium dome that protects Montana Keep rests frowningly on the
bottom. Within the Keep is carnival, for the Montanans celebrate
the four-hundred-year anniversary of Earthman's landing on
Venus. Under the great dome that houses the city all is light and
color and gaiety. Masked men and women, bright in celoflex and
silks, wander through the broad streets, laughing, drinking the
strong native wines of Venus. The sea bottom has been combed,
like the hydroponic tanks, for rare delicacies to grace the tables
of the nobles.*

*Through the festival grim shadows stalk, men whose faces mark
them unmistakably as members of a Free Company. Their finery
cannot disguise that stamp, hard-won through years of battle. Under the domino masks their mouths are hard and harsh. Unlike
the undersea dwellers, their skins are burned black with the ultraviolet rays that filter through the cloud layer of Venus. They are
skeletons at the feast. They are respected but resented. They are
Free Companions—*

*We are on Venus, nine hundred years ago, beneath the Sea
of Shoals, not much north of the equator. But there is a wide
range in time and space. All over the cloud planet the underwater
Keeps are dotted, and life will not change for many centuries.
Looking back, as we do now, from the civilized days of the
Thirty-fourth Century, it is too easy to regard the men of the
Keeps as savages, groping, stupid and brutal. The Free Companies have long since vanished. The islands and continents of Venus have been tamed, and there is no war.*

But in periods of transition, of desperate rivalry, there is always war. The Keeps fought among themselves, each striving to draw the fangs of the others by depriving them of their reserves of korium, the power source of the day. Students of that era find pleasure in sifting the legends and winnowing out the basic social and geopolitical truths. It is fairly well known that only one factor saved the Keeps from annihilating one another—the gentlemen's agreement that left war to the warriors, and allowed the undersea cities to develop their science and social cultures. That particular compromise was, perhaps, inevitable. And it caused the organization of the Free Companies, the roving bands of mercenaries, highly trained for their duties, who hired themselves out to fight for whatever Keeps were attacked or wished to attack.

Ap Towrn, in his monumental "Cycle of Venus," tells the saga through symbolic legends. Many historians have recorded the sober truth, which, unfortunately, seems often Mars-dry. But it is not generally realized that the Free Companions were almost directly responsible for our present high culture. War, because of them, was not permitted to usurp the place of peace-time social and scientific work. Fighting was highly specialized, and, because of technical advances, manpower was no longer important. Each band of Free Companions numbered a few thousand, seldom more.

It was a strange, lonely life they must have led, shut out from the normal life of the Keeps. They were vestigian but necessary, like the fangs of the marsupians who eventually evolved into Homo sapiens. But without those warriors, the Keeps would have been plunged completely into total war, with fatally destructive results.

Harsh, gallant, indomitable, serving the god of battles so that it might be destroyed—working toward their own obliteration—the Free Companies roar down the pages of history, the banner of Mars streaming above them in the misty air of Venus. They were doomed as Tyrannosaur Rex was doomed, and they fought on as he did, serving, in their strange way, the shape of Minerva that stood behind Mars.

Now they are gone. We can learn much by studying the place they held in the Undersea Period. For, because of them, civilization rose again to the heights it had once reached on Earth, and far beyond.

"These lords shall light the mystery
Of mastery or victory,
And these ride high in history,
But these shall not return."

*The Free Companions hold their place in interplanetary litera-
ture. They are a legend now, archaic and strange. For they were
fighters, and war has gone with unification. But we can understand them a little more than could the people of the Keeps.*

*This story, built on legends and fact, is about a typical warrior
of the period—Captain Brian Scott of Doone's Free Companions.
He may never have existed—*

I

*O, it's Tommy this, an' Tommy that, an' "Tommy, go away";
But it's "Thank you, Mr. Atkins," when the band begins to play,
The band begins to play, my boys, the band begins to play—
O, it's "Thank you, Mr. Atkins," when the band begins to play.*
                                        —R. Kipling circa 1900

Scott drank stinging uisqueplus and glowered across the smoky
tavern. He was a hard, stocky man, with thick gray-shot brown
hair and the scar of an old wound crinkling his chin. He was
thirty-odd, looking like the veteran he was, and he had sense
enough to wear a plain suit of blue celoflex, rather than the garish
silks and rainbow fabrics that were all around him.

Outside, through the transparent walls, a laughing throng was
carried to and fro along the movable ways. But in the tavern it
was silent, except for the low voice of a harpman as he chanted
some old ballad, accompanying himself on his complicated instrument. The song came to an end. There was scattered applause, and from the hot-box overhead the blaring music of an
orchestra burst out. Instantly the restraint was gone. In the booths
and at the bar men and women began to laugh and talk with
casual unrestraint. Couples were dancing now.

The girl beside Scott, a slim, tan-skinned figure with glossy
black ringlets cascading to her shoulders, turned inquiring eyes
to him.

"Want to, Brian?"

Scott's mouth twisted in a wry grimace. "Suppose so, Jeana.
Eh?" He rose, and she came gracefully into his arms. Brian did
not dance too well, but what he lacked in practice he made up
in integration. Jeana's heart-shaped face, with its high cheekbones
and vividly crimson lips, lifted to him.

"Forget Bienne. He's just trying to ride you."

Scott glanced toward a distant booth, where two girls sat with
a man—Commander Fredric Bienne of the Doones. He was a
gaunt, tall, bitter-faced man, his regular features twisted into a

perpetual sneer, his eyes somber under heavy dark brows. He was pointing, now, toward the couple on the floor.

"I know," Scott said. "He's doing it, too. Well, the hell with him. So I'm a captain now and he's still a commander. That's tough. Next time he'll obey orders and not send his ship out of the line, trying to ram."

"That was it, eh?" Jeana asked. "I wasn't sure. There's plenty of talk."

"There always is. Oh, Bienne's hated me for years. I reciprocate. We simply don't get on together. Never did. Every time I got a promotion, he chewed his nails. Figured he had a longer service record than I had, and deserved to move up faster. But he's too much of an individualist—at the wrong times."

"He's drinking a lot," Jeana said.

"Let him. Three months we've been in Montana Keep. The boys get tired of inaction—being treated like this." Scott nodded toward the door, where a Free Companion was arguing with the keeper. "No noncoms allowed in here. Well, the devil with it."

They could not hear the conversation above the hubbub, but its importance was evident. Presently the soldier shrugged, his mouth forming a curse, and departed. A fat man in scarlet silks shouted encouragement.

"—want any . . . Companions here!"

Scott saw Commander Bienne, his eyes half closed, get up and walk toward the fat man's booth. His shoulder moved in an imperceptible shrug. The hell with civilians, anyhow. Serve the lug right if Bienne smashed his greasy face. And that seemed the probable outcome. For the fat man was accompanied by a girl, and obviously wasn't going to back down, though Bienne, standing too close to him, was saying something insulting, apparently.

The auxiliary hot-box snapped some quick syllables, lost in the general tumult. But Scott's trained ear caught the words. He nodded to Jeana, made a significant clicking noise with his tongue, and said, "This is it."

She, too, had heard. She let Scott go. He headed toward the fat man's booth just in time to see the beginning of a brawl. The civilian, red as a turkey cock, had struck out suddenly, landing purely by accident on Bienne's gaunt cheek. The commander, grinning tightly, stepped back a pace, his fist clenching. Scott caught the other's arm.

"Hold it, commander."

Bienne swung around, glaring. "What business is it of yours? Let—"

The fat man, seeing his opponent's attention distracted,

acquired more courage and came in swinging. Scott reached past Bienne, planted his open hand in the civilian's face, and pushed hard. The fat man almost fell backward on his table.

As he rebounded, he saw a gun in Scott's hand. The captain said curtly, " 'Tend to your knitting, mister."

The civilian licked his lips, hesitated, and sat down. Under his breath he muttered something about too-damn-cocky Free Companions.

Bienne was trying to break free, ready to swing on the captain. Scott holstered his gun. "Orders," he told the other, jerking his head toward the hot-box. "Get it?"

"—mobilization. Doonemen report to headquarters. Captain Scott to Administration. Immediate mobilization—"

"Oh," Bienne said, though he still scowled. "O.K. I'll take over. There was time for me to take a crack at that louse, though."

"You know what instant mobilization means," Scott grunted. "We may have to leave at an instant's notice. Orders, commander."

Bienne saluted halfheartedly and turned away. Scott went back to his own booth. Jeana had already gathered her purse and gloves and was applying lip juice.

She met his eyes calmly enough.

"I'll be at the apartment, Brian. Luck."

He kissed her briefly, conscious of a surging excitement at the prospect of a new venture. Jeana understood his emotion. She gave him a quick, wry smile, touched his hair lightly, and rose. They went out into the gay tumult of the ways.

Perfumed wind blew into Scott's face. He wrinkled his nose disgustedly. During carnival seasons the Keeps were less pleasant to the Free Companions than otherwise; they felt more keenly the gulf that lay between them and the undersea dwellers. Scott pushed his way through the crowd and took Jeana across the ways to the center fast-speed strip. They found seats.

At a clover-leaf intersection Scott left the girl, heading toward Administration, the cluster of taller buildings in the city's center. The technical and political headquarters were centered here, except for the laboratories, which were in the suburbs near the base of the Dome. There were a few small test-domes a mile or so distant from the city, but these were used only for more precarious experiments. Glancing up, Scott was reminded of the catastrophe that had unified science into something like a freemasonry. Above him, hanging without gravity over a central plaza, was the globe of the Earth, half shrouded by the folds of a black plastic pall. In every Keep on Venus there was a similar ever-present reminder of the lost mother planet.

Scott's gaze went up farther, to the Dome, as though he could penetrate the impervium and the mile-deep layer of water and the clouded atmosphere to the white star that hung in space, one quarter as brilliant as the Sun. A star—all that remained of Earth, since atomic power had been unleashed there two centuries ago. The scourge had spread like flame, melting continents and leveling mountains. In the libraries there were wire-tape pictorial records of the Holocaust. A religious cult—Men of the New Judgment—had sprung up, and advocated the complete destruction of science; followers of that dogma still existed here and there. But the cult's teeth had been drawn when technicians unified, outlawing experiments with atomic power forever, making use of that force punishable by death, and permitting no one to join their society without taking the Minervan Oath.

"—to work for the ultimate good of mankind . . . taking all precaution against harming humanity and science . . . requiring permission from those in authority before undertaking any experiment involving peril to the race . . . remembering always the extent of the trust placed in us and remembering forever the death of the mother planet through misuse of knowledge—"

The Earth. A strange sort of world it must have been, Scott thought. Sunlight, for one thing, unfiltered by the cloud layer. In the old days, there had been few unexplored areas left on Earth. But here on Venus, where the continents had not yet been conquered—there was no need, of course, since everything necessary to life could be produced under the Domes—here on Venus, there was still a frontier. In the Keeps, a highly specialized social culture. Above the surface, a primeval world, where only the Free Companions had their fortresses and navies—the navies for fighting, the forts to house the technicians who provided the latter-day sinews of war, science instead of money. The Keeps tolerated visits from the Free Companions, but would not offer them headquarters, so violent the feeling, so sharp the schism, in the public mind, between war and cultural progress.

Under Scott's feet the sliding way turned into an escalator, carrying him into the Administration Building. He stepped to another way which took him to a lift, and, a moment or two later, was facing the door-curtain bearing the face of President Dane Crosby of Montana Keep.

Crosby's voice said, "Come in, captain," and Scott brushed through the curtain, finding himself in a medium-sized room with muraled walls and a great window overlooking the city. Crosby, a white-haired, thin figure in blue silks, was at his desk. He looked like a tired old clerk out of Dickens, Scott thought suddenly, entirely undistinguished and ordinary. Yet Crosby was one of the greatest socio-politicians on Venus.

Cinc Rhys, leader of Doone's Free Companions, was sitting in a relaxer, the apparent antithesis of Crosby. All the moisture in Rhys' body seemed to have been sucked out of him years ago by ultraviolet actinic, leaving a mummy of brown leather and whipcord sinew. There was no softness in the man. His smile was a grimace. Muscles lay like wire under the swarthy cheeks.

Scott saluted. Rhys waved him to a relaxer. The look of subdued eagerness in the cinc's eyes was significant—an eagle poising himself, smelling blood. Crosby sensed that, and a wry grin showed on his pale face.

"Every man to his trade," he remarked, semi-ironically. "I suppose I'd be bored stiff if I had too long a vacation. But you'll have quite a battle on your hands this time, Cinc Rhys."

Scott's stocky body tensed automatically. Rhys glanced at him.

"Virginia Keep is attacking, captain. They've hired the Helldivers—Flynn's outfit."

There was a pause. Both Free Companions were anxious to discuss the angles, but unwilling to do so in the presence of a civilian, even the president of Montana Keep. Crosby rose.

"The money settlement's satisfactory, then?"

Rhys nodded. "Yes, that's all right. I expect the battle will take place in a couple of days. In the neighborhood of Venus Deep, at a rough guess."

"Good. I've a favor to ask, so if you'll excuse me for a few minutes, I'll—" He left the sentence unfinished and went out through the door-curtain. Rhys offered Scott a cigarette.

"You get the implications, captain—the Helldivers?"

"Yes, sir. Thanks. We can't do it alone."

"Right. We're short on manpower and armament both. And the Helldivers recently merged with O'Brien's Legion, after O'Brien was killed in that polar scrap. They're a strong outfit, plenty strong. Then they've got their specialty—submarine attack. I'd say we'll have to use H-plan 7."

Scott closed his eyes, remembering the files. Each Free Company kept up-to-date plans of attack suited to the merits of every other Company of Venus. Frequently revised as new advances were made, as groups merged, and as the balance of power changed on each side, the plans were so detailed that they could be carried into action at literally a moment's notice. H-plan 7,

Scott recalled, involved enlisting the aid of the Mob, a small but well-organized band of Free Companions led by Cinc Tom Mendez.

"Right," Scott said. "Can you get him?"

"I think so. We haven't agreed yet on the bonus. I've been telaudioing him on a tight beam, but he keeps putting me off—waiting till the last moment, when he can dictate his own terms."

"What's he asking, sir?"

"Fifty thousand cash and a fifty percent cut on the loot."

"I'd say thirty percent would be about right."

Rhys nodded. "I've offered him thirty-five. I may send you to his fort—carte blanche. We can get another Company, but Mendez has got beautiful sub-detectors—which would come in handy against the Helldivers. Maybe I can settle things by audio. If not, you'll have to fly over to Mendez and buy his services, at less than fifty per if you can."

Scott rubbed the old scar on his chin with a calloused forefinger. "Meantime Commander Bienne's in charge of mobilization. When—"

"I telaudioed our fort. Air transports are on the way now."

"It'll be quite a scrap," Scott said, and the eyes of the two men met in perfect understanding. Rhys chuckled dryly.

"And good profits. Virginia Keep has a big supply of korium . . . dunno how much, but plenty."

"What started the fracas this time?"

"The usual thing, I suppose," Rhys said disinterestedly. "Imperialism. Somebody in Virginia Keep worked out a new plan for annexing the rest of the Keeps. Same as usual."

They stood up as the door-curtain swung back, admitting President Crosby, another man, and a girl. The man looked young, his boyish face not yet toughened under actinic burn. The girl was lovely in the manner of a plastic figurine, lit from within by vibrant life. Her blond hair was cropped in the prevalent mode, and her eyes, Scott saw, were an unusual shade of green. She was more than merely pretty—she was instantly exciting.

Crosby said, "My niece, Ilene Kane—and my nephew, Norman Kane." He performed introductions, and they found seats.

"What about drinks?" Ilene suggested. "This is rather revoltingly formal. The fight hasn't started yet, after all."

Crosby shook his head at her. "You weren't invited here anyway. Don't try to turn this into a party—there isn't too much time, under the circumstances."

"O. K.," Ilene murmured. "I can wait." She eyed Scott interestedly.

Norman Kane broke in. "I'd like to join Doone's Free Companions, sir. I've already applied, but now that there's a battle coming up, I hate to wait till my application's approved. So I thought—"

Crosby looked at Cinc Rhys. "A personal favor, but the decision's up to you. My nephew's a misfit—a romanticist. Never liked the life of a Keep. A year ago he went off and joined Starling's outfit."

Rhys raised an eyebrow. "That gang? It's not a recommendation, Kane. They're not even classed as Free Companions. More like a band of guerrillas, and entirely without ethics. There've even been rumors they're messing around with atomic power."

Crosby looked startled. "I hadn't heard that."

"It's no more than a rumor. If it's ever proved, the Free Companions—all of them—will get together and smash Starling in a hurry."

Norman Kane looked slightly uncomfortable. "I suppose I was rather a fool. But I wanted to get in the fighting game, and Starling's group appealed to me—"

The cinc made a sound in his throat. "They would. Swashbuckling romantics, with no idea of what war means. They've not more than a dozen technicians. And they've no discipline—it's like a pirate outfit. War today, Kane, isn't won by romantic animals dashing at forlorn hopes. The modern soldier is a tactician who knows how to think, integrate, and obey. If you join our Company, you'll have to forget what you learned with Starling."

"Will you take me, sir?"

"I think it would be unwise. You need the training course."

"I've had experience—"

Crosby said, "It would be a favor, Cinc Rhys, if you'd skip the red tape. I'd appreciate it. Since my nephew wants to be a soldier, I'd much prefer to see him with the Doones."

Rhys shrugged. "Very well. Captain Scott will give you your orders, Kane. Remember that discipline is vitally important with us."

The boy tried to force back a delighted grin. "Thank you, sir."

"Captain—"

Scott rose and nodded to Kane. They went out together. In the anteroom was a telaudio set, and Scott called the Doone's local headquarters in Montana Keep. An integrator answered, his face looking inquiringly from the screen.

"Captain Scott calling, subject induction."

"Yes, sir. Ready to record."

Scott drew Kane forward. "Photosnap this man. He'll report to headquarters immediately. Name, Norman Kane. Enlist him without training course—special orders from Cinc Rhys."

"Acknowledged, sir."

Scott broke the connection. Kane couldn't quite repress his grin.

"All right," the captain grunted, a sympathetic gleam in his eyes. "That fixes it. They'll put you in my command. What's your specialty?"

"Flitterboats, sir."

"Good. One more thing. Don't forget what Cinc Rhys said, Kane. Discipline is damned important, and you may not have realized that yet. This isn't a cloak-and-sword war. There are no Charges of Light Brigades. No grandstand plays—that stuff went out with the Crusades. Just obey orders, and you'll have no trouble. Good luck."

"Thank you, sir." Kane saluted and strode out with a perceptible swagger. Scott grinned. The kid would have *that* knocked out of him pretty soon.

A voice at his side made him turn quickly. Ilene Kane was standing there, slim and lovely in her celoflex gown.

"You seem pretty human after all, captain," she said. "I heard what you told Norman."

Scott shrugged. "I did that for his own good—and the good of the Company. One man off the beam can cause plenty of trouble, Mistress Kane."

"I envy Norman," she said. "It must be a fascinating life you lead. I'd like it—for a while. Not for long. I'm one of the useless offshoots of this civilization, not much good for anything. So I've perfected one talent."

"What's that?"

"Oh, hedonism, I suppose you'd call it. I enjoy myself. It's not often too boring. But I'm a bit bored now. I'd like to talk to you, captain."

"Well, I'm listening," Scott said.

Ilene Kane made a small grimace. "Wrong semantic term. I'd like to get inside of you psychologically. But painlessly. Dinner and dancing. Can do?"

"There's no time," Scott told her. "We may get our orders any moment." He wasn't sure he wanted to go out with this girl of the Keeps, though there was definitely a subtle fascination for him, an appeal he could not analyze. She typified the most pleasurable part of a world he did not know. The other facets of that world could not impinge on him; geopolitics or nonmilitary science held no appeal, were too alien. But all worlds touch at one point—pleasure. Scott could understand the relaxations of the undersea groups, as he could not understand or feel sympathy for their work or their social impulses.

Cinc Rhys came through the door-curtain, his eyes narrowed. "I've some telaudioing to do, captain," he said. Scott knew what implications the words held: the incipient bargain with Cinc Mendez. He nodded.

"Yes, sir. Shall I report to headquarters?"

Rhys' harsh face seemed to relax suddenly as he looked from Ilene to Scott. "You're free till dawn. I won't need you till then, but report to me at six a.m. No doubt you've a few details to clean up."

"Very well, sir." Scott watched Rhys go out. The cinc had meant Jeana, of course. But Ilene did not know that.

"So?" she asked. "Do I get a turn-down? You might buy me a drink, anyway."

There was plenty of time. Scott said, "It'll be a pleasure," and Ilene linked her arm with his. They took the dropper to ground-level.

As they came out on one of the ways, Ilene turned her head and caught Scott's glance. "I forgot something, captain. You may have a previous engagement. I didn't realize—"

"There's nothing," he said. "Nothing important."

It was true; he felt a mild gratitude toward Jeana at the realization. His relationship with her was the peculiar one rendered advisable by his career. Free-marriage was the word for it; Jeana was neither his wife nor his mistress, but something midway between. The Free Companions had no firmly grounded foundation for social life; in the Keeps they were visitors, and in their coastal forts they were—well, soldiers. One would no more bring a woman to a fort than aboard a ship of the line. So the women of the Free Companions lived in the Keeps, moving from one to another as their men did; and because of the ever-present shadow of death, ties were purposely left loose. Jeana and Scott had been free-married for five years now. Neither made demands on the other. No one expected fidelity of a Free Companion. Soldiers lived under such iron disciplines that when they were released, during the brief peacetimes, the pendulum often swung far in the opposite direction.

To Scott, Ilene Kane was a key that might unlock the doors of the Keep—doors that opened to a world of which he was not a part, and which he could not quite understand.

II

I, a stranger and afraid
In a world I never made.
                          —Housman

There were nuances, Scott found, which he had never known existed. A hedonist like Ilene devoted her life to such nuances; they were her career. Such minor matters as making the powerful, insipid Moonflower Cocktails more palatable by filtering them through lime-soaked sugar held between the teeth. Scott was a uisqueplus man, having the average soldier's contempt for what he termed hydroponic drinks, but the cocktails Ilene suggested were quite as effective as acrid, burning amber uisqueplus. She taught him, that night, such tricks as pausing between glasses to sniff lightly at happy-gas, to mingle sensual excitement with mental by trying the amusement rides designed to give one the violent physical intoxication of breathless speed. Nuances all, which only a girl with Ilene's background could know. She was not representative of Keep life. As she had said, she was an offshoot, a casual and useless flower on the great vine that struck up inexorably to the skies, its strength in its tough, reaching tendrils—scientists and technicians and socio-politicians. She was doomed in her own way, as Scott was in his. The undersea folk served Minerva; Scott served Mars; and Ilene served Aphrodite—not purely the sexual goddess, but the patron of arts and pleasure. Between Scott and Ilene was the difference between Wagner and Strauss; the difference between crashing chords and tinkling arpeggios. In both was a muted bittersweet sadness, seldom realized by either. But that undertone was brought out by their contact. The sense of dim hopelessness in each responded to the other.

It was carnival, but neither Ilene nor Scott wore masks. Their faces were masks enough, and both had been trained to reserve, though in different ways. Scott's hard mouth kept its tight grimness even when he smiled. And Ilene's smiles came so often that they were meaningless.

Through her, Scott was able to understand more of the undersea life than he had ever done before. She was for him a catalyst. A tacit understanding grew between them, not needing words. Both realized that, in the course of progress, they would eventually die out. Mankind tolerated them because that was necessary for a little time. Each responded differently. Scott served Mars;

he served actively; and the girl, who was passive, was attracted by the antithesis.

Scott's drunkenness struck psychically deep. He did not show it. His stiff silver-brown hair was not disarranged, and his hard, burned face was impassive as ever. But when his brown eyes met Ilene's green ones a spark of—something—met between them.

Color and light and sound. They began to form a pattern now, were not quite meaningless to Scott. They were, long past midnight, sitting in an Olympus, which was a private cosmos. The walls of the room in which they were seemed nonexistent. The gusty tides of gray, faintly luminous clouds seemed to drive chaotically past them, and, dimly, they could hear the muffled screaming of an artificial wind. They had the isolation of the gods.

And the Earth was without form, and void; and darkness was upon the face of the deep— That was, of course, the theory of the Olympus room. No one existed, no world existed, outside of the chamber; values automatically shifted, and inhibitions seemed absurd.

Scott relaxed on a translucent cushion like a cloud. Beside him, Ilene lifted the bit of a happy-gas tube to his nostrils. He shook his head.

"Not now, Ilene."

She let the tube slide back into its reel. "Nor I. Too much of anything is unsatisfactory, Brian. There should always be something untasted, some anticipation left— You have that. I haven't."

"How?"

"Pleasures—well, there's a limit. There's a limit to human endurance. And eventually I build up a resistance psychically, as I do physically, to everything. With you, there's always the last adventure. You never know when death will come. You can't plan. Plans are dull; it's the unexpected that's important."

Scott shook his head slightly. "Death isn't important either. It's an automatic cancellation of values. Or, rather—" He hesitated, seeking words. "In this life you can plan, you can work out values, because they're all based on certain conditions. On—let's say—arithmetic. Death is a change to a different plane of conditions, quite unknown. Arithmetical rules don't apply as such to geometry."

"You think death has its rules?"

"It may be a lack of rules, Ilene. One lives realizing that life is subject to death; civilization is based on that. That's why civilization concentrates on the race instead of the individual. Social self-preservation."

She looked at him gravely. "I didn't think a Free Companion could theorize that way."

Scott closed his eyes, relaxing. "The Keeps know nothing about Free Companions. They don't want to. We're men. Intelligent men. Our technicians are as great as the scientists under the Domes."

"But they work for war."

"War's necessary," Scott said. "Now, anyway."

"How did you get into it? Should I ask?"

He laughed a little at that. "Oh, I've no dark secrets in my past. I'm not a runaway murderer. One—drifts. I was born in Australia Keep. My father was a tech, but my grandfather had been a soldier. I guess it was in my blood. I tried various trades and professions. Meaningless. I wanted something that . . . hell, I don't know. Something, maybe, that needs all of a man. Fighting does. It's like a religion. Those cultists—Men of the New Judgment—they're fanatics, but you can see that their religion is the only thing that matters to them."

"Bearded, dirty men with twisted minds, though."

"It happens to be a religion based on false premises. There are others, appealing to different types. But religion was too passive for me, in these days."

Ilene examined his harsh face. "You'd have preferred the church militant—the Knights of Malta, fighting Saracens."

"I suppose. I had no values. Anyhow, I'm a fighter."

"Just how important is it to you? The Free Companions?"

Scott opened his eyes and grinned at the girl. He looked unexpectedly boyish.

"Damn little, really. It has emotional appeal. Intellectually, I know that it's a huge fake. Always has been. As absurd as the Men of the New Judgment. Fighting's doomed. So we've no real purpose. I suppose most of us know there's no future for the Free Companions. In a few hundred years—well!"

"And still you go on. Why? It isn't money."

"No. There is a . . . a drunkenness to it. The ancient Norsemen had their berserker madness. We have something similar. To a Dooneman, his group is father, mother, child, and God Almighty. He fights the other Free Companions when he's paid to do so, but he doesn't hate the others. They serve the same toppling idol. And it *is* toppling, Ilene. Each battle we win or lose brings us closer to the end. We fight to protect the culture that eventually will wipe us out. The Keeps—when they finally unify, will they need a military arm? I can see the trend. If war was an essential part of civilization, each Keep would maintain its own military.

But they shut us out—a necessary evil. If they would end war now!" Scott's fist unconsciously clenched. "So many men would find happier places in Venus—undersea. But as long as the Free Companions exist, there'll be new recruits."

Ilene sipped her cocktail, watching the gray chaos of clouds flow like a tide around them. In the dimly luminous light Scott's face seemed like dark stone, flecks of brightness showing in his eyes. She touched his hand gently.

"You're a soldier, Brian. You wouldn't change."

His laugh was intensely bitter. "Like hell I wouldn't, Mistress Ilene Kane! Do you think fighting's just pulling a trigger? I'm a military strategist. That took ten years. Harder cramming than I'd have had in a Keep Tech-Institute. I have to know everything about war from trajectories to mass psychology. This is the greatest science the System has ever known, and the most useless. Because war will die in a few centuries at most. Ilene—you've never seen a Free Company's fort. It's science, marvelous science, aimed at military ends only. We have our psych-specialists. We have our engineers, who plan everything from ordnance to the frictional quotient on flitterboats. We have the foundries and mills. Each fortress is a city made for war, as the Keeps are made for social progress."

"As complicated as that?"

"Beautifully complicated and beautifully useless. There are so many of us who realize that. Oh, we fight—it's a poison. We worship the Company—that is an emotional poison. But we live only during wartime. It's an incomplete life. Men in the Keeps have full lives; they have their work, and their relaxations are geared to fit them. We don't fit."

"Not all the undersea races," Ilene said. "There's always the fringe that doesn't fit. At least you have a *raison d'être*. You're a soldier. I can't make a lifework out of pleasure. But there's nothing else for me."

Scott's fingers tightened on hers. "You're the product of a civilization, at least. I'm left out."

"With you, Brian, it might be better. For a while. I don't think it would last for long."

"It might."

"You think so now. It's quite a horrible thing, feeling yourself a shadow."

"I know."

"I want you, Brian," Ilene said, turning to face him. "I want you to come to Montana Keep and stay here. Until our experiment fails. I think it'll fail presently. But, perhaps, not for some time. I need your strength. I can show you how to get the most out of this sort of life—how to enter into it. True hedonism. You can give me—companionship perhaps. For me the companionship of hedonists who know nothing else isn't enough."

Scott was silent. Ilene watched him for a while.

"Is war so important?" she asked at last.

"No," he said, "it isn't at all. It's a balloon. And it's empty, I know that. Honor of the regiment!" Scott laughed. "I'm not hesitating, really. I've been shut out for a long time. A social unit shouldn't be founded on an obviously doomed fallacy. Men and women are important, nothing else, I suppose."

"Men and women—or the race?"

"Not the race," he said with abrupt violence. "Damn the race! It's done nothing for me. I can fit myself into a new life. Not necessarily hedonism. I'm an expert in several lines; I have to be. I can find work in Montana Keep."

"If you like. I've never tried. I'm more of a fatalist, I suppose. But . . . what about it, Brian?"

Her eyes were almost luminous, like shining emerald, in the ghostly light.

"Yes," Scott said. "I'll come back. To stay."

Ilene said, "Come back? Why not stay now?"

"Because I'm a complete fool, I guess. I'm a key man, and Cinc Rhys needs me just now."

"Is it Rhys or the Company?"

Scott smiled crookedly. "Not the Company. It's just a job I have to do. When I think how many years I've been slaving, pretending absurdities were important, knowing that I was bowing to a straw dummy— *No!* I want your life—the sort of life I didn't know could exist in the Keeps. I'll be back, Ilene. It's something more important than love. Separately we're halves. Together we may be a complete whole."

She didn't answer. Her eyes were steady on Scott's. He kissed her.

Before morning bell he was back in the apartment. Jeana had already packed the necessary light equipment. She was asleep, her dark hair cascading over the pillow, and Scott did not waken her. Quietly he shaved, showered, and dressed. A heavy, waiting silence seemed to fill the city like a cup brimmed with stillness.

As he emerged from the bathroom, buttoning his tunic, he saw the table had been let down and two places set at it. Jeana came in, wearing a cool morning frock. She set cups down and poured coffee.

"Morning, soldier," she said. "You've time for this, haven't you?"

"Uh-huh." Scott kissed her, a bit hesitantly. Up till this moment, the breaking with Jeana had seemed easy enough. She would raise no objections. That was the chief reason for free-marriage. However—

She was sitting in the relaxer, sweeting the coffee, opening a fresh celopack of cigarettes. "Hung over?"

"No. I vitamized. Feel pretty good." Most bars had a vitamizing chamber to nullify the effects of too much stimulant. Scott was, in fact, feeling fresh and keenly alert. He was wondering how to broach the subject of Ilene to Jeana.

She saved him the trouble.

"If it's a girl, Brian, just take it easy. No use doing anything till this war's over. How long will it take?"

"Oh, not long. A week at most. One battle may settle it, you know. The girl—"

"She's not a Keep girl."

"Yes."

Jeana looked up, startled. "You're crazy."

"I started to tell you," Scott said impatiently. "It isn't just—her. I'm sick of the Doones. I'm going to quit."

"Hm-m-m. Like that?"

"Like that."

Jeana shook her head. "Keep women aren't tough."

"They don't need to be. Their men aren't soldiers."

"Have it your own way. I'll wait till you get back. Maybe I've got a hunch. You see, Brian, we've been together for five years. We fit. Not because of anything like philosophy or psychology— it's a lot more personal. It's just us. As man and woman, we get along comfortably. There's love, too. Those close emotional feelings are more important, really, than the long view. You can get excited about futures, but you can't live them."

Scott shrugged. "Could be I'm starting to forget about futures. Concentrating on Brian Scott."

"More coffee . . . there. Well, for five years now I've gone with you from Keep to Keep, waiting every time you went off to war, wondering if you'd come back, knowing that I was just a part of your life, but—I sometimes thought—the most important part. Soldiering's seventy-five percent. I'm the other quarter. I think you need that quarter—you need the whole thing, in that proportion, actually. You could find another woman, but she'd have to be willing to take twenty-five percent."

Scott didn't answer. Jeana blew smoke through her nostrils.

"O.K., Brian. I'll wait."

"It isn't the girl so much. She happens to fit into the pattern of what I want. You—"

"I'd never be able to fit that pattern," Jeana said softly. "The Free Companions need women who are willing to be soldiers' wives. Free-wives, if you like. Chiefly it's a matter of not being too demanding. But there are other things. No, Brian. Even if you wanted that, I couldn't make myself over into one of the Keep people. It wouldn't be me. I wouldn't respect myself, living a life that'd be false to me; and you wouldn't like me that way either. I couldn't and wouldn't change. I'll have to stay as I am. A soldier's wife. As long as you're a Dooneman, you'll need me. But if *you* change—" She didn't finish.

Scott lit a cigarette, scowling. "It's hard to know, exactly."

"I may not understand you, but I don't ask questions and I don't try to change you. As long as you want that, you can have it from me. I've nothing else to offer you. It's enough for a Free Companion. It's not enough—or too much—for a Keep-dweller."

"I'll miss you," he said.

"That'll depend, too. I'll miss you." Under the table her fingers writhed together, but her face did not change. "It's getting late. Here, let me check your chronometer." Jeana leaned across the table, lifted Scott's wrist, and compared his watch with the central-time clock on the wall. "O.K. On your way, soldier."

Scott stood up, tightening his belt. He bent to kiss Jeana, and, though she began to turn her face away, after a moment she raised her lips to his.

They didn't speak. Scott went out quickly, and the girl sat motionless, the cigarette smoldering out unheeded between her fingers. Somehow it did not matter so much, now, that Brian was leaving her for another woman and another life. As always, the one thing of real importance was that he was going into danger.

Guard him from harm, she thought, not knowing that she was praying. *Guard him from harm!*

And now there would be silence, and waiting. That, at least, had not changed. Her eyes turned to the clock.

Already the minutes were longer.

III

'E's the kind of a giddy harumfrodite—soldier an' sailor too!
> —Kipling

Commander Bienne was superintending the embarkation of the last Dooneman when Scott arrived at headquarters. He saluted the captain briskly, apparently untired by his night's work of handling the transportation routine.

"All checked, sir."

Scott nodded. "Good. Is Cinc Rhys here?"

"He just arrived." Bienne nodded toward a door-curtain. As Scott moved away, the other followed.

"What's up, commander?"

Bienne pitched his voice low. "Bronson's laid up with endemic fever." He forgot to say "sir." "He was to handle the left wing of the fleet. I'd appreciate that job."

"I'll see if I can do it."

Bienne's lips tightened, but he said nothing more. He turned back to his men, and Scott went on into the cinc's office. Rhys was at the telaudio. He looked up, his eyes narrowed.

"Morning, captain. I've just heard from Mendez."

"Yes, sir?"

"He's still holding out for a fifty percent cut on the korium ransom from Virginia Keep. You'll have to see him. Try and get the Mob for less than fifty if you can. Telaudio me from Mendez's fort."

"Check, sir."

"Another thing. Bronson's in sick bay."

"I heard that. If I may suggest Commander Bienne to take his place at left-wing command—"

But Cinc Rhys raised his hand. "Not this time. We can't afford individualism. The commander tried to play a lone hand in the last war. You know we can't risk it till he's back in line—thinking of the Doones instead of Fredric Bienne."

"He's a good man, sir. A fine strategist."

"But not yet a good integrating factor. Perhaps next time. Put Commander Geer on the left wing. Keep Bienne with you. He needs discipline. And—take a flitterboat to Mendez."

"Not a plane?"

"One of the technicians just finished a new tight-beam camouflager for communications. I'm having it installed immediately on all our planes and gliders. Use the boat; it isn't far to the Mob's fort—that long peninsula on the coast of Southern Hell."

Even on the charts that continent was named Hell—for obvious reasons. Heat was only one of them. And, even with the best equipment, a party exploring the jungle there would soon find itself suffering the tortures of the damned. On the land of Venus, flora and fauna combined diabolically to make the place uninhabitable to Earthmen. Many of the plants even exhaled poisonous gases. Only the protected coastal forts of the Free Companies could exist—and that was because they *were* forts.

Cinc Rhys frowned at Scott. "We'll use H-plan 7 if we can get the Mob. Otherwise we'll have to fall back on another outfit, and I don't want to do that. The Helldivers have too many subs, and we haven't enough detectors. So do your damnedest."

Scott saluted. "I'll do that, sir." Rhys waved him away, and he went out into the next room, finding Commander Bienne alone. The officer turned an inquiring look toward him.

"Sorry," Scott said. "Geer gets the left-wing command this time."

Bienne's sour face turned dark red. "I'm sorry I didn't take a crack at you before mobilization," he said. "You hate competition, don't you?"

Scott's nostrils flared. "If it had been up to me, you'd have got that command, Bienne."

"Sure. I'll bet. All right, captain. Where's my bunk? A flitter-boat?"

"You'll be on right wing, with me. Control ship *Flintlock*."

"With you. Under you, you mean," Bienne said tightly. His eyes were blazing. "Yeah."

Scott's dark cheeks were flushed too. "Orders, commander," he snapped. "Get me a flitterboat pilot. I'm going topside."

Without a word Bienne turned to the telaudio. Scott, a tight, furious knot in his stomach, stamped out of headquarters, trying to fight down his anger. Bienne was a jackass. A lot he cared about the Doones—

Scott caught himself and grinned sheepishly. Well, he cared little about the Doones himself. But while he was in the Company, discipline was important—integration with the smoothly running fighting machine. No place for individualism. One thing he and Bienne had in common; neither had any sentiment about the Company.

He took a lift to the ceiling of the Dome. Beneath him Montana Keep dropped away, shrinking to doll size. Somewhere down there, he thought, was Ilene. He'd be back. Perhaps this war would be a short one—not that they were ever much longer than a week, except in unusual cases where a Company developed new strategies.

He was conducted through an air lock into a bubble, a tough, transparent sphere with a central vertical core through which the cable ran. Except for Scott, the bubble was empty. After a moment it started up with a slight jar. Gradually the water outside the curving walls changed from black to deep green, and thence to translucent chartreuse. Sea creatures were visible, but they were nothing new to Scott; he scarcely saw them.

The bubble broke surface. Since air pressure had been constant, there was no possibility of the bends, and Scott opened the panel and stepped out on one of the buoyant floats that dotted the water above Montana Keep. A few sightseers crowded into the chamber he had left, and presently it was drawn down, out of sight.

In the distance Free Companions were embarking from a larger float to an air ferry. Scott glanced up with a weather eye. No storm, he saw, though the low ceiling was, as usual, torn and twisted into boiling currents by the winds. He remembered, suddenly, that the battle would probably take place over Venus Deep. That would make it somewhat harder for the gliders—there would be few of the thermals found, for instance, above the Sea of Shallows here.

A flitterboat, low, fast, and beautifully maneuverable, shot in toward the quay. The pilot flipped back the overhead shell and saluted Scott. It was Norman Kane, looking shipshape in his tight-fitting gray uniform, and apparently ready to grin at the slightest provocation.

Scott jumped lightly down into the craft and seated himself beside the pilot. Kane drew the transparent shell back over them. He looked at Scott.

"Orders, captain?"

"Know where the Mob's fort is? Good. Head there. Fast."

Kane shot the flitterboat out from the float with a curtain of v-shaped spray rising from the bow. Drawing little water, maneuverable, incredibly fast, these tiny craft were invaluable in naval battle. It was difficult to hit one, they moved so fast. They had no armor to slow them down. They carried high-explosive bullets fired from small-caliber guns, and were, as a rule, two-man craft. They complemented the heavier ordnance of the battle-wagons and destroyers.

Scott handed Kane a cigarette. The boy hesitated.

"We're not under fire," the captain chuckled. "Discipline clamps down during a battle, but it's O. K. for you to have a smoke with me. Here!" He lit the white tube for Kane.

"Thanks, sir. I guess I'm a bit—over-anxious?"

"Well, war has its rules. Not many, but they mustn't be broken." Both men were silent for a while, watching the blank gray surface of the ocean ahead. A transport plane passed them, flying low.

"Is Ilene Kane your sister?" Scott asked presently.

Kane nodded. "Yes, sir."

"Thought so. If she'd been a man, I imagine she'd have been a Free Companion."

The boy shrugged. "Oh, I don't know. She doesn't have the— I don't know. She'd consider it too much effort. She doesn't like discipline."

"Do you?"

"It's fighting that's important to me. Sir." That was an afterthought. "Winning, really."

"You can lose a battle even though you win it," Scott said rather somberly.

"Well, I'd rather be a Free Companion than do anything else I know of. Not that I've had much experience—"

"You've had experience of war with Starling's outfit, but you probably learned some dangerous stuff at the same time. War isn't swashbuckling piracy these days. If the Doones tried to win battles by that sort of thing, there'd be no more Doones in a week or so."

"But—" Kane hesitated. "Isn't that sort of thing rather necessary? Taking blind chances, I mean—"

"There are desperate chances," Scott told him, "but there are no blind chances in war—not to a good soldier. When I was green in the service, I ran a cruiser out of the line to ram. I was demoted, for a very good reason. The enemy ship I rammed wasn't as important to the enemy as our cruiser was to us. If I'd stayed on course, I'd have helped sink three or four ships instead of disabling one and putting my cruiser out of action. It's the great god integration we worship, Kane. It's much more important now than it ever was on Earth, because the military has consolidated. Army, navy, air, undersea—they're all part of one organization now. I suppose the only important change was in the air."

"Gliders, you mean? I knew powered planes couldn't be used in battle."

"Not in the atmosphere of Venus," Scott agreed. "Once powered planes get up in the cloud strata, they're fighting crosscurrents and pockets so much they've got no time to do accurate firing. If they're armored, they're slow. If they're light, detectors can spot them and antiaircraft can smash them. Unpowered gliders are valuable not for bombing but for directing attacks. They get into the clouds, stay hidden, and use infrared telecameras which are broadcast on a tight beam back to the control ships. They're the eyes of the fleet. They can tell us— *White water ahead, Kane! Swerve!*"

The pilot had already seen the ominous boiling froth foaming out in front of the bow. Instinctively he swung the flitterboat in a wrenching turn. The craft heeled sidewise, throwing its occupants almost out of their seats.

"Sea beast?" Scott asked, and answered his own question. "No, not with those spouts. It's volcanic. And it's spreading fast."

"I can circle it, sir," Kane suggested.

Scott shook his head. "Too dangerous. Backtrack."

Obediently the boy sent the flitterboat racing out of the area of danger. Scott had been right about the extent of the danger; the boiling turmoil was widening almost faster than the tiny ship could flee. Suddenly the line of white water caught up with them. The flitterboat jounced like a chip, the wheel being nearly torn from Kane's grip. Scott reached over and helped steady it. Even with two men handling the wheel, there was a possibility that it might wrench itself free. Steam rose in veils beyond the transparent shell. The water had turned a scummy brown under the froth.

Kane jammed on the power. The flitterboat sprang forward like a ricocheting bullet, dancing over the surface of the seething waves. Once they plunged head-on into a swell, and a screaming of outraged metal vibrated through the craft. Kane, tight-lipped, instantly slammed in the auxiliary, cutting out the smashed motor unit. Then, unexpectedly, they were in clear water, cutting back toward Montana Keep.

Scott grinned. "Nice handling. Lucky you didn't try to circle. We'd never have made it."

"Yes, sir." Kane took a deep breath. His eyes were bright with excitement.

"Circle now. Here." He thrust a lighted cigarette between the boy's lips. "You'll be a good Dooneman, Kane. Your reactions are good and fast."

"Thanks, sir."

Scott smoked silently for a while. He glanced toward the north, but, with the poor visibility, he could not make out the towering range of volcanic peaks that were the backbone of Southern Hell. Venus was a comparatively young planet, the internal fires still bursting forth unexpectedly. Which was why no forts were ever built on islands—they had an unhappy habit of disappearing without warning!

The flitterboat rode hard, at this speed, despite the insulating system of springs and shock absorbers. After a ride in one of these "spankers"—the irreverent name the soldiers had for them—a man needed arnica if not a chiropractor. Scott shifted his weight on the soft air cushions under him, which felt like cement.

Under his breath he hummed:

"It ain't the 'eavy 'aulin' that 'urts the 'orses' 'oofs,
It's the 'ammer, 'ammer, 'ammer on the 'ard 'ighway!"

The flitterboat scooted on, surrounded by monotonous sea and cloud, till finally the rampart of the coast grew before the bow, bursting suddenly from the fog-veiled horizon. Scott glanced at his chronometer and sighed with relief. They had made good time, in spite of the slight delay caused by the sub-sea volcano.

The fortress of the Mob was a huge metal and stone castle on the tip of the peninsula. The narrow strip that separated it from the mainland had been cleared, and the pockmarks of shell craters showed where guns had driven back onslaughts from the jungle—the reptilian, ferocious giants of Venus, partially intelligent but absolutely untractable because of the gulf that existed between their methods of thinking and the culture of mankind. Overtures had been made often enough; but it had been found that the reptile-folk were better left alone. They would not parley. They were blindly bestial savages, with whom it was impossible to make truce. They stayed in the jungle, emerging only to hurl furious attacks at the forts—attacks doomed to failure, since fang and talon were matched against lead-jacketed bullet and high explosive.

As the flitterboat shot in to a jetty, Scott kept his eyes straight ahead—it was not considered good form for a Free Companion to seem too curious when visiting the fort of another Company. Several men were on the quay, apparently waiting for him. They saluted as Scott stepped out of the boat.

He gave his name and rank. A corporal stepped forward.

"Cinc Mendez is expecting you, sir. Cinc Rhys telaudioed an hour or so back. If you'll come this way—"

"All right, corporal. My pilot—"

"He'll be taken care of, sir. A rubdown and a drink, perhaps, after a spanker ride."

Scott nodded and followed the other into the bastion that thrust out from the overhanging wall of the fort. The sea gate was open, and he walked swiftly through the courtyard in the corporal's wake, passing a door-curtain, mounting an escalator, and finding himself, presently, before another curtain that bore the face of Cinc Mendez, plump, hoglike, and bald as a bullet.

Entering, he saw Mendez himself at the head of a long table, where nearly a dozen officers of the Mob were also seated. In person Mendez was somewhat more prepossessing than in effigy. He looked like a boar rather than a pig—a fighter, not a gourmand. His sharp black eyes seemed to drive into Scott with the impact of a physical blow.

He stood up, his officers following suit. "Sit down, captain. There's a place at the foot of the table. No reflections on rank, but I prefer to be face to face with the man I'm dealing with. But first—you just arrived? If you'd like a quick rubdown, we'll be glad to wait."

Scott took his place. "Thank you, no, Cinc Mendez. I'd prefer not to lose time."

"Then we'll waste none on introductions. However, you can probably stand a drink." He spoke to the orderly at the door, and presently a filled glass stood at Scott's elbow.

His quick gaze ran along the rows of faces. Good soldiers, he thought—tough, well trained, and experienced. They had been under fire. A small outfit, the Mob, but a powerful one.

Cinc Mendez sipped his own drink. "To business. The Doonemen wish to hire our help in fighting the Helldivers. Virginia Keep has bought the services of the Helldivers to attack Montana Keep." He enumerated on stubby fingers. "You offer us fifty thousand cash and thirty-five percent of the korium ransom. So?"

"That's correct."

"We ask fifty percent."

"It's high. The Doones have superior manpower and equipment."

"To us, not to the Helldivers. Besides, the percentage is contingent. If we should lose, we get only the cash payment."

Scott nodded. "That's correct, but the only real danger from the Helldivers is their submarine corps. The Doones have plenty of surface and air equipment. We might lick the Helldivers without you."

"I don't think so." Mendez shook his bald head. "They have some new underwater torpedoes that make hash out of heavy armor plate. But *we* have new sub-detectors. We can blast the Helldivers' subs for you before they get within torpedo range."

Scott said bluntly, "You've been stalling, Cinc Mendez. We're not that bad off. If we can't get you, we'll find another outfit."

"With sub-detectors?"

"Yardley's Company is good at undersea work."

A major near the head of the table spoke up. "That's true, sir.

They have suicide subs—not too dependable, but they have them."

Cinc Mendez wiped his bald head with his palms in a slow circular motion. "Hm-m-m. Well, captain, I don't know. Yardley's Company isn't as good as ours for this job."

"All right," Scott said, "I've *carte blanche*. We don't know how much korium Virginia Keep has in her vaults. How would this proposition strike you: the Mob gets fifty percent of the korium ransom up to a quarter of a million; thirty-five percent above that."

"Forty-five."

"Forty, above a quarter of a million; forty-five below that sum."

"Gentlemen?" Cinc Mendez asked, looking down the table. "Your vote?"

There were several ayes, and a scattering of nays. Mendez shrugged.

"Then I have the deciding vote. Very well. We get forty-five percent of the Virginia Keep ransom up to a quarter of a million; forty percent on any amount above that. Agreed. We'll drink to it."

Orderlies served drinks. As Mendez rose, the others followed his example. The cinc nodded to Scott.

"Will you propose a toast, captain?"

"With pleasure. Nelson's toast, then—a willing foe and sea room!"

They drank to that, as Free Companions had always drunk that toast on the eve of battle. As they seated themselves once more, Mendez said, "Major Matson, please telaudio Cinc Rhys and arrange details. We must know his plans."

"Yes, sir."

Mendez glanced at Scott. "Now how else may I serve you?"

"Nothing else. I'll get back to our fort. Details can be worked out on the telaudio, on tight beam."

"If you're going back in that flitterboat," Mendez said sardonically, "I strongly advise a rubdown. There's time to spare, now we've come to an agreement."

Scott hesitated. "Very well. I'm . . . uh . . . starting to ache." He stood up. "Oh, one thing I forgot. We've heard rumors that Starling's outfit is using atomic power."

Mendez's mouth twisted into a grimace of distaste. "Hadn't heard that. Know anything about it, gentlemen?"

Heads were shaken. One officer said, "I've heard a little talk about it, but only talk, so far."

Mendez said, "After this war, we'll investigate further. If there's truth in the story, we'll join you, of course, in mopping up the Starlings. No court-martial is necessary for *that* crime!"

"Thanks. I'll get in touch with other Companies and see what they've heard. Now, if you'll excuse me—"

He saluted and went out, exultation flaming within him. The bargain had been a good one—for the Doonemen badly needed the Mob's help against the Helldivers. Cinc Rhys would be satisfied with the arrangement.

An orderly took him to the baths, where a rubdown relaxed his aching muscles. Presently he was on the quay again, climbing into the flitterboat. A glance behind him showed that the gears of war were beginning to grind. There was little he could see, but men were moving about through the courtyard with purposeful strides, to the shops, to administration, to the laboratories. The battlewagons were anchored down the coast, Scott knew, in a protected bay, but they would soon move out to their rendezvous with the Doones.

Kane, at the controls of the flitterboat, said, "They repaired the auxiliary unit for us, sir."

"Courtesies of the trade." Scott lifted a friendly hand to the men on the quay as the boat slid toward open water. "The Doone fort, now. Know it?"

"Yes, sir. Are . . . are the Mob fighting with us, if I may ask?"

"They are. And they're a grand lot of fighters. You're going to see action, Kane. When you hear battle stations next, it's going to mean one of the sweetest scraps that happened on Venus. Push down that throttle—we're in a hurry!"

The flitterboat raced southwest at top speed, its course marked by the flying V of spray.

"One last fight," Scott thought to himself. "I'm glad it's going to be a good one."

IV

We eat and drink our own damnation.
—The Book of Common Prayer

The motor failed when they were about eight miles from the Doone fort.

It was a catastrophe rather than merely a failure. The overstrained and overheated engine, running at top speed, blew back. The previous accident, at the subsea volcano, had brought out hidden flaws in the alloy which the Mob's repair men had failed to detect, when they replaced the smashed single unit. Sheer luck had the flitterboat poised on a swell when the crack-up happened. The engine blew out and down, ripping the bow to shreds. Had they been bow-deep, the blast would have been unfortunate for Scott and the pilot—more so than it was.

They were perhaps a half mile from the shore. Scott was deafened by the explosion and simultaneously saw the horizon swinging in a drunken swoop. The boat turned turtle, the shell smacking into water with a loud cracking sound. But the plastic held. Both men were tangled together on what had been their ceiling, sliding forward as the flitterboat began to sink bow first. Steam sizzled from the ruined engine.

Kane managed to touch one of the emergency buttons. The shell was, of course, jammed, but a few of the segments slid aside, admitting a gush of acrid sea water. For a moment they struggled there, fighting the crosscurrents till the air had been displaced. Scott, peering through cloudy green gloom, saw Kane's dark shadow twist and kick out through a gap. He followed.

Beneath him the black bulk of the boat dropped slowly and was gone. His head broke surface, and he gasped for breath, shaking droplets from his lashes and glancing around. Where was Kane?

The boy appeared, his helmet gone, sleek hair plastered to his forehead. Scott caught his eye and pulled the trigger on his life vest, the inflatable undergarment which was always worn under the blouse on sea duty. As chemicals mixed, light gas rushed into the vest, lifting Scott higher in the water. He felt the collar cushion inflate against the back of his head—the skull-fitting pillow that allowed shipwrecked men to float and rest without danger of drowning in their sleep. But he had no need for this now.

Kane, he saw, had triggered his own life vest. Scott hurled himself up, searching for signs of life. There weren't any. The gray-green sea lay desolate to the misty horizon. A half mile away was a mottled chartreuse wall that marked the jungle. Above and beyond that dim sulphurous red lit the clouds.

Scott got out his leaf-bladed smatchet, gesturing for Kane to do the same. The boy did not seem worried. No doubt this was merely an exciting adventure for him, Scott thought wryly. Oh, well.

Gripping the smatchet between his teeth, the captain began to swim shoreward. Kane kept at his side. Once Scott warned his companion to stillness and bent forward, burying his face in the water and peering down at a great dim shadow that coiled away and was gone—a sea snake, but, luckily, not hungry. The oceans of Venus were perilous with teeming, ferocious life. Precautions were fairly useless. When a man was once in the water, it was up to him to get out of it as rapidly as possible.

Scott touched a small cylinder attached to his belt and felt bubbles rushing against his palm. He was slightly relieved. When he had inflated the vest, this tube of compressed gas had automatically begun to release, sending out a foul-smelling vapor that permeated the water for some distance around. The principle was that of the skunk adjusted to the environment of the squid, and dangerous undersea life was supposed to be driven away by the Mellison tubes; but it didn't work with carrion eaters like the snakes. Scott averted his nose. The gadgets were named Mellison tubes, but the men called them Stinkers, a far more appropriate term.

Tides on Venus are unpredictable. The clouded planet has no moon, but it is closer to the Sun than Earth. As a rule the tides are mild, except during volcanic activity, when tidal waves sweep the shores. Scott, keeping a weather eye out for danger, rode the waves in toward the beach, searching the strip of dull blackness for signs of life.

Nothing.

He scrambled out at last, shaking himself like a dog, and instantly changed the clip in his automatic for high explosive. The weapon, of course, was watertight—a necessity on Venus. As Kane sat down with a grunt and deflated his vest, Scott stood eying the wall of jungle thirty feet away. It stopped there abruptly, for nothing could grow on black sand.

The rush and whisper of the waves made the only sound. Most of the trees were liana-like, eking out a precarious existence, as the saying went, by taking in each other's washing. The moment one of them showed signs of solidity, it was immediately assailed by parasitic vines flinging themselves madly upward to reach the filtered sunlight of Venus. The leaves did not begin for thirty feet above the ground; they made a regular roof up there, lying like crazy shingles, and would have shut out all light had they not been of light translucent green. Whitish tendrils crawled like reaching serpents from tree to tree, tentacles of vegetable octopi. There were two types of Venusian fauna: the giants who could crash through the forest, and the supple, small ground-dwellers—insects and reptiles mostly—who depended on poison sacs for self-protection. Neither kind was pleasant company.

There were flying creatures, too, but these lived in the upper strata, among the leaves. And there were ambiguous horrors that lived in the deep mud and the stagnant pools under the forest, but no one knew much about these.

"Well," Scott said, "that's that."

Kane nodded. "I guess I should have checked the motors."

"You wouldn't have found anything. Latent flaws—it would have taken black night to bring 'em out. Just one of those things. Keep your gas mask handy, now. If we get anywhere near poison flowers and the wind's blowing this way, we're apt to keel over like that." Scott opened a waterproof wallet and took out a strip of sensitized litmus, which he clipped to his wrist. "If this turns blue, that means gas, even if we don't smell it."

"Yes, sir. What now?"

"We-el—the boat's gone. We can't telaudio for help." Scott fingered the blade of his smatchet and slipped it into the belt sheath. "We head for the fort. Eight miles. Two hours, if we can stick to the beach and if we don't run into trouble. More than that if Signal Rock's ahead of us, because we'll have to detour inland in that case." He drew out a collapsible single-lenser telescope and looked southwest along the shore. "Uh-huh. We detour."

A breath of sickening sweetness gusted down from the jungle roof. From above, Scott knew, the forest looked surprisingly lovely. It always reminded him of an antique candlewick spread he had once bought Jeana—immense rainbow flowers scattered over a background of pale green. Even among the flora competition was keen; the plants vied in producing colors and scents that would attract the winged carriers of pollen.

There would always be frontiers, Scott thought. But they might remain unconquered for a long time, here on Venus. The Keeps were enough for the undersea folk; they were self-sustaining. And the Free Companions had no need to carve out empires on the continents. They were fighters, not agrarians. Land hunger was no longer a part of the race. It might come again, but not in the time of the Keeps.

The jungles of Venus held secrets he would never know. Men can conquer lands from the air, but they cannot hold them by that method. It would take a long, slow period of encroachment, during which the forest and all it represented would be driven back, step by painful step—and that belonged to a day to come, a time Scott would not know. The savage world would be tamed. But not now—not yet.

At the moment it was untamed and very dangerous. Scott

stripped off his tunic and wrung water from it. His clothing would not dry in this saturated air, despite the winds. His trousers clung to him stickily, clammy coldness in their folds.

"Ready, Kane?"

"Yes, sir."

"Then let's go."

They went southwest, along the beach, at a steady, easy lope that devoured miles. Speed and alertness were necessary in equal proportion. From time to time Scott scanned the sea with his telescope, hoping to sight a vessel. He saw nothing. The ships would be in harbor, readying for the battle; and planes would be grounded for installation of the new telaudio device Cinc Rhys had mentioned.

Signal Rock loomed ahead, an outthrust crag with eroded, unscalable sides towering two hundred feet and more. The black strip of sand ended there. From the rock there was a straight drop into deep water, cut up by a turmoil of currents. It was impossible to take the sea detour; there was nothing else for it but to swerve inland, a dangerous but inevitable course. Scott postponed the plunge as long as possible, till the scarp of Signal Rock, jet black with leprous silvery patches on its surface, barred the way. With a quizzical look at Kane he turned sharply to his right and headed for the jungle.

"Half a mile of forest equals a hundred miles of beach hiking," he remarked.

"That bad, sir? I've never tackled it."

"Nobody does, unless they have to. Keep your eyes open and your gun ready. Don't wade through water, even when you can see bottom. There are some little devils that are pretty nearly transparent—vampire fish. If a few of those fasten on you, you'll need a transfusion in less than a minute. I wish the volcanoes would kick up a racket. The beasties generally lie low when that happens."

Under a tree Scott stopped, seeking a straight, long limb. It took a while to find a suitable one, in that tangle of coiling lianas, but finally he succeeded, using his smatchet blade to hack himself a light five-foot pole. Kane at his heels, he moved on into the gathering gloom.

"We may be stalked," he told the boy. "Don't forget to guard the rear."

The sand had given place to sticky whitish mud that plastered the men to their calves before a few moments had passed. A patina of slickness seemed to overlay the ground. The grass was

colored so much like the mud itself that it was practically invisible, except by its added slipperiness. Scott slowly advanced
keeping close to the wall of rock on his left where the tangle was
not so thick. Nevertheless he had to use the smatchet more than
once to cut a passage through vines.

He stopped, raising his hand, and the squelch of Kane's feet
in the mud paused. Silently Scott pointed. Ahead of them in the
cliff base, was the mouth of a burrow.

The captain bent down, found a small stone, and threw it toward the den. He waited, one hand lightly on his gun, ready to
see something flash out of that burrow and race toward them. In
the utter silence a new sound made itself heard—tiny goblin
drums, erratic and resonant in a faraway fashion. Water, dropping from leaf to leaf, in the soaked jungle ceiling above them.
Tink, tink, tink-tink, tink, tink-tink—

"O. K.," Scott said quietly. "Watch it, though." He went on, gun
drawn, till they were level with the mouth of the burrow. "Turn,
Kane. Keep your eye on it till I tell you to stop." He gripped the
boy's arm and guided him, holstering his own weapon. The pole,
till now held between biceps and body, slipped into his hand.
He used it to probe the slick surface of the mud ahead. Sinkhole
and quicksands were frequent, and so were traps, camouflaged
pits built by mud-wolves—which, of course, were not wolves, and
belonged to no known genus. On Venus, the fauna had more sub-
divisions than on old Earth, and lines of demarcation were more
subtle.

"All right now."

Kane, sighing with relief, turned his face forward again. "What
was it?"

"You never know what may come out of those holes," Scott
told him. "They come fast, and they're usually poisonous. So you
can't take chances with the critters. Slow down here. I don't like
the looks of that patch ahead."

Clearings were unusual in the forest. There was one here,
twenty feet wide, slightly saucer-shaped. Scott gingerly extended
the pole and probed. A faint ripple shook the white mud, and
almost before it had appeared the captain had unholstered his
pistol and was blasting shot after shot at the movement.

"Shoot, Kane!" he snapped. "Quick! Shoot at it!"

Kane obeyed, though he had to guess at his target. Mud gey-
sered up, suddenly crimson-stained. Scott, still firing, gripped the
boy's arm and ran him back at a breakneck pace.

The echoes died. Once more the distant elfin drums whispered
through the green gloom.

"We got it," Scott said, after a pause.

"We did?" the other asked blankly. "What—"

"Mud-wolf, I think. The only way to kill those things is to get 'em before they get out of the mud. They're fast and they die hard. However—" He warily went forward. There was nothing to see. The mud had collapsed into a deeper saucer, but the holes blasted by the high-x bullets had filled in. Here and there were traces of thready crimson.

"Never a dull moment," Scott remarked. His crooked grin eased the tension. Kane chuckled and followed the captain's example in replacing his half-used clip with a full one.

The narrow spine of Signal Rock extended inland for a quarter mile before it became scalable. They reached that point finally, helping each other climb, and finding themselves, at the summit, still well below the leafy ceiling of the trees. The black surface of the rock was painfully hot, stinging their palms as they climbed, and even striking through their shoe soles.

"Halfway point, captain?"

"Yeah. But don't let that cheer you. It doesn't get any better till we hit the beach again. We'll probably need some fever shots when we reach the fort, just in case. Oh-oh. Mask, Kane, quick." Scott lifted his arm. On his wrist the band of litmus had turned blue.

With trained accuracy they donned the respirators. Scott felt a faint stinging on his exposed skin, but that wasn't serious. Still, it would be painful later. He beckoned to Kane, slid down the face of the rock, used the pole to test the mud below, and jumped lightly. He dropped in the sticky whiteness and rolled over hastily, plastering himself from head to foot. Kane did the same. Mud wouldn't neutralize the poison flowers' gas, but it would absorb most of it before it reached the skin.

Scott headed toward the beach, a grotesque figure. Mud dripped on the eye plate, and he scrubbed it away with a handful of white grass. He used the pole constantly to test the footing ahead.

Nevertheless the mud betrayed him. The pole broke through suddenly, and as Scott automatically threw his weight back, the ground fell away under his feet. He had time for a crazy feeling of relief that this was quicksand, not a mud-wolf's den, and then the clinging, treacherous stuff had sucked him down knee-deep. He fell back, keeping his grip on the pole and swinging the other end in an arc toward Kane.

The boy seized it in both hands and threw himself flat. His

foot hooked over an exposed root. Scott, craning his neck at a painfully awkward angle and trying to see through the mud-smeared vision plates, kept a rattrap grip on his end of the pole, hoping its slickness would not slip through his fingers.

He was drawn down farther, and then Kane's anchorage began to help. The boy tried to pull the pole toward him, hand over hand. Scott shook his head. He was a good deal stronger than Kane, and the latter would need all his strength to keep a tight grip on the pole.

Something stirred in the shadows behind Kane. Scott instinctively let go with one hand, and, with the other, got out his gun. It had a sealed mechanism, so the mud hadn't harmed the firing, and the muzzle had a one-way trap. He fired at the movement behind Kane, heard a muffled tumult, and waited till it had died. The boy, after a startled look behind him, had not stirred.

After that, rescue was comparatively easy. Scott simply climbed along the pole, spreading his weight over the surface of the quicksand. The really tough part was pulling his legs free of that deadly grip. Scott had to rest for five minutes after that.

But he got out. That was the important thing.

Kane pointed inquiringly into the bushes where the creature had been shot, but Scott shook his head. The nature of the beast wasn't a question worth deciding, as long as it was apparently *hors de combat*. Readjusting his mask, Scott turned toward the beach, circling the quicksand, and Kane kept at his heels.

Their luck had changed. They reached the shore with no further difficulty and collapsed on the black sand to rest. Presently Scott used a litmus, saw that the gas had dissipated, and removed his mask. He took a deep breath.

"Thanks, Kane," he said. "You can take a dip now if you want to wash off that mud. But stay close inshore. No, don't strip. There's no time."

The mud clung like glue and the black sand scratched like pumice. Still, Scott felt a good deal cleaner after a few minutes in the surf, while Kane stayed on guard. Slightly refreshed, they resumed the march.

An hour later a convoy plane, testing, sighted them, telaudioed the fort, and a flitterboat came racing out to pick them up. What Scott appreciated most of all was the stiff shot of uisqueplus the pilot gave him.

Yeah. It was a dog's life, all right!

He passed the flask to Kane.

Presently the fort loomed ahead, guarding Doone Harbor.

Large as the landlocked bay was, it could scarcely accommodate the fleet. Scott watched the activity visible with an approving eye. The flitterboat rounded the sea wall, built for protection against tidal waves, and shot toward a jetty. Its almost inaudible motor died; the shell swung back.

Scott got out, beckoning to an orderly.

"Yes, sir?"

"See that this soldier gets what he needs. We've been in the jungle."

The man didn't whistle sympathetically, but his mouth pursed. He saluted and helped Kane climb out of the flitterboat. As Scott hurried along the quay, he could hear an outburst of friendly profanity from the men on the dock, gathering around Kane.

He nodded imperceptibly. The boy would make a good Free Companion—always granted that he could stand the gaff under fire. That was the acid test. Discipline was tightened then to the snapping point. If it snapped—well, the human factor always remained a variable, in spite of all the psychologists could do.

He went directly to his quarters, switching on the telaudio to call Cinc Rhys. The cinc's seamed, leathery face resolved itself on the screen.

"Captain Scott reporting for duty, sir."

Rhys looked at him sharply. "What happened?"

"Flitterboat crack-up. Had to make it in here on foot."

The cinc called on his God in a mild voice. "Glad you made it. Any accident?"

"No, sir. The pilot's unharmed, too. I'm ready to take over, after I've cleaned up."

"Better take a rejuvenation—you probably need it. Everything's going like clockwork. You did a good job with Mendez—a better bargain than I'd hoped for. I've been talking with him on the telaudio, integrating our forces. We'll go into that later, though. Clean up and then make general inspection."

"Check, sir."

Rhys clicked off. Scott turned to face his orderly.

"Hello, Briggs. Help me off with these duds. You'll probably have to cut 'em off."

"Glad to see you back, sir. I don't think it'll be necessary to cut—" Blunt fingers flew deftly over zippers and clasps. "You were in the jungle?"

Scott grinned wryly. "Do I look as if I'd been gliding?"

"Not all the way, sir—no."

Briggs was like an old bulldog—one of those men who proved the truth of the saying: "Old soldiers never die; they only fade away." Briggs could have been pensioned off ten years ago, but he hadn't wanted that. There was alway a place for old soldiers in the Free Companies, even those who were unskilled. Some became technicians; others, military instructors; the rest, orderlies. The forts were their homes. Had they retired to one of the Keeps, they would have died for lack of interests.

Briggs, now—he had never risen above the ranks, and knew nothing of military strategy, ordnance, or anything except plain fighting. But he had been a Dooneman for forty years, twenty-five of them on active service. He was sixty-odd now, his squat figure slightly stooped like an elderly bear, his ugly face masked with scar tissue.

"All right. Start the shower, will you?"

Briggs stumped off, and Scott, stripped of his filthy, sodden garments, followed. He luxuriated under the stinging spray, first hot soapy water, then alcomix, and after that plain water, first hot, then cold. That was the last task he had to do himself. Briggs took over, as Scott relaxed on the slab, dropping lotion into the captain's burning eyes, giving him a deft but murderous rubdown, combining osteopathic and chiropractic treatment, adjusting revitalizing lamps, and measuring a hypo shot to nullify fatigue toxins. When the orderly was finished, Scott was ready to resume his duties with a clear brain and a refreshed body.

Briggs appeared with fresh clothing. "I'll have the old uniform cleaned, sir. No use throwing it away."

"You can't clean that," Scott remarked, slipping into a singlet. "Not after I rolled in mud. But suit yourself. I won't be needing it for long."

The orderly's fingers, buttoning Scott's tunic, stopped briefly and then resumed their motion. "Is that so, sir?"

"Yeah. I'm taking out discharge papers."

"Another Company, sir?"

"Don't get on your high horse," Scott told the orderly. "It's not that. What would you do if it were? Court-martial me yourself and shoot me at sunrise?"

"No, sir. Begging your pardon, sir, I'd just think you were crazy."

"Why I stand you only the Lord knows," Scott remarked. "You're too damn independent. There's no room for new ideas in that plastic skull of yours. You're the quintessence of dogmatism."

Briggs nodded. "Probably, sir. When a man's lived by one set of rules for as long as I have, and those rules work out, I suppose he might get dogmatic."

"Forty years for you—about twelve for me."

"You came up fast, captain. You'll be cinc here yet."

"That's what you think."

"You're next in line after Cinc Rhys."

"But I'll be out of the Doones," Scott pointed out. "Keep that under your belt, Briggs."

The orderly grunted. "Can't see it, sir. If you don't join another Company, where'll you go?"

"Ever heard of the Keeps?"

Briggs permitted himself a respectful snort. "Sure. They're fine for a binge, but—"

"I'm going to live in one. Montana Keep."

"The Keeps were built with men and machines. I helped at the building of Doone fort. Blood's mixed with the plastic here. We had to hold back the jungle while the technicians were working. Eight months, sir, and never a day passed without some sort of attack. And attacks always meant casualties then. We had only breastworks. The ships laid down a barrage, but barrages aren't impassable. That was a fight, captain."

Scott thrust out a leg so that Briggs could lace his boots. "And a damn good one. I know." He looked down at the orderly's baldish, brown head where white hairs straggled.

"You know, but you weren't there, captain. I was. First we dynamited. We cleared a half circle where we could dig in behind breastworks. Behind us were the techs, throwing up a plastic wall as fast as they could. The guns were brought in on barges. Lying offshore were the battlewagons. We could hear the shells go whistling over our heads—it sounded pretty good, because we knew things were O. K. as long as the barrage kept up. But it couldn't be kept up day and night. The jungle broke through. For months the smell of blood hung here, and that drew the enemy."

"But you held them off."

"Sure, we did. Addison Doone was cinc then—he'd formed the Company years before, but we hadn't a fort. Doone fought with us. Saved my life once, in fact. Anyhow—we got the fort built, or rather the techs did. I won't forget the kick I got out of it when the first big gun blasted off from the wall behind us. There was a lot to do after that, but when that shell was fired, we knew we'd done the job."

Scott nodded. "You feel a proprietary interest in the fort, I guess."

Briggs looked puzzled. "The fort? Why, that doesn't mean much, captain. There are lots of forts. It's something more than that; I don't quite know what it is. It's seeing the fleet out there—breaking in the rookies—giving the old toasts at mess—knowing that—" He stopped, at a loss.

Scott's lips twisted wryly. "You don't really know, do you, Briggs?"

"Know what, sir?"

"Why you stay here. Why you can't believe I'd quit."

Briggs gave a little shrug. "Well—it's the Doones," he said. "That's all, captain. It's just that."

"And what the devil will it matter, in a few hundred years?"

"I suppose it won't. No, sir. But it isn't our business to think about that. We're Doonemen, that's all."

Scott didn't answer. He could easily have pointed out the fallacy of Briggs' argument, but what was the use? He stood up, the orderly whisking invisible dust off his tunic.

"All set, sir. Shipshape."

"Check, Briggs. Well, I've one more scrap, anyhow. I'll bring you back a souvenir, eh?"

The orderly saluted, grinning. Scott went out, feeling good. Inwardly he was chuckling rather sardonically at the false values he was supposed to take seriously. Of course many men had died when Doone fort had been built. But did that, in itself, make a tradition? What good was the fort? In a few centuries it would have outlived its usefulness. Then it would be a relic of the past. Civilization moved on, and, these days, civilization merely tolerated the military.

So—what was the use? Sentiment needed a valid reason for its existence. The Free Companions fought, bitterly, doggedly, with insane valor, in order to destroy themselves. The ancient motives for war had vanished.

What was the use? All over Venus the lights of the great forts were going out—and, this time, they would never be lit again—not in a thousand lifetimes!

V

And we are here as on a darkling plain
Swept with confused alarms of struggle and flight,
Where ignorant armies clash by night.

—Arnold circa 1870

The fort was a completely self-contained unit, military rather than social. There was no need for any agrarian development, since a state of complete siege never existed. Food could be brought in from the Keeps by water and air.

But military production was important, and, in the life of the fort, the techs played an important part, from the experimental physicist to the spot welder. There were always replacements to be made, for, in battle, there were always casualties. And it was necessary to keep the weapons up-to-date, continually striving to perfect new ones. But strategy and armament were of equal importance. An outnumbered fleet had been known to conquer a stronger one by the use of practical psychology.

Scott found Commander Bienne at the docks, watching the launching of a new sub. Apparently Bienne hadn't yet got over his anger, for he turned a scowling, somber face to the captain as he saluted.

"Hello, commander," Scott said. "I'm making inspection. Are you free?"

Bienne nodded. "There's not much to do."

"Well—routine. We got that sub finished just in time, eh?"

"Yes." Bienne couldn't repress his pleasure at sight of the trim, sleek vessel beginning to slide down the ways. Scott, too, felt his pulses heighten as the sub slipped into the water, raising a mighty splash, and then settling down to a smooth, steady riding on the waves. He looked out to where the great battlewagons stood at anchor, twelve of them, gray-green monsters of plated metal. Each of them carried launching equipment for gliders, but the collapsible aircraft were stowed away out of sight as yet. Smaller destroyers lay like lean-flanked wolves among the battleships. There were two fast carriers, loaded with gliders and flitterboats. There were torpedo boats and one low-riding monitor, impregnable, powerfully armed, but slow. Only a direct hit could disable a monitor, but the behemoths had their disadvantages. The battle was usually over before they lumbered into sight. Like all monitors, this one—the *Armageddon*—was constructed on the principle of a razorback hog, covered, except for the firing ports, by a tureen-shaped shield, strongly braced from within. The *Armageddon* was divided into groups of compartments and had several auxiliary engines, so that, unlike the legendary *Rover,* when a monitor died, it did *not* die all over. It was, in effect, a dinosaur. You could blow off the monster's head, and it would continue to fight with talons and lashing tail. Its heavy guns made up in mobility for the giant's unwieldness—but the trouble was to get the monitor into battle. It was painfully slow.

Scott scowled. "We're fighting over Venus Deep, eh?"

"Yes," Bienne nodded. "That still goes. The Helldivers are already heading toward Montana Keep, and we'll intercept them over the Deep."

"When's zero hour?"

"Midnight tonight."

Scott closed his eyes, visualizing their course on a mental chart. Not so good. When battle was joined near island groups, it was sometimes possible for a monitor to slip up under cover of the islets, but that trick wouldn't work now. Too bad—for the Helldivers were a strong outfit, more so since their recent merger with O'Brien's Legion. Even with the Mob to help, the outcome of the scrap would be anyone's guess. The *Armageddon* might be the decisive factor.

"I wonder—" Scott said. "No. It'd be impossible."

"What?"

"Camouflaging the *Armageddon*. If the Helldivers see the monitor coming, they'll lead the fight away from it, faster than that tub can follow. I was thinking we might get her into the battle without the enemy realizing it."

"She's camouflaged now."

"Paint, that's all. She can be spotted. I had some screwy idea about disguising her as an island or a dead whale."

"She's too big for a whale and floating islands look a bit suspicious."

"Yeah. But if we *could* slip the *Armageddon* in without scaring off the enemy— Hm-m-m. Monitors have a habit of turning turtle, don't they?"

"Right. They're top-heavy. But a monitor can't fight upside down. It's not such a bright idea, captain." Briefly Bienne's sunken eyes gleamed with sneering mockery. Scott grunted and turned away.

"All right. Let's take a look around."

The fleet was shipshape. Scott went to the shops. He learned that several new hulls were under way, but would not be completed by zero hour. With Bienne, he continued to the laboratory offices. Nothing new. No slip-ups; no surprises. The machine was running smoothly.

By the time inspection was completed, Scott had an idea. He told Bienne to carry on and went to find Cinc Rhys. The cinc was in his office, just clicking off the telaudio as Scott appeared.

"That was Mendez," Rhys said. "The Mob's meeting our fleet a hundred miles off the coast. They'll be under our orders, of course. A good man, Mendez, but I don't entirely trust him."

"You're not thinking of a double cross, sir?"

Cinc Rhys made disparaging noises. "Brutus is an honorable man. No, he'll stick to his bargain. But I wouldn't cut cards with Mendez. As a Free Companion, he's trustworthy. Personally— Well, how do things look?"

"Very good, sir. I've an idea about the *Armageddon*."

"I wish I had," Rhys said frankly. "We can't get that damned scow into the battle in any way I can figure out. The Helldivers will see it coming, and lead the fight away."

"I'm thinking of camouflage."

"A monitor's a monitor. It's unmistakable. You can't make it look like anything else."

"With one exception, sir. You can make it look like a disabled monitor."

Rhys sat back, giving Scott a startled glance. "That's interesting. Go on."

"Look here, sir." The captain used a stylo to sketch the outline of a monitor on a convenient pad. "Above the surface, the *Armageddon's* dome-shaped. Below, it's a bit different, chiefly because of the keel. Why can't we put a fake superstructure on the monitor—build a false keel on it, so it'll seem capsized?"

"It's possible."

"Everybody knows a monitor's weak spot—that it turns turtle under fire sometimes. If the Helldivers saw an apparently capsized *Armageddon* drifting toward them, they'd naturally figure the tub was disabled."

"It's crazy," Rhys said. "One of those crazy ideas that might work." He used the local telaudio to issue crisp orders. "Got it? Good. Get the *Armageddon* under way as soon as the equipment's aboard. Alterations will be made at sea. We can't waste time. If we had them made in the yards, she'd never catch up with the fleet."

The cinc broke the connection, his seamed, leathery face twisting into a grin. "I hope it works. We'll see."

He snapped his fingers. "Almost forgot. President Crosby's nephew—Kane?—he was with you when you cracked up, wasn't he? I've been wondering whether I should have waived training for him. How did he show up in the jungle?"

"Quite well," Scott said. "I had my eye on him. He'll make a good soldier."

Rhys looked keenly at the captain. "What about discipline? I felt that was his weak spot."

"I've no complaint to make."

"So. Well, maybe. Starling's outfit is bad training for anyone—

especially a raw kid. Speaking of Starling, did Cinc Mendez know anything about his using atomic power?"

"No, sir. If Starling's doing that, he's keeping it plenty quiet."

"We'll investigate after the battle. Can't afford that sort of thing —we don't want another holocaust. It was bad enough to lose Earth. It decimated the race. If it happened again, it'd wipe the race out."

"I don't think there's much danger of that. On Earth, it was the big atomic-power stations that got out of control. At worst, Starling can't have more than hand weapons."

"True. You can't blow up a world with those. But you know the law—no atomic power on Venus."

Scott nodded.

"Well, that's all." Rhys waved him away. "Clear weather."

Which, on this perpetually clouded world, had a tinge of irony.

After mess Scott returned to his quarters, for a smoke and a brief rest. He waved away Briggs' suggestion of a rubdown and sent the orderly to the commissary for fresh tobacco. "Be sure to get Twenty Star," he cautioned. "I don't want that green hydroponic cabbage."

"I know the brand, sir." Briggs looked hurt and departed. Scott settled back in his relaxer, sighing.

Zero hour at twelve. The last zero hour he'd ever know. All through the day he had been conscious that he was fulfilling his duties for the last time.

His mind went back to Montana Keep. He was living again those other-worldly moments in the cloud-wrapped Olympus with Ilene. Curiously, he found it difficult to visualize the girl's features. Perhaps she was a symbol—her appearance did not matter. Yet she was very lovely.

In a different way from Jeana. Scott glanced at Jeana's picture on the desk, three-dimensional and tinted after life. By pressing a button on the frame, he could have given it sound and motion. He leaned forward and touched the tiny stud. In the depths of the picture the figure of Jeana stirred, smiling. The red lips parted.

Her voice, though soft, was quite natural.

"Hello, Brian," the recording said. "Wish I were with you now. Here's a present, darling." The image blew him a kiss, and then faded back to immobility.

Scott sighed again. Jeana was a comfortable sort of person. But— Oh, hell! She wasn't willing to change. Very likely she couldn't. Ilene perhaps was equally dogmatic, but she represented the life of the Keeps—and that was what Scott wanted now.

It was an artificial life Ilene lived, but she was honest about it. She knew its values were false. At least she didn't pretend, like the Free Companions, that there were ideals worth dying for. Scott remembered Briggs. The fact that men had been killed during the building of Doone fort meant a lot to the old orderly. He never asked himself—*why?* Why had they died? Why was Doone fort built in the first place? For war. And war was doomed.

One had to believe in an ideal before devoting one's life to it. One had to feel he was helping the ideal to survive—watering the plant with his blood so eventually it would come to flower. The red flower of Mars had long since blown. How did that old poem go?

> *One thing is certain, and the rest is lies;*
> *The flower that once has blown forever dies.*

It was true. But the Free Companions blindly pretended that the flower was still in blazing scarlet bloom, refusing to admit that even the roots were withered and useless, scarcely able now to suck up the blood sacrificed to its hopeless thirst.

New flowers bloomed; new buds opened. But in the Keeps, not in the great doomed forts. It was the winter cycle, and, as the last season's blossoms faded, the buds of the next stirred into life. Life questing and intolerant. Life that fed on the rotting petals of the rose of war.

But the pretense went on, in the coastal forts that guarded the Keeps. Scott made a grimace of distaste. Blind, stupid folly! He was a man first, not a soldier. And man is essentially a hedonist, whether he identifies himself with the race or not.

Scott could not. He was not part of the undersea culture, and he could never be. But he could lose himself in the hedonistic backwash of the Keeps, the froth that always overlies any social unit. With Ilene, he could, at least, seek happiness, without the bitter self-mockery he had known for so long. Mockery at his own emotional weaknesses in which he did not believe.

Ilene was honest. She knew she was damned, because unluckily she had intelligence.

So—Scott thought—they would make a good pair.

Scott looked up as Commander Bienne came into the room. Bienne's sour, mahogany face was flushed deep red under the bronze. His lids were heavy over angry eyes. He swung the door-curtain shut after him and stood rocking on his heels, glowering at Scott.

He called Scott something unprintable.

The captain rose, an icy knot of fury in his stomach. Very softly he said, "You're drunk, Bienne. Get out. Get back to your quarters."

"Sure—you little tinhorn soldier. You like to give orders, don't you? You like to chisel, too. The way you chiseled me out of that left-wing command today. I'm pretty sick of it, Captain Brian Scott."

"Don't be a damned fool! I don't like you personally any more than you like me, but that's got nothing to do with the Company. I recommended you for that command."

"You lie," Bienne said, swaying. "And I hate your guts."

Scott went pale, the scar on his cheek flaming red. Bienne came forward. He wasn't too drunk to co-ordinate. His fist lashed out suddenly and connected agonizingly with Scott's molar.

The captain's reach was less than Bienne's. He ducked inside of the next swing and carefully smashed a blow home on the point of the other's jaw. Bienne was driven back, crashing against the wall and sliding down in a limp heap, his head lolling forward.

Scott, rubbing his knuckles, looked down, considering. Presently he knelt and made a quick examination. A knockout, that was all.

Oh, well.

Briggs appeared, showing no surprise at sight of Bienne's motionless body. The perfect orderly walked across to the table and began to refill the humidor with the tobacco he had brought.

Scott almost chuckled.

"Briggs."

"Yes, sir?"

"Commander Bienne's had a slight accident. He—slipped. Hit his chin on something. He's a bit tight, too. Fix him up, will you?"

"With pleasure, sir." Briggs hoisted Bienne's body across his brawny shoulders.

"Zero hour's at twelve. The commander must be aboard the *Flintlock* by then. And sober. Can do?"

"Certainly, sir," Briggs said, and went out.

Scott returned to his chair, filling his pipe. He should have confined Bienne to his quarters, of course. But—well, this was a personal matter. One could afford to stretch a point, especially since Bienne was a valuable man to have aboard during action.

Scott vaguely hoped the commander would get his thick head blown off.

After a time he tapped the dottle from his pipe and went off for a final inspection.

At midnight the fleet hoisted anchor.

By dawn the Doones were nearing the Venus Deep.

The ships of the Mob had already joined them, seven battleships, and assorted cruisers, destroyers, and one carrier. No monitor. The Mob didn't own one—it had capsized two months before, and was still undergoing repairs.

The combined fleets sailed in crescent formation, the left wing, commanded by Scott, composed of his own ship, the *Flintlock*, and the *Arquebus*, the *Arrow*, and the *Misericordia*, all Doone battlewagons. There were two Mob ships with him, the *Navaho* and the *Zuni*, the latter commanded by Cinc Mendez. Scott had one carrier with him, the other being at right wing. Besides these, there were the lighter craft.

In the center were the battleships *Arbalest*, *Lance*, *Gatling*, and *Mace*, as well as three of Mendez's. Cinc Rhys was aboard the *Lance*, controlling operations. The camouflaged monitor *Armageddon* was puffing away valiantly far behind, well out of sight in the mists.

Scott was in his control room, surrounded by telaudio screens and switchboards. Six operators were perched on stools before the controls, ready to jump to action when orders came through their earphones. In the din of battle spoken commands often went unheard, which was why Scott wore a hush-mike strapped to his chest.

His eyes roved over the semicircle of screens before him.

"Any report from the gliders yet?"

"No, sir."

"Get me air-spotting command."

One of the screens flamed to life; a face snapped into view on it.

"Report."

"Nothing yet, captain. Wait." There was a distant thunder. "Detectors clamped on a telaudio tight-beam directly overhead."

"Enemy glider in the clouds?"

"Apparently. It's out of the focus now."

"Try to relocate it."

A lot of good that would do. Motored planes could easily be detected overhead, but a glider was another matter. The only way to spot one was by clamping a detector focus directly on the glider's telaudio beam—worse than a needle in a haystack. Luckily the crates didn't carry bombs.

"Report coming in, sir. One of our gliders."

Another screen showed a face. "Pilot reporting, sir. Located enemy."

"Good. Switch in the telaudio, infra. What sector?"

"V. D. eight hundred seven northwest twenty-one."

Scott said into his hush-mike, "Get Cinc Rhys and Commander Geer on tight-beam. And Cinc Mendez."

Three more screens lit up, showing the faces of the three officers.

"Cut in the pilot."

Somewhere over Venus Deep the glider pilot was arcing his plane through the cloud-layer, the automatic telaudio-camera, lensed to infrared, penetrating the murk and revealing the ocean below. On the screen ships showed, driving forward in battle formation.

Scott recognized and enumerated them mentally. The *Orion*, the *Sirius*, the *Vega*, the *Polaris*—uh-huh. Lighter ships. Plenty of them. The scanner swept on.

Cinc Rhys said, "We're outnumbered badly. Cinc Mendez, are your sub-detectors in operation?"

"They are. Nothing yet."

"We'll join battle in half an hour, I judge. We've located them, and they've no doubt located us."

"Check."

The screens blanked out. Scott settled back, alertly at ease. Nothing to do now but wait, keeping ready for the unexpected. The *Orion* and the *Vega* were the Helldivers' biggest battleships, larger than anything in the line of the Doones—or the Mob. Cinc Flynn was no doubt aboard the *Orion*. The Helldivers owned a monitor, but it had not showed on the infrared aërial scanner. Probably the behemoth wouldn't even show up in time for the battle.

But even without the monitor, the Helldivers had an overwhelming surface display. Moreover, their undersea fleet was an important factor. The sub-detectors of Cinc Mendez might—probably would—cut down the odds. But possibly not enough.

The *Armageddon*, Scott thought, might be the point of decision, the ultimate argument. And, as yet, the camouflaged monitor was lumbering through the waves far in the wake of the Doones.

Commander Bienne appeared on a screen. He had frozen into

a disciplined, trained robot, personal animosities forgotten for the time. Active duty did that to a man.

Scott expected nothing different, however, and his voice was completely impersonal as he acknowledged Bienne's call.

"The flitterboats are ready to go, captain."

"Send them out in fifteen minutes. Relay to left wing, all ships carrying flitters."

"Check."

For a while there was silence. A booming explosion brought Scott to instant alertness. He glanced up at the screens.

A new face appeared. "Helldivers opening up. Testing for range. They must have gliders overhead. We can't spot 'em."

"Get the men under cover. Send up a test barrage. Prepare to return fire. Contact our pilots over the Helldivers."

It was beginning now—the incessant, racking thunder that would continue till the last shot was fired. Scott cut in to Cinc Rhys as the latter signaled.

"Reporting, sir."

"Harry the enemy. We can't do much yet. Change to R-8 formation."

Cinc Mendez said, "We've got three enemy subs. Our detectors are tuned up to high pitch."

"Limit the range so our subs will be outside the sphere of influence."

"Already did that. The enemy's using magnetic depth charges, laying an undersea barrage as they advance."

"I'll talk to the sub command." Rhys cut off. Scott listened to the increasing fury of explosions. He could not yet hear the distinctive *clap-clap* of heat rays, but the quarters were not yet close enough for those undependable, though powerful, weapons. It took time for a heat ray to warm up, and during that period a well-aimed bullet could smash the projector lens.

"Casualty, sir. Direct hit aboard destroyer *Bayonet*."

"Extent of damage?"

"Not disabled. Complete report later."

After a while a glider pilot came in on the beam.

"Shell landed on the *Polaris*, sir."

"Use the scanner."

It showed the Helldivers' battlewagon, part of the superstructure carried away, but obviously still in fighting trim. Scott nodded. Both sides were getting the range now. The hazy clouds still hid each fleet from the other, but they were nearing.

The sound of artillery increased. Problems of trajectory were increased by the violent winds of Venus, but accurate aiming was possible. Scott nodded grimly as a crash shook the *Flintlock*.

They were getting it now. Here, in the brain of the ship, he was as close to the battle as any member of a firing crew. The screens were his eyes.

They had the advantage of being able to use infrared, so that Scott, buried here, could see more than he could have on deck, with his naked eye. Something loomed out of the murk and Scott's breath stopped before he recognized the lines of the Doone battlewagon *Misericordia*. She was off course. The captain used his hush-mike to snap a quick reprimand.

Flitterboats were going out now, speedy hornets that would harry the enemy fleet. In one of them, Scott remembered, was Norman Kane. He thought of Ilene and thrust the thought back, out of his mind. No time for that now.

Battle stations allowed no time for wool gathering.

The distant vanguard of the Helldivers came into sight on the screens. Cinc Mendez called.

"Eleven more subs. One got through. Seems to be near the *Flintlock*. Drop depth bombs."

Scott nodded and obeyed. Shuddering concussions shook the ship. Presently a report came in: fuel slick to starboard.

Good. A few well-placed torpedoes could do a lot of damage.

The *Flintlock* heeled incessantly under the action of the heavy guns. Heat rays were lancing out. The big ships could not easily avoid the searing blasts that could melt solid metal, but the flitterboats, dancing around like angry insects, sent a rain of bullets at the projectors. But even that took integration. The rays themselves were invisible, and could only be traced from their targets. The camera crews were working overtime, snapping shots of the enemy ships, tracing the rays' points of origin, and telaudioing the information to the flitterboats.

"Helldivers' *Rigel* out of action."

On the screen the big destroyer swung around, bow pointing forward. She was going to ram. Scott snapped orders. The *Flintlock* went hard over, guns pouring death into the doomed *Rigel*.

The ships passed, so close that men on the *Flintlock's* decks could see the destroyer lurching through the haze. Scott judged her course and tried desperately to get Mendez. There was a delay.

"QM—QM—emergency! Get the *Zuni!*"

"Here she answers, sir."

Scott snapped, "Change course. QM. Destroyer *Rigel* bearing down on you."

"Check." The screen blanked. Scott used a scanner. He

groaned at the sight. The *Zuni* was swinging fast, but the *Rigel* was too close—too damned close.

She rammed.

Scott said, "Hell." That put the *Zuni* out of action. He reported to Cinc Rhys.

"All right, captain. Continue R-8 formation."

Mendez appeared on a screen. "Captain Scott. We're disabled. I'm coming aboard. Have to direct sub-strafing operations. Can you give me a control board?"

"Yes, sir. Land at Port Sector 7."

Hidden in the mist, the fleets swept on in parallel courses, the big battlewagons keeping steady formation, pouring heat rays and shells across the gap. The lighter ships strayed out of line at times, but the flitterboats swarmed like midges, dog-fighting when they were not harrying the larger craft. Gliders were useless now, at such close quarters.

The thunder crashed and boomed. Shudders rocked the *Flint-lock*.

"Hit on Helldivers' *Orion*. Hit on *Sirius*."

"Hit on Mob ship *Apache*."

"Four more enemy subs destroyed."

"Doone sub *X-16* fails to report."

"Helldivers' *Polaris* seems disabled."

"Send out auxiliary flitterboats, units nine and twenty."

Cinc Mendez came in, breathing hard. Scott waved him to an auxiliary control unit seat.

"Hit on *Lance*. Wait a minute. Cinc Rhys a casualty, sir."

Scott froze. "Details."

"One moment— Dead, sir."

"Very well," Scott said after a moment. "I'm assuming command. Pass it along."

He caught a sidelong glance from Mendez. When a Company's cinc was killed, one of two things happened—promotion of a new cinc, or a merger with another Company. In this case Scott was required, by his rank, to assume temporarily the fleet's command. Later, at the Doone fort, there would be a meeting and a final decision.

He scarcely thought of that now. Rhys dead! Tough, unemotional old Rhys, killed in action. Rhys had a free-wife in some Keep, Scott remembered. The Company would pension her. Scott had never seen the woman. Oddly, he wondered what she was like. The question had never occurred to him before.

The screens were flashing. Double duty now—or triple. Scott forgot everything else in directing the battle.

It was like first-stage anæsthesia—it was difficult to judge time. It might have been an hour or six since the battle had started. Or less than an hour, for that matter.

"Destroyer disabled. Cruiser disabled. Three enemy subs out of action—"

It went on, endlessly. At the auxiliaries Mendez was directing substrafing operations. Where in hell's the *Armageddon,* Scott thought? The fight would be over before that overgrown tortoise arrived.

Abruptly a screen flashed QM. The lean, beak-nosed face of Cinc Flynn of the Helldivers showed.

"Calling Doone command."

"Acknowledging," Scott said. "Captain Scott, emergency command."

Why was Flynn calling? Enemy fleets in action never communicated, except to surrender.

Flynn said curtly, "You're using atomic power. Explanation, please."

Mendez jerked around. Scott felt a tight band around his stomach.

"Done without my knowledge or approval, of course, Cinc Flynn. My apologies. Details?"

"One of your flitterboats fired an atomic-powered pistol at the *Orion.*"

"Damage?"

"One seven-unit gun disabled."

"One of ours, of the same caliber, will be taken out of action immediately. Further details, sir?"

"Use your scanner, captain, on Sector Mobile 18 south *Orion.* Your apology is accepted. The incident will be erased from our records."

Flynn clicked off. Scott used the scanner, catching a Doone flitterboat in its focus. He used the enlarger.

The little boat was fleeing from enemy fire, racing back toward the Doone fleet, heading directly toward the *Flintlock,* Scott saw. Through the transparent shell he saw the bombardier slumped motionless, his head blown half off. The pilot, still gripping an atomic-fire pistol in one hand, was Norman Kane. Blood streaked his boyish, strained face.

So Starling's outfit did have atomic power, then. Kane must have smuggled the weapon out with him when he left. And, in the excitement of battle, he had used it against the enemy.

Scott said coldly, "Gun crews starboard. Flitterboat Z-19-4. Blast it."

Almost immediately a shell burst near the little craft. On the screen Kane looked up, startled by his own side firing upon him. Comprehension showed on his face. He swung the flitterboat off course, zigzagging, trying desperately to dodge the barrage.

Scott watched, his lips grimly tight. The flitterboat exploded in a rain of spray and debris.

Automatic court-martial.

After the battle, the Companies would band together and smash Starling's outfit.

Meantime, this was action. Scott returned to his screens, erasing the incident from his mind.

Very gradually, the balance of power was increasing with the Helldivers. Both sides were losing ships, put out of action rather than sunk, and Scott thought more and more often of the monitor *Armageddon*. She could turn the battle now. But she was still far astern.

Scott never felt the explosion that wrecked the control room. His senses blacked out without warning.

He could not have been unconscious for long. When he opened his eyes, he stared up at a shambles. He seemed to be the only man left alive. But it could not have been a direct hit, or he would not have survived either.

He was lying on his back, pinned down by a heavy crossbeam. But no bones were broken. Blind, incredible luck had helped him there. The brunt of the damage had been borne by the operators. They were dead, Scott saw at a glance.

He tried to crawl out from under the beam, but that was impossible. In the thunder of battle his voice could not be heard.

There was a movement across the room, halfway to the door. Cinc Mendez stumbled up and stared around, blinking. Red smeared his plump cheeks.

He saw Scott and stood, rocking back and forth, staring.

Then he put his hand on the butt of his pistol.

Scott could very easily read the other's mind. If the Doone captain died now, the chances were that Mendez could merge with the Doones and assume control. The politico-military balance lay that way.

If Scott lived, it was probable that he would be elected cinc.

It was, therefore, decidedly to Mendez's advantage to kill the imprisoned man.

A shadow crossed the doorway. Mendez, his back to the newcomer, did not see Commander Bienne halt on the threshold, scowling at the tableau. Scott knew that Bienne understood the situation as well as he himself did. The commander realized that in a very few moments Mendez would draw his gun and fire.

Scott waited. The cinc's fingers tightened on his gun butt.

Bienne, grinning crookedly, said, "I thought that shell had finished you, sir. Guess it's hard to kill a Dooneman."

Mendez took his hand off the gun, instantly regaining his poise. He turned to Bienne.

"I'm glad you're here, commander. It'll probably take both of us to move that beam."

"Shall we try, sir?"

Between the two of them, they managed to shift the weight off Scott's torso. Briefly the latter's eyes met Bienne's. There was still no friendliness in them, but there was a look of wry self-mockery.

Bienne hadn't saved Scott's life, exactly. It was, rather, a question of being a Dooneman. For Bienne was, first of all, a soldier, and a member of the Free Company.

Scott tested his limbs; they worked.

"How long was I out, commander?"

"Ten minutes, sir. The *Armageddon's* in sight."

"Good. Are the Helldivers veering off?"

Bienne shook his head. "So far they're not suspicious."

Scott grunted and made his way to the door, the others at his heels. Mendez said, "We'll need another control ship."

"All right. The *Arquebus.* Commander, take over here. Cinc Mendez—"

A flitterboat took them to the *Arquebus,* which was still in good fighting trim. The monitor *Armageddon,* Scott saw, was rolling helplessly in the trough of the waves. In accordance with the battle plan, the Doone ships were leading the Helldivers toward the apparently capsized giant. The technicians had done a good job; the false keel looked shockingly convincing.

Aboard the *Arquebus,* Scott took over, giving Mendez the auxiliary control for his substrafers. The Cinc beamed at Scott over his shoulder.

"Wait till that monitor opens up, captain."

"Yeah . . . we're in bad shape, though."

Neither man mentioned the incident that was in both their minds. It was tacitly forgotten—the only thing to do now.

Guns were still bellowing. The Helldivers were pouring their fire into the Doone formation, and they were winning. Scott scowled at the screens. If he waited too long, it would be just too bad.

Presently he put a beam on the *Armageddon*. She was in a beautiful position now, midway between two of the Helldivers' largest battleships.

"Unmask. Open fire."

Firing ports opened on the monitor. The sea titan's huge guns snouted into view. Almost simultaneously they blasted, the thunder drowning out the noise of the lighter guns.

"All Doone ships attack," Scott said. "Plan R-7."

This was it. *This was it!*

The Doones raced in to the kill. Blasting, bellowing, shouting, the guns tried to make themselves heard above the roaring of the monitor. They could not succeed, but that savage, invincible onslaught won the battle.

It was nearly impossible to maneuver a monitor into battle formation, but, once that was accomplished, the only thing that could stop the monster was atomic power.

But the Helldivers fought on, trying strategic formation. They could not succeed. The big battlewagons could not get out of range of the *Armageddon's* guns. And that meant—

Cinc Flynn's face showed on the screen.

"Capitulation, sir. Cease firing."

Scott gave orders. The roar of the guns died into humming, incredible silence.

"You gave us a great battle, cinc."

"Thanks. So did you. Your strategy with the monitor was excellent."

So—that was that. Scott felt something go limp inside of him. Flynn's routine words were meaningless; Scott was drained of the vital excitement that had kept him going till now.

The rest was pure formula.

Token depth charges would be dropped over Virginia Keep. They would not harm the Dome, but they were the rule. There would be the ransom, paid always by the Keep which backed the losing side. A supply of korium, or its negotiable equivalent. The Doone treasury would be swelled. Part of the money would go into replacements and new keels. The life of the forts would go on.

Alone at the rail of the *Arquebus*, heading for Virginia Keep, Scott watched slow darkness change the clouds from pearl to gray, and then to invisibility. He was alone in the night. The wash of waves came up to him softly as the *Arquebus* rushed to her destination, three hundred miles away.

Warm yellow lights gleamed from ports behind him, but he did not turn. This, he thought, was like the cloud-wrapped Olympus in Montana Keep, where he had promised Ilene—many things.

Yet there was a difference. In an Olympus a man was like a god, shut away completely from the living world. Here, in the unbroken dark, there was no sense of alienage. Nothing could be seen—Venus has no moon, and the clouds hid the stars. And the seas are not phosphorescent.

Beneath these waters stand the Keeps, Scott thought. They hold the future. Such battles as were fought today are fought so that the Keeps may not be destroyed.

And men will sacrifice. Men have always sacrificed, for a social organization or a military unit. Man must create his own ideal. "If there had been no God, man would have created Him."

Bienne had sacrificed today, in a queer, twisted way of loyalty to his fetish. Yet Bienne still hated him, Scott knew.

The Doones meant nothing. Their idea was a false one. Yet, because men were faithful to that ideal, civilization would rise again from the guarded Keeps. A civilization that would forget its doomed guardians, the watchers of the seas of Venus, the Free Companions yelling their mad, futile battle cry as they drove on— as this ship was driving—into a night that would have no dawn.

Ilene.

Jeana.

It was no such simple choice. It was, in fact, no real choice at all. For Scott knew, very definitely, that he could never, as long as he lived, believe wholeheartedly in the Free Companions. Always a sardonic devil deep within him would be laughing in bitter self-mockery.

The whisper of the waves drifted up.

It wasn't sensible. It was sentimental, crazy, stupid, sloppy thinking.

But Scott knew, now, that he wasn't going back to Ilene.

He was a fool.

But he was a soldier.

1943

FOUR/

· The Storm
· City
· First Contact

Things kept getting better.

Perhaps that was part of the ASF confidence trick. This month was great. And you knew next month would be even greater.

It always was.

Part of the recipe for success was that new ideas were founded upon a now established tradition. Campbell's authors built up a dialogue with their editor and with each other—so much so, so intricately so, that one sometimes fancied that a new reader, venturing in during, say, 1943, would be in the position of a newcomer arriving late at a party, quite unable to comprehend what was going on, or to get with it. The whole business was fantastically in-group, and that was part of its attraction; though the slight flavor of persecution and paranoia which went with the in-group feeling was perhaps less attractive.

Anyhow, paranoia and persecution were meat and drink to the raging young van Vogt of the period. Like some terrible fragment of one's own id, he came raving at you in story after story with something well-nigh incomprehensible—something just too big for you ever to get properly in focus. One thinks of the typical Campbell story as something compact and slightly chilled, like a Heinlein or a Hal Clement. But Campbell had the inspiration to give A. E. van Vogt his head, knowing surely that the man was not making sense on the Heinlein-realism level at all.

But what music he made! "The Storm" is one of three linked stories full of van Vogtian complexities all about robots and Mixed-Men, with concealments and crazy

*searches going on all over the galaxy. There was a peck of
Kafka in the early van Vogt, as well a pinch of E. E. Smith.*

*"The Storm" contains a really fantastic storm in space,
no less than nine light years wide, and a romance—kisses
were a rarity in ASF. The whole package, with centaurs,
towering IQs, three-dimensional hypnotic spells
comes hot and fresh from sf's most unafraid magician.*

*By contrast, what a delicate little tale is "City"!
Sensitive, well-thought, expressed in rather ricketty prose.
Almost self-contained.*

*Yet it was the start of one of ASF's long-lived and most
well-loved series, eventually published in book form under
that same four-letter word, "City". It was the beginning of a
trail leading from the here-and-now into the otherwhere,
otherwhen which Simak so loved. His otherwhere, otherwhen
would never find more poetic expression than in this series
about the Websters, unless perhaps in a later novel, "Ring
Around the Sun".*

*By 1944, Simak's name was well-known to ASF readers, and
his uncertain grasp on prose improved. Among more
high-powered authors, Simak stood out like a healthy
thumb. He was almost the only writer of the time who
allowed himself to dwell on the Great Outdoors—ASF's typical
environment was the Great Indoors; even the air was
generally recycled. Simak kept to the woods. His characters
were to be found sitting on rocking-chairs on verandahs,
or leaning on fences. When aliens came along, those
same characters would just stay right where they
were and dicker, and in the end—well, maybe mankind
would score a victory, but more like both sides would strike a
bargain and profit by it.*

*Meanwhile, on all sides of Simak's peaceful tale, the blasters
were going off and aliens were being fried from here to
Betelgeuse. Simak was the first ASF writer to make
Deals not War.*

*Almost all the stories in ASF were revelations to their
young readers in those days. They built on the traditions
of the magazine and turned them through just a few
degrees. You might say that all three stories in this
section deal with obsessional questions asked and
answered over and over again: "What will it be like in
space?", "What's going to happen to people?", and
"What would happen if we meet aliens?"*

To this last question, the famous story "First Contact"

seemed for many years to be the definitive answer (indeed, it was because ASF was delivering so many definitive answers to these sorts of questions that eventually sf had to go away and start up business somewhere else!).

In the tremendous roll call of sf authors, the name of Murray Leinster has a place of peculiar honor. He had science fiction stories published before the first science fiction magazine was launched in 1926, and is still writing today. He wrote many stories for Campbell, and seemed always capable of renewing himself. But this story was one of his best; although world experience since its publication, and particularly the long confrontation between East and West, suggests that coming to terms with aliens can never be as simple as Leinster hints, such an argument should not be allowed to spoil the consistent internal logic of a fine story.

Here one may add that "First Contact" has another and intriguing claim to fame. Perhaps because the Russians were also conscious of the story's relevance or otherwise to the East-West confrontation, it was one in which they took a great deal of interest. It is mentioned by name in Yefremov's "Andromeda," one of the most famous sf novels in the U.S.S.R. The context implies that Leinster's tale is well known still to cosmonauts many centuries into the future. Fame indeed!

The Storm/

by A. E. VAN VOGT

The combined military powers of all the people of that galaxy could could not stand up to the tremendous might of the battleship of space. But there was one force their galaxy held that could smash that or any other ship!

Over the miles and the years, the gases drifted. Waste matter from ten thousand suns, a diffuse miasm of spent explosions, of dead hell fires and the furies of a hundred million raging sunspots —formless, purposeless.

But it was the beginning.

Into the great dark the gases crept. Calcium was in them, and sodium, and hydrogen; and the speed of the drift varied up to twenty miles a second.

There was a timeless period while gravitation performed its function. The inchoate mass became masses. Great blobs of gas took a semblance of shape in widely separate areas, and moved on and on and on.

They came finally to where a thousand flaring seetee suns had long before doggedly "crossed the street" of the main stream of terrene suns. Had crossed, and left *their* excrement of gases.

The first clash quickened the vast worlds of gas. The electron haze of terrene plunged like spurred horses and sped deeper into the equally violently reacting positron haze of contraterrene. Instantly, the lighter orbital positrons and electrons went up in a blaze of hard radiation.

The storm was on.

The stripped seetee nuclei carried now terrific and unbalanced negative charges and repelled electrons, but tended to attract terrene atom nuclei. In their turn the stripped terrene nuclei attracted contraterrene.

Violent beyond all conception were the resulting cancellations of charges.

The two opposing masses heaved and spun in a cataclysm of partial adjustment. They had been heading in different directions. More and more they became one tangled, seething whirlpool.

The new course, uncertain at first, steadied and became a line drive through the midnight heavens. On a front of nine light years, at a solid fraction of the velocity of light, the storm roared toward its destiny.

Suns were engulfed for half a hundred years—and left behind with only a hammering of cosmic rays to show that they had been the centers of otherwise invisible, impalpable atomic devastation.

In its four hundred and ninetieth Sidereal year, the storm intersected the orbit of a Nova at the flash moment.

It began to move!

On the three-dimensional map at weather headquarters on the planet Kaider III, the storm was colored orange. Which meant it was the biggest of the four hundred odd storms raging in the Fifty Suns region of the Lesser Magellanic Cloud.

It showed as an uneven splotch fronting at Latitude 473, Longitude 228, Center 190 parsecs, but that was a special Fifty Suns degree system which had no relation to the magnetic center of the Magellanic Cloud as a whole.

The report about the Nova had not yet been registered on the map. When that happened the storm color would be changed to an angry red.

They had stopped looking at the map. Maltby stood with the councilors at the great window staring up at the Earth ship.

The machine was scarcely more than a dark sliver in the distant sky. But the sight of it seemed to hold a deadly fascination for the older men.

Maltby felt cool, determined, but also sardonic. It was funny, these—these people of the Fifty Suns in this hour of their danger calling upon *him.*

He unfocused his eyes from the ship, fixed his steely, laconic gaze on the plump, perspiring chairman of the Kaider III government—and, tensing his mind, forced the man to look at him. The councilor, unaware of the compulsion, conscious only that he had turned, said:

"You understand your instructions, Captain Maltby?"

Maltby nodded. "I do."

The curt words must have evoked a vivid picture. The fat face rippled like palsied jelly and broke out in a new trickle of sweat.

"The worst part of it all," the man groaned, "is that the people of the ship found us by the wildest accident. They had run into one of our meteorite stations and captured its attendant. The attendant sent a general warning and then forced them to kill him before they could discover which of the fifty million suns of the Lesser Magellanic Cloud was us.

"Unfortunately, they did discover that he and the rest of us were all descendants of the robots who had escaped the massacre of the robots in the main galaxy fifteen thousand years ago.

"But they were baffled, and without a clue. They started home, stopping off at planets on the way on a chance basis. The seventh stop was us. Captain Maltby—"

The man looked almost beside himself. He shook. His face was as colorless as a white shroud. He went on hoarsely:

"Captain Maltby, you must not fail. They have asked for a meteorologist to guide them to Cassidor VII, where the central government is located. They mustn't reach there. You must drive them into the great storm at 473.

"We have commissioned you to do this for us because you have the two minds of the Mixed Men. We regret that we have not always fully appreciated your services in the past. But you must admit that, after the wars of the Mixed Men, it was natural that we should be careful about—"

Maltby cut off the lame apology. "Forget it," he said. "The Mixed Men are robots, too, and therefore as deeply involved, as I see it, as the Dellians and non-Dellians. Just what the Hidden Ones of my kind think, I don't know, nor do I care. I assure you I shall do my best to destroy this ship."

"Be careful!" the chairman urged anxiously. "This ship could destroy us, our planet, our sun in a single minute. We never dreamed that Earth could have gotten so far ahead of us and produced such a devastatingly powerful machine. After all, the non-Dellian robots and, of course, the Mixed Men among us are capable of research work; the former have been laboring feverishly for thousands of years.

"But, finally, remember that you are not being asked to commit suicide. The battleship is absolutely invincible. Just how it will survive a real storm we were not told when we were shown around. But it will. What happens, however, is that everyone aboard becomes unconscious.

"As a Mixed Man you will be the first to revive. Our combined fleets will be waiting to board the ship the moment you open the doors. Is that clear?"

It had been clear the first time it was explained, but these non-Dellians had a habit of repeating themselves, as if thoughts kept growing vague in their minds. As Maltby closed the door of the great room behind him, one of the councilors said to his neighbor:

"Has he been told that the storm has gone Nova?"

The fat man overheard. He shook his head. His eyes gleamed

as he said quietly: "No. After all, he is one of the Mixed Men. We can't trust him too far no matter what his record."

All morning the reports had come in. Some showed progress, some didn't. But her basic good humor was untouched by the failures.

The great reality was that her luck had held. She had found a planet of the robots. Only one planet so far, but—

Grand Captain Laurr smiled grimly. It wouldn't be long now. Being a supreme commander was a terrible business. But she had not shrunk from making the deadly threat: provide all required information, or the entire planet of Kaider III would be destroyed.

The information was coming in: Population of Kaider III two billion, one hundred million, two-fifths Dellian, three-fifths non-Dellian robots.

Dellians physically and mentally the higher type, but completely lacking in creative ability. Non-Dellians dominated in the research laboratories.

The forty-nine other suns whose planets were inhabited were called, in alphabetical order: Assora, Atmion, Bresp, Buraco, Cassidor, Corrab— They were located at (1) Assora: Latitude 931, Longitude 27, Center 201 parsecs; (2) Atmion—

It went on and on. Just before noon she noted with steely amusement that there was still nothing coming through from the meteorology room, nothing at all about storms.

She made the proper connection and flung her words: "What's the matter, Lieutenant Cannons? Your assistants have been making prints and duplicates of various Kaider maps. Aren't you getting anything?"

The old meteorologist shook his head. "You will recall, noble lady, that when we captured that robot in space, he had time to send out a warning. Immediately on every Fifty Suns planet, all maps were despoiled, civilian meteorologists were placed aboard spaceships, that were stripped of receiving radios, with orders to go to a planet on a chance basis, and stay there for ten years.

"To my mind, all this was done before it was clearly grasped that their navy hadn't a chance against us. Now they are going to provide us with a naval meteorologist, but we shall have to depend on our lie detectors as to whether or not he is telling us the truth."

"I see." The woman smiled. "Have no fear. They don't dare oppose us openly. No doubt there is a plan being built up against us, but it cannot prevail now that we can take action to enforce our unalterable will. Whoever they send must tell us the truth. Let me know when he comes."

Lunch came, but she ate at her desk, watching the flashing pictures on the astro, listening to the murmur of voices, storing the facts, the general picture, into her brain.

"There's no doubt, Captain Turgess," she commented once, savagely, "that we're being lied to on a vast scale. But let it be so. We can use psychological tests to verify all the vital details.

"For the time being it is important that you relieve the fears of everyone you find it necessary to question. We must convince these people that Earth will accept them on an equal basis without bias or prejudice of any kind because of their robot orig—"

She bit her lip. "That's an ugly word, the worst kind of propaganda. We must eliminate it from our thoughts."

"I'm afraid," the officer shrugged, "not from our thoughts."

She stared at him, narrow-eyed, then cut him off angrily. A moment later she was talking into the general transmitter: "The word robot must not be used—by any of our personnel—under pain of fine—"

Switching off, she put a busy signal on her spare receiver, and called Psychology House. Lieutenant Neslor's face appeared on the plate.

"I heard your order just now, noble lady," the woman psychologist said. "I'm afraid, however, that we're dealing with the deepest instincts of the human animal—hatred or fear of the stranger, the alien.

"Excellency, we come from a long line of ancestors who, in their time, have felt superior to others because of some slight variation in the pigmentation of the skin. It is even recorded that the color of the eyes has influenced the egoistic in historical decisions. We have sailed into very deep waters, and it will be the crowning achievement of our life if we sail out in a satisfactory fashion."

There was an eager lilt in the psychologist's voice; and the grand captain experienced a responsive thrill of joy. If there was one thing she appreciated, it was the positive outlook, the kind of people who faced all obstacles short of the recognizably impossible with a youthful zest, a will to win. She was still smiling as she broke the connection.

The high thrill sagged. She sat cold with her problem. It was a problem. Hers. All aristocratic officers had *carte blanche* powers, and were expected to solve difficulties involving anything up to whole groups of planetary systems.

After a minute she dialed the meteorology room again.

"Lieutenant Cannons, when the meteorology officer of the Fifty Suns navy arrives, please employ the following tactics—"

Maltby waved dismissal to the driver of his car. The machine pulled away from the curb and Maltby stood frowning at the flaming energy barrier that barred farther progress along the street. Finally, he took another look at the Earth ship.

It was directly above him now that he had come so many miles across the city toward it. It was tremendously high up, a long, black torpedo shape almost lost in the mist of distance.

But high as it was it was still visibly bigger than anything ever seen by the Fifty Suns, an incredible creature of metal from a world so far away that, almost, it had sunk to the status of myth.

Here was the reality. There would be tests, he thought, penetrating tests before they'd accept any orbit he planned. It wasn't that he doubted the ability of his double mind to overcome anything like that, but—

Well to remember that the frightful gap of years which separated the science of Earth from that of the Fifty Suns had already shown unpleasant surprises. Maltby shook himself grimly and gave his full attention to the street ahead.

A fan-shaped pink fire spread skyward from two machines that stood in the center of the street. The flame was a very pale pink and completely transparent. It looked electronic, deadly.

Beyond it were men in glittering uniforms. A steady trickle of them moved in and out of buildings. About three blocks down the avenue a second curtain of pink fire flared up.

There seemed to be no attempt to guard the sides. The men he could see looked at ease, confident. There was murmured conversation, low laughter and—they weren't all men.

As Maltby walked forward, two fine-looking young women in uniform came down the steps of the nearest of the requisitioned buildings. One of the guards of the flame said something to them. There was a twin tinkle of silvery laughter. Still laughing, they strode off down the street.

It was suddenly exciting. There was an air about these people of far places, of tremendous and wonderful lands beyond the farthest horizons of the staid Fifty Suns.

He felt cold, then hot, then he glanced up at the fantastically big ship; and the chill came back. One ship, he thought, but so big, so mighty that thirty billion people didn't dare send their own fleets against it. They—

He grew aware that one of the brilliantly arrayed guards was staring at him. The man spoke into a wrist radio, and after a moment a second man broke off his conversation with a third soldier and came over. He stared through the flame barrier at Maltby.

"Is there anything you desire? Or are you just looking?"

He spoke English, curiously accented—but English! His manner was mild, almost gentle, cultured. The whole effect had a naturalness, an unalienness that was pleasing. After all, Maltby thought, he had never had the fear of these people that the others had. His very plan to defeat the ship was based upon his own fundamental belief that the robots were indestructible in the sense that no one could ever wipe them out completely.

Quietly, Maltby explained his presence.

"Oh, yes," the man nodded, "we've been expecting you. I'm to take you at once to the meteorological room of the ship. Just a moment—"

The flame barrier went down and Maltby was led into one of the buildings. There was a long corridor, and the transmitter that projected him into the ship must have been focused somewhere along it.

Because abruptly he was in a very large room. Maps floated in half a dozen antigravity pits. The walls shed light from millions of tiny point sources. And everywhere were tables with curved lines of very dim but sharply etched light on their surfaces.

Maltby's guide was nowhere to be seen. Coming toward him, however, was a tall, fine-looking old man. The oldster offered his hand.

"My name is Lieutenant Cannons, senior ship meteorologist. If you will sit down here we can plan an orbit and the ship can start moving within the hour. The grand captain is very anxious that we get started."

Maltby nodded casually. But he was stiff, alert. He stood quite still, feeling around with that acute second mind of his, his Dellian mind, for energy pressures that would show secret attempts to watch or control his mind.

But there was nothing like that.

He smiled finally, grimly. It was going to be as simple as this, was it? Like hell it was.

As he sat down, Maltby felt suddenly cozy and alive. The pure exhilaration of existence burned through him like a flame. He recognized the singing excitement for the battle thrill it was and felt a grim joy that for the first time in fifteen years he could do something about it.

During his long service in the Fifty Suns navy, he had faced hostility and suspicion because he was a Mixed Man. And always he had felt helpless, unable to do anything about it. Now, here was a far more basic hostility, however veiled, and a suspicion that must be like a burning fire.

And this time he could fight. He could look this skillfully voluble, friendly old man squarely in the eye and—

Friendly?

"It makes me smile sometimes," the old man was saying, "when I think of the unscientific aspects of the orbit we have to plan now. For instance, what is the time lag on storm reports out here?"

Maltby could not suppress a smile. So Lieutenant Cannons wanted to know things, did he? To give the man credit, it wasn't really a lame opening. The truth was, the only way to ask a question was—well—to ask it. Maltby said:

"Oh, three, four months. Nothing unusual. Each space meteorologist takes about that length of time to check the bounds of the particular storm in his area, and then he reports, and we adjust our maps.

"Fortunately"—he pushed his second mind to the fore as he coolly spoke the great basic lie—"there are no major storms between the Kaider and Cassidor suns."

He went on, sliding over the untruth like an eel breasting wet rock:

"However, several suns prevent a straight line movement. So if you would show me some of your orbits for twenty-five hundred light years, I'll make a selection of the best ones."

He wasn't, he realized instantly, going to slip over his main point as easily as that.

"No intervening storms?" the old man said. He pursed his lips. The fine lines in his long face seemed to deepen. He looked genuinely nonplused; and there was no doubt at all that he hadn't expected such a straightforward statement. "Hm-m-m, no storms. That does make it simple, doesn't it?"

He broke off. "You know, the important thing about two"—he hesitated over the word, then went on—"two people, who have been brought up in different cultures, under different scientific standards, is that they make sure they are discussing a subject from a common viewpoint.

"Space is so big. Even this comparatively small system of stars, the Lesser Magellanic Cloud, is so vast that it defies our reason. We on the battleship *Star Cluster* have spent ten years surveying it, and now we are able to say glibly that it comprises two hundred sixty billion cubic light years, and contains fifty millions of suns.

"We located the magnetic center of the Cloud, fixed our zero line from center to the great brightest star, S Doradus; and now, I suppose, there are people who would be fools enough to think we've got the system stowed away in our brainpans."

Maltby was silent because he himself was just such a fool. This was warning. He was being told in no uncertain terms that they were in a position to check any orbit he gave them with respect to all intervening suns.

It meant much more. It showed that Earth was on the verge of extending her tremendous sway to the Lesser Magellanic Cloud. Destroying this ship now would provide the Fifty Suns with precious years during which they would have to decide what they intended to do.

But that would be all. Other ships would come; the inexorable pressure of the stupendous populations of the main galaxy would burst out even farther into space. Always under careful control, shepherded by mighty hosts of invincible battleships, the great transports would sweep into the Cloud, and every planet everywhere, robot or non-robot, would acknowledge Earth suzerainty.

Imperial earth recognized no separate nations of any description anywhere. The robots, Dellian, non-Dellian and Mixed, would need every extra day, every hour; and it was lucky for them all that he was not basing his hope of destroying this ship on an orbit that would end inside a sun.

Their survey had magnetically placed all the suns for them. But they couldn't know about the storms. Not in ten years or in a hundred was it possible for one ship to locate possible storms in an area that involved twenty-five hundred light years of length.

Unless their psychologists could uncover the special qualities of his double brain, he had them. He grew aware that Lieutenant Cannons was manipulating the controls of the orbit table.

The lines of light on the surface flickered and shifted. Then settled like the balls in a game of chance. Maltby selected six that ran deep into the great storm. Ten minutes after that he felt the faint jar as the ship began to move. He stood up, frowning. Odd that they should act without *some* verification of his—

"This way," said the old man.

Maltby thought sharply: This couldn't be all. Any minute now they'd start on him and—

His thought ended.

He was in space. Far, far below was the receding planet of Kaider III. To one side gleamed the vast dark hull of the battleship;

and on every other side, and up, and down, were stars and the distances of dark space.

In spite of all his will, the shock was inexpressibly violent.

His active mind jerked. He staggered physically; and he would have fallen like a blindfolded creature except that, in the movement of trying to keep on his feet, he recognized that he *was* still on his feet.

His whole being steadied. Instinctively, he—tilted—his second mind awake, and pushed it forward. Put its more mechanical and precise qualities, its Dellian strength, between his other self and whatever the human beings might be doing against him.

Somewhere in the mist of darkness and blazing stars, a woman's clear and resonant voice said:

"Well, Lieutenant Neslor, did the surprise yield any psychological fruits?"

The reply came from a second, an older-sounding woman's voice:

"After three seconds, noble lady, his resistance leaped to I. Q. 900. Which means they've sent us a Dellian. Your excellency, I thought you specifically asked that their representative be not a Dellian."

Maltby said swiftly into the night around him: "You're quite mistaken. I am not a Dellian. And I assure you that I will lower my resistance to zero if you desire. I reacted instinctively to surprise, naturally enough."

There was a click. The illusion of space and stars snapped out of existence. Maltby saw what he had begun to suspect, that he was, had been all the time, in the meteorology room.

Nearby stood the old man, a thin smile on his lined face. On a raised dais, partly hidden behind a long instrument board, sat a handsome young woman. It was the old man who spoke. He said in a stately voice:

"You are in the presence of Grand Captain, the Right Honorable Gloria Cecily, the Lady Laurr of Noble Laurr. Conduct yourself accordingly."

Maltby bowed but he said nothing. The grand captain frowned at him, impressed by his appearance. Tall, magnificent-looking body—strong, supremely intelligent face. In a single flash she noted all the characteristics common to the first-class human being and robot.

These people might be more dangerous than she had thought. She said with unnatural sharpness for her:

"As you know, we have to question you. We would prefer that

you do not take offense. You have told us that Cassidor VII, the chief planet of the Fifty Suns, is twenty-five hundred light years from here. Normally, we would spend more than sixty years *feeling* our way across such an immense gap of uncharted, star-filled space. But you have given us a choice of orbits.

"We must make sure those orbits are honest, offered without guile or harmful purpose. To that end we have to ask you to open your mind and answer our questions under the strictest psychological surveillance."

"I have orders," said Maltby, "to co-operate with you in every way."

He had wondered how he would feel, now that the hour of decision was upon him. But there was nothing unnormal. His body was a little stiffer, but his minds—

He withdrew his *self* into the background and left his Dellian mind to confront all the questions that came. His Dellian mind that he had deliberately kept apart from his thoughts. That curious mind, which had no will of its own, but which, by remote control, reacted with the full power of an I. Q. of 191.

Sometimes, he marveled himself at that second mind of his. It had no creative ability, but its memory was machinelike, and its resistance to outside pressure was, as the woman psychologist had so swiftly analyzed, over nine hundred. To be exact, the equivalent of I. Q. 917.

"What is your name?"

That was the way it began: His name, distinction— He answered everything quietly, positively, without hesitation. When he had finished, when he had sworn to the truth of every word about the storms, there was a long moment of dead silence. And then a middle-aged woman stepped out of the nearby wall.

She came over and motioned him into a chair. When he was seated she tilted his head and began to examine it. She did it gently; her fingers were caressing as a lover's. But when she looked up she said sharply:

"You're not a Dellian or a non-Dellian. And the molecular structure of your brain and body is the most curious I've ever seen. All the molecules are twins. I saw a similar arrangement once in an artificial electronic structure where an attempt was being made to balance an unstable electronic structure. The parallel isn't exact, but—mm-m-m, I must try to remember what the end result was of that experiment."

She broke off: "What is your explanation? What are you?"

Maltby sighed. He had determined to tell only the one main

lie. Not that it mattered so far as his double brain was concerned. But untruths effected slight variations in blood pressure, created neural spasms and disturbed muscular integration. He couldn't take the risk of even one more than was absolutely necessary.

"I'm a Mixed Man," he explained. He described briefly how the cross between the Dellian and non-Dellian, so long impossible, had finally been brought about a hundred years before. The use of cold and pressure—

"Just a moment," said the psychologist.

She disappeared. When she stepped again out of the wall transmitter, she was thoughtful.

"He seems to be telling the truth," she confessed, almost reluctantly.

"What is this?" snapped the grand captain. "Ever since we ran into that first citizen of the Fifty Suns, the psychology department has qualified every statement it issues. I thought psychology was the only perfect science. Either he is telling the truth or he isn't."

The older woman looked unhappy. She stared very hard at Maltby, seemed baffled by his cool gaze, and finally faced her superior, said:

"It's that double molecule structure of his brain. Except for that, I see no reason why you shouldn't order full acceleration."

The grand captain smiled. "I shall have Captain Maltby to dinner tonight. I'm sure he will co-operate then with any further studies you may be prepared to make at that time. Meanwhile I think—"

She spoke into a communicator: "Central engines, step up to half light year a minute on the following orbit—"

Maltby listened, estimating with his Dellian mind. Half a light year a minute; it would take a while to attain that speed, but—in eight hours they'd strike the storm.

In eight hours he'd be having dinner with the grand captain. Eight hours!

The full flood of a contraterrene Nova impinging upon terrene gases already infuriated by seetee gone insane—that was the new, greater storm.

The exploding, giant sun added weight to the diffuse, maddened thing. And it added something far more deadly.

Speed! From peak to peak of velocity the tumult of ultrafire leaped. The swifter crags of the storm danced and burned with an absolutely hellish fury.

The sequence of action was rapid almost beyond the bearance of matter. First raced the light of the Nova, blazing its warning at more than a hundred and eighty-six thousand miles a second to all who knew that it flashed from the edge of an interstellar storm.

But the advance glare of warning ws nullified by the colossal speed of the storm. For weeks and months it drove through the vast night at a velocity that was only a bare measure short of that of light itself.

The dinner dishes had been cleared away. Maltby was thinking: In half an hour—*half an hour!*

He was wondering shakily just what did happen to a battleship suddenly confronted by thousands of gravities of deceleration. Aloud he was saying:

"My day? I spent it in the library. Mainly, I was interested in the recent history of Earth's interstellar colonization. I'm curious as to what is done with groups like the Mixed Men. I mentioned to you that, after the war in which they were defeated largely because there was so few of them, the Mixed Men hid themselves from the Fifty Suns. I was one of the captured children who—"

There was an interruption, a cry from the wall communicator: *"Noble lady, I've solved it!"*

A moment fled before Maltby recognized the strained voice of the woman psychologist. He had almost forgotten that she was supposed to be studying him. Her next words chilled him:

"Two minds! I thought of it a little while ago and rigged up a twin watching device. Ask him, *ask* him the question about the storms. Meanwhile stop the ship. At once!"

Maltby's dark gaze clashed hard with the steely, narrowed eyes of the grand captain. Without hesitation he concentrated his two minds on her, forced her to say:

"Don't be silly, lieutenant. One person can't have two brains. Explain yourself further."

His hope was delay. They had ten minutes in which they could save themselves. He must waste every second of that time, resist all their efforts, try to control the situation. If only his special three-dimensional hypnotism worked through communicators—

It didn't. Lines of light leaped at him from the wall and crisscrossed his body, held him in his chair like so many unbreakable cables. Even as he was bound hand and foot by palpable energy, a second complex of forces built up before his face, barred his thought pressure from the grand captain, and finally coned over his head like a dunce cap.

He was caught as neatly as if a dozen men had swarmed with

their strength and weight over his body. Maltby relaxed and laughed.

"Too late," he taunted. "It'll take at least an hour for this ship to reduce to a safe speed; and at this velocity you can't turn aside in time to avoid the greatest storm in this part of the Universe."

That wasn't strictly true. There was still time and room to sheer off before the advancing storm in any of the fronting directions. The impossibility was to turn toward the storm's tail or its great, bulging sides.

His thought was interrupted by the first cry from the young woman; a piercing cry: "Central engines! Reduce speed! Emergency!"

There was a jar that shook the walls and a pressure that tore at his muscles. Maltby adjusted and then stared across the table at the grand captain. She was smiling, a frozen mask of a smile; and she said from between clenched teeth:

"Lieutenant Neslor, use any means physical or otherwise, but make him talk. There must be something."

"His second mind is the key," the psychologist's voice came. "It's not Dellian. It has only normal resistance. I shall subject it to the greatest concentration of conditioning ever focused on a human brain, using the two basics: sex and logic. I shall have to use you, noble lady, as the object of his affections."

"Hurry!" said the young woman. Her voice was like a metal bar.

Maltby sat in a mist, mental and physical. Deep in his mind was awareness that he was an entity, and that irresistible machines were striving to mold his thought.

He resisted. The resistance was as strong as his life, as intense as all the billions and quadrillions of impulses that had shaped his being, could make it.

But the outside thought, the pressure, grew stronger. How silly of him to resist Earth—when this lovely woman of Earth loved him, loved him, loved him. Glorious was that civilization of Earth and the main galaxy. Three hundred million billion people. The very first contact would rejuvenate the Fifty Suns. How lovely she is; I must save her. She means everything to me.

As from a great distance, he began to hear his own voice, explaining what must be done, just how the ship must be turned, in what direction, how much time there was. He tried to stop himself, but inexorably his voice went on, mouthing the words that spelled defeat for the Fifty Suns.

The mist began to fade. The terrible pressure eased from his straining mind. The damning stream of words ceased to pour from his lips. He sat up shakily, conscious that the energy cords and the energy cap had been withdrawn from his body. He heard the grand captain say into a communicator:

"By making a point 0100 turn we shall miss the storm by seven light weeks. I admit it is an appallingly sharp curve, but I feel that we should have at least that much leeway."

She turned and stared at Maltby: "Prepare yourself. At half a light year a minute even a hundredth of a degree turn makes some people black out."

"Not me," said Maltby, and tensed his Dellian muscles.

She fainted three times during the next four minutes as he sat there watching her. But each time she came to within seconds. "We human beings," she said wanly, finally, "are a poor lot. But at least we know how to endure."

The terrible minutes dragged. And dragged. Maltby began to feel the strain of that infinitesimal turn. He thought at last: Space! How could these people ever hope to survive a direct hit on a storm?

Abruptly, it was over; a man's voice said quietly: "We have followed the prescribed course, noble lady, and are now out of dang—"

He broke off with a shout: "Captain, the light of a Nova sun has just flashed from the direction of the storm. We—"

In those minutes before disaster struck, the battleship *Star Cluster,* glowed like an immense and brilliant jewel. The warning glare from the Nova set off an incredible roar of emergency clamor through all of her hundred and twenty decks.

From end to end her lights flicked on. They burned row by row straight across her four thousand feet of length with the hard tinkle of cut gems. In the reflection of that light, the black mountain that was her hull looked like the fabulous planet of Cassidor, her destination, as seen at night from a far darkness, sown with diamond shining cities.

Silent as a ghost, grand and wonderful beyond all imagination, glorious in her power, the great ship slid through the blackness along the special river of time and space which was her plotted course.

Even as she rode into the storm there was nothing visible. The space ahead looked as clear as any vacuum. So tenuous were the gases that made up the storm that the ship would not even have been aware of them if it had been traveling at atomic speeds.

Violent the disintegration of matter in that storm might be, and the sole source of cosmic rays the hardest energy in the known universe. But the immense, the cataclysmic danger to the *Star Cluster* was a direct result of her own terrible velocity.

If she had had time to slow, the storm would have meant nothing.

Striking that mass of gas at half a light year a minute was like running into an unending solid wall. The great ship shuddered in every plate as the deceleration tore at her gigantic strength.

In seconds she had run the gamut of all the recoil systems her designers had planned for her as a unit.

She began to break up.

And still everything was according to the original purpose of the superb engineering firm that had built her. The limit of unit strain reached, she dissolved into her nine thousand separate sections.

Streamlined needles of metal were those sections, four hundred feet long, forty feet wide; sliverlike shapes that sinuated cunningly through the gases, letting the pressure of them slide off their smooth hides.

But it wasn't enough. Metal groaned from the torture of deceleration. In the deceleration chambers, men and women lay at the bare edge of consciousness, enduring agony that seemed on the verge of being beyond endurance.

Hundreds of the sections careened into each other in spite of automatic screens, and instantaneously fused into white-hot coffins.

And still, in spite of the hideously maintained velocity, that mass of gases was not bridged; light years of thickness had still to be covered.

For those sections that remained, once more all the limits of human strength were reached. The final action was chemical, directly on the human bodies that remained of the original thirty thousand. Those bodies for whose sole benefit all the marvelous safety devices had been conceived and constructed, the poor, fragile, human beings who through all the ages had persisted in dying under normal conditions from a pressure of something less than fifteen gravities.

The prompt reaction of the automatics in rolling back every floor, and plunging every person into the deceleration chambers of each section—that saving reaction was abruptly augmented as the deceleration chamber was flooded by a special type of gas.

Wet was that gas, and clinging. It settled thickly on the clothes of the humans, soaked through to the skin and *through* the skin, into every part of the body.

Sleep came gently, and with it a wonderful relaxation. The blood grew immune to shock; muscles that, in a minute before, had been drawn with anguish—loosened; the brain impregnated with life-giving chemicals that relieved it of all shortages remained untroubled even by dreams.

Everybody grew enormously flexible to gravitation pressures— a hundred—a hundred and fifty gravities of deceleration; and still the life force clung.

The great heart of the Universe beat on. The storm roared along its inescapable artery, creating the radiance of life, purging the dark of its poisons—and at last the tiny ships in their separate courses burst its great bounds.

They began to come together, to seek each other, as if among them there was an irresistible passion that demanded intimacy of union.

Automatically, they slid into their old positions; the battleship *Star Cluster* began again to take form—but there were gaps. Segments destroyed, and segments lost.

On the third day Acting Grand Captain Rutgers called the surviving captains to the forward bridge, where he was temporarily making his headquarters. After the conference a communique was issued to the crew:

At oo8 hours this morning a message was received from Grand Captain, the Right Honorable Gloria Cecily, the Lady Laurr of Noble Laurr, I. C., C. M., G. K. R. She has been forced down on the planet of a yellow-white sun. Her ship crashed on landing, and is unrepairable. As all communication with her has been by nondirectional sub-space radio, and as it will be utterly impossible to locate such an ordinary type sun among so many millions of other suns, the Captains in Session regret to report that our noble lady's name must now be added to that longest of all lists of naval casualties: the list of those who have been lost forever on active duty.

The admiralty lights will burn blue until further notice.

Her back was to him as he approached. Maltby hesitated, then tensed his mind, and held her there beside the section of ship that had been the main bridge of the *Star Cluster*.

The long metal shape lay half buried in the marshy ground of the great valley, its lower end jutting down into the shimmering deep yellowish black waters of a sluggish river.

Maltby paused a few feet from the tall, slim woman, and, still holding her unaware of him, examined once again the environment that was to be their life.

The fine spray of dark rain that had dogged his exploration walk was retreating over the yellow rim of valley to the "west."

As he watched, a small yellow sun burst out from behind a curtain of dark, ocherous clouds and glared at him brilliantly. Below it an expanse of jungle glinted strangely brown and yellow.

Everywhere was that dark-brown and intense, almost liquid yellow.

Maltby sighed—and turned his attention to the woman, willed her not to see him as he walked around in front of her.

He had given a great deal of thought to the Right Honorable Gloria Cecily during his walk. Basically, of course, the problem of a man and a woman who were destined to live the rest of their lives together, alone, on a remote planet, was very simple. Particularly in view of the fact that one of the two had been conditioned to be in love with the other.

Maltby smiled grimly. He could appreciate the artificial origin of that love. But that didn't dispose of the profound fact of it.

The conditioning machine had struck to his very core. Unfortunately, it had not touched her at all; and two days of being alone with her had brought out one reality:

The Lady Laurr of Noble Laurr was not even remotely thinking of yielding herself to the normal requirements of the situation.

It was time that she was made aware, not because an early solution was necessary or even desirable, but because she had to realize that the problem existed.

He stepped forward and took her in his arms.

She was a tall, graceful woman; she fitted into his embrace as if she belonged there; and, because his control of her made her return the kiss, its warmth had an effect beyond his intention.

He had intended to free her mind in the middle of the kiss. He didn't.

When he finally released her, it was only a physical release. Her mind was still completely under his domination.

There was a metal chair that had been set just outside one of the doors. Maltby walked over, sank into it and stared up at the grand captain.

He felt shaken. The flame of desire that had leaped through him was a telling tribute to the conditioning he had undergone. But it was entirely beyond his previous analysis of the intensity of his own feelings.

He had thought he was in full control of himself, and he wasn't. Somehow, the sardonicism, the half detachment, the objectivity, which he had fancied was the keynote of his own reaction to this situation, didn't apply at all.

The conditioning machine had been thorough.

He loved this woman with such a violence that the mere touch of her was enough to disconnect his will from operations immediately following.

His heart grew quieter; he studied her with a semblance of detachment.

She was lovely in a handsome fashion; though almost all robot women of the Dellian race were better-looking. Her lips, while medium full, were somehow a trifle cruel; and there was a quality in her eyes that accentuated that cruelty.

There were built-up emotions in this woman that would not surrender easily to the idea of being marooned for life on an unknown planet.

It was something he would have to think over. Until then—

Maltby sighed. And released her from the three-dimensional hypnotic spell that his two minds had imposed on her.

He had taken the precaution of turning her away from him. He watched her curiously as she stood, back to him, for a moment, very still. Then she walked over to a little knob of trees above the springy, soggy marsh land.

She climbed up it and gazed in the direction from which he had come a few minutes before. Evidently looking for him.

She turned finally, shaded her face against the yellow brightness of the sinking sun, came down from the hillock and saw him.

She stopped; her eyes narrowed. She walked over slowly. She said with an odd edge in her voice:

"You came very quietly. You must have circled and walked in from the west."

"No," said Maltby deliberately, "I stayed in the east."

She seemed to consider that. She was silent, her lean face creased into a frown. She pressed her lips together, finally; there was a bruise there that must have hurt, for she winced, then she said:

"What did you discover? Did you find any—"

She stopped. Consciousness of the bruise on her lip must have penetrated at that moment. Her hand jerked up, her fingers touched the tender spot. Her eyes came alive with the violence of her comprehension. Before she could speak, Maltby said:

"Yes, you're quite right."

She stood looking at him. Her stormy gaze quietened. She said finally, in a stony voice:

"If you try that again I shall feel justified in shooting you."

Maltby shook his head. He said, unsmiling:

"And spend the rest of your life here alone? You'd go mad."

He saw instantly that her basic anger was too great for that kind of logic. He went on swiftly:

"Besides, you'd have to shoot me in the back. I have no doubt you could do that in the line of duty. But not for personal reasons."

Her compressed lips—separated. To his amazement there were suddenly tears in her eyes. Anger tears, obviously. But tears!

She stepped forward with a quick movement and slapped his face.

"You robot!" she sobbed.

Maltby stared at her ruefully; then he laughed. Finally he said, a trace of mockery in his tone:

"If I remember rightly, the lady who just spoke is the same one who delivered a ringing radio address to all the planets of the Fifty Suns swearing that in fifteen thousand years Earth people had forgotten all their prejudices against robots.

"Is it possible," he finished, "that the problem on *closer* investigation is proving more difficult?"

There was no answer. The Honorable Gloria Cecily brushed past him and disappeared into the interior of the ship.

She came out again a few minutes later.

Her expression was more serene; Maltby noted that she had removed all trace of the tears. She looked at him steadily, said:

"What did you discover when you were out? I've been delaying my call to the ship till you returned."

Maltby said: "I thought they asked you to call at 010 hours."

The woman shrugged; and there was an arrogant note in her voice as she replied:

"They'll take my calls when I make them. Did you find any sign of intelligent life?"

Maltby allowed himself brief pity for a human being who had as many shocks still to absorb as had Grand Captain Laurr.

One of the books he had read while aboard the battleship about colonists of remote planets had dealt very specifically with castaways.

He shook himself and began his description. "Mostly marsh land in the valley and there's jungle, very old. Even some of the trees are immense, though sections show no growth rings—some interesting beasts and a four-legged, two-armed thing that watched me from a distance. It carried a spear but it was too far away for me to use my hypnotism on it. There must be a village somewhere, perhaps on the valley rim. My idea is that during the next months I'll cut the ship into small sections and transport it to drier ground.

"I would say that we have the following information to offer the ship's scientists: We're on a planet of a G-type sun. The sun must be larger than the average yellow-white type and have a larger surface temperature.

"It must be larger and hotter because, though it's far away, it is hot enough to keep the northern hemisphere of this planet in a semitropical condition.

"The sun was quite a bit north at midday, but now it's swinging back to the south. I'd say offhand the planet must be tilted at about forty degrees, which means there's a cold winter coming up, though that doesn't fit with the age and type of the vegetation."

The Lady Laurr was frowning. "It doesn't seem very helpful," she said. "But, of course, I'm only an executive."

"And I'm only a meteorologist."

"Exactly. Come in. Perhaps my astrophysicist can make something of it."

"*Your* astrophysicist!" said Maltby. But he didn't say it aloud. He followed her into the segment of ship and closed the door.

Maltby examined the interior of the main bridge with a wry smile as the young woman seated herself before the astroplate.

The very imposing glitter of the instrument board that occupied one entire wall was ironical now. All the machines it had controlled were far away in space. Once it had dominated the entire Lesser Magellanic Cloud; now his own hand gun was a more potent instrument.

He grew aware that Lady Laurr was looking up at him.

"I don't understand it," she said. "They don't answer."

"Perhaps"—Maltby could not keep the faint sardonicism out of his tone—"perhaps they may really have had a good reason for wanting you to call at 010 hours."

The woman made a faint, exasperated movement with her facial muscles but she did not answer. Maltby went on coolly:

"After all, it doesn't matter. They're only going through routine motions, the idea being to leave no loophole of rescue unlooked through. I can't even imagine the kind of miracle it would take for anybody to find us."

The woman seemed not to have heard. She said, frowning:

"How is it that we've never heard a single Fifty Suns broadcast? I intended to ask about that before. Not once during our ten years in the Lesser Cloud did we catch so much as a whisper of radio energy."

Maltby shrugged. "All radios operate on an extremely complicated variable wave length—changes every twentieth of a second. Your instruments would register a tick once every ten minutes, and—"

He was cut off by a voice from the astroplate. A man's face was there—Acting Grand Captain Rutgers.

"Oh, there you are, captain," the woman said. "What kept you?"

"We're in the process of landing our forces on Cassidor VII," was the reply. "As you know, regulations require that the grand captain—"

"Oh, yes. Are you free now?"

"No. I've taken a moment to see that everything is right with you, and then I'll switch you over to Captain Planston."

"How is the landing proceeding?"

"Perfectly. We have made contact with the government. They seem resigned. But now I must leave. Good-by, my lady."

His face flickered and was gone. The plate went blank. It was about as curt a greeting as anybody had ever received. But Maltby, sunk in his own gloom, scarcely noticed.

So it was all over. The desperate scheming of the Fifty Suns leaders, his own attempt to destroy the great battleship, proved futile against an invincible foe.

For a moment he felt very close to the defeat, with all its implications. Consciousness came finally that the fight no longer mattered in his life. But the knowledge failed to shake his dark mood.

He saw that the Right Honorable Gloria Cecily had an expression of mixed elation and annoyance on her fine, strong face; and there was no doubt that she didn't *feel*—disconnected—from the mighty events out there in space. Nor had she missed the implications of the abruptness of the interview.

The astroplate grew bright and a face appeared on it—one that Maltby hadn't seen before. It was of a heavy-jowled, oldish man with a ponderous voice that said:

"Privilege your ladyship—hope we can find something that will enable us to make a rescue. Never give up hope, I say, until the last nail's driven in your coffin."

He chuckled; and the woman said: "Captain Maltby will give you all the information he has, then no doubt you can give him some advice, Captain Planston. Neither he nor I, unfortunately, are astrophysicists."

"Can't be experts on every subject," Captain Planston puffed. "Er, Captain Maltby, what do you know?"

Maltby gave his information briefly, then waited while the other gave instructions. There wasn't much:

"Find out length of seasons. Interested in that yellow effect of the sunlight and the deep brown. Take the following photographs, using orthosensitive film—use three dyes, a red sensitive, a blue and a yellow. Take a spectrum reading—what I want to check on is that maybe you've got a strong blue sun there, with the ultraviolet barred by a heavy atmosphere, and all the heat and light coming in on the yellow band.

"I'm not offering much hope, mind you—the Lesser Cloud is packed with blue suns—five hundred thousand of them brighter than Sirius.

"Finally, get that season information from the natives. Make a point of it. Good-by!"

The native was wary. He persisted in retreating elusively into the jungle; and his four legs gave him a speed advantage of which he seemed to be aware. For he kept coming back, tantalizingly.

The woman watched with amusement, then exasperation.

"Perhaps," she suggested, "if we separated, and I drove him toward you?"

She saw the frown on the man's face as Maltby nodded reluctantly. His voice was strong, tense.

"He's leading us into an ambush. Turn on the sensitives in your helmet and carry your gun. Don't be too hasty about firing, but don't hesitate in a crisis. A spear can make an ugly wound; and we haven't got the best facilities for handling anything like that."

His orders brought a momentary irritation. He seemed not to be aware that she was as conscious as he of the requirements of the situation.

The Right Honorable Gloria sighed. If they had to stay on this planet there would have to be some major psychological adjustments, and not—she thought grimly—only by herself.

"Now!" said Maltby beside her, swiftly. "Notice the way the ravine splits in two. I came this far yesterday and they join about two hundred yards farther on. He's gone up the left fork. I'll take the right. You stop here, let him come back to see what's happened, then drive him on."

He was gone, like a shadow, along a dark path that wound under thick foliage.

Silence settled.

She waited. After a minute she felt herself alone in a yellow and black world that had been lifeless since time began.

She thought: This was what Maltby had meant yesterday when he had said she wouldn't dare shoot him—and remain alone. It hadn't penetrated then.

It did now. Alone, on a nameless planet of a mediocre sun, one woman waking up every morning on a moldering ship that rested its unliving metal shape on a dark, muggy, yellow marsh land.

She stood somber. There was no doubt that the problem of robot and human being would have to be solved here as well as out there.

A sound pulled her out of her gloom. As she watched, abruptly more alert, a catlike head peered cautiously from a line of bushes a hundred yards away across the clearing.

It was an interesting head; its ferocity not the least of its fascinating qualities. The yellowish body was invisible now in the underbrush, but she had caught enough glimpses of it earlier to recognize that it was the CC type, of the almost universal Centaur family. Its body was evenly balanced between its hind and forelegs.

It watched her, and its great glistening black eyes were round with puzzlement. Its head twisted from side to side, obviously searching for Maltby.

She waved her gun and walked forward. Instantly the creature disappeared. She could hear it with her sensitives, running into distance. Abruptly, it slowed; then there was no sound at all.

"He's got it," she thought.

She felt impressed. These two-brained Mixed Men, she thought, were bold and capable. It would really be too bad if antirobot prejudice prevented them from being absorbed into the galactic civilization of Imperial Earth.

She watched him a few minutes later, using the block system of communication with the creature. Maltby looked up, saw her. He shook his head as if puzzled.

"He says it's always been warm like this, and that he's been alive for thirteen hundred moons. And that a moon is forty suns—forty days. He wants us to come up a little farther along this valley, but that's too transparent for comfort. Our move is to make a cautious, friendly gesture, and—"

He stopped short. Before she could even realize anything was wrong, her mind was caught, her muscles galvanized. She was thrown sideways and downward so fast that the blow of striking the ground was pure agony.

She lay there stunned, and out of the corner of her eye she saw the spear plunge through the air where she had been.

She twisted, rolled over—her own free will now—and jerked her gun in the direction from which the spear had come. There was a second centaur there, racing away along a bare slope. Her finger pressed on the control; and then—

"Don't!" It was Maltby, his voice low. "It was a scout the others sent ahead to see what was happening. He's done his work. It's all over."

She lowered her gun and saw with annoyance that her hand was shaking, her whole body trembling. She parted her lips to say: "Thanks for saving my life!" Then she closed them again. Because the words would have quavered. And because—

Saved her life! Her mind poised on the edge of blankness with the shock of the thought. Incredibly—she had never before been in personal danger from an individual creature.

There had been the time when her battleship had run into the outer fringes of a sun; and there was the cataclysm of the storm, just past.

But those had been impersonal menaces to be met with technical virtuosities and the hard training of the service.

This was different.

All the way back to the segment of ship she tried to fathom what the difference meant.

It seemed to her finally that she had it.

"Spectrum featureless." Maltby gave his findings over the astro. "No dark lines at all; two of the yellow bands so immensely intense that they hurt my eyes. As you suggested, apparently what we have here is a blue sun whose strong violet radiation is cut off by the atmosphere.

"However," he finished, "the uniqueness of that effect is confined to our planet here, a derivation of the thick atmosphere. Any questions?"

"No-o!" The astrophysicist looked thoughtful. "And I can give you no further instructions. I'll have to examine this material. Will you ask Lady Laurr to come in? Like to speak to her privately, if you please."

"Of course."

When she had come, Maltby went outside and watched the moon come up. Darkness—he had noticed it the previous night —brought a vague, overall violet haze. Explained now!

An eighty-degree temperature on a planet that, the angular diameter of the sun being what it was, would have been minus one hundred eighty degrees, if the sun's apparent color had been real.

A blue sun, one of five hundred thousand— Interesting but— Maltby smiled savagely—Captain Planston's "No further instructions!" had a finality about it that—

He shivered involuntarily. And after a moment tried to picture himself sitting, like this, a year hence, staring up at an unchanged moon. Ten years, twenty—

He grew aware that the woman had come to the doorway and was gazing at him where he sat on the chair.

Maltby looked up. The stream of white light from inside the ship caught the queer expression on her face, gave her a strange, bleached look after the yellowness that had seemed a part of her complexion all day.

"We shall receive no more astroradio calls," she said and, turning, went inside.

Maltby nodded to himself, almost idly. It was hard and brutal, this abrupt cutting off of communication. But the regulations governing such situations were precise.

The marooned ones must realize with utter clarity, without false hopes and without the curious illusions produced by radio communication, that they were cut off forever. Forever on their own.

Well, so be it. A fact was a fact, to be faced with resolution. There had been a chapter on castaways in one of the books he had read on the battleship. It had stated that nine hundred million human beings had, during recorded history, been marooned on then undiscovered planets. Most of these planets had eventually been found; and on no less than ten thousand of them great populations had sprung from the original nucleus of castaways.

The law prescribed that a castaway could not withhold himself or herself from participating in such population increases—regardless of previous rank. Castaways must forget considerations of sensitivity and individualism, and think of themselves as instruments of race expansion.

There were penalties; naturally inapplicable if no rescue was effected, but ruthlessly applied whenever recalcitrants were found.

Conceivably the courts might determine that a human being and a robot constituted a special case.

Half an hour must have passed while he sat there. He stood up finally, conscious of hunger. He had forgotten all about supper.

He felt a qualm of self-annoyance. Damn it, this was not the night to appear to be putting pressure on her. Sooner or later she would have to be convinced that she ought to do her share of the cooking.

But not tonight.

He hurried inside, toward the compact kitchen that was part of every segment of ship. In the corridor, he paused.

A blaze of light streamed from the kitchen door. Somebody was whistling softly and tunelessly but cheerfully; and there was an odor of cooking vegetables, and hot *lak* meat.

They almost bumped in the doorway. "I was just going to call you," she said.

The supper was a meal of silences, quickly over. They put the dishes into the automatic and went and sat in the great lounge; Maltby saw finally that the woman was studying him with amused eyes.

"Is there any possibility," she said abruptly, "that a Mixed Man and a human woman can have children?"

"Frankly," Maltby confessed, "I doubt it."

He launched into a detailed description of the cold and pressure process that had molded the protoplasm to make the original Mixed Men. When he finished he saw that her eyes were still regarding him with a faint amusement. She said in an odd tone:

"A very curious thing happened to me today, after that native threw his spear. I realized"—she seemed for a moment to have difficulty in speaking—"I realized that I had, so far as I personally was concerned, solved the robot problem.

"Naturally," she finished quietly, "I would not have withheld myself in any event. But it is pleasant to know that I like you without"—she smiled—"qualifications."

Blue sun that looked yellow. Maltby sat in the chair the following morning puzzling over it. He half expected a visit from the natives, and so he was determined to stay near the ship that day.

He kept his eyes aware of the clearing edges, the valley rims, the jungle trails, but—

There was a law, he remembered, that governed the shifting of light to other wave bands, to yellow for instance. Rather complicated, but in view of the fact that all the instruments of the main bridge were controls of instruments, not the machines themselves, he'd have to depend on mathematics if he ever hoped to visualize the kind of sun that was out there.

Most of the heat probably came through the ultraviolet range.

But that was uncheckable. So leave it alone and stick to the yellow.

He went into the ship. Gloria was nowhere in sight, but her bedroom door was closed. Maltby found a notebook, returned to his chair and began to figure.

An hour later he stared at the answer: One million three hundred thousand million miles. About a fifth of a light year.

He laughed curtly. That was that. He'd have to get better data than he had or—

Or would he?

His mind poised. In a single flash of understanding, the stupendous truth burst upon him.

With a cry he leaped to his feet, whirled to race through the door as a long, black shadow slid across him.

The shadow was so vast, instantly darkening the whole valley, that, involuntarily, Maltby halted and looked up.

The battleship *Star Cluster* hung low over the yellow-brown jungle planet, already disgorging a lifeboat that glinted a yellowish silver as it circled out into the sunlight, and started down.

Maltby had only a moment with the woman before the lifeboat landed. "To think," he said, "that I just now figured out the truth."

She was, he saw, not looking at him. Her gaze seemed far away. He went on:

"As for the rest, the best method, I imagine, is to put me in the conditioning chamber, and—"

Still without looking at him, she cut him off:

"Don't be ridiculous. You must not imagine that I feel embarrassed because you have kissed me. I shall receive you later in my quarters."

A bath, new clothes—at last Maltby stepped through the transmitter into the astrophysics department. His own first realization of the tremendous truth, while generally accurate, had lacked detailed facts.

"Ah, Maltby!" The chief of the department came forward, shook hands. "Some sun you picked there—we suspected from your first description of the yellowness and the black. But naturally we couldn't rouse your hopes— Forbidden, you know.

"The axial tilt, the apparent length of a summer in which jungle trees of great size showed no growth rings—very suggestive. The featureless spectrum with its complete lack of dark lines— almost conclusive. Final proof was that the orthosensitive film was overexposed, while the blue and red sensitives were badly underexposed.

"This star-type is so immensely hot that practically all of its energy radiation is far in the ultravisible. A secondary radiation—a sort of fluorescence in the star's own atmosphere—produces the visible yellow when a minute fraction of the appalling ultraviolet radiation is transformed into longer wave lengths by helium atoms. A fluorescent lamp, in a fashion—but on a scale that is more than ordinarily cosmic in its violence. The total radiation reaching the planet was naturally tremendous; the surface radiation, after passing through miles of absorbing ozone, water vapor, carbondioxide and other gases, was very different.

"No wonder the native said it had always been hot. The summer lasts four thousand years. The normal radiation of that special appalling star type—the æon-in-æon-out radiation rate—is about equal to a full-fledged Nova at its catastrophic maximum of violence. It has a period of a few hours, and is equivalent to approximately a hundred million ordinary suns. Nova O, we call that brightest of all stars; and there's only one in the Lesser Magellanic Cloud, the great and glorious S-Doradus.

"When I asked you to call Grand Captain Laurr, and I told her that out of thirty million suns she had picked—"

It was at that point that Maltby cut him off. "Just a minute," he said, "did you say you told Lady Laurr *last night?*"

"Was it night down there?" Captain Planston said, interested. "Well, well— By the way, I almost forgot—this marrying and giving in marriage is not so important to me now that I am an old man. But congratulations."

The conversation was too swift for Maltby. His minds were still examining the first statement. That she had known all the time. He came up, groping, before the new words.

"Congratulations?" he echoed.

"Definitely time she had a husband," boomed the captain. "She's been a career woman, you know. Besides, it'll have a revivifying effect on the other robots . . . pardon me. Assure you, the name means nothing to me.

"Anyway, Lady Laurr herself made the announcement a few minutes ago, so come down and see me again."

He turned away with a wave of a thick hand.

Maltby headed for the nearest transmitter. She would probably be expecting him by now.

She would not be disappointed.

1943

City/

by CLIFFORD D. SIMAK

A City is a place where men gather together for mutual protection, and to help each other with the work of living. But there's a point at which the city ceases to serve—

Gramp Stevens sat in a lawn chair, watching the mower at work, feeling the warm, soft sunshine seep into his bones. The mower reached the edge of the lawn, clucked to itself like a contented hen, made a neat turn and trundled down another swath. The bag holding the clippings bulged.

Suddenly the mower stopped and clicked excitedly. A panel in its side snapped open and a cranelike arm reached out. Grasping steel fingers fished around in the grass, came up triumphantly with a stone clutched tightly, dropped the stone into a small container, disappeared back into the panel again. The lawn mower gurgled, purred on again, following its swath.

Gramp grumbled at it with suspicion.

"Some day," he told himself, "that dadburned thing is going to miss a lick and have a nervous breakdown."

He lay back in the chair and stared up at the sun-washed sky. A helicopter skimmed far overhead. From somewhere inside the house a radio came to life and a torturing clash of music poured out. Gramp, hearing it, shivered and hunkered lower in the chair.

Young Charlie was settling down for a twitch session. Dadburn the kid.

The lawn mower chuckled past and Gramp squinted at it maliciously.

"Automatic," he told the sky. "Ever' blasted thing is automatic now. Getting so you just take a machine off in a corner and whisper in its ear and it scurries off to do the job."

His daughter's voice came to him out the window, pitched to carry above the music.

"Father!"

Gramp stirred uneasily. "Yes, Betty."

"Now, father, you see you move when that lawn mower gets

to you. Don't try to out-stubborn it. After all, it's only a machine. Last time you just sat there and made it cut around you. I never saw the beat of you."

He didn't answer, letting his head nod a bit, hoping she would think he was asleep and let him be.

"Father," she shrilled, "did you hear me?"

He saw it was no good. "Sure, I heard you," he told her. "I was just fixing to move."

He rose slowly to his feet, leaning heavily on his cane. Might make her feel sorry for the way she treated him when she saw how old and feeble he was getting. He'd have to be careful, though. If she knew he didn't need the cane at all, she'd be finding jobs for him to do and, on the other hand, if he laid it on too thick, she'd be having that fool doctor in to pester him again.

Grumbling, he moved the chair out into that portion of the lawn that had been cut. The mower, rolling past, chortled at him fiendishly.

"Some day," Gramp told it, "I'm going to take a swipe at you and bust a gear or two."

The mower hooted at him and went serenely down the lawn.

From somewhere down the grassy street came a jangling of metal, a stuttered coughing.

Gramp, ready to sit down, straightened up and listened.

The sound came more clearly, the rumbling backfire of a balky engine, the clatter of loose metallic parts.

"An automobile!" yelped Gramp. "An automobile, by cracky!"

He started to gallop for the gate, suddenly remembered that he was feeble and subsided to a rapid hobble.

"Must be that crazy Ole Johnson," he told himself. "He's the only one left that's got a car. Just too dadburned stubborn to give it up."

It was Ole.

Gramp reached the gate in time to see the rusty, dilapidated old machine come bumping around the corner, rocking and chugging along the unused street. Steam hissed from the over-heated radiator and a cloud of blue smoke issued from the exhaust, which had lost its muffler five years or more ago.

Ole sat stolidly behind the wheel, squinting his eyes, trying to duck the roughest places, although that was hard to do, for weeds and grass had overrun the streets and it was hard to see what might be underneath them.

Gramp waved his cane.

"Hi, Ole," he shouted.

Ole pulled up, setting the emergency brake. The car gasped, shuddered, coughed, died with a horrible sigh.

"What you burning?" asked Gramp.

"Little bit of everything," said Ole. "Kerosene, some old tractor oil I found out in a barrel, some rubbing alcohol."

Gramp regarded the fugitive machine with forthright admiration. "Them was the days," he said. "Had one myself; used to be able to do a hundred miles an hour."

"Still O.K.," said Ole, "if you could only find the stuff to run them or get the parts to fix them. Up to three, four years ago I used to be able to get enough gasoline, but ain't seen none for a long time now. Quit making it, I guess. No use having gasoline, they tell me, when you have atomic power."

"Sure," said Gramp. "Guess maybe that's right, but you can't smell atomic power. Sweetest thing I know, the smell of burning gasoline. These here helicopters and other gadgets they got took all the romance out of traveling, somehow."

He squinted at the barrels and baskets piled in the back seat.

"Got some vegetables?" he asked.

"Yup," said Ole. "Some sweet corn and early potatoes and a few baskets of tomatoes. Thought maybe I could sell them."

Gramp shook his head. "You won't, Ole. They won't buy them. Folks has got the notion that this new hydroponics stuff is the only garden sass that's fit to eat. Sanitary, they say, and better flavored."

"Wouldn't give a hoot in a tin cup for all they grow in them tanks they got," Ole declared, belligerently. "Don't taste right to me, somehow. Like I tell Martha, food's got to be raised in the soil to have any character."

He reached down to turn over the ignition switch.

"Don't know as it's worth trying to get the stuff to town," he said, "the way they keep the roads. Or the way they don't keep them, rather. Twenty years ago the state highway out there was a strip of good concrete and they kept it patched and plowed it every winter. Did anything, spent any amount of money to keep it open. And now they just forgot about it. The concrete's all broken up and some of it has washed out. Brambles are growing in it. Had to get out and cut away a tree that fell across it one place this morning."

"Ain't it the truth," agreed Gramp.

The car exploded into life, coughing and choking. A cloud of dense blue smoke rolled out from under it. With a jerk it stirred to life and lumbered down the street.

Gramp clumped back to his chair and found it dripping wet. The automatic mower, having finished its cutting job, had rolled out the hose, was sprinkling the lawn.

Muttering venom, Gramp stalked around the corner of the house and sat down on the bench beside the back porch. He didn't like to sit there, but it was the only place he was safe from the hunk of machinery out in front.

For one thing, the view from the bench was slightly depressing, fronting as it did on street after street of vacant, deserted houses and weed-grown, unkempt yards.

It had one advantage, however. From the bench he could pretend he was slightly deaf and not hear the twitch music the radio was blaring out.

A voice called from the front yard.

"Bill! Bill, where be you?"

Gramp twisted around.

"Here I am, Mark. Back of the house. Hiding from that dad-burned mower."

Mark Bailey limped around the corner of the house, cigarette threatening to set fire to his bushy whiskers.

"Bit early for the game, ain't you?" asked Gramp.

"Can't play no game today," said Mark.

He hobbled over and sat down beside Gramp on the bench. "We're leaving," he said.

Gramp whirled on him. "You're leaving!"

"Yeah. Moving out into the country. Lucinda finally talked Herb into it. Never gave him a minute's peace, I guess. Said everyone was moving away to one of them nice country estates and she didn't see no reason why we couldn't."

Gramp gulped. "Where to?"

"Don't rightly know," said Mark. "Ain't been there myself. Up north some place. Up on one of the lakes. Got ten acres of land. Lucinda wanted a hundred, but Herb put down his foot and said ten was enough. After all, one city lot was enough for all these years."

"Betty was pestering Johnny, too," said Gramp, "but he's holding out against her. Says he simply can't do it. Says it wouldn't look right, him the secretary of the Chamber of Commerce and all, if he went moving away from the city."

"Folks are crazy," Mark declared. "Plumb crazy."

"That's a fact," Gramp agreed. "Country crazy, that's what they are. Look across there."

He waved his hand at the streets of vacant houses. "Can remember the time when those places were as pretty a bunch of homes as you ever laid your eyes on. Good neighbors, they were. Women ran across from one back door to another to trade recipes. And the men folks would go out to cut the grass and pretty soon the mowers would all be sitting idle and the men would be ganged up, chewing the fat. Friendly people, Mark. But look at it now."

Mark stirred uneasily. "Got to be getting back, Bill. Just sneaked over to let you know we were lighting out. Lucinda's got me packing. She'd be sore if she knew I'd run out."

Gramp rose stiffly and held out his hand. "I'll be seeing you again? You be over for one last game?"

Mark shook his head. "Afraid not, Bill."

They shook hands awkwardly, abashed. "Sure will miss them games," said Mark.

"Me, too," said Gramp. "I won't have nobody once you're gone."

"So long, Bill," said Mark.

"So long," said Gramp.

He stood and watched his friend hobble around the house, felt the cold claw of loneliness reach out and touch him with icy fingers. A terrible loneliness. The loneliness of age—of age and the outdated. Fiercely, Gramp admitted it. He was outdated. He belonged to another age. He had outstripped his time, lived beyond his years.

Eyes misty, he fumbled for the cane that lay against the bench, slowly made his way toward the sagging gate that opened onto the deserted street back of the house.

The years had moved too fast. Years that had brought the family plane and helicopter, leaving the auto to rust in some forgotten place, the unused roads to fall into disrepair. Years that had virtually wiped out the tilling of the soil with the rise of hydroponics. Years that had brought cheap land with the disappearance of the farm as an economic unit, had sent city people scurrying out into the country where each man, for less than the price of a city lot, might own broad acres. Years that had revolutionized the construction of homes to a point where families simply walked away from their old homes to the new ones that could be bought, custom-made, for less than half the price of a prewar structure and could be changed at small cost, to accommodate need of additional space or just a passing whim.

Gramp sniffed. Houses that could be changed each year, just like one would shift around the furniture. What kind of living was that?

He plodded slowly down the dusty path that was all that remained of what a few years before had been a busy residential street. A street of ghosts, Gramp told himself—of furtive, little ghosts that whispered in the night. Ghosts of playing children, ghosts of upset tricycles and canted coaster wagons. Ghosts of gossiping housewives. Ghosts of shouted greetings. Ghosts of flaming fireplaces and chimneys smoking of a winter night.

Little puffs of dust rose around his feet and whitened the cuffs of his trousers.

There was the old Adams place across the way. Adams had been mighty proud of it, he remembered. Gray field stone front and picture windows. Now the stone was green with creeping moss and the broken windows gaped with ghastly leer. Weeds choked the lawn and blotted out the stoop. An elm tree was pushing its branches against the gable. Gramp could remember the day Adams had planted that elm tree.

For a moment he stood there in the grass-grown street, feet in the dust, both hands clutching the curve of his cane, eyes closed.

Through the fog of years he heard the cry of playing children, the barking of Conrad's yapping pooch from down the street. And there was Adams, stripped to the waist, plying the shovel, scooping out the hole, with the elm tree, roots wrapped in burlap, lying on the lawn.

May, 1946. Forty-four years ago. Just after he and Adams had come home from the war together.

Footsteps padded in the dust and Gramp, startled, opened his eyes.

Before him stood a young man. A man of thirty, perhaps. Maybe a bit less.

"Good morning," said Gramp.

"I hope," said the young man, "that I didn't startle you."

"You saw me standing here," asked Gramp, "like a danged fool, with my eyes shut?"

The young man nodded.

"I was remembering," said Gramp.

"You live around here?"

"Just down the street. The last one in this part of the city."

"Perhaps you can help me then."

"Try me," said Gramp.

The young man stammered. "Well, you see, it's like this. I'm on a sort of . . . well, you might call it a sentimental pilgrimage—"

"I understand," said Gramp. "So am I."

"My name is Adams," said the young man. "My grandfather used to live around here somewhere. I wonder—"

"Right over there," said Gramp.

Together they stood and stared at the house.

"It was a nice place once," Gramp told him. "Your granddaddy planted that tree right after he came home from the war. I was with him all through the war and we came home together. That was a day for you . . ."

"It's a pity," said young Adams. "A pity . . ."

But Gramp didn't seem to hear him. "Your granddaddy?" he asked. "I seem to have lost track of him."

"He's dead," said young Adams. "Quite a number of years ago."

"He was messed up with atomic power," said Gramp.

"That's right," said Adams proudly. "Got into it just as soon as it was released to industry. Right after the Moscow agreement."

"Right after they decided," said Gramp, "they couldn't fight a war."

"That's right," said Adams.

"It's pretty hard to fight a war," said Gramp, "when there's nothing you can aim at."

"You mean the cities," said Adams.

"Sure," said Gramp, "and there's a funny thing about it. Wave all the atom bombs you wanted to and you couldn't scare them out. But give them cheap land and family planes and they scattered just like so many dadburned rabbits."

John J. Webster was striding up the broad stone steps of the city hall when the walking scarecrow carrying a rifle under his arm caught up with him and stopped him.

"Howdy, Mr. Webster," said the scarecrow.

Webster stared, then recognition crinkled his face.

"It's Levi," he said. "How are things going, Levi?"

Levi Lewis grinned with snagged teeth. "Fair to middling. Gardens are coming along and the young rabbits are getting to be good eating."

"You aren't getting mixed up in any of the hell raising that's being laid to the *houses?*" asked Webster.

"No, sir," declared Levi. "Ain't none of us Squatters mixed up in any wrongdoing. We're law-abiding, God-fearing people, we are. Only reason we're there is we can't make a living no place else. And us living in them places other people up and left ain't harming no one. Police are just blaming us for the thievery and other things that's going on, knowing we can't protect ourselves. They're making us the goats."

"I'm glad to hear that," said Webster. "The chief wants to burn the *houses.*"

"If he tries that," said Levi, "he'll run against something he ain't counting on. They run us off our farms with this tank farming of theirs but they ain't going to run us any farther."

He spat across the steps.

"Wouldn't happen you might have some jingling money on you?" he asked. "I'm fresh out of cartridges and with them rabbits coming up—"

Webster thrust his fingers into a vest pocket, pulled out a half dollar.

Levi grinned. "That's obliging of you, Mr. Webster. I'll bring a mess of squirrels, come fall."

The Squatter touched his hat with two fingers and retreated down the steps, sun glinting on the rifle barrel. Webster turned up the steps again.

The city council session already was in full swing when he walked into the chamber.

Police Chief Jim Maxwell was standing by the table and Mayor Paul Carter was talking.

"Don't you think you may be acting a bit hastily, Jim, in urging such a course of action with the *houses?*"

"No, I don't," declared the chief. "Except for a couple of dozen or so, none of those houses are occupied by their rightful owners, or rather, their original owners. Every one of them belongs to the city now through tax forfeiture. And they are nothing but an eyesore and a menace. They have no value. Not even salvage value. Wood? We don't use wood any more. Plastics are better. Stone? We use steel instead of stone. Not a single one of those houses have any material of marketable value.

"And in the meantime they are becoming the haunts of petty criminals and undesirable elements. Grown up with vegetation as the residential sections are, they make a perfect hideout for all types of criminals. A man commits a crime and heads straight for the *houses*—once there he's safe, for I could send a thousand men in there and he could elude them all.

"They aren't worth the expense of tearing down. And yet they are, if not a menace, at least a nuisance. We should get rid of them and fire is the cheapest, quickest way. We'd use all precautions."

"What about the legal angle?" asked the mayor.

"I checked into that. A man has a right to destroy his own property in any way he may see fit so long as it endangers no one else's. The same law, I suppose, would apply to a municipality."

Alderman Thomas Griffin sprang to his feet.

"You'd alienate a lot of people," he declared. "You'd be burn-

ing down a lot of old homesteads. People still have some sentimental attachments—"

"If they cared for them," snapped the chief, "why didn't they
pay the taxes and take care of them? Why did they go running
off to the country, just leaving the houses standing. Ask Webster
here. He can tell you what success he had trying to interest the
people in their ancestral homes."

"You're talking about that Old Home Week farce," said Griffin.
"It failed. Of course, it failed. Webster spread it on so thick that
they gagged on it. That's what a Chamber of Commerce mentality always does."

Alderman Forrest King spoke up angrily. "There's nothing
wrong with a Chamber of Commerce, Griffin. Simply because
you failed in business is no reason . . ."

Griffin ignored him. "The day of high pressure is over, gentlemen. The day of high pressure is gone forever. Ballyhoo is something that is dead and buried.

"The day when you could have tall-corn days or dollar days
or dream up some fake celebration and deck the place up with
bunting and pull in big crowds that were ready to spend money
is past these many years. Only you fellows don't seem to know
it.

"The success of such stunts as that was its appeal to mob psychology and civic loyalty. You can't have civic loyalty with a city
dying on its feet. You can't appeal to mob psychology when there
is no mob—when every man, or nearly every man has the soli-
tude of forty acres."

"Gentlemen," pleaded the mayor. "Gentlemen, this is distinctly
out of order."

King sputtered into life, walloped the table.

"No, let's have it out. Webster is over there. Perhaps he can
tell us what he thinks."

Webster stirred uncomfortably. "I scarcely believe," he said,
"I have anything to say."

"Forget it," snapped Griffin and sat down.

But King still stood, his face crimson, his mouth trembling with
anger.

"Webster!" he shouted.

Webster shook his head. "You came here with one of your big
ideas," shouted King. "You were going to lay it before the council. Step up, man, and speak your piece."

Webster rose slowly, grim-lipped.

"Perhaps you're too thick-skulled," he told King, "to know why
I resent the way you have behaved."

King gasped, then exploded. "Thick-skulled! You would say that to me. We've worked together and I've helped you. You've never called me that before . . . you've—"

"I've never called you that before," said Webster, levelly. "Naturally not. I wanted to keep my job."

"Well, you haven't got a job," roared King. "From this minute on, you haven't got a job."

"Shut up," said Webster.

King stared at him, bewildered, as if someone had slapped him across the face.

"And sit down," said Webster, and his voice bit through the room like a sharp-edged knife.

King's knees caved beneath him and he sat down abruptly. The silence was brittle.

"I have something to say," said Webster. "Something that should have been said long ago. Something all of you should hear. That I should be the one who would tell it to you is the one thing that astounds me. And yet, perhaps, as one who has worked in the interests of this city for almost fifteen years, I am the logical one to speak the truth.

"Alderman Griffin said the city is dying on its feet and his statement is correct. There is but one fault I would find with it and that is its understatement. The city . . . this city, any city . . . already is dead.

"The city is an anachronism. It has outlived its usefulness. Hydroponics and the helicopter spelled its downfall. In the first instance the city was a tribal place, an area where the tribe banded together for mutual protection. In later years a wall was thrown around it for additional protection. Then the wall finally disappeared but the city lived on because of the conveniences which it offered trade and commerce. It continued into modern times because people were compelled to live close to their jobs and the jobs were in the city.

"But today that is no longer true. With the family plane, one hundred miles today is a shorter distance than five miles back in 1930. Men can fly several hundred miles to work and fly home when the day is done. There is no longer any need for them to live cooped up in a city.

"The automobile started the trend and the family plane finished it. Even in the first part of the century the trend was noticeable—a movement away from the city with its taxes and its stuffiness, a move toward the suburb and close-in acreages. Lack of adequate transportation, lack of finances held many to the city. But now, with tank farming destroying the value of land, a man can buy a huge acreage in the country for less than he could a city lot forty years ago. With planes powered by atomics there is no longer any transportation problem."

He paused and the silence held. The mayor wore a shocked look. King's lips moved, but no words came. Griffin was smiling.

"So what have we?" asked Webster. "I'll tell you what we have. Street after street, block after block, of deserted houses, houses that the people just up and walked away from. Why should they have stayed? What could the city offer them? None of the things that it offered the generations before them, for progress had wiped out the need of the city's benefits. They lost something, some monetary consideration, of course, when they left the houses. But the fact that they could buy a house twice as good for half as much, the fact that they could live as they wished to live, that they could develop what amounts to family estates after the best tradition set them by the wealthy of a generation ago—all these things outweighed the leaving of their homes.

"And what have we left? A few blocks of business houses. A few acres of industrial plants. A city government geared to take care of a million people without the million people. A budget that has run the taxes so high that eventually even business houses will move to escape those taxes. Tax forfeitures that have left us loaded with worthless property. That's what we have left.

"If you think any Chamber of Commerce, any ballyhoo, any hare-brained scheme will give you the answers, you're crazy. There is only one answer and that is simple. The city as a human institution is dead. It may struggle on a few more years, but that is all."

"Mr. Webster—" said the mayor.

But Webster paid him no attention.

"But for what happened today," he said, "I would have stayed on and played doll house with you. I would have gone on pretending that the city was a going concern. Would have gone on kidding myself and you. But there is, gentlemen, such a thing as human dignity."

The icy silence broke down in the rustling of papers, the muffled cough of some embarrassed listener.

But Webster was not through.

"The city failed," he said, "and it is well it failed. Instead of sitting here in mourning above its broken body you should rise to your feet and shout your thanks it failed.

"For if this city had not outlived its usefulness, as did every other city—if the cities of the world had not been deserted, they would have been destroyed. There would have been a war, gentlemen, an atomic war. Have you forgotten the 1950s and the 60s? Have you forgotten waking up at night and listening for the bomb to come, knowing that you would not hear it when it came, knowing that you would never hear again, if it did come?

"But the cities were deserted and industry was dispersed and there were no targets and there was no war.

"Some of you gentlemen," he said, "many of you gentlemen, are alive today because the people left your city.

"Now, for God's sake, let it stay dead. Be happy that it's dead. It's the best thing that ever happened in all human history."

John J. Webster turned on his heel and left the room.

Outside on the broad stone steps, he stopped and stared up at the cloudless sky, saw the pigeons wheeling above the turrets and spires of the city hall.

He shook himself mentally, like a dog coming out of a pool.

He had been a fool, of course. Now he'd have to hunt for a job and it might take time to find one. He was getting a bit old to be hunting for a job.

But despite his thoughts, a little tune rose unbidden to his lips. He walked away briskly, lips pursed, whistling soundlessly.

No more hypocrisy. No more lying awake nights wondering what to do—knowing that the city was dead, knowing that what he did was a useless task, feeling like a heel for taking a salary that he knew he wasn't earning. Sensing the strange, nagging frustration of a worker who knows his work is nonproductive.

He strode toward the parking lot, heading for his helicopter.

Now, maybe he told himself, they could move out into the country the way Betty wanted to. Maybe he could spend his evenings tramping land that belonged to him. A place with a stream. Definitely it had to have a stream he could stock with trout.

He made a mental note to go up into the attic and check his fly equipment.

Martha Johnson was waiting at the barnyard gate when the old car chugged down the lane.

Ole got out stiffly, face rimmed with weariness.

"Sell anything?" asked Martha.

Ole shook his head. "It ain't no use. They won't buy farm-raised stuff. Just laughed at me. Showed me ears of corn twice as big as the ones I had, just as sweet and with more even rows. Showed me melons that had almost no rind at all. Better tasting, too, they said."

He kicked at a clod and it exploded into dust.

"There ain't no getting around it," he declared. "Tank farming sure has ruined us."

"Maybe we better fix to sell the farm," suggested Martha.

Ole said nothing.

"You could get a job on a tank farm," she said. "Harry did. Likes it real well."

Ole shook his head.

"Or maybe a gardener," said Martha. "You would make a right smart gardener. Ritzy folks that's moved out to big estates like to have gardeners to take care of flowers and things. More classy than doing it with machines."

Ole shook his head again. "Couldn't stand to mess around with flowers," he declared. "Not after raising corn for more than twenty years."

"Maybe," said Martha, "we could have one of them little planes. And running water in the house. And a bathtub instead of taking a bath in the old washtub by the kitchen fire."

"Couldn't run a plane," objected Ole.

"Sure you could," said Martha. "Simple to run, they are. Why, them Anderson kids ain't no more than knee-high to a cricket and they fly one all over. One of them got fooling around and fell out once, but—"

"I got to think about it," said Ole desperately. "I got to think."

He swung away, vaulted a fence, headed for the fields. Martha stood beside the car and watched him go. One lone tear rolled down her dusty cheek.

"Mr. Taylor is waiting for you," said the girl.

John J. Webster stammered. "But I haven't been here before. He didn't know I was coming."

"Mr. Taylor," insisted the girl, "is waiting for you."

She nodded her head toward the door. It read:

Bureau of Human Adjustment

"But I came here to get a job," protested Webster. "I didn't come to be adjusted or anything. This is the World Committee's placement service, isn't it?"

"That is right," the girl declared. "Won't you see Mr. Taylor?"

"Since you insist," said Webster.

The girl clicked over a switch, spoke into the intercommunicator. "Mr. Webster is here, sir."

"Send him in," said a voice.

Hat in hand, Webster walked through the door.

The man behind the desk had white hair but a young man's face. He motioned toward a chair.

"You've been trying to find a job," he said.

"Yes," said Webster, "but—"

"Please sit down," said Taylor. "If you're thinking about that sign on the door, forget it. We'll not try to adjust you."

"I couldn't find a job," said Webster. "I've hunted for weeks and no one would have me. So, finally, I came here."

"You didn't want to come here?"

"No, frankly, I didn't. A placement service. It has, well . . . it has an implication I do not like."

Taylor smiled. "The terminology may be unfortunate. You're thinking of the employment services of the old days. The places where men went when they were desperate for work. The government operated places that tried to find work for men so they wouldn't become public charges."

"I'm desperate enough," confessed Webster. "But I still have a pride that made it hard to come. But, finally, there was nothing else to do. You see, I turned traitor—"

"You mean," said Taylor, "that you told the truth. Even when it cost you your job. The business world, not only here, but all over the world is not ready for that truth. The businessman still clings to the city myth, to the myth of salesmanship. In time to come he will realize he doesn't need the city, that service and honest values will bring him more substantial business than salesmanship ever did.

"I've wondered, Webster, just what made you do what you did?"

"I was sick of it," said Webster. "Sick of watching men blundering along with their eyes tight shut. Sick of seeing an old tradition being kept alive when it should have been laid away. Sick of King's simpering civic enthusiasm when all cause for enthusiasm had vanished."

Taylor nodded. "Webster, do you think you could adjust human beings?"

Webster merely stared.

"I mean it," said Taylor. "The World Committee has been doing it for years, quietly, unobtrusively. Even many of the people who have been adjusted don't know they have been adjusted.

"Changes such as have come since the creation of the World Committee out of the old United Nations has meant much human maladjustment. The advent of workable atomic power took jobs away from hundreds of thousands. They had to be trained and guided into new jobs, some with the new atomics, some into other lines of work. The advent of tank farming swept the farmers off their land. They, perhaps, have supplied us with our greatest problem, for other than the special knowledge needed to grow crops and handle animals, they had no skills. Most of them had no wish for acquiring skills. Most of them were bitterly resentful at having been forced from the livelihood which they inherited from their forebears. And being natural individualists, they offered the toughest psychological problems of any other class."

"Many of them," declared Webster, "still are at loose ends. There's a hundred or more of them squatting out in the *houses*, living from hand to mouth. Shooting a few rabbits and a few squirrels, doing some fishing, raising vegetables and picking wild fruit. Engaging in a little petty thievery now and then and doing occasional begging on the uptown streets."

"You know these people?" asked Taylor.

"I know some of them," said Webster. "One of them brings me squirrels and rabbits on occasions. To make up for it, he bums ammunition money."

"They'd resent being adjusted, wouldn't they?"

"Violently," said Webster.

"You know a farmer by the name of Ole Johnson? Still sticking to his farm, still unreconstructed?"

Webster nodded.

"What if you tried to adjust him?"

"He'd run me off the farm," said Webster.

"Men like Ole and the Squatters," said Taylor, "are our special problems now. Most of the rest of the world is fairly well-adjusted, fairly well settled into the groove of the present. Some of them are doing a lot of moaning about the past, but that's just for effect. You couldn't drive them back to their old ways of life.

"Years ago, with the advent of industrial atomics in fact, the World Committee faced a hard decision. Should changes that spelled progress in the world be brought about gradually to allow the people to adjust themselves naturally, or should they be developed as quickly as possible, with the committee aiding in the necessary human adjustment? It was decided, rightly or wrongly, that progress should come first, regardless of its effect upon the people. The decision in the main has proved a wise one.

"We knew, of course, that in many instances, this readjustment could not be made too openly. In some cases, as in large groups of workers who had been displaced, it was possible, but in most individual cases, such as our friend Ole, it was not. These people must be helped to find themselves in this new world, but they must not know that they're being helped. To let them know would destroy confidence and dignity, and human dignity is the key-stone of any civilization."

"I knew, of course, about the readjustments made within industry itself," said Webster, "but I had not heard of the individual cases."

"We could not advertise it," Taylor said. "It's practically undercover."

"But why are you telling me all this now?"

"Because we'd like you to come in with us. Have a hand at adjusting Ole to start with. Maybe see what could be done about the Squatters next."

"I don't know—" said Webster.

"We'd been waiting for you to come in," said Taylor. "We knew you'd finally have to come here. Any chance you might have had at any kind of job would have been queered by King. He passed the word along. You're blackballed by every Chamber of Commerce and every civic group in the world today."

"Probably I have no choice," said Webster.

"We don't want you to feel that way about it," Taylor said. "Take a while to think it over, then come back. Even if you don't want the job we'll find you another one—in spite of King."

Outside the office, Webster found a scarecrow figure waiting for him. It was Levi Lewis, snaggle-toothed grin wiped off, rifle under his arm.

"Some of the boys said they seen you go in here," he explained. "So I waited for you."

"What's the trouble?" Webster asked, for Levi's face spoke eloquently of trouble.

"It's them police," said Levi. He spat disgustedly.

"The police," said Webster, and his heart sank as he said the words. For he knew what the trouble was.

"Yeah," said Levi. "They're fixing to burn us out."

"So the council finally gave in," said Webster.

"I just came from police headquarters," declared Levi. "I told them they better go easy. I told them there'd be guts strewed all over the place if they tried it. I got the boys posted all around the place with orders not to shoot till they're sure of hitting."

"You can't do that, Levi," said Webster, sharply.

"I can't!" retorted Levi. "I done it already. They drove us off the farms, forced us to sell because we couldn't make a living. And they aren't driving us no farther. We either stay here or we die here. And the only way they'll burn us out is when there's no one left to stop them."

He shucked up his pants and spat again.

"And we ain't the only ones that feel that way," he declared. "Gramp is out there with us."

"Gramp!"

"Sure, Gramp. The old guy that lives with you. He's sort of taken over as our commanding general. Says he remembers tricks from the war them police have never heard of. He sent some of the boys over to one of them Legion halls to swipe a cannon. Says he knows where we can get some shells for it from the museum. Says we'll get it all set up and then send word that if the police make a move we'll shell the loop."

"Look, Levi, will you do something for me?"

"Sure will, Mr. Webster."

"Will you go in and ask for a Mr. Taylor? Insist on seeing him. Tell him I'm already on the job."

"Sure will, but where are you going?"

"I'm going up to the city hall."

"Sure you don't want me along?"

"No," declared Webster. "I'll do better alone. And, Levi—"

"Yes."

"Tell Gramp to hold up his artillery. Don't shoot unless he has to—but if he has, to lay it on the line."

"The mayor is busy," said Raymond Brown, his secretary.

"That's what you think," said Webster, starting for the door.

"You can't go in there, Webster," yelled Brown.

He leaped from his chair, came charging around the desk, reaching for Webster. Webster swung broadside with his arm, caught Brown across the chest, swept him back against the desk. The desk skidded and Brown waved his arms, lost his balance, thudded to the floor.

Webster jerked open the mayor's door.

The mayor's feet thumped off his desk. "I told Brown—" he said.

Webster nodded. "And Brown told me. What's the matter, Carter. Afraid King might find out I was here? Afraid of being corrupted by some good ideas?"

"What do you want?" snapped Carter.

"I understand the police are going to burn the *houses*."

"That's right," declared the mayor, righteously. "They're a menace to the community."

"What community?"

"Look here, Webster—"

"You know there's no community. Just a few of you lousy politicians who stick around so you can claim residence, so you can be sure of being elected every year and drag down your salaries. It's getting to the point where all you have to do is vote for one another. The people who work in the stores and shops, even those who do the meanest jobs in the factories, don't live inside the city limits. The businessmen quit the city long ago. They do business here, but they aren't residents."

"But this is still a city," declared the mayor.

"I didn't come to argue that with you," said Webster. "I came to try to make you see that you're doing wrong by burning those houses. Even if you don't realize it, the *houses* are homes to people who have no other homes. People who have come to this city to seek sanctuary, who have found refuge with us. In a measure, they are our responsibility."

"They're not our responsibility," gritted the mayor. "Whatever happens to them is their own hard luck. We didn't ask them here. We don't want them here. They contribute nothing to the community. You're going to tell me they're misfits. Well, can I help that? You're going to say they can't find jobs. And I'll tell you they could find jobs if they tried to find them. There's work to be done, there's always work to be done. They've been filled up with this new world talk and they figure it's up to someone to find the place that suits them and the job that suits them."

"You sound like a rugged individualist," said Webster.

"You say that like you think it's funny," yapped the mayor.

"I do think it's funny," said Webster. "Funny, and tragic, that anyone should think that way today."

"The world would be a lot better off with some rugged individualism," snapped the mayor. "Look at the men who have gone places—"

"Meaning yourself?" asked Webster.

"You might take me, for example," Carter agreed. "I worked hard. I took advantage of opportunity. I had some foresight. I did—"

"You mean you licked the correct boots and stepped in the proper faces," said Webster. "You're the shining example of the kind of people the world doesn't want today. You positively smell musty, your ideas are so old. You're the last of the politicians, Carter, just as I was the last of the Chamber of Commerce secretaries. Only you don't know it yet. I did. I got out. Even when it cost me something, I got out, because I had to save my self-respect. Your kind of politics is dead. They are dead because any tinhorn with a loud mouth and a brassy front could gain power by appeal to mob psychology. And you haven't got mob psychology any more. You can't have mob psychology when people don't give a damn what happens to a thing that's dead already—a political system that broke down under its own weight."

"Get out of here," screamed Carter. "Get out before I have the cops come and throw you out."

"You forget," said Webster, "that I came in to talk about the *houses*."

"It won't do you any good," snarled Carter. "You can stand and talk till doomsday for all the good it does. Those houses burn. That's final."

"How would you like to see the loop a mass of rubble?" asked Webster.

"Your comparison," said Carter, "is grotesque."

"I wasn't talking about comparisons," said Webster.

"You weren't—" The mayor stared at him. "What were you talking about then?"

"Only this," said Webster. "The second the first torch touches the *houses*, the first shell will land on the city hall. And the second one will hit the First National. They'll go down the line, the biggest targets first."

Carter gaped. Then a flush of anger crawled from his throat up into his face.

"It won't work, Webster," he snapped. "You can't bluff me. Any cock-and-bull story like that—"

"It's no cock-and-bull story," declared Webster. "Those men have cannon out there. Pieces from in front of Legion halls, from the museums. And they have men who know how to work them. They wouldn't need them, really. It's practically point-blank range. Like shooting the broadside of a barn."

Carter reached for the radio, but Webster stopped him with an upraised hand.

"Better think a minute, Carter, before you go flying off the handle. You're on a spot. Go ahead with your plan and you have a battle on your hands. The *houses* may burn but the loop is wrecked. The businessmen will have your scalp for that."

Carter's hand retreated from the radio.

From far away came the sharp crack of a rifle.

"Better call them off," warned Webster.

Carter's face twisted with indecision.

Another rifle shot, another and another.

"Pretty soon," said Webster, "it will have gone too far. So far that you can't stop it."

A thudding blast rattled the windows of the room. Carter leaped from his chair.

Webster felt suddenly cold and weak. But he fought to keep his face straight and his voice calm.

Carter was staring out the window, like a man of stone.

"I'm afraid," said Webster, "that it's gone too far already."

The radio on the desk chirped insistently, red light flashing. Carter reached out a trembling hand and snapped it on.

"Carter," a voice was saying. "Carter. Carter."

Webster recognized that voice—the bull-throated tone of Police Chief Jim Maxwell.

"What is it?" asked Carter.

"They had a big gun," said Maxwell. "It exploded when they tried to fire it. Ammunition no good, I guess."

"One gun?" asked Carter. "Only one gun?"

"I don't see any others."

"I heard rifle fire," said Carter.

"Yeah, they did some shooting at us. Wounded a couple of the boys. But they've pulled back now. Deeper into the brush. No shooting now."

"O.K.," said Carter, "go ahead and start the fires."

Webster started forward. "Ask him, ask him—"

But Carter clicked the switch and the radio went dead.

"What was it you want to ask?"

"Nothing," said Webster. "Nothing that amounted to anything."

He couldn't tell Carter that Gramp had been the one who knew about firing big guns. Couldn't tell him that when the gun exploded Gramp had been there.

He'd have to get out of here, get over to the gun as quickly as possible.

"It was a good bluff, Webster," Carter was saying. "A good bluff, but it petered out."

The mayor turned to the window that faced toward the *houses.*

"No more firing," he said. "They gave up quick."

"You'll be lucky," snapped Webster, "if six of your policemen come back alive. Those men with the rifles are out in the brush and they can pick the eye out of a squirrel at a hundred yards."

Feet pounded in the corridor outside, two pairs of feet racing toward the door.

The mayor whirled from his window and Webster pivoted around.

"Gramp!" he yelled.

"Hi, Johnny," puffed Gramp, skidding to a stop.

The man behind Gramp was a young man and he was waving

something in his hand—a sheaf of papers that rustled as he waved them.

"What do you want?" asked the mayor.

"Plenty," said Gramp.

He stood for a moment, catching back his breath, and said between puffs:

"Meet my friend, Henry Adams."

"Adams?" asked the mayor.

"Sure," said Gramp. "His granddaddy used to live here. Out on Twenty-seventh Street."

"Oh," said the mayor and it was as if someone had smacked him with a brick. "Oh, you mean F. J. Adams."

"Bet your boots," said Gramp. "Him and me, we were in the war together. Used to keep me awake nights telling me about his boy back home."

Carter nodded to Henry Adams. "As mayor of the city," he said, trying to regain some of his dignity, "I welcome you to—"

"It's not a particularly fitting welcome," Adams said. "I understand you are burning my property."

"Your property!" The mayor choked and his eyes stared in disbelief at the sheaf of papers Adams waved at him.

"Yeah, his property," shrilled Gramp. "He just bought it. We just come from the treasurer's office. Paid all the back taxes and penalties and all the other things you legal thieves thought up to slap against them houses."

"But, but—" the mayor was grasping for words, gasping for breath. "Not all of it. Perhaps just the old Adams property."

"Lock, stock and barrel," said Gramp, triumphantly.

"And now," said Adams to the mayor, "if you would kindly tell your men to stop destroying my property."

Carter bent over the desk and fumbled at the radio, his hands suddenly all thumbs.

"Maxwell," he shouted. "Maxwell. Maxwell."

"What do you want?" Maxwell yelled back.

"Stop setting those fires," yelled Carter. "Start putting them out. Call out the fire department. Do anything. But stop those fires."

"Cripes," said Maxwell, "I wish you'd make up your mind."

"You do what I tell you," screamed the mayor. "You put out those fires."

"All right," said Maxwell. "All right. Keep your shirt on. But the boys won't like it. They won't like getting shot at to do something you change your mind about."

Carter straightened from the radio.

"Let me assure you, Mr. Adams," he said, "that this is all a big mistake."

"It is," Adams declared solemnly. "A very great mistake, mayor. The biggest one you ever made."

For a moment the two of them stood there, looking across the room at one another.

"Tomorrow," said Adams, "I shall file a petition with the courts asking dissolution of the city charter. As owner of the greatest portion of the land included in the corporate limits, both from the standpoint of area and valuation, I understand I have a perfect legal right to do that."

The mayor gulped, finally brought out some words.

"Upon what grounds?" he asked.

"Upon the grounds," said Adams, "that there is no further need of it. I do not believe I shall have too hard a time to prove my case."

"But . . . but . . . that means . . ."

"Yeah," said Gramp, "you know what it means. It means you are out right on your ear."

"A park," said Gramp, waving his arm over the wilderness that once had been the residential section of the city. "A park so that people can remember how their old folks lived."

The three of them stood on Tower Hill, with the rusty old water tower looming above them, its sturdy steel legs planted in a sea of waist-high grass.

"Not a park, exactly," explained Henry Adams. "A memorial, rather. A memorial to an era of communal life that will be forgotten in another hundred years. A preservation of a number of peculiar types of construction that arose to suit certain conditions and each man's particular tastes. No slavery to any archirural concepts, but an effort made to achieve better living. In another hundred years men will walk through those houses down there with the same feeling of respect and awe they have when they go into a museum today. It will be to them something out of what amounts to a primeval age, a stepping-stone on the way to the better, fuller life. Artists will spend their lives transferring those old houses to their canvasses. Writers of historical novels will come here for the breath of authenticity."

"But you said you meant to restore all the houses, make the lawns and gardens exactly like they were before," said Webster. "That will take a fortune. And, after that, another fortune to keep them in shape."

"I have too much money," said Adams. "Entirely too much

money. Remember, my grandfather and father got into atomics
on the ground floor."

"Best crap player I ever knew, your granddaddy was," said
Gramp. "Used to take me for a cleaning every pay day."

"In the old days," said Adams, "when a man had too much
money, there were other things he could do with it. Organized
charities, for example. Or medical research or something like that.
But there are no organized charities today. Not enough business
to keep them going. And since the World Committee has hit its
stride, there is ample money for all the research, medical or otherwise, anyone might wish to do.

"I didn't plan this thing when I came back to see my grandfather's old house. Just wanted to see it, that was all. He'd told
me so much about it. How he planted the tree in the front lawn.
And the rose garden he had out back.

"And then I saw it. And it was a mocking ghost. It was something that had been left behind. Something that had meant a lot
to someone and had been left behind. Standing there in front of
that house with Gramp that day, it came to me that I could do
nothing better than preserve for posterity a cross section of the
life their ancestors lived."

A thin blue thread of smoke rose above the trees far below.
Webster pointed to it. "What about them?"

"The Squatters stay," said Adams, "if they want to. There will
be plenty of work for them to do. And there'll always be a house
or two that they can have to live in.

"There's just one thing that bothers me. I can't be here all the
time myself. I'll need someone to manage the project. It'll be a
lifelong job."

He looked at Webster.

"Go ahead, Johnny," said Gramp.

Webster shook his head. "Betty's got her heart set on that
place out in the country."

"You wouldn't have to stay here," said Adams. "You could fly
in every day."

From the foot of the hill came a hail.

"It's Ole," yelled Gramp.

He waved his cane. "Hi, Ole. Come on up."

They watched Ole striding up the hill, waiting for him, silently.

"Wanted to talk to you, Johnny," said Ole. "Got an idea. Waked
me out of a sound sleep last night."

"Go ahead," said Webster.

Ole glanced at Adams. "He's all right," said Webster. "He's
Henry Adams. Maybe you remember his grandfather, old F. J."

"I remember him," said Ole. "Nuts about atomic power, he was. How did he make out?"

"He made out rather well," said Adams.

"Glad to hear that," Ole said. "Guess I was wrong. Said he never would amount to nothing. Daydreamed all the time."

"How about that idea?" Webster asked.

"You heard about dude ranches, ain't you?" Ole asked.

Webster nodded.

"Place," said Ole, "where people used to go and pretend they were cowboys. Pleased them because they really didn't know all the hard work there was in ranching and figured it was romantic-like to ride horses and—"

"Look," asked Webster, "you aren't figuring on turning your farm into a dude ranch, are you?"

"Nope," said Ole. "Not a dude ranch. Dude farm, maybe. Folks don't know too much about farms any more, since there ain't hardly no farms. And they'll read about the frost being on the pumpkin and how pretty a—"

Webster stared at Ole. "They'd go for it, Ole," he declared. "They'd kill one another in the rush to spend their vacation on a real, honest-to-God, old-time farm."

Out of a clump of bushes down the hillside burst a shining thing that chattered and gurgled and screeched, blades flashing, a cranelike arm waving.

"What the—" asked Adams.

"It's that dadburned lawn mower!" yelped Gramp. "I always knew the day would come when it would strip a gear and go completely off its nut!"

1944

First Contact /

by MURRAY LEINSTER

An expedition from Earth had gone to investigate the Crab Nebula. And—an expedition from Somewhere was already there! Now what is a spaceship skipper to do under such circumstances? Lead the possibly deadly aliens home? Try to destroy them? What can he do?

I

Tommy Dort went into the captain's room with his last pair of stereophotos and said:

"I'm through, sir. These are the last two pictures I can take."

He handed over the photographs and looked with professional interest at the visiplates which showed all space outside the ship. Subdued, deep-red lighting indicated the controls and such instruments as the quartermaster on duty needed for navigation of the spaceship *Llanvabon*. There was a deeply cushioned control chair. There was the little gadget of oddly angled mirrors—remote descendant of the back-view mirrors of twentieth century motorists—which allowed a view of all the visiplates without turning the head. And there were the huge plates which were so much more satisfactory for a direct view of space.

The *Llanvabon* was a long way from home. The plates, which showed every star of visual magnitude and could be stepped up to any desired magnification, portrayed stars of every imaginable degree of brilliance, in the startlingly different colors they show outside of atmosphere. But every one was unfamiliar. Only two constellations could be recognized as seen from Earth, and they were shrunken and distorted. The Milky Way seemed vaguely out of place. But even such oddities were minor compared to a sight in the forward plates.

There was a vast, vast mistiness ahead. A luminous mist. It seemed motionless. It took a long time for any appreciable nearing to appear in the vision plates, though the spaceship's velocity indicator showed an incredible speed. The mist was the Crab Nebula, six light-years long, three and a half light-years thick, with outward-reaching members that in the telescopes of Earth gave it some resemblance to the creature for which it was named. It was a cloud of gas, infinitely tenuous, reaching half again as far as from Sol to its nearest neighbor-sun. Deep within it burned two stars; a double star; one component the familiar yellow of the sun of Earth, the other an unholy white.

Tommy Dort said meditatively:

"We're heading into a deep, sir?"

The skipper studied the last two plates of Tommy's taking, and put them aside. He went back to his uneasy contemplation of the vision plates ahead. The *Llanvabon* was decelerating at full force. She was a bare half light-year from the nebula. Tommy's work was guiding the ship's course, now, but the work was done. During all the stay of the exploring ship in the nebula, Tommy Dort would loaf. But he'd more than paid his way so far.

He had just completed a quite unique first—a complete photographic record of the movement of a nebula during a period of four thousand years, taken by one individual with the same apparatus and with control exposures to detect and record any systematic errors. It was an achievement in itself worth the journey from Earth. But in addition, he had also recorded four thousand years of the history of a double star, and four thousand years of the history of a star in the act of degenerating into a white dwarf.

It was not that Tommy Dort was four thousand years old. He was, actually, in his twenties. But the Crab Nebula is four thousand light-years from Earth, and the last two pictures had been taken by light which would not reach Earth until the sixth millennium A. D. On the way here—at speeds incredible multiples of the speed of light—Tommy Dort had recorded each aspect of the nebula by the light which had left it from forty centuries since to a bare six months ago.

The *Llanvabon* bored on through space. Slowly, slowly, slowly, the incredible luminosity crept across the vision plates. It blotted out half the universe from view. Before was glowing mist, and behind was a star-studded emptiness. The mist shut off three-fourths of all the stars. Some few of the brightest shone dimly through it near its edge, but only a few. Then there was only an irregularly shaped patch of darkness astern against which stars shone unwinking. The *Llanvabon* dived into the nebula, and it seemed as if it bored into a tunnel of darkness with walls of shining fog.

Which was exactly what the spaceship was doing. The most distant photographs of all had disclosed structural features in the nebula. It was not amorphous. It had form. As the *Llanvabon* drew nearer, indications of structure grew more distinct, and Tommy Dort had argued for a curved approach for photographic reasons. So the spaceship had come up to the nebula on a vast logarithmic curve, and Tommy had been able to take successive photographs from slightly different angles and get stereo-pairs which showed the nebula in three dimensions; which disclosed billowings and hollows and an actually complicated shape. In places, the nebula displayed convolutions like those of a human brain. It was into one of those hollows that the spaceship now plunged. They had been called "deeps" by analogy with crevasses in the ocean floor. And they promised to be useful.

The skipper relaxed. One of a skipper's functions, nowadays, is to think of things to worry about, and then worry about them. The skipper of the *Llanvabon* was conscientious. Only after a certain instrument remained definitely nonregistering did he ease himself back in his seat.

"It was just barely possible," he said heavily, "that those deeps might be nonluminous gas. But they're empty. So we'll be able to use overdrive as long as we're in them."

It was a light-year-and-a-half from the edge of the nebula to the neighborhood of the double star which was its heart. That was the problem. A nebula is a gas. It is so thin that a comet's tail is solid by comparison, but a ship traveling on overdrive—above the speed of light—does not want to hit even a merely hard vacuum. It needs pure emptiness, such as exists between the stars. But the *Llanvabon* could not do much in this expanse of mist if it was limited to speeds a merely hard vacuum will permit.

The luminosity seemed to close in behind the spaceship, which slowed and slowed and slowed. The overdrive went off with the sudden *pinging* sensation which goes all over a person when the overdrive field is released.

Then, almost instantly, bells burst into clanging, strident uproar all through the ship. Tommy was almost deafened by the alarm bell which rang in the captain's room before the quartermaster shut it off with a flip of his hand. But other bells could be heard ringing throughout the rest of the ship, to be cut off as automatic doors closed one by one.

Tommy Dort stared at the skipper. The skipper's hands clenched. He was up and staring over the quartermaster's shoulder. One indicator was apparently having convulsions. Others strained to record their findings. A spot on the diffusedly bright mistiness of a bow-quartering visiplate grew brighter as the automatic scanner focused on it. That was the direction of the object which had sounded collision-alarm. But the object locator itself—. According to its reading, there was one solid object some eighty thousand miles away—an object of no great size. But there was another object whose distance varied from extreme range to zero, and whose size shared its impossible advance and retreat.

"Step up the scanner," snapped the skipper.

The extra-bright spot on the scanner rolled outward, obliterating the undifferentiated image behind it. Magnification increased. But nothing appeared. Absolutely nothing. Yet the radio locator insisted that something monstrous and invisible made lunatic dashes toward the *Llanvabon,* at speeds which inevitably implied collision, and then fled coyly away at the same rate.

The visiplate went up to maximum magnification. Still nothing. The skipper ground his teeth. Tommy Dort said meditatively:

"D'you know, sir, I saw something like this on a liner on the Earth-Mars run once, when we were being located by another ship. Their locator beam was the same frequency as ours, and every time it hit, it registered like something monstrous, and solid."

"That," said the skipper savagely, "is just what's happening now. There's something like a locator beam on us. We're getting that beam and our own echo besides. But the other ship's invisible! Who is out here in an invisible ship with locator devices? Not men, certainly!"

He pressed the button in his sleeve communicator and snapped:

"Action stations! Man all weapons! Condition of extreme alert in all departments immediately!"

His hands closed and unclosed. He stared again at the visiplate which showed nothing but a formless brightness.

"Not men?" Tommy Dort straightened sharply. "You mean—"

"How many solar systems in our galaxy?" demanded the skipper bitterly. "How many planets fit for life? And how many kinds of life could there be? If this ship isn't from Earth—and it isn't—it has a crew that isn't human. And things that aren't human but are up to the level of deep-space travel in their civilization could mean anything!"

The skipper's hands were actually shaking. He would not have talked so freely before a member of his own crew, but Tommy Dort was of the observation staff. And even a skipper whose duties include worrying may sometimes need desperately to unload his worries. Sometimes, too, it helps to think aloud.

"Something like this has been talked about and speculated about for years," he said softly. "Mathematically, it's been an odds-on bet that somewhere in our galaxy there'd be another race with a civilization equal to or further advanced than ours. Nobody could ever guess where or when we'd meet them. But it looks like we've done it now!"

Tommy's eyes were very bright.

"D'you suppose they'll be friendly, sir?"

The skipper glanced at the distance indicator. The phantom object still made its insane, nonexistent swoops toward and away from the *Llanvabon*. The secondary indication of an object at eighty thousand miles stirred ever so slightly.

"It's moving," he said curtly. "Heading for us. Just what we'd do if a strange spaceship appeared in our hunting grounds! Friendly? Maybe! We're going to try to contact them. We have to. But I suspect this is the end of this expedition. Thank God for the blasters!"

The blasters are those beams of ravening destruction which take care of recalcitrant meteorites in a spaceship's course when the deflectors can't handle them. They are not designed as weapons, but they can serve as pretty good ones. They can go into action at five thousand miles, and draw on the entire power output of a whole ship. With automatic aim and a traverse of five degrees, a ship like the *Llanvabon* can come very close to blasting a hole through a small-sized asteroid which gets in its way. But not on overdrive, of course.

Tommy Dort had approached the bow-quartering visiplate. Now he jerked his head around.

"Blasters, sir? What for?"

The skipper grimaced at the empty visiplate.

"Because we don't know what they're like and can't take a chance! I know!" he added bitterly. "We're going to make contacts and try to find out all we can about them—especially where they come from. I suppose we'll try to make friends—but we haven't much chance. We can't trust them the fraction of an inch. We daren't! They've locators. Maybe they've tracers better than any we have. Maybe they could trace us all the way home without our knowing it! We can't risk a nonhuman race knowing where Earth is unless we're sure of them! And how can we be sure? They could come to trade, of course—or they could swoop down on overdrive with a battle fleet that could wipe us out before we knew what happened. We wouldn't know which to expect, or when!"

Tommy's face was startled.

"It's all been thrashed out over and over, in theory," said the skipper. "Nobody's ever been able to find a sound answer, even on paper. But you know, in all their theorizing, no one considered the crazy, rank impossibility of a deep-space contact, with neither side knowing the other's home world! But we've got to find an answer in fact! What are we going to do about them? Maybe these creatures will be aesthetic marvels, nice and friendly and polite—and underneath with the sneaking brutal ferocity of a Japanese. Or maybe they'll be crude and gruff as a Swedish farmer—and just as decent underneath. Maybe they're something in between. But am I going to risk the possible future of the human race on a guess that it's safe to trust them? God knows it would be worth while to make friends with a new civilization! It would be bound to stimulate our own, and maybe we'd gain enormously. But I can't take chances. The one thing I won't risk is having them know how to find Earth! Either I know they can't follow me, or I don't go home! And they'll probably feel the same way!"

He pressed the sleeve-communicator button again.

"Navigation officers, attention! Every star map on this ship is to be prepared for instant destruction. This includes photographs and diagrams from which our course or starting point could be deduced. I want all astronomical data gathered and arranged to be destroyed in a split second, on order. Make it fast and report when ready!"

He released the button. He looked suddenly old. The first contact of humanity with an alien race was a situation which had been foreseen in many fashions, but never one quite so hopeless of solution as this. A solitary Earth-ship and a solitary alien, meeting in a nebula which must be remote from the home planet of each. They might wish peace, but the line of conduct which best prepared a treacherous attack was just the seeming of friendliness. Failure to be suspicious might doom the human race,—and a peaceful exchange of the fruits of civilization would be the greatest benefit imaginable. Any mistake would be irreparable, but a failure to be on guard would be fatal.

The captain's room was very, very quiet. The bow-quartering visiplate was filled with the image of a very small section of the nebula. A very small section indeed. It was all diffused, featureless, luminous mist. But suddenly Tommy Dort pointed.

"There, sir!"

There was a small shape in the mist. It was far away. It was a black shape, not polished to mirror-reflection like the hull of the *Llanvabon*. It was bulbous—roughly pear-shaped. There was much thin luminosity between, and no details could be observed, but it was surely no natural object. Then Tommy looked at the distance indicator and said quietly:

"It's headed for us at very high acceleration, sir. The odds are that they're thinking the same thing, sir, that neither of us will dare let the other go home. Do you think they'll try a contact with us, or let loose with their weapons as soon as they're in range?"

The *Llanvabon* was no longer in a crevasse of emptiness in the nebula's thin substance. She swam in luminescence. There were no stars save the two fierce glows in the nebula's heart. There was nothing but an all-enveloping light, curiously like one's imagining of underwater in the tropics of Earth.

The alien ship had made one sign of less than lethal intention. As it drew near the *Llanvabon,* it decelerated. The *Llanvabon* itself had advanced for a meeting and then come to a dead stop. Its movement had been a recognition of the nearness of the other ship. Its pausing was both a friendly sign and a precaution against attack. Relatively still, it could swivel on its own axis to present the least target to a slashing assault, and it would have a longer firing-time than if the two ships flashed past each other at their combined speeds.

The moment of actual approach, however, was tenseness itself. The *Llanvabon's* needle-pointed bow aimed unwaveringly at the alien bulk. A relay to the captain's room put a key under his hand which would fire the blasters with maximum power. Tommy Dort watched, his brow wrinkled. The aliens must be of a high degree of civilization if they had spaceships, and civilization does not develop without the development of foresight. These aliens must recognize all the implications of this first contact of two civilized races as fully as did the humans on the *Llanvabon.*

The possibility of an enormous spurt in the development of both, by peaceful contact and exchange of their separate technologies, would probably appeal to them as to the man. But when dissimilar human cultures are in contact, one must usually be subordinate or there is war. But subordination between races arising on separate planets could not be peacefully arranged. Men, at least, would never consent to subordination, nor was it likely that any highly developed race would agree. The benefits to be derived from commerce could never make up for a condition of inferiority. Some races—men, perhaps—would prefer commerce to conquest. Perhaps—perhaps!—these aliens would also. But some types even of human beings would have craved red war. If the alien ship now approaching the *Llanvabon* returned to its home base with news of humanity's existence and of ships like the *Llanvabon,* it would give its race the choice of trade or battle. They might want trade, or they might want war. But it takes two to make trade, and only one to make war. They could not be sure of men's peacefulness, nor could men be sure of theirs. The only safety for either civilization would lie in the destruction of one or both of the two ships here and now.

But even victory would not be really enough. Men would need to know where this alien race was to be found, for avoidance if not for battle. They would need to know its weapons, and its resources, and if it could be a menace and how it could be eliminated in case of need. The aliens would feel the same necessities concerning humanity.

So the skipper of the *Llanvabon* did not press the key which might possibly have blasted the other ship to nothingness. He dared not. But he dared not fire either. Sweat came out on his face.

A speaker muttered. Someone from the range room.

"The other ship's stopped, sir. Quite stationary. Blasters are centered on it, sir."

It was an urging to fire. But the skipper shook his head, to himself. The alien ship was no more than twenty miles away. It was dead-black. Every bit of its exterior was an abysmal, nonreflecting sable. No details could be seen except by minor variations in its outline against the misty nebula.

"It's stopped dead, sir," said another voice. "They've sent a modulated short wave at us, sir. Frequency modulated. Apparently a signal. Not enough power to do any harm."

The skipper said through tight-locked teeth:

"They're doing something now. There's movement on the outside of their hull. Watch what comes out. Put the auxiliary blasters on it."

Something small and round came smoothly out of the oval outline of the black ship. The bulbous hulk moved.

"Moving away, sir," said the speaker. "The object they let out is stationary in the place they've left."

Another voice cut in:

"More frequency modulated stuff, sir. Unintelligible."

Tommy Dort's eyes brightened. The skipper watched the visiplate, with sweat-droplets on his forehead.

"Rather pretty, sir," said Tommy, meditatively. "If they sent anything toward us, it might seem a projectile or a bomb. So they came close, let out a lifeboat, and went away again. They figure we can send a boat or a man to make contact without risking our ship. They must think pretty much as we do."

The skipper said, without moving his eyes from the plate:

"Mr. Dort, would you care to go out and look the thing over? I can't order you, but I need all my operating crew for emergencies. The observation staff—"

"Is expendable. Very well, sir," said Tommy briskly. "I won't take a lifeboat, sir. Just a suit with a drive in it. It's smaller and the arms and legs will look unsuitable for a bomb. I think I should carry a scanner, sir."

The alien ship continued to retreat. Forty, eighty, four hundred miles. It came to a stop and hung there, waiting. Climbing into his atomic-driven spacesuit just within the *Llanvabon's* air lock, Tommy heard the reports as they went over the speakers throughout the ship. That the other ship had stopped its retreat at four hundred miles was encouraging. It might not have weapons effective at a greater distance than that, and so felt safe. But just as the thought formed itself in his mind, the alien retreated precipitately still farther. Which, as Tommy reflected as he emerged from the lock, might be because the aliens had realized they were giving themselves away, or might be because they wanted to give the impression that they had done so.

He swooped away from the silvery-mirror *Llanvabon*, through a brightly glowing emptiness which was past any previous experience of the human race. Behind him, the *Llanvabon* swung about and darted away. The skipper's voice came in Tommy's helmet phones.

"We're pulling back, too, Mr. Dort. There is a bare possibility that they've some explosive atomic reaction they can't use from their own ship, but which might be destructive even as far as this. We'll draw back. Keep your scanner on the object."

The reasoning was sound, if not very comforting. An explosive which would destroy anything within twenty miles was theoretically possible, but humans didn't have it yet. It was decidedly safest for the *Llanvabon* to draw back.

But Tommy Dort felt very lonely. He sped through emptiness toward the tiny black speck which hung in incredible brightness. The *Llanvabon* vanished. Its polished hull would merge with the glowing mist at a relatively short distance, anyhow. The alien ship was not visible to the naked eye, either. Tommy swam in nothingness, four thousand light-years from home, toward a tiny black spot which was the only solid object to be seen in all of space.

It was a slightly distorted sphere, not much over six feet in diameter. It bounced away when Tommy landed on it, feet-first. There were small tentacles, or horns, which projected in every direction. They looked rather like the detonating horns of a submarine mine, but there was a glint of crystal at the tip-end of each.

"I'm here," said Tommy into his helmet phone.

He caught hold of a horn and drew himself to the object. It was all metal, dead-black. He could feel no texture through his space gloves, of course, but he went over and over it, trying to discover its purpose.

"Deadlock, sir," he said presently. "Nothing to report that the scanner hasn't shown you."

Then, through his suit, he felt vibrations. They translated themselves as clankings. A section of the rounded hull of the object opened out. Two sections. He worked his way around to look in and see the first nonhuman civilized beings that any man had ever looked upon.

But what he saw was simply a flat plate on which dim-red glows crawled here and there in seeming aimlessness. His helmet phones emitted a startled exclamation. The skipper's voice:

"Very good, Mr. Dort. Fix your scanner to look into that plate. They dumped out a robot with an infrared visiplate for communication. Not risking any personnel. Whatever we might do would damage only machinery. Maybe they expect us to bring it on board—and it may have a bomb charge that can be detonated when they're ready to start for home. I'll send a plate to face one of its scanners. You return to the ship."

"Yes, sir," said Tommy. "But which way is the ship, sir?"

There were no stars. The nebula obscured them with its light. The only thing visible from the robot was the double star at the nebula's center. Tommy was no longer oriented. He had but one reference point.

"Head straight away from the double star," came the order in his helmet phone. "We'll pick you up."

He passed another lonely figure, a little later, headed for the alien sphere with a vision plate to set up. The two spaceships, each knowing that it dared not risk its own race by the slightest lack of caution, would communicate with each other through this small round robot. Their separate vision systems would enable them to exchange all the information they dared give, while they debated the most practical way of making sure that their own civilization would not be endangered by this first contact with another. The truly most practical method would be the destruction of the other ship in a swift and deadly attack—in self-defense.

II

The *Llanvabon*, thereafter, was a ship in which there were two separate enterprises on hand at the same time. She had come out from Earth to make close-range observations on the smaller component of the double star at the nebula's center. The nebula itself was the result of the most titanic explosion of which men have any knowledge. The explosion took place sometime in the year 2946 B. C., before the first of the seven cities of long-dead Ilium was even thought of. The light of that explosion reached Earth in the year 1054 A. D., and was duly recorded in ecclesiastic annals and somewhat more reliably by Chinese court astronomers. It was bright enough to be seen in daylight for twenty-three successive days. Its light—and it was four thousand light-years away —was brighter than that of Venus.

From these facts, astronomers could calculate nine hundred years later the violence of the detonation. Matter blown away from the center of the explosion would have traveled outward at the rate of two million three hundred thousand miles an hour; more than thirty-eight thousand miles a minute; something over six hundred thirty-eight miles per second. When twentieth-century telescopes were turned upon the scene of this vast explosion, only a double star remained—and the nebula. The brighter star of the doublet was almost unique in having so high a surface temperature that it showed no spectrum lines at all. It had a continuous spectrum. Sol's surface temperature is about 7,000° Absolute. That of the hot white star is 500,000 degrees. It has nearly the mass of the sun, but only one fifth its diameter, so that its density is one hundred seventy-three times that of water, sixteen times that of lead, and eight times that of iridium—the heaviest substance known on Earth. But even this density is not that of a dwarf white star like the companion of Sirius. The white star in the Crab Nebula is an incomplete dwarf; it is a star still in the act of collapsing. Examination—including the survey of a four-thousand-year column of its light—was worth while. The *Llanvabon* had come to make that examination. But the finding of an alien spaceship upon a similar errand had implications which overshadowed the original purpose of the expedition.

A tiny bulbous robot floated in the tenuous nebular gas. The normal operating crew of the *Llanvabon* stood at their posts with a sharp alertness which was productive of tense nerves. The observation staff divided itself, and a part went half-heartedly about the making of the observations for which the *Llanvabon* had come. The other half applied itself to the problem the spaceship offered.

It represented a culture which was up to space travel on an interstellar scale. The explosion of a mere five thousand years since must have blasted every trace of life out of existence in the area now filled by the nebula. So the aliens of the black spaceship came from another solar system. Their trip must have been, like that of the Earth ship, for purely scientific purposes. There was nothing to be extracted from the nebula.

They were, then, at least near the level of human civilization, which meant that they had or could develop arts and articles of commerce which men would want to trade for, in friendship. But they would necessarily realize that the existence and civilization of humanity was a potential menace to their own race. The two races could be friends, but also they could be deadly enemies. Each, even if unwillingly, was a monstrous menace to the other. And the only safe thing to do with a menace is to destroy it.

In the Crab Nebula the problem was acute and immediate. The future relationship of the two races would be settled here and now. If a process for friendship could be established, one race, otherwise doomed, would survive and both would benefit immensely. But that process had to be established, and confidence built up, without the most minute risk of danger from treachery. Confidence would need to be established upon a foundation of necessarily complete distrust. Neither dared return to its own base if the other could do harm to its race. Neither dared risk any of the necessities to trust. The only safe thing for either to do was destroy the other or be destroyed.

But even for war, more was needed than mere destruction of the other. With interstellar traffic, the aliens must have atomic power and some form of overdrive for travel above the speed of light. With radio location and visiplates and short-wave communication they had, of course, many other devices. What weapons did they have? How widely extended was their culture? What were their resources? Could there be a development of trade and friendship, or were the two races so unlike that only war could exist between them? If peace was possible, how could it be begun?

The men on the *Llanvabon* needed facts—and so did the crew of the other ship. They must take back every morsel of information they could. The most important information of all would be of the location of the other civilization, just in case of war. That one bit of information might be the decisive factor in an interstellar war. But other facts would be enormously valuable.

The tragic thing was that there could be no possible information which could lead to peace. Neither ship could stake its own race's existence upon any conviction of the good will or the honor of the other.

So there was a strange truce between the two ships. The alien went about its work of making observations, as did the *Llanvabon*. The tiny robot floated in bright emptiness. A scanner from the *Llanvabon* was focused upon a vision plate from the alien. A scanner from the alien regarded a vision plate from the *Llanvabon*. Communication began.

It progressed rapidly. Tommy Dort was one of those who made the first progress report. His special task on the expedition was over. He had now been assigned to work on the problem of communication with the alien entities. He went with the ship's solitary psychologist to the captain's room to convey the news of success. The captain's room, as usual, was a place of silence and dull-red indicator lights and the great bright visiplates on every wall and on the ceiling.

"We've established fairly satisfactory communication, sir," said the psychologist. He looked tired. His work on the trip was supposed to be that of measuring personal factors of error in the observation staff, for the reduction of all observations to the nearest possible decimal to the absolute. He had been pressed into service for which he was not especially fitted, and it told upon him. "That is, we can say almost anything we wish, to them, and can understand what they say in return. But of course we don't know how much of what they say is the truth."

The skipper's eyes turned to Tommy Dort.

"We've hooked up some machinery," said Tommy, "that amounts to a mechanical translator. We have vision plates, of course, and then short-wave beams direct. They use frequency-modulation plus what is probably variation in wave forms—like our vowel and consonant sounds in speech. We've never had any use for anything like that before, so our coils won't handle it, but we've developed a sort of code which isn't the language of either set of us. They shoot over short-wave stuff with frequency-modulation, and we record it as sound. When we shoot it back, it's reconverted into frequency-modulation."

The skipper said, frowning:

"Why wave-form changes in short waves? How do you know?"

"We showed them our recorder in the vision plates, and they showed us theirs. They record the frequency-modulation direct. I think," said Tommy carefully, "they don't use sound at all, even in speech. They've set up a communications room, and we've watched them in the act of communicating with us. They make no perceptible movement of anything that corresponds to a speech organ. Instead of a microphone, they simply stand near something that would work as a pick-up antenna. My guess, sir, is that they use microwaves for what you might call person-to-person conversation. I think they make short-wave trains as we make sounds."

The skipper stared at him:

"That means they have telepathy?"

"M-m-m. Yes, sir," said Tommy. "Also it means that we have telepathy too, as far as they are concerned. They're probably deaf. They've certainly no idea of using sound waves in air for communication. They simply don't use noises for any purpose."

The skipper stored the information away.

"What else?"

"Well, sir," said Tommy doubtfully, "I think we're all set. We agreed on arbitrary symbols for objects, sir, by way of the visiplates, and worked out relationships and verbs and so on with diagrams and pictures. We've a couple of thousand words that have mutual meanings. We set up an analyzer to sort out their short-wave groups, which we feed into a decoding machine. And then the coding end of the machine picks out recordings to make the wave groups we want to send back. When you're ready to talk to the skipper of the other ship, sir, I think we're ready."

"H-m-m. What's your impression of their psychology?" The skipper asked the question of the psychologist.

"I don't know, sir," said the psychologist harassedly. "They seem to be completely direct. But they haven't let slip even a hint of the tenseness we know exists. They act as if they were simply setting up a means of communication for friendly conversation. But there is . . . well . . . an overtone—"

The psychologist was a good man at psychological mensuration, which is a good and useful field. But he was not equipped to analyze a completely alien thought-pattern.

"If I may say so, sir—" said Tommy uncomfortably.

"What?"

"They're oxygen breathers," said Tommy, "and they're not too dissimilar to us in other ways. It seems to me, sir, that parallel evolution has been at work. Perhaps intelligence evolves in parallel lines, just as . . . well . . . basic bodily functions. I mean," he added conscientiously, "any living being of any sort must ingest, metabolize, and excrete. Perhaps any intelligent brain must per-

ceive, apperceive, and find a personal reaction. I'm sure I've detected irony. That implies humor, too. In short, sir, I think they
could be likable."

The skipper heaved himself to his feet.

"H-m-m." He said profoundly, "We'll see what they have to say."

He walked to the communications room. The scanner for the
vision plate in the robot was in readiness. The skipper walked in
front of it. Tommy Dort sat down at the coding machine and
tapped at the keys. Highly improbable noises came from it, went
into a microphone, and governed the frequency-modulation of a
signal sent through space to the other spaceship. Almost instantly
the vision screen which with one relay—in the robot—showed the
interior of the other ship lighted up. An alien came before the
scanner and seemed to look inquisitively out of the plate. He was
extraordinarily manlike, but he was not human. The impression
he gave was of extreme baldness and a somehow humorous frankness.

"I'd like to say," said the skipper heavily, "the appropriate things
about this first contact of two dissimilar civilized races, and of my
hopes that a friendly intercourse between the two peoples will
result."

Tommy Dort hesitated. Then he shrugged and tapped expertly
upon the coder. More improbable noises.

The alien skipper seemed to receive the message. He made a
gesture which was wryly assenting. The decoder on the *Llanvabon* hummed to itself and word-cards dropped into the message
frame. Tommy said dispassionately:

"He says, sir, 'That is all very well, but is there any way for us to
let each other go home alive? I would be happy to hear of such a
way if you can contrive one. At the moment it seems to me that
one of us must be killed.'"

III

The atmosphere was of confusion. There were too many questions to be answered all at once. Nobody could answer any of
them. And all of them had to be answered.

The *Llanvabon* could start for home. The alien ship might or
might not be able to multiply the speed of light by one more
unit than the Earth vessel. If it could, the *Llanvabon* would get
close enough to Earth to reveal its destination—and then have to
fight. It might or might not win. Even if it did win, the aliens might
have a communication system by which the *Llanvabon's* destination might have been reported to the aliens' home planet before

battle was joined. But the *Llanvabon* might lose in such a fight. If she was to be destroyed, it would be better to be destroyed here, without giving any clue to where human beings might be found by a forewarned, forearmed alien battle fleet.

The black ship was in exactly the same predicament. It, too, could start for home. But the *Llanvabon* might be faster, and an overdrive field can be trailed, if you set to work on it soon enough. The aliens, also, would not know whether the *Llanvabon* could report to its home base without returning. If the alien was to be destroyed, it also would prefer to fight it out here, so that it could not lead a probable enemy to its own civilization.

Neither ship, then, could think of flight. The course of the *Llanvabon* into the nebula might be known to the black ship, but it had been the end of a logarithmic curve, and the aliens could not know its properties. They could not tell from that form what direction the Earth ship had started. As of the moment, then, the two ships were even. But the question was and remained, "What now?"

There was no specific answer. The aliens traded information for information—and did not always realize what information they gave. The humans traded information for information—and Tommy Dort sweated blood in his anxiety not to give any clue to the whereabouts of Earth.

The aliens saw by infrared light, and the vision plates and scanners in the robot communication-exchange had to adapt their respective images up and down an optical octave each, for them to have any meaning at all. It did not occur to the aliens that their eyesight told that their sun was a red dwarf, yielding light of greatest energy just below the part of the spectrum visible to human eyes. But after that fact was realized on the *Llanvabon,* it was realized that the aliens, also, should be able to deduce the Sun's spectral type by the light to which men's eyes were best adapted.

There was a gadget for the recording of short-wave trains which was as casually in use among the aliens as a sound-recorder is among men. The humans wanted that, badly. And the aliens were fascinated by the mystery of sound. They were able to perceive noise, of course, just as a man's palm will perceive infrared light by the sensation of heat it produces, but they could no more differentiate pitch or tone-quality than a man is able to distinguish between two frequencies of heat-radiation even half an octave apart. To them, the human science of sound was a remarkable discovery. They would find uses for noises which humans had never imagined—if they lived.

But that was another question. Neither ship could leave without first destroying the other. But while the flood of information was in passage, neither ship could afford to destroy the other. There was the matter of the outer coloring of the two ships. The *Llanvabon* was mirror-bright exteriorly. The alien ship was dead-black by visible light. It absorbed heat to perfection, and should radiate it away again as readily. But it did not. The black coating was not a "black body" color or lack of color. It was a perfect reflector of certain infrared wave lengths while simultaneously it fluoresced in just those wave bands. In practice, it absorbed the higher frequencies of heat, converted them to lower frequencies it did not radiate—and stayed at the desired temperature even in empty space.

Tommy Dort labored over his task of communications. He found the alien thought-processes not so alien that he could not follow them. The discussion of technics reached the matter of interstellar navigation. A star map was needed to illustrate the process. It would have been logical to use a star map from the chart room—but from a star map one could guess the point from which the map was projected. Tommy had a map made specially, with imaginary but convincing star images upon it. He translated directions for its use by the coder and decoder. In return, the aliens presented a star map of their own before the visiplate. Copied instantly by photograph, the Nav officers labored over it, trying to figure out from what spot in the galaxy the stars and Milky Way would show at such an angle. It baffled them.

It was Tommy who realized finally that the aliens had made a special star map for their demonstration too, and that it was a mirror-image of the faked map Tommy had shown them previously.

Tommy could grin, at that. He began to like these aliens. They were not human, but they had a very human sense of the ridiculous. In course of time Tommy essayed a mild joke. It had to be translated into code numerals, these into quite cryptic groups of short-wave, frequency-modulated impulses, and these went to the other ship and into heaven knew what to become intelligible. A joke which went through such formalities would not seem likely to be funny. But the aliens did see the point.

There was one of the aliens to whom communication became as normal a function as Tommy's own code-handlings. The two of them developed a quite insane friendship, conversing by coder, decoder and short-wave trains. When technicalities in the official messages grew too involved, that alien sometimes threw in strictly nontechnical interpolations akin to slang. Often, they cleared up the confusion. Tommy, for no reason whatever, had filed a code-name of "Buck" which the decoder picked out regularly when this particular operator signed his own symbol to a message.

In the third week of communication, the decoder suddenly presented Tommy with a message in the message frame.

You are a good guy. It is too bad we have to kill each other.—Buck.

Tommy had been thinking much the same thing. He tapped off the rueful reply:

We can't see any way out of it. Can you?

There was a pause, and the message frame filled up again.

If we could believe each other, yes. Our skipper would like it. But we can't believe you, and you can't believe us. We'd trail you home if we got a chance, and you'd trail us. But we feel sorry about it. —Buck.

Tommy Dort took the messages to the skipper.

"Look here, sir!" he said urgently. "These people are almost human, and they're likable cusses."

The skipper was busy about his important task of thinking things to worry about, and worrying about them. He said tiredly:

"They're oxygen breathers. Their air is twenty-eight per cent oxygen instead of twenty, but they could do very well on Earth. It would be a highly desirable conquest for them. And we still don't know what weapons they've got or what they can develop. Would you tell them how to find Earth?"

"N-no," said Tommy, unhappily.

"They probably feel the same way," said the skipper dryly. "And if we did manage to make a friendly contact, how long would it stay friendly? If their weapons were inferior to ours, they'd feel that for their own safety they had to improve them. And we, knowing they were planning to revolt, would crush them while we could—for our own safety! If it happened to be the other way about, they'd have to smash us before we could catch up to them."

Tommy was silent, but he moved restlessly.

"If we smash this black ship and get home," said the skipper, "Earth Government will be annoyed if we don't tell them where it came from. But what can we do? We'll be lucky enough to get back alive with our warning. It isn't possible to get out of those creatures any more information than we give them, and we surely won't give them our address! We've run into them by accident. Maybe—if we smash this ship—there won't be another contact for thousands of years. And it's a pity, because trade could mean so much! But it takes two to make a peace, and we can't risk trusting them. The only answer is to kill them if we can, and if we can't, to make sure that when they kill us they'll find out nothing that will lead them to Earth. I don't like it," added the skipper tiredly, "but there simply isn't anything else to do!"

IV

On the *Llanvabon,* the technicians worked frantically in two divisions. One prepared for victory, and the other for defeat. The ones working for victory could do little. The main blasters were the only weapons with any promise. Their mountings were cautiously altered so that they were no longer fixed nearly dead ahead, with only a 5° traverse. Electronic controls which followed a radio-locator master-finder would keep them trained with absolute precision upon a given target regardless of its maneuverings. More; a hitherto unsung genius in the engine room devised a capacity-storage system by which the normal full-output of the ship's engines could be momentarily accumulated and released in surges of stored power far above normal. In theory, the range of the blasters should be multiplied and their destructive power considerably stepped up. But there was not much more that could be done.

The defeat crew had more leeway. Star charts, navigational instruments carrying telltale notations, the photographic record Tommy Dort had made on the six months' journey from Earth, and every other memorandum offering clues to Earth's position, were prepared for destruction. They were put in sealed files, and if any one of them was opened by one who did not know the exact, complicated process, the contents of all the files would flash into ashes and the ashes be churned past any hope of restoration. Of course, if the *Llanvabon* should be victorious, a carefully not-indicated method of reopening them in safety would remain.

There were atomic bombs placed all over the hull of the ship. If its human crew should be killed without complete destruction of the ship, the atomic-power bombs should detonate if the *Llanvabon* were brought alongside the alien vessel. There were no ready-made atomic bombs on board, but there were small spare atomic-power units on board. It was not hard to trick them so that when they were turned on, instead of yielding a smooth flow of power they would explode. And four men of the earth ship's crew remained always in spacesuits with closed helmets, to fight the ship should it be punctured in many compartments by an unwarned attack.

Such an attack, however, would not be treacherous. The alien skipper had spoken frankly. His manner was that of one who wryly admits the uselessness of lies. The skipper and the *Llanvabon*, in turn, heavily admitted the virtue of frankness. Each insisted—perhaps truthfully—that he wished for friendship between the two races. But neither could trust the other not to make every conceivable effort to find out the one thing he needed most desperately to conceal—the location of his home planet. And neither dared believe that the other was unable to trail him and find out. Because each felt it his own duty to accomplish that unbearable —to the other—act, neither could risk the possible extinction of his race by trusting the other. They must fight because they could not do anything else.

They could raise the stakes of the battle by an exchange of information beforehand. But there was a limit to the stake either would put up. No information on weapons, population, or resources would be given by either. Not even the distance of their home bases from the Crab Nebula would be told. They exchanged information, to be sure, but they knew a battle to the death must follow, and each strove to represent his own civilization as powerful enough to give pause to the other's ideas of possible conquest —and thereby increased its appearance of menace to the other, and made battle more unavoidable.

It was curious how completely such alien brains could mesh, however. Tommy Dort, sweating over the coding and decoding machines, found a personal equation emerging from the at first stilted arrays of word-cards which arranged themselves. He had seen the aliens only in the vision screen, and then only in light at least one octave removed from the light they saw by. They, in turn, saw him very strangely, by transposed illumination from what to them would be the far ultraviolet. But their brains worked alike. Amazingly alike. Tommy Dort felt an actual sympathy and even something close to friendship for the gill-breathing, bald, and dryly ironic creatures of the black space vessel.

Because of that mental kinship he set up—though hopelessly— a sort of table of the aspects of the problem before them. He did not believe that the aliens had any instinctive desire to destroy man. In fact, the study of communications from the aliens had produced on the *Llanvabon* a feeling of tolerance not unlike that between enemy soldiers during a truce on Earth. The men felt no enmity, and probably neither did the aliens. But they had to kill or be killed for strictly logical reasons.

Tommy's table was specific. He made a list of objectives the men must try to achieve, in the order of their importance. The first was the carrying back of news of the existence of the alien culture. The second was the location of that alien culture in the galaxy. The third was the carrying back of as much information as possible about that culture. The third was being worked on but the second was probably impossible. The first—and all—would depend on the result of the fight which must take place.

The aliens' objectives would be exactly similar, so that the men must prevent, first, news of the existence of Earth's culture from being taken back by the aliens, second, alien discovery of the location of Earth, and third, the acquiring by the aliens of information which would help them or encourage them to attack humanity. And again the third was in train, and the second was probably taken care of, and the first must await the battle.

There was no possible way to avoid the grim necessity of the destruction of the black ship. The aliens would see no solution to their problems but the destruction of the *Llanvabon*. But Tommy Dort, regarding his tabulation ruefully, realized that even complete victory would not be a perfect solution. The ideal would be for the *Llanvabon* to take back the alien ship for study. Nothing less would be a complete attainment of the third objective. But Tommy realized that he hated the idea of so complete a victory, even if it could be accomplished. He would hate the idea of killing even nonhuman creatures who understood a human joke. And beyond that, he would hate the idea of Earth fitting out a fleet of fighting ships to destroy an alien culture because its existence was dangerous. The pure accident of this encounter, between peoples who could like each other, had created a situation which could only result in wholesale destruction.

Tommy Dort soured on his own brain which could find no answer which would work. But there had to be an answer! The gamble was too big! It was too absurd that two spaceships should fight—neither one primarily designed for fighting—so that the survivor could carry back news which would set one side to frenzied preparation for war against the unwarned other.

If both races could be warned, though, and each knew that the other did not want to fight, and if they could communicate with each other but not locate each other until some grounds for mutual trust could be reached—

It was impossible. It was chimerical. It was a daydream. It was nonsense. But it was such luring nonsense that Tommy Dort ruefully put it into the coder to his gill-breathing friend Buck, then some hundred thousand miles off in the misty brightness of the nebula.

"Sure," said Buck, in the decoder's word-cards flicking into place in the message frame. "That is a good dream. But I like you and still won't believe you. If I said that first, you would like me but not believe me either. I tell you the truth more than you believe, and maybe you tell me the truth more than I believe. But there is no way to know. I am sorry."

Tommy Dort stared gloomily at the message. He felt a very horrible sense of responsibility. Everyone did, on the *Llanvabon*. If they failed in this encounter, the human race would run a very good chance of being exterminated in time to come. If they succeeded, the race of the aliens would be the one to face destruction, most likely. Millions or billions of lives hung upon the actions of a few men.

Then Tommy Dort saw the answer.

It would be amazingly simple, if it worked. At worst it might give a partial victory to humanity and the *Llanvabon*. He sat quite still, not daring to move lest he break the chain of thought that followed the first tenuous idea. He went over and over it, excitedly finding objections here and meeting them, and overcoming impossibilities there. It was the answer! He felt sure of it.

He felt almost dizzy with relief when he found his way to the captain's room and asked leave to speak.

It is the function of a skipper, among others, to find things to worry about. But the *Llanvabon*'s skipper did not have to look. In the three weeks and four days since the first contact with the alien black ship, the skipper's face had grown lined and old. He had not only the *Llanvabon* to worry about. He had all of humanity.

"Sir," said Tommy Dort, his mouth rather dry because of his enormous earnestness, "may I offer a method of attack on the black ship? I'll undertake it myself, sir, and if it doesn't work our ship won't be weakened."

The skipper looked at him unseeingly.

"The tactics are all worked out, Mr. Dort," he said heavily. "They're being cut on tape now, for the ship's handling. It's a terrible gamble, but it has to be done."

"I think," said Tommy carefully, "I've worked out a way to take the gamble out. Suppose, sir, we send a message to the other ship, offering—"

His voice went on in the utterly quiet captain's room, with the visiplates showing only a vast mistiness outside and the two fiercely burning stars in the nebula's heart.

V

The skipper himself went through the air lock with Tommy. For one reason, the action Tommy had suggested would need his authority behind it. For another, the skipper had worried more intensively than anybody else on the *Llanvabon,* and he was tired of it. If he went with Tommy, he would do the thing himself, and if he failed he would be the first one killed—and the taps for the Earth ship's maneuvering were already fed into the control board and correlated with the master-timer. If Tommy and the skipper were killed, a single control pushed home would throw the *Llanvabon* into the most furious possible all-out attack, which would end in the complete destruction of one ship or the other—or both. So the skipper was not deserting his post.

The outer airlock door swung wide. It opened upon that shining emptiness which was the nebula. Twenty miles away, the little round robot hung in space, drifting in an incredible orbit about the twin central suns, and floating ever nearer and nearer. It would never reach either of them, of course. The white star alone was so much hotter than Earth's sun that its heat-effect would produce Earth's temperature on an object five times as far from it as Neptune is from Sol. Even removed to the distance of Pluto, the little robot would be raised to cherry-red heat by the blazing white dwarf. And it could not possibly approach to the ninety-odd million miles which is the Earth's distance from the sun. So near, its metal would melt and boil away as vapor. But, half a light-year out, the bulbous object bobbed in emptiness.

The two spacesuited figures soared away from the *Llanvabon.* The small atomic drives which made them minute spaceships on their own had been subtly altered, but the change did not interfere with their functioning. They headed for the communication robot. The skipper, out in space, said gruffly:

"Mr. Dort, all my life I have longed for adventure. This is the first time I could ever justify it to myself."

His voice came through Tommy's space-phone receivers. Tommy wetted his lips and said:

"It doesn't seem like adventure to me, sir. I want terribly for the plan to go through. I thought adventure was when you didn't care."

"Oh, no," said the skipper. "Adventure is when you toss your life on the scales of chance and wait for the pointer to stop."

They reached the round object. They clung to its short, scanner-tipped horns.

"Intelligent, those creatures," said the skipper heavily. "They must want desperately to see more of our ship than the communications room, to agree to this exchange of visits before the fight."

"Yes, sir," said Tommy. But privately, he suspected that Buck— his gill-breathing friend—would like to see him in the flesh before one or both of them died. And it seemed to him that between the two ships had grown up an odd tradition of courtesy, like that between two ancient knights before a tourney, when they admired each other wholeheartedly before hacking at each other with all the contents of their respective armories.

They waited.

Then, out of the mist, came two other figures. The alien spacesuits were also power-driven. The aliens themselves were shorter than men, and their helmet openings were coated with a filtering material to cut off visible and ultraviolet rays which to them would be lethal. It was not possible to see more than the outline of the heads within.

Tommy's helmet phone said, from the communications room on the *Llanvabon:*

"They say that their ship is waiting for you, sir. The air lock door will be open."

The skipper's voice said heavily:

"Mr. Dort, have you seen their spacesuits before? If so, are you sure they're not carrying anything extra, such as bombs?"

"Yes, sir," said Tommy. "We've showed each other our space equipment. They've nothing but regular stuff in view, sir."

The skipper made a gesture to the two aliens. He and Tommy Dort plunged on for the black vessel. They could not make out the ship very clearly with the naked eye, but directions for change of course came from the communication room.

The black ship loomed up. It was huge; as long as the *Llanvabon* and vastly thicker. The air lock did stand open. The two spacesuited men moved in and anchored themselves with magnetic-soled boots. The outer door closed. There was a rush of air and simultaneously the sharp quick tug of artificial gravity. Then the inner door opened.

All was darkness. Tommy switched on his helmet light at the same instant as the skipper. Since the aliens saw by infrared, a white light would have been intolerable to them. The men's helmet lights were, therefore, of the deep-red tint used to illuminate instrument panels so there will be no dazzling of eyes that must be able to detect the minutest specks of white light on a navigating vision plate. There were aliens waiting to receive them. They blinked at the brightness of the helmet lights. The space-phone receivers said in Tommy's ear:

"They say, sir, their skipper is waiting for you."

Tommy and the skipper were in a long corridor with a soft flooring underfoot. Their lights showed details of which every one was exotic.

"I think I'll crack my helmet, sir," said Tommy.

He did. The air was good. By analysis it was thirty per cent oxygen instead of twenty for normal air on Earth, but the pressure was less. It felt just right. The artificial gravity, too, was less than that maintained on the *Llanvabon*. The home planet of the aliens would be smaller than Earth, and—by the infrared data— circling close to a nearly dead, dull-red sun. The air had smells in it. They were utterly strange, but not unpleasant.

An arched opening. A ramp with the same soft stuff underfoot. Lights which actually shed a dim, dull-red glow about. The aliens had stepped up some of their illuminating equipment as an act of courtesy. The light might hurt their eyes, but it was a gesture of consideration which made Tommy even more anxious for his plan to go through.

The alien skipper faced them, with what seemed to Tommy a gesture of wryly humorous deprecation. The helmet phones said:

"He says, sir, that he greets you with pleasure, but he has been able to think of only one way in which the problem created by the meeting of these two ships can be solved."

"He means a fight," said the skipper. "Tell him I'm here to offer another choice."

The *Llanvabon's* skipper and the skipper of the alien ship were face to face, but their communication was weirdly indirect. The aliens used no sound in communication. Their talk, in fact, took place on microwaves and approximated telepathy. But they could not hear, in any ordinary sense of the word, so the skipper's and Tommy's speech approached telepathy, too, as far as they were concerned. When the skipper spoke, his space phone sent his words back to the *Llanvabon*, where the words were fed into the coder and short-wave equivalents sent back to the black ship. The alien skipper's reply went to the *Llanvabon* and through the decoder, and was retransmitted by space phone in words read from the message frame. It was awkward, but it worked.

The short and stocky alien skipper paused. The helmet phones relayed his translated, soundless reply.

"He is anxious to hear, sir."

The skipper took off his helmet. He put his hands at his belt in a belligerent pose.

"Look here!" he said truculently to the bald, strange creature in the unearthly red glow before him. "It looks like we have to fight and one batch of us get killed. We're ready to do it if we have to. But if you win, we've got it fixed so you'll never find out where Earth is, and there's a good chance we'll get you anyhow! If we win, we'll be in the same fix. And if we win and go back home, our government will fit out a fleet and start hunting your planet. And if we find it we'll be ready to blast it to hell! If you win, the same thing will happen to us! And it's all foolishness! We've stayed here a month, and we've swapped information, and we don't hate each other. There's no reason for us to fight except for the rest of our respective races!"

The skipper stopped for breath, scowling. Tommy Dort inconspicuously put his own hands on the belt of his spacesuit. He waited, hoping desperately that the trick would work.

"He says, sir," reported the helmet phones, "that all you say is true. But that his race has to be protected, just as you feel that yours must be."

"Naturally!" said the skipper angrily, "but the sensible thing to do is to figure out how to protect it! Putting its future up as a gamble in a fight is not sensible. Our races have to be warned of each other's existence. That's true. But each should have proof that the other doesn't want to fight, but wants to be friendly. And we shouldn't be able to find each other, but we should be able to communicate with each other to work out grounds for a common trust. If our governments want to be fools, let them! But we should give them the chance to make friends, instead of starting a space war out of mutual funk!"

Briefly, the space phone said:

"He says that the difficulty is that of trusting each other now. With the possible existence of his race at stake, he cannot take any chance, and neither can you, of yielding an advantage."

"But my race," boomed the skipper, glaring at the alien captain, "my race has an advantage now. We came here to your ship in atom-powered spacesuits! Before we left, we altered the drives! We can set off ten pounds of sensitized fuel apiece, right here in this ship, or it can be set off by remote control from our ship! It will be rather remarkable if your fuel store doesn't blow up with us! In other words, if you don't accept my proposal for a commonsense approach to this predicament, Dort and I blow up in an atomic explosion, and your ship will be wrecked if not destroyed—and the *Llanvabon* will be attacking with everything it's got within two seconds after the blast goes off!"

The captain's room of the alien ship was a strange scene, with its dull-red illumination and the strange, bald, gill-breathing aliens watching the skipper and waiting for the inaudible translation of the harangue they could not hear. But a sudden tensity appeared in the air. A sharp, savage feeling of strain. The alien skipper made a gesture. The helmet phones hummed.

"He says, sir, what is your proposal?"

"Swap ships!" roared the skipper. "Swap ships and go on home! We can fix our instruments so they'll do no trailing, he can do the same with his. We'll each remove our star maps and records. We'll each dismantle our weapons. The air will serve, and we'll take their ship and they'll take ours, and neither one can harm or trail the other, and each will carry home more information than can be taken otherwise! We can agree on this same Crab Nebula as a rendezvous when the double-star has made another circuit, and if our people want to meet them they can do it, and if they are scared they can duck it! That's my proposal! And he'll take it, or Dort and I blow up their ship and the *Llanvabon* blasts what's left!"

He glared about him while he waited for the translation to reach the tense small stocky figures about him. He could tell when it came because the tenseness changed. The figures stirred. They made gestures. One of them made convulsive movements. It lay down on the soft floor and kicked. Others leaned against its walls and shook.

The voice in Tommy Dort's helmet phones had been strictly crisp and professional, before, but now it sounded blankly amazed.

"He says, sir, that it is a good joke. Because the two crew members he sent to our ship, and that you passed on the way, have their spacesuits stuffed with atomic explosive too, sir, and he intended to make the very same offer and threat! Of course he accepts, sir. Your ship is worth more to him than his own, and his is worth more to you than the *Llanvabon*. It appears, sir, to be a deal."

Then Tommy Dort realized what the convulsive movements of the aliens were. They were laughter.

It wasn't quite as simple as the skipper had outlined it. The actual working-out of the proposal was complicated. For three days the crews of the two ships were intermingled, the aliens learning the workings of the *Llanvabon's* engines, and the men learning the controls of the black spaceship. It was a good joke— but it wasn't all a joke. There were men on the black ship, and aliens on the *Llanvabon,* ready at an instant's notice to blow up the vessels in question. And they would have done it in case of need, for which reason the need did not appear. But it was, actually, a better arrangement to have two expeditions return to two civilizations, under the current arrangement, than for either to return alone.

There were differences, though. There was some dispute about the removal of records. In most cases the dispute was settled by the destruction of the records. There was more trouble caused by the *Llanvabon's* books, and the alien equivalent of a ship's library, containing works which approximated the novels of Earth. But those items were valuable to possible friendship, because they would show the two cultures, each to the other, from the viewpoint of normal citizens and without propaganda.

But nerves were tense during those three days, Aliens unloaded and inspected the foodstuffs intended for the men on the black ship. Men transshipped the foodstuffs the aliens would need to return to their home. There were endless details, from the exchange of lighting equipment to suit the eyesight of the exchanging crews, to a final check-up of apparatus. A joint inspection party of both races verified that all detector devices had been smashed but not removed, so that they could not be used for trailing and had not been smuggled away. And of course, the aliens were anxious not to leave any useful weapon on the black ship, nor the men upon the *Llanvabon.* It was a curious fact that each crew was best qualified to take exactly the measures which made an evasion of the agreement impossible.

There was a final conference before the two ships parted, back in the communication room of the *Llanvabon.*

"Tell the little runt," rumbled the *Llanvabon's* former skipper, "that he's got a good ship and he'd better treat her right."

The message frame flicked word-cards into position.

"I believe," it said on the alien skipper's behalf, "that your ship is just as good. I will hope to meet you here when the double star has turned one turn."

The last man left the *Llanvabon*. It moved away into the misty nebula before they had returned to the black ship. The vision plates in that vessel had been altered for human eyes, and human crewmen watched jealously for any trace of their former ship as their new craft took a crazy, evading course to a remote part of the nebula. It came to a crevasse of nothingness, leading to the stars. It rose swiftly to clear space. There was the instant of breathlessness which the overdrive field produces as it goes on, and then the black ship whipped away into the void at many times the speed of light.

Many days later, the skipper saw Tommy Dort poring over one of the strange objects which were the equivalent of books. It was fascinating to puzzle over. The skipper was pleased with himself. The technicians of the *Llanvabon's* former crew were finding out desirable things about the ship almost momently. Doubtless the aliens were as pleased with their discoveries in the *Llanvabon*. But the black ship would be enormously worth while —and the solution that had been found was by any standard much superior even to a combat in which the Earthmen had been overwhelmingly victorious.

"Hm-m-m, Mr. Dort," said the skipper profoundly. "You've no equipment to make another photographic record on the way back. It was left on the *Llanvabon*. But fortunately, we have your record taken on the way out, and I shall report most favorably on your suggestion and your assistance in carrying it out. I think very well of you, sir."

"Thank you, sir," said Tommy Dort.

He waited. The skipper cleared his throat.

"You . . . ah . . . first realized the close similarity of mental processes between the aliens and ourselves," he observed. "What do you think of the prospects of a friendly arrangement if we keep a rendezvous with them at the nebula as agreed?"

"Oh, we'll get along all right, sir," said Tommy. "We've got a good start toward friendship. After all, since they see by infrared, the planets they'd want to make use of wouldn't suit us. There's no reason why we shouldn't get along. We're almost alike in psychology."

"Hm-m-m. Now just what do you mean by that?" demanded the skipper.

"Why, they're just like us, sir!" said Tommy. "Of course they breathe through gills and they see by heat waves, and their blood has a copper base instead of iron and a few little details like that. But otherwise we're just alike! There were only men in their crew, sir, but they have two sexes as we have, and they have families, and . . . er . . . their sense of humor— In fact—"

Tommy hesitated.

"Go on, sir," said the skipper.

"Well— There was the one I called Buck, sir, because he hasn't any name that goes into sound waves," said Tommy. "We got along very well. I'd really call him my friend, sir. And we were together for a couple of hours just before the two ships separated and we'd nothing in particular to do. So I became convinced that humans and aliens are bound to be good friends if they have only half a chance. You see, sir, we spent those two hours telling dirty jokes."

FIVE/

- **Giant Killer**
- **Vintage Season**
- **Placet Is a Crazy Place**

*These three stories appeared in the mid-forties, which
is in many ways a good place at which to close the first volume.
Astounding had already established itself as the sf
magazine par* excellence, *but many good years and many
good stories lay ahead—though we are soon to notice
a change of tone.*

*Meanwhile, both "Giant Killer" and "Placet" have
the characteristic flavor of the times, slightly acid, slightly
sour. "Giant Killer" enjoys another quality which makes
it typical. Look at the first paragraph, with its talk of "old, gray
Sterret, Judge of the Newborn" and of some children being
condemned as Different Ones. Very ominous, those capitals
initial letters! Where are we, what's going on?*

*That Kafkaesque sense of disorientation—what a delight
it was. The ASF writers loved to begin a story in total
obscurity, so that the reader never knew if he was in this
universe or the next, in the past or the future, following
humans, mutants, or some ghastly life-form of which
he had never previously heard. Chandler maintains this
sense of alienation expertly, and for several pages, as we become
involved with the desperate struggle going on in his
story—a struggle at once horribly strange and yet familiar.
The fact that Chandler was a ship's officer who spent
most of his time at sea lent the whole thing bitter authority.
He had a point: you can never kill all the rats.*

*The cover to the issue containing "Giant Killer" gave away
much of the disorientation, but it was faithful to Chandler's
image of the spaceship, which was the dominant image
in common use by writers—a great cavernous place with
high ceilings, echoing corridors, and a good many
miles of naked pipe running everywhere. Only a few years*

*earlier, Schneeman had illustrated the stokehold of one
of Commander Bullard's spaceships!*

*The image of that sort of ship, roomy as a cathedral,
silent as a morgue, and something of a cross between both,
was embodied in Dick Calkins's spirited drawings
for the Buck Rogers comic strip of the period. Sunken
under the realities of economy-class spaceflight of today,
that old image of a starship is now as much a period piece as the
"Titanic." But still recalled with affection by all of us
who sailed in her . . .*

*The echoing functionalism of those old ships was
matched by the functional men who manned them. It
must be admitted that the typical ASF hero of the early
forties was somewhat robot-like. In fact, he resembled Rogers's
ikon-like cover of the Grey Lensman, full of muscle, but
with his emotional life anaesthetised. How could it
be otherwise, when he had to live through mind-numbing
wonders, or survive many tedious years simply blasting
through space? The sensuous world, the world of the arts, was
closed to him; no vibrations got through but the pulse
of atomic engines.*

*Of course there were exceptions. "Vintage Season" provides
one of many. This time, the name O'Donnell conceals
Mrs. Henry Kuttner, the incomparable Catherine L. Moore.
It is an amazing story to find in Astounding, just as it
would have been an astounding story to find in Amazing;
for such sensuous delights were hardly reckoned standard
fare for an audience traditionally shy of sex. The amorous
Kleph, langorous, effete, and part dipso, is a portrait
of a type of vampire, and her affair with the doomed
hero gains strength from its suggestion of incest. It
remains a mature and effective tale, as contemporary today
as it was in 1946.*

*"Placet" is comedy, one of the best pieces of humor ever
to appear in Campbell's magazine. Comedy traditionally
needs no commentary, but it is worth noticing how in
fact Brown's story contains all the standard ingredients of
an ASF yarn: a planet laboring under cosmological
difficulties, distortions of human senses, unpleasant
indigenous flora and fauna, and trouble at the local base.
Fredric Brown shakes them up and—look out, here come those
damn widgie birds again, flying through the foundations!*

Giant Killer/

by A. BERTRAM CHANDLER

We've read of mutant supermen, of strange and alien races on other worlds. But never have we had a tale of quite so homely, yet so utterly alien a race, nor of quite such a super-mutant. Chandler has a yarn to tell—

Shrick should have died before his baby eyes had opened on his world. Shrick would have died, but Weena, his mother, was determined that he, alone of all her children should live. Three previous times since her mating with Skreer had she borne, and on each occasion the old, gray Sterret, Judge of the Newborn, had condemned her young as Different Ones.

Weena had no objection to the Law when it did not affect her or hers. She, as much as any other member of the Tribe, keenly enjoyed the feasts of fresh, tasty meat following the ritual slaughter of the Different Ones. But when those sacrificed were the fruit of her own womb it wasn't the same.

It was quiet in the cave where Weena awaited the coming of her lord. Quiet, that is, save for the sound of her breathing and an occasional plaintive, mewling cry from the newborn child. And even these sounds were deadened by the soft spongy walls and ceiling.

She sensed the coming of Skreer long before his actual arrival. She anticipated his first question and, as he entered the cave, said quietly, "One. A male."

"A male?" Skreer radiated approval. Then she felt his mood change to one of questioning, of doubt. "Is it . . . he—?"

"Yes."

Skreer caught the tiny, warm being in his arms. There was no light, but he, like all his race, was accustomed to the dark. His fingers told him all that he needed to know. The child was hairless. The legs were too straight. And—this was worst of all—the head was a great, bulging dome.

"Skreer!" Weena's voice was anxious. "Do you—?"

"There is no doubt. Sterret will condemn it as a Different One."

"But—"

"There is no hope." Weena sensed that her mate shuddered,

heard the faint, silken rustle of his fur as he did so. "His head! He is like the Giants!"

The mother sighed. It was hard, but she knew the Law. And yet— This was her fourth child-bearing, and she was never to know, perhaps, what it was to watch and wait with mingled pride and terror whilst her sons set out with the other young males to raid the Giants' territory, to bring back spoils from the great Cave-of-Food, the Place-of-Green-Growing-Things or, even, precious scraps of shiny metal from the Place of Life-That-Is-Not-Life.

She clutched at a faint hope.

"His head is like a Giant's? Can it be, do you think, that the Giants are Different Ones? I have heard it said."

"What if they are?"

"Only this. Perhaps he will grow to be a Giant. Perhaps he will fight the other Giants for us, his own people. Perhaps—"

"Perhaps Sterret will let him live, you mean." Skreer made the short, unpleasant sound that passed among his people for a laugh. "No, Weena. He must die. And it is long since we feasted—"

"But—"

"Enough. Or do *you* wish to provide meat for the Tribe also? I may wish to find a mate who will bear me sturdy sons, not monsters!"

The Place-of-Meeting was almost deserted when Skreer and Weena, she with Shrick clutched tightly in her arms, entered. Two more couples were there, each with newborn. One of the mothers was holding two babies, each of whom appeared to be normal. The other had three, her mate holding one of them.

Weena recognized her as Teeza, and flashed her a little half smile of sympathy when she saw that the child carried by Teeza's mate would certainly be condemned by Sterret when he chose to appear. For it was, perhaps, even more revolting than her own Different One, having two hands growing from the end of each arm.

Skreer approached one of the other males, he unburdened with a child.

"How long have you been waiting?" he asked.

"Many heartbeats. We—"

The guard stationed at the doorway through which light entered from Inside hissed a warning:

"Quiet! A Giant is coming!"

The mothers clutched their children to them yet more tightly, their fur standing on end with superstitious dread. They knew that if they remained silent there was no danger, that even if they should betray themselves by some slight noise there was no immediate peril. It was not size alone that made the Giants dreaded, it was the supernatural powers that they were known to possess. The food-that-kills had slain many an unwary member of the Tribe, also their fiendishly cunning devices that crushed and mangled any of the People unwise enough to reach greedily for the savory morsels left exposed on a kind of little platform. Although there were those who averred that, in the latter case, the risk was well worth it, for the yellow grains from the many bags in the Cave-of-Food were as monotonous as they were nourishing.

"The Giant has passed!"

Before those in the Place-of-Meeting could resume their talk, Sterret drifted out from the entrance of his cave. He held in his right hand his wand of office, a straight staff of the hard, yet soft, stuff dividing the territory of the People from that of the Giants. It was tipped with a sharp point of metal.

He was old, was Sterret.

Those who were themselves grandparents had heard their grandparents speak of him. For generations he had survived attacks by young males jealous of his prerogatives as chief, and the more rare assaults by parents displeased by his rulings as Judge of the Newborn. In this latter case, however, he had had nothing to fear, for on those isolated occasions the tribe had risen as one and torn the offenders to pieces.

Behind Sterret came his personal guards and then, floating out from the many cave entrances, the bulk of the Tribe. There had been no need to summon them; they *knew.*

The chief, deliberate and unhurried, took his position in the center of the Place-of-Meeting. Without orders, the crowd made way for the parents and their newborn. Weena winced as she saw their gloating eyes fixed on Shrick's revolting baldness, his misshapen skull. She knew what the verdict would be.

She hoped that the newborn of the others would be judged before her own, although that would merely delay the death of her own child by the space of a very few heartbeats. She hoped—

"Weena! Bring the child to me that I may see and pass judgment!"

The chief extended his skinny arms, took the child from the mother's reluctant hands. His little, deep-set eyes gleamed at the thought of the draught of rich, red blood that he was soon to enjoy. And yet he was reluctant to lose the savor of a single heartbeat of the mother's agony. Perhaps she could be provoked into an attack—

"You insult us," he said slowly, "by bringing forth *this!*" He held Shrick, who squalled feebly, at arm's length. "Look, oh People, at this *thing* the miserable Weena has brought for my judgment!"

"He has a Giant's head," Weena's timid voice was barely audible. "Perhaps—"

"—his father was a Giant!"

A tittering laugh rang through the Place-of-Meeting.

"No. But I have heard it said that perhaps the Giants, or their fathers and mothers, were Different Ones. And—"

"Who said that?"

"Strela."

"Yes, Strela the Wise. Who, in his wisdom, ate largely of the food-that-kills!"

Again the hateful laughter rippled through the assembly.

Sterret raised the hand that held the spear, shortening his grip on the haft. His face puckered as he tasted in anticipation the bright bubble of blood that would soon well from the throat of the Different One. Weena screamed. With one hand she snatched her child from the hateful grasp of the chief, with the other she seized his spear.

Sterret was old, and generations of authority had made him careless. Yet, old as he was, he evaded the vicious thrust aimed at him by the mother. He had no need to cry orders, from all sides the People converged upon the rebel.

Already horrified by her action, Weena knew that she could expect no mercy. And yet life, even as lived by the Tribe, was sweet. Gaining a purchase from the gray, spongy floor of the Place-of-Meeting she jumped. The impetus of her leap carried her up to the doorway through which streamed the light from Inside. The guard there was unarmed, for of what avail would a puny spear be against the Giants? He fell back before the menace of Weena's bright blade and bared teeth. And then Weena was Inside.

She could, she knew, hold the doorway indefinitely against pursuit. But this was Giant country. In an agony of indecision she clung to the rim of the door with one hand, the other still holding the spear. A face appeared in the opening, and then vanished, streaming with blood. It was only later that she realized that it had been Skreer's.

She became acutely conscious of the fierce light beating around and about her, of the vast spaces on all sides of a body that was accustomed to the close quarters of the caves and tunnels. She felt naked and, in spite of her spear, utterly defenseless.

Then that which she dreaded came to pass.

Behind her, she sensed the approach of two of the Giants. Then she could hear their breathing, and the low, infinitely menacing rumble of their voices as they talked one with the other. They hadn't seen her—of that she was certain but it was only a matter of heartbeats before they did so. The open doorway, with the certainty of death that lay beyond, seemed infinitely preferable to the terror of the unknown. Had it been only her life at stake she would have returned to face the righteous wrath of her chief, her mate and her Tribe.

Fighting down her blind panic, she forced herself to a clarity of thought normally foreign to her nature. If she yielded to instinct, if she fled madly before the approaching Giants, she would be seen. Her only hope was to remain utterly still. Skreer, and others of the males who had been on forays Inside, had told her that the Giants, careless in their size and power, more often than not did not notice the People unless they made some betraying movement.

The Giants were very close.

Slowly, cautiously, she turned her head.

She could see them now, two enormous figures floating through the air with easy arrogance. They had not seen her, and she knew that they would not see her unless she made some sudden movement to attract their attention. Yet it was hard not to yield to the impulse to dive back into the doorway to the Place-of-Meeting, there to meet certain death at the hands of the outraged Tribe. It was harder still to fight the urge to relinquish her hold on the rim of the doorway and flee—anywhere—in screaming panic.

But she held on.

The Giants passed.

The dull rumble of their voices died in the distance, their acrid, unpleasant odor, of which she had heard but never before experienced, diminished. Weena dared to raise her head once more.

In the confused, terrified welter of her thoughts one idea stood out with dreadful clarity. Her only hope of survival, pitifully slim though it was, lay in following the Giants. There was no time to lose, already she could hear the rising clamor of voices as those in the caves sensed that the Giants had passed. She relinquished her hold on the edge of the door and floated slowly up.

When Weena's head came into sudden contact with something hard she screamed. For long seconds she waited, eyes close shut in terror, for the doom that would surely descend upon her. But nothing happened. The pressure upon the top of her skull neither increased nor diminished.

Timidly, she opened her eyes.

As far as she could see, in two directions, stretched a long, straight shaft or rod. Its thickness was that of her own body, and it was made, or covered with, a material not altogether strange to the mother. It was like the ropes woven by the females with fibers from the Place-of-Green-Growing-Things—but incomparably finer. Stuff such as this was brought back sometimes by the males from their expeditions. It had been believed, once, that it was the fur of the Giants, but now it was assumed that it was made by them for their own purposes.

On three sides of the shaft was the glaring emptiness so terrifying to the people of the caves. On the fourth side was a flat, shiny surface. Weena found that she could insinuate herself into the space between the two without discomfort. She discovered, also, that with comforting solidity at her back and belly she could make reasonably fast progress along the shaft. It was only when she looked to either side that she felt a return of her vertigo. She soon learned not to look.

It is hard to estimate the time taken by her journey in a world where time was meaningless. Twice she had to stop and feed Shrick—fearful lest his hungry wailings betray their presence either to Giants or any of the People who might—although this was highly improbable—have followed her. Once she felt the shaft vibrating and froze to its matt surface in utter and abject terror. A Giant passed, pulling himself rapidly along with his two hands. Had either of those hands fallen upon Weena it would have been the finish. For many heartbeats after his passing she clung there limp and helpless, scarcely daring to breathe.

It seemed that she passed through places of which she had heard the males talk. This may have been so—but she had no means of knowing. For the world of the People, with its caves and tunnels, was familiar territory, whilst that of the Giants was known only in relation to the doorways through which a daring explorer could enter.

Weena was sick and faint with hunger and thirst when, at last, the long shaft led her into a place where she could smell the tantalizing aroma of food. She stopped, looked in all directions. But here, as everywhere in this alien country, the light was too dazzling for her untrained eyes. She could see, dimly, vast shapes beyond her limited understanding. She could see no Giants, nor anything that moved.

Cautiously, keeping a tight hold on the rough surface of the shaft, she edged out to the side away from the polished, flat surface along which she had been traveling. Back and forth her head swung, her sensitive nostrils dilated. The bright light confused her, so she shut her eyes. Once again her nose sought the source of the savory smell, swinging ever more slowly as the position was determined with reasonable accuracy.

She was loathe to abandon the security of her shaft, but hunger overruled all other considerations. Orienting her body, she jumped. With a thud she brought up against another flat surface. Her free hand found a projection, to which she clung. This she almost relinquished as it turned. Then a crack appeared, with disconcerting suddenness, before her eyes, widening rapidly. Behind this opening was black, welcome darkness. Weena slipped inside, grateful for relief from the glaring light of the Inside. It wasn't until later that she realized that this was a door such as was made by her own people in the Barrier, but a door of truly gigantic proportions. But all that mattered at first was the cool, refreshing shade.

Then she took stock of her surroundings.

Enough light came in through the barely open doorway for her to see that she was in a cave. It was the wrong shape for a cave, it is true, having flat, perfectly regular walls and floor and ceiling. At the far end, each in its own little compartment, were enormous, dully shining globes. From them came a smell that almost drove the famishing mother frantic.

Yet she held back. She knew that smell. It was that of fragments of food that had been brought into the caves, won by stealth and guile from the killing platforms of the Giants. Was this a killing platform? She wracked her brains to recall the poor description of these devices given by the males, decided that this, after all, must be a Cave-of-Food. Relinquishing her hold of Shrick and Sterret's spear she made for the nearest globe.

At first she tried to pull it from its compartment, but it appeared to be held. But it didn't matter. Bringing her face against the surface of the sphere she buried her teeth in its thin skin. There was flesh beneath the skin, and blood—a thin, sweet, faintly acid juice. Skreer had, at times, promised her a share of this food when next he won some from a killing platform, but that promise had never been kept. And now Weena had a whole cave of this same food all to herself.

Gorged to repletion, she started back to pick up the now loudly complaining Shrick. He had been playing with the spear and had cut himself on the sharp point. But it was the spear that Weena snatched, swinging swiftly to defend herself and her child. For a voice said, understandable, but with an oddly slurred intonation, "Who are you? What are you doing in our country?"

It was one of the People, a male. He was unarmed, otherwise it is certain that he would never have asked questions. Even so, Weena knew that the slightest relaxation of vigilance on her part would bring a savage, tooth and nail attack.

She tightened her grasp on the spear, swung it so that its point was directed at the stranger.

"I am Weena," she said, "of the Tribe of Sterret."

"Of the Tribe of Sterret? But the Tribe of Sessa holds the ways between our countries."

"I came Inside. But who are you?"

"Tekka. I am one of Skarro's people. You are a spy."

"So I brought my child with me."

Tekka was looking at Shrick.

"I see," he said at last. "A Different One. But how did you get through Sessa's country?"

"I didn't. I came Inside."

It was obvious that Tekka refused to believe her story.

"You must come with me," he said, "to Skarro. He will judge."

"And if I come?"

"For the Different One, death. For you, I do not know. But we have too many females in our Tribe already."

"This says that I will not come." Weena brandished her spear.

She would not have defied a male of her own tribe thus—but this Tekka was not of her people. And she had always been brought up to believe that even a female of the Tribe of Sterret was superior to a male—even a chief—of any alien community.

"The Giants will find you here." Tekka's voice showed an elaborate unconcern. Then— "That is a fine spear."

"Yes. It belonged to Sterret. With it I wounded my mate. Perhaps he is dead."

The male looked at her with a new respect. If her story were true—this was a female to be handled with caution. Besides—

"Would you give it to me?"

"Yes." Weena laughed nastily. There was no mistaking her meaning.

"Not that way. Listen. Not long ago, in our Tribe, many mothers, two whole hands of mothers with Different Ones, defied the Judge of the Newborn. They fled along the tunnels, and live outside the Place-of-Little-Lights. Skarro has not yet led a war party against them. Why, I do not know, but there is always a Giant in that place. It may be that Skarro fears that a fight behind the Barrier would warn the Giants of our presence—"

"And you will lead me there?"

"Yes. In return for the spear."

Weena was silent for the space of several heartbeats. As long as Tekka preceded her she would be safe. It never occurred to her that she could let the other fulfill his part of the bargain, and then refuse him his payment. Her people were a very primitive race.

"I will come with you," she said.

"It is well."

Tekka's eyes dwelt long and lovingly upon the fine spear. Skarro would not be chief much longer.

"First," he said, "we must pull what you have left of the good-to-eat-ball into our tunnel. Then I must shut the door lest a Giant should come—"

Together they hacked and tore the sphere to pieces. There was a doorway at the rear of one of the little compartments, now empty. Through this they pushed and pulled their fragrant burden. First Weena went into the tunnel, carrying Shrick and the spear, then Tekka. He pushed the round door into place, where it fitted with no sign that the Barrier had been broken. He pushed home two crude locking bars.

"Follow me," he ordered the mother.

The long journey through the caves and tunnels was heaven after the Inside. Here there was no light—or, at worst, only a feeble glimmer from small holes and cracks in the Barrier. It seemed that Tekka was leading her along the least frequented ways and tunnels of Skarro's country, for they met none of his people. Nevertheless, Weena's perceptions told her that she was in densely populated territory. From all around her beat the warm, comforting waves of the routine, humdrum life of the People. She knew that in snug caves males, females and children were living in cozy intimacy. Briefly she regretted having thrown away all this for the ugly, hairless bundle in her arms. But she could never return to her own Tribe, and should she wish to throw in her lot with this alien community the alternatives would be death or slavery.

"Careful!" hissed Tekka. "We are approaching Their country."

"You will—?"

"Not me. They will kill me. Just keep straight along this tunnel and you will find Them. Now, give me the spear."

"But—"

"*You* are safe. There is your pass." He lightly patted the uneasy, squirming Shrick. "Give me the spear, and I will go."

Reluctantly, Weena handed over the weapon. Without a word Tekka took it. Then he was gone. Briefly the mother saw him in the dim light that, in this part of the tunnel, filtered through the Barrier—a dim, gray figure rapidly losing itself in the dim grayness. She felt very lost and lonely and frightened. But the die was cast. Slowly, cautiously, she began to creep along the tunnel.

When They found her she screamed. For many heartbeats she had sensed their hateful presence, had felt that beings even more alien than the Giants were closing in on her. Once or twice she called, crying that she came in peace, that she was the mother of a Different One. But not even echo answered her, for the soft, spongy tunnel walls deadened the shrill sound of her voice. And the silence that was not silence was, if that were possible, more menacing than before.

Without warning the stealthy terror struck. Weena fought with the courage of desperation, but she was overcome by sheer weight of numbers. Shrick, protesting feebly, was torn from her frantic grasp. Hands—and surely there were far too many hands for the number of her assailants—pinned her arms to her sides, held her ankles in a vicelike grip. No longer able to struggle she looked at her captors. Then she screamed again. Mercifully, the dim light spared her the full horror of their appearance, but what she saw would have been enough to haunt her dreams to her dying day had she escaped.

Softly, almost caressingly, the hateful hands ran over her body with disgusting intimacy.

Then— "She is a Different One."

She allowed herself to hope.

"And the child?"

"Two-Tails has newborn. She can nurse him."

And as the sharp blade found her throat Weena had time to regret most bitterly ever having left her snug, familiar world. It was not so much the forfeit of her own life—that she had sacrificed when she defied Sterret—it was the knowledge that Shrick, instead of meeting a clean death at the hands of his own people, would live out his life among these unclean monstrosities.

Then there was a sharp pain and a feeling of utter helplessness as the tide of her life swiftly ebbed—and the darkness that Weena had loved so well closed about her for evermore.

No-Fur—who, at his birth, had been named Shrick—fidgetted impatiently at his post midway along what was known to his people as Skarro's Tunnel. It was time that Long-Nose came to relieve him. Many heartbeats had passed since he had heard the sounds on the other side of the Barrier proclaiming that the Giant in the Place-of-Little-Lights had been replaced by another of his kind. It was a mystery what the Giants did there—but the New People had come to recognize a strange regularity in the actions of the monstrous beings, and to regulate their time accordingly.

No-Fur tightened his grip on his spear—of Barrier material it was, roughly sharpened at one end—as he sensed the approach of somebody along the tunnel, coming from the direction of Tekka's country. It could be a Different One bearing a child who would become one of the New People, it could be attack. But, somehow, the confused impressions that his mind received did not bear out either of these assumptions.

No-Fur shrank against the wall of the tunnel, his body sinking deep into the spongy material. Now he could dimly see the intruder—a solitary form flittering furtively through the shadows. His sense of smell told him that it was a female. Yet he was certain that she had no child with her. He tensed himself to attack as soon as the stranger should pass his hiding place.

Surprisingly, she stopped.

"I come in peace," she said. "I am one of you. I am," here she paused a little, "one of the New People."

Shrick made no reply, no betraying movement. It was barely possible, he knew, that this female might be possessed of abnormally keen eyesight. It was even more likely that she had smelled him out. But then—how was it that she had known the name by which the New People called themselves? To the outside world they were Different Ones—and had the stranger called herself such she would at once have proclaimed herself an alien whose life was forfeit.

"You do not know," the voice came again, "how it is that I called myself by the proper name. In my own Tribe I am called a Different One—"

"Then how is it," No-Fur's voice was triumphant, "that you were allowed to live?"

"Come to me! No, leave your spear. Now come!"

No-Fur stuck his weapon into the soft cavern wall. Slowly, almost fearfully, he advanced to where the female was waiting. He could see her better now—and she seemed no different from those fugitive mothers of Different Ones—at whose slaughter he had so often assisted. The body was well proportioned and covered with fine, silky fur. The head was well shaped. Physically she was so normal as to seem repugnant to the New People.

And yet—No-Fur found himself comparing her with the females of his own Tribe, to the disadvantage of the latter. Emotion rather than reason told him that the hatred inspired by the sight of an ordinary body was the result of a deep-rooted feeling of inferiority rather than anything else. And he wanted this stranger.

"No," she said slowly, "it is not my body that is different. It is in my head. I didn't know myself until a little while—about two hands of feeding—ago. But I can tell, now, what is going on inside your head, or the head of any of the People—"

"But," asked the male, "how did they—"

"I was ripe for mating. I was mated to Trillo, the son of Tekka, the chief. And in our cave I told Trillo things of which he only knew. I thought that I should please him, I thought that he would like to have a mate with magical powers that he could put to good use. With my aid he could have made himself chief. But he was angry—and very frightened. He ran to Tekka, who judged me as a Different One. I was to have been killed, but I was able to escape. They dare not follow me too far into this country—"

Then— "You want me."

It was a statement rather than a question.

"Yes. But—"

"No-Tail? She can die. If I fight her and win, I become your mate."

Briefly, half regretfully, No-Fur thought of his female. She had been patient, she had been loyal. But he saw that, with this stranger for a mate there were no limits to his advancement. It was not that he was more enlightened than Trillo had been, it was that as one of the New People he regarded abnormality as the norm.

"Then you will take me." Once again there was no hint of questioning. Then— "My name is Wesel."

The arrival of No-Fur, with Wesel in tow, at the Place-of-Meeting could not have been better timed. There was a trial in progress, a young male named Big-Ears having been caught red-handed in the act of stealing a coveted piece of metal from the cave of one Four-Arms. Long-Nose, who should have relieved No-Fur, had found the spectacle of a trial with the prospect of a feast to follow far more engrossing than the relief of the lonely sentry.

It was he who first noticed the newcomers.

"Oh, Big-Tusk," he called, "No-Fur has deserted his post!"

The chief was disposed to be lenient.

"He has a prisoner," he said. "A Different One. We shall feast well."

"*He is afraid of you,*" hissed Wesel. "*Defy him!*"

"It is no prisoner." No-Fur's voice was arrogant. "It is my new mate. And you, Long-Nose, go at once to the tunnel."

"Go, Long-Nose. My country must not remain unguarded. No-Fur, hand the strange female over to the guards that she may be slaughtered."

No-Fur felt his resolution wavering under the stern glare of the chief. As two of Big-Tusk's bullies approached he slackened his grip on Wesel's arm. She turned to him, pleading and desperation in her eyes.

"No, no. He is afraid of you, I say. Don't give in to him. Together we can—"

Ironically, it was No-Tail's intervention that turned the scales. She confronted her mate, scorn written large on her unbeautiful face, the shrewish tongue dreaded by all the New People, even the chief himself, fast getting under way.

"So," she said, "you prefer this drab, common female to me. Hand her over, so that she may, at least, fill our bellies. As for you, my bucko, you will pay for this insult!"

No-Fur looked at the grotesque, distorted form of No-Tail, and then at the slim, sleek Wesel. Almost without volition he spoke.

"Wesel is my mate," he said. "She is one of the New People!"

Big-Tusk lacked the vocabulary to pour adequate scorn upon the insolent rebel. He struggled for words, but could find none to cover the situation. His little eyes gleamed redly, and his hideous tusks were bared in a vicious snarl.

"*Now!*" prompted the stranger. "His head is confused. He will be rash. His desire to tear and maul will cloud his judgment. Attack!"

No-Fur went into the fight coldly, knowing that if he kept his head he must win. He raised his spear to stem the first rush of the infuriated chief. Just in time Big-Tusk saw the rough point and, using his tail as a rudder, swerved. He wasn't fast enough, although his action barely saved him from immediate death. The spear caught him in the shoulder and broke off short, leaving the end in the wound. Mad with rage and pain the chief was now a most dangerous enemy—and yet, at the same time, easy meat for an adversary who kept his head.

No-Fur was, at first, such a one. But his self-control was racking fast. Try as he would he could not fight down the rising tides of hysterical fear, of sheer, animal blood lust. As the enemies circled, thrust and parried, he with his almost useless weapon, Big-Tusk with a fine, metal tipped spear, it took all his will power to keep himself from taking refuge in flight or closing to grapple with his more powerful antagonist. His reason told him that both courses of action would be disastrous—the first would end in his being hunted down and slaughtered by the Tribe, the second would bring him within range of the huge, murderous teeth that had given Big-Tusk his name.

So he thrust and parried, thrust and parried, until the keen edge of the chief's blade nicked his arm. The stinging pain made him all animal, and with a shrill scream of fury he launched himself at the other.

But if Nature had provided Big-Tusk with a fine armory she had not been niggardly with the rebel's defensive equipment. True, he had nothing outstanding in the way of teeth or claws, had not the extra limbs possessed by so many of his fellow New People. His brain may have been a little more nimble—but at this stage of the fight that counted for nothing. What saved his life was his hairless skin.

Time afer time the chief sought to pull him within striking distance, time after time he pulled away. His slippery hide was crisscrossed with a score of scratches, many of them deep but none immediately serious. And all the time he himself was scratching and pummeling with both hands and feet, biting and gouging.

It seemed that Big-Tusk was tiring, but he was tiring too. And the other had learned that it was useless to try to grab a handful of fur, that he must try to take his enemy in an unbreakable embrace. Once he succeeded. No-Fur was pulled closer and closer to the slavering fangs, felt the foul breath of the other in his face, knew that it was a matter of heartbeats before his throat was torn out. He screamed, threw up his legs and lunged viciously at Big-Tusk's belly. He felt his feet sink into the soft flesh, but the chief grunted and did not relax his pressure. Worse—the failure of his desperate counterattack had brought No-Fur even closer to death.

With one arm, his right, he pushed desperately against the other's chest. He tried to bring his knees up in a crippling blow, but they were held in a vicelike grip by Big-Tusk's heavily muscled legs. With his free, left arm he flailed viciously and desperately, but he might have been beating against the Barrier itself.

The People, now that the issue of the battle was decided, were yelling encouragement to the victor. No-Fur heard among the cheers the voice of his mate, No-Tail. The little, cold corner of his brain in which reason was still enthroned told him that he couldn't blame her. If she were vociferous in *his* support, she could expect only death at the hands of the triumphant chief. But he forgot that he had offered her insult and humiliation, remembered only that she was his mate. And the bitterness of it kept him fighting when others would have relinquished their hold on a life already forfeit.

The edge of his hand came down hard just where Big-Tusk's thick neck joined his shoulder. He was barely conscious that the other winced, that a little whimper of pain followed the blow. Then, high and shrill, he heard Wesel.

"Again! Again! That is his weak spot!"

Blindly groping, he searched for the same place. And Big-Tusk was afraid, of that there was no doubt. His head twisted, trying to cover his vulnerability. Again he whimpered, and No-Fur knew that the battle was his. His thin, strong fingers with their sharp nails dug and gouged. There was no fur here, and the flesh was soft. He felt the warm blood welling beneath his hand as the chief screamed dreadfully. Then the iron grip was abruptly relaxed. Before Big-Tusk could use hands or feet to cast his enemy from him No-Fur had twisted and, each hand clutching skin and fur, had buried his teeth in the other's neck. They found the jugular. Almost at once the chief's last, desperate struggles ceased.

No-Fur drank long and satisfyingly.

Then, the blood still clinging to his muzzle, he wearily surveyed the People.

"I am chief," he said.

"You are the chief!" came back the answering chorus.

"And Wesel is my mate."

This time there was hesitation on the part of the People. The new chief heard mutters of "*The feast . . . Big-Tusk is old and tough. . . . are we to be cheated–?*"

"Wesel is my mate," he repeated. Then– "There is your feast–"

At the height of his power he was to remember No-Tail's stricken eyes, the dreadful feeling that by his words he had put himself outside all custom, all law.

"*Above* the Law," whispered Wesel.

He steeled his heart.

"There is your feast," he said again.

It was Big-Ears who, snatching a spear from one of the guards, with one swift blow dispatched the cringing No-Tail.

"I am your mate," said Wesel.

No-Fur took her in his arms. They rubbed noses. It wasn't the old chief's blood that made her shudder ever so slightly. It was the feel of the disgusting, hairless body against her own.

Already the People were carving and dividing the two corpses and wrangling over an even division of the succulent spoils.

There was one among the New People who, had her differences from the racial stock been only psychological, would have been slaughtered long since. Her three eyes notwithstanding, the imprudent exercise of her gift would have brought certain doom. But, like her sisters in more highly civilized communities, she was careful to tell those who came to her only that which they desired to hear. Even then, she exercised restraint. Experience had taught her that foreknowledge of coming events on the part of the participants often resulted in entirely unforeseen results. This annoyed her. Better misfortune on the main stream of Time than well-being on one of its branches.

To this Three-Eyes came No-Fur and Wesel.

Before the chief could ask his questions the seeress raised one emaciated hand.

"You are Shrick," she said. "So your mother called you. Shrick the Giant Killer."

"But—"

"Wait. You came to ask me about your war against Tekka's people. Continue with your plans. You will win. You will then fight the Tribe of Sterret the Old. Again you will win. You will be Lord of the Outside. And then—"

"And then?"

"The Giants will know of the People. Many, but not all, of the People will die. You will fight the Giants. And the last of the Giants you will kill, but he will plunge the world into— Oh, if I could make you see! But we have no words."

"What—?"

"No, you cannot know. You will never know till the end is upon you. But this I can tell you. The People are doomed. Nothing you or they can do will save them. But you will kill those who will kill us, and that is good."

Again No-Fur pleaded for enlightenment. Abruptly, his pleas became threats. He was fast lashing himself into one of his dreaded fits of blind fury. But Three-Eyes was oblivious of his presence. Her two outer eyes were tight shut and that strange, dreaded inner one was staring at *something*, something outside the limits of the cave, outside the framework of things as they are.

Deep in his throat the chief growled.

He raised the fine spear that was the symbol of his office and buried it deep in the old female's body. The inner eye shut and the two outer ones flickered open for the last time.

"I am spared the End—" she said.

Outside the little cavern the faithful Big-Ears was waiting.

"Three-Eyes is dead," said his master. "Take what you want, and give the rest to the People—"

For a little there was silence.

Then— "I am glad you killed her," said Wesel. "She frightened me. I got inside her head—and I was lost!" Her voice had a hysterical edge. "I was lost! It was mad, mad. *What Was* was a *place*, a *PLACE*, and *Now*, and *What Will Be*. And I saw the End."

"What did you see?"

"A great light, far brighter than the Giants' lights Inside. And heat, stronger than the heat of the floors of the Far Outside caves and tunnels. And the People gasping and dying and the great light bursting into our world and eating them up—"

"But the Giants?"

"I did not see. I was lost. All I saw was the End."

No-Fur was silent. His active, nimble mind was scurrying down the vistas opened up by the dead prophetess. Giant Killer *Giant Killer*. Even in his most grandiose dreams he had never seen himself thus. And what was that name? Shrick? He repeated it to himself—Shrick the Giant Killer. It had a fine swing to it. As for the rest, the End, if he could kill the Giants then, surely, he could stave off the doom that they would mete out to the People. Shrick, the Giant Killer—

"It is a name that I like better than No-Fur," said Wesel.

"Shrick, Lord of the Outside. Shrick, Lord of the World. Shrick, the Giant Killer—"

"Yes," he said, slowly. "But the End—"

"You will go through that door when you come to it."

The campaign against Tekka's People had opened.

Along the caves and tunnels poured the nightmare hordes of Shrick. The dim light but half revealed their misshapen bodies, limbs where no limbs should be, heads like something from a half forgotten bad dream.

All were armed. Every male and female carried a spear, and that in itself was a startling innovation in the wars of the People.

For sharp metal, with which the weapons were tipped, was hard to come by. True, a staff of Barrier material could be sharpened, but it was a liability rather than an asset in a pitched battle. With the first thrust the point would break off, leaving the fighter with a weapon far inferior to his natural armory of teeth and claws.

Fire was new to the People—and it was Shrick who had brought them fire. For long periods he had spied upon the Giants in the Place-of-Little-Lights, had seen them bring from the pouches in their fur little, glittering devices from which when a projection was pressed, issued a tiny, naked light. And he had seen them bring this light to the end of strange, white sticks that they seemed to be sucking. And the end of the stick would glow, and there would be a cloud like the cloud that issued from the mouths of the People in some of the Far Outside caverns where it was very cold. But this cloud was fragrant, and seemed to be strangely soothing.

And one of the Giants had lost his little, hot light. He had put it to one of the white sticks, had made to return it to his pouch, and his hand had missed the opening. The Giant did not notice. He was doing something which took all his attention—and strain his eyes and his imagination as he might Shrick could not see what it was. There were strange glittering machines through which he peered intently at the glittering Little Lights beyond their transparent Barrier. Or were they on the inside of the Barrier? Nobody had ever been able to decide. There was something alive that wasn't alive that clicked. There were sheets of fine, white skin on which the Giant was making black marks with a pointed stick.

But Shrick soon lost interest in these strange rites that he could never hope to comprehend. All his attention was focused on the glittering prize that was drifting ever so slowly towards him on the wings of some vagrant eddy.

When it seemed that it would surely fall right into the doorway where Shrick crouched waiting it swerved. And, much as he dreaded the pseudo life that hummed and clicked, Shrick came out. The Giant, busy with his sorcery, did not notice him. One swift leap carried him to the drifting trophy. And then he had it, tight clasped to his breast. It was bigger than he had thought, it having appeared so tiny only in relationship to its previous owner. But it wasn't too big to go through the door in the Barrier. In triumph Shrick bore it to his cave.

Many were the experiments that he, eager but fumbling, performed. For a while both he and Wesel nursed painful burns. Many were the experiments that he intended to perform in the future. But he had stumbled on one use for the hot light that was to be of paramount importance in his wars.

Aping the Giants, he had stuck a long splinter of Barrier material in his mouth. The end he had brought to the little light. There was, as he had half expected, a cloud. But it was neither fragrant nor soothing. Blinded and coughing, Wesel snatched at the glowing stick, beat out its strange life with her hands.

Then— "It is hard," she said. "It is almost as hard as metal—"

And so Shrick became the first mass producer of armaments that his world had known. The first few sharpened staves he treated himself. The rest he left to Wesel and the faithful Big-Ears. He dare not trust his wonderful new power to any who were not among his intimates.

Shrick's other innovation was a direct violation of all the rules of war. He had pressed the females into the fighting line. Those who were old and infirm, together with the old and infirm males, brought up the rear with bundles of the mass produced spears. The New People had been wondering for some little time why their chief had refused to let them slaughter those of their number who had outlived their usefulness. Now they knew.

The caves of the New People were deserted save for those few females with newborn.

And through the tunnels poured the hordes of Shrick.

There was little finesse in the campaign against Tekka's people. The outposts were slaughtered out of hand, but not before they had had time to warn the Tribe of the attack.

Tekka threw a body of picked spearmen into his van, confident that he, with better access to those parts of Inside where metal could be obtained, would be able to swamp the motley horde of the enemy with superior arms and numbers.

When Tekka saw, in the dim light, only a few betraying gleams of metal scattered among Shrick's massed spears he laughed.

"This No-Fur is mad," he said. "And I shall kill him with this." He brandished his own weapon. "His mother gave it to me many, many feedings ago."

"Is Wesel—?"

"Perhaps, my son. You shall eat her heart, I promise you."

And then Shrick struck.

His screaming mob rushed along the wide tunnel. Confident the Tekkan spearmen waited, knowing that the enemy's weapons were good for only one thrust, and that almost certainly not lethal.

Tekka scowled as he estimated the numbers of the attackers.

There couldn't be that many males among the New People. There couldn't—And then the wave struck.

In the twinkling of an eye the tunnel was tightly packed with struggling bodies. Here was no dignified, orderly, series of single combats such as had always, in the past, graced the wars of the People. And with growing terror Tekka realized that the enemy spears were standing up to the strain of battle at least as well as his own few metal-tipped weapons.

Slowly, but with ever mounting momentum, the attackers pressed on, gaining impetus from the many bodies that now lay behind them. Gasping for air in the effluvium of sweat and newly shed blood Tekka and the last of his guards were pressed back and ever back.

When one of the New People was disarmed he fell to the rear of his own front line. As though by magic a fresh fighter would appear to replace him.

Then— "He's using females!" cried Trillo. "He's—"

But Tekka did not answer. He was fighting for his life with a four-armed monster. Every hand held a spear—and every spear was bright with blood. For long heart-beats he parried the other's thrusts, then his nerve broke. Screaming, he turned his back on the enemy. It was the last thing he did.

And so the remnant of the fighting strength of the Tribe of Tekka was at last penned up against one wall of their Place-of-Meeting. Surrounding them was a solid hemisphere of the New People. Snarl was answered by snarl. Trillo and his scant half dozen guards knew that there was no surrender. All they could do was to sell their lives as dearly as possible.

And so they waited for the inevitable, gathering the last reserves of their strength in this lull of the battle, gasping the last sweet mouthfuls of air that they would ever taste. From beyond the wall of their assailants they could hear the cries and screams as the females and children, who had hidden in their caves, were hunted out and slaughtered. They were not to know that the magnanimous Shrick was sparing most of the females. They, he hoped, would produce for him more New People.

And then Shrick came, elbowing his way to the forefront of his forces. His smooth, naked body was unmarked, save by the old scars of his battle with Big-Tusk. And with him was Wesel, not a hair of her sleek fur out of place. And Big-Ears—but he, obviously, had been in the fight. With them came more fighters, fresh and eager.

"Finish them!" ordered Shrick.

"Wait!" Wesel's voice was imperative. "I want Trillo."

Him she pointed out to the picked fighters, who raised their spears—weapons curiously slender and light, too fragile for hand-to-hand combat. A faint hope stirred in the breasts of the last defenders.

"Now!"

Trillo and his guards braced themselves to meet the last rush. It never came. Instead, thrown with unerring aim, came those sharp, flimsy spears, pinning them horribly against the gray, spongy wall of the Place-of-Meeting.

Spared in this final slaughter, Trillo looked about him with wide, fear-crazed eyes. He started to scream, then launched himself at the laughing Wesel. But she slipped back through the packed masses of the New People. Blind to all else but that hateful figure, Trillo tried to follow. And the New People crowded about him, binding his arms and legs with their strong cords, snatching his spear from him before its blade drank blood.

Then again the captive saw she who had been his mate.

Shamelessly, she was caressing Shrick.

"My Hairless One," she said. "I was once mated to *this*. You shall have his fur to cover your smooth body." And then— "Big-Ears! You know what to do!"

Grinning, Big-Ears found the sharp blade of a spear that had become detached from its haft. Grinning, he went to work. Trillo started to whimper, then to scream. Shrick felt a little sick.

"Stop!" he said. "He is not dead. You must—"

"What does it matter?" Wesel's eyes were avid, and her little, pink tongue came out to lick her thin lips. Big-Ears had hesitated in his work but, at her sign, continued.

"What does it matter?" she said again.

As had fared the Tribe of Tekka so fared the Tribe of Sterret, and a hand or more of smaller communities owing a loose allegiance to these two.

But it was in his war with Sterret that Shrick almost met disaster. To the cunning oldster had come survivors from the massacre of Tekka's army. Most of these had been slaughtered out of hand by the frontier guards, but one or two had succeeded in convincing their captors that they bore tidings of great importance.

Sterret heard them out.

He ordered that they be fed and treated as his own people, for he knew that he would need every ounce of fighting strength that he could muster.

Long and deeply he pondered upon their words, and then sent

foray after foray of his young males to the Place-of-Life-That-is-Not-Life. Careless he was of detection by the Giants. They might or might not act against him—but he had long been convinced that, for all their size, they were comparatively stupid and harmless. Certainly, at this juncture, they were not such a menace as Shrick, already self-styled Lord of the Outside.

And so his store of sharp fragments of metal grew, whilst his armorers worked without cessation binding these to hafts of Barrier stuff. And he, too, could innovate. Some of the fragments were useless as spearheads, being blunt, rough, and irregular. But, bound like a spearhead to a shaft, they could deliver a crushing blow. Of this Sterret was sure after a few experiments on old and unwanted members of his Tribe.

Most important, perhaps, his mind, rich in experience but not without a certain youthful zest, busied itself with problems of strategy. In the main tunnel from what had been Tekka's country his females hacked and tore at the spongy wall, the material being packed tightly and solidly into another small tunnel that was but rarely used.

At last his scouts brought the word that Shrick's forces were on the move. Careless in the crushing weight of his military power, Shrick disdained anything but a direct frontal attack. Perhaps he should have been warned by the fact that all orifices admitting light from the Inside had been closed, that the main tunnel along which he was advancing was in total darkness.

This, however, hampered him but little. The body of picked spearmen opposing him fought in the conventional way, and these, leaving their dead and wounded, were forced slowly but surely back. Each side relied upon smell, and hearing, and a certain perception possessed by most, if not all, of the People. At such close quarters these were ample.

Shrick himself was not in the van—that honor was reserved for Big-Ears, his fighting general. Had the decision rested with him alone he would have been in the forefront of the battle—but Wesel averred that the leader was of far greater importance than a mere spear bearer, should be shielded from needless risk. Not altogether unwillingly, Shrick acquiesced.

Surrounded by his guard, with Wesel at his side, the leader followed the noise of the fighting. He was rather surprised at the reports back to him concerning the apparent numbers of the enemy, but assumed that this was a mere delaying action and that Sterret would make his last stand in the Place-of-Meeting. It never occurred to him in his arrogance that others could innovate.

Abruptly, Wesel clutched his arm.

"Shrick! Danger—from the side!"

"From the side? But—"

There was a shrill cry, and a huge section of the tunnel wall fell inwards. The spongy stuff was in thin sheets, and drifted among the guard, hampering their every movement. Then, led by Sterret in person, the defenders came out. Like mountaineers they were roped together, for in this battle in the darkness their best hope lay in keeping in one, compact body. Separated, they would fall easy prey to the superior numbers of the hordes of Shrick.

With spear and mace they lay about them lustily. The first heartbeat of the engagement would have seen the end of Shrick, and it was only the uncured hide of Trillo, stiff and stinking, that saved his life. Even so, the blade of Sterret penetrated the crude armor, and, sorely wounded, Shrick reeled out of the battle.

Ahead, Big-Ears was no longer having things all his own way. Reinforcements had poured along the tunnel and he dare not return to the succor of his chief. And Sterret's maces were having their effect. Stabbing and slashing the People could understand—but a crushing blow was, to them, something infinitely horrible.

It was Wesel who saved the day. With her she had brought the little, hot light. It had been her intention to try its effect on such few prisoners as might be taken in this campaign—she was too shrewd to experiment on any of the New People, even those who had incurred the displeasure of herself or her mate.

Scarce knowing what she did she pressed the stud.

With dazzling suddenness the scene of carnage swam into full view. From all sides came cries of fear.

"Back!" cried Wesel. "Back! Clear a space!"

In two directions the New People retreated.

Blinking but dogged, Sterret's phalanx tried to follow, tried to turn what was a more or less orderly withdrawl into a rout. But the cords that had, at first, served them so well now proved their undoing. Some tried to pursue those making for the Place-of-Meeting, others those of the New People retiring to their own territory. Snarling viciously, blood streaming from a dozen minor wounds, Sterret at last cuffed and bullied his forces into a semblance of order. He attempted to lead a charge to where Wesel, the little, hot light still in her hand, was retreating among her personal, amazon guards.

But again the cunning—too cunning—ropes defeated his purpose. Not a few corpses were there to hamper fast movement, and almost none of his fighters had the intelligence to cut them free.

And the spear throwers of Shrick came to the fore, and, one

by one, the people of Sterret were pinned by the slim deadly shafts to the tunnel walls. Not all were killed outright, a few unfortunates squirmed and whimpered, plucking at the spears with ineffectual hands.

Among these was Sterret.

Shrick came forward, spear in hand, to administer the *coup de grace*. The old chief stared wildly, then—"Weena's hairless one!" he cried.

Ironically it was his own spear—the weapon that, in turn, had belonged to Weena and to Tekka—that slit his throat.

Now that he was Lord of the Outside Shrick had time in which to think and to dream. More and more his mind harked back to Three-Eyes and her prophesy. It never occurred to him to doubt that he was to be the Giant Killer—although the vision of the End he dismissed from his mind as the vaporings of a half-crazed old female.

And so he sent his spies to the Inside to watch the Giants in their mysterious comings and goings, tried hard to find some pattern for their incomprehensible behavior. He himself often accompanied these spies—and it was with avid greed that he saw the vast wealth of beautiful, shining things to which the Giants were heir. More than anything he desired another little hot light, for his own had ceased to function, and all the clumsy, ignorant tinkerings of himself and Wesel could not produce more than a feeble, almost heatless spark from its baffling intricacies.

It seemed, too, that the Giants were now aware of the swarming, fecund life surrounding them. Certain it was that their snares increased in number and ingenuity. And the food-that-kills appeared in new and terrifying guise. Not only did those who had eaten of it die, but their mates and—indeed all who had come into contact with them.

It smacked of sorcery, but Shrick had learned to associate cause and effect. He made the afflicted ones carry those already dead into a small tunnel. One or two of them rebelled—but the spear throwers surrounded them, their slim, deadly weapons at the ready. And those who attempted to break through the cordon of guards were run through repeatedly before ever they laid their defiling hands on any of the unafflicted People.

Big-Ears was among the sufferers. He made no attempt to quarrel with his fate. Before he entered the yawning tunnel that was to be his tomb he turned and looked at his chief. Shrick made to call him to his side—even though he knew that his friend's life could not be saved, and that by associating with him he would almost certainly lose his own.

But Wesel was at his side.

She motioned to the spear throwers, and a full two hands of darts transfixed the ailing Big-Ears.

"It was kinder this way," she lied.

But, somehow, the last look that his most loyal supporter had given him reminded him of No-Tail. With a heavy heart he ordered his people to seal the tunnel. Great strips of the spongy stuff were brought and stuffed into the entrance. The cries of those inside grew fainter and ever fainter. Then there was silence. Shrick ordered guards posted at all points where, conceivably, the doomed prisoners might break out. He returned to his own cave. Wesel, when one without her gift would have intruded, let him go in his loneliness. Soon he would want her again.

It had long been Wesel's belief that, given the opportunity, she could get inside the minds of the Giants just as she could those of the People. And if she could—who knew what prizes might be hers? Shrick, still inaccessible and grieving for his friend, she missed more than she cared to admit. The last of the prisoners from the last campaign had been killed, ingeniously, many feedings ago. Though she had no way of measuring time it hung heavily on her hands.

And so, accompanied by two of her personal attendants, she roamed those corridors and tunnels running just inside the Barrier. Through spyhole after spyhole she peered, gazing in wonderment that long use could not stale at the rich and varied life of the Inside.

At last she found that for which she was searching—a Giant, alone and sleeping. Experience among the People had taught her that from a sleeping mind she could read the most secret thoughts.

For a heartbeat she hesitated. Then—"Four-Arms, Little-Head, wait here for me. Wait and watch."

Little-Head grunted an affirmative, but Four-Arms was dubious. "Lady Wesel," she said, "what if the Giant should wake? What—?"

"What if you should return to the Lord of the Outside without me? Then he would, without doubt, have your hides. The one he is wearing now is old, and the fur is coming out. But do as I say."

There was a door in the Barrier here, a door but rarely used. This was opened, and Wesel slipped through. With the ease that all the People were acquiring with their more frequent ventures to the Inside she floated up to the sleeping Giant. Bonds held him in a sort of framework, and Wesel wondered if, for some offense, he had been made prisoner by his own kind. She would soon know.

And then a glittering object caught her eye. It was one of the little, hot lights, its polished metal case seeming to Wesel's covetous eyes the most beautiful thing in the world. Swiftly she made her decision. She could take the shining prize now, deliver it to her two attendants, and then return to carry out her original intentions.

In her eagerness she did not see that it was suspended in the middle of an interlacing of slender metal bars—or she did not care. And as her hands grabbed the bait something not far away began a shrill, not unmusical metallic beating. The Giant stirred and awoke. What Wesel had taken for bonds fell away from his body. In blind panic she turned to flee back to her own world. But, somehow, more of the metal bars had fallen into place and she was a prisoner.

She started to scream.

Surprisingly, Four-Arms and Little-Head came to her aid. It would be nice to be able to place on record that they were actuated by devotion to their mistress—but Four-Arms knew that her life was forfeit. And she had seen those who displeased either Shrick or Wesel flayed alive. Little-Head blindly followed the other's leadership. Hers not to reason why—

Slashing with their spears they assailed the Giant. He laughed —or so Wesel interpreted the deep, rumbling sound that came from his throat. Four-Arms he seized first. With one hand he grasped her body, with the other her head. He twisted. And that was the end of Four-Arms.

Anybody else but Little-Head would have turned and fled. But her dim mind refused to register that which she had seen. Perhaps a full feeding or so after the event the horror of it all would have stunned her with its impact—perhaps not. Be that as it may, she continued her attack. Blindly, instinctively, she went for the Giant's throat. Wesel sensed that he was badly frightened. But after a short struggle one of his hands caught the frenzied, squealing Little-Head. Violently, he flung her from him. She heard the thud as her attendant's body struck something hard and unyielding. And the impressions that her mind had been receiving from that of the other abruptly ceased.

Even in her panic fear she noticed that the Giant had not come out of the unequal combat entirely unscathed. One of his hands had been scratched, and was bleeding freely. And there were deep scratches on the hideous, repulsively naked face. The Giants, then, were vulnerable. There might have been some grain of truth after all in Three-Eyes' insane babbling.

And then Wesel forgot her unavailing struggle against the bars of her cage. With sick horror she watched what the Giant was doing. He had taken the limp body of Four-Arms, had secured it to a flat surface. From somewhere he had produced an array of glittering instruments. One of these he took, and drew it down the body from throat to crotch. On either side of the keen blade the skin fell away, leaving the flesh exposed.

And the worst part of it was that it was not being done in hate or anger, neither was the unfortunate Four-Arms being divided up that she might be eaten. There was an impersonal quality about the whole business that sickened Wesel—for, by this time, she had gained a certain limited access to the mind of the other.

The Giant paused in his work. Another of his kind had come, and for many heartbeats the two talked together. They examined the mutilated carcass of Four-Arms, the crushed body of Little-Head. Together, they peered into the cage where Wesel snarled impotently.

But, in spite of her hysterical fear, part of her mind was deadly cold, was receiving and storing impressions that threw the uninhibited, animal part of her into still greater panic. Whilst the Giants talked the impressions were clear—and whilst their great, ungainly heads hung over her cage, scant handsbreadths away, they were almost overpowering in their strength. She knew who she and the People were, what their world was. She had not the ability to put it into words—but she *knew*. And she saw the doom that the Giants were preparing for the People.

With a few parting words to his fellow the second Giant left. The first one resumed his work of dismembering Four-Arms. At last he was finished. What was left of the body was put into transparent containers.

The Giant picked up Little-Head. For many heartbeats he examined her, turning her over and over in his great hands. Wesel thought that he would bind the body to the flat surface, do with it as he had done with that of Four-Arms. But, at last he put the body to one side. Over his hands he pulled something that looked like a thick, additional skin. Suddenly, the metal bars at one end of the cage fell away, and one of those enormous hands came groping for Wesel.

After the death of Big-Ears, Shrick slept a little. It was the only way in which he could be rid of the sense of loss, of the feeling that he had betrayed his most loyal follower. His dreams were troubled, haunted by ghosts from his past. Big-Ears was in them, and Big-Tusk, and a stranger female with whom he felt a sense of oneness, whom he knew to be Weena, his mother.

And then all these phantasms were gone, leaving only the image of Wesel. It wasn't the Wesel he had always known, cool, self-assured, ambitious. This was a terrified Wesel—Wesel descending into a black abyss of pain and torture even worse than that which she had, so often, meted out to others. And she wanted him.

Shrick awoke, frightened by his dreams. But he knew that ghosts had never hurt anybody, could not hurt him, Lord of the Outside. He shook himself, whimpering a little, and then tried to compose himself for further sleep.

But the image of Wesel persisted. At last Shrick abandoned his attempts to seek oblivion and, rubbing his eyes, emerged from his cave.

In the dim, half-light of the Place-of-Meeting little knots of the People hung about, talking in low voices. Shrick called to the guards. There was a sullen silence. He called again. At last one answered.

"Where is Wesel?"

"I do not know . . . lord." The last word came out grudgingly.

Then one of the others volunteered the information that she had been seen, in company with Four-Arms and Little-Head, proceeding along the tunnels that led to that part of the Outside in the way of the Place-of-Green-Growing-Things.

Shrick hesitated.

He rarely ventured abroad without his personal guards, but then, Big-Ears was always one of them. And Big-Ears was gone.

He looked around him, decided that he could trust none of those at present in the Place-of-Meeting. The People had been shocked and horrified by his necessary actions in the case of those who had eaten of the food-that-kills and regarded him, he knew, as a monster even worse than the Giants. Their memories were short—but until they forgot he would have to walk with caution.

"Wesel is my mate. I will go alone," he said.

At his words he sensed a change of mood, was tempted to demand an escort. But the instinct that—as much as any mental superiority—maintained him in authority warned him against throwing away his advantage.

"I go alone," he said.

One Short-Tail, bolder than his fellows, spoke up.

"And if you do not return, Lord of the Outside? Who is to be—?"

"I shall return," said Shrick firmly, his voice displaying a confidence he did not feel.

In the more populous regions the distinctive scent of Wesel was overlaid by that of many others. In tunnels but rarely frequented it was strong and compelling—but now he had no need to use his olfactory powers. For the terrified little voice in his brain—from outside his brain—was saying *hurry, HURRY*—and some power beyond his ken was guiding him unerringly to where his mate was in such desperate need of him.

From the door in the Barrier through which Wesel had entered the Inside—it had been left open—streamed a shaft of light. And now Shrick's natural caution reasserted itself. The voice inside his brain was no less urgent, but the instinct of self-preservation was strong. Almost timorously, he peered through the doorway.

He smelled death. At first he feared that he was too late, then identified the personal odors of Four-Arms and Little-Head. That of Wesel was there too—intermingled with the acrid scent of terror and agony. But she was still alive.

Caution forgotten, he launched himself from the doorway with all the power of his leg muscles. And he found Wesel, stretched supine on a flat surface that was slippery with blood. Most of it was Four-Arms', but some of it was hers.

"Shrick!" she screamed. "The Giant!"

He looked away from his mate and saw hanging over him, pale and enormous, the face of the Giant. He screamed, but there was more of fury than terror in the sound. He saw, not far from where he clung to Wesel, a huge blade of shining metal. He could see that its edge was keen. The handle had been fashioned for a hand far larger than his, nevertheless he was just able to grasp it. It seemed to be secured. Feet braced against Wesel's body for purchase, he tugged desperately.

Just as the Giant's hand, fingers outstretched to seize him, came down the blade pulled free. As Shrick's legs suddenly and involuntarily straightened he was propelled away from Wesel. The Giant grabbed at the flying form, and howled in agony as Shrick swept the blade around and lopped off a finger.

He heard Wesel's voice: "You are the Giant Killer!"

Now he was level with the Giant's head. He swerved, and with his feet caught a fold of the artificial skin covering the huge body. And he hung there, swinging his weapon with both hands, cutting and slashing. Great hands swung wildly and he was bruised and buffeted. But not once did they succeed in finding a grip. Then there was a great and horrid spurting of blood and a wild threshing of mighty limbs. This ceased, but it was only the voice of Wesel that called him from the fury of his slaughter lust.

So he found her again, still stretched out for sacrifice to the Giants' dark gods, still bound to that surface that was wet with her blood and that of her attendant. But she smiled up at him, and in her eyes was respect that bordered on awe.

"Are you hurt?" he demanded, a keen edge of anxiety to his voice.

"Only a little. But Four-Arms was cut in pieces . . . I should have been had you not come. And," her voice was a hymn of praise, "you killed the Giant!"

"It was foretold. Besides," for once he was honest, "it could not have been done without the Giant's weapon."

With its edge he was cutting Wesel's bonds. Slowly she floated away from the place of sacrifice. Then: "I can't move my legs!" Her voice was terror-stricken. "I can't move!"

Shrick guessed what was wrong. He knew a little of anatomy— his knowledge was that of the warrior who may be obliged to immobilize his enemy prior to his slaughter—and he could see that the Giant's keen blade had wrought this damage. Fury boiled up in him against these cruel, monstrous beings. And there was more than fury. There was the feeling, rare among his people, of overwhelming pity for his crippled mate.

"The blade . . . it is very sharp . . . I shall feel nothing."

But Shrick could not bring himself to do it.

Now they were floating up against the huge bulk of the dead Giant. With one hand he grasped Wesel's shoulder—the other still clutched his fine, new weapon—and kicked off against the gigantic carcass. Then he was pushing Wesel through the doorway in the Barrier, and sensed her relief as she found herself once more in familiar territory. He followed her, then carefully shut and barred the door.

For a few heartbeats Wesel busied herself smoothing her bedraggled fur. He couldn't help noticing that she dare not let her hands stray to the lower part of her body where were the wounds, small but deadly, that had robbed her of the power of her limbs. Dimly, he felt that something might be done for one so injured, but knew that it was beyond his powers. And fury—not helpless now—against the Giants returned again, threatening to choke him with its intensity.

"Shrick!" Wesel's voice was grave. "We must return at once to the People. We must warn the People. The Giants are making a sorcery to bring the End."

"The great, hot light?"

"No. But wait! First I must tell you of what I learned. Otherwise, you would not believe. I have learned what we are, what the world is. And it is strange and wonderful beyond all our beliefs.

"What is Outside?" She did not wait for his answer, read it in his mind before his lips could frame the words. "The world is but a bubble of emptiness in the midst of a vast piece of metal, greater than the mind can imagine. But it is not so! Outside the metal that lies outside the Outside there is nothing. *Nothing!* There is no air."

"But there must be air, at least."

"No, I tell you. There is *nothing.*

"And the world—how can I find words? Their name for the world is—*ship,* and it seems to mean something big going from one place to another place. And all of us—Giants and People—are inside the ship. The Giants made the ship."

"Then it is not alive?"

"I cannot say. *They* seem to think that it is a female. It must have some kind of life that is not life. And it is going from one world to another world."

"And these other worlds?"

"I caught glimpses of them. They are dreadful, dreadful. *We* find the open spaces of the Inside frightening—but these other worlds are *all* open space except for one side."

"But what are we?" In spite of himself, Shrick at least half believed Wesel's fantastic story. Perhaps she possessed, to some slight degree, the power of projecting her own thoughts into the mind of another with whom she was intimate. "What are we?"

She was silent for the space of many heartbeats. Then: *"Their* name for us is—*mutants.* The picture was . . . not clear at all. It means that we—the People—have changed. And yet their picture of the People before the change was like the Different Ones before we slew them all.

"Long and long ago—many hands of feedings—the first People, our parents' parents' parents, came into the world. They came from that greater world—the world of dreadful, open spaces. They came with the food in the great Cave-of-Food—and that is being carried to another world.

"Now, in the horrid, empty space outside the Outside there is—light that is not light. And this light—changes persons. No, not the grown person or the child, but the child before the birth. Like the dead and gone chiefs of the People, the Giants fear change in themselves. So they have kept the light that is not light from the Inside.

"And this is how. Between the Barrier and the Far Outside they filled the space with the stuff in which we have made our caves and tunnels. The first People left the great Cave-of-Food, they tunneled through the Barrier and into the stuff Outside. It was their nature. And some of them mated in the Far Outside caves. Their children were—*Different.*"

"That is true," said Shrick slowly. "It has always been thought that children born in the Far Outside were never like their parents, and that those born close to the Barrier were—"

"Yes.

"Now, the Giants always knew that the People were here, but they did not fear them. They did not know our numbers, and they regarded us as beings much lower than themselves. They were content to keep us down with their traps and the food-that-kills. Somehow, they found that we had changed. Like the dead chiefs they feared us then—and like the dead chiefs they will try to kill us all before we conquer them."

"And the End?"

"Yes, the End." She was silent again, her big eyes looking past Shrick at something infinitely terrible. "Yes," she said again, "the End. *They* will make it, and *They* will escape it. *They* will put on artificial skins that will cover *Their* whole bodies, even *Their* heads, and *They* will open huge doors in the . . . skin of the ship, and all the air will rush out into the terrible empty space outside the Outside. And all the People will die."

"I must go," said Shrick. "I must kill the Giants before this comes to pass."

"No! There was one hand of Giants—now that you have killed Fat-Belly there are four of them left. And they know, now, that they can be killed. They will be watching for you.

"Do you remember when we buried the People with the sickness? That is what we must do to all the People. And then when the Giants fill the world with air again from their store we can come out."

Shrick was silent awhile. He had to admit that she was right. One unsuspecting Giant had fallen to his blade—but four of them, aroused, angry and watchful, he could not handle. In any case there was no way of knowing when the Giants would let the air from the world. The People must be warned—and fast.

Together, in the Place-of-Meeting, Shrick and Wesel faced the People. They had told their stories, only to be met with blank incredulity. True, there were some who, seeing the fine, shining blade that Shrick had brought from the Inside, were inclined to believe. But they were shouted down by the majority. It was when he tried to get them to immure themselves against the End that he met with serious opposition. The fact that he had so treated those suffering from the sickness still bulked big in the mob memory.

It was Short-Tail who precipitated the crisis.

"He wants the world to himself!" he shouted. "He has killed Big-Tusk and No-Tail, he has killed all the Different Ones, and Big-Ears he slew because he would have been chief. He and his ugly, barren mate want the world to themselves!"

Shrick tried to argue, but Big-Ears' following shouted him down. He squealed with rage and, raising his blade with both hands, rushed upon the rebel. Short-Tail scurried back out of reach. Shrick found himself alone in a suddenly cleared space. From somewhere a long way off he heard Wesel screaming his name. Dazedly, he shook his head, and then the red mist cleared from in front of his eyes.

All around him were the spear throwers, their slender weapons poised. He had trained them himself, had brought their specialized art of war into being. And now—

"Shrick!" Wesel was saying, "don't fight! They will kill you, and I shall be alone. I shall have the world to myself. Let them do as they will with us, and *we* shall live through the End."

At her words a tittering laugh rippled through the mob.

"*They* will live through the End! They will die as Big-Ears and his friends died!"

"I want your blade," said Short-Tail.

"Give it to him," cried Wesel. "You will get it back after the End!"

Shrick hesitated. The other made a sign. One of the throwing spears buried itself in the fleshy part of his arm. Had it not been for Wesel's voice, pleading, insistent, he would have charged his tormenters and met his end in less than a single heartbeat. Reluctantly, he released his hold upon the weapon. Slowly—as though loath to leave its true owner—it floated away from him. And then the People were all around him, almost suffocating him with the pressure of their bodies.

The cave into which Shrick and Wesel were forced was their own dwelling place. They were in pitiable state when the mob retreated to the entrance—Wesel's wounds had reopened and Shrick's arm was bleeding freely. Somebody had wrenched out the spear—but the head had broken off.

Outside, Short-Tail was laying about him with the keen blade he had taken from his chief. Under its strokes great masses of the spongy stuff of the Outside were coming free, and many willing hands were stuffing this tight into the cave entrance.

"We will let you out after the End!" called somebody. There was a hoot of derision. Then: "I wonder which will eat the other first?"

"Never mind," said Wesel softly. "We shall laugh last."

"Perhaps. But . . . the People. *My* People. And you are barren. The Giants have won—"

Wesel was silent. Then he heard her voice again. She was whimpering to herself in the darkness. Shrick could guess her thoughts. All their grandiose dreams of world dominion had come to this— a tiny, cramped space in which there was barely room for either of them to stir a finger.

And now they could no longer hear the voices of the People outside their prison. Shrick wondered if the Giants had already struck, then reassured himself with the memory of how the voices of those suffering from the sickness had grown fainter and fainter and then, at the finish, ceased altogether. And he wondered how he and Wesel would know when the End had come, and how they would know when it was safe to dig themselves out. It would be a long, slow task with only their teeth and claws with which to work.

But he had a tool.

The fingers of the hand of his uninjured arm went to the spearhead still buried in the other. He knew that by far the best way of extracting it would be one, quick pull—but he couldn't bring himself to do it. Slowly, painfully, he worked away at the sharp fragment of metal.

"Let me do it for you."

"No." His voice was rough. "Besides, there is no haste."

Slowly, patiently, he worried at the wound. He was groaning a little, although he was not conscious of doing so. And then, suddenly, Wesel screamed. The sound was so unexpected, so dreadful in that confined space, that Shrick started violently. His hand jerked away from his upper arm, bringing with it the spearhead.

His first thought was that Wesel, telepath as she was, had chosen this way to help him. But he felt no gratitude, only a dull resentment.

"What did you do that for?" he demanded angrily.

She didn't answer his question. She was oblivious of his presence.

"The People . . ." she whispered, "the People . . . I can feel their thoughts . . . I can feel what they are feeling. And they are gasping for air . . . they are gasping and dying . . . and the cave of Long-Fur the spearmaker . . . but they are dying, and the blood is coming out of their mouths and noses and ears . . . I can't bear it . . . I can't—"

And then a terrifying thing happened. The sides of the cave pressed in upon them. Throughout the world, throughout the ship, the air cells in the spongy insulation were expanding as the air pressure dropped to zero. It was this alone that saved Shrick and Wesel, although they never knew it. The rough plug sealing their cave that, otherwise, would have blown out swelled to meet the expanding walls of the entrance, making a near perfect air-tight joint.

But the prisoners were in no state to appreciate this, even had they been in possession of the necessary knowledge. Panic seized them both. Claustrophobia was unknown among the People—but walls that closed upon them were outside their experience.

Perhaps Wesel was the more level-headed of the pair. It was she who tried to restrain her mate as he clawed and bit savagely, madly, at the distended, bulging walls. He no longer knew what lay outside the cave, had he known it would have made no difference. His one desire was to get out.

At first he made little headway, then he bethought himself of the little blade still grasped in his hand. With it he attacked the pulpy mass. The walls of the cells were stretched thin, almost to bursting, and under his onslaught they put up no more resistance than so many soap bubbles. A space was cleared, and Shrick was able to work with even greater vigor.

"Stop! Stop, I tell you! There is only the choking death outside the cave. And you will kill us both!"

But Shrick paid no heed, went on stabbing and hacking. It was only slowly, now, that he was able to enlarge upon the original impression he had made. As the swollen surfaces burst and withered beneath his blade, so they bulged and bellied in fresh places.

"Stop!" cried Wesel again.

With her arms, her useless legs trailing behind her, she pulled herself towards her mate. And she grappled with him, desperation lending her strength. So for many heartbeats they fought—silent, savage, forgetful of all that each owed to the other. And yet, perhaps, Wesel never quite forgot. For all her blind, frantic will to survive her telepathic powers were at no time entirely in abeyance. In spite of herself she, as always, shared the other's mind.

And this psychological factor gave her an advantage that off-set the paralysis of the lower half of her body—and at the same time inhibited her from pressing that advantage home to its logical conclusion.

But it did not save her when her fingers, inadvertently, dug into the wound in Shrick's arm. His ear-splitting scream was compounded of pain and fury, and he drew upon reserves of strength that the other never even guessed that he possessed. And the hand gripping the blade came round with irresistible force.

For Wesel there was a heartbeat of pain, of sorrow for herself and Shrick, of blind anger against the Giants who, indirectly, had brought this thing to pass.

And then the beating of her heart was stilled forever.

With the death of Wesel Shrick's frenzy left him.

There, in the darkness, he ran his sensitive fingers over the lifeless form, hopelessly hoping for the faintest sign of life. He called her name, he shook her roughly. But at last the knowledge that she was dead crept into his brain—and stayed there. In his short life he had known many times this sense of loss, but never with such poignancy.

And worst of all was the knowledge that *he* had killed her.

He tried to shift the burden of blame. He told himself that she would have died, in any case, of the wounds received at the hands of the Giants. He tried to convince himself that, wounds or no wounds, the Giants were directly responsible for her death. And he knew that he was Wesel's murderer, just as he knew that all that remained for him in life was to bring the slayers of his people to a reckoning.

This made him cautious.

For many heartbeats he lay there in the thick darkness, not daring to renew his assault on the walls of his prison. He told himself that, somehow, he would know when the Giants let the air back into the world. How he would know he could not say, but the conviction persisted.

And when at last, with returning pressure, the insulation resumed its normal consistency, Shrick took this as a sign that it was safe for him to get out. He started to hack at the spongy material, then stopped. He went back to the body of Wesel. Just once he whispered her name, and ran his hands over the stiff, silent form in a last caress.

He did not return.

And when, at last, the dim light of the Place-of-Meeting broke through she was buried deep in the debris that he had thrown behind him as he worked.

The air tasted good after the many times breathed atmosphere of the cave. For a few heartbeats Shrick was dizzy with the abrupt increase of pressure, for much of the air in his prison had escaped before the plug expanded to seal the entrance. It is probable that had it not been for the air liberated from the burst cells of the insulation he would long since have asphyxiated.

But this he was not to know—and if he had known it would not have worried him overmuch. He was alive, and Wesel and all the People were dead. When the mist cleared from in front of his eyes he could see them, their bodies twisted in the tortuous attitudes of their last agony, mute evidence of the awful powers of the Giants.

And now that he saw them he did not feel the overwhelming sorrow that he knew he should have done. He felt instead a kind of anger. By their refusal to heed his warning they had robbed him of his kingdom. None now could dispute his mastery of the Outside—but with no subjects, willing or unwilling, the vast territory under his sway was worthless.

With Wesel alive it would have been different.

What was it that she had said—? . . . *and the cave of Long-Fur the spear maker* . . .

He could hear her voice as she said it . . . *and the cave of Long-Fur the spear maker.*

Perhaps— But there was only one way to make sure.

He found the cave, saw that its entrance had been walled up. He felt a wild upsurge of hope. Frantically, with tooth and claw, he tore at the insulation. The fine blade that he had won from the Inside gleamed dully not a dozen handsbreadths from where he was working, but such was his blind, unreasoning haste that he ignored the tool that would have made his task immeasurably shorter. At last the entrance was cleared. A feeble cry greeted the influx of air and light. For a while Shrick could not see who was within, and then could have screamed in his disappointment.

For here were no tough fighting males, no sturdy, fertile females, but two hands or so of weakly squirming infants. Their mothers must have realized, barely in time, that he and Wesel had been right, that there was only one way to ward off the choking death. Themselves they had not been able to save.

But they will grow up, Shrick told himelf. *It won't be long before they are able to carry a spear for the Lord of the Outside, before the females are able to bear his children.*

Conquering his repugnance, he dragged them out. There was

a hand of female infants, all living, and a hand of males. Three of these were dead. But here, he knew, was the nucleus of the army with which he would re-establish his rule over the world, Inside as well as Outside.

But first, they had to be fed.

He saw, now, his fine blade, and seizing it he began to cut up the three lifeless male children. The scent of their blood made him realize that he was hungry. But it was not until the children, now quieted, were all munching happily that he cut a portion for himself.

When he had finished it he felt much better.

It was some time before Shrick resumed his visits to the Inside. He had the pitiful remnant of his people to nurse to maturity and, besides, there was no need to make raids upon the Giants' stocks of food. They themselves had provided him with sustenance beyond his powers of reckoning. He knew, too, that it would be unwise to let his enemies know that there had been any survivors from the cataclysm that they had launched. The fact that he had survived the choking death did not mean that it was the only weapon that the Giants had at their disposal.

But as time went on he felt an intense longing to watch once more the strange life beyond the Barrier. Now that he had killed a Giant he felt a strange sense of kinship with the monstrous beings. He thought of the Thin-One, Loud-Voice, Bare-Head and the Little Giant almost as old friends. At times he even caught himself regretting that he must kill them all. But he knew that in this lay the only hope for the survival of himself and his people.

And then, at last, he was satisfied that he could leave the children to fend for themselves. Even should he fail to return from the Inside they would manage. No-Toes, the eldest of the female children, had already proved to be a capable nurse.

And so he roamed once more the maze of caves and tunnels just outside the Barrier. Through his doorways and peepholes he spied upon the bright, fascinating life of the Inner World. From the Cave-of-Thunders—though how it had come by its name none of the People has ever known—to the Place-of-Little-Lights he ranged. Many feedings passed, but he was not obliged to return to his own food store. For the corpses of the People were everywhere. True, they were beginning to stink a little, but like all his race Shrick was never a fastidious eater.

And he watched the Giants going about the strange, ordered routine of their lives. Often he was tempted to show himself, to shout defiance. But this action had to remain in the realm of wish-fulfillment dreams—he knew full well that it would bring sure and speedy calamity.

And then, at last, came the opportunity for which he had been waiting. He had been in the Place-of-Little-Lights, watching the Little Giant going about his mysterious, absorbing business. He had wished that he could understand its purport, that he could ask the Little Giant in his own tongue what it was that he was doing. For, since the death of Wesel, there had been none with whom a communion of mind was possible. He sighed, so loudly that the Giant must have heard.

He started uneasily and looked up from his work. Hastily Shrick withdrew into his tunnel. For many heartbeats he remained there, occasionally peeping out. But the other was still alert, must have known in some way that he was not alone. And so, eventually, Shrick had retired rather than risk incurring the potent wrath of the Giants once more.

His random retreat brought him to a doorway but rarely used. On the other side of it was a huge cavern in which there was nothing of real interest or value. In it, as a rule, at least one of the Giants would be sleeping, and others would be engaged in one of their incomprehensible pastimes.

This time there was no deep rumble of conversation, no movement whatsoever. Shrick's keen ears could distinguish the breathing of three different sleepers. The Thin-One was there, his respiration, like himself, had a meager quality. Loud-Voice was loud even in sleep. And Bare-Head, the chief of the Giants, breathed with a quiet authority.

And the Little Giant who, alone of all his people, was alert and awake was in the Place-of-Little-Lights.

Shrick knew that it was now or never. Any attempt to deal with the Giants singly must surely bring the great, hot light foretold by Three-Eyes. Now, with any luck at all, he could deal with the three sleepers and then lay in wait for the Little Giant. Unsuspecting, unprepared, he could be dealt with as easily as had Fat-Belly.

And yet—he did not want to do it.

It wasn't fear; it was that indefinable sense of kinship, the knowledge that, in spite of gross physical disparities, the Giants and the People were as one. For the history of Man, although Shrick was not to know this, is but the history of the fire-making, tool-using animal.

Then he forced himself to remember Wesel, and Big-Ears, and the mass slaughter of almost all his race. He remembered Three-Eyes' words—*but this I can tell you, the People are doomed. Noth-*

*ing you or they can do will save them. But you will kill those who
will kill us, and that is good.*

But you will kill those who will like us—

But if I kill all the Giants before they kill us, he thought, then
the world, all the world, will belong to the People . . .

And still he hung back.

It was not until the Thin-One, who must have been in the
throes of a bad dream, murmured and stirred in his sleep that
Shrick came out of his doorway. The keen blade with which he
had slain Fat-Belly was grasped in both his hands. He launched
himself towards the uneasy sleeper. His weapon sliced down once
only—how often had he rehearsed this in his imagination!—and
for the Thin-One the dream was over.

The smell of fresh blood, as always, excited him. It took him all
of his will power to restrain himself from hacking and slashing
at the dead Giant. But he promised himself that this would come
later. And he jumped from the body of the Thin-One to where
Loud-Voice was snoring noisily.

The abrupt cessation of that all too familiar sound must have
awakened Bare-Head. Shrick saw him shift and stir, saw his hands
go out to loosen the bonds that held him to his sleeping place.
And when the Giant Killer, his feet scrabbling for a hold, landed
on his chest he was ready. And he was shouting in a great Voice,
so that Shrick knew that it was only a matter of heartbeats before
the Little Giant came to his assistance.

Fat-Belly had been taken off guard, the Thin-One and Loud-
Voice had been killed in their sleep. But here was no easy victory
for the Giant Killer.

For a time it looked as though the chief of the Giants would
win. After a little he ceased his shouting and fought with grim,
silent desperation. Once one of his great hands caught Shrick in a
bone-crushing grip, and it seemed as though the battle was over.
Shrick could feel the blood pounding in his head, his eyeballs
almost popping out of their sockets. It took him every ounce of
resolution he possessed to keep from dropping his blade and
scratching frenziedly at the other's wrist with ineffectual hands.

Something gave—it was his ribs—and in the fleeting instant of
relaxed pressure he was able to twist, to turn and slash at the monstrous, hairy wrist. The warm blood spurted and the Giant cried
aloud. Again and again Shrick plied his blade, until it became
plain that the Giant would not be able to use that hand again.

He was single-handed now against an opponent as yet—insofar
as his limbs were concerned—uncrippled. True, every movement

of the upper part of his body brought spears of pain lancing through Shrick's chest. But he could move, and smite—and slay.

For Bare-Head weakened as the blood flowed from his wounds. No longer was he able to ward off the attacks on his face and neck. Yet he fought, as his race had always fought, to his dying breath. His enemy would have given no quarter—this much was obvious —but he could have sought refuge with the Little Giant in the Place-of-Little-Lights.

Towards the end he started shouting again.

And as he died, the Little Giant came into the cave.

It was sheer, blind luck that saved the Giant Killer from speedy death at the intruder's hands. Had the Little Giant known of the pitifully small forces arrayed against him it would have gone hard with Shrick. But No-Toes, left with her charges, had grown bored with the Place-of-Meeting. She had heard Shrick talk of the wonders of the Inside; and now, she thought, was her chance to see them for herself.

Followed by her charges she wandered aimlessly along the tunnels just outside the Barrier. She did not know the location of the doors to the Inside, and the view through the occasional peepholes was very circumscribed.

Then she came upon the doorway which Shrick had left open when he made his attack on the sleeping Giants. Bright light streamed through the aperture—light brighter than any No-Toes had seen before in her short life. Like a beacon it lured her on.

She did not hesitate when she came to the opening. Unlike her parents, she had not been brought up to regard the Giants with superstitious awe. Shrick was the only adult she could remember having known—and he, although he had talked of the Giants, had boasted of having slain one in single combat. He had said, also, that he would, at some time or other, kill all the Giants.

In spite of her lack of age and experience, No-Toes was no fool. Woman-like, already she had evaluated Shrick. Much of his talk she discounted as idle bragging, but she had never seen any reason to disbelieve his stories of the deaths of Big-Tusk, Sterret, Tekka, Fat-Belly—and all the myriads of the People who had perished with them.

So it was that—foolhardy in her ignorance—she sailed through the doorway. Behind her came the other children, squealing in their excitement. Even if the Little Giant had not at first seen them he could not have failed to hear the shrill tumult of their irruption.

There was only one interpretation that he could put upon the evidence of his eyes. The plan to suffocate the People had failed. They had sallied out from their caves and tunnels to the massacre of his fellow Giants—and now fresh reinforcements were arriving to deal with him.

He turned and fled.

Shrick rallied his strength, made a flying leap from the monstrous carcass of Bare-Head. But in mid flight a hard, polished surface interposed itself between him and the fleeing Giant. Stunned, he hung against it for many heartbeats before he realized that it was a huge door which had shut in his face.

He knew that the Little Giant was not merely seeking refuge in flight—for where in the world could he hope to escape the wrath of the People? He had gone, perhaps, for arms of some kind. Or—and at the thought Shrick's blood congealed—he had gone to loose the final doom foretold by Three-Eyes. Now that his plans had begun to miscarry he remembered the prophecy in its entirety, was no longer able to ignore those parts that, in his arrogance, he had found displeasing.

And then No-Toes, her flight clumsy and inexpert in these—to her—strange, vast spaces was at his side.

"Are you hurt?" she gasped. "They are so big—and you fought them."

As she spoke, the world was filled with a deep humming sound. Shrick ignored the excited female. That noise could mean only one thing. The Little Giant was back in the Place-of-Little-Lights, was setting in motion vast, incomprehensible forces that would bring to pass the utter and irrevocable destruction of the People.

With his feet against the huge door he kicked off, sped rapidly down to the open doorway in the Barrier. He put out his hand to break the shock of his landing, screamed aloud as his impact sent a sickening wave of pain through his chest. He started to cough—and when he saw the bright blood that was welling from his mouth he was very frightened.

No-Toes was with him again. "You are hurt, you are bleeding. Can I—?"

"No!" He turned a snarling mask to her. "No! Leave me alone!"

"But where are you going?"

Shrick paused. Then: "I am going to save the world," he said slowly. He savored the effect of his words. They made him feel better, they made him bulk big in his own mind, bigger, perhaps, than the Giants. "I am going to save you all."

"But how—?"

This was too much for the Giant Killer. He screamed again,

but this time with anger. With the back of his hand he struck the young female across the face.

"Stay here!" he ordered.

And then he was gone along the tunnel.

The gyroscopes were still singing their quiet song of power when Shrick reached the Control Room. Strapped in his chair, the navigator was busy over his plotting machine. Outside the ports the stars wheeled by in orderly succession.

And Shrick was frightened.

He had never quite believed Wesel's garbled version of the nature of the world until now. But he could see, at last, that the ship was moving. The fantastic wonder of it all held him spellbound until a thin edge of intolerable radiance crept into view from behind the rim of one of the ports. The navigator touched something and, suddenly, screens of dark blue glass mitigated the glare. But it was still bright, too bright, and the edge became a rapidly widening oval and then, at last, a disk.

The humming of the gyroscope stopped.

Before the silence had time to register a fresh sound assailed Shrick's ears. It was the roar of the main drive.

A terrifying force seized him and slammed him down upon the deck. He felt his bones crack under the acceleration. True child of free fall as he was, all this held for him the terror of the supernatural. For a while he lay there, weakly squirming, whimpering a little. The navigator looked down at him and laughed. It was this sound more than anything else that stung Shrick to his last, supreme effort. He didn't want to move. He just wanted to lie there on the deck, slowly coughing his life away. But the Little Giant's derision tapped unsuspected reserves of strength, both moral and physical.

The navigator went back to his calculations, handling his instruments for the last time with a kind of desperate elation. He knew that the ship would never arrive at her destination, neither would her cargo of seed grain. But she would not—and this outweighed all other considerations—drift forever among the stars carrying within her hull the seeds of the destruction of Man and all his works.

He knew that—had he not taken this way out—he must have slept at last, and then death at the hands of the mutants would inevitably have been his portion. And with the mutants in full charge anything might happen.

The road he had taken was the best.

Unnoticed, inch by inch Shrick edged his way along the deck. Now, he could stretch his free hand and touch the Giant's foot.

In the other he still held his blade, to which he had clung as the one thing sure and certain in this suddenly crazy world.

Then he had a grip on the artificial skin covering the Giant's leg. He started to climb, although every movement was unadulterated agony. He did not see the other raise his hand to his mouth, swallow the little pellet that he held therein.

So it was that when, at long last, he reached the soft, smooth throat of the Giant, the Giant was dead.

It was a very fast poison.

For a while he clung there. He should have felt elation at the death of the last of his enemies but—instead—he felt cheated. There was so much that he wanted to know, so much that only the Giants could have told him. Besides—it was his blade that should have won the final victory. He knew that, somewhere, the Little Giant was still laughing at him.

Through the blue-screened ports blazed the sun. Even at this distance, even with the intervening filters, its power and heat were all too evident. And aft the motors still roared, and would roar until the last ounce of fuel had been fed into the hungry main drive.

Shrick clung to the dead man's neck, looked long and longingly at the glittering instruments, the shining switches and levers, whose purpose he would never understand, whose inertia would have defeated any attempt of his fast ebbing strength to move them. He looked at the flaming doom ahead, and knew that this was what had been foretold.

Had the metaphor existed in his language, he would have told himelf that he and the few surviving People were caught like rats in a trap.

But even the Giants would not have used that phrase in its metaphorical sense.

For that is all that the People were—rats in a trap.

Vintage Season /
by LAWRENCE O'DONNELL

*Everybody seemed to want the old house during May—and seemed
willing to pay fantastic prices for the privilege. Strange tourists they
were, too. The Café Society of another time.*

Three people came up the walk to the old mansion just at dawn
on a perfect May morning. Oliver Wilson in his pyjamas watched
them from an upper window through a haze of conflicting emotions, resentment predominant. He didn't want them there.

They were foreigners. He knew only that much about them.
They had the curious name of Sancisco, and their first names,
scrawled in loops on the lease, appeared to be Omerie, Kleph
and Klia, though it was impossible as he looked down upon them
to sort them out by signature. He hadn't even been sure whether
they would be men or women, and he had expected something a
little less cosmopolitan.

Oliver's heart sank a little as he watched them follow the taxi
driver up the walk. He had hoped for less self-assurance in his
unwelcome tenants, because he meant to force them out of the
house if he could. It didn't look very promising from here.

The man went first. He was tall and dark, and he wore his
clothes and carried his body with that peculiar arrogant assurance that comes from perfect confidence in every phase of one's
being. The two women were laughing as they followed him. Their
voices were light and sweet, and their faces were beautiful, each
in its own exotic way, but the first thing Oliver thought of when
he looked at them was, Expensive!

It was not only that patina of perfection that seemed to dwell
in every line of their incredibly flawless garments. There are degrees of wealth beyond which wealth itself ceases to have significance. Oliver had seen before, on rare occasions, something like
this assurance that the earth turning beneath their well-shod feet
turned only to their whim.

It puzzled him a little in this case, because he had the feeling
as the three came up the walk that the beautiful clothing they
wore so confidently was not clothing they were accustomed to.

There was a curious air of condescension in the way they moved. Like women in costume. They minced a little on their delicate high heels, held out an arm to stare at the cut of a sleeve, twisted now and then inside their garments as if the clothing sat strangely on them, as if they were accustomed to something entirely different.

And there was an elegance about the way the garments fitted them which even to Oliver looked strikingly unusual. Only an actress on the screen, who can stop time and the film to adjust every disarrayed fold so that she looks perpetually perfect, might appear thus elegantly clad. But let these women move as they liked, and each fold of their clothing followed perfectly with the movement and fell perfectly into place again. One might almost suspect the garments were not cut of ordinary cloth, or that they were cut according to some unknown, subtle scheme, with many artful hidden seams placed by a tailor incredibly skilled at his trade.

They seemed excited. They talked in high, clear, very sweet voices, looking up at the perfect blue and transparent sky in which dawn was still frankly pink. They looked at the trees on the lawn, the leaves translucently green with an under colour of golden newness, the edges crimped from constriction in the recent bud.

Happily and with excitement in their voices they called to the man, and when he answered his own voice blended so perfectly in cadence with theirs that it sounded like three people singing together. Their voices, like their clothing, seemed to have an elegance far beyond the ordinary, to be under a control such as Oliver Wilson had never dreamed of before this morning.

The taxi driver brought up the luggage, which was of a beautiful pale stuff that did not look quite like leather, and had curves in it so subtle it seemed square until you saw how two or three pieces of it fitted together when carried, into a perfectly balanced block. It was scuffed, as if from much use. And though there was a great deal of it, the taxi man did not seem to find his burden heavy. Oliver saw him look down at it now and then and heft the weight incredulously.

One of the women had very black hair and skin like cream, and the smoke-blue eyes heavy-lidded with the weight of her lashes. It was the other woman Oliver's gaze followed as she came up the walk. Her hair was a clear, pale red, and her face had a softness that he thought would be like velvet to touch. She was tanned to a warm amber darker than her hair.

Just as they reached the porch steps the fair woman lifted her head and looked up. She gazed straight into Oliver's eyes and he saw that hers were very blue, and just a little amused, as if she had known he was there all along. Also they were frankly admiring.

Feeling a bit dizzy, Oliver hurried back to his room to dress.

"We are here on a vacation," the dark man said, accepting the keys. "We will not wish to be disturbed, as I made clear in our correspondence. You have engaged a cook and housemaid for us, I understand? We will expect you to move your own belongings out of the house, then, and——"

"Wait," Oliver said uncomfortably. "Something's come up. I——" He hesitated, not sure just how to present it. These were such increasingly odd people. Even their speech was odd. They spoke so distinctly, not slurring any of the words into contractions. English seemed as familiar to them as a native tongue, but they all spoke as trained singers sing, with perfect breath control and voice placement.

And there was a coldness in the man's voice, as if some gulf lay between him and Oliver, so deep no feeling of human contact could bridge it.

"I wonder," Oliver said, "if I could find you better living quarters somewhere else in town. There's a place across the street that——"

The dark woman said, "Oh, no!" in a lightly horrified voice, and all three of them laughed. It was cool, distant laughter that did not include Oliver.

The dark man said, "We chose this house carefully, Mr. Wilson. We would not be interested in living anywhere else."

Oliver said desperately, "I don't see why. It isn't even a modern house. I have two others in much better condition. Even across the street you'd have a fine view of the city. Here there isn't anything. The other houses cut off the view, and——"

"We engaged rooms here, Mr. Wilson," the man said with finality. "We expect to use them. Now will you make arrangements to leave as soon as possible."

Oliver said, "No," and looked stubborn. "That isn't in the lease. You can live here until next month, since you paid for it, but you can't put me out. I'm staying."

The man opened his mouth to say something. He looked coldly at Oliver and closed it again. The feeling of aloofness was chill between them. There was a moment's silence. Then the man said, "Very well. Be kind enough to stay out of our way."

It was a little odd that he didn't inquire into Oliver's motives.

Oliver was not yet sure enough of the man to explain. He couldn't very well say, "Since the lease was signed, I've been offered three times what the house is worth if I'll sell it before the end of May." He couldn't say, "I want the money, and I'm going to use my own nuisance-value to annoy you until you're willing to move out." After all, there seemed no reason why they shouldn't. After seeing them, there seemed doubly no reason, for it was clear they must be accustomed to surroundings infinitely better than this time-worn old house.

It was very strange, the value this house had so suddenly acquired. There was no reason at all why two groups of semi-anonymous people should be so eager to possess it for the month of May.

In silence Oliver showed his tenants upstairs to the three big bedrooms across the front of the house. He was intensely conscious of the red-haired woman and the way she watched him with a sort of obviously covert interest, quite warmly, and with a curious undertone to her interest that he could not quite place. It was familiar, but elusive. He thought how pleasant it would be to talk to her alone, if only to try to capture that elusive attitude and put a name to it.

Afterwards he went down to the telephone and called his fiancée.

Sue's voice squeaked a little with excitement over the wire.

"Oliver, so early? Why, it's hardly six yet. Did you tell them what I said? Are they going to go?"

"Can't tell yet. I doubt it. After all, Sue, I did take their money, you know."

"Oliver, they've got to go! You've got to do something!"

"I'm trying, Sue. But I don't like it."

"Well, there isn't any reason why they shouldn't stay somewhere else. And we're going to need that money. You'll just have to think of something, Oliver."

Oliver met his own worried eyes in the mirror above the telephone and scowled at himself. His straw-coloured hair was tangled and there was a shining stubble on his pleasant, tanned face. He was sorry the red-haired woman had first seen him in his untidy condition. Then his conscience smote him at the sound of Sue's determined voice and he said:

"I'll try, darling. I'll try. But I did take their money."

They had, in fact, paid a great deal of money, considerably more than the rooms were worth even in that year of high prices and high wages. The country was just moving into one of those fabulous eras which are later referred to as the Gay Forties or the Golden Sixties—a pleasant period of national euphoria. It was a stimulating time to be alive—while it lasted.

"All right," Oliver said resignedly. "I'll do my best."

But he was conscious, as the next few days went by, that he was not doing his best. There were several reasons for that. From the beginning the idea of making himself a nuisance to his tenants had been Sue's, not Oliver's. And if Oliver had been a little determined the whole project would never have got under way. Reason was on Sue's side, but——

For one thing, the tenants were so fascinating. All they said and did had a queer sort of inversion to it, as if a mirror had been held up to ordinary living and in the reflection showed strange variations from the norm. Their minds worked on a different basic premise, Oliver thought, from his own. They seemed to derive covert amusement from the most unamusing things; they patronized, they were aloof with a quality of cold detachment which did not prevent them from laughing inexplicably far too often for Oliver's comfort.

He saw them occasionally, on their way to and from their rooms. They were polite and distant, not he suspected, from anger at his presence but from sheer indifference.

Most of the day they spent out of the house. The perfect May weather held unbroken and they seemed to give themselves up wholeheartedly to admiration of it, entirely confident that the warm, pale-gold sunshine and the scented air would not be interrupted by rain or cold. They were so sure of it that Oliver felt uneasy.

They took only one meal a day in the house, a late dinner. And their reactions to the meal were unpredictable. Laughter greeted some of the dishes, and a sort of delicate disgust others. No one would touch the salad, for instance. And the fish seemed to cause a wave of queer embarrassment around the table.

They dressed elaborately for each dinner. The man—his name was Omerie—looked extremely handsome in his dinner clothes, but he seemed a little sulky and Oliver twice heard the women laughing because he had to wear black. Oliver entertained a sudden vision, for no reason, of the man in garments as bright and subtly cut as the women's, and it seemed somehow very right for him. He wore even the dark clothing with a certain flamboyance, as if cloth-of-gold would be more normal for him.

When they were in the house at other mealtimes, they ate in their rooms. They must have brought a great deal of food with them, from whatever mysterious place they had come. Oliver wondered with increasing curiosity where it might be. Delicious odours drifted into the hall sometimes, at odd hours, from their closed doors. Oliver could not identify them, but almost always they smelled irresistible. A few times the food smell was rather shockingly unpleasant, almost nauseating. It takes a connoisseur, Oliver reflected, to appreciate the decadent. And these people, most certainly, were connoisseurs.

Why they lived so contentedly in this huge ramshackle old house was a question that disturbed his dreams at night. Or why they refused to move. He caught some fascinating glimpses into their rooms, which appeared to have been changed almost completely by additions he could not have defined very clearly from the brief sights he had of them. The feeling of luxury which his first glance at them had evoked was confirmed by the richness of the hangings they had apparently brought with them, the half-glimpsed ornaments, the pictures on the walls, even the whiffs of exotic perfume that floated from half-open doors.

He saw the women go by him in the halls, moving softly through the brown dimness in their gowns so uncannily perfect in fit, so lushly rich, so glowingly coloured they seemed unreal. That poise born of confidence in the subservience of the world gave them an imperious aloofness, but more than once Oliver, meeting the blue gaze of the woman with the red hair and the soft, tanned skin, thought he saw quickened interest. She smiled at him in the dimness and went by in a haze of fragrance and a halo of incredible richness, and the warmth of the smile lingered after she had gone.

He knew she did not mean this aloofness to last between them. From the very first he was sure of that. When the time came she would make the opportunity to be alone with him. The thought was confusing and tremendously exciting. There was nothing he could do but wait, knowing she would see him when it suited her.

On the third day he lunched with Sue in a little downtown restaurant overlooking the great sweep of the metropolis across the river far below. Sue had shining brown curls and brown eyes, and her chin was a bit more prominent than is strictly accordant with beauty. From childhood Sue had known what she wanted and how to get it, and it seemed to Oliver just now that she had never wanted anything quite so much as the sale of this house.

"It's such a marvellous offer for the old mausoleum," she said, breaking into a roll with a gesture of violence. "We'll never have a chance like that again, and prices are so high we'll need the money to start housekeeping. Surely you can do *something,* Oliver!"

"I'm trying," Oliver assured her uncomfortably.

"Have you heard anything more from that madwoman who wants to buy it?"

Oliver shook his head. "Her attorney phoned again yesterday. Nothing new. I wonder who she is."

"I don't think even the attorney knows. All this mystery—I don't like it, Oliver. Even those Sancisco people——What did they do today?"

Oliver laughed. "They spent about an hour this morning telephoning movie theatres in the city, checking up on a lot of third-rate films they want to see parts of."

"Parts of? But why?"

"I don't know. I think . . . oh, nothing. More coffee?"

The trouble was, he thought he did know. It was too unlikely a guess to tell Sue about, and without familiarity with the Sancisco oddities she would only think Oliver was losing his mind. But he had from their talk, a definite impression that there was an actor in bit parts in all these films whose performances they mentioned with something very near to awe. They referred to him as Golconda, which didn't appear to be his name, so that Oliver had no way of guessing which obscure bit player it was they admired so deeply. Golconda might have been the name of a character he had once played—and with superlative skill, judging by the comments of the Sanciscos—but to Oliver it meant nothing at all.

"They do funny things," he said, stirring his coffee reflectively. "Yesterday Omerie—that's the man—came in with a book of poems published about five years ago, and all of them handled it like a first edition of Shakespeare. I never even heard of the author, but he seems to be a tin god in their country, wherever that is."

"You still don't know? Haven't they even dropped any hints?"

"We don't do much talking," Oliver reminded her with some irony.

"I know, but—— Oh, well I guess it doesn't matter. Go on, what else do they do?"

"Well, this morning they were going to spend studying 'Golconda' and his great art, and this afternoon I think they're taking a trip up the river to some sort of shrine I never heard of. It isn't very far, wherever it is, because I know they're coming back for dinner. Some great man's birthplace, I think—they promised to take home souvenirs of the place if they could get any. They're typical tourists, all right—if I could only figure out what's behind the whole thing. It doesn't make sense."

"Nothing about that house makes sense any more. I do wish——"

She went on in a petulant voice, but Oliver ceased suddenly to hear her, because just outside the door, walking with imperial elegance on her high heels, a familiar figure passed. He did not see her face, but he thought he would know that poise, that richness of line and motion, anywhere on earth.

"Excuse me a minute," he muttered to Sue, and was out of his chair before she could speak. He made the door in half a dozen long strides, and the beautifully elegant passerby was only a few steps away when he got there. Then, with the words he had meant to speak already half uttered, he fell silent and stood there staring.

It was not the red-haired woman. It was not her dark companion. It was a stranger. He watched, speechless, while the lovely, imperious creature moved on through the crowd and vanished, moving with familiar poise and assurance and an equally familiar strangeness as if the beautiful and exquisitely fitted garments she wore were an exotic costume to her, as they had always seemed to the Sancisco women. Every other woman on the street looked untidy and ill at ease beside her. Walking like a queen, she melted into the crowd and was gone.

She came from *their* country, Oliver told himself dizzily. So someone else nearby had mysterious tenants in this month of perfect May weather. Someone else was puzzling in vain today over the strangeness of the people from the nameless land.

In silence he went back to Sue.

The door stood invitingly ajar in the brown dimness of the upper hall. Oliver's steps slowed as he drew near it, and his heart began to quicken correspondingly. It was the red-haired woman's room, and he thought the door was not open by accident. Her name, he knew now, was Kleph.

The door creaked a little on its hinges and from within a very sweet voice said lazily, "Won't you come in?"

The room looked very different indeed. The big bed had been pushed back against the wall, and a cover thrown over it that brushed the floor all around looked like soft-haired fur except that it was pale blue-green and sparkled as if every hair were tipped with invisible crystals. Three books lay open on the fur, and a very curious-looking magazine with faintly luminous printing and a page of pictures that at first glance appeared three-dimensional.

Also a tiny porcelain pipe encrusted with porcelain flowers, and a thin wisp of smoke floating from the bowl.

Above the bed a broad picture hung, framing a square of blue water so real Oliver had to look twice to be sure it was not rippling gently from left to right. From the ceiling swung a crystal globe on a glass cord. It turned gently, the light from the windows making curved rectangles in its sides.

Under the centre window a sort of chaise-longue stood which Oliver had not seen before. He could only assume it was at least partly pneumatic and had been brought in the luggage. There was a very rich-looking quilted cloth covering and hiding it, embossed all over in shining metallic patterns.

Kleph moved slowly from the door and sank upon the chaise-longue with a little sigh of content. The couch accommodated itself to her body with what looked like delightful comfort. Kleph wriggled a little and then smiled up at Oliver.

"Do come on in. Sit over there, where you can see out the window. I love your beautiful spring weather. You know, there never was a May like it in civilized times." She said that quite seriously, her blue eyes on Oliver's, and there was a hint of patronage in her voice, as if the weather had been arranged especially for her.

Oliver started across the room and then paused and looked down in amazement at the floor, which felt unstable. He had not noticed before that the carpet was pure white, unspotted, and sank about an inch under the pressure of the feet. He saw then that Kleph's feet were bare, or almost bare. She wore something like gossamer buskins of filmy net, fitting her feet exactly. The bare soles were pink as if they had been rouged, and the nails had a liquid gleam like tiny mirrors. He moved closer, and was not as surprised as he should have been to see that they really were tiny mirrors, painted with some lacquer that gave them reflecting surfaces.

"Do sit down," Kleph said again, waving a white-sleeved arm towards a chair by the window. She wore a garment that looked like short, soft down, loosely cut but following perfectly every motion she made. And there was something curiously different about her very shape today. When Oliver saw her in street clothes, she had the square-shouldered, slim-flanked figure that all women strove for, but here in the lounging robe she looked— well, different. There was an almost swan-like slope to her shoulders today, a roundness and softness to her body that looked unfamiliar and very appealing.

"Will you have some tea?" Kleph asked, and smiled charmingly.

A low table beside her held a tray and several small covered cups, lovely things with an inner glow like rose quartz, the colour shining deeply as if from within layer upon layer of translucence. She took up one of the cups—there were no saucers—and offered it to Oliver.

It felt fragile and thin as paper in his hand. He could not see the contents because of the cup's cover, which seemed to be one with the cup itself and left only a thin open crescent at the rim. Steam rose from the opening.

Kleph took up a cup of her own and tilted it to her lips, smiling at Oliver over the rim. She was very beautiful. The pale red hair lay in shining loops against her head and the corona of curls like a halo above her forehead might have been pressed down like a wreath. Every hair kept order as perfectly as if it had been painted on, though the breeze from the window stirred now and then among the softly shining strands.

Oliver tried the tea. Its flavour was exquisite, very hot, and the taste that lingered upon his tongue was like the scent of flowers. It was an extremely feminine drink. He sipped again, surprised to find how much he liked it.

The scent of flowers seemed to increase as he drank, swirling through his head like smoke. After the third sip there was a faint buzzing in his ears. The bees among the flowers, perhaps, he thought incoherently—and sipped again.

Kleph watched him, smiling.

"The others will be out all afternoon," she told Oliver comfortably. "I thought it would give us a pleasant time to be acquainted."

Oliver was rather horrified to hear himself saying, "What makes you talk like that?" He had had no idea of asking the question; something seemed to have loosened his control over his own tongue.

Kleph's smile deepened. She tipped the cup to her lips and there was indulgence in her voice when she said, "What do you mean 'like that'?"

He waved his hand vaguely, noting with some surprise that at a glance it seemed to have six or seven fingers as it moved past his face.

"I don't know—precision, I guess. Why don't you say 'don't', for instance?"

"In our country we are trained to speak with precision," Kleph explained. "Just as we are trained to move and dress and think with precision. Any slovenliness is trained out of us in childhood. With you, of course——" She was polite. "With you, this does not happen to be a national fetish. With us, we have time for the amenities. We like them."

Her voice had grown sweeter and sweeter as she spoke, until by now it was almost indistinguishable from the sweetness of the flower-scent in Oliver's head, and the delicate flavour of the tea.

"What country do you come from?" he asked, and tilted the cup again to drink, mildly surprised to notice that it seemed inexhaustible.

Kleph's smile was definitely patronizing this time. It didn't irritate him. Nothing could irritate him just now. The whole room swam in a beautiful rosy glow as fragrant as the flowers.

"We must not speak of that, Mr. Wilson."

"But—" Oliver paused. After all, it was, of course, none of his business. "This is a vacation?" he asked vaguely.

"Call it a pilgrimage, perhaps."

"Pilgrimage?" Oliver was so interested that for an instant his mind came back into sharp focus. "To—what?"

"I should not have said that, Mr. Wilson. Please forget it. Do you like the tea?"

"Very much."

"You will have guessed by now that it is not only tea, but an euphoriac."

Oliver stared. "Euphoriac?"

Kleph made a descriptive circle in the air with one graceful hand, and laughed. "You do not feel the effects yet? Surely you do?"

"I feel," Oliver said, "the way I'd feel after four whiskies."

Kleph shuddered delicately. "We get our euphoria less painfully. And without the after-effects your barbarous alcohol used to have." She bit her lip. "Sorry. I must be euphoric myself to speak so freely. Please forgive me. Shall we have some music?"

Kleph leaned backward on the chaise-longue and reached towards the wall beside her. The sleeve, falling away from her round tanned arm, left bare the inside of the wrist, and Oliver was startled to see there a long, rosy streak of fading scar. His inhibitions had dissolved in the fumes of the fragrant tea; he caught his breath and leaned forward to stare.

Kleph shook the sleeve back over the scar with a quick gesture. Colour came into her face beneath the softly tinted tan and she would not meet Oliver's eyes. A queer shame seemed to have fallen upon her.

Oliver said tactlessly, "What is it? What's the matter?"

Still she would not look at him. Much later he understood that shame and knew she had reason for it. Now he listened blankly as she said:

"Nothing . . . nothing at all. A . . . an inoculation. All of us . . . oh, never mind. Listen to the music."

This time she reached out with the other arm. She touched nothing, but when she had held her hand near the wall a sound breathed through the room. It was the sound of water, the sighing of waves receding upon long, sloped beaches. Oliver followed Kleph's gaze towards the picture of the blue water above the bed.

The waves there were moving. More than that, the point of vision moved. Slowly the seascape drifted past, moving with the waves, following them towards shore. Oliver watched, half-hypnotized by a motion that seemed at the time quite acceptable and not in the least surprising.

The waves lifted and broke in creaming foam and ran seething up a sandy beach. Then through the sound of the water music began to breathe, and through the water itself a man's face dawned in the frame, smiling intimately into the room. He held an oddly archaic musical instrument, lute-shaped, its body striped light and dark like a melon and its long neck bent back over his shoulder. He was singing, and Oliver felt mildly astonished at the song. It was very familiar and very odd indeed. He groped through the unfamiliar rhythms and found at last a thread to catch the tune by —it was "Make-Believe" from "Showboat," but certainly a showboat that had never steamed up the Mississippi.

"What's he doing to it?" he demanded after a few moments of outraged listening. "I never heard anything like it!"

Kleph laughed and stretched out her arm again. Enigmatically she said: "We call it kyling. Never mind. How do you like this?"

It was a comedian, a man in semi-clown make-up, his eyes exaggerated so that they seemed to cover half his face. He stood by a broad glass pillar before a dark curtain and sang a gay, staccato song interspersed with patter that sounded impromptu, and all the while his left hand did an intricate, musical tattoo of the nailtips on the glass of the column. He strolled around and around it as he sang. The rhythms of his fingernails blended with the song and swung widely away into patterns of their own, and blended again without a break.

It was confusing to follow. The song made even less sense than the monologue, which had something to do with a lost slipper and was full of allusions which made Kleph smile, but were utterly unintelligible to Oliver. The man had a dry, brittle style that was not very amusing, though Kleph seemed fascinated. Oliver was interested to see in him an extension and a variation of that extreme smooth confidence which marked all three of the Sanciscos. Clearly a racial trait, he thought.

Other performances followed, some of them fragmentary as if lifted out of a completer version. One he knew. The obvious, stirring melody struck his recognition before the figures—marching men against a haze, a great banner rolling backward above them in the smoke, foreground figures striding gigantically and shouting in rhythm, "Forward, forward the lily banners go!"

The music was tinny, the images blurred and poorly coloured, but there was a gusto about the performance that caught at Oliver's imagination. He stared, remembering the old film from long ago. Dennis King and a ragged chorus, singing "The Song of the Vagabonds" from—was it "Vagabond King"?

"A very old one," Kleph said apologetically. "But I like it."

The steam of the intoxicating tea swirled between Oliver and the picture. Music swelled and sank through the room and the fragrant fumes and his own euphoric brain. Nothing seemed strange. He had discovered how to drink the tea. Like nitrous oxide, the effect was not cumulative. When you reached a peak of euphoria, you could not increase the peak. It was best to wait for a slight dip in the effect of the stimulant before taking more.

Otherwise it had most of the effects of alcohol—everything after a while dissolved into a delightful fog through which all he saw was uniformly enchanting and partook of the qualities of a dream. He questioned nothing. Afterwards he was not certain how much of it he really had dreamed.

There was the dancing doll, for instance. He remembered it quite clearly, in sharp focus—a tiny, slender woman with a long-nosed, dark-eyed face and a pointed chin. She moved delicately across the white rug—knee-high, exquisite. Her features were as mobile as her body, and she danced lightly, with resounding strokes of her toes, each echoing like a bell. It was a formalized sort of dance, and she sang breathlessly in accompaniment, making amusing little grimaces. Certainly it was a portrait-doll, animated to mimic the original perfectly in voice and motion. Afterwards, Oliver knew he must have dreamed it.

What else happened he was quite unable to remember later. He knew Kleph had said some curious things, but they all made sense at the time, and afterwards he couldn't remember a word. He knew he had been offered little glittering candies in a transparent dish, and that some of them had been delicious and one or two so bitter his tongue still curled the next day when he recalled them, and one—Kleph sucked luxuriantly on the same kind —of a taste that was actively nauseating.

As for Kleph herself—he was frantically uncertain the next day what had really happened. He thought he could remember the softness of her white-downed arms clasped at the back of his neck, while she laughed up at him and exhaled into his face the flowery fragrance of the tea. But beyond that he was totally unable to recall anything for a while.

There was a brief interlude later, before the oblivion of sleep. He was almost sure he remembered a moment when the other two Sanciscos stood looking down at him, the man scowling, the smoky-eyed woman smiling a derisive smile.

The man said, from a vast distance, "Kleph, you know this is against every rule——" His voice began in a thin hum and soared in fantastic flight beyond the range of hearing. Oliver thought he remembered the dark woman's laughter, thin and distant too, and the hum of her voice like bees in flight.

"Kleph, Kleph, you silly little fool, can we never trust you out of sight?"

Kleph's voice then said something that seemed to make no sense. "What does it matter, *here?*"

The man answered in that buzzing, faraway hum. "The matter of giving your bond before you leave, not to interfere. You know you signed the rules——"

Kleph's voice, nearer and more intelligible: "But here the difference is . . . it does not matter *here!* You both know that. How could it matter?"

Oliver felt the downy brush of her sleeve against his cheek, but he saw nothing except the slow, smoke-like ebb and flow of darkness past his eyes. He heard the voices wrangle musically from far away, and he heard them cease.

When he woke the next morning, alone in his own room, he woke with the memory of Kleph's eyes upon him very sorrowfully, her lovely tanned face looking down on him with the red hair falling fragrantly on each side of it and sadness and compassion in her eyes. He thought he had probably dreamed that. There was no reason why anyone should look at him with such sadness.

Sue telephoned that day.

"Oliver, the people who want to buy the house are here. That madwoman and her husband. Shall I bring them over?"

Oliver's mind all day had been hazy with the vague, bewildering memories of yesterday. Kleph's face kept floating before him, blotting out the room. He said, "What? I . . . oh, well, bring them if you want to. I don't see what good it'll do."

"Oliver, what's wrong with you? We agreed we needed the money, didn't we? I don't see how you can think of passing up such a wonderful bargain without even a struggle. We could get married and buy our own house right away, and you know we'll never get such an offer again for that old trash-heap. Wake up, Oliver!"

Oliver made an effort. "I know, Sue—I know. But——"

"Oliver, you've got to think of something!" Her voice was imperious.

He knew she was right. Kleph or no Kleph, the bargain shouldn't be ignored if there was any way at all of getting the tenants out. He wondered again what made the place so suddenly priceless to so many people. And what the last week in May had to do with the value of the house.

A sudden sharp curiosity pierced even the vagueness of his mind today. May's last week was so important that the whole sale of the house stood or fell upon occupancy by then. Why? *Why?*

"What's going to happen next week?" he asked rhetorically of the telephone. "Why can't they wait till these people leave? I'd knock a couple of thousand off the price if they'd——"

"You would not, Oliver Wilson! I can buy all our refrigeration units with that extra money. You'll just have to work out some way to give possession by next week, and that's that. You hear me?"

"Keep your shirt on," Oliver said practically. "I'm only human, but I'll try."

"I'm bringing the people over right away," Sue told him. "While the Sanciscos are still out. Now you put your mind to work and think of something, Oliver." She paused, and her voice was reflective when she spoke again. "They're . . . awfully odd people, darling."

"Odd?"

"You'll see."

It was an elderly woman and a very young man who trailed Sue up the walk. Oliver knew immediately what had struck Sue about them. He was somehow not at all surprised to see that both wore their clothing with the familiar air of elegant self-consciousness he had come to know so well. They, too, looked around them at the beautiful, sunny afternoon with conscious enjoyment and an air of faint condescension. He knew before he heard them speak how musical their voices would be and how meticulously they would pronounce each word.

There was no doubt about it. The people of Kleph's mysterious country were arriving here in force—for something. For the last week of May? He shrugged mentally; there was no way of guessing—yet. One thing only was sure: all of them must come from that nameless land where people controlled their voices like singers and their garments like actors who could stop the reel of time itself to adjust every disordered fold.

The elderly woman took full charge of the conversation from the start. They stood together on the rickety, unpainted porch, and Sue had no chance even for introductions.

"Young man, I am Madame Hollia. This is my husband." Her voice had an underrunning current of harshness, which was perhaps age. And her face looked almost corseted, the loose flesh coerced into something like firmness by some invisible method Oliver could not guess at. The make-up was so skilful he could not be certain it was make-up at all, but he had a definite feeling that she was much older than she looked. It would have taken a lifetime of command to put so much authority into the harsh, deep, musically controlled voice.

The young man said nothing. He was very handsome. His type, apparently, was one that does not change much no matter in what culture or country it may occur. He wore beautifully tailored garments and carried in one gloved hand a box of red leather, about the size and shape of a book.

Madame Hollia went on: "I understand your problem about the house. You wish to sell to me, but are legally bound by your lease with Omerie and his friends. Is that right?"

Oliver nodded. "But——"

"Let me finish. If Omerie can be forced to vacate before next week, you will accept our offer. Right? Very well. Hara!" She nodded to the young man beside her. He jumped to instant attention, bowed slightly, said, "Yes, Hollia," and slipped a gloved hand into his coat.

Madame Hollia took the little object offered on his palm, her gesture as she reached for it almost imperial, as if royal robes swept from her outstretched arm.

"Here," she said, "is something that may help us. My dear——" She held it out to Sue—"if you can hide this somewhere about the house, I believe your unwelcome tenants will not trouble you much longer."

Sue took the thing curiously. It looked like a tiny silver box, no more than an inch square, indented at the top and with no line to show it could be opened.

"Wait a minute," Oliver broke in uneasily. "What is it?"

"Nothing that will harm anyone, I assure you."

"Then what——"

Madame Hollia's imperious gesture at one sweep silenced him and commanded Sue forward. "Go on, my dear. Hurry, before Omerie comes back. I can assure you there is no danger to anyone."

Oliver broke in determinedly. "Madame Hollia, I'll have to know what your plans are. I——"

"Oh, Oliver, please!" Sue's fingers closed over the silver cube. "Don't worry about it. I'm sure Madame Hollia knows best. Don't you *want* to get those people out?"

"Of course I do. But I don't want the house blown up or——"

Madame Hollia's deep laughter was indulgent. "Nothing so crude, I promise you, Mr. Wilson. Remember, we want the house! Hurry, my dear."

Sue nodded and slipped hastily past Oliver into the hall. Outnumbered, he subsided uneasily. The young man, Hara, tapped a negligent foot and admired the sunlight as they waited. It was an afternoon as perfect as all of May had been, translucent gold, balmy with an edge of chill lingering in the air to point up a perfect contrast with the summer to come. Hara looked around him confidently, like a man paying just tribute to a stage-set provided wholly for himself. He even glanced up at a drone from above and followed the course of a big transcontinental plane half dissolved in golden haze high in the sun. "Quaint," he murmured in a gratified voice.

Sue came back and slipped her hand through Oliver's arm, squeezing excitedly. "There," she said. "How long will it take, Madame Hollia?"

"That will depend, my dear. Not very long. Now, Mr. Wilson, one word with you. You live here also, I understand? For your own comfort, take my advice and——"

Somewhere within the house a door slammed and a clear high voice rang wordlessly up a rippling scale. Then there was the sound of feet on the stairs, and single line of song, *"Come hider, love, to me——"*

Hara started, almost dropping the red leather box he held.

"Kleph!" he said in a whisper. "Or Klia. I know they both just came on from Canterbury. But I thought——"

"Huh." Madame Hollia's features composed themselves into an imperious blank. She breathed triumphantly through her nose, drew back upon herself and turned an imposing façade to the door.

Kleph wore the same softly downy robe Oliver had seen before, except that today it was not white, but a pale, clear blue that gave her tan an apricot flush. She was smiling.

"Why, Hollia!" Her tone was at its most musical. "I thought I recognized voices from home. How nice to see you. No one knew you were coming to the——" She broke off and glanced at Oliver and then away again. "Hara, too," she said. "What a pleasant surprise."

Sue said flatly, "When did *you* get back?"

Kleph smiled at her. "You must be the little Miss Johnson. Why, I did not go out at all. I was tired of sightseeing. I have been napping in my room."

Sue drew in her breath in something that just escaped being a disbelieving sniff. A look flashed between the two women, and for an instant held—and that instant was timeless. It was an extraordinary pause in which a great deal of wordless interplay took place in the space of a second.

Oliver saw the quality of Kleph's smile at Sue, that same look of quiet confidence he had noticed so often about all of these strange people. He saw Sue's quick inventory of the other woman, and he saw how Sue squared her shoulders and stood up straight, smoothing down her summer frock over her flat hips so that for an instant she stood posed consciously, looking down on Kleph. It was deliberate. Bewildered, he glanced again at Kleph.

Kleph's shoulders sloped softly, her robe was belted to a tiny waist and hung in deep folds over frankly rounded hips. Sue's was the fashionable figure—but Sue was the first to surrender.

Kleph's smile did not falter. But in the silence there was an abrupt reversal of values, based on no more than the measureless quality of Kleph's confidence in herself, the quiet, assured smile. It was suddenly made very clear that fashion is not a constant. Kleph's curious, out-of-mode curves without warning became the norm, and Sue was a queer, angular, half-masculine creature beside her.

Oliver had no idea how it was done. Somehow the authority passed in a breath from one woman to the other. Beauty is almost wholly a matter of fashion; what is beautiful today would have been grotesque a couple of generations ago and will be grotesque a hundred years ahead. It will be worse than grotesque; it will be outmoded and therefore faintly ridiculous.

Sue was that. Kleph had only to exert her authority to make it clear to everyone on the porch. Kleph was a beauty, suddenly and very convincingly, beautiful in the accepted mode, and Sue was amusingly old-fashioned, an anachronism in her lithe, square-shouldered slimness. She did not belong. She was grotesque among these strangely immaculate people.

Sue's collapse was complete. But pride sustained her, and bewilderment. Probably she never did grasp entirely what was wrong. She gave Kleph one glance of burning resentment and when her eyes came back to Oliver there was suspicion in them, and mistrust.

Looking backward later, Oliver thought that in that moment, for the first time clearly, he began to suspect the truth. But he had no time to ponder it, for after the brief instant of enmity the three people from—elsewhere—began to speak all at once, as if in a belated attempt to cover something they did not want noticed.

Kleph said, "This beautiful weather——" and Madame Hollia said "So fortunate to have this house——" and Hara, holding up the red leather box, said loudest of all, "Cenbe sent you this, Kleph. His latest."

Kleph put out both hands for it eagerly, the eiderdown sleeves falling back from her rounded arms. Oliver had a quick glimpse of that mysterious scar before the sleeve fell back, and it seemed to him that there was the faintest trace of a similar scar vanishing into Hara's cuff as he let his own arm drop.

"Cenbe!" Kleph cried, her voice high and sweet and delighted. "How wonderful! What period?"

"From November 1664," Hara said. "London, of course, though I think there may be some counterpoint from the 1347 November. He hasn't finished—of course." He glanced almost nervously at Oliver and Sue. "A wonderful example," he said quickly. "Marvellous. If you have the taste for it, of course."

Madame Hollia shuddered with ponderous delicacy. "That man!" she said. "Fascinating, of course—a great man. But—so *advanced!*"

"It takes a connoisseur to appreciate Cenbe's work fully," Kleph said in a slightly tart voice, "We all admit that."

"Oh yes, we all bow to Cenbe," Hollia conceded. "I confess the man terrifies me a little, my dear. Do we expect him to join us?"

"I suppose so," Kleph said. "If his—work—is not yet finished, then of course. You know Cenbe's tastes."

Hollia and Hara laughed together. "I know when to look for him, then," Hollia said. She glanced at the staring Oliver and the subdued but angry Sue, and with a commanding effort brought the subject back into line.

"So fortunate, my dear Kleph, to have this house," she declared heavily. "I saw a tridimensional of it—afterwards—and it was still quite perfect. Such a fortunate coincidence. Would you consider

parting with your lease, for a consideration? Say, a coronation
seat at——"

"Nothing could buy us, Hollia," Kleph told her gaily, clasping
the red box to her bosom.

Hollia gave her a cool stare. "You may change your mind, my
dear Kleph," she said pontifically. "There is still time. You can always reach us through Mr. Wilson here. We have rooms up the
street in the Montgomery House—nothing like yours, of course, but
they will do. For us, they will do."

Oliver blinked. The Montgomery House was the most expensive
hotel in town. Compared to this collapsing old ruin, it was a palace. There was no understanding these people. Their values
seemed to have suffered a complete reversal.

Madame Hollia moved majestically towards the steps.

"Very pleasant to see you, my dear," she said over one well-
padded shoulder. "Enjoy your stay. My regards to Omerie and
Klia. Mr. Wilson——" she nodded towards the walk. "A word with
you."

Oliver followed her down towards the street. Madame Hollia
paused half-way there and touched his arm.

"One word of advice," she said huskily. "You say you sleep
here? Move out, young man. Move out before tonight."

Oliver was searching in a half-desultory fashion for the hiding
place Sue had found for the mysterious silver cube, when the first
sounds from above began to drift down the stairwell towards him.
Kleph had closed her door, but the house was old, and strange
qualities in the noise overhead seemed to seep through the wood-
work like an almost visible stain.

It was music, in a way. But much more than music. And it was a
terrible sound, the sounds of calamity and of all human reaction
to calamity, everything from hysteria to heartbreak, from irra-
tional joy to rationalized acceptance.

The calamity was—single. The music did not attempt to correlate all human sorrows; it focused sharply upon one and followed
the ramifications out and out. Oliver recognized these basics to
the sounds in a very brief moment. They were essentials, and
they seemed to beat into his brain with the first strains of the
music which was so much more than music.

But when he lifted his head to listen he lost all grasp upon the
meaning of the noise and it was sheer medley and confusion. To
think of it was to blur it hopelessly in the mind, and he could not
recapture that first instant of unreasoning acceptance.

He went upstairs almost in a daze, hardly knowing what he was doing. He pushed Kleph's door open. He looked inside——

What he saw there he could not afterwards remember except in a blurring as vague as the blurred ideas the music roused in his brain. Half the room had vanished behind a mist, and the mist was a three-dimensional screen upon which were projected—— He had no words for them. He was not even sure if the projections were visual. The mist was spinning with motion and sound, but essentially it was neither sound nor motion that Oliver saw.

This was a work of art. Oliver knew no name for it. It transcended all art-forms he knew, blended them, and out of the blend produced subtleties his mind could not begin to grasp. Basically, this was the attempt of a master composer to correlate every essential aspect of a vast human experience into something that could be conveyed in a few moments to every sense at once.

The shifting visions on the screen were not pictures in themselves, but hints of pictures, subtly selected outlines that plucked at the mind and with one deft touch set whole chords ringing through the memory. Perhaps each beholder reacted differently, since it was in the eye and the mind of the beholder that the truth of the picture lay. No two would be aware of the same symphonic panorama, but each would see essentially the same terrible story unfold.

Every sense was touched by that deft and merciless genius. Colour and shape and motion flickered in the screen, hinting much, evoking unbearable memories deep in the mind; odours floated from the screen and touched the heart of the beholder more poignantly than anything visual could do. The skin scrawled sometimes as if to a tangible cold hand laid upon it. The tongue curled with remembered bitterness and remembered sweet.

It was outrageous. It violated the innermost privacies of a man's mind, called up secret things long ago walled off behind mental scar tissue, forced its terrible message upon the beholder relentlessly though the mind might threaten to crack beneath the stress of it.

And yet, in spite of all this vivid awareness, Oliver did not know what calamity the screen portrayed. That it was real, vast, overwhelmingly dreadful he could not doubt. That it had once happened was unmistakable. He caught flashing glimpses of human faces distorted with grief and disease and death—real faces, faces that had once lived and were seen now in the instant of dying. He saw men and women in rich clothing superimposed in panorama upon reeling thousands of ragged folk, great throngs of them swept past the sight in an instant, and he saw that death made no distinction among them.

He saw lovely women laugh and shake their curls, and the laughter shriek into hysteria and the hysteria into music. He saw one man's face, over and over—a long, dark saturnine face, deeply lined, sorrowful, the face of a powerful man wise in worldliness, urbane—and helpless. That face was for a while a recurring motif, always more tortured, more helpless than before.

The music broke off in the midst of a rising glide. The mist vanished and the room reappeared before him. The anguished dark face for an instant seemed to Oliver printed everywhere he looked, like after-vision on the eyelids. He knew that face. He had seen it before, not often, but he should know its name——

"Oliver, Oliver——" Kleph's sweet voice came out of a fog at him. He was leaning dizzily against the doorpost looking down into her eyes. She, too, had that dazed blankness he must show on his own face. The power of the dreadful symphony still held them both. But even in this confused moment Oliver saw that Kleph had been enjoying the experience.

He felt sickened to the depths of his mind, dizzy with sickness and revulsion because of the superimposing of human miseries he had just beheld. But Kleph—only appreciation showed upon her face. To her it had been magnificence, and magnificence only.

Irrelevantly Oliver remembered the nauseating candies she had enjoyed, the nauseating odours of strange food that drifted sometimes through the hall from her room.

What was it she had said downstairs a little while ago? Connoisseur, that was it. Only a connoisseur could appreciate work as—as *advanced*—as the work of someone called Cenbe.

A whiff of intoxicating sweetness curled past Oliver's face. Something cool and smooth was pressed into his hand.

"Oh, Oliver, I am so sorry," Kleph's voice murmured contritely. "Here, drink the euphoriac and you will feel better. Please drink!"

The familiar fragrance of the hot sweet tea was on his tongue before he knew he had complied. Its relaxing fumes floated up through his brain and in a moment or two the world felt stable around him again. The room was as it had always been. And Kleph——

Her eyes were very bright. Sympathy showed in them for him, but for herself she was still brimmed with the high elation of what she had just been experiencing.

"Come and sit down," she said gently, tugging at his arm. "I am so sorry—I should not have played that over, where you could hear it. I have no excuse, really. It was only that I forgot what the effect might be on one who had never heard Cenbe's symphonies before. I was so impatient to see what he had done with . . . with his new subject. I am so very sorry, Oliver!"

"What was it?" His voice sounded steadier than he had expected. The tea was responsible for that. He sipped again, glad of the consoling euphoria its fragrance brought.

"A . . . a composite interpretation of . . . oh, Oliver, you know I must not answer questions!"

"But——"

"No—drink your tea and forget what it was you saw. Think of other things. Here, we will have music—another kind of music, something gay——"

She reached for the wall beside the window, and as before, Oliver saw the broad framed picture of blue water above the bed ripple and grow pale. Through it another scene began to dawn like shapes rising beneath the surface of the sea.

He had a glimpse of a dark-curtained stage upon which a man in a tight dark tunic and hose moved with a restless, sidelong pace, his hands and face startlingly pale against the black about him. He limped; he had a crooked back and he spoke familiar lines. Oliver had seen John Barrymore once as the crook-backed Richard, and it seemed vaguely outrageous to him that any other actor should essay that difficult part. This one he had never seen before, but the man had a fascinatingly smooth manner and his interpretation of the Plantagenet king was quite new and something Shakespeare probably never dreamed of.

"No," Kleph said, "not this. Nothing gloomy." And she put out her hand again. The nameless new Richard faded and there was a swirl of changing pictures and changing voices, all blurred together, before the scene steadied upon a stageful of dancers in pastel ballet skirts, drifting effortlessly through some complicated pattern of motion. The music that went with it was light and effortless too. The room filled up with the clear, floating melody.

Oliver set down his cup. He felt much surer of himself now, and he thought the euphoriac had done all it could for him. He didn't want to blur again mentally. There were things he meant to learn about. Now. He considered how to begin.

Kleph was watching him. "That Hollia," she said suddenly. "She wants to buy the house?"

Oliver nodded. "She's offering a lot of money. Sue's going to be awfully disappointed if——" He hesitated. Perhaps, after all, Sue would not be disappointed. He remembered the little silver cube with the enigmatic function and he wondered if he should mention it to Kleph. But the euphoriac had not reached that level of his brain, and he remembered his duty to Sue and was silent.

Kleph shook her head, her eyes upon his warm with—was it sympathy?

"Believe me," she said, "you will not find that—important—after all. I promise you, Oliver."

He stared at her. "I wish you'd explain."

Kleph laughed on a note more sorrowful than amused. But it occurred to Oliver suddenly that there was no longer condescension in her voice. Imperceptibly that air of delicate amusement had vanished from her manner towards him. The cool detachment that still marked Omerie's attitude, and Klia's, was not in Kleph's any more. It was a subtlety he did not think she could assume. It had to come spontaneously or not at all. And for no reason he was willing to examine, it became suddenly very important to Oliver that Kleph should not condescend to him, that she should feel towards him as he felt towards her. He would not think of it.

He looked down at his cup, rose-quartz, exhaling a thin plume of steam from its crescent-slit opening. This time, he thought, maybe he could make the tea work for him. For he remembered how it loosened the tongue, and there was a great deal he needed to know. The idea that had come to him on the porch in the instant of silent rivalry between Kleph and Sue seemed not too fantastic to entertain. But some answer there must be.

Kleph herself gave him the opening.

"I must not take too much euphoriac this afternoon," she said, smiling at him over her pink cup. "It will make me drowsy, and we are going out this evening with friends."

"More friends?" Oliver asked. "From your country?"

Kleph nodded. "Very dear friends we have expected all this week."

"I wish you'd tell me," Oliver said bluntly, "where it is you come from. It isn't from here. Your culture is too different from ours— even your names——" He broke off as Kleph shook her head.

"I wish I could tell you. But that is against all the rules. It is even against the rules for me to be here talking to you now."

She made a helpless gesture. "You must not ask me, Oliver." She leaned back on the chaise-longue, which adjusted itself luxuriously to the motion, and smiled very sweetly at him. "We must not talk about things like that. Forget it, listen to the music, enjoy yourself if you can——" She closed her eyes and laid her head back against the cushions. Oliver saw the round tanned throat swell as she began to hum a tune. Eyes still closed, she sang again the words she had sung upon the stairs. *"Come hider, love, to me——"*

A memory clicked over suddenly in Oliver's mind. He had never heard the queer, lagging tune before, but he thought he knew the words. He remembered what Hollia's husband had said when he heard that line of song, and he leaned forward. She would not answer a direct question, but perhaps——

"Was the weather this warm in Canterbury?" he asked, and held his breath. Kleph hummed another line of the song and shook her head, eyes still closed.

"It was autumn there," she said. "But bright, wonderfully bright. Even their clothing, you know . . . everyone was singing that new song, and I can't get it out of my head." She sang another line, and the words were almost unintelligible—English, yet not an English Oliver could understand.

He stood up. "Wait," he said. "I want to find something. Back in a minute."

She opened her eyes and smiled mistily at him, still humming. He went downstairs as fast as he could—the stairway swayed a little, though his head was nearly clear now—and into the library. The book he wanted was old and battered, interlined with the pencilled notes of his college days. He did not remember very clearly where the passage he wanted was, but he thumbed fast through the columns and by sheer luck found it within a few minutes. Then he went back upstairs, feeling a strange emptiness in his stomach because of what he almost believed now.

"Kleph," he said firmly, "I know that song. I know the year it was new."

Her lids rose slowly; she looked at him through a mist of euphoriac. He was not sure she had understood. For a long moment she held him with her gaze. Then she put out one downy-sleeved arm and spread her tanned fingers towards him. She laughed deep in her throat.

"Come hider, love, to me," she said.

He crossed the room slowly, took her hand. The fingers closed warmly about his. She pulled him down so that he had to kneel beside her. Her other arm lifted. Again she laughed, very softly, and closed her eyes, lifting her face to his.

The kiss was warm and long. He caught something of her own euphoria from the fragrance of the tea breathed into his face. And he was startled at the end of the kiss, when the clasp of her arms loosened about his neck, to feel the sudden rush of her breath against his cheek. There were tears on her face, and the sound she made was a sob.

He held her off and looked down in amazement. She sobbed once more, caught a deep breath, and said, "Oh, Oliver, Oliver——" Then she shook her head and pulled free, turning away to hide her face. "I . . . I am sorry," she said unevenly. "Please forgive me. It does not matter . . . I *know* it does not matter . . . but——"

"What's wrong? What doesn't matter?"

"Nothing. Nothing . . . please forget it. Nothing at all." She got a handkerchief from the table and blew her nose, smiling at him with an effect of radiance through the tears.

Suddenly he was very angry. He had heard enough evasions and mystifying half-truths. He said roughly, "Do you think I'm crazy? I know enough now to——"

"Oliver, please!" She held up her own cup, steaming fragrantly. "Please, no more questions. Here, euphoria is what you need, Oliver. Euphoria, not answers."

"What year was it when you heard that song in Canterbury?" he demanded, pushing the cup aside.

She blinked at him, tears bright on her lashes. "Why . . . what year do you think?"

"I know," Oliver told her grimly. "I know the year that song was popular. I know you just came from Canterbury—Hollia's husband said so. It's May now, but it was autumn in Canterbury, and you just came from there, so lately the song you heard is still running through your head. Chaucer's Pardoner sang that song some time around the end of the fourteenth century. Did you see Chaucer, Kleph? What was it like in England that long ago?"

Kleph's eye fixed his for a silent moment. Then her shoulders drooped and her whole body went limp with resignation beneath the soft blue robe. "I am a fool," she said gently. "It must have been easy to trap me. You really believe—what you say?"

Oliver nodded.

She said in a low voice, "Few people do believe it. That is one of our maxims, when we travel. We are safe from much suspicion because people before The Travel began will not believe."

The emptiness in Oliver's stomach suddenly doubled in volume. For an instant the bottom dropped out of time itself and the universe was unsteady about him. He felt sick. He felt naked and helpless. There was a buzzing in his ears and the room dimmed before him.

He had not really believed—not until this instant. He had expected some rational explanation from her that would tidy all his wild half-thoughts and suspicions into something a man could accept as believable. Not this.

Kleph dabbed at her eyes with the pale-blue handkerchief and smiled tremulously.

"I know," she said. "It must be a terrible thing to accept. To have all your concepts turned upside down—— We know it from childhood, of course, but for you . . . here, Oliver. The euphoriac will make it easier."

He took the cup, the faint stain of her lip rouge still on the crescent opening. He drank, feeling the dizzy sweetness spiral through his head, and his brain turned a little in his skull as the volatile fragrance took effect. With that turning, focus shifted and all his values with it.

He began to feel better. The flesh settled on his bones again, and the warm clothing of temporal assurance settled upon his flesh, and he was no longer naked and in the vortex of unstable time.

"The story is very simple, really," Kleph said. "We—travel. Our own time is not terribly far ahead of yours. No. I must not say how far. But we still remember your songs and poets and some of your great actors. We are a people of much leisure, and we cultivate the art of enjoying ourselves.

"This is a tour we are making—a tour of a year's seasons. Vintage seasons. That autumn in Canterbury was the most magnificent autumn our researchers could discover anywhere. We rode in a pilgrimage to the shrine—it was a wonderful experience, though the clothing was a little hard to manage.

"Now this month of May is almost over—the loveliest May in recorded times. A perfect May in a wonderful period. You have no way of knowing what a good, gay period you live in, Oliver. The very feeling in the air of the cities—that wonderful national confidence and happiness—everything going as smoothly as a dream. There were other Mays with fine weather, but each of them had a war or a famine, or something else wrong." She hesitated, grimaced and went on rapidly. "In a few days we are to meet at a coronation in Rome," she said. "I think the year will be 800—Christmastime. We——"

"But why," Oliver interrupted, "did you insist on this house? Why do the others want to get it away from you?"

Kleph stared at him. He saw the tears rising again in small bright crescents that gathered above her lower lids. He saw the look of obstinacy that came upon her soft, tanned face. She shook her head.

"You must not ask me that." She held out the steaming cup. "Here, drink and forget what I have said. I can tell you no more. No more at all."

When he woke, for a little while he had no idea where he was. He did not remember leaving Kleph or coming to his own room. He didn't care, just then. For he woke to a sense of overwhelming terror.

The dark was full of it. His brain rocked on waves of fear and pain. He lay motionless, too frightened to stir, some atavistic memory warning him to lie quiet until he knew from which direction the danger threatened. Reasonless panic broke over him in a tidal flow; his head ached with its violence and the dark throbbed to the same rhythms.

A knock sounded at the door. Omerie's deep voice said, "Wilson! Wilson, are you awake?"

Oliver tried twice before he had breath to answer. "Y-yes—what is it?"

The knob rattled. Omerie's dim figure groped for the light switch and the room sprang into visibility. Omerie's face was drawn with strain, and he held one hand to his head as if it ached in rhythm with Oliver's.

It was in that moment, before Omerie spoke again, that Oliver remembered Hollia's warning. "Move out, young man—move out before tonight." Wildly he wondered what threatened them all in this dark house that throbbed with the rhythms of pure terror.

Omerie in an angry voice answered the unspoken question. "Someone has planted a subsonic in the house, Wilson. Kleph thinks you may know where it is."

"S-subsonic?"

"Call it a gadget," Omerie interpreted impatiently. "Probably a small metal box that——"

Oliver said, "Oh," in a tone that must have told Omerie everything.

"Where is it?" he demanded. "Quick. Let's get this over."

"I don't know." With an effort Oliver controlled the chattering of his teeth. "Y-you mean all this—all this is just from the little box?"

"Of course. Now tell me how to find it before we all go crazy."

Oliver got shakily out of bed, groping for his robe with nerveless hands. "I s-suppose she hid it somewhere downstairs," he said. "S-she wasn't gone long."

Omerie got the story out of him in a few brief questions. He clicked his teeth in exasperation when Oliver had finished it.

"That stupid Hollia——"

"Omerie!" Kleph's plaintive voice wailed from the hall. "Please hurry, Omerie! This is too much to stand! Oh, Omerie, please!"

Oliver stood up abruptly. Then a redoubled wave of the inexplicable pain seemed to explode in his skull at the motion, and he clutched the bedpost and reeled.

"Go find the thing yourself," he heard himself saying dizzily. "I can't even walk——"

Omerie's own temper was drawn wire-tight by the pressure in the room. He seized Oliver's shoulder and shook him, saying in a tight voice, "You let it in—now help us get it out, or——"

"It's a gadget out of your world, not mine!" Oliver said furiously.

And then it seemed to him there was a sudden coldness and silence in the room. Even the pain and the senseless terror paused for a moment. Omerie's pale, cold eyes fixed upon Oliver a stare so chill he could almost feel the ice in it.

"What do you know about our—world?" Omerie demanded.

Oliver did not speak a word. He did not need to; his face must have betrayed what he knew. He was beyond concealment in the stress of night-time terror he still could not understand.

Omerie bared his white teeth and said three perfectly unintelligible words. Then he stepped to the door and snapped, "Kleph!"

Oliver could see the two women huddled together in the hall, shaking violently with involuntary waves of that strange, synthetic terror. Klia, in a luminous green gown, was rigid with control, but Kleph made no effort whatever at repression. Her downy robe had turned soft gold tonight; she shivered in it and the tears ran down her face unchecked.

"Kleph," Omerie said in a dangerous voice, "you were euphoric again yesterday?"

Kleph darted a scared glance at Oliver and nodded guiltily.

"You talked too much." It was a complete indictment in one sentence. "You know the rules, Kleph. You will not be allowed to travel again if anyone reports this to the authorities."

Kleph's lovely creamy face creased suddenly into impenitent dimples.

"I know it was wrong. I am very sorry—but you will not stop me if Cenbe says no."

Klia flung out her arms in a gesture of helpless anger. Omerie shrugged. "In this case, as it happens, no great harm is done," he said, giving Oliver an unfathomable glance. "But it might have been serious. Next time perhaps it will be. I must have a talk with Cenbe."

"We must find the subsonic first of all," Klia reminded them, shivering. "If Kleph is afraid to help, she can go out for a while. I confess I am very sick of Kleph's company just now."

"We could give up the house!" Kleph cried wildly. "Let Hollia have it! How can you stand this long enough to hunt——"

"Give up the house?" Klia echoed. "You must be mad! With all our invitations out?"

"There will be no need for that," Omerie said. "We can find it if we all hunt. You feel able to help?" He looked at Oliver.

With an effort Oliver controlled his own senseless panic as the waves of it swept through the room. "Yes," he said. "But what about me? What are you going to do?"

"That should be obvious," Omerie said, his pale eyes in the dark face regarding Oliver impassively. "Keep you in the house until we go. We can certainly do no less. You understand that. And there is no reason for us to do more, as it happens. Silence is all we promised when we signed our travel papers."

"But——" Oliver groped for the fallacy in that reasoning. It was no use. He could not think clearly. Panic surged insanely through his mind from the very air around him. "All right," he said. "Let's hunt."

It was dawn before they found the box, tucked inside the ripped seam of a sofa cushion. Omerie took it upstairs without a word. Five minutes later the pressure in the air abruptly dropped and peace fell blissfully upon the house.

"They will try again," Omerie said to Oliver at the door of the back bedroom. "We must watch for that. As for you, I must see that you remain in the house until Friday. For your own comfort, I advise you to let me know if Hollia offers any further tricks. I confess I am not quite sure how to enforce your staying indoors. I could use methods that would make you very uncomfortable. I would prefer to accept your word on it."

Oliver hesitated. The relaxing of pressure upon his brain had left him exhausted and stupid, and he was not at all sure what to say.

Omerie went on after a moment. "It was partly our fault for not ensuring that we had the house to ourselves," he said. "Living here with us, you could scarcely help suspecting. Shall we say that in return for your promise, I reimburse you in part for losing the sale price on this house?"

Oliver thought that over. It would pacify Sue a little. And it meant only two days indoors. Besides, what good would escaping do? What could he say to outsiders that would not lead him straight to a padded cell?

"All right," he said wearily. "I promise."

By Friday morning there was still no sign from Hollia. Sue telephoned at noon. Oliver knew the crackle of her voice over the wire when Kleph took the call. Even the crackle sounded hysterical; Sue saw her bargain slipping hopelessly through her grasping little fingers.

Kleph's voice was soothing. "I am sorry," she said many times, in the intervals when the voice paused. "I am truly sorry. Believe me, you will find it does not matter. I know. I am sorry—"

She turned from the phone at last. "The girl says Hollia has given up," she told the others.

"Not Hollia," Klia said firmly.

Omerie shrugged. "We have very little time left. If she intends anything more, it will be tonight. We must watch for it."

"Oh, not tonight!" Kleph's voice was horrified. "Not even Hollia would do that."

"Hollia, my dear, in her own way is quite as unscrupulous as you are," Omerie told her with a smile.

"But—would she spoil things for us just because she can't be here?"

"What do you think?" Klia demanded.

Oliver ceased to listen. There was no making sense out of their talk, but he knew that by tonight whatever the secret was must surely come into the open at last. He was willing to wait and see.

For two days excitement had been building up in the house and the three who shared it with him. Even the servants felt it and were nervous and unsure of themselves. Oliver had given up asking questions—it only embarrassed his tenants—and watched.

All the chairs in the house were collected in the three front bedrooms. The furniture was rearranged to make room for them, and dozens of covered cups had been set out on trays. Oliver recognized Kleph's rose-quartz set among the rest. No steam rose from the thin crescent-openings, but the cups were full. Oliver lifted one and felt a heavy liquid move within it, like something half-solid, sluggishly.

Guests were obviously expected, but the regular dinner hour of nine came and went, and no one had yet arrived. Dinner was finished; the servants went home. The Sanciscos went to their rooms to dress, amid a feeling of mounting tension.

Oliver stepped out on the porch after dinner, trying in vain to guess what it was that had wrought such a pitch of expectancy in the house. There was a quarter moon swimming in haze on the horizon, but the stars which had made every night of May thus far a dazzling translucency were very dim tonight. Clouds had begun to gather at sundown, and the undimmed weather of the whole month seemed ready to break at last.

Behind Oliver the door opened a little, and closed. He caught Kleph's fragrance before he turned, and a faint whiff of the fragrance of the euphoriac she was much too fond of drinking. She came to his side and slipped a hand into his, looking up into his face in the darkness.

"Oliver," she said very softly. "Promise me one thing. Promise me not to leave the house tonight."

"I've already promised that," he said a little irritably.

"I know. But tonight—I have a very particular reason for wanting you indoors tonight." She leaned her head against his shoulder for a moment, and despite himself his irritation softened. He had not seen Kleph alone since that last night of her revelations; he supposed he never would be alone with her again for more than a few minutes at a time. But he knew he would not forget those two bewildering evenings. He knew too, now, that she was very weak and foolish—but she was still Kleph and he had held her in his arms, and was not likely ever to forget it.

"You might be—hurt—if you went out tonight," she was saying in a muffled voice. "I know it will not matter, in the end, but—remember you promised, Oliver."

She was gone again, and the door had closed behind her, before he could voice the futile questions in his mind.

The guests began to arrive just before midnight. From the head of the stairs Oliver saw them coming in by twos and threes, and was astonished at how many of these people from the future must have gathered here in the past weeks. He could see quite clearly now how they differed from the norm in his own period. Their physical elegance was what one noticed first—perfect grooming, meticulous manners, meticulously controlled voices. But because they were all idle, all, in a way, sensation-hunters, there was a certain shrillness underlying their voices, especially when heard all together. Petulance and self-indulgence showed beneath the good manners. And tonight, an all-pervasive excitement.

By one o'clock everyone had gathered in the front rooms. The teacups had begun to steam, apparently of themselves, around midnight, and the house was full of the faint, thin fragrance that induced a sort of euphoria all through the rooms, breathed in with the perfume of the tea.

It made Oliver feel light and drowsy. He was determined to

sit up as long as the others did, but he must have dozed off in his own room, by the window, an unopened book in his lap.

For when it happened he was not sure for a few minutes whether or not it was a dream.

The vast, incredible crash was louder than sound. He felt the whole house shake under him, felt rather than heard the timbers grind upon one another like broken bones, while he was still in the borderland of sleep. When he woke fully he was on the floor among the shattered fragments of the window.

How long or short a time he had lain there he did not know. The world was still stunned with that tremendous noise, or his ears still deaf from it, for there was no sound anywhere.

He was half-way down the hall towards the front rooms when sound began to return from outside. It was a low, indescribable rumble at first, prickled with countless tiny distant screams. Oliver's eardrums ached from the terrible impact of the vast unheard noise, but the numbness was wearing off and he heard before he saw it the first voices of the stricken city.

The door to Kleph's room resisted him for a moment. The house had settled a little from the violence of the—the explosion? —and the frame was out of line. When he got the door open he could only stand blinking stupidly into the darkness within. All the lights were out, but there was a breathless sort of whispering going on in many voices.

The chairs were drawn around the broad front windows so that everyone could see out; the air swam with the fragrance of euphoria. There was light enough here from outside for Oliver to see that a few onlookers still had their hands to their ears, but all were craning eagerly forward to see.

Through a dream-like haze Oliver saw the city spread out with impossible distinctness below the window. He knew quite well that a row of houses across the street blocked the view—yet he was looking over the city now, and he could see it in a limitless panorama from here to the horizon. The houses between had vanished.

On the far skyline fire was already a solid mass, painting the low clouds crimson. That sulphurous light reflecting back from the sky upon the city made clear the rows upon rows of flattened houses with flame beginning to lick up among them, and farther out the formless rubble of what had been houses a few minutes ago and was now nothing at all.

The city had begun to be vocal. The noise of the flames rose loudest, but you could hear a rumble of human voices like the beat of surf a long way off, and staccato noises of screaming made a sort of pattern that came and went continuously through the web of sound. Threading it in undulating waves the shrieks of sirens knit the web together into a terrible symphony that had, in its way, a strange, inhuman beauty.

Briefly through Oliver's stunned incredulity went the memory of that other symphony Kleph had played here one day, another catastrophe retold in terms of music and moving shapes.

He said hoarsely: "Kleph——"

The tableau by the window broke. Every head turned, and Oliver saw the faces of strangers staring at him, some few in embarrassment avoiding his eyes, but most seeking them out with that avid, inhuman curiosity which is common to a type in all crowds at accident scenes. But these people were here by design, audience at a vast disaster timed almost for their coming.

Kleph got up unsteadily, her velvet dinner gown tripping her as she rose. She set down a cup and swayed a little as she came towards the door, saying, "Oliver . . . Oliver——" in a sweet, uncertain voice. She was drunk, he saw, and wrought up by the catastrophe to a pitch of stimulation in which she was not very sure what she was doing.

Oliver heard himself saying in a thin voice not his own, "W-what was it, Kleph? What happened? What——" But *happened* seemed so inadequate a word for the incredible panorama below that he had to choke back hysterical laughter upon the struggling questions, and broke off entirely, trying to control the shaking that had seized his body.

Kleph made an unsteady stoop and seized a steaming cup. She came to him, swaying, holding it out—her panacea for all ills.

"Here, drink it, Oliver—we are all quite safe here, quite safe." She thrust the cup to his lips and he gulped automatically, grateful for the fumes that began their slow, coiling surcease in his brain with the first swallow.

"It was a meteor," Kleph was saying. "Quite a small meteor, really. We are perfectly safe here. This house was never touched."

Out of some cell of the unconscious Oliver heard himself saying incoherently, "Sue? Is Sue——" he could not finish.

Kleph thrust the cup at him again. "I think she may be safe—for a while. Please, Oliver—forget about all that and drink."

"But you *knew!*" Realization of that came belatedly to his stunned brain. "You could have given warning, or——"

"How could we change the past?" Kleph asked. "We knew—

but could we stop the meteor? Or warn the city? Before we come
we must give our word never to interfere——"

Their voices had risen imperceptibly to be audible above the
rising volume of sound from below. The city was roaring now,
with flames and cries and the crash of falling buildings. Light in
the room turned lurid and pulsed upon the walls and ceiling in
red light and redder dark.

Downstairs a door slammed. Someone laughed. It was high,
hoarse, angry laughter. Then from the crowd in the room someone gasped and there was a chorus of dismayed cries. Oliver tried
to focus upon the window and the terrible panorama beyond,
and found he could not.

It took several seconds of determined blinking to prove that
more than his own vision was at fault. Kleph whimpered softly
and moved against him. His arms closed about her automatically,
and he was grateful for the warm, solid flesh against him. This
much at least he could touch and be sure of, though everything
else that was happening might be a dream. Her perfume and the
heady perfume of the tea rose together in his head, and for an
instant, holding her in this embrace that must certainly be the
last time he ever held her, he did not care that something had
gone terribly wrong with the very air of the room.

It was blindness—not continuous, but a series of swift, widening ripples between which he could catch glimpses of the other
faces in the room, strained and astonished in the flickering light
from the city.

The ripples came faster. There was only a blink of sight between them now, and the blinks grew briefer and briefer, the
intervals of darkness more broad.

From downstairs the laughter rose again up the stairwell. Oliver thought he knew the voice. He opened his mouth to speak,
but a door nearby slammed open before he could find his
tongue, and Omerie shouted down the stairs.

"Hollia?" he roared above the roaring of the city. "Hollia, is
that you?"

She laughed again, triumphantly. "I warned you!" her hoarse,
harsh voice called. "Now come out in the street with the rest of
us if you want to see any more!"

"Hollia!" Omerie shouted desperately. "Stop this or——"

The laughter was derisive. "What will you do, Omerie? This
time I hid it too well—come down in the street if you want to
watch the rest."

There was angry silence in the house. Oliver could feel Kleph's quick, excited breathing light upon his cheek, feel the soft motions of her body in his arms. He tried consciously to make the moment last, stretch it out to infinity. Everything had happened too swiftly to impress very clearly on his mind anything except what he could touch and hold. He held her in an embrace made consciously light, though he wanted to clasp her in a tight, despairing grip, because he was sure this was the last embrace they would ever share.

The eye-straining blinks of light and blindness went on. From far away below the roar of the burning city rolled on, threaded together by the long, looped cadences of the sirens that linked all sounds into one.

Then in the bewildering dark another voice sounded from the hall downstairs. A man's voice, very deep, very melodious, saying:

"What is this? What are you doing here? Hollia—is that you?"

Oliver felt Kleph stiffen in his arms. She caught her breath, but she said nothing in the instant while heavy feet began to mount the stairs, coming up with a solid, confident tread that shook the old house to each step.

Then Kleph thrust herself hard out of Oliver's arms. He heard her high, sweet, excited voice crying, "Cenbe! Cenbe!" and she ran to meet the newcomer through the waves of dark and light that swept the shaken house.

Oliver staggered a little and felt a chair seat catching the back of his legs. He sank into it and lifted to his lips the cup he still held. Its steam was warm and moist in his face, though he could scarcely make out the shape of the rim.

He lifted it with both hands and drank.

When he opened his eyes it was quite dark in the room. Also it was silent except for a thin, melodious humming almost below the threshold of sound. Oliver struggled with the memory of a monstrous nightmare. He put it resolutely out of his mind and sat up, feeling an unfamiliar bed creak and sway under him.

This was Kleph's room. But no—Kleph's no longer. Her shining hangings were gone from the walls, her white resilient rug, her pictures. The room looked as it had looked before she came, except for one thing.

In the far corner was a table—a block of translucent stuff—out of which light poured softly. A man sat on a low stool before it, leaning forward, his heavy shoulders outlined against the glow.

He wore earphones and he was making quick, erratic notes upon a pad on his knee, swaying a little as if to the tune of unheard music.

The curtains were drawn, but from beyond them came a distant, muffled roaring that Oliver remembered from his nightmare. He put a hand to his face, aware of a feverish warmth and a dipping of the room before his eyes. His head ached, and there was a deep malaise in every limb and nerve.

As the bed creaked, the man in the corner turned, sliding the earphones down like a collar. He had a strong, sensitive face above a dark beard, trimmed short. Oliver had never seen him before, but he had that air Oliver knew so well by now, of remoteness which was the knowledge of time itself lying like a gulf between them.

When he spoke his deep voice was impersonally kind.

"You had too much euphoriac, Wilson," he said, aloofly sympathetic. "You slept a long while."

"How long?" Oliver's throat felt sticky when he spoke.

The man did not answer. Oliver shook his head experimentally. He said, "I thought Kleph said you don't get hangovers from——" Then another thought interrupted the first, and he said quickly, "Where is Kleph?" He looked confusedly towards the door.

"They should be in Rome by now. Watching Charlemagne's coronation at St. Peter's on Christmas Day a thousand years from here."

That was not a thought Oliver could grasp clearly. His aching brain sheered away from it; he found thinking at all was strangely difficult. Staring at the man, he traced an idea painfully to its conclusion.

"So they've gone on—but you stayed behind? Why? You . . . you're Cenbe? I heard your—symphonia, Kleph called it."

"You heard part of it. I have not finished yet. I needed—this." Cenbe inclined his head towards the curtains beyond which the subdued roaring still went on.

"You needed—the meteor?" The knowledge worked painfully through his dulled brain until it seemed to strike some area still untouched by the aching, an area still alive to implication. "The *meteor?* But——"

There was a power implicit in Cenbe's raised hand that seemed to push Oliver down upon the bed again. Cenbe said patiently, "The worst of it is past now, for a while. Forget if you can. That was days ago. I said you were asleep for some time. I let you rest. I knew this house would be safe—from the fire at least."

"Then—something more's to come?" Oliver only mumbled his

question. He was not sure he wanted an answer. He had been curious so long, and now that knowledge lay almost within reach, something about his brain seemed to refuse to listen. Perhaps this weariness, this feverish, dizzy feeling would pass as the effect of the euphoriac wore off.

Cenbe's voice ran on smoothly, soothingly, almost as if Cenbe too did not want him to think. It was easiest to lie here and listen.

"I am a composer," Cenbe was saying. "I happen to be interested in interpreting certain forms of disaster into my own terms. That is why I stayed on. The others were dilettantes. They came for the May weather and the spectacle. The aftermath—well why should they wait for that? As for myself—I suppose I am a connoisseur. I find the aftermath rather fascinating. And I need it. I need to study it at first hand, for my own purposes."

His eyes dwelt upon Oliver for an instant very keenly, like a physician's eyes, impersonal and observing. Absently he reached for his stylus and the note pad. And as he moved, Oliver saw a familiar mark on the underside of the thick, tanned wrist.

"Kleph had that scar, too," he heard himself whisper. "And the others."

Cenbe nodded. "Inoculation. It was necessary, under the circumstances. We did not want disease to spread in our own time-world."

"Disease?"

Cenbe shrugged. "You would not recognize the name."

"But, if you can inoculate against disease——" Oliver thrust himself up on an aching arm. He had a half-grasp upon a thought now which he did not want to let go. Effort seemed to make the ideas come more clearly through his mounting confusion. With enormous effort he went on.

"I'm getting it now," he said. "Wait. I've been trying to work this out. You can change history? You can! I know you can. Kleph said she had to promise not to interfere. You all had to promise. Does that mean you really could change your own past—our time?"

Cenbe laid down his pad again. He looked at Oliver thoughtfully, a dark, intent look under heavy brows. "Yes," he said. "Yes, the past can be changed, but not easily. And it changes the future, too, necessarily. The lines of probability are switched into new patterns—but it is extremely difficult, and it has never been allowed. The physio-temporal course tends to slide back to its norm, always. That is why it is so hard to force any alteration." He shrugged. "A theoretical science. We do not change history,

Wilson. If we changed our past, our present would be altered, too. And our time-world is entirely to our liking. There may be a few malcontents there, but they are not allowed the privilege of temporal travel."

Oliver spoke louder against the roaring from beyond the windows. "But you've got the power! Your could alter history, if you wanted to—wipe out all the pain and suffering and tragedy——"

"All of that passed away long ago," Cenbe said.

"Not—*now*! Not—*this*!"

Cenbe looked at him enigmatically for a while. Then—"This, too," he said.

And suddenly Oliver realized from across what distances Cenbe was watching him. A vast distance, as time is measured. Cenbe was a composer and a genius, and necessarily strongly empathic, but his psychic locus was very far away in time. The dying city outside, the whole world of *now* was not quite real to Cenbe, falling short of reality because of that basic variance in time. It was merely one of the building blocks that had gone to support the edifice on which Cenbe's culture stood in a misty, unknown, terrible future.

It seemed terrible to Oliver now. Even Kleph—all of them had been touched with a pettiness, the faculty that had enabled Hollia to concentrate on her malicious, small schemes to acquire a ringside seat while the meteor thundered in towards Earth's atmosphere. They were all dilettantes, Kleph and Omerie and the others. They toured time, but only as onlookers. Were they bored —sated—with their normal existence?

Not sated enough to wish change, basically. Their own time-world was a fulfilled womb, a perfection made manifest for their needs. They dared not change the past—they could not risk flawing their own present.

Revulsion shook him. Remembering the touch of Kleph's lips, he felt a sour sickness on his tongue. Alluring she had been: he knew that too well. But the aftermath——

There was something about this race from the future. He had felt it dimly at first, before Kleph's nearness had drowned caution and buffered his sensibilities. Time travelling purely as an escape mechanism seemed almost blasphemous. A race with such power——

Kleph—leaving him for the barbaric, splendid coronation at Rome a thousand years ago—*how had she seen him?* Not as a living, breathing man. He knew that, very certainly Kleph's race were spectators.

But he read more than casual interest in Cenbe's eyes now. There was an avidity there, a bright, fascinated probing. The man had replaced his earphones—he was different from the others. He was a connoisseur. After the vintage season came the aftermath—and Cenbe.

Cenbe watched and waited, light flickering softly in the translucent block before him, his fingers poised over the note pad. The ultimate connoisseur waited to savour the rarities that no non-gourmet could appreciate.

Those thin, distant rhythms of sound that was almost music began to be audible again above the noises of the distant fire. Listening, remembering. Oliver could very nearly catch the pattern of the symphonia as he had heard it, all intermingled with the flash of changing faces and the rank upon rank of the dying—

He lay back on the bed letting the room swirl away into the darkness behind his closed and aching lids. The ache was implicit in every cell of his body, almost a second ego taking possession and driving him out of himself, a strong, sure ego taking over as he himself let go.

Why, he wondered dully, should Kleph have lied? She had said there was no aftermath to the drink she had given him. No aftermath—and yet this painful possession was strong enough to edge him out of his own body.

Kleph had not lied. It was no aftermath to drink. He knew that —but the knowledge no longer touched his brain or his body. He lay still, giving them up to the power of the illness which was aftermath to something far stronger than the strongest drink. The illness that had no name—yet.

Cenbe's new symphonia was a crowning triumph. It had its première from Antares Hall, and the applause was an ovation. History itself, of course, was the artist—opening with the meteor that forecast the great plagues of the fourteenth century and closing with the climax Cenbe had caught on the threshold of modern times. But only Cenbe could have interpreted it with such subtle power.

Critics spoke of the masterly way in which he had chosen the face of the Stuart king as a recurrent motif against the montage of emotion and sound and movement. But there were other faces, fading through the great sweep of the composition, which helped to build up to the tremendous climax. One face in particular, one moment that the audience absorbed greedily. A moment in which one man's face loomed huge in the screen, every feature clear.

Cenbe had never caught an emotional crisis so effectively, the critics agreed. You could almost read the man's eyes.

After Cenbe had left, he lay motionless for a long while. He was thinking feverishly——

I've got to find some way to tell people. If I'd known in advance, maybe something could have been done. We'd have forced them to tell us how to change the probabilities. We could have evacuated the city.

If I could leave a message——

Maybe not for today's people. But later. They visit all through time. If they could be recognized and caught somewhere, some time, and made to change destiny——

It wasn't easy to stand up. The room kept tilting. But he managed it. He found pencil and paper and through the swaying of the shadows he wrote down what he could. Enough. Enough to warn, enough to save.

He put the sheets on the table, in plain sight, and weighted them down before he stumbled back to bed through closing darkness.

The house was dynamited six days later, part of the futile attempt to halt the relentless spread of the Blue Death.

1946

Placet Is a Crazy Place/

by FREDRIC BROWN

It wasn't that Placet itself was so crazy; it was just that the things Placet's gravitic situation did to human sensory organs was really remarkable. You could even solve impossible problems quite unintentionally—

Even when you're used to it, it gets you down sometimes. Like that morning—if you can call it a morning. Really it was night. But we go by Earth time on Placet because Placet time would be as screwy as everything else on that goofy planet. I mean, you'd have a six-hour day and then a two-hour night and then a fifteen-hour day and a one-hour night and—well, you just couldn't keep time on a planet that does a figure-eight orbit around two dissimilar suns, going like a bat out of hell around and between them, and the suns going around each other so fast and so comparatively close that Earth astronomers thought it was only one sun until the Blakeslee expedition landed here twenty years ago.

You see, the rotation of Placet isn't any even fraction of the period of its orbit and there's the Blakeslee Field in the middle between the suns—a field in which light rays slow down to a crawl and get left behind and—well——

If you've not read the Blakeslee reports on Placet, hold on to something while I tell you this:

Placet is the only known planet that can eclipse itself twice at the same time, run headlong into itself every forty hours, and then chase itself out of sight.

I don't blame you.

I didn't believe it either, and it scared me stiff the first time I stood on Placet and saw Placet coming head-on to run into us. And yet I'd read the Blakeslee reports and knew what was really happening, and why. It's rather like those early movies when the camera was set up in front of a train and the audience saw the locomotive heading right toward them and would feel an impulse to run even though they knew the locomotive wasn't really there.

But I started to say, like that morning. I was sitting at my desk, the top of which was covered with grass. My feet were—or seemed to be—resting on a sheet of rippling water. But it wasn't wet.

On top of the grass of my desk lay a pink flowerpot, into which, nose-first, stuck a bright green Saturnian lizard. That—reason and not my eyesight told me—was my pen and inkwell. Also an embroidered sampler that said, "God Bless Our Home" in neat cross-stitching. It actually was a message from Earth Centre which had just come in on the radiotype. I didn't know what it said because I'd come into my office after the B. F. effect had started. I didn't think it really said, "God Bless Our Home" because it seemed to. And just then I was mad, I was fed up, and I didn't care a holler what it actually did say.

You see—maybe I'd better explain—the Blakeslee Field effect occurs when Placet is in mid-position between Argyle I and Argyle II, the two suns it figure eights around. There's a scientific explanation of it, but it must be expressed in formulas, not in words. It boils down to this; Argyle I is terrene matter and Argyle II is contraterrene, or negative matter. Half-way between them— over a considerable stretch of territory—is a field in which light rays are slowed down, way down. They move at about the speed of sound. The result is that if something is moving faster than sound—as Placet itself does—you can still see it coming after it has passed you. It takes the visual image of Placet twenty-six hours to get through the field. By that time, Placet has rounded one of its suns and meets its own image on the way back. In midfield, there's an image coming and an image going, and it eclipses itself twice, occulting both suns at the same time. A little farther on, it runs into itself coming from the opposite direction— and scares you stiff if you're watching, even if you know it's not really happening.

Let me explain it this way before you get dizzy. Say an old-fashioned locomotive is coming toward you, only at a speed much faster than sound. A mile away, it whistles. It passes you and *then* you hear the whistle, coming from the point a mile back where the locomotive isn't any more. That's the auditory effect of an object travelling faster than sound; what I've just described is the visual effect of an object travelling—in a figure-eight orbit— faster than its own visual image.

That isn't the worst of it; you can stay indoors and avoid the eclipsing and the head-on collisions, but you can't avoid the physio-psychological effect of the Blakeslee Field.

And that, the physio-psychological effect, is something else again. The field does something to the optic nerve centres, or to the part of the brain to which the optic nerves connect, something similar to the effect of certain drugs. You have—you can't exactly call them hallucinations, because you don't ordinarily see things that aren't there, but you get an illusory picture of what *is* there.

I knew perfectly well that I was sitting at a desk the top of which was glass, and not grass; that the floor under my feet was ordinary plastiplate and not a sheet of rippling water; that the objects on my desk were not a pink flowerpot with a Saturnian lizard sticking in it, but an antique twentieth-century inkwell and pen—and that the "God Bless Our Home" sampler was a radiotype message on ordinary radiotype paper. I could verify any of those things by my sense of touch, which the Blakeslee Field doesn't affect.

You can close your eyes, of course, but you don't—because even at the height of the effect, your eyesight gives you the relative size and distance of things and if you stay in familiar territory your memory and your reason tell you what they are.

So when the door opened and a two-headed monster walked in, I knew it was Reagan. Reagan isn't a two-headed monster, but I could recognise the sound of his walk.

I said, "Yes, Reagan?"

The two-headed monster said, "Chief, the machine shop is wobbling. We may have to break the rule not to do any work in midperiod."

"Birds?" I asked.

Both of his heads nodded. "The underground part of those walls must be like sieves from the birds flying through 'em, and we'd better pour concrete quick. Do you think those new alloy reinforcing bars the *Ark*'ll bring will stop them?"

"Sure," I lied. Forgetting the field, I turned to look at the clock, but there was a funeral wreath of white lilies on the wall where the clock should have been. You can't tell time from a funeral wreath. I said, "I was hoping we wouldn't have to reinforce those walls till we had the bars to sink in them. The *Ark*'s about due; they're probably hovering outside right now waiting for us to come out of the field. You think we could wait till——"

There was a crash.

"Yeah, we can wait," Reagan said. "There went the machine shop, so there's no hurry at all."

"Nobody was in there?"

"Nope, but I'll make sure." He ran out.

That's what life on Placet is like. I'd had enough of it; I'd had too much of it. I made up my mind while Reagan was gone.

When he came back, he was a bright blue articulated skeleton. He said, "O.K., Chief. Nobody was inside."

"Any of the machines badly smashed?"

He laughed. "Can you look at a rubber beach horse with purple polka dots and tell whether it's an intact lathe or a busted one? Say, Chief, you know what you look like?"

I said, "If you tell me, you're fired."

I don't know whether I was kidding or not; I was plenty on edge. I opened the drawer of my desk and put the "God Bless Our Home" sampler in it and slammed the drawer shut. I was fed up. Placet is a crazy place and if you stay there long enough you go crazy yourself. One out of ten of Earth's Centre's Placet employees has to go back to Earth for psychopathic treatment after a year or two on Placet. And I'd been there three years, almost. My contract was up. I made my mind up, too.

"Reagan," I said.

He'd been heading for the door. He turned. "Yeah, Chief?"

I said, "I want you to send a message on the radiotype to Earth Centre. And get it straight, two words: *I quit.*"

He said, "O.K., Chief." He went on out and closed the door.

I sat back and closed my eyes to think. I'd done it now. Unless I ran after Reagan and told him not to send the message, it was done and over and irrevocable. Earth Centre's funny that way; the board is plenty generous in some directions, but once you resign they never let you change your mind. It's an ironclad rule and ninety-nine times out of a hundred it's justified on interplanetary and intragalactic projects. A man must be 100 per cent enthusiastic about his job to make a go of it, and once he's turned against it, he's lost the keen edge.

I knew the midperiod was about over, but I sat there with my eyes closed just the same. I didn't want to open them to look at the clock until I could see the clock *as* a clock and not as whatever it might be this time. I sat there and thought.

I felt a bit hurt about Reagan's casualness in accepting the message. He'd been a good friend of mine for ten years; he could at least have said he was sorry I was going to leave. Of course there was a fair chance that he might get the promotion, but even if he was thinking that, he could have been diplomatic about it. At least, he could have——

Oh, quit feeling sorry for yourself, I told myself. *You're through with Placet and you're through with Earth Centre, and you're going back to Earth pretty soon now, as soon as they relieve you, and you can get another job there, probably teaching again.*

But damn Reagan, just the same. He'd been my student at

Earth City Poly, and I'd got him this Placet job and it was a good one for a youngster his age, assistant administrator of a planet with nearly a thousand population. For that matter, my job was a good one for a man *my* age—I'm only thirty-one myself. An excellent job, except that you couldn't put up a building that wouldn't fall down again and—*Quit crabbing,* I told myself; *you're through with it now. Back to Earth and a teaching job again. Forget it.*

I was tired. I put my head on my arms on top of the desk, and I must have dozed off for a minute.

I looked up at the sound of footsteps coming through the doorway; they weren't Reagan's footsteps. The illusions were getting better now, I saw. It was—or appeared to be—a gorgeous redhead. It couldn't be, of course. There are a few women on Placet, mostly wives of technicians, but——

She said, "Don't you remember me, Mr. Rand?" It was a woman; her voice was a woman's voice, and a beautiful voice. Sounded vaguely familiar, too.

"Don't be silly," I said; "how can I recognise you at midper——" My eyes suddenly caught a glimpse of the clock past her shoulder, and it was a clock and not a funeral wreath or a cuckoo's nest, and I realised suddenly that everything else in the room was back to normal. And that meant midperiod was over, and I wasn't seeing things.

My eyes went back to the redhead. She must be real, I realised. And suddenly I knew her, although she'd changed, changed plenty. All changes were improvements, although Michaelina Witt had been a very pretty girl when she'd been in my extra-terrestrial Botany III class at Earth City Polytech four—no, five years ago.

She'd been pretty, then. Now she was beautiful. She was stunning. How had the teletalkies missed her? Or had they? What was she doing *here?* She must have just got off the *Ark,* but—I realised I was still gawking at her. I stood up so fast I almost fell across the desk.

"Of course I remember you, Miss Witt," I stammered. "Won't you sit down? How did you come here? Have they relaxed the no-visitors rule?"

She shook her head, smiling. "I'm not a visitor, Mr. Rand. Centre advertised for a technician-secretary for you, and I tried for the job and got it, subject to your approval, of course. I'm on probation for a month, that is."

"Wonderful," I said. It was a masterpiece of understatement. I started to elaborate on it: "Marvellous——"

There was the sound of someone clearing his throat. I looked around; Reagan was in the doorway. This time not as a blue skeleton or a two-headed monster. Just plain Reagan.

He said, "Answer to your radiotype just came." He crossed over and dropped it on my desk. I looked at it. "O.K. August 19th," it read. My momentary wild hope that they'd failed to accept my resignation went down among the widgie birds. They'd been as brief about it as I'd been.

August 19th—the next arrival of the *Ark.* They certainly weren't wasting any time—mine or theirs. Four days!

Reagan said, "I thought you'd want to know right away, Phil."

"Yeah," I told him. I glared at him. "Thanks." With a touch of spite—or maybe more than a touch—I thought, *well, my bucko, you don't get the job, or that message would have said so; they're sending a replacement on the next shuttle of the* Ark.

But I didn't say that; the veneer of civilisation was too thick. I said, "Miss Witt, I'd like you to meet——" They looked at each other and started to laugh, and I remembered. Of course, Reagan and Michaelina had both been in my botany class, as had Michaelina's twin brother, Ichabod. Only, of course, no one ever called the redheaded twins Michaelina and Ichabod. It was Mike and Ike, once you knew them.

Reagan said, "I met Mike getting off the *Ark.* I told her how to find your office, since you weren't there to do the honours."

"Thanks," I said. "Did the reinforcing bars come?"

"Guess so. They unloaded some crates. They were in a hurry to pull out again. They've gone."

I grunted.

Reagan said, "Well, I'll check the ladings. Just came to give you the radiotype; thought you'd want the good news right away."

He went out, and I glared after him. The louse. The——

Michaelina said, "Am I to start to work right away, Mr. Rand?"

I straightened out my face and managed a smile. "Of course not," I told her. "You'll want to look around the place first. See the scenery and get acclimated. Want to stroll into the village for a drink?"

"Of course."

We strolled down the path toward the little cluster of buildings, all small, one-story, and square.

She said, "It's—it's nice. Feels like I'm walking on air, I'm so light. Exactly what is the gravity?"

"Point seven four," I said. "If you weigh—um-m, a hundred

twenty pounds on Earth, you weigh about eighty-nine pounds here. And on you, it looks good."

She laughed. "Thank you, Professor—— Oh, that's right; you're not a professor now. You're now my boss, and I must call you Mr. Rand."

"Unless you're willing to make it Phil, Michaelina."

"If you'd called me Mike; I detest Michaelina, almost as much as Ike hates Ichabod."

"How is Ike?"

"Fine. Has a student-instructor job at Poly, but he doesn't like it much." She looked ahead at the village. "Why so many small buildings instead of a few bigger ones?"

"Because the average life of a structure of any kind on Placet is about three weeks. And you never know when one is going to fall down—with someone inside. It's our biggest problem. All we can do is make them small and light, except the foundations, which we make as strong as possible. Thus far, nobody has been hurt seriously in the collapse of a building, for that reason, but—— Did you feel that?"

"The vibration? What was it, an earthquake?"

"No," I said. "It was a flight of birds."

"What?"

I had to laugh at the expression on her face. I said, "Placet is a crazy place. A minute ago, you said you felt as though you were walking on air. Well, in a way, you are doing just exactly that. Placet is one of the rare objects in the Universe that is composed of both ordinary and *heavy* matter. Matter with a collapsed molecular structure, so heavy you couldn't lift a pebble of it. Placet has a core of that stuff; that's why this tiny planet, which has an area about twice the size of Manhattan Island, has a gravity three-quarters that of Earth. There is life—animal life, not intelligent—living on the core. There are birds, whose molecular structure is like that of the planet's core, so dense that ordinary matter is as tenuous to them as air is to us. They actually *fly* through it, as birds on Earth fly through the air. From their standpoint, we're walking on top of Placet's atmosphere."

"And the vibration of their flight under the surface makes the houses collapse?"

"Yes, and worse—they fly right through the foundations, no matter what we make them of. Any matter we can work with is just so much gas to them. They fly through iron or steel as easily as through sand or loam. I've just got a shipment of some specially tough stuff from Earth—the special alloy steel you heard me ask Reagan about—but I haven't much hope of it doing any good."

"But aren't those birds dangerous? I mean, aside from making the buildings fall down. Couldn't one get up enough momentum flying to carry it out of the ground and into the air a little way? And wouldn't it go right through anyone who happened to be there?"

"It would," I said, "but it doesn't. I mean, they never fly closer to the surface than a few inches. Some sense seems to tell them when they're nearing the top of their 'atmosphere.' Something analogous to the supersonics a bat uses. You know, of course, how a bat can fly in utter darkness and never fly into a solid object."

"Like radar, yes."

"Like radar, yes, except a bat uses sound waves instead of radio waves. And the widgie birds must see something that works on the same principle, in reverse; turns them back a few inches before they approach what to them would be the equivalent of a vacuum. Being heavy-matter, they could no more exist or fly in air than a bird could exist or fly in a vacuum."

While we were having a cocktail apiece in the village, Michaelina mentioned her brother again. She said, "Ike doesn't like teaching at all, Phil. Is there any chance at all that you could get him a job here on Placet?"

I said, "I've been badgering Earth Centre for another administrative assistant. The work is increasing plenty since we've got more of the surface under cultivation. Reagan really needs help. I'll——"

Her whole face was alight with eagerness. And I remembered. I was through. I'd resigned, and Earth Centre would pay as much attention to any recommendation of mine as though I were a widgie bird. I finished weakly, "I'll—I'll see if I can do anything about it."

She said, "Thanks—Phil." My hand was on the table beside my glass, and for a second she put hers over it. All right, it's a hackneyed metaphor to say it felt as though a high-voltage current went through me. But it did, and it was a mental shock as well as a physical one, because I realised then and there that I was head over heels. I'd fallen harder than any of Placet's buildings ever had. The thump left me breathless. I wasn't watching Michaelina's face, but from the way she pressed her hand harder against mine for a millisecond and then jerked it away as though from a flame, she must have felt a little of that current, too.

I stood up a little shakily and suggested that we walk back to headquarters.

Because the situation was completely impossible, now. Now that Centre had accepted my resignation and I was without visible or invisible means of support. In a psychotic moment, I'd cooked my own goose. I wasn't even sure I could get a teaching job. Earth Centre is the most powerful organisation in the Universe and has a finger in every pie. If they blacklisted me——

Walking back, I let Michaelina do most of the talking; I had some heavy thinking to do. I wanted to tell her the truth—and I didn't want to.

Between monosyllabic answers, I fought it out with myself. And, finally lost. Or won. I'd not tell her—until just before the next coming of the *Ark*. I'd pretend everything was O.K. and normal for that long, give myself that much chance to see if Michaelina would fall for me. That much of a break I'd give myself. A chance, for four days.

And then—well, if by then she'd come to feel about me the way I did about her, I'd tell her what a fool I'd been and tell her I'd like to—— No, I wouldn't let her return to Earth with me, even if she wanted to, until I saw light ahead through a foggy future. All I could tell her was that if and when I had a chance of working my way up again to a decent job—and after all I was still only thirty-one and might be able to——

That sort of thing.

Reagan was waiting in my office, looking as mad as a wet hornet. He said, "Those saps at Earth Centre shipping department gummed things again. Those crates of special steel aren't."

"Aren't what?"

"Aren't anything. They're empty crates. Something went wrong with the crating machine and they never knew it."

"Are you sure that's what those crates were supposed to contain?"

"Sure I'm sure. Everything else on the order came, and the ladings specified the steel for those particular crates." He ran a hand through his tousled hair. It made him look more like an Airedale than he usually does.

I grinned at him. "Maybe it's invisible steel."

"Invisible, weightless and intangible. Can *I* word the message to Centre telling them about it?"

"Go as far as you like," I told him. "Wait here a minute, though. I'll show Mike where her quarters are and then I want to talk to you a minute."

I took Michaelina to the best available sleeping cabin of the cluster around headquarters. She thanked me again for trying to get Ike a job here, and I felt lower than a widgie bird's grave when I went back to my office.

"Yeah, Chief?" Reagan said.

"About that message to Earth," I told him. "I mean the one I sent this morning. I don't want you to say anything about it to Michaelina."

He chuckled. "Want to tell her yourself, huh? O.K. I'll keep my yap shut."

I said, a bit wryly, "Maybe I was foolish sending it."

"Huh?" he said. "I'm sure glad you did. Swell idea."

He went out, and I managed not to throw anything at him.

The next day was a Tuesday, if that matters. I remember it as the day I solved one of Placet's two major problems. An ironic time to do it, maybe.

I was dictating some notes on greenwort culture—Placet's importance to Earth is, of course, the fact that certain plants native to the place and which won't grow anywhere else yield derivatives that have become important to the pharmacopoeia. I was having heavy sledding because I was watching Michaelina take the notes; she'd insisted on starting work her second day on Placet.

And suddenly, out of a clear sky and out of a muggy mind, came an idea. I stopped dictating and rang for Reagan. He came in.

"Reagan," I said, "order five thousand ampoules of J-17 Conditioner. Tell 'em to rush it."

"Chief, don't you remember? We tried the stuff. Thought it might condition us to see normally in midperiod, but it didn't affect the optic nerves. We still saw screwy. It's great for conditioning people to high or low temperatures or——"

"Or long or short waking-sleeping periods," I interrupted him. "That's what I'm talking about, Reagan. Look, revolving around two suns, Placet had such short irregular periods of light and dark that we never took them seriously. Right?"

"Sure, but——"

"But since there's no logical Placet day and night we could use, we made ourselves slaves to a sun so far away we can't see it. We use a twenty-four hour day. But midperiod occurs every twenty hours, regularly. We can use conditioner to adapt ourselves to a *twenty*-hour day—six hours sleep, twelve awake—with everybody blissfully sleeping through the period when their eyes play tricks on them. And in a darkened sleeping room so you couldn't see anything, even if you woke up. More and shorter days per year—and nobody goes psychopathic on us. Tell me what's wrong with it."

His eyes went bleak and blank and he hit his forehead a resounding whack with the palm of his hand.

He said, "Too simple, that's what's wrong with it. So darned simple only a genius could see it. For two years I've been going slowly nuts and the answer so easy nobody could see it. I'll put the order in right away."

He started out and then turned back. "Now how do we keep the buildings up? Quick, while you're fey or whatever you are."

I laughed. I said, "Why not try that invisible steel of yours in the empty crates?"

He said, "Nuts," and closed the door.

And the next day was a Wednesday and I knocked off work and took Michaelina on a walking tour around Placet. Once around is just a nice day's hike. But with Michaelina Witt, any day's hike would be a nice day's hike. Except, of course, that I knew I had only one more full day to spend with her. The world would end on Friday.

Tomorrow the *Ark* would leave Earth, with the shipment of conditioner that would solve one of our problems—and with whomever Earth Centre was sending to take my place. It would warp through space to a point a safe distance outside the Argyle I-II system and come in on rocket power from there. It would be here Friday, and I'd go back with it. But I tried not to think about that.

I pretty well managed to forget it until we got back to headquarters and Reagan met me with a grin that split his homely mug into horizontal halves. He said, "Chief, you did it."

"Swell," I said, "I did what?"

"Gave me the answer what to use for reinforcing foundations. You solved the problem."

"Yeah?" I said.

"Yeah. Didn't he, Mike?"

Michaelina looked as puzzled as I must have. She said, "He was kidding. He said to use the stuff in the empty crates, didn't he?"

Reagan grinned again. "He just thought he was kidding. That's what we're going to use from now on. Nothing. Look, Chief, it's like the conditioner—so simple we never thought of it. Until you told me to use what was in the empty crates, and I got to thinking it over."

I stood thinking a moment myself, and then I did what Reagan had done the day before—hit myself a whack on the forehead with the heel of my palm.

Michaelina still looked puzzled.

"Hollow foundations," I told her. "What's the one thing widgie birds won't fly through? *Air*. We can make buildings as big as we need them, now. For foundations, we sink double walls with a wide air space between. We can——"

I stopped, because it wasn't "we" any more. *They* could do it after I was back on Earth looking for a job.

And Thursday went and Friday came.

I was working, up till the last minute, because it was the easiest thing to do. With Reagan and Michaelina helping me, I was making out material lists for our new construction projects. First, a three-story building of about forty rooms for a headquarters building.

We were working fast, because it would be midperiod shortly, and you can't do paper work when you can't read and can write only by feel.

But my mind was on the *Ark*. I picked up the phone and called the radiotype shack to ask about it.

"Just got a call from them," said the operator. "They've warped in, but not close enough to land before midperiod. They'll land right after."

"O.K.," I said, abandoning the hope that they'd be a day late.

I got up and walked to the window. We were nearing mid-position, all right. Up in the sky to the north I could see Placet coming toward us.

"Mike," I said. "Come here."

She joined me at the window and we stood there, watching. My arm was around her. I don't remember putting it there, but I didn't take it away, and she didn't move.

Behind us, Reagan cleared his throat. He said, "I'll give this much of the list to the operator. He can get it on the ether right after midperiod." He went out and shut the door behind him.

Michaelina seemed to move a little closer. We were both looking out the window at Placet rushing toward us. She said, "Beautiful, isn't it, Phil?"

"Yes," I said. But I turned, and I was looking at her face as I said it. Then—I hadn't meant to—I kissed her.

I went back, and sat down at my desk. She said, "Phil, what's the matter? You haven't got a wife and six kids hidden away somewhere, or something, have you? You were single when I had a crush on you at Earth Polytech—and I waited five years to get over it and didn't, and finally wangled a job on Placet just to—— Do I have to do the proposing?"

I groaned. I didn't look at her. I said, "Mike, I'm nuts about you. But—just before you came, I sent a two-word radio-type to Earth. It said, 'I quit.' So I've got to leave Placet on this shuttle of the *Ark*, and I doubt if I can even get a teaching job, now that I've got Earth Centre down on me, and——"

She said, "But, Phil!" and took a step toward me.

There was a knock on the door, Reagan's knock. I was glad, for once, of the interruption. I called out for him to come in, and he opened the door.

He said, "You told Mike yet, Chief?"

I nodded, glumly.

Reagan grinned. "Good," he said; "I've been busting to tell her. It'll be swell to see Ike again."

"Huh?" I said. "Ike who?"

Reagan's grin faded. He said, "Phil, are you slipping, or something? Don't you remember giving me the answer to that Earth Centre radiotype four days ago, just before Mike got here?"

I stared at him with my mouth open. I hadn't even read that radiotype, let alone answered it. Had Reagan gone psychopathic, or had I? I remembered shoving it in the drawer of my desk. I jerked open the drawer and pulled it out. My hand shook a little as I read it:

REQUEST FOR ADDITIONAL ASSISTANT GRANTED. WHOM DO YOU WANT FOR THE JOB?

I looked up at Reagan again. I said, "You're trying to tell me I sent an answer to this?"

He looked as dumbfounded as I felt.

"You told me to," he said.

"What did I tell you to send?"

"Ike Witt." He stared at me. "Chief, are you feeling all right?"

I felt so all right something seemed to explode in my head. I stood up and started for Michaelina. I said, "Mike, will you marry me?" I got my arms around her, just in time, before midperiod closed down on us, so I couldn't see what she looked like, and vice versa. But over her shoulder, I could see what must be Reagan. I said, "Get out of here, you ape," and I spoke quite literally because that's exactly what he appeared to be. A bright yellow ape.

The floor was shaking under my feet, but other things were happening to me, too, and I didn't realise what the shaking meant until the ape turned back and yelled, "A flight of birds going under us, Chief! Get out quick, before——"

But that was as far as he got before the house fell down around us and the tin roof hit my head and knocked me out. Placet is a crazy place. I like it.

1946